MADAME BOVARY

BACKGROUNDS AND SOURCES
ESSAYS IN CRITICISM

NORTON CRITICAL EDITIONS

≫ A NORTON CRITICAL EDITION ≪

GUSTAVE FLAUBERT

MADAME BOVARY

BACKGROUNDS AND SOURCES
ESSAYS IN CRITICISM

≫≪

*Edited with a substantially
new translation by*

PAUL DE MAN

CORNELL UNIVERSITY

W · W · NORTON & COMPANY · INC · New York

≫≫ ≪≪

≫≫ W. W. Norton & Company, Inc. is also the publisher of *The Norton Anthology of English Literature*, edited by M. H. Abrams, Robert M. Adams, David Daiches, E. Talbot Donaldson, George H. Ford, Samuel Holt Monk, and Hallett Smith; *The American Tradition in Literature*, edited by Sculley Bradley, Richmond Croom Beatty, and E. Hudson Long; *World Masterpieces*, edited by Maynard Mack, Kenneth Douglas, Howard E. Hugo, Bernard M. W. Knox, John C. McGalliard, P. M. Pasinetti, and René Wellek; and *The Norton Reader*, edited by Arthur M. Eastman, Caesar R. Blake, Hubert M. English, Jr., Alan B. Howes, Robert T. Leneghan, Leo F. McNamara, and James Rosier.

Contents

Essays in Criticism

Introduction

Ever since its publication in 1857, *Madame Bovary* has been one of the most discussed books in the history of world literature. Despite the distinction and importance of his other novels, Flaubert had to reconcile himself to the fact that he became known, once and forever, as the author of *Madame Bovary*. The popularity of the novel has increased rather than diminished with time. Numberless translations exist in various languages; the word "bovarysme" has became part of the French language; the myth surrounding the figure of Emma Bovary is so powerful that, as in the case of Don Quixote, or Don Juan, or Faust, one has to remind oneself that she is a fiction and not an actual historical person; the literary influence on subsequent novelists in France and elsewhere is of determining importance and the critical response to the book is of such high quality that it can be said, without exaggeration, that contemporary criticism of fiction owes more to this novel than to any other nineteenth century work.

Why this extraordinary response to a work which, for its author, was to be primarily an exercise preparatory to later novels? The first notoriety of *Madame Bovary* was due to a *succès de scandale*, the curiosity awakened by a publication judged scandalous enough to excite the ire of the censors. The twenty or thirty thousand readers who bought the earliest edition published by Michel Lévy may have been somewhat disappointed to discover a book that was severe rather than salacious. But the universality of the theme, the quality of the style, the truthfulness of the realistic and satirical detail, have kept their appeal long after extra-literary motives for attracting attention to *Madame Bovary* had died down. Something in the destiny of the heroine and of the main supporting characters, as well as in the destiny of the book itself, surrounds it with the aura of immortality that belongs only to truly major creations. Though some critics have expressed their preference for *The Sentimental Education* over *Madame Bovary*, something exemplary about the latter novel makes it into a main articulation of literary history, perhaps because, like its model *Don Quixote*, it captures the full intricacy of the relationship between reality and fiction out of which the entire genre of the novel originates.

The genesis of *Madame Bovary* is well known and abundantly documented in Flaubert's letters, as well as in numerous eye-witness accounts from his friends and contemporaries. Flaubert was thirty years old and far from a beginner at his craft when he started out on *Madame Bovary:* he had completed the first versions of the *Sentimental Education* and of the *Temptation of Saint Anthony*, and written several shorter tales, many of them rich enough to be considered first outlines for complete novels. But he had never published, although his literary vocation had asserted itself since his adolescence in the form of an irrevocable decision to be a writer.

His correspondence allows us to follow the progress of the novel with unusual precision. During the more than four years that he worked at *Madame Bovary* Flaubert was in daily contact with his close friend and collaborator Louis Bouilhet. The letters to Bouilhet reveal the painstaking care with which he documented every single detail of the story, as well as the torture to which he submitted himself to achieve the stylistic perfection for which he strove. On a more personal and intimate level, the letters to Louise Colet are like the private diary of his creative effort, a chronicle of the labors, sacrifices, and satisfactions involved in the elaboration of a master-piece. This correspondence shows Flaubert's complete immersion in his project at the exclusion of any other activity, over a long period of agonizingly slow progress. Unlike such writers as Balzac, Dickens, or Dostoevsky who had to write at great speed, Flaubert's obsessive concern with stylistic perfection never allowed him to produce more than a few paragraphs a day, and he would submit these to endless revision. Certain passages of the novel exist in as many as eleven different versions.

When the work was finally completed in 1856, its publication nearly ended in disaster. It appeared in serial form in the *Revue de Paris*, a journal directed by Flaubert's close friend Maxime DuCamp in collaboration with Laurent-Pichat. For a book that painted such a merciless picture of reality, the time and the place were hardly safe: the government of Napoleon III was anything but permissive towards the press, and the republican tendencies of the *Revue de Paris* made it into an easy target for censorship. Even from a purely literary point of view, realistic writers such as Duranty or Champfleury, or the painter Courbet, were under steady attack from conservative critics. The editors of the review thus had some reason to view the particularly audacious aspects of the novel with alarm. Their tactics in trying to protect themselves, however, were inept. Hoping that the suppression of certain passages might tone down the shock-effect of the whole, they made a series of clumsy and useless emendations that damaged the unity of the book but failed to appease the authorities. Flaubert protested against the arbitrary suppressions: "You lose your time attacking details. The element of brutality is not at the surface but at the heart of the book * * * one cannot change the *blood* of a work. All you can do is make it poorer."[1] He was right. The scandal broke in spite of last-minute changes. Using *Madame Bovary* in part as a pretext to attack a politically hostile periodical, the administration suspended the review and started a legal action against Flaubert and his publishers. An enlightened judge, an eloquent defense attorney (Sénard), and an inept prosecutor turned the tide. Flaubert and the *Revue de Paris* were acquitted on February 7, 1856, and the novel was allowed to appear in book form without suppressions. No publisher could have dreamt of a better publicity to promote the book and when it appeared in April of the same year, it was immensely successful. But it would take many years before the textual errors of the first edition would be corrected and an accurate edition of *Madame Bovary* made available.

The critical reception of the book was mixed, though on the whole not unfavorable. The violence of tone and action upset many critics, but their strictures were almost always accompanied by expressions of admiration for the style. Cuvillier-Fleury, the rival of Sainte-Beuve at the *Journal des Débats,* was one of the few critics to attack Flaubert's style as marred by a romantic flamboyance that does not blend with the harshness of the realism. Most of the other hostile critics preferred to attack the political subversiveness associated with realism rather than *Madame Bovary* itself: "*Madame Bovary,*" writes A. de Pontmartin in the *Correspondant,* "is the pathological glorification of the senses and of the imagination in a disappointed democracy * * * it proves once and for all that realism means literary democracy."[2] Sainte-Beuve's own article reflects many of the hesitations with which a late romantic temperament reacts to the new sound of the novel; he did, however, recognize the historical importance of the occasion. Flaubert's fellow-Norman, the novelist and critic Barbey d'Aurevilly (who was to react very negatively to Flaubert's later work), wrote a penetrating article in which he rather overemphasizes the impersonal objectivity of the style in terms that are reminiscent of some of Flaubert's own statements in his correspondence. The deepest understanding was to come from Baudelaire, whose article was the only one to satisfy Flaubert completely: "You have penetrated the inner mystery of the work as if you and I shared the same mind," he wrote to Baudelaire. "You have felt and understood me entirely."[3]

Flaubert remained aloof from the public debates stirred up by *Madame Bovary.* He was to go on to even harsher, more ironic and uncompromising works, *The Sentimental Education* and *Bouvard*

---

1. *Correspondence,* III, 87.
2. Quoted by René Descharmes and René Dumesnil in *Autour de Flaubert. Etudes historiques et documentaires* (Paris: Mercure, 1922).
3. *Correspondence,* III, 148.

and Pécuchet, none of which found an even remotely comparable response among the general public.

Ever since the articles by Sainte-Beuve, Barbey d'Aurevilly, and Baudelaire, the amount of critical and scholarly publications on *Madame Bovary* has reached staggering proportions. Scholarship and literary erudition have put the criticism of *Madame Bovary* on a sound basis: the critical edition established by René Dumesnil (1945–48) gives an authoritative text; the publication of the *Correspondence* has considerably extended our insight into the mind of Flaubert and in the genesis of his novel. The Conard edition already contained samples of Flaubert's voluminous notes for *Madame Bovary,* and several specialists of Flaubert studies, among them most prominently D. L. Demorest in his 1931 thesis on *Figurative and Symbolic Expression in the Work of Flaubert,* had drawn attention to the wealth of material contained in these early drafts. Some of Flaubert's most original writing was to be found in discarded notes that the author, with fierce integrity, had ruthlessly eliminated from the pared down and rigidly economical final version. A highly technical edition of the early drafts was published in 1936 by Mlle. Gabrielle Leleu, librarian at Rouen, entitled *Madame Bovary, Sketches and Unpublished Fragments.* Later, with the assistance of the eminent Flaubert scholar Jean Pommier, the same author compiled a so-called "new version" of *Madame Bovary,* a composite text that prints the fragments in continuous succession. This highly readable version never actually existed in this form, but it has nevertheless provided recent critics of *Madame Bovary* with invaluable source material. In the present edition, we are able to include a selection of letters relevant to *Madame Bovary,* based on the selection made by Frances Steegmuller in his edition of Flaubert's letters in English, and a selection of some of the most characteristic samples of the early versions, together with an evaluation of these versions by the critic Albert Béguin.

The historical and factual sources of the novel have been subjected to an equally thorough-going investigation. It had been known from the start that Flaubert had used life-models in writing *Madame Bovary.* With a characteristic mixture of historical precision combined with a vivid interest in other people's love life, French scholars have spent a great deal of ingenuity tracking down the "real" sources of *Madame Bovary.* As is often the case in such investigations, the more the research progressed, the more complicated and inconclusive the results became: it seems clearly established that Flaubert used as a model a certain Deslauriers, a doctor whose wife Delphine Couturier committed suicide by poison and who lived in a Norman town called Ry that has much in common with Yonville l'Abbaye. But many other sources have been proposed, and the entire question is far from being clearly settled. Moreover, the whole problem of the exegetic value of such investigations has been raised. Rather than involving the student in the minutia of source investigation (quite fascinating when conducted by specialists such as Pommier or Dumesnil), we have preferred to include the essays by Jean-Paul Sartre and René Dumesnil in which the importance of source material for an understanding of *Madame Bovary* is discussed in more general terms.

The Sartre essay may seem difficult to follow for readers who are not familiar with Sartre's recent thought and vocabulary. Yet it indicates how sociological or psychological methods of interpretation can be combined with intrinsic or stylistic analysis to reach a full understanding of Flaubert's project when he undertook to write *Madame Bovary*. Sartre blueprints a method that moves backwards and forwards between the work and the life, with a high degree of awareness of the complex relationship between both. We are far removed from oversimplified deterministic schemes that consider the work as the result of outside forces. Still, Sartre's inquiry is in the last analysis oriented towards the man Flaubert rather than towards the work *Madame Bovary*. One may think that relationships such as those indicated by René Dumesnil, when he points out the similarity between the early story *Passion et Vertu* and the later *Madame Bovary*, are even more revealing than the relationships between Flaubert's milieu, his childhood, and his novels that Sartre hopes to discover by means of his regressive-progressive method.

The selection of the Essays in Criticism, has been, for the present Critical Edition, a nearly hopeless task. Between 1857 and the present, all leading French writers and critics have something noteworthy to say about *Madame Bovary*: Brunetière, Faguet, Jules de Gaultier (who coined the expression "bovarysme" in a book by that name), but also the Goncourts, Maupassant, Zola, Paul Bourget, and later Gide, Mauriac, and Proust. None of this material could be included, sometimes because the statements apply to Flaubert as a whole rather than to *Madame Bovary*, sometimes because they are too general or, on the contrary (as in the case of Proust) too technical and particular to be translated into English. One can consider the fragment from Thibaudet as a good example of French criticism during the period between the two world wars. But the principle of our selection has very definitely been oriented towards problems of method that are important in the contemporary criticism of fiction. *Madame Bovary* is a starting-point for many of these techniques, and it was thought interesting to let students compare for themselves the results achieved by some of these methods. The close interdependence between several of the essays (a critic will frequently take off from a remark made by one of his predecessors and carry it further) gives insight into the unified development of critical thought in the twentieth century. This opportunity for comparative criticism also permits us to introduce to American students some examples of recent European criticism not yet available in translation.

Recent criticism of *Madame Bovary* has for its main concern the study of narrative and metaphorical structures in the novel. In his essays on Flaubert, Henry James commented on the "point of view" of the narrator in relation to his characters, a concept that was to dominate the contemporary theory of fiction. The same issue was raised, in a more technical way, by Proust in a 1920 controversy with Albert Thibaudet, in connection with Flaubert's use in dialogues of reported (rather than directly quoted) speech. This aspect of Flaubert's style (also stressed by linguists such as Bally or, more recently, by Stephen Ullmann in his *Style in the French Novel*) is too technical to be included here, except for a brief introductory statement by von Wartburg that serves as a reminder of the importance of linguistic analysis in the description of Flaubert's style. On the other hand, James's own remarks and their subsequent elaboration by the English critic Percy Lubbock still constitute a useful exposition of Flaubert's use of point of view. The existence in *Madame Bovary* of long passages without identifiable narrative function indicates that certain elements of the novel lie beyond the reach of the point of view technique. At least two kinds of diction seem to alternate and to interact subtly throughout the book: that of an objective narrator who can stand back and observe while maintaining an ironic distance, and that of a subjective consciousness without "point of view" that freely espouses the reveries and spontaneously uses the richly metaphorical style that seems to be Flaubert's natural idiom. French critics have been, on the whole, most interested in exploring this subjective voice, whereas English and American critics have paid most attention to the objective narrative techniques. This implies that the French concentrate on the metaphorical and figural elements of the style that abound especially in the early versions. As Harry Levin's essay demonstrates, American commentators have by no means ignored the thematic importance of recurrent metaphorical patterns, but their efforts are primarily directed towards a description of the novel's form. In his epoch-making essay on "The Interior Environment in Flaubert" the French critic Charles du Bos recaptures the creative consciousness of the writer from the inside, by an act of sympathetic understanding. Jean-Pierre Richard refines and expands du Bos's suggestions in his detailed description of Flaubert's material imagination. Combining du Bos's insight into Flaubert's subjectivity with Auerbach's awareness of the complex structures of consciousness at work in *Madame Bovary*, Georges Poulet was able to break through the narrative surface of the novel and to reveal a deeper pattern that reproduces the very pulsations of Flaubert's mind. It is clear that a fully inclusive study of *Madame Bovary* would have to combine the French study of metaphors with the American study of narrative structures in the novel. The concluding essay by Jean Rousset, which juxtaposes a Jamesian examination of point of view with a thematic study of a central metaphor, reveals some of the possibilities contained in such a combination of European with American critical methods.

I feel particularly indebted to Prof. D. L. Demorest of Ohio State University, whose exhaustive knowledge of Flaubert and of the Flaubert bibliography has been of considerable assistance in preparing this edition. He brought to my attention several articles and essays that are not generally known, including the article by Albert Béguin on the early versions of the novel. Even highly specialized students of this important critic had failed to record this text. My only regret is that lack of space made it impossible to incorporate more of his valuable suggestions.

PAUL DE MAN

The Text of
Madame Bovary

A Substantially New Translation by Paul de Man
Based on the Version by Eleanor Marx Aveling

A Note on the Translation

There are several English translations of *Madame Bovary* in existence. Although none can be called really perfect, more than one achieves a reasonable degree of accuracy and stylistic felicity. The text here reproduced is an extensively revised version of one of the older translations of *Madame Bovary*, done by Eleanor Marx Aveling, the daughter of Karl Marx.

Like most translations, the Marx Aveling text has advantages and drawbacks. One of its main virtues is the relatively high degree of fidelity in rendering the cadence of Flaubert's sentence. Other translators have produced versions that are a great deal more fluent and idiomatic. But Flaubert himself is neither fluent nor really idiomatic (except in conversations), and by adhering more closely to his rhythm, Mrs. Aveling sometimes succeeds in conveying Flaubert's carefully controlled syntax. A certain number of revisions, however, were unavoidable. The Victorian diction has, in part, been modernized. Flaubert's original paragraphs, a fundamental and subtly measured unit of composition, have been restored throughout. Several misleading inaccuracies and mistranslations have been corrected. Especially in Part II and III of the novel entire pages had, at times, to be rewritten; Mrs. Aveling often loses track of the meaning in the meditative, inward passages and renders the already obscure original altogether opaque. One feels about this patching and mending job the way a surgeon must feel about a difficult operation: the patient is by no means as good as new, but he should at least feel some relief. Students of this text should be a little closer to Flaubert's original intention than when the Marx Aveling translation was sprung upon them without warning.

Some of Flaubert's stylistic devices cannot be rendered in translation. He italicizes certain words, especially when he is reporting someone's speech, in order to catch a nuance which is particularly important to him: the use of stilted, inert speech that reveals the degradation of the character's relation towards language. Sometimes entire expressions are italicized (the "received ideas" of which Flaubert compiled a dictionary as a monument to human stupidity), but at other times it is a single word, quite inconspicuous at first sight, whose cliché-like nature is revealed only by the use of this typographical device. It often takes an ear finely attuned to colloquial French to catch the derisive intent introduced in this way, one of the means by which Flaubert establishes ironic distance between himself and his characters. Except in some more obvious instances, the effect is irrevocably lost in translation.

Since literary and historical allusions do not figure very prominently in *Madame Bovary*, annotation could be kept down to a minimum. The notes are exclusively aimed at factual comprehension and avoid all suggestion of critical commentary. In revising the Marx Aveling translation, the text has been checked against authoritative editions of *Madame Bovary*: the Dumesnil critical edition, the Conard edition, and the current Garnier edition established by Edouard Maynial.

Madame Bovary

TO

MARIE-ANTOINE-JULES SENARD,[1]
MEMBER OF THE PARIS BAR,
EX-PRESIDENT OF THE NATIONAL ASSEMBLY, AND
FORMER MINISTER OF THE INTERIOR.

DEAR AND ILLUSTRIOUS FRIEND,—

PERMIT me to inscribe your name at the head of this book, and above its dedication; for it is to you, before all, that I owe its publication. By becoming part of your magnificent defence, my work has acquired for myself, as it were, an unexpected authority. Accept, then, here, the homage of my gratitude, which, however great, will never attain to the level of your eloquence and your devotion.

GUSTAVE FLAUBERT.

Paris, April 12th 1857

Part One

I

We were in class when the headmaster came in, followed by a new boy, not wearing the school uniform, and a school servant carrying a large desk. Those who had been asleep woke up, and every one rose as if just surprised at his work.

The headmaster made a sign to us to sit down. Then, turning to the teacher, he said to him in a low voice:

"Monsieur Roger, here is a pupil whom I recommend to your care; he'll be in the second. If his work and conduct are satisfactory, he will go into one of the upper classes, as becomes his age."

The new boy, standing in the corner behind the door so that he could hardly be seen, was a country lad of about fifteen, and taller than any of us. His hair was cut square on his forehead like a village choir boy; he looked reliable, but very ill at ease. Although he was not broad-shouldered, his short jacket of green cloth with black

1. Senard was the lawyer whose brilliant defense saved the day for Flaubert when *Madame Bovary* came up for trial on January 31 and February 7, 1857. The original dedication, when the novel appeared in serial form in the *Revue de Paris* was to Louis Bouilhet, Flaubert's lifelong friend and close collaborator who, as the *Correspondence* shows, played an important part in the composition of the novel.

buttons must have been tight about the armholes, and showed at the opening of the cuffs red wrists accustomed to being bare. His legs, in blue stockings, looked out from beneath yellowish trousers, drawn tight by suspenders. He wore stout, ill-cleaned, hob-nailed boots.

We began reciting the lesson. He listened with all his ears, as attentive as if at a sermon, not daring even to cross his legs or lean on his elbow; and when at two o'clock the bell rang, the master was obliged to tell him to fall into line with the rest of us.

When we came back to work, we were in the habit of throwing our caps on the ground so as to have our hands more free; we used from the door to toss them under the desk, so that they hit against the wall and made a lot of dust: it was the fad of the moment.

But, whether he had not noticed the trick, or did not dare to attempt it, the new boy was still holding his cap on his knees even after prayers were over. It was one of those head-gears of composite order, in which we can find traces of the bear- and the coonskin, the shako, the bowler, and the cotton nightcap; one of those poor things, in fine, whose dumb ugliness has depths of expression, like an imbecile's face. Ovoid and stiffened with whalebone, it began with three circular strips; then came in succession lozenges of velvet and rabbit fur separated by a red band; after that a sort of bag that ended in a cardboard polygon covered with complicated braiding, from which hung, at the end of a long thin cord, small twisted gold threads in the manner of a tassel. The cap was new; its peak shone.[2]

"Rise," said the master.

He stood up; his cap fell. The whole class began to laugh. He stooped to pick it up. A neighbour knocked it down again with his elbow; he picked it up once more.

"Get rid of your helmet," said the master, who liked to joke.

There was a burst of laughter from the boys, which so thoroughly put the poor lad out of countenance that he did not know whether to keep his cap in his hand, leave it on the ground, or put it on his head. He sat down again and placed it on his knee.

"Rise," repeated the master, "and tell me your name."

The new boy articulated in a stammering voice an unintelligible name.

"Again!"

The same sputtering of syllables was heard, drowned by the tittering of the class.

"Louder!" cried the master; "louder!"

2. The description of this amazing head-gear is based on a drawing that appeared in the satirical paper *Charivari* of June 21, 1833. The relationship between *Charivari* and "Charbovari" a few lines further may or may not be a mere coincidence.

The new boy then took a supreme resolution, opened an inordinately large mouth, and shouted at the top of his voice as if calling some one, the word "Charbovari."

A hubbub broke out, rose in *crescendo* with bursts of shrill voices (they yelled, barked, stamped, repeated "Charbovari! Charbovari!), then died away into single notes, growing quieter only with great difficulty, and now and again suddenly recommencing along the line of a seat from where rose here and there, like a damp cracker going off, a stifled laugh.

However, amid a rain of penalties, order was gradually reestablished in the class; and the master having succeeded in catching the name of "Charles Bovary," having had it dictated to him, spelt out, and re-read, at once ordered the poor devil to go and sit down on the punishment form at the foot of the master's desk. He got up, but before going hesitated.

"What are you looking for?" asked the master.

"My c-c-c-cap," said the new boy shyly, casting troubled looks round him.

"Five hundred verses for all the class!" shouted in a furious voice, stopped, like the *Quos ego*,[3] a fresh outburst. "Silence!"continued the master indignantly, wiping his brow with his handkerchief, which he had just taken from his cap. As to you, Bovary, you will conjugate '*ridiculus sum*' twenty times." Then, in a gentler tone, "Come, you'll find your cap again; it hasn't been stolen."

Quiet was restored. Heads bent over desks, and the new boy remained for two hours in an exemplary attitude, although from time to time some paper pellet flipped from the tip of a pen came bang in his face. But he wiped his face with one hand and continued motionless, his eyes lowered.

In the evening, at study hall, he pulled out his sleeveguards from his desk, arranged his small belongings, and carefully ruled his paper. We saw him working conscientiously, looking up every word in the dictionary, and taking the greatest pains. Thanks, no doubt, to the willingness he showed, he had not to go down to the class below. But though he knew his rules passably, he lacked all elegance in composition. It was the curé of his village who had taught him his first Latin; his parents, from motives of economy, having sent him to school as late as possible.

His father, Monsieur Charles Denis Bartolomé Bovary, retired assistant-surgeon-major, compromised about 1812 in certain conscription scandals, and forced at this time to leave the service, had taken advantage of his fine figure to get hold of a dowry of sixty thousand francs in the person of a hosier's daughter who had fallen in love with his good looks. He was a fine man, a great talker,

3. Neptune becalming the winds in the *Aeneid* (I.135)

making his spurs ring as he walked, wearing whiskers that ran into his moustache, his fingers always garnished with rings; he dressed in loud colours, had the dash of a military man with the easy go of a commercial traveller. Once married, he lived for three or four years on his wife's fortune, dining well, rising late, smoking long porcelain pipes, not coming in at night till after the theatre, and haunting cafés. The father-in-law died, leaving little; he was indignant at this, tried his hand at the textile business, lost some money in it, then retired to the country, where he thought he would make the land pay off. But, as he knew no more about farming than calico, as he rode his horses instead of sending them to plough, drank his cider in bottle instead of selling it in cask, ate the finest poultry in his farmyard, and greased his hunting-boots with the fat of his pigs, he was not long in finding out that he would do better to give up all speculation.

For two hundred francs[4] a year he managed to rent on the border of the provinces of Caux and Picardy, a kind of place half farm, half private house; and here, soured, eaten up with regrets, cursing his luck, jealous of every one, he shut himself up at the age of forty-five, sick of men, he said, and determined to live in peace.

His wife had adored him once on a time; she had loved him with a thousand servilities that had only estranged him the more. Lively once, expansive and affectionate, in growing older she had become (after the fashion of wine that, exposed to air, turns to vinegar) ill-tempered, grumbling, irritable. She had suffered so much without complaint at first, when she had seen him going after all the village harlots, and when a score of bad houses sent him back to her at night, weary, stinking drunk. Then her pride revolted. After that she was silent, burying her anger in a dumb stoicism that she maintained till her death. She was constantly going about looking after business matters. She called on the lawyers, the judges, remembered when notes fell due, got them renewed, and at home ironed, sewed, washed, looked after the workmen, paid the accounts, while he, troubling himself about nothing, eternally besotted in a sleepy sulkiness from which he only roused himself to say nasty things to her, sat smoking by the fire and spitting into the cinders.

When she had a child, it had to be sent out to nurse. When he came home, the lad was spoilt as if he were a prince. His mother stuffed him with jam; his father let him run about barefoot, and, playing the philosopher, even said he might as well go about quite

<hr />

4. It is very difficult to transpose monetary values from 1840 into present-day figures, since relationships between the actual value of the franc, the cost of living, and the relative cost of specific items (such as rent, real estate, etc.) have undergone fundamental changes. One would not be too far off the mark by reading present-day dollars for Flaubert's francs; that would show Madame Bovary destroyed, at the end of the book, by an 8,000-dollar debt.

naked like the young of animals. As opposed to the maternal ideas, he had a certain virile idea of childhood on which he sought to mould his son, wishing him to be brought up hardily, like a Spartan, to give him a strong constitution. He sent him to bed without any fire, taught him to drink off large draughts of rum and to jeer at religious processions. But, peaceable by nature, the boy responded poorly to his attempts. His mother always kept him near her; she cut out cardboard pictures for him, told him tales, entertained him with monologues full of melancholy gaiety, chatting and fondling in endless baby-talk. In her life's isolation she transferred on the child's head all her scattered, broken little vanities. She dreamed of high station; she already saw him, tall, handsome, clever, settled as an engineer or in the law. She taught him to read, and even on an old piano she had taught him two or three sentimental ballads. But to all this Monsieur Bovary, caring little for arts and letters, said "It was not worth while. Would they ever have the means to send him to a public school, to buy him a practice, or start him in business? Besides, with brashness a man can always make his way in the world." Madame Bovary bit her lips, and the child knocked about the village.

He followed the farm laborers, drove away with clods of earth the ravens that were flying about. He ate blackberries along the hedges, minded the geese with a long switch, went hay-making during harvest, ran about in the woods, played hopscotch under the church porch on rainy days, and at great fêtes begged the beadle to let him toll the bells, that he might hang all his weight on the long rope and feel himself borne upward by it in its swing.

So he grew like an oak; he was strong of hand, ruddy of complexion.

When he was twelve years old his mother had her own way; he began his lessons. The curé took him in hand; but the lessons were so short and irregular that they could not be of much use. They were given at spare moments in the sacristy, standing up, hurriedly, between a baptism and a burial; or else the curé, if he had not to go out, sent for his pupil after the *Angelus.* They went up to his room and settled down; the flies and moths fluttered round the candle. It was close, the child fell asleep, and the good man, beginning to doze with his hands on his stomach, was soon snoring with his mouth wide open. On other occasions, when Monsieur le Curé, on his way back after administering the holy oil to some sick person in the neighborhood, caught sight of Charles playing about the fields, he called him, lectured him for a quarter of an hour, and took advantage of the occasion to make him conjugate his verb at the foot of a tree. The rain interrupted them or an acquaintance passed. All the same he was always pleased with him, and even said the "young man" had a very good memory.

Charles could not go on like this. Madame Bovary took strong steps. Ashamed, or rather tired out, Monsieur Bovary gave in without a struggle, and they waited one year longer, so that the child could take his first communion.

Six months more passed, and the year after Charles was finally sent to school at Rouen. His father took him there towards the end of October, at the time of the St. Romain fair.

It would now be impossible for any of us to remember any thing about him. He was a youth of even temperament, who played in playtime, worked in school-hours, was attentive in class, slept well in the dormitory, and ate well in the refectory. He had for guardian a hardware merchant in the Rue Ganterie, who took him out once a month on Sundays after his shop was shut, sent him for a walk on the quay to look at the boats, and then brought him back to college at seven o'clock before supper. Every Thursday evening he wrote a long letter to his mother with red ink and three wax seals; then he went over his history note-books, or read an old volume of "Anarchasis"[5] that was lying about the study. When he went for walks he talked to the servant, who, like himself, came from the country.

By dint of hard work he kept always about the middle of the class; once even he got an honor mark in natural history. But at the end of his third year his parents withdrew him from the school to make him study medicine, convinced that he could make it to the bachelor's degree by himself.

His mother chose a room for him on the fourth floor of a dyer's she knew, overlooking the Eau-de-Robec.[6] She made arrangements for his board, got him furniture, table and two chairs, sent home for an old cherry-tree bedstead, and bought besides a small cast-iron stove with the supply of wood that was to warm her poor child. Then at the end of a week she departed, after a thousand injunctions to be good now that he was going to be left to himself.

The course list that he read on the notice-board stunned him: lectures on anatomy, lectures on pathology, lectures on physiology, lectures on pharmacy, lectures on botany and clinical medicine, and therapeutics, without counting hygiene and materia medica—all names of whose etymologies he was ignorant, and that were to him as so many doors to sanctuaries filled with magnificent darkness.

He understood nothing of it all; it was all very well to listen—he did not follow. Still he worked; he had bound note-books, he attended all the courses, never missed a single lecture. He did his little

---

5. Dialogue by Lucian (A.D. 125–85) in which the usefulness of gymnastic exercises for young people is discussed.
6. Small river, now covered up, that flows through the poorest neighborhood of Rouen, used as a sewer by the factories that border it, thus suggesting Flaubert's description as *"une ignoble petite Venise."*

daily task like a mill-horse, who goes round and round with his eyes bandaged, not knowing what work it is grinding out.

To spare him expense his mother sent him every week by the carrier a piece of veal baked in the oven,[7] with which he lunched when he came back from the hospital, while he sat kicking his feet against the wall. After this he had to run off to lectures, to the operation-room, to the hospital, and return to his home at the other end of the town. In the evening, after the poor dinner of his landlord, he went back to his room and set to work again in his wet clothes, that smoked as he sat in front of the hot stove.

On the fine summer evenings, at the time when the close streets are empty, when the servants are playing shuttle-cock at the doors, he opened his window and leaned out. The river, that makes of this quarter of Rouen a wretched little Venice, flowed beneath him, between the bridges and the railings, yellow, violet, or blue. Working men, kneeling on the banks, washed their bare arms in the water. On poles projecting from the attics, skeins of cotton were drying in the air. Opposite, beyond the roofs, spread the pure sky with the red sun setting. How pleasant it must be at home! How fresh under the beech-tree! And he expanded his nostrils to breathe in the sweet odours of the country which did not reach him.

He grew thin, his figure became taller, his face took a saddened look that made it almost interesting.

Passively, through indifference, he abandoned all the resolutions he had made. Once he missed a lecture; the next day all the lectures; and, enjoying his idleness, little by little he gave up work altogether.

He got into the habit of going to the cafés, and had a passion for dominoes. To shut himself up every evening in the dirty public room, to push about on marble tables the small sheep-bones with black dots, seemed to him a fine proof of his freedom, which raised him in his own esteem. It was beginning to see life, the sweetness of stolen pleasures; and when he entered, he put his hand on the door-handle with a joy almost sensual. Then many things compressed within him expanded; he learned by heart student songs and sang them at gatherings, became enthusiastic about Béranger, learnt how to make punch, and, finally how to make love.

Thanks to these preparatory labors, he failed completely in his examination for his degree of *officier de santé*.[8] He was expected

7. The editors of the *Revue de Paris*, intent on removing all traces of excessive sordidity, suppressed this innocent *"morceau de veau cuit au four."* It is the first in a long series of emendations demanded by the editors of the review, most of which aimed at more obviously shocking passages than this one. The Belles Lettres and the Garnier editions

of *Madame Bovary* (see Bibliography) give the full list of suppressions.
8. The degree of Officier de Santé, instituted during the Revolution, was a kind of second-class medical degree, well below the doctorate. The student was allowed to attend a medical school without having passed the equivalence of the *baccalauréat*. He could only practice in

home the same night to celebrate his success.

He started on foot, stopped at the beginning of the village, sent for his mother, and told her all. She excused him, threw the blame of his failure on the injustice of the examiners, encouraged him a little, and took upon herself to set matters straight. It was only five years later that Monsieur Bovary knew the truth; it was old then, and he accepted it. Moreover, he could not believe that a man born of him could be a fool.

So Charles set to work again and crammed for his examination, ceaselessly learning all the old questions by heart. He passed pretty well. What a happy day for his mother! They gave a grand dinner.

Where should he go to practise? To Tostes, where there was only one old doctor. For a long time Madame Bovary had been on the look-out for his death, and the old fellow had barely been packed off when Charles was installed, opposite his place, as his successor.

But it was not everything to have brought up a son, to have had him taught medicine, and discovered Tostes, where he could practise it; he must have a wife. She found him one—the widow of a bailiff at Dieppe, who was forty-five and had an income of twelve hundred francs.

Though she was ugly, as dry as a bone, her face with as many pimples as the spring has buds, Madame Dubuc had no lack of suitors. To attain her ends Madame Bovary had to oust them all, and she even succeeded in very cleverly baffling the intrigues of a pork-butcher backed up by the priests.

Charles had seen in marriage the advent of an easier life, thinking he would be more free to do as he liked with himself and his money. But his wife was master; he had to say this and not say that in company, to fast every Friday, dress as she liked, harass at her bidding those patients who did not pay. She opened his letters, watched his comings and goings, and listened at the partition-wall when women came to consult him in his surgery.

She had to have her chocolate every morning, attentions without end. She constantly complained of her nerves, her chest, her liver. The noise of footsteps made her ill; when people went away, solitude became odious to her; if they came back, it was doubtless to see her die. When Charles returned in the evening, she stretched forth two long thin arms from beneath the sheets, put them round his neck, and having made him sit down on the edge of the bed, began to talk to him of her troubles: he was neglecting her, he loved another. She had been warned she would be unhappy; and she ended by asking him for a dose of medicine and a little more love.

---

the department in which the diploma had been conferred (Bovary is thus tied down to the vicinity of Rouen) and was not allowed to perform major operations except in the presence of a full-fledged doctor. The diploma was suppressed in 1892.

II

One night towards eleven o'clock they were awakened by the noise of a horse pulling up outside their door. The maid opened the garret-window and parleyed for some time with a man in the street below. He came for the doctor, had a letter for him. Nastasie came downstairs shivering and undid the locks and bolts one after the other. The man left his horse, and, following the servant, suddenly came in behind her. He pulled out from his wool cap with grey top-knots a letter wrapped up in a rag and presented it gingerly to Charles, who rested on his elbow on the pillow to read it. Nastasie, standing near the bed, held the light. Madame in modesty had turned to the wall and showed only her back.

This letter, sealed with a small seal in blue wax, begged Monsieur Bovary to come immediately to the farm of the Bertaux to set a broken leg. Now from Tostes to the Bertaux was a good fifteen miles across country by way of Longueville and Saint-Victor. It was a dark night; Madame Bovary junior was afraid of accidents for her husband. So it was decided the stable-boy should go on first; Charles would start three hours later when the moon rose. A boy was to be sent to meet him, in order to show him the way to the farm and open the gates for him.

Towards four o'clock in the morning, Charles, well wrapped up in his cloak, set out for the Bertaux. Still sleepy from the warmth of his bed, he let himself be lulled by the quiet trot of his horse. When it stopped of its own accord in front of those holes surrounded with thorns that are dug on the margin of furrows, Charles awoke with a start, suddenly remembered the broken leg, and tried to call to mind all the fractures he knew. The rain had stopped, day was breaking, and on the branches of the leafless trees birds roosted motionless, their little feathers bristling in the cold morning wind. The flat country stretched as far as eye could see, and the tufts of trees around the farms seemed, at long intervals, like dark violet stains on the vast grey surface, fading on the horizon into the gloom of the sky. Charles from time to time opened his eyes but his mind grew weary, and sleep coming upon him, he soon fell into a doze wherein his recent sensations blending with memories, he became conscious of a double self, at once student and married man, lying in his bed as but now, and crossing the operation theatre as of old. The warm smell of poultices mingled in his brain with the fresh odour of dew; he heard the iron rings rattling along the curtain-rods of the bed and saw his wife sleeping . . . As he passed Vassonville he came upon a boy sitting on the grass at the edge of a ditch.

"Are you the doctor?" asked the child.

And on Charles's answer he took his wooden shoes in his hands and ran on in front of him.

The *officier de santé*, riding along, gathered from his guide's talk that Monsieur Rouault must be one of the well-to-do farmers. He had broken his leg the evening before on his way home from a Twelfth-night feast at a neighbor's. His wife had been dead for two years. There was only his daughter, who helped him to keep house, with him.

The ruts were becoming deeper; they were approaching the Bertaux. The little farmboy, slipping through a hole in the hedge, disappeared; then he came back to the end of a courtyard to open the gate. The horse slipped on the wet grass; Charles had to stoop to pass under the branches. The watchdogs in their kennels barked, dragging at their chains. As he entered the Bertaux the horse took fright and stumbled.

It was a substantial-looking farm. In the stables, over the top of the open doors, one could see great cart-horses quietly feeding from new racks. Right along the outbuildings extended a large dunghill, smoking at the top, while amidst fowls and turkeys five or six peacocks, the luxury of Cauchois farmyards, were foraging around. The sheepfold was long, the barn high, with walls smooth as a hand. Under the cart-shed were two large carts and four ploughs, with their whips, shafts and harnesses complete, whose fleeces of blue wool were getting soiled by the fine dust that fell from the graneries. The courtyard sloped upwards, planted with trees set out symmetrically, and the chattering noise of a flock of geese was heard near the pond.

A young woman in a blue merino dress with three flounces came to the threshold of the door to receive Monsieur Bovary; she led him to the kitchen, where a large fire was blazing. The servants' breakfast was boiling beside it in small pots of all sizes. Some damp clothes were drying inside the chimney-corner. The shovel, tongs, and the nozzle of the bellows, all of colossal size, shone like polished steel, while along the walls hung many pots and pans in which the clear flame of the hearth, mingling with the first rays of the sun coming in through the window, was mirrored fitfully.

Charles went up to the first floor to see the patient. He found him in his bed, sweating under his bed-clothes, having thrown his cotton nightcap right away from him. He was a fat little man of fifty, with white skin and blue eyes, the fore part of his head bald, and he wore ear-rings. By his side on a chair stood a large decanter of brandy, from which he poured himself out a little from time to time to keep up his spirits; but as soon as he caught sight of the doctor his elation subsided, and instead of swearing, as he had been doing for the last twelve hours, he began to groan feebly.

The fracture was a simple one, without any kind of complication. Charles could not have hoped for an easier case. Then calling to mind the devices of his masters at the bedside of patients, he comforted the sufferer with all sorts of kindly remarks, those caresses of the surgeon that are like the oil they put on scalpels. In order to make some splints a bundle of laths was brought up from the carthouse. Charles selected one, cut it into two pieces and planed it with a fragment of windowpane, while the servant tore up sheets to make bandages, and Mademoiselle Emma tried to sew some pads. As she was a long time before she found her workcase, her father grew impatient; she did not answer, but as she sewed she pricked her fingers, which she then put to her mouth to suck them.

Charles was surprised at the whiteness of her nails. They were shiny, delicate at the tips, more polished than the ivory of Dieppe, and almond-shaped. Yet her hand was not beautiful, perhaps not white enough, and a little hard at the knuckles; besides, it was too long, with no soft inflections in the outlines. Her real beauty was in her eyes. Although brown, they seemed black because of the lashes, and her look came at you frankly, with a candid boldness.

The bandaging over, the doctor was invited by Monsieur Rouault himself to have a bite before he left.

Charles went down into the room on the ground-floor. Knives and forks and silver goblets were laid for two on a little table at the foot of a huge bed that had a canopy of printed cotton with figures representing Turks. There was an odor of iris-root and damp sheets that escaped from a large oak chest opposite the window. On the floor in corners were sacks of flour stuck upright in rows. These were the overflow from the neighboring granary, to which three stone steps led. By way of decoration for the apartment, hanging to a nail in the middle of the wall, whose green paint scaled off from the effects of the saltpeter, was a crayon head of Minerva in a gold frame, underneath which was written in Gothic letters "To my dear Papa."

First they spoke of the patient, then of the weather, of the great cold, of the wolves that infested the fields at night. Mademoiselle Rouault did not at all like the country, especially now that she had to look after the farm almost alone. As the room was chilly, she shivered as she ate. This showed something of her full lips, that she had a habit of biting when silent.

Her neck stood out from a white turned-down collar. Her hair, whose two black folds seemed each of a single piece, so smooth were they, was parted in the middle by a delicate line that curved slightly with the curve of the head; and, just showing the tip of the ear, it was joined behind in a thick chignon, with a wavy movement at the temples that the country doctor saw now for the first time in his life. The upper part of her cheek was rose-coloured. Like a man, she wore a tortoise-shell eyeglass thrust between two buttons of her blouse.

When Charles, after bidding farewell to old Rouault, returned to the room before leaving, he found her standing, her forehead against the window, looking into the garden, where the beanpoles had been knocked down by the wind. She turned around. "Are you looking for something?" she asked.

"My riding crop, if you please," he answered.

He began rummaging on the bed, behind the doors, under the chairs. It had fallen to the ground, between the sacks and the wall. Mademoiselle Emma saw it, and bent over the flour sacks. Charles out of politeness made a dash also, and as he stretched out his arm, at the same moment felt his breast brush against the back of the young girl bending beneath him. She drew herself up, scarlet, and looked at him over her shoulder as she handed him his riding crop.

Instead of returning to the Bertaux in three days as he had promised, he went back the very next day, then regularly twice a week, without counting the visits he paid now and then as if by accident.

Everything, moreover, went well; the patient progressed favorably; and when, at the end of forty-six days, old Rouault was seen trying to walk alone in his "den," Monsieur Bovary began to be looked upon as a man of great capacity. Old Rouault said that he could not have been cured better by the first doctor of Yvetot, or even of Rouen.

As to Charles, he did not stay to ask himself why it was a pleasure to him to go to the Bertaux. Had he done so, he would, no doubt have attributed his zeal to the importance of the case, or perhaps to the money he hoped to make by it. Was it for this, however, that his visits to the farm formed a delightful exception to the barren occupations of his life? On these days he rose early, set off at a gallop, urging on his horse, then got down to wipe his boots in the grass and put on black gloves before entering. He liked seeing himself enter the courtyard, and noticing the gate turn against his shoulder, the cock crow on the wall, the farmboys run to meet him. He liked the granary and the stables; he liked old Rouault, who pressed his hand and called him his saviour; he liked the small wooden shoes of Mademoiselle Emma on the scoured flags of the kitchen—her high heels made her a little taller; and when she walked in front of him, the wooden soles springing up quickly struck with a sharp sound against the leather of her boots.

She always reconducted him to the first step of the porch. When his horse had not yet been brought round she stayed there. They had said "Good-bye"; there was no more talking. The open air wrapped her round, playing with the soft down on the back of her neck, or blew to and fro on her hips her apron-strings, that fluttered like streamers. Once, during a thaw, the bark of the trees in the yard was oozing, the snow melted on the roofs of the buildings; she stood on the threshold, went to fetch her sunshade and opened it. The parasol, made of an iridescent silk that let the sunlight sift through, colored the white skin of her face with shifting reflections. Beneath it, she smiled at the gentle warmth; drops of water fell one by one on the taut silk.

During the first period of Charles's visits to the Bertaux, the younger Madame Bovary never failed to inquire after the invalid, and she had even chosen in the book that she kept on a system of double entry a clean blank page for Monsieur Rouault. But when she heard he had a daughter, she began to make inquiries, and she learnt that Mademoiselle Rouault, brought up at the Ursuline Convent, had received what is called "a good education"; and so knew dancing, geography, drawing, how to embroider and play the piano. That was the last straw.

"So that's why he looks so beaming when he goes to see her," she thought. "That's why he puts on his new waistcoat regardless of the rain. Ah! that woman! that woman!"

And she detested her instinctively. At first she solaced herself by allusions that Charles did not understand, then by casual observations that he let pass for fear of a storm, finally by open apostrophes to which he knew no reply.—Why did he go back to the Bertaux now that Monsieur Rouault was cured and that the bill was still unpaid? Ah! it was because a certain person was there, some one who knew how to talk, to embroider, to be witty. So that was what he liked; he wanted city girls! And she went on:

"Imagine old Rouault's daughter being taken for a city girl! The grandfather was a shepherd and a cousin of theirs barely escaped being sentenced for nearly killing someone in a brawl. Hardly a reason to put on airs, or showing herself in church dressed in silk, like a countess. If it hadn't been for the colza crop last year, the old fellow would have been hard put paying his arrears."

For very weariness Charles left off going to the Bertaux. Héloïse made him swear, his hand on the prayer-book, that he would go there no more, after much sobbing and many kisses, in a great outburst of love. He obeyed then, but the strength of his desire protested against the servility of his conduct; and he thought, with a kind of naïve hypocrisy, that this interdict to see her gave him a sort of right to love her. And then the widow was thin; she had long teeth; wore in all weathers a little black shawl, the edge of which hung down between her shoulder-blades; her bony figure was sheathed in her clothes as if they were a scabbard; they were too short, and displayed her ankles with the laces of her large boots crossed over grey stockings.

Charles's mother came to see them from time to time, but after a few days the daughter-in-law seemed to put her own edge on her, and then, like two knives, they scarified him with their reflections and observations. It was wrong of him to eat so much. Why did he always offer a free drink to everyone who came along? How stubborn of him not to put on flannel underwear!

In the spring it came about that a notary at Ingouville, who managed the widow Dubuc's property, one fine day vanished, taking with him all the money in his office. Héloïse, it is true, still owned, besides a share in a boat valued at six thousand francs, her house in the Rue St. François; and yet, with all this fortune that had been so trumpeted abroad, nothing, excepting perhaps a little furniture and a few clothes, had appeared in the household. The matter had to be gone into. The house at Dieppe was found to be eaten up with mortgages to its foundations; what she had placed with the notary God only knew, and her share in the boat did not exceed three thousand francs. She had lied, the good lady! In his exasperation, Monsieur Bovary the elder, smashing a chair on the stone floor, accused his wife of having caused the misfortune of their son by harnessing him to such a harridan, whose harness wasn't worth her hide. They came to Tostes. Explanations followed. There were scenes. Héloïse in tears, throwing her arms about her husband, conjured him to defend her from his parents. Charles tried to speak up for her. They grew angry and left the house.

But "the blow had struck home." A week after, as she was hanging up some washing in her yard, she was seized with a spitting of blood, and the next day, while Charles had his back turned and was closing the window curtains, she said, "O God!" gave a sigh and fainted. She was dead! What a surprise!

When all was over at the cemetery Charles went home. He found no one downstairs; he went up to the first floor to their room; saw her dress still hanging at the foot of the alcove; then leaning against the writing-table, he stayed until the evening, buried in a sorrowful reverie. She had loved him after all!

III

One morning old Rouault brought Charles the money for setting his leg—seventy-five francs in forty-sou pieces, and a turkey. He had heard of his loss, and consoled him as well as he could.

"I know what it is," said he, clapping him on the shoulder; "I've been through it. When I lost my poor wife, I went into the field to be alone. I fell at the foot of a tree; I cried; I called on God; I talked nonsense to Him. I wanted to be like the moles that I saw on the branches, their insides swarming with maggots, in short, dead, and an end of it. And when I thought that there were others at that very moment, with their wives in their arms, I struck great blows on the earth with my stick. I almost went out of my mind, to the point of not eating; the very idea of going to a café disgusted me—you wouldn't believe it. Well, very slowly, one day following another, a spring on a winter, and an autumn after a summer, this wore away, piece by piece, crumb by crumb; it passed away, it is gone, I should say it has sunk; for something always remains inside, as we would say—a weight here, at one's heart. But since it is the lot of all of us, one must not give way altogether, and, because others have died, want to die too. You must pull yourself together, Monsieur Bovary. It will pass away. Come and see us; my daughter thinks of you time and again, you know, and she says you are forgetting her. Spring will soon be here. We'll have you shoot a rabbit in the field to help you get over your sorrows."

Charles followed his advice. He went back to the Bertaux. He found all as he had left it, that is to say, as it was five months ago. The pear trees were already in blossom, and Farmer Rouault, on his legs again, came and went, making the farm more lively.

Thinking it his duty to heap the greatest attention upon the doctor because of his sad situation, he begged him not to take his hat off, spoke to him in whispers as if he had been ill, and even pretended to be angry because nothing lighter had been prepared for him than for the others, such as a little custard or stewed pears. He told stories. Charles found himself laughing, but the remembrance of his wife suddenly coming back to him depressed him. Coffee was brought in; he thought no more about her.

He thought less of her as he grew accustomed to living alone. The new delight of independence soon made his loneliness bearable. He could now change his meal-times, go in or out without explanation, and when he was very tired stretch himself at full length on his bed. So he nursed and coddled himself and accepted the consolations that were offered him. On the other hand, the death of his wife had not served him ill in his business, since for a month people had been saying, "The poor young man! what a loss!" His name had been talked about, his practice had increased; and, moreover, he could go to the Bertaux just as he liked. He had an aimless hope, and a vague happiness; he thought himself better looking as he brushed his whiskers before the looking-glass.

One day he got there about three o'clock. Everybody was in the fields. He went into the kitchen, but did not at once catch sight of Emma; the outside shutters were closed. Through the chinks of the wood the sun sent across the flooring long fine rays that were broken at the corners of the furniture and trembled along the ceiling. Some flies on the table were crawling up the glasses that had been used, and buzzing as they drowned themselves in the dregs of the cider. The daylight that came in by the chimney made velvet of the soot at the back of the fireplace, and touched with blue the cold cinders. Between the window and the hearth Emma was sewing; she wore no scarf; he could see small drops of perspiration on her bare shoulders.

After the fashion of country folks she asked him to have something to drink. He said no; she insisted, and at last laughingly offered to have a glass of liqueur with him. So she went to fetch a bottle of curaçoa from the cupboard, reached down two small glasses, filled one to the brim, poured scarcely anything into the other, and, after having clinked glasses, carried hers to her mouth. As it was almost empty she bent back to drink, her head thrown back, her lips pouting, her neck straining. She laughed at getting none, while with the tip of her tongue passing between her small teeth she licked drop by drop the bottom of her glass.

She sat down again and took up her work, a white cotton stocking she was darning. She worked with her head bent down; she did not speak, nor did Charles. The air coming in under the door blew a little dust over the stone floor; he watched it drift along, and heard nothing but the throbbing in his head and the faint clucking of a hen that had laid an egg in the yard. Emma from time to time cooled her cheeks with the palms of her hands, and cooled these again on the knobs of the huge fire-dogs.

She complained of suffering since the beginning of the spring from giddiness; she asked if sea-baths would do her any good; she began talking of her convent, Charles of his school; words came to them. They went up into her bed-room. She showed him her old music-books, the little prizes she had won, and the oak-leaf crowns, left at the bottom of a cupboard. She spoke to him, too, of her mother, of the country, and even showed him the bed in the garden where, on the first Friday of every month, she gathered flowers to put on her mother's tomb. But their gardener understood nothing about it; servants were so careless. She would have dearly liked, if only for the winter, to live in town, although the length of the fine days made the country perhaps even more wearisome in the summer. And, according to what she was saying, her voice was clear, sharp, or, suddenly all languor, lingering out in modulations that ended almost in murmurs as she spoke to herself, now joyous, opening big naïve eyes, then with her eyelids half closed, her look full of boredom, her thoughts wandering.

Going home at night, Charles went over her words one by one, trying to recall them, to fill out their sense, that he might piece out the life she had lived before he knew her. But he never saw her in his thoughts other than he had seen her the first time, or as he had just left her. Then he asked himself what would become of her—if she would be married, and to whom? Alas! old Rouault was rich, and she!—so beautiful! But Emma's face always rose before his eyes, and a monotone, like the humming of a top, sounded in his ears, "If you should marry after all! if you should marry!" At night he could not sleep; his throat was parched; he was thirsty. He got up to drink from the water-bottle and opened the window. The night was covered with stars, a warm wind blowing in the distance; the dogs were barking. He turned his head towards the Bertaux.

Thinking that, after all, he had nothing to lose, Charles promised himself to ask her in marriage at the earliest opportunity, but each time the fear of not finding the right words sealed his lips.

Old Rouault would not have been sorry to be rid of his daughter, who was of no use to him in the house. In his heart he excused her, thinking her too clever for farming, a calling under the ban of Heaven, since one never saw a millionaire in it. Far from having made a fortune, the old man was losing every year; for if he was good at bargaining and enjoyed the dodges of the trade, he was the poorest of growers or farm managers. He did not willingly take his hands out of his pockets, and did not spare expense for his own comforts, liking to eat and to sleep well, and never to suffer from the cold. He liked old cider, underdone legs of mutton, brandied coffee well beaten up. He took his meals in the kitchen, alone, opposite the fire on a little table brought to him already laid as on the stage.

When, therefore, he perceived that Charles's cheeks grew flushed if near his daughter, which meant that he would propose one of these days, he mulled over the entire matter beforehand. He certainly thought him somewhat weak, not quite the son-in-law he would have liked, but he was said to be well-behaved, prudent with his money as well as learned, and no doubt would not make too many difficulties about the dowry. Now, as old Rouault would soon be forced to sell twenty-two acres of his land as he owed a good deal to the mason, to the harnessmaker, and as the shaft of the cider-press wanted renewing, "If he asks for her," he said to himself, "I'll give her to him."

In the early fall Charles went to spend three days at the Bertaux. The last had passed like the others in procrastinating from hour to hour. Old Rouault was seeing him off; they were walking along a dirt road full of ruts; they were about to part. This was the time. Charles gave himself as far as to the corner of the hedge, and at last, when past it . . .

"Monsieur Rouault," he murmured, "I should like to say something to you."

They stopped. Charles was silent.

"Well, tell me your story. Don't I know all about it?" said old

Rouault, laughing softly.

"Monsieur Rouault—Monsieur Rouault," stammered Charles.

"I ask nothing better," the farmer went on. "Although, no doubt, the little one agrees with me, still we must ask her opinion. So you get off—I'll go back home. If it is 'yes,' you needn't return because of all the people around, and besides it would upset her too much. But so that you may not be biting your fingernails with impatience, I'll open wide the outer shutter of the window against the wall; you can see it from the back by leaning over the hedge."

And he went off.

Charles fastened his horse to a tree; he ran into the road and waited. Half-an-hour passed, then he counted nineteen minutes by his watch. Suddenly a noise was heard against the wall; the shutter had been thrown back; the hook was still quivering.

The next day by nine o'clock he was at the farm. Emma blushed as he entered, and she gave a little forced laugh to hide her embarrassment. Old Rouault embraced his future son-in-law. The discussion of money matters was put off; moreover, there was plenty of time before them, as the marriage could not decently take place till Charles was out of mourning, that is to say, about the spring of the next year.

The winter passed waiting for this. Mademoiselle Rouault was busy with her trousseau. Part of it was ordered at Rouen, and she made herself slips and nightcaps after fashionplates that she borrowed. When Charles visited the farmer, the preparations for the wedding were talked over; they wondered in what room they should have dinner; they dreamed of the number of dishes that would be wanted, and what should be the entrées.

Emma would, on the contrary, have preferred to have a midnight wedding with torches, but old Rouault could not understand such an idea. So there was a wedding at which forty-three persons were present, at which they remained sixteen hours at table, began again the next day, and even carried a little into the following days.

IV

The guests arrived early in carriages, in one-horse chaises, two-wheeled cars, old open gigs, vans with leather curtains, and the young people from the nearer villages in carts, in which they stood up in rows, holding on to the sides so as not to fall, going at a trot and well shaken up. Some came from a distance of thirty miles, from Goderville, from Normanville, and from Cany. All the relatives of both families had been invited, old quarrels had been patched up and near-forgotten acquaintances written to for the occasion.

From time to time one heard the crack of a whip behind the hedge; then the gates opened, a chaise entered. Galloping up to the foot of the steps, it stopped short and emptied its load. They got down from all sides, rubbing knees and stretching arms. The ladies, wearing bonnets, had on dresses in the town fashion, gold watch chains, pelerines with the ends tucked into belts, or little coloured scarfs fastened down behind with a pin, and that left the back of the neck bare. The boys, dressed like their papas, seemed uncomfortable in their new clothes (many that day were wearing their first pair of boots), and by their sides, speaking never a word, wearing the white dress of their first communion lengthened for the occasion, were some big girls of fourteen or sixteen, cousins or elder sisters no doubt, scarlet, bewildered, their hair greasy with rose-pomade, and very much afraid of dirtying their gloves. As there were not enough stable-boys to unharness all the carriages, the gentlemen turned up their sleeves and set about it themselves. According to their different social positions they wore tail-coats, overcoats, shooting-jackets, cutaway-coats: fine tail-coats, redolent of family respectability, that only came out of the wardrobe on state occasions; overcoats with long tails flapping in the wind and round capes and pockets like sacks; shooting-jackets of coarse cloth, generally worn with a cap with a brass-bound peak; very short cutaway-coats with two small buttons in the back, close together like a pair of eyes, and the tails of which seemed cut out of one piece by a carpenter's hatchet. Some, too (but these, you may be sure, would sit at the bottom of the table), wore their best smocks—that is to say, with collars turned down to the shoulders, the back gathered into small plaits and the waist fastened very low down with a stitched belt.

And the shirts stood out from the chests like armour breastplates! Everyone had just had his hair cut; ears stood out from the heads; they had been close-shaven; a few, even, who had had to get up before daybreak, and not been able to see to shave, had diagonal gashes under their noses or cuts the size of a three-franc piece along the jaws, which the fresh air had enflamed during the trip, so that the great white beaming faces were mottled here and there with red spots.

The mairie was a mile and a half from the farm, and they went there on foot, returning in the same way after the ceremony in the church. The procession, first united like one long coloured scarf that undulated across the fields, along the narrow path winding amid the green wheat, soon lengthened out, and broke up into different groups that loitered to talk. The fiddler walked in front with his violin, gay with ribbons at its pegs. Then came the married pair, the relatives, the friends, all following pell-mell; the children stayed behind amusing themselves plucking the bell-flowers from oat-ears, or playing amongst themselves unseen. Emma's dress, too long, trailed a little on the ground; from time to time she stopped to pull it up, and then delicately, with her gloved hands, she picked off the coarse grass and the thistles, while Charles, empty handed, waited till she had finished. Old Rouault, with a new silk hat and the cuffs of his black coat covering his hands up to the nails, gave his arm to Madame Bovary senior. As to Monsieur Bovary senior, who, heartily despising all these people, had come simply in a frock-coat of military cut with one row of buttons—he was exchanging barroom banter with a blond young farmgirl. She bowed, blushed, and did not know what to say. The other wedding guests talked business or played tricks behind each other's backs, egging each other on in advance for the fun that was to come. Those who listened could always catch the squeaking of the fiddler, who went on playing across the fields. When he saw that the rest were far behind he stopped to take breath, slowly rosined his bow, so that the strings should squeak all the louder, then set off again, by turns lowering and raising the neck of his violin, the better to mark time for himself. The noise of the instrument drove away the little birds from afar.

The table was laid under the cart-shed. On it were four roasts of beef, six chicken fricassées, stewed veal, three legs of mutton, and in the middle a fine roast sucking-pig, flanked by four pork sausages with sorrel. At the corners were decanters of brandy. Sweet bottled-cider frothed round the corks, and all the glasses had been filled to the brim with wine beforehand. Large dishes of yellow cream, that trembled with the least shake of the table, had designed on their smooth surface the initials of the newly wedded pair in nonpareil arabesques. A confectioner of Yvetot had been entrusted with the pies and candies. As he had only just started out in the neighborhood, he had taken a lot of trouble, and at dessert he himself brought in a wedding cake that provoked loud cries of wonderment. At its base there was a square of blue cardboard, representing a temple with porticoes, colonnades, and stucco statuettes all round, and in the niches constellations of gilt paper stars; then on the second level was a dungeon of Savoy cake, surrounded by many fortifications in candied angelica, almonds, raisins, and quarters of oranges; and finally, on the upper platform a green field with rocks set in lakes of jam, nutshell boats, and a small Cupid balancing himself in a chocolate swing whose two uprights ended in real roses for balls at the top.

Until night they ate. When any of them were too tired of sitting, they went out for a stroll in the yard, or for a game of darts in the granary, and then returned to table. Some towards the end went to sleep and snored. But with the coffee every one woke up. Then they began songs, showed off tricks, raised heavy weights, competed to see who could pass his head under his arm while keeping a thumb on the table, tried lifting carts on their shoulders, made bawdy jokes, kissed the women. At night when they left, the horses, stuffed up to the nostrils with oats, could hardly be got into the shafts; they kicked, reared, the harness broke, their masters laughed or swore; and all night in the light of the moon along country roads there were runaway carts at full gallop plunging into the ditches, jumping over yard after yard of stones, clambering up the hills, with women leaning out from the tilt to catch hold of the reins.

Those who stayed at the Bertaux spent the night drinking in the kitchen. The children had fallen asleep under the seats.

The bride had begged her father to be spared the usual marriage pleasantries. However, a fishmonger, one of their cousins (who had brought a pair of soles for his wedding present), began to squirt water from his mouth through the keyhole, when old Rouault came up just in time to stop him, and explain to him that the distinguished position of his son-in-law would not allow of such liberties. The cousin was not easily convinced. In his heart he accused old Rouault of being proud, and he joined four or five other guests in a corner, who, through mere chance, had been served the poorer cuts of meat several times over and also considered themselves ill-treated. They were whispering about their host, hoping with covered hints that he would ruin himself.

Madame Bovary, senior, had not opened her mouth all day. She had been consulted neither as to the dress of her daughter-in-law nor as to the arrangement of the feast; she went to bed early. Her husband, instead of following her, sent to Saint-Victor for some cigars, and smoked till daybreak, drinking kirsch-punch, a mixture unknown to the company that added even more to the consideration in which he was held.

Charles, who was anything but quick-witted, did not shine at the wedding. He answered feebly to the puns, *doubles entendres*, compliments, and the customary pleasantries that were dutifully aimed at him as soon as the soup appeared.

The next day, on the other hand, he seemed another man. It was he who might rather have been taken for the virgin of the evening before, whilst the bride gave no sign that revealed anything. The shrewdest did not know what to make of it, and they looked at her when she passed near them with an unbounded concentration of mind. But Charles concealed nothing. He called her "my wife," addressed her by the familiar "tu," asked for her of everyone, looked for her everywhere, and often he dragged her into the yards, where he could be seen from far between the trees, putting his arm round her waist, and walking half-bending over her, ruffling the collar of her blouse with his head.

Two days after the wedding the married pair left. Charles, on account of his patients, could not be away longer. Old Rouault had them driven back in his cart, and himself accompanied them as far as Vassonville. Here he embraced his daughter for the last time, got down, and went his way. When he had gone about a hundred paces he stopped, and as he saw the cart disappearing, its wheels turning in the dust, he gave a deep sigh. Then he remembered his wedding, the old times, the first pregnancy of his wife; he, too, had been very happy the day when he had taken her from her father to his home, and had carried her off riding pillion, trotting through the snow, for it was near Christmas-time, and the country was all white. She held him by one arm, her basket hanging from the other; the wind blew the long lace of her Cauchois headdress so that it sometimes flapped across his mouth, and when he turned his head he saw near him, on his shoulder, her little rosy face, smiling silently under the gold bands of her cap. To warm her hands she put them from time to time in his breast. How long ago it all was! Their son would have been thirty by now. Then he looked back and saw nothing on the road. He felt dreary as an empty house; and tender memories mingling with sad thoughts in his brain, addled by the fumes of the feast, he felt inclined for a moment to take a turn towards the church. As he was afraid, however, that this sight would make him even sadder, he went right away home.

Monsieur and Madame Charles arrived at Tostes about six o'clock. The neighbors came to the windows to see their doctor's new wife.

The old servant presented herself, curtsied to her, apologised for not having dinner ready, and suggested that madame, in the meantime, should look over her house.

V

The brick front was just in a line with the street, or rather the road. Behind the door hung a cloak with a small collar, a bridle, and a black leather cap, and on the floor, in a corner, were a pair of leggings, still covered with dry mud. On the right was the one room that was both dining and sitting room. A canary-yellow paper, relieved at the top by a garland of pale flowers, was puckered everywhere over the badly-stretched canvas; white calico curtains with a red border hung crossways the length of the window; and on the narrow mantelpiece a clock with a head of Hippocrates shone resplendent between two plate candlesticks under oval shades. On the other side of the passage was Charles's consulting-room, a little room about six paces wide, with a table, three chairs, and an office-chair. Volumes of the "Dictionary of Medical Science," uncut, but the binding rather the worse for the successive sales through which they had gone, occupied almost alone the six shelves of a pinewood bookcase. The smell of sauces penetrated through the walls when he saw patients, just as in the kitchen one could hear the people coughing in the consulting-room and recounting their whole histories. Then, opening on the yard, where the stable was, came a large dilapidated room with a stove, now used as a wood-house, cellar, and pantry, full of old rubbish, of empty casks, discarded garden tools, and a mass of dusty things whose use it was impossible to guess.

The garden, longer than wide, ran between two mud walls covered with espaliered apricot trees, to a thorn hedge that separated it from the field. In the middle was a slate sundial on a brick pedestal; four flower-beds with eglantines surrounded symmetrically the more useful vegetable garden. Right at the bottom, under the spruce bushes, a plaster priest was reading his breviary.

Emma went upstairs. The first room was not furnished, but in the second, the conjugal bedroom, was a mahogany bedstead in an alcove with red drapery. A shell-box adorned the chest of drawers, and on the secretary near the window a bouquet of orange blossoms tied with white satin ribbons stood in a bottle. It was a bride's bouquet: the other one's. She looked at it. Charles noticed; he took the bouquet, carried it to the attic, while Emma seated in an armchair (they were putting her things down around her) thought of her bridal flowers packed up in a bandbox, and wondered, dreaming, what would be done with them if she were to die.

During the first days she kept busy thinking about changes in the house. She took the shades off the candlesticks, had new wall-paper put up, the staircase repainted, and seats made in the garden round the sundial; she even inquired how she could get a basin with a jet fountain and fishes. Finally her husband, knowing that she liked to drive out, picked up a second-hand dogcart, which, with new lamps and a splashboard in striped leather, looked almost like a tilbury.

He was happy then, and without a care in the world. A meal together, a walk in the evening on the highroad, a gesture of her hands over her hair, the sight of her straw hat hanging from the window-fastener, and many other things of which he had never suspected how pleasant they could be, now made up the endless round of his happiness. In bed, in the morning, by her side, on the pillow, he watched the sunlight sinking into the down on her fair cheek, half hidden by the ribbons of her nightcap. Seen thus closely, her eyes looked to him enlarged, especially when, on waking up, she opened and shut her eyelids rapidly many times. Black in the shade, dark blue in broad daylight, they had, as it were, depths of successive colors that, more opaque in the center, grew more transparent towards the surface of the eye. His own eyes lost themselves in these depths and he could see himself mirrored in miniature, down to his shoulders, with his scarf round his head and the top of his shirt open. He rose. She came to the window to see him off, and stayed leaning on the sill between two pots of geranium, clad in her dressing-gown hanging loosely about her. Charles, in the street, buckled his spurs, his foot on the mounting stone, while she talked to him from above, picking with her mouth some scrap of flower or leaf that she blew out at him and which, eddying, floating, described semicircles in the air like a bird, caught before it reached the ground in the ill-groomed mane of the old white mare standing motionless at the door. Charles from horseback threw her a kiss; she answered with a nod; she shut the window, and he set off. And then, along the endless dusty ribbon of the highroad, along the deep lanes that the trees bent over as in arbours, along paths where the wheat reached to the knees, with the sun on his back and the morning air in his nostrils, his heart full of the joys of the past night, his mind at rest, his flesh at ease, he went on, re-chewing his happiness, like those who after dinner taste again the truffles which they are digesting.

Until now what good had he had of his life? His time at school, when he remained shut up within the high walls, alone, in the midst of companions richer than he or cleverer at their work, who laughed at his accent, who jeered at his clothes, and whose mothers came to the school with cakes in their muffs? Later on, when he studied medicine, and never had his purse full enough to take out dancing some little work-girl who would have become his mistress? Afterwards, he had lived fourteen months with the widow, whose feet in bed were cold as icicles. But now he had for life this beautiful woman whom he adored. For him the universe did not extend beyond the silky circumference of her petticoat. He reproached himself for not loving her enough; he wanted to see her again, turned back quickly, ran up the stairs with a beating heart. Emma, in her room, was dressing; he came up on tiptoe, kissed her back; she cried out in surprise.

He could not keep from constantly touching her comb, her rings, her scarf; sometimes he gave her great sounding kisses with all his mouth on her cheeks, or else little kisses in a row all along her bare arm from the tip of her fingers up to her shoulder, and she put him away half-smiling, half-annoyed, as one does with a clinging child.

Before marriage she thought herself in love; but since the happiness that should have followed failed to come, she must, she thought, have been mistaken. And Emma tried to find out what one meant exactly in life by the words *bliss*, *passion*, *ecstasy*, that had seemed to her so beautiful in books.

VI

She had read "Paul and Virginia," and she had dreamed of the little bamboo-house, the negro Domingo, the dog Fidèle, but above all of the sweet friendship of some dear little brother, who seeks red fruit for you on trees taller than steeples, or who runs barefoot over the sand, bringing you a bird's nest.

When she was thirteen, her father himself took her to town to place her in the convent. They stopped at an inn in the St. Gervais quarter, where, at their supper, they used painted plates that set forth the story of Mademoiselle de la Vallière.[9] The explanatory legends, chipped here and there by the scratching of knives, all glorified religion, the tendernesses of the heart, and the pomps of court.

Far from being bored at first at the convent, she took pleasure in the society of the good sisters, who, to amuse her, took her to the chapel, which one entered from the refectory by a long corridor. She played very little during recreation hours, knew her catechism well, and it was she who always answered the Vicar's difficult questions. Living thus, without ever leaving the warm atmosphere of the class-rooms, and amid these pale-faced women wearing rosaries with brass crosses, she was softly lulled by the mystic languor exhaled in the perfumes of the altar, the freshness of the holy water, and the lights of the tapers. Instead of following mass, she looked at the pious vignettes with their azure borders in her book, and she loved the sick lamb, the sacred heart pierced with sharp arrows, or the poor Jesus sinking beneath the cross he carried. She tried, by way of mortification, to eat nothing a whole day. She puzzled her head to find some vow to fulfil.

When she went to confession, she invented little sins in order that she might stay there longer, kneeling in the shadow, her hands joined, her face against the grating beneath the whispering of the priest. The comparisons of betrothed, husband, celestial lover, and eternal marriage, that recur in sermons, stirred within her soul depths of unexpected sweetness.

In the evening, before prayers, there was some religious reading in the study. On week-nights it was some abstract of sacred history or the Lectures of the Abbé Frayssinous, and on Sundays passages from the "Génie du Christianisme," as a recreation. How she listened at first to the sonorous lamentations of romantic melancholy re-echoing through the world and eternity! If her childhood had been spent in the shops of a busy city section, she might perhaps have opened her heart to those lyrical invasions of Nature, which usually come to us only through translation in books. But she knew the country too well; she knew the lowing of cattle, the milking, the ploughs. Accustomed to the quieter aspects of life, she turned instead to its tumultuous parts. She loved the sea only for the sake of

9. One of Louis XIV's mistresses, whose mythologized character is familiar to all readers of Alexandre Dumas's *Le Vicomte de Bragelonne* (a sequel to *The Three Musketeers*).

its storms, and the green only when it was scattered among ruins. She had to gain some personal profit from things and she rejected as useless whatever did not contribute to the immediate satisfaction of her heart's desires—being of a temperament more sentimental than artistic, looking for emotions, not landscapes.

At the convent there was an old maid who came for a week each month to mend the linen. Patronised by the clergy, because she belonged to an ancient family of noblemen ruined by the Revolution, she dined in the refectory at the table of the good sisters, and after the meal chatted with them for a while before going back to her work. The girls often slipped out from the study to go and see her. She knew by heart the love-songs of the last century, and sang them in a low voice as she stitched away. She told stories, gave them news, ran their errands in the town, and on the sly lent the big girls some of the novels, that she always carried in the pockets of her apron, and of which the lady herself swallowed long chapters in the intervals of her work. They were all about love, lovers, sweethearts, persecuted ladies fainting in lonely pavilions, postilions killed at every relay, horses ridden to death on every page, sombre forests, heart-aches, vows, sobs, tears and kisses, little boatrides by moonlight, nightingales in shady groves, gentlemen brave as lions, gentle as lambs, virtuous as no one ever was, always well dressed, and weeping like fountains. For six months, then, a fifteen year old Emma dirtied her hands with the greasy dust of old lending libraries. With Walter Scott, later on, she fell in love with historical events, dreamed of guardrooms, old oak chests and minstrels. She would have liked to live in some old manor-house, like those long-waisted chatelaines who, in the shade of pointed arches, spent their days leaning on the stone, chin in hand, watching a white-plumed knight galloping on his black horse from the distant fields. At this time she had a cult for Mary Stuart and enthusiastic veneration for illustrious or unhappy women. Joan of Arc, Héloïse, Agnès Sorel, the beautiful Ferronière, and Clémence Isaure[1] stood out to her like comets in the dark immensity of history, where also were seen, lost in shadow, and all unconnected, St. Louis with his oak, the dying Bayard, some cruelties of Louis XI, a little of St. Bartholomew's, the plume of the Béarnais, and always the remembrance of the painted plates glorifying Louis XIV.

In the music-class, the ballads she sang were all about little angels with golden wings, madonnas, lagunes, gondoliers; harmless-

---

1. Agnès Sorel (1422–50) was a mistress of Charles VII, rumored to have been poisoned by the future Louis XI; *"la belle Ferronière"* (died in 1540) was one of François I's mistresses, wife of the lawyer Le Ferron who is said to have contracted syphilis for the mere satisfaction of passing it on to the king; Clémence Isaure is a half-fictional lady from Toulouse (fourteenth century), popularized in a novel by Florian as an incarnation of the mystical poetry of the troubadours.

sounding compositions that, in spite of the inanity of the style and the vagueness of the melody, enabled one to catch a glimpse of the tantalizing phantasmagoria of sentimental realities. Some of her companions brought keepsakes given them as new year's gifts to the convent. These had to be hidden; it was quite an undertaking; they were read in the dormitory. Delicately handling the beautiful satin bindings, Emma looked with dazzled eyes at the names of the unknown authors, who had signed their verses for the most part as counts or viscounts.

She trembled as she blew back the thin transparent paper over the engraving and saw it folded in two and fall gently against the page. Here behind the balustrade of a balcony was a young man in a short cloak, holding in his arms a young girl in a white dress who was wearing an alms-bag at her belt; or there were nameless portraits of English ladies with fair curls, who looked at you from under their round straw hats with their large clear eyes. Some could be seen lounging in their carriages, gliding through parks, a greyhound bounding along ahead of the equipage, driven at a trot by two small postilions in white breeches. Others, dreaming on sofas with an open letter, gazed at the moon through a slightly open window half draped by a black curtain. The innocent ones, a tear on their cheeks, were kissing doves through the bars of a Gothic cage, or, smiling, their heads on one side, were plucking the leaves of a marguerite with their taper fingers, that curved at the tips like peaked shoes. And you, too, were there, Sultans with long pipes reclining beneath arbours in the arms of Bayadères; Giaours, curved swords, fezzes; and you especially, pale landscapes of dithyrambic lands, that often show us at once palm-trees and firs, tigers on the right, a lion to the left, Tartar minarets on the horizon, Roman ruins in the foreground with some kneeling camels besides; the whole framed by a very neat virgin forest, and with a great perpendicular sunbeam trembling in the water, where, sharply edged on a steel-grey background, white swans are swimming here and there.

And the shade of the oil lamp fastened to the wall above Emma's head lighted up all these pictures of the world, that passed before her one by one in the silence of the dormitory, and to the distant noise of some belated carriage still rolling down the Boulevards.

When her mother died she cried much the first few days. She had a funeral picture made with the hair of the deceased, and, in a letter sent to the Bertaux full of sad reflections on life, she asked to be buried later on in the same grave. The old man thought she must be ill, and came to see her. Emma was secretly pleased that she had reached at a first attempt the rare ideal of delicate lives, never attained by mediocre hearts. She let herself meander along with Lamartine, listened to harps on lakes, to all the songs of dying swans, to the falling of the leaves, the pure virgins ascending to heaven, and the voice of the Eternal discoursing down the valleys. She soon grew tired but wouldn't admit it, continued from habit first, then out of vanity, and at last was surprised to feel herself consoled, and with no more sadness at heart than wrinkles on her brow.

The good nuns, who had been so sure of her vocation, perceived with great astonishment that Mademoiselle Rouault seemed to be slipping from them. They had indeed been so lavish to her of prayers, retreats, novenas, and sermons, they had so often preached the respect due to saints and martyrs, and given so much good advice as to the modesty of the body and the salvation of her soul, that she did as tightly reigned horses: she pulled up short and the bit slipped from her teeth. This nature, positive in the midst of its enthusiasms, that had loved the church for the sake of the flowers, and music for the words of the songs, and literature for the passions it excites, rebelled against the mysteries of faith as it had rebelled against discipline, as something alien to her constitution. When her father took her from school, no one was sorry to see her go. The Lady Superior even thought that she had of late been less than reverent toward the community.

Emma, at home once more, first took pleasure in ruling over servants, then grew disgusted with the country and missed her convent. When Charles came to the Bertaux for the first time, she thought herself quite disillusioned, with nothing more to learn, and nothing more to feel.

But the uneasiness of her new position, or perhaps the disturbance caused by the presence of this man, had sufficed to make her believe that she at last felt that wondrous passion which, till then, like a great bird with rose-coloured wings, hung in the splendor of poetic skies;—and now she could not think that the calm in which she lived was the happiness of her dreams.

VII

She thought, sometimes, that, after all, this was the happiest time of her life: the honeymoon, as people called it. To taste the full sweetness of it, it would no doubt have been necessary to fly to those lands with sonorous names where the days after marriage are full of the most suave laziness! In post-chaises behind blue silken curtains, one rides slowly up steep roads, listening to the song of the postilion re-echoed by the mountains, along with the bells of goats and the muffled sound of a waterfall. At sunset on the shores of gulfs one breathes in the perfume of lemon-trees; then in the evening on the villa-terraces above, one looks hand in hand at the stars, making plans for the future. It seemed to her that certain places on earth must bring happiness, as a plant peculiar to the soil, and that cannot thrive elsewhere. Why could not she lean over balconies in Swiss châlets, or enshrine her melancholy in a Scotch cottage, with a husband dressed in a black velvet coat with long tails, and thin shoes, a pointed hat and frills?

Perhaps she would have liked to confide all these things to some one. But how tell an undefinable uneasiness, changing as the clouds, unstable as the winds? Words failed her and, by the same token, the opportunity, the courage.

If Charles had but wished it, if he had guessed, if his look had but once met her thought, it seemed to her that a sudden bounty would have come from her heart, as the fruit falls from a tree when shaken by a hand. But as the intimacy of their life became deeper, the greater became the gulf that kept them apart.

Charles's conversation was commonplace as a street pavement, and every one's ideas trooped through it in their everyday garb, without exciting emotion, laughter, or thought. He had never had the curiosity, he said, while he lived at Rouen, to go to the theatre to see the actors from Paris. He could neither swim, nor fence, nor shoot, and one day he could not explain some term of horsemanship to her that she had come across in a novel.

A man, on the contrary, should he not know everything, excel in manifold activities, initiate you into the energies of passion, the refinements of life, all mysteries? But this one taught nothing, knew nothing, wished nothing. He thought her happy; and she resented this easy calm, this serene heaviness, the very happiness she gave him.

Sometimes she would draw; and it was great amusement to Charles to stand there bolt upright and watch her bend over her paper, with eyes half-closed the better to see her work, or rolling, between her fingers, little bread-pellets. As to the piano, the more quickly her fingers glided over it the more he wondered. She struck the notes with aplomb, and ran from top to bottom of the key-board without a break. Thus shaken up, the old instrument, whose strings buzzed,[2] could be heard at the other end of the village when the window was open, and often the bailiff's clerk, passing along the highroad bareheaded and in slippers, stopped to listen, his sheet of paper in his hand.

Emma, on the other hand, knew how to look after her house. She sent the patients' accounts in well-phrased letters that had no suggestion of a bill. When they had a neighbor to dinner on Sundays, she managed to have some tasty dish, knew how to pile the plums in pyramids on vine-leaves, how to serve jam turned out on a plate,

2. The unusual French term *friser*, according to Littré, means that the vibrations are so strong that they communicate themselves to the neighboring strings.

and even spoke of buying finger bowls for dessert. From all this much consideration was extended to Bovary.

Charles finished by rising in his own esteem for possessing such a wife. He showed with pride in the sitting-room two small pencil sketches by her that he had had framed in very large frames, and hung up against the wall-paper by long green cords. People returning from mass saw him standing on his doorstep, wearing beautiful carpet slippers.

He came home late—at ten o'clock, at midnight sometimes. Then he asked for something to eat, and as the servant had gone to bed, Emma waited on him. He took off his coat to dine more at his ease. He told her, one after the other, the people he had met, the villages where he had been, the prescriptions he had written, and, well pleased with himself, he finished the remainder of the boiled beef, peeled the crust of his cheese, munched an apple, finished the wine, and then went to bed, lay on his back and snored.

As he had been for a long time accustomed to wear nightcaps, his handkerchief would not keep down over his ears, so that his hair in the morning was all dishevelled and whitened with the feathers of the pillow, whose strings came untied during the night. He always wore thick boots that had two long creases over the instep running obliquely towards the ankle, while the upper part continued in a straight line as if stretched on a wooden foot. He said that this was quite good enough for someone who lived in the country.

His mother approved of his thrift, for she came to see him as before, after there had been some violent row at her place; and yet the elder Madame Bovary seemed prejudiced against her daughter-in-law. She thought she was living above her means; the wood, sugar and candles vanished as in a large establishment, and the amount of stovewood used in the kitchen would have been enough for twenty-five courses. She straightened the linen chests, and taught her to keep an eye on the butcher when he brought the meat. Emma had to accept these lessons lavished upon her, and the words "daughter" and "mother" were exchanged all day long, accompanied by little quiverings of the lips, each one uttering sweet words in a voice trembling with anger.

In Madame Dubuc's time the old woman felt that she was still the favourite; but now the love of Charles for Emma seemed to her a desertion from her tenderness, an encroachment upon what was hers, and she watched her son's happiness in sad silence, as a ruined man looks through the windows at people dining in his old house. She recalled to him as remembrances her troubles and her sacrifices, and, comparing these with Emma's casual ways, came to the conclusion that it was not reasonable to adore her so exclusively.

Charles knew not what to answer: he respected his mother, and he loved his wife infinitely; he considered the judgment of the one infallible, and yet he thought the conduct of the other irreproachable. When Madame Bovary had gone, he tried timidly and in the same terms to hazard one or two of the more anodyne observations he had heard from his mamma. Emma proved to him with a word that he was mistaken, and sent him off to his patients.

And yet, in accord with theories she believed right, she wanted to experience love with him. By moonlight in the garden she recited all the passionate rhymes she knew by heart, and, sighing, sang to him many melancholy adagios; but she found herself as calm after this as before, and Charles seemed neither more amorous, nor more moved.

When she had thus for a while struck the flint on her heart without getting a spark, incapable, moreover, of understanding what she did not experience or of believing anything that did not take on a conventional form, she persuaded herself without difficulty that Charles's passion was no longer very ardent. His outbursts became regular; he embraced her at certain fixed times. It was one habit among other habits, like a familiar dessert after the monotony of dinner.

A gamekeeper, whom the doctor had cured of a lung infection, had given madame a little Italian greyhound; she took her out walking, for she went out sometimes in order to be alone for a moment, and not to see before her eyes the eternal garden and the dusty road.

She went as far as the beeches of Banneville, near the deserted pavilion which forms an angle on the field side of the wall. Amidst the grass of the ditches grow long reeds with sharp-edged leaves that cut you.

She began by looking round her to see if nothing had changed since she had last been there. She found again in the same places the foxgloves and wallflowers, the beds of nettles growing round the big stones, and the patches of lichen along the three windows, whose shutters, always closed, were rotting away on their rusty iron bars. Her thoughts, aimless at first, wandered at random, like her greyhound, who ran round and round in the fields, yelping after the yellow butterflies, chasing the field-mice, or nibbling the poppies on the edge of a wheatfield. Then gradually her ideas took definite shape, and, sitting on the grass that she dug up with little pricks of her sunshade, Emma repeated to herself:—Why, for Heaven's sake, did I marry?

She asked herself if by some other chance combination it would not have been possible to meet another man; and she tried to imagine what would have been these unrealised events, this different life, this unknown husband. All, surely, could not be like this one. He might have been handsome, witty, distinguished, attractive, like, no doubt, the men her old companions of the convent had married. What were they doing now? In town, among the crowded streets, the buzzing theatres and the lights of the ball-room, they were living lives where the heart expands and the senses blossom out. As for her, her life was cold as a garret facing north, and ennui, the silent spider, was weaving its web in the darkness, in every corner of her heart. She recalled graduation day, when she mounted the platform to receive her little wreaths. With her hair in long plaits, in her white frock and open prunella shoes she had a pretty way, and when she went back to her seat, the gentlemen bent over to congratulate her; the courtyard was full of carriages; farewells were called to her through their windows; the music-master with his violin-case bowed in passing by. How far off all this! How far away!

She called Djali, took her between her knees, and smoothed the long, delicate head, saying, "Come, kiss your mistress, you who are free of cares."

Then noting the melancholy face of the graceful animal, who yawned slowly, she softened, and comparing her to herself, spoke to her aloud as to somebody in pain whom one is consoling.

Occasionally there came gusts of wind, breezes from the sea rolling in one sweep over the whole plateau of the Caux country, which brought to these fields a salt freshness. The rushes, close to the ground, whistled; the branches of the beech trees trembled in a swift rustling, while their crowns, ceaselessly swaying, kept up a deep murmur. Emma drew her shawl round her shoulders and rose.

In the avenue a green light dimmed by the leaves lit up the short moss that crackled softly beneath her feet. The sun was setting; the sky showed red between the branches, and the trunks of the trees, uniform, and planted in a straight line, seemed a brown colonnade standing out against a background of gold. A fear took hold of her; she called Djali, and hurriedly returned to Tostes by the highroad, threw herself into an armchair, and for the rest of the evening did not speak.

But towards the end of September something extraordinary befell her: she was invited by the Marquis d'Andervilliers to Vaubyessard.

Secretary of State under the Restoration, the Marquis, anxious to re-enter political life, had long since been preparing for his candidature to the Chamber of Deputies. In the winter he distributed a great deal of firewood, and in the Conseil Général always enthusiastically demanded new roads for his arrondissement. During the height of the Summer heat he had suffered from an abcess in the mouth, which Charles had cured as if by miracle by giving a timely little touch with the lancet. The steward sent to Tostes to pay for the operation reported in the evening that he had seen some superb cherries in the doctor's little garden. Now cherry-trees did not thrive at Vaubyessard; the Marquis asked Bovary for some offshoots. He made it his business to thank him personally and, on that occasion, saw Emma. He thought she had a pretty figure, and that she did not greet him like a peasant; so that he did not think he was going beyond the bounds of condescension, nor, on the other hand, making a mistake, in inviting the young couple.

One Wednesday at three o'clock, Monsieur and Madame Bovary, seated in their dog-cart, set out for Vaubyessard, with a great trunk strapped on behind and a hat-box in front on the apron. Besides these Charles held a carton between his knees.

They arrived at nightfall, just as the lamps in the park were being lit to show the way for the carriages.

VIII

The château, a modern building in Italian style, with two projecting wings and three flights of steps, lay at the foot of an immense lawn, on which some cows were grazing among clumps of large trees set out at regular intervals, while large beds of arbutus, rhododendron, syringas and snowballs bulged out their irregular clusters of green along the curve of the gravel path. A river flowed under a bridge; through the mist one could distinguish buildings with thatched roofs scattered over the field bordered by two gently-sloping well-timbered hillocks, and in the background amid the trees rose in two parallel lines the coach-houses and stables, all that was left of the ruined old château.

Charles's dog-cart pulled up before the middle flight of steps; servants appeared; the Marquis came forward, and offering his arm to the doctor's wife, conducted her to the vestibule.

It was paved with marble slabs and seemed very lofty; the sound of footsteps and that of voices re-echoed through it as in a church. Opposite rose a straight staircase, and on the left a gallery overlooking the garden led to the billiard room, from where the click of the ivory balls could be heard immediately upon entering. As she crossed it to go to the drawing-room, Emma saw standing round the table men with grave faces, their chins resting on high cravats. They all wore orders, and smiled silently as they made their strokes. On the dark wainscoting of the walls large gold frames bore at the bottom names written in black letters. She read: "Jean-Antoine d'Andervilliers d'Yverbonville, Count de la Vaubyessard and Baron de la Fresnaye, killed at the battle of Coutras on the 20th of October 1587." And on another: "Jean-Antoine-Henry-Guy d'Andervilliers de la Vaubyessard, Admiral of France and Chevalier of the Order of St. Michael, wounded at the battle of the Hougue-

Saint-Vaast on the 29th of May 1692; died at Vaubyessard on the 23rd of January 1693." One could hardly make out the next ones, for the light of the lamps lowered over the green cloth threw a dim shadow round the room. Burnishing the horizontal pictures, it broke up in delicate lines among the cracks in the varnish, and from all these great black squares framed in gold stood out here and there some lighter portion of the painting—a pale brow, two eyes that looked at you, wigs resting on the powdered shoulder of red coats, or the buckle of a garter above a well-rounded calf.

The Marquis opened the drawing-room door; one of the ladies (the Marquise herself) came to meet Emma. She made her sit down by her on an ottoman, and began talking to her as amicably as if she had known her a long time. She was a woman of about forty, with fine shoulders, a hook nose, a drawling voice, and on this evening she wore over her brown hair a simple guipure fichu that fell in a point at the back. A blond young woman sat by her side in a high-backed chair, and gentlemen with flowers in their button-holes were talking to ladies round the fire.

At seven dinner was served. The men, who were in the majority, sat down at the first table in the vestibule; the ladies at the second in the dining-room with the Marquis and Marquise.

Emma, on entering, felt herself wrapped round as by a warm breeze, a blending of the perfume of flowers and of the fine linen, of the fumes of the roasts and the odour of the truffles. The candles in the candelabra threw their lights on the silver dish covers; the cut crystal, covered with a fine mist of steam, reflected pale rays of light; bouquets were placed in a row the whole length of the table; and in the large-bordered plates each napkin, arranged after the fashion of a bishop's mitre, held between its two gaping folds a small oval-shaped roll. The red claws of lobsters hung over the dishes; rich fruit in woven baskets was piled up on moss; the quails were dressed in their own plumage, smoke was rising; and in silk stockings, knee-breeches, white cravat, and frilled shirt, the steward, grave as a judge, passed between the shoulders of the guests, offering ready-carved dishes and, with a flick of the spoon, landed on one's plate the piece one had chosen. On the large porcelain stove inlaid with copper baguettes the statue of a woman, draped to the chin, gazed motionless on the crowded room.

Madame Bovary noticed that many ladies had not put their gloves in their glasses.[3]

At the upper end of the table, alone amongst all these women, bent over his full plate, and his napkin tied round his neck like a

---

3. Frances Steegmuller explains this sentence in his introduction to his translation of *Madame Bovary*. The ladies in the provinces, unlike their Paris counterparts, did not drink wine at public dinner parties, and signified their intention by putting their gloves in their wine-glasses. The fact that they fail to to do so suggests to Emma the high degree of sophistication of the company.

child, an old man sat eating, letting drops of gravy drip from his
mouth. His eyes were bloodshot, and he wore his hair in a little
queue tied with a black ribbon. He was the Marquis's father-in-law,
the old Duke de Laverdière, once on a time favourite of the Count
d'Artois, in the days of the Marquis de Conflans' hunting-parties at
le Vaudreuil, and had been, it was said, the lover of Queen Marie
Antoinette, between Monsieur de Coigny and Monsieur de Lauzun.
He had lived a life of loud dissipation, full of duels, bets, elope-
ments; he had squandered his fortune and frightened all his family.
A servant behind his chair shouted in his ear, in reply to his mutter-
ings, the names of the dishes that he pointed to, and constantly
Emma's eyes turned involuntarily to this old man with hanging lips,
as to something extraordinary. He had lived at court and slept in
the bed of queens!

Iced champagne was poured out. Emma shivered all over as she
felt its cold in her mouth. She had never seen pomegranates nor
tasted pineapples. Even the powdered sugar seemed to her whiter
and finer than elsewhere.

The ladies afterwards retired to their rooms to prepare for the
ball.

Emma made her toilette with the fastidious care of an actress on
her début. She did her hair according to the directions of the
hairdresser, and put on the barege dress spread out upon the bed.
Charles's trousers were tight across the belly.

"My trouser-straps will be rather awkward for dancing," he said.

"Dancing?" repeated Emma.

"Yes!"

"Why, you must be mad! They would make fun of you; stay in
your place, as it becomes a doctor."

Charles was silent. He walked up and down waiting for Emma to
finish dressing.

He saw her from behind in the mirror between two lights. Her
black eyes seemed blacker than ever. Her hair, gently undulating
towards the ears, shone with a blue lustre; a rose in her chignon
trembled on its mobile stalk, with artificial dewdrops on the tip of
the leaves. She wore a gown of pale saffron trimmed with three
bouquets of pompon roses mixed with green.

Charles came and kissed her on her shoulder.

"Don't touch me!" she cried; "I'll be all rumpled."

One could hear the flourish of the violin and the notes of a horn.
She went downstairs restraining herself from running.

Dancing had begun. Guests were arriving and crowding the
room. She sat down on a bench near the door.

The quadrille over, the floor was occupied by groups of talking
men and by servants in livery bearing large trays. Along the line of

seated women painted fans were fluttering, bouquets half-hid smiling faces, and gold-stoppered scent-bottles were turned in half-clenched hands, with white gloves outlining the nail and tightening on the flesh at the wrists. Lace trimmings, diamond brooches, medallion bracelets trembled on blouses, gleamed on breasts, clinked on bare arms. The hair, well smoothed over the temples and knotted at the nape, bore crowns, or bunches, or sprays of myosotis, jasmine, pomegranate blossoms, wheat-sprays and corn-flowers. Calmly seated in their places, mothers with forbidding countenances were wearing red turbans.

Emma's heart beat rather faster when, her partner holding her by the tips of the fingers, she took her place in a line with the dancers, and waited for the first note to start. But her emotion soon vanished, and, swaying to the rhythm of the orchestra, she glided forward with slight movements of the neck. A smile rose to her lips at certain delicate phrases of the violin, that sometimes played alone while the other instruments were silent; one could hear the clear clink of the louis d'or that were being thrown down upon the card-tables in the next room; then all struck in again, the trumpet uttered its sonorous note, feet marked time, skirts swelled and rustled, hands touched and parted; the same eyes that had been lowered returned to gaze at you again.

A few men (some fifteen or so), of twenty-five to forty, scattered here and there among the dancers or talking at the doorways, distinguished themselves from the crowd by a certain family-air, whatever their differences in age, dress, or countenance.

Their clothes, better made, seemed of finer cloth, and their hair, brought forward in curls towards the temples, glossy with more delicate pomades. They had the complexion of wealth,—that clear complexion that is heightened by the pallor of porcelain, the shimmer of satin, the veneer of old furniture, and that a well-ordered diet of exquisite food maintains at its best. Their necks moved easily in their low cravats, their long whiskers fell over their turned-down collars, they wiped their lips upon handkerchiefs with embroidered initials that gave forth a subtle perfume. Those who were beginning to grow old had an air of youth, while there was something mature in the faces of the young. Their indifferent eyes had the appeased expression of daily-satiated passions, and through all their gentleness of manner pierced that peculiar brutality that stems from a steady command over half-tame things, for the exercise of one's strength and the amusement of one's vanity—the handling of thoroughbred horses and the society of loose women.

A few steps from Emma a gentleman in a blue coat was talking of Italy with a pale young woman wearing a parure of pearls. They were praising the width of the columns of St. Peter's, Tivoli,

Vesuvius, Castellamare, and the Cascines, the roses of Genoa, the Coliseum by moonlight. With her other ear Emma was listening to a conversation full of words she did not understand. A circle gathered round a very young man who the week before had beaten "Miss Arabella" and "Romolus," and won two thousand louis jumping a ditch in England. One complained that his racehorses were growing fat; another of the printers' errors that had disfigured the name of his horse.

The atmosphere of the ball was heavy; the lamps were growing dim. Guests were flocking to the billiard-room. A servant got upon a chair and broke the window-panes. At the crash of the glass Madame Bovary turned her head and saw in the garden the faces of peasants pressed against the window looking in at them. Then the memory of the Bertaux came back to her. She saw the farm again, the muddy pond, her father in his apron under the apple-trees, and she saw herself again as formerly, skimming with her finger the cream off the milk-pans in the dairy. But in the splendor of the present hour her past life, so distinct until then, faded away completely, and she almost doubted having lived it. She was there; beyond the ball was only shadow overspreading all the rest. She was eating a maraschino ice that she held with her left hand in a silver-gilt cup, her eyes half-closed, and the spoon between her teeth.

A lady near her dropped her fan. A gentleman was passing.

"Would you be good enough," said the lady, "to pick up my fan that has fallen behind the sofa?"

The gentleman bowed, and as he moved to stretch out his arm, Emma saw the hand of the young woman throw something white, folded in a triangle, into his hat. The gentleman picking up the fan, respectfully offered it to the lady; she thanked him with a nod and breathed in the smell of her bouquet.

After supper, consisting of plenty of Spanish and Rhine wines, bisque and almond-cream soups, Trafalgar puddings and all sorts of cold meats with jellies that trembled in the dishes, the carriages began to leave one after the other. Raising the corners of the muslin curtain, one could see the light of their lanterns glimmering through the darkness. The seats began to empty, some card-players were still left; the musicians were cooling the tips of their fingers on their tongues. Charles was half asleep, his back propped against a door.

At three o'clock the cotillion began. Emma did not know how to waltz. Every one was waltzing, Mademoiselle d'Andervilliers herself and the Marquis; only the guests staying at the castle were still there, about a dozen persons.

One of the waltzers, however, who was addressed as Viscount, and whose low cut waistcoat seemed moulded to his chest, came a second time to ask Madame Bovary to dance, assuring her that he would guide her, and that she would get through it very well.

They began slowly, then increased in speed. They turned; all around them was turning, the lamps, the furniture, the wainscoting, the floor, like a disc on a pivot. On passing near the doors the train of Emma's dress caught against his trousers. Their legs intertwined; he looked down at her; she raised her eyes to his. A torpor seized her and she stopped. They started again, at an even faster pace; the Viscount, sweeping her along, disappeared with her to the end of the gallery, where, panting, she almost fell, and for a moment rested her head upon his breast. And then, still turning, but more slowly, he guided her back to her seat. She leaned back against the wall and covered her eyes with her hands.

When she opened them again, in the middle of the drawing-room three waltzers were kneeling before a lady sitting on a stool. She chose the Viscount, and the violin struck up once more.

Every one looked at them. They kept passing by, she with rigid body, her chin bent down, and he always in the same pose, his figure curved, his elbow rounded, his chin thrown forward. That woman knew how to waltz! They kept it up a long time, and tired out all the others.

Then they talked a few moments longer, and after the good-nights, or rather good-mornings, the guests of the château retired to bed.

Charles dragged himself up by the banister. His knees were giving way under him. For five consecutive hours, he had stood bolt upright at the card-tables, watching them play whist, without understanding anything about it, and it was with a deep sigh of relief that he pulled off his boots.

Emma threw a shawl over her shoulders, opened the window, and leant out.

The night was dark; some drops of rain were falling. She breathed in the damp wind that refreshed her eyelids. The music of the ball was still echoing in her ears, and she tried to keep herself awake in order to prolong the illusion of this luxurious life that she would soon have to give up.

Day began to break. She looked long at the windows of the château, trying to guess which were the rooms of all those she had noticed the evening before. She would have wanted to know their lives, to penetrate into them, to blend with them.

But she was shivering with cold. She undressed, and cowered down between the sheets against Charles, who was asleep.

There were a great many people to luncheon. The meal lasted ten minutes; to the doctor's astonishment, no liqueurs were served. Next, Mademoiselle d'Andervilliers collected some rolls in a small basket to take them to the swans on the ornamental waters, and they went for a walk in the hothouses, where strange plants, bristling with hairs, rose in pyramids under hanging vases from where fell, as from overfilled nests of serpents, long green cords interlacing. The orangery, at the other end, led by a covered way to the tenant houses of the château. The Marquis, to amuse the young woman, took her to see the stables. Above the basket-shaped racks porcelain slabs bore the names of the horses in black letters. Each animal in its stall whisked its tail when any one came near and clicked his tongue. The boards of the harness-room shone like the flooring of a drawing-room. The carriage harness was piled up in the middle against two twisted columns, and the bits, the whips, the spurs, the curbs, were lined up in a line all along the wall.

Charles, meanwhile, went to ask a groom to harness his horse. The dog-cart was brought to the foot of the steps, and all the parcels being crammed in, the Bovarys paid their respects to the Marquis and the Marquise and set out again for Tostes.

Emma watched the turning wheels in silence. Charles, on the extreme edge of the seat, held the reins with his arms spread far apart, and the little horse ambled along in the shafts that were too big for him. The loose reins hanging over his crupper were wet with foam, and the box fastened behind bumped regularly against the cart.

They were on the heights of Thibourville when suddenly some horsemen with cigars between their lips passed, laughing. Emma thought she recognised the Viscount, turned back, and caught on the horizon only the movement of the heads rising or falling with the unequal cadence of the trot or gallop.

A mile farther on they had to stop to mend with some string the traces that had broken.

But Charles, giving a last look to the harness, saw something on the ground between his horse's legs, and he picked up a cigar-case with a green silk border and a crest in the centre like the door of a carriage.

"There are even two cigars in it," said he; "they'll do for this evening after dinner."

"Since when do you smoke?" she asked.

"Sometimes, when I get a chance."

He put his find in his pocket and whipped up the nag.

When they reached home the dinner was not ready. Madame lost her temper. Nastasie answered rudely.

"Leave the room!" said Emma. "You are being insolent. I'll dismiss you."

For dinner there was onion soup and a piece of veal with sorrel. Charles, seated opposite Emma, rubbed his hands gleefully.

"How good it is to be at home again!"

Nastasie could be heard crying. He was rather fond of the poor girl. She had formerly, during the wearisome time of his widowhood, kept him company many an evening. She had been his first patient, his oldest acquaintance in the place.

"Have you dismissed her for good?" he asked at last.

"Yes. Who is to prevent me?" she replied.

Then they warmed themselves in the kitchen while their room was being made ready. Charles began to smoke. He smoked with lips protruded, spitting every moment, drawing back at every puff.

"You'll make yourself ill," she said scornfully.

He put down his cigar and ran to swallow a glass of cold water at the pump. Seizing the cigar case, Emma threw it quickly to the back of the cupboard.

The next day was a long one. She walked about her little garden, up and down the same walks, stopping before the beds, before the fruit tree, before the plaster priest, looking with amazement at all these things of the past that she knew so well. How far off the ball seemed already! What was it that thus set so far asunder the morning of the day before yesterday and the evening of to-day? Her journey to Vaubyessard had made a gap in her life, like the huge crevasses that a thunderstorm will sometimes carve in the mountains, in the course of a single night. Still she was resigned. She devoutly put away in her drawers her beautiful dress, down to the satin shoes whose soles were yellowed with the slippery wax of the dancing floor. Her heart resembled them: in its contact with wealth, something had rubbed off on it that could not be removed.

The memory of this ball, then, became an occupation for Emma. Whenever Wednesday came round she said to herself as she awoke, "Ah! I was there a week—a fortnight—three weeks ago." And little by little the faces grew confused in her remembrance. She forgot the tune of the quadrilles; she no longer saw the liveries and the guest-houses so distinctly; some of the details faded but the wistful feeling remained with her.

IX

Often when Charles was out she took from the cupboard, between the folds of the linen where she had left it, the green silk cigar-case.

She looked at it, opened it, and even smelt the odour of the lining, a mixture of verbena and tobacco. Whose was it? . . . The Viscount's? Perhaps it was a present from his mistress. It had been embroidered on some rosewood frame, a pretty piece of furniture, hidden from all eyes, that had occupied many hours, and over which had fallen the soft curls of the pensive worker. A breath of love had passed over the stitches on the canvas; each prick of the

needle had fixed there a hope or a memory, and all those interwoven threads of silk were but the continued extension of the same
silent passion. And then one morning the Viscount had taken it
away with him. Of what had they spoken when it lay upon the wide-
mantelled chimneys between flower-vases and Pompadour clocks?
She was at Tostes; he was at Paris now, far away! What was this
Paris like? What a boundless name! She repeated it in a low voice,
for the mere pleasure of it; it rang in her ears like a great cathedral
bell; it shone before her eyes, even on the labels of her jars of
pomade.

At night, when the carts passed under her windows, carrying fish
to Paris to the tune of "la Marjolaine," she awoke, and listened to
the noise of the iron-bound wheels, which, as they gained the country road, was soon deadened by the earth. "They will be there to-
morrow!" she said to herself.

And she followed them in thought up and down the hills, crossing villages, gliding along the highroads by the light of the stars. At
the end of some indefinite distance there was always a confused
spot, into which her dream died.

She bought a plan of Paris, and with the tip of her finger on the
map she walked about the capital. She went up the boulevards,
stopping at every turn, between the lines of the streets, in front of
the white squares that represented the houses. At last she would
close the lids of her weary eyes, and see in the darkness the gas jets
flaring in the wind and the steps of carriages lowered noisily in
front of the theatre-entrances.

She subscribed to "La Corbeille," a ladies' magazine, and the
"Sylphe des Salons." She devoured, without skipping a word, all the
accounts of first nights, races, and soirées, took an interest in the
début of a singer, in the opening of a new shop. She knew the latest
fashions, the addresses of the best tailors, the days of the Bois
and the Opera. In Eugène Sue[4] she studied descriptions of furniture; she read Balzac and George Sand, seeking in them imaginary
satisfaction for her own desires. She even brought her book to the
table, and turned over the pages while Charles ate and talked to
her. The memory of the Viscount always cropped up in everything
she read. She made comparisons between him and the fictional
characters in her books. But the circle of which he was the centre
gradually widened round him, and the aureole that he bore, fading
from his form and extending beyond his image, lit up her other
dreams.

Paris, more vague than the ocean, glimmered before Emma's eyes
with a silvery glow. The many lives that stirred amid this tumult

4. Eugène Sue (1804–57) a popular
novelist, extremely successful at that
period, both as a writer and as a fashionable dandy.

were, however, divided into parts, classed as distinct pictures. Emma perceived only two or three that hid from her all the rest, and in themselves represented all humanity. The world of ambassadors moved over polished floors in drawing-rooms lined with mirrors, round oval tables covered with velvet and gold-fringed cloths. There were dresses with trains, deep mysteries, anguish hidden beneath smiles. Then came the society of the duchesses; all were pale; all got up at four o'clock; the women, poor angels, wore English point on their petticoats; and the men, their talents hidden under a frivolous appearance, rode horses to death at pleasure parties, spent the summer season at Baden, and ended up, on reaching their forties, by marrying heiresses. In the private rooms of restaurants, where one dines after midnight by the light of wax candles, the colorful crowd of writers and actresses held sway. They were prodigal as kings, full of ambitious ideals and fantastic frenzies. They lived far above all others, among the storms that rage between heaven and earth, partaking of the sublime. As for the rest of the world, it was lost, with no particular place, and as if non-existent. Anyway, the nearer things were the more her thoughts turned away from them. All her immediate surroundings, the wearisome countryside, the petty-bourgeois stupidity, the mediocrity of existence seemed to her the exception, an exception in which she had been caught by a stroke of faith, while beyond stretched as far as eye could see an immense land of joys and passions. In her wistfulness, she confused the sensuous pleasures of luxury with the delights of the heart, elegance of manners with delicacy of sentiment. Did not love, like Indian plants, need a special soil, a special temperature? Sighs by moonlight, long embraces, tears flowing over yielded hands, all the passions of the flesh and the languors of tenderness seemed to her inseparable from the balconies of great castles where life flows idly by, from boudoirs with silken curtains and thick carpets, well-filled flower-stands, a bed on a raised daïs, and from the flashing of precious stones and the golden braids of liveries.

The boy from the post-office who came to groom the mare every morning passed through the passage with his heavy wooden shoes; there were holes in his apron; his feet were bare in his slippers. And this was the groom in knee-breeches with whom she had to be content! His work done, he did not come back again all day, for Charles on his return put up his horse himself, unsaddled it and put on the halter, while the maid brought a bundle of straw and threw it as best she could into the manger.

To replace Nastasie (who finally left Tostes shedding torrents of tears) Emma hired a young girl of fourteen, an orphan with a sweet face. She forbade her wearing cotton caps, taught her to address her in the third person, to bring a glass of water on a plate, to knock before coming into a room, to iron, starch, and to dress her; she wanted to make a lady's-maid of her. The new servant obeyed without a murmur, so as not to be dismissed; and as madame usually left the key in the sideboard, Félicité every evening took a small supply of sugar that she ate alone in her bed after she had said her prayers.

Sometimes in the afternoon she went across the road to chat with the coachmen. Madame stayed upstairs.

She wore an open dressing-gown, that showed under the shawl-shaped collar a pleated blouse with three gold buttons. Her belt was a corded girdle with great tassels, and her small wine-red slippers had a large knot of ribbon that fell over her instep. She had bought herself a blotter, writing-case, pen-holder, and envelopes although she had no one to write to; she dusted her shelf, looked at herself in the mirror, picked up a book, and then, dreaming between the lines, let it drop on her knees. She longed to travel or to go back to her convent. She wanted to die, but she also wanted to live in Paris.

Charles trotted over the country-roads in snow and rain. He ate omelettes on farmhouse tables, poked his arm into damp beds, received the tepid spurt of blood-letting in his face, listened to death-rattles, examined basins, turned over a good deal of dirty linen; but every evening he found a blazing fire, his dinner ready, easy-chairs, and a well-dressed woman, charming and so freshly scented that it was impossible to say where the perfume came from; it might have been her skin that communicated its fragrance to her blouse.

She delighted him by numerous attentions; now it was some new way of arranging paper sconces for the candles, a flounce that she altered on her gown, or an extraordinary name for some very simple dish that the servant had spoilt, but that Charles swallowed with pleasure to the last mouthful. At Rouen she saw some ladies who wore a bundle of charms hanging from their watch-chains; she bought some. She wanted for her mantelpiece two large blue glass vases, and some time after an ivory nécessaire with a silver-gilt thimble. The less Charles understood these refinements the more they seduced him. They added something to the pleasure of the senses and to the comfort of his fireside. It was like a golden dust sanding all along the narrow path of his life.

He was well, looked well; his reputation was firmly established. The country-folk loved him because he was not proud. He petted the children, never went to the public-house, and, moreover, his good behavior inspired confidence. He was specially successful with heavy colds and chest ailments. Being much afraid of killing his patients, Charles, in fact, only prescribed sedatives, from time to time an emetic, a footbath, or leeches. It was not that he was afraid of surgery; he bled people copiously like horses, and for the pulling of teeth the strength of his grasp was second to no one.

Finally, to keep up with the times, he subscribed to "La Ruche Médicale," a new journal whose prospectus had been sent him. He read it a little after dinner, but in about five minutes, the warmth of the room added to the effect of his dinner sent him to sleep; and he sat there, his chin on his two hands and his hair spreading like a mane to the foot of the lamp. Emma looked at him and shrugged her shoulders. Why at least, was not her husband one of those silently determined men who work at their books all night, and at last, when at sixty the age of rhumatism was upon them, wear a string of medals on their ill-fitting black coat? She would have wished this name of Bovary, which was hers, to be illustrious, to see it displayed at the booksellers', repeated in the newspapers, known to all France. But Charles had no ambition. An Yvetot doctor whom he had lately met in consultation had somewhat humiliated him at the very bedside of the patient, before the assembled relatives. When, in the evening, Charles told this incident Emma inveighed loudly against his colleague. Charles was much touched. He kissed her forehead with a tear in his eyes. But she was angered with shame; she felt a wild desire to strike him; she went to open the window in the passage and breathed in the fresh air to calm herself.

"What a man! what a man!" she said in a low voice, biting her lips.

She was becoming more irritated with him. As he grew older his manner grew coarser; at dessert he cut the corks of the empty bottles; after eating he cleaned his teeth with his tongue; in eating his soup he made a gurgling noise with every spoonful; and, as he was getting fatter, the puffed-out cheeks seemed to push the eyes, always small, up to the temples.

Sometimes Emma tucked the red borders of his undervest into his waistcoat, rearranged his cravat, and threw away the faded gloves he was going to put on; and this was not, as he fancied, for his sake; it was for herself, by an expansion of selfishness, of nervous irritation. At other times, she told him what she had been reading, some passage in a novel, a new play, or an anecdote from high society found in a newspaper story; for, after all, Charles was someone to talk to, an ever-open ear, an ever-ready approbation. She even confided many a thing to her greyhound! She would have done so to the logs in the fireplace or to the pendulum of the clock.

All the while, however, she was waiting in her heart for something to happen. Like shipwrecked sailors, she turned despairing eyes upon the solitude of her life, seeking afar some white sail in the mists of the horizon. She did not know what this act of fortune would be, what wind would bring it, towards what shore it would drive her, if it would be a rowboat or an ocean liner with three decks, carrying anguish or laden to the gunwales with bliss. But each morning, as she awoke, she hoped it would come that day; she listened to every sound, sprang up with a start, wondered that it did not come; then at sunset, always more saddened, she longed for the next day.

Spring came round. With the first warm weather, when the pear-trees began to blossom, she had fainting-spells.

From the beginning of July she counted off on her fingers how many weeks there were to October, thinking that perhaps the Marquis d'Andervilliers would give another ball at Vaubyessard. But all September passed without letters or visits.

After the shock of this disappointment her heart once more remained empty, and then the same series of identical days recommenced.

So now they would keep following one another, always the same, immovable, and bringing nothing new. Other lives, however flat, had at least the chance of some event. One adventure sometimes brought with it infinite consequences and the scene changed. But nothing happened to her; God had willed it so! The future was a dark corridor, with its door at the end shut tight.

She gave up music. What was the good of playing? Who would hear her? Since she could never, in a velvet gown with short sleeves, striking with her light fingers the ivory keys of an Erard concert piano, feel the murmur of ecstasy envelop her like a breeze, it was not worth while boring herself with practising. Her drawing cardboard and her embroidery she left in the cupboard. What was the use? What was the use? Sewing irritated her.

"I have read everything," she said to herself.

And she sat there, letting the tongs grow red-hot or looking at the rain falling.

How sad she was on Sundays when vespers sounded! She listened with dull attention to each stroke of the cracked bell. A cat slowly walking over some roof put up his back in the pale rays of the sun. The wind on the highroad blew up clouds of dust. A dog sometimes howled in the distance; and the bell, keeping time, continued at regular intervals its monotonous ringing that died away over the fields.

Then the people came out from church. The women had waxed their wooden shoes, the farmers wore new smocks, and with the little bareheaded children skipping along in front of them, all were going home. And till nightfall, five or six men, always the same, stayed playing at corks in front of the large door of the inn.

The winter was severe. Every morning, the windows were covered with rime, and the light that shone through them, dim as through ground-glass, sometimes did not change the whole day long. At four o'clock the lamp had to be lighted.

On fine days she went down into the garden. The dew had left a silver lace on the cabbages with long transparent threads spreading from one to the other. No birds were to be heard; everything seemed asleep, the fruit tree covered with straw, and the vine, like a great sick serpent under the coping of the wall, along which, on drawing near, one saw the many-footed woodlice crawling. Under the spruce by the hedgerow, the curé in the three-cornered hat reading his breviary had lost his right foot, and the very plaster, scaling off with the frost, had left white scabs on his face.

Then she went up again, shut her door, put on coals, and fainting with the heat of the hearth, felt her boredom weigh more heavily than ever. She would have liked to go down and talk to the maid, but a sense of shame restrained her.

Every day at the same time the schoolmaster in a black skull-cap opened the shutters of his house, and the village policeman, wearing his sword over his blouse, passed by. Night and morning the post-horses, three by three, crossed the street to water at the pond. From time to time the bell of a café would tinkle, and when it was windy one could hear the little brass basins that served as signs for the hairdresser's shop creaking on their two rods. The shop was decorated with an old engraving of a fashion-plate stuck against a window-pane and with the wax bust of a woman with yellow hair. He, too, the hairdresser, lamented his wasted calling, his hopeless future, and dreaming of some shop in a big town—at Rouen, for example, overlooking the harbour, near the theatre—he walked up and down all day from the mairie to the church, sombre and waiting for customers. When Madame Bovary looked up, she always saw him there, like a sentinel on duty, with his skull-cap over his ears and his woolen jacket.

Sometimes in the afternoon outside the window of her room, the head of a man appeared, a swarthy head with black whiskers, smiling slowly, with a broad, gentle smile that showed his white teeth. A waltz began, and on the barrel-organ, in a little drawing-room, dancers the size of a finger, women in pink turbans, Tyrolians in jackets, monkeys in frock-coats, gentlemen in knee breeches, turned and turned between the armchairs, the sofas and the tables, reflected in small pieces of mirror that strips of golf paper held together at the corners. The man turned the handle, looking to the right, to the left and up at the windows. Now and again, while he shot out a long squirt of brown saliva against the milestone, he lifted his instrument with his knee, to relieve his shoulder from the pressure of the hard straps; and now, doleful and drawling, or merry and hurried, the music issued forth from the box, droning through a curtain of pink taffeta underneath an ornate brass grill. They were airs played in other places at the theatres, sung in drawing-rooms, danced to at night under lighted lustres, echoes of the world that reached even to Emma. Endless sarabands ran through her head, and, like an Oriental dancing-girl on the flowers of a carpet, her thoughts leapt with the notes, swung from dream to dream, from sadness to sadness. When the man had caught some pennies in his cap he drew down an old cover of blue cloth, hitched his organ on to his back, and went off with a heavy tread. She watched him going.

But it was above all the meal-times that were unbearable to her, in this small room on the ground-floor, with its smoking stove, its creaking door, the walls that sweated, the damp pavement; all the bitterness of life seemed served up on her plate, and with the smoke of the boiled beef there rose from her secret soul waves of nauseous disgust. Charles was a slow eater; she played with a few nuts, or, leaning on her elbow, amused herself drawing lines along the oil-cloth table-cover with the point of her knife.

She now let everybody in her household go its own way, and the elder Madame Bovary, when she came to spend part of Lent at Tostes, was much surprised at the change. She who was formerly so careful, so dainty, now spent whole days without dressing, wore grey cotton stockings, and used tallow candles to light the house. She kept saying they must be economical since they were not rich, adding that she was very contented, very happy, that Tostes pleased her very much, and other such statements that left her mother-in-law speechless. Besides, Emma no longer seemed inclined to follow her advice; on one occasion, when Madame Bovary had thought fit to maintain that masters ought to keep an eye on the religion of their servants, she had answered with a look so angry and a smile so cold that the old lady preferred to let the matter drop.

Emma was growing difficult, capricious. She ordered dishes for herself, then she did not touch them; one day drank only pure milk, and the next cups of tea by the dozen. Often she persisted in not going out, then, stifling, threw open the windows and put on light dresses. After she had well scolded her maid she gave her presents or sent her out to see neighbors. She sometimes threw beggars all the silver in her purse, although she was by no means tender-hearted or easily accessible to the feelings of others; like most country-bred people, she always retained in her soul something of the horny hardness of the paternal hands.

Towards the end of February old Rouault, in memory of his cure, personally brought a superb turkey to his son-in-law, and stayed three days at Tostes. Charles being with his patients, Emma kept him company. He smoked in the room, spat on the andirons, talked farming, calves, cows, poultry, and municipal council, so that when he left she closed the door on him with a feeling of satisfaction that surprised even herself. Moreover she no longer concealed her contempt for anything or anybody, and at times expressed singular opinions, finding fault with whatever others approved, and approving things perverse and immoral, all of which left her husband wide-eyed.

Would this misery last for ever? Would she never escape from it? Yet she was the equal of all the women who were living happily. She had seen duchesses at Vaubyessard with clumsier waists and commoner ways, and she hated the divine injustice of God. She leant her head against the walls to weep; she longed for lives of adventure, for masked balls, for shameless pleasures that were bound, she thought, to initiate her to ecstacies she had not yet experienced.

She grew pale and suffered from palpitations of the heart. Charles prescribed valerian drops and camphor baths. Everything that was tried only seemed to irritate her the more.

On certain days she chattered with feverish profusion, and this overexcitement was suddenly followed by a state of torpor, in which she remained without speaking, without moving. What then revived her was to pour a bottle of eau-de-cologne over her arms.

As she was constantly complaining about Tostes, Charles fancied that her illness was no doubt due to some local cause, and, struck by this idea, he began to think seriously of setting up practice elsewhere.

From that moment she drank vinegar to lose weight, contracted a sharp little cough, and lost all appetite.

It cost Charles much to give up Tostes after living there four years, just when he was beginning to get somewhere. Yet if it must be! He took her to Rouen to see his old master. It was a nervous condition; she needed a change of air.

After some looking around, Charles discovered that the doctor of a considerable market-town in the arrondissement of Neufchâtel, a former Polish refugee, had vanished a week earlier. Then he wrote to the local pharmacist to ask the size of the population, the distance from the nearest doctor, how much his predecessor had earned in a year, and so forth; and the answer being satisfactory, he made up his mind to move towards the spring, if Emma's health did not improve.

One day when, in view of her departure, she was tidying a drawer, something pricked her finger. It was a wire of her wedding-bouquet. The orange blossoms were yellow with dust and the silver-bordered satin ribbons frayed at the edges. She threw it into the fire. It flared up more quickly than dry straw. Then it was like a red bush in the cinders, slowly shrinking away. She watched it burn. The little pasteboard berries burst, the wire twisted, the gold lace melted; and the shrivelled paper petals, fluttering like black butter-flies at the back of the stove, at last flew up the chimney.

When they left Tostes in the month of March, Madame Bovary was pregnant.

Part Two

I

Yonville-l'Abbaye (named after an old Capuchin abbey of which not even the ruins remain), is a market-town some twenty miles from Rouen, between the Abbeville and Beauvais roads. It lies at the foot of a valley watered by the Rieule, a little river that runs into the Andelle after turning three water-mills near its mouth; it contains a few trout and, on Sundays, the village boys entertain themselves by fishing.

Leaving the main road at la Boissière, one reaches the height of les Leux from where the valley comes into view. The river that runs through it has divided the area into two very distinct regions: on the left are pastures, while the right consists of tilled land. The meadow stretches under a bulge of low hills to join at the back with the pasture land of the Bray country, while on the eastern side, the plain, gently rising, broadens out, showing as far as the eye can reach its blond wheatfields. The water, flowing through the grass, divides with a white line the color of the meadows from that of the ploughed fields, and the country is like a great unfolded mantle with a green velvet cape bordered with a fringe of silver.

On the horizon rise the oaks of the forest of Argueil, with the steeps of the Saint-Jean hills scarred from top to bottom with red irregular lines; they are rain-tracks, and these brick-tones standing out in narrow streaks against the grey colour of the mountain are due to the high iron content of the springs that flow beyond in the neighboring country.

These are the confines of Normandy, Picardy, and the Ile-de-France, a mongrel land whose language, like its landscape, is with-out accent or character. The worst Neufchâtel cheeses in the arron-dissement are made here; and, on the other hand, farming is costly because so much manure is needed to enrich this brittle soil, full of sand and stones.

Up to 1835 no practicable road for getting to Yonville existed, but about this time a cross-road was cut, joining the Abbeville to the Amiens highway; it is occasionally used by the Rouen teamsters on their way to Flanders. Yonville-l'Abbaye has remained stationary in spite of its "new outlet." Instead of improving the soil they persist in keeping up the pasture lands, however depreciated they may be in value, and the lazy village, growing away from the plain, has naturally spread riverwards. It is seen from afar sprawling along the banks like a cowherd taking a nap by the side of the river.

At the foot of the hill beyond the bridge begins a roadway, planted with young aspens that leads in a straight line to the first houses in the place. These, fenced in by hedges, are in the middle of courtyards full of straggling buildings, wine-presses, cart-sheds, and distilleries scattered under thick trees, with ladders, poles, or scythes hooked over the branches. The thatched roofs, like fur caps drawn over eyes, reach down over about a third of the low windows, whose coarse convex glasses have bull's eyes in the middle, like the bottom of a bottle. A meagre pear-tree may be found leaning against some plaster wall crossed by black beams, and one enters the ground-floors through a door with a small swing-gate that keeps out the chicks when they pilfer, on the threshold, crumbs of bread steeped in cider. Gradually the courtyards grow narrower, the houses closer together, and the fences disappear; a bundle of ferns swings under a window from the end of a broom-stick; there is a blacksmith's forge and then a wheelwright's, with two or three new carts outside that partly block the way. Then across an open space appears a white house at the end of a round lawn ornamented by a Cupid, his finger on his lips. Two cast-iron jars flank the high porch, copper signs gleam on the door. It is the notary's house, the finest in the place.

The church is on the other side of the street, twenty paces farther down, at the entrance of the square. The little graveyard that surrounds it, closed in by a breast-high wall, is so full of graves that the old stones, level with the ground, form a continuous pavement, on which the grass has, by itself, marked out regular green squares. The church was rebuilt during the last years of the reign of Charles X. The wooden roof is beginning to rot from the top, and here and there black hollows appear in the blue paint. Over the door, where the organ should be, is a gallery for the men, with a spiral staircase that reverberates under the weight of their wooden shoes.

The daylight coming through the plain glass windows falls obliquely upon the pews perpendicular to the walls, here and there adorned with a straw mat inscribed, in large letters, with the name of some parishioner. Further on, where the nave grows narrow, the confessional faces a small Madonna, clothed in satin, wearing a tulle veil sprinkled with silver stars and with cheeks stained red like an idol of the Sandwich Islands; finally, a painted copy entitled "The Holy Family, a gift from the Minister of the Interior," flanked by four candlesticks, crowns the main altar and rounds off the view. The choir stalls, of pine wood, have been left unpainted.

The market, that is to say, a tiled roof supported by some twenty posts, occupies by itself about half the public square of Yonville. The town hall, constructed "after the designs of a Paris architect," is a sort of Greek temple that forms the corner next to the pharmacy. On the ground-floor are three Ionic columns and on the first floor a gallery with arched windows, while the crowning frieze is occupied by a Gallic cock, resting one foot upon the Charter[1] and holding in the other the scales of Justice.

But what catches the eye most of all is Mr. Homais' pharmacy, right across from the Lion d'Or. In the evening especially its lamp is lit up and the red and green jars that embellish his shop-front cast their colored reflection far across the street; beyond them, as in a Bengal light, the silhouette of the pharmacist can be seen leaning over his desk. His house is plastered from top to bottom with inscriptions written in longhand, in round, in lower case: "Vichy, Seltzer and Barrège waters, depurative gum drops, Raspail patent medicine, Arabian racahout, Darcet lozenges, Regnault ointment, trusses, baths, laxative chocolate, etc." And the signboard, which stretches all the breadth of the shop, bears in gold letters "Homais, Pharmacist." Then at the back of the shop, behind the great scales fixed to the counter, the word "Laboratory" appears on a scroll above a glass door on which, about half-way up, the word Homais is once more repeated in gold letters on a black ground.

Beyond this there is nothing to see at Yonville. The street (the only one) a gunshot long and flanked by a few shops on either side stops short at the turn of the high road. Turning right and following the foot of the Saint-Jean hills one soon reaches the graveyard.

At the time of the cholera epidemic, a piece of wall was pulled down and three acres of land purchased in order to make more room, but the new area is almost deserted; the tombs, as heretofore, continue to crowd together towards the gate. The keeper, who is at once gravedigger and church sexton (thus making a double profit out of the parish corpses), has taken advantage of the unused plot of ground to plant potatoes. From year to year, however, his small field grows smaller, and when there is an epidemic, he does not know whether to rejoice at the deaths or regret the added graves.

"You feed on the dead, Lestiboudois!" the curé told him one day.

This grim remark made him reflect; it checked him for some time; but to this day he carries on the cultivation of his little tubers, and even maintains stoutly that they grow naturally.

Since the events about to be narrated, nothing in fact has changed at Yonville. The tin tricolour flag still swings at the top of

1. The *Charte constitutionelle de la France*, basis of the French constitution after the Revolution, bestowed in 1814 by Louis XVIII and revised in 1830, after the downfall of Charles X.

the church-steeple; the two streamers at the novelty store still flutter in the wind; the spongy white lumps, the pharmacist's foetuses, rot more and more in their cloudy alcohol, and above the big door of the inn the old golden lion, faded by rain, still shows passers-by its poodle mane.

On the evening when the Bovarys were to arrive at Yonville, the widow Lefrançois, the landlady of this inn, was so busy that she sweated great drops as she moved her saucepans around. To-morrow was market-day. The meat had to be cut beforehand, the chickens drawn, the soup and coffee made. Moreover, she had the boarders' meal to see to, and that of the doctor, his wife, and their maid; the billiard-room was echoing with bursts of laughter; three millers in the small parlour were calling for brandy; the wood was blazing, the charcoal crackling, and on the long kitchen-table, amid the quarters of raw mutton, rose piles of plates that rattled with the shaking of the block on which spinach was being chopped. From the poultry-yard was heard the screaming of the chickens whom the servant was chasing in order to wring their necks.

A slightly pockmarked man in green leather slippers, and wearing a velvet cap with a gold tassel, was warming his back at the chimney. His face expressed nothing but self-satisfaction, and he appeared as calmly established in life as the gold-finch suspended over his head in its wicker cage: he was the pharmacist.

"Artémise!" shouted the innkeeper, "chop some wood, fill the water bottles, bring some brandy, hurry up! If only I knew what dessert to offer the guests you are expecting! Good heavens! Those furniture-movers are beginning their racket in the billiard-room again; and their van has been left before the front door! The 'Hirondelle' might crash into it when it draws up. Call Polyte and tell him to put it away . . . Imagine, Monsieur Homais, that since morning they have had about fifteen games, and drunk eight pots of cider! . . . Why they'll tear my billiard-cloth to pieces!" she went on, looking at them from a distance, her strainer in her hand.

"That wouldn't be much of a loss," replied Monsieur Homais. "You would buy another."

"Another billiard-table!" exclaimed the widow.

"Since that one is coming to pieces, Madame Lefrançois. I tell you again you are doing yourself harm, much harm! And besides, players now want narrow pockets and heavy cues. They don't play the way they used to, everything is changed! One must keep pace with the times! Just look at Tellier!"

The hostess grew red with anger. The pharmacist added:

"You may say what you like; his table is better than yours; and if one were to think, for example, of getting up a patriotic tournament for Polish independence or for the victims of the Lyon floods . . ."[2]

"It isn't beggars like him that'll frighten us," interrupted the landlady, shrugging her fat shoulders. "Come, come, Monsieur Homais; as long as the 'Lion d'Or' exists people will come to it. We are no fly-by-nights, we have feathered our nest! While one of these days you'll find the 'Café Français' closed with a fine poster on the shutters. Change my billiard-table!" she went on, speaking to herself, "the table that comes in so handy for folding the washing, and on which, in the hunting season, I have slept six visitors! . . . But what can be keeping the slowpoke of a Hivert?"

"Are you waiting for him to serve your gentlemen's dinner?"

"Wait for him! And what about Monsieur Binet? As the clock strikes six you'll see him come in, for he hasn't his equal under the sun for punctuality. He must always have his seat in the small parlour. He'd rather die than eat anywhere else. And he is finicky! and particular about his cider! Not like monsieur Léon; he sometimes comes at seven, or even half-past, and he doesn't so much as look at what he eats. Such a nice young man! Never speaks a cross word!"

"Well, you see, there's a great difference between an educated man and a former army man who is now a tax-collector."

Six o'clock struck. Binet came in.

He was dressed in a blue frock-coat falling in a straight line round his thin body, and his leather cap, with its lappets knotted over the top of his head with string, showed under the turned-up peak a bald forehead, flattened by the constant wearing of a helmet. He wore a black cloth vest, a hair collar, grey trousers, and, all the year round, well-blacked boots, that had two parallel swellings where the big toes protruded. Not a hair stood out from the regular line of fair whiskers, which, encircling his jaws, framed like a garden border his long, wan face, with smallish eyes and a hooked nose. Clever at all games of cards, a good hunter, and writing a fine hand, he had at home a lathe, and amused himself by turning napkin-rings, with which he crammed his house, jealous as an artist and selfish as a bourgeois.

He went to the small parlour, but the three millers had to be got out first, and during the whole time necessary for resetting the table, Binet remained silent in his place near the stove. Then he shut the door and took off his cap as usual.

"Politeness will not wear out his tongue," said the pharmacist, as soon as he was alone with the hostess.

"He never talks more," she replied. "Last week I had two travel-

2. The allusion dates the action of the novel as taking place in 1840; during the winter of 1840, the Rhône overflowed with catastrophic results. At the same time, Louis Philippe was under steady attack for his failure to offer sufficient assistance to the victims of the repression that followed the insurrection of Warsaw.

ling salesmen here selling cloth, really a cheerful pair, who spent the night telling jokes. They made me weep with laughter but he, he stood there mute as a fish, never opened his mouth."

"Yes," said the pharmacist, "no imagination, no wit, nothing that makes a man shine in society."

"Yet they say he is a man of means," objected the landlady.

"Of means?" replied the pharmacist. "He? In his own line, perhaps," he added in a calmer tone. And he went on:

"Now, that a businessman with numerous connections, a lawyer, a doctor, a pharmacist, should be thus absent-minded, that they should become whimsical or even peevish, I can understand; such cases are cited in history. But at least it is because they are thinking of something. How often hasn't it happened to me, for instance, to look on my desk for my pen when I had to write out a label, merely to discover, at last, that I had put it behind my ear?"

Madame Lefrançois just then went to the door to see if the "Hirondelle" was not coming. She started. A man dressed in black suddenly came into the kitchen. By the last gleam of the twilight one could see that he was red-faced and powerfully built.

"What can I do for you, Monsieur le curé?" asked the hostess, as she reached down a copper candlestick from the row of candles. "Will you have something to drink? A thimbleful of *Cassis*? A glass of wine?"

The priest declined very politely. He had come for his umbrella, that he had forgotten the other day at the Ernemont convent, and after asking Madame Lefrançois to have it sent to him at the rectory in the evening, he left for the church; the Angelus was ringing.

When the pharmacist no longer heard the noise of his boots along the square, he confessed that he had found the priest's behaviour just now very unbecoming. This refusal to take any refreshment seemed to him the most odious hypocrisy; all priests tippled on the sly, and were trying to bring back the days of the tithe.

The landlady took up the defence of her curé.

"Besides, he could double up four men like you over his knee. Last year he helped our people to bring in the hay, he carried as many as six bales at once, he is so strong."

"Bravo!" said the pharmacist. "Now just send your daughters to confess to such vigorous fellows! I, if I were the Government, I'd have the priests bled once a month. Yes, Madame Lefrançois, every month—a good phlebotomy, in the interests of the police and morals."

"Be quiet, Monsieur Homais. You are a godless man! You have no religion."

The chemist replied:

"I have a religion, my religion, and I even have more than all these others with their mummeries and their juggling. I adore God, on the contrary. I believe in the Supreme Being, in a Creator, whatever he may be. I care little who has placed us here below to fulfill our duties as citizens and parents; but I don't need to go to church to kiss silver plates, and fatten, out of my pocket, a lot of good-for-nothings who live better than we do. For one can know him as well in a wood, in a field, or even contemplating the ethereal heavens like the ancients. My God is the God of Socrates, of Franklin, of Voltaire, and of Béranger! I support the *Profession de Foi du Vicaire savoyard* and the immortal principles of '89! And I can't admit of an old boy of a God who takes walks in his garden with a cane in his hand, who lodges his friends in the belly of whales, dies uttering a cry, and rises again at the end of three days; things absurd in themselves, and completely opposed, moreover, to all physical laws, which proves to us, by the way, that priests have always wallowed in squalid ignorance, and tried to drag whole nations down after them."

He stopped, looked around as if expecting to find an audience, for in his enthusiasm the pharmacist had for a moment fancied himself in the midst of the town council. But the landlady no longer heard him; she was listening to a distant rolling. One could distinguish the noise of a carriage mingled with the clattering of loose horseshoes that beat against the ground, and at last the "Hirondelle" stopped at the door.

It was a yellow box on two large wheels, that, reaching to the tilt, prevented travellers from seeing the road and dirtied their shoulders. The small panes of narrow windows rattled in their frames when the coach was closed, and retained here and there patches of mud amid the old layers of dust, that not even storms of rain had altogether washed away. It was drawn by three horses, the first a leader, and when it came down-hill its lower side jolted against the ground.

Some of the inhabitants of Yonville came out into the square; they all spoke at once, asking for news, for explanations of the delay, for their orders. Hivert did not know whom to answer first. He ran the errands in town for the entire village. He went to the shops and brought back rolls of leather for the shoemaker, old iron for the farrier, a barrel of herrings for his mistress, hats from the hat-shop and wigs from the hairdresser, and all along the road on his return journey he distributed his parcels, throwing them over fences as he stood upright on his seat and shouted at the top of his voice, while his horses went their own way.

An accident had delayed him. Madame Bovary's greyhound had escaped across the field. They had whistled for him a quarter of an hour; Hivert had even gone back a mile and a half expecting every moment to catch sight of her; but they had been forced to resume the journey. Emma had wept, grown angry; she had accused Charles of this misfortune. Monsieur Lheureux, a draper, who happened to be in the coach with her, had tried to console her by a number of examples of lost dogs recognising their masters at the end of long years. He had been told of one, he said, who had come back to Paris from Constantinople. Another had gone one hundred and fifty miles in a straight line, and swum four rivers; and his own father had owned a poodle, which, after twelve years of absence, had all of a sudden jumped on his back in the street as he was going to dine in town.

II

Emma got out first, then Félicité, Monsieur Lheureux, and a nurse, and they had to wake up Charles in his corner, where he had slept soundly since night set in.

Homais introduced himself; he offered his homages to madame and his respects to monsieur; said he was charmed to have been able to render them some slight service, and added cordially that he had taken the liberty to join them at dinner, his wife being away.

When Madame Bovary entered the kitchen she went up to the fireplace. With two fingertips she caught her dress at the knee, and having thus pulled it up to her ankle, held out her black-booted foot to the fire above the revolving leg of mutton. The flame lit up the whole of her, casting its harsh light over the pattern of her gown, the fine pores of her fair skin, and even her eyelids, when she blinked from time to time. A great red glow passed over her with the wind, blowing through the half-open door.

On the other side of the fireplace, a fair-haired young man watched her in silence.

As he was frequently bored at Yonville, where he was a clerk at Maître Guilleumin, the notary, Monsieur Léon Dupuis (the second of the *Lion d'Or*'s daily customers) often delayed his dinner-hour in the hope that some traveller might come to the inn, with whom he could chat in the evening. On the days when his work was done early, he had, for want of something else to do, to come punctually, and endure from soup to cheese a *tête-à-tête* with Binet. It was therefore with delight that he accepted the hostess's suggestion that he should dine in company with the newcomers, and they passed into the large parlour where Madame Lefrançois, hoping to make an impression, had had the table laid for four.

Homais asked to be allowed to keep on his skull-cap, for fear of catching cold; then, turning to his neighbor:

"Madame is no doubt a little fatigued; one gets so frightfully shaken up in out *Hirondelle*."

"That is true," replied Emma; "but moving about always amuses me. I like a change."

"It is so tedious," sighed the clerk, "to be always riveted to the same places."

"If you were like me," said Charles, "constantly obliged to be in the saddle" . . .

"But," Leon went on, addressing himself to Madame Bovary, "nothing, it seems to me, is more pleasant—when one can," he added.

"Moreover," said the pharmacist, "the practice of medicine is not very hard work in our part of the world, for the state of our roads allows us the use of gigs, and generally, as the farmers are well off, they pay pretty well. We have, medically speaking, besides the ordinary cases of enteritis, bronchitis, bilious affections, &c., now and then a few intermittent fevers at harvest-time; but on the whole, little of a serious nature, nothing special to note, unless it be a great deal of scrofula, due, no doubt, to the deplorable hygienic conditions of our peasant dwellings. Ah! you will find many prejudices to combat, Monsieur Bovary, much obstinacy of routine, with which all the efforts of your science will daily come into collision; for people still have recourse to novenas, to relics, to the priest, rather than come straight to the doctor or the pharmacist. The climate, however, is truly not too bad, and we even have a few nonagenarians in our parish. The thermometer (I have made some observations) falls in winter to 4 degrees, and in the hottest season rises to 25 or 30 degrees Centigrade at the outside, which gives us 24 degrees Réaumur as the maximum, or otherwise stated 54 degrees Fahrenheit (English scale), not more. And, as a matter of fact, we are sheltered from the north winds by the forest of Argueil on the one side, from the west winds by the Saint Jean hills on the other; and this heat, moreover, which, on account of the watery vapours given off by the river and the considerable number of cattle in the fields, which, as you know, exhale much ammonia, that is to say, nitrogen, hydrogen, and oxygen (no, nitrogen and hydrogen alone), and which sucking up the humus from the soil, mixing together all those different emanations, unites them into a single bundle, so to speak, and combining with the electricity diffused through the atmosphere, when there is any, might in the long-run, as in tropical countries, engender poisonous fumes,—this heat, I say, finds itself perfectly tempered on the side from where it comes, or rather from where it ought to come, that is the south side, by the south-eastern winds, which, having cooled themselves in crossing the Seine, reach us sometimes all at once like blasts from Russia!"

"Do you at least have some walks in the neighborhood?" continued Madame Bovary, speaking to the young man.

"Oh, very few," he answered. "There is a place they call La Pâture, on the top of the hill, on the edge of the forest. Sometimes, on Sundays, I go and stay there with a book, watching the sunset."

"I think there is nothing so beautiful as sunsets," she resumed; "but especially by the seashore."

"Oh, I love the sea!" said Monsieur Léon.

"And doesn't it seem to you," continued Madame Bovary, "that the mind travels more freely on this limitless expanse, of which the contemplation elevates the soul, gives ideas of the infinite, the ideal?"

"It is the same with mountainous landscapes," continued Léon. "A cousin of mine who travelled in Switzerland last year told me that one could not picture to oneself the poetry of the lakes, the charm of the waterfalls, the gigantic effect of the glaciers. One sees pines of incredible size across torrents, cottages suspended over precipices, and, a thousand feet below one, whole valleys when the clouds open. Such spectacles must stir to enthusiasm, incline to prayer, to ecstasy; and I no longer wonder why a celebrated musician, in order to stimulate his imagination, was in the habit of playing the piano before some imposing view."

"Do you play?" she asked.

"No, but I am very fond of music," he replied.

"Ah! don't you listen to him, Madame Bovary," interrupted Homais, bending over his plate. "That's sheer modesty. Why, my friend, the other day in your room you were singing 'L'Ange Gardien'[3] to perfection. I heard you from the laboratory. You articulated with the skill of an actor."

Léon rented a small room at the pharmacist's, on the second floor overlooking the Square. He blushed at the compliment of his landlord, who had already turned to the doctor, and was enumerating to him, one after the other, all the principal inhabitants of Yonville. He was telling anecdotes, giving information; no one knew just how wealthy the notary was and there were, of course, the Tuvaches who put up a considerable front.

Emma continued, "And what music do you prefer?"

"Oh, German music; that which makes you dream."

"Have you been to the opera?"

"Not yet; but I shall go next year, when I'll be living in Paris to get a law degree."

"As I had the honour of putting it to your husband," said the pharmacist, "with regard to this poor Yanoda who has run away, you will find yourself, thanks to his extravagance, in the possession of one of the most comfortable houses of Yonville. Its greatest

3. A sentimental romance written by Mme. Pauline Duchambre, author of several such songs that appeared in the keepsakes.

convenience for a doctor is a door giving on the Walk, where one can go in and out unseen. Moreover, it contains everything that is useful in a household—a laundry, kitchen with pantry, sitting-room, fruit bins, etc. He was a gay dog, who didn't care what he spent. At the end of the garden, by the side of the water, he had an arbour built just for the purpose of drinking beer in summer; and if madame is fond of gardening she will be able . . . "

"My wife doesn't care to," said Charles; "although she has been advised to take exercise, she prefers always sitting in her room reading."

"Just like me," replied Léon. "And indeed, what is better than to sit by one's fireside in the evening with a book, while the wind beats against the window and the lamp is burning? . . ."

"What, indeed?" she said, fixing her large black eyes wide open upon him.

"One thinks of nothing," he continued; "the hours slip by. Without having to move, we walk through the countries of our imagination, and your thought, blending with the fiction, toys with the details, follows the outline of the adventures. It mingles with the characters, and it seems you are living their lives, that your own heart beats in their breast."

"That is true! that is true!" she said.

"Has it ever happened to you," Léon went on, "to discover some vague idea of one's own in a book, some dim image that comes back to you from afar, and as the fullest expression of your own slightest sentiment?"

"I have experienced it," she replied.

"That is why," he said, "I especially love the poets. I think verse more tender than prose, and that it makes one weep more easily."

"Still in the long-run it is tiring," continued Emma, "and now, on the contrary, I have come to love stories that rush breath-lessly along, that frighten one. I detest commonplace heroes and moderate feelings, as one finds them in nature."

"You are right," observed the clerk, "since these works fail to touch the heart, they miss, it seems to me, the true end of art. It is so sweet, amid all the disenchantments of life, to be able to dwell in thought upon noble characters, pure affections, and pictures of happiness. For myself, living here far from the world, this is my one distraction. But there is so little to do in Yonville!"

"Like Tostes, no doubt," replied Emma; "and so I always sub-scribed to a lending library."

"If madame will do me the honor of making use of it," said the pharmacist, who had just caught the last words, "I have at her disposal a library composed of the best authors, Voltaire, Rousseau, Delille, Walter Scott, the 'Echo des Feuilletons'; and in addition I receive various periodicals, among them the 'Fanal de Rouen' daily, being privileged to act as its correspondent for the districts of Buchy, Forges, Neufchâtel, Yonville, and vicinity."

They had been at the table for two hours and a half, for Artémise, the maid, listlessly dragged her slippered feet over the tile-floor, brought in the plates one by one, forgot everything, understood nothing and constantly left the door of the billiard-room half open, so that the handle kept beating against the wall with its hooks.

Unconsciously, Léon, while talking, had placed his foot on one of the bars of the chair on which Madame Bovery was sitting. She wore a small blue silk necktie, which held upright, stiff as a ruff, a pleated batiste collar, and with the movements of her head the lower part of her face gently sunk into the linen or rose from it. Thus side by side, while Charles and the pharmacist chatted, they entered into one of those vague conversations where the hazard of all that is said brings you back to the fixed centre of a common sympathy. The Paris theatres, titles of novels, new quadrilles, and the world they did not know; Tostes, where she had lived, and Yonville, where they were; they examined all, talked of everything till the end of dinner.

When coffee was served Félicité left to prepare the room in the new house, and the guests soon rose from the table. Madame Lefrançois was asleep near the cinders, while the stable-boy, lantern in hand, was waiting to show Monsieur and Madame Bovary the way home. Bits of straw stuck in his red hair, and his left leg had a limp. When he had taken in his other hand the curé's umbrella, they started.

The town was asleep; the pillars of the market threw great shadows; the earth was all grey as on a summer's night.

But as the doctor's house was only some fifty paces from the inn, they had to say good-night almost immediately, and the company dispersed.

As soon as she entered the hallway, Emma felt the cold of the plaster fall about her shoulders like damp linen. The walls were new and the wooden stairs creaked. In their bedroom, on the first floor, a whitish light passed through the curtainless windows. She could catch glimpses of tree-tops, and beyond, the fields, half-drowned in the fog that lay like smoke over the course of the river. In the middle of the room, pell-mell, were scattered drawers, bottles, curtain-rods, gilt poles, with mattresses on the chairs and basins on the floor—the two men who had brought the furniture had left everything about carelessly.

This was the fourth time that she had slept in a strange place. The first was the day she went to the convent; the second, of her arrival at Tostes; the third, at Vaubyessard; and this was the fourth; and it so happened that each one had marked in her life a new beginning. She did not believe that things could remain the same in different places, and since the portion of her life that lay behind her had been bad, no doubt that which remained to be lived would be better.

III

The next day, as she was getting up, she saw the clerk on the Place. She had on a dressing-gown. He looked up and bowed. She nodded quickly and reclosed the window.

Léon waited all day for six o'clock in the evening to come, but on going to the inn, he found only Monsieur Binet already seated at the table.

The dinner of the evening before had been a considerable event for him; he had never till then talked for two hours consecutively to a "lady." How then had he been able to express, and in such language, so many things that he could not have said so well before? He was usually shy, and maintained that reserve which partakes at once of modesty and dissimulation. At Yonville, his manners were generally admired. He listened to the opinions of the older people, and seemed to have moderate political views, a rare thing for a young man. Then he had some accomplishments; he painted in water-colours, could read music, and readily talked literature after dinner when he did not play cards. Monsieur Homais respected him for his education; Madame Homais liked him for his good-nature, for he often took the little Homais into the garden—little brats who were always dirty, very much spoilt, and somewhat slow-moving, like their mother. They were looked after by the maid and by Justin, the pharmacist's apprentice, a second cousin of Monsieur Homais, who had been taken into the house out of charity and was also being put to work as a servant.

The druggist proved the best of neighbors. He advised Madame Bovary as to the tradespeople, sent expressly for his own cider merchant, tasted the wine himself, and saw that the casks were properly placed in the cellar; he explained how to stock up cheaply on butter, and made an arrangement with Lestiboudois, the sacristan, who, besides his ecclesiastical and funereal functions, looked after the main gardens at Yonville by the hour or the year, according to the wishes of the customers.

The need of looking after others was not the only thing that urged the pharmacist to such obsequious cordiality; there was a plan underneath it all.

He had infringed the law of the 19th Ventôse, year xi., article 1, which forbade all persons not having a diploma to practise medicine; so that, after certain anonymous denunciations, Homais had been summoned to Rouen to see the royal prosecutor in his private office; the magistrate receiving him standing up, ermine on shoulder and cap on head. It was in the morning, before the court opened. In the corridors one heard the heavy boots of the gendarmes walking past, and like a far-off noise great locks that were shut. The druggist's ears tingled as if he were about to have a stroke; he saw the depths of dungeons, his family in tears, his shop sold, all the jars dispersed; and he was obliged to enter a café and take a glass of rum and soda water to recover his spirits.

Little by little the memory of this reprimand grew fainter, and he continued, as heretofore, to give anodyne consultations in his back-parlour. But the mayor resented it, his colleagues were jealous, he had everything and everyone to fear; gaining over Monsieur Bovary by his attentions was to earn his gratitude, and prevent his speaking out later on, should he notice anything. So every morning Homais brought him the paper, and often in the afternoon left his shop for a few moments to have a chat with the Doctor.

Charles was depressed: he had no patients. He remained seated for hours without speaking, went into his consulting-room to sleep, or watched his wife sewing. Then for diversion he tried to work as a handyman around the house; he even tried to decorate the attic with some paint that had been left behind by the painters. But money matters worried him. He had spent so much for repairs at Tostes, for madame's toilette, and for the moving, that the whole dowry, over three thousand écus, had slipped away in two years. Then how many things had been spoilt or lost during their move from Tostes to Yonville, without counting the plaster curé, who, thrown out of the carriage by a particularly severe jolt, had broken in a thousand pieces on the pavement of Quincampoix!

A more positive worry came to distract him, namely, the pregnancy of his wife. As the time of birth approached he cherished her more. It was another bond of the flesh between them, and, as it were, a continued sentiment of a more complex union. When he caught sight of her indolent walk or watched her figure filling out over her uncorseted hips, when he had the opportunity to look at her undisturbed taking tired poses in her armchair, then his happiness knew no bounds; he got up, embraced her, passed his hands over her face, called her little mamma, wanted to make her dance, and, half-laughing, half-crying, uttered all kinds of caressing pleasantries that came into his head. The idea of having begotten a child delighted him. Now he wanted nothing more. He knew all there was to know of human life and sat down to enjoy it serenely, his elbows planted on the table as for a good meal.

Emma at first felt a great astonishment; then was anxious to be delivered that she might know what it felt like to be a mother. But not being able to spend as much as she would have liked on a suspended cradle with rose silk curtains, and embroidered caps, in a fit of bitterness she gave up looking for the layette altogether and had it all made by a village seamstress, without choosing or discussing anything.

Thus she did not amuse herself with those preparations that stimulate the tenderness of mothers, and so her affection was perhaps impaired from the start.

As Charles, however, spoke of the baby at every meal, she soon began to think of him more steadily.

She hoped for a son; he would be strong and dark; she would call him George; and this idea of having a male child was like an expected revenge for all her impotence in the past. A man, at least, is free; he can explore all passions and all countries, overcome obstacles, taste of the most distant pleasures. But a woman is always hampered. Being inert as well as pliable, she has against her the weakness of the flesh and the inequity of the law. Like the veil held to her hat by a ribbon, her will flutters in every breeze; she is always drawn by some desire, restrained by some rule of conduct.

She gave birth on a Sunday at about six o'clock, as the sun was rising.

"It is a girl!" said Charles.

She turned her head away and fainted.

Madame Homais, as well as Madame Lefrançois of the Lion d'Or, almost immediately came running in to embrace her. The pharmacist, as a man of discretion, only offered a few provisional felicitations through the half-opened door. He asked to see the child, and thought it well made.

During her recovery, she spent much time seeking a name for her daughter. First she went over all names that have Italian endings, such as Clara, Louisa, Amanda, Atala; she liked Galsuinde pretty well, and Yseult or Léocadie still better. Charles wanted the child to be called after her mother; Emma opposed this. They ran over the calendar from end to end, and then consulted outsiders.

"Monsieur Léon," said the chemist, "with whom I was talking about it the other day, wonders why you do not choose Madeleine. It is very much in fashion just now."

But Monsieur Bovary's mother protested loudly against this name of a sinner. As to Monsieur Homais, he had a preference for all names that recalled some great man, an illustrious fact, or a generous idea, and it was in accordance with this system that he had baptized his four children. Thus Napoleon represented glory and Franklin liberty; Irma was perhaps a concession to romanticism, but Athalie was a homage to the greatest masterpiece of the French stage. For his philosophical convictions did not interfere with his

artistic tastes; in him the thinker did not stifle the man of sentiment; he could make distinctions, make allowances for imagination
and fanaticism. In this tragedy, for example, he found fault with
the ideas, but admired the style; he detested the conception, but
applauded all the details, and loathed the characters while he grew
enthusiastic over their dialogue. When he read the fine passages he
was transported, but when he thought that the Catholics would use
it to their advantage, he was disconsolate; and in this confusion of
sentiments in which he was involved he would have liked both to
crown Racine with both his hands and take him to task for a good
quarter of an hour.

At last Emma remembered that at the château of Vaubyessard
she had heard the Marquise call a young lady Berthe; from that
moment this name was chosen; and as old Rouault could not come,
Monsieur Homais was requested to be godfather. His gifts were all
products from his establishment, to wit: six boxes of jujubes, a
whole jar of racahout, three cakes of marsh-mallow paste, and six
sticks of sugar-candy that he had come across in a cupboard. On the
evening of the ceremony there was a grand dinner; the curé was
present; there was much excitement. Towards liqueur time, Monsieur
Homais began singing "Le Dieu des bonnes gens." Monsieur Léon
sang a barcarolle, and the elder Madame Bovary, who was god-
mother, a romance of the time of the Empire; finally, M. Bovary,
senior, insisted on having the child brought down, and began bap-
tizing it with a glass of champagne that he poured over its head.
This mockery of the first of the sacraments aroused the indignation
of the Abbé Bournisien; Father Bovary replied by a quotation from
"La Guerre des Dieux"; the curé wanted to leave; the ladies implored, Homais interfered; they succeeded in making the priest sit
down again, and he quietly went on with the half-finished coffee in
his saucer.

Monsieur Bovary père stayed at Yonville a month, dazzling the
natives by a superb soldier's cap with silver tassels that he wore in
the morning when he smoked his pipe in the square. Being also in
the habit of drinking a good deal of brandy, he often sent the
servant to the Lion d'Or to buy him a bottle, which was put down
to his son's account, and to perfume his handkerchiefs he used up
his daughter-in-law's whole supply of eau-de-cologne.

The latter did not at all dislike his company. He had knocked
about the world, he talked about Berlin, Vienna, and Strasbourg, of
his soldier times, of his mistresses, of the brilliant dinner-parties he
had attended; then he was amiable, and sometimes even, either on
the stairs or in the garden, would catch her by the waist, exclaiming:

"Charles, you better watch out!"

Then the elder Madame Bovary became alarmed for her son's happiness, and fearing that her husband might in the long run have an immoral influence upon the ideas of the young woman, she speeded up their departure. Perhaps she had more serious reasons for uneasiness. Monsieur Bovary was the man to stop at nothing.

One day Emma was suddenly seized with the desire to see her little girl, who had been put to nurse with the carpenter's wife, and, without looking at the calendar to see whether the six weeks of the Virgin[4] were yet passed, she set out for the Rollets' house, situated at the extreme end of the village, between the highroad and the fields.

It was mid-day, the shutters of the houses were closed, and the slate roofs that glittered beneath the fierce light of the blue sky seemed to strike sparks from the crest of their gables. A heavy wind was blowing; Emma felt weak as she walked; the stones of the pavement hurt her; she was doubtful whether she would not go home again, or enter somewhere to rest.

At that moment Monsieur Léon came out from a neighboring door with a bundle of papers under his arm. He came to greet her, and stood in the shade in front of Lheureux's shop under the projecting grey awning.

Madame Bovary said she was going to see her baby, but that she was getting tired.

"If . . ." said Léon, not daring to go on.

"Have you any business to attend to?" she asked.

And on the clerk's negative answer, she begged him to accompany her. That same evening this was known in Yonville, and Madame Tuvache, the mayor's wife, declared in the presence of her maid that Madame Bovary was jeopardizing her good name.

To get to the nurse's it was necessary to turn to the left on leaving the street, as if heading for the cemetery, and to follow between little houses and yards a small path bordered with privet hedges. They were in bloom, and so were the speedwells, eglantines, thistles, and the sweetbriar that sprang up from the thickets. Through openings in the hedges one could see into the huts, some pig on a dung-heap, or tethered cows rubbing their horns against the trunk of trees. The two, side by side, walked slowly, she leaning upon him, and he restraining his pace, which he regulated by hers; in front of them flies were buzzing in the warm air.

They recognised the house by an old walnut-tree which shaded it. Low and covered with brown tiles, there hung outside it, beneath the attic-window, a string of onions. Faggots upright against a thorn fence surrounded a bed of lettuces, a few square feet of lavender,

4. Originally the six weeks that separate Christmas from Purification (Feb.
2nd); in those days, the normal period
of confinement for a woman after childbirth.

and sweet peas strung on sticks. Dirty water was running here and there on the grass, and all round were several indefinite rags, knitted stockings, a red flannel undershirt, and a large sheet of coarse linen spread over the hedge. At the noise of the gate the wet nurse appeared with a baby she was suckling on one arm. With her other hand she was pulling along a poor puny little boy, his face covered with a scrofulous rash, the son of a Rouen hosier, whom his parents, too taken up with their business, left in the country.

"Go in," she said; "your baby is there asleep."

The room on the ground-floor, the only one in the dwelling, had at its farther end, against the wall, a large bed without curtains, while a kneading-trough took up the side by the window, one pane of which was mended with a piece of blue paper. In the corner behind the door, shining hob-nailed shoes stood in a row under the slab of the washstand, near a bottle of oil with a feather stuck in its mouth; a Mathieu Laensberg[5] lay on the dusty mantelpiece amid gunflints, candle-ends, and bits of tinder. Finally, the last extravagance in the room was a picture representing Fame blowing her trumpets, cut out, no doubt, from some perfumer's prospectus and nailed to the wall with six wooden shoe-pegs.

Emma's child was asleep in a wicker-cradle. She took it up in the wrapping that enveloped it and began singing softly as she rocked it to and fro.

Léon walked up and down the room; it seemed strange to him to see this beautiful woman in her silk dress in the midst of all this poverty. Madame Bovary blushed; he turned away, thinking perhaps there had been an impertinent look in his eyes. Then she put back the little girl, who had just thrown up over her collar. The nurse at once came to dry her, protesting that it wouldn't show.

"You should see some of the other tricks she plays on me," she said. "I always seem to be sponging her off. If you would have the goodness to order Camus, the grocer, to let me have a little soap; it would really be more convenient for you, as I needn't trouble you then."

"All right, all right!" said Emma. "Good-bye, Madame Rollet."

And she went out, wiping her shoes at the door.

The woman accompanied her to the end of the garden, complaining all the time of the trouble she had getting up nights.

"I'm so worn out sometimes that I drop asleep on my chair. You could at least give me a pound of ground coffee; that'd last me a month, and I'd take it in the morning with some milk."

After having submitted to her thanks, Madame Bovary left. She had gone a little way down the path when, at the sound of wooden shoes, she turned round. It was the nurse.

5. A farmer's almanac, begun in 1635 by Mathieu Laensberg, frequently found in farms and country houses.

"What is it?"

Then the peasant woman, taking her aside behind an elm tree, began talking to her of her husband, who with his trade and six francs a year that the captain . . .

"Hurry up with your story," said Emma.

"Well," the nurse went on, heaving sighs between each word, "I'm afraid he'll be put out seeing me have coffee alone, you know men . . ."

"But I just told you you'll get some," Emma repeated; "I will give you some. Leave me alone!"

"Oh, my dear lady! you see, his wounds give him terrible cramps in the chest. He even says that cider weakens him."

"Do make haste, Mère Rollet!"

"Well," the latter continued, making a curtsey, "if it weren't asking too much," and she curtsied once more, "if you would"— and her eyes begged—"a jar of brandy," she said at last, "and I'd rub your little one's feet with it; they're as tender as your tongue."

Once they were rid of the nurse, Emma again took Monsieur Léon's arm. She walked fast for some time, then more slowly, and looking straight in front of her, her eyes rested on the shoulder of the young man, whose frock-coat had a black-velvet collar. His brown hair fell over it, straight and carefully combed. She noticed his nails, which were longer than one wore them in Yonville. It was one of the clerk's chief concerns to trim them, and for this purpose he kept a special knife in his writing-desk.

They returned to Yonville by the water-side. In the warm season the bank, wider than at other times, showed to their foot the garden walls from where a few steps led to the river. It flowed noiselessly, swift, and cold to the eye; long, thin grasses huddled together in it as the current drove them, and spread themselves upon the limpid water like streaming hair. Sometimes at the top of the reeds or on the leaf of a water-lily an insect with fine legs crawled or rested. The sun pierced with a ray the small blue bubbles of the waves that broke successively on the bank; branchless old willows mirrored their grey barks in the water; beyond, all around, the meadows seemed empty. It was the dinner-hour at the farms, and the young woman and her companion heard nothing as they walked but the fall of their steps on the earth of the path, the words they spoke, and the sound of Emma's dress rustling round her.

The walls of the gardens, crested with pieces of broken bottle, were heated like the glass roof of a hothouse. Wallflowers had sprung up between the bricks, and with the tip of her open parasol Madame Bovary, as she passed, made some of their faded flowers crumble into yellow dust, or else a spray of overhanging honeysuckle and clematis would catch in the fringe of the parasol and scrape for a moment over the silk.

They were talking of a troupe of Spanish dancers who were expected shortly at the Rouen theatre.

"Are you going?" she asked.

"If I can," he answered.

Had they nothing else to say to one another? Yet their eyes were full of more serious speech, and while they forced themselves to find trivial phrases, they felt the same languor stealing over them both; it was like the deep, continuous murmur of the soul dominating that of their voices. Surprised with wonder at this strange sweetness, they did not think of speaking of the sensation or of seeking its cause. Future joys are like tropical shores; like a fragrant breeze, they extend their innate softness to the immense inland world of past experience, and we are lulled by this intoxication into forgetting the unseen horizons beyond.

In one place the ground had been trodden down by the cattle; they had to step on large green stones put here and there in the mud. She often stopped a moment to look where to place her foot, and tottering on the stone that shook, her arms outspread, her form bent forward with a look of indecision, she would laugh, afraid of falling into the puddles of water.

When they arrived in front of her garden, Madame Bovary opened the little gate, ran up the steps and disappeared.

Léon returned to his office. His employer was away; he just glanced at the briefs, then cut himself a pen, and finally took up his hat and went out.

He went to La Pâture at the top of the Argueil hills at the beginning of the forest; he stretched out under the pines and watched the sky through his fingers.

"How bored I am!" he said to himself, "how bored I am!"

He thought he was to be pitied for living in this village, with Homais for a friend and Monsieur Guillaumin for master. The latter, entirely absorbed by his business, wearing gold-rimmed spectacles and red whiskers over a white cravat, understood nothing of mental refinements, although he affected a stiff English manner, which in the beginning had impressed the clerk.

As for Madame Homais, she was the best wife in Normandy, gentle as a sheep, loving her children, her father, her mother, her cousins, weeping for others' woes, letting everything go in her household, and detesting corsets; but so slow of movement, such a bore to listen to, so common in appearance, and of such restricted conversation, that although she was thirty and he only twenty, although they slept in rooms next each other and he spoke to her daily, he never thought that she might be a woman to anyone, or that she possessed anything else of her sex than the gown.

And what else was there? Binet, a few shopkeepers, two or three innkeepers, the curé, and, finally, Monsieur Tuvache, the mayor, with his two sons, rich, haughty, obtuse people, who farmed their own lands and had feasts among themselves, devout Christians at that, but altogether unbearable as companions.

But from the general background of all these human faces the figure of Emma stood out isolated and yet farthest off; for between her and him he seemed to sense a vague abyss.

In the beginning he had called on her several times along with the pharmacist. Charles had not appeared particularly anxious to see him again, and Léon did not know what to do between his fear of being indiscreet and the desire for an intimacy that seemed almost impossible.

IV

When the first cold days set in Emma left her bedroom for the parlour, a long, low-ceilinged room, with on the mantelpiece a large bunch of coral spread out against the looking-glass. Seated in her armchair near the window, she could see the villagers pass along the pavement.

Twice a day Léon went from his office to the Lion d'Or. Emma could watch him coming from afar; she leant forward listening, and the young man glided past the curtain, always dressed in the same way, and without turning his head. But in the twilight, when, her chin resting on her left hand, she let her begun embroidery fall on her knees, she often shuddered at the apparition of this shadow suddenly gliding past. She would get up and order the table to be laid.

Monsieur Homais called at dinner-time. Skull-cap in hand, he came in on tiptoe, in order to disturb no one, always repeating the same phrase, "Good evening, everybody." Then, when he had taken his seat at table between them, he asked the doctor about his patients, and the latter consulted him as to the probability of their payment. Next they talked of "what was in the paper." By this hour of the day, Homais knew it almost by heart, and he repeated from beginning to end, including the comments of the journalist, all the stories of individual catastrophes that had occurred in France or abroad. But the subject becoming exhausted, he was not slow in throwing out some remarks on the dishes before him. Sometimes even, half-rising, he delicately pointed out to madame the tenderest morsel, or turning to the maid, gave her some advice on the manipulation of stews and the hygiene of seasoning. He talked aroma, osmazome, juices, and gelatine in a bewildering manner. Moreover, Homais, with his head fuller of recipes than his shop of jars, excelled in making all kinds of preserves, vinegars, and sweet liqueurs; he knew also all the latest inventions in economic stoves, together with the art of preserving cheeses and of curing sick wines.

At eight o'clock Justin came to fetch him to shut up the shop. Then Monsieur Homais gave him a sly look, especially if Félicité was there, for he had noticed that his apprentice was fond of the doctor's house.

"The young man," he said, "is beginning to have ideas, and the devil take me if I don't believe he's in love with your maid!"

But a more serious fault with which he reproached Justin was his constantly listening to conversation. On Sunday, for example, one could not get him out of the parlor, even when Madame Homais called him to fetch the children, who had fallen asleep in the arm-chairs, dragging down with their backs the overwide slip-covers.

Not many people came to the pharmacist's evening parties, his scandal-mongering and political opinions having successfully alienated various persons. The clerk never failed to be there. As soon as he heard the bell he ran to meet Madame Bovary, took her shawl, and put away under the shop-counter the heavy overshoes she wore when it snowed.

First they played some hands at trente-et-un; next Monsieur Homais played écarté with Emma; Léon standing behind her, gave advice. Standing up with his hands on the back of her chair, he saw the teeth of her comb that bit into her chignon. With every movement that she made to throw her cards the right side of her dress was drawn up. From her turned-up hair a dark colour fell over her back, and growing gradually paler, lost itself little by little in the shade. Her dress dropped on both sides of her chair, blowing out into many folds before it spread on the floor. When Léon occasionally felt the sole of his boot resting on it, he drew back as if he had trodden on something alive.

When the game of cards was over, the pharmacist and the Doctor played dominoes, and Emma, changing her place, leant her elbow on the table, turning over the pages of "L'Illustration." She had brought her ladies' journal with her. Léon sat down near her; they looked at the engravings together, and waited for one another at the bottom of the pages. She often begged him to read her the verses; Léon declaimed them in a languid voice, to which he carefully gave a dying fall in the love passages. But the noise of the dominoes annoyed him. Monsieur Homais was strong at the game; he could beat Charles and give him a double-six. Then the three hundred finished, they both stretched in front of the fire, and were soon asleep. The fire was dying out in the cinders; the teapot was empty, Léon was still reading. Emma listened to him, mechanically turning round the lampshade, its gauze decorated with painted clowns in carriages, and tightrope dancers with balancing-poles.

Léon stopped, pointing with a gesture to his sleeping audience; then they talked in low tones, and their conversation seemed the sweeter to them because it was unheard.

Thus a kind of bond was established between them, a constant exchange of books and of romances. Little inclined to jealousy, Monsieur Bovary thought nothing of it.

On his birthday he received a beautiful phrenological head, all marked with figures to the thorax and painted blue. This was a gift of the clerk's. He showed him many other attentions, to the point of running errands for him at Rouen: and a novel having made the mania for cactuses fashionable, Léon bought some for Madame Bovary, bringing them back on his knees in the "Hirondelle," pricking his fingers on their hard spikes.

She had a railed shelf suspended against her window to hold the pots. The clerk, too, had his small hanging garden; they saw each other tending their flowers at their windows.

One of the village windows was even more often occupied; for on Sundays from morning to night, and every morning when the weather was bright, one could see at an attic-window the profile of Monsieur Binet bending over his lathe: its monotonous humming could be heard at the Lion d'Or.

One evening on coming home Léon found in his room a rug in velvet and wool with leaves on a pale ground. He called Madame Homais, Monsieur Homais, Justin, the children, the cook; he spoke of it to his employer; every one wanted to see this rug. Why did the doctor's wife give the clerk presents? It looked odd; and they decided that he must be her lover.

He gave plenty of reason for this belief, so ceaselessly did he talk of her charms and of her wit; so much so, that Binet once roughly interrupted him:

"What do I care since I'm not one of her friends?"

He tortured himself to find out how he could make his declaration to her, and always halting between the fear of displeasing her and the shame of being such a coward, he wept with discouragement and desire. Then he took energetic resolutions, wrote letters that he tore up, put it off to times that he again deferred. Often he set out with the determination to dare all; but this resolution soon deserted him in Emma's presence; and when Charles, dropping in, invited him to jump into his carriage to go with him to see some patient in the neighborhood, he at once accepted, bowed to madame, and left. Wasn't the husband also a part of her after all?

As for Emma, she did not ask herself whether she loved him. Love, she thought, must come suddenly, with great outbursts and lightnings,—a hurricane of the skies, which sweeps down on life, upsets everything, uproots the will like a leaf and carries away the heart as in an abyss. She did not know that on the terrace of houses the rain makes lakes when the pipes are choked, and she would thus have remained safe in her ignorance when she suddenly discovered a rent in the wall.

V

It was a Sunday in February, an afternoon when the snow was falling.

Monsieur and Madame Bovary, Homais, and Monsieur Léon had all gone to see a yarn-mill that was being built in the valley a mile and a half from Yonville. The druggist had taken Napoleon and Athalie to give them some exercise, and Justin accompanied them, carrying the umbrellas over his shoulder.

Nothing, however, could be less worth seeing than this sight. A great piece of waste ground, on which, amid a mass of sand and stones, were scattered a few rusty cogwheels, surrounded by a long rectangular building pierced with numerous little windows. The building was unfinished; the sky could be seen through the beams of the roofing. Attached to the ridgepole of the gable a bunch of straw mixed with corn-ears fluttered its tricoloured ribbons in the wind.

Homais was talking. He explained to the company the future importance of this establishment, computed the strength of the floorings, the thickness of the walls, and regretted extremely not having a yard-stick such as Monsieur Binet possessed for his own special use.

Emma, who had taken his arm, bent lightly against his shoulder, and she looked at the sun's disc shining afar through the mist with pale splendour. She turned; there was Charles. His cap was drawn down over his eyebrows, and his two thick lips were trembling, which added a look of stupidity to his face; his very back, his calm back, was irritating to behold, and she saw all his platitude spelled out right there, on his very coat.

While she was considering him thus, savoring her irritation with a sort of depraved pleasure, Léon made a step forward. The cold that made him pale seemed to add a more gentle languor to his face; between his cravat and his neck the somewhat loose collar of his shirt showed the skin; some of his ear was showing beneath a lock of hair, and his large blue eyes, raised to the clouds, seemed to Emma more limpid and more beautiful than those mountain-lakes which mirror the heavens.

"Look out there!" suddenly cried the pharmacist.

And he ran to his son, who had just jumped into a pile of lime in order to whiten his boots. Overcome by his father's reproaches, Napoleon began to howl, while Justin dried his shoes with a wisp of straw. But a knife was needed; Charles offered his.

"Ah!" she said to herself, "he carries a knife in his pocket like a peasant."

It was beginning to snow and they turned back to Yonville.

In the evening Madame Bovary did not go to her neighbor's, and when Charles had left and she felt herself alone, the comparison again forced itself upon her, almost with the clarity of direct sensation, and with that lengthening of perspective which memory gives to things. Looking from her bed at the bright fire that was burning, she still saw, as she had down there, Léon standing up with one hand bending his cane, and with the other holding Athalie, who was quietly sucking a piece of ice. She thought him charming; she could not tear herself away from him; she recalled his other attitudes on other days, the words he had spoken, the sound of his voice, his whole person; and she repeated, pouting out her lips as if for a kiss:

"Yes, charming! charming! Is he not in love?" . . . she asked herself; "but with whom? . . . With me!"

All the evidence asserted itself at once; her heart leapt. The flame of the fire threw a joyous light upon the ceiling; she turned on her back, stretched out her arms.

Then began the eternal lamentation: "Oh, if Heaven had but willed it! And why not? What prevented it?"

When Charles came home at midnight, she seemed to have just awakened, and as he made a noise undressing, she complained of a headache, then asked casually what had happened that evening.

"Monsieur Léon," he said, "went to his room early."

She could not help smiling, and she fell asleep, her soul filled with a new delight.

The next day, at dusk, she received a visit from Monsieur Lheureux, the owner of the local general store.

He was a smart man, this shopkeeper.

Born in Gascony but bred a Norman, he grafted upon his southern volubility the cunning of the Cauchois. His fat, flabby, beardless face seemed dyed by a decoction of liquorice, and his white hair made even more vivid the keen brilliance of his small black eyes. No one knew what he had been formerly; some said he was a peddler, others that he was a banker at Routot. One thing was certain: he could make complex figurings in his head that would have frightened Binet himself. Polite to obsequiousness, he always held himself with his back bent in the attitude of one who bows or who invites.

After leaving at the door his black-bordered hat, he put down a green cardboard box on the table, and began by complaining to madame, with many civilities, that he should have remained till that day without the benefit of her confidence. A poor shop like his was not made to attract a lady of fashion; he stressed the words; yet she had only to command, and he would undertake to provide her with anything she might wish, whether it be lingerie or knitwear, hats or dresses, for he went to town regularly four times a month. He was connected with the best houses. His name could be mentioned at the "Trois Frères," at the "Barbe d'Or," or at the "Grand Sauvage"; all these gentlemen knew him inside out. To-day, then, he had come to show madame, in passing, various articles he happened to have by an unusual stroke of luck. And he pulled out half-a-dozen embroidered collars from the box.

Madame Bovary examined them.

"I don't need anything," she said.

Then Monsieur Lheureux delicately exhibited three Algerian scarves, several packages of English needles, a pair of straw slippers, and, finally, four eggcups in cocoa-nut wood, carved in open work by convicts. Then, with both hands on the table, his neck stretched out, leaning forward with open mouth, he watched Emma's gaze wander undecided over the merchandise. From time to time, as if to remove some dust, he flicked his nail against the silk of the scarves spread out at full length, and they rustled with a little noise, making the gold spangles of the material sparkle like stars in the greenish twilight.

"How much are they?"

"A mere trifle," he replied, "a mere trifle. But there's no hurry; whenever it's convenient. We are no Jews."

She reflected for a few moments, and ended by again declining Monsieur Lheureux's offer. Showing no concern, he replied:

"Very well! Better luck next time. I have always got on with ladies . . . even if I didn't with my own!"

Emma smiled.

"I wanted to tell you," he went on good-naturedly, after his joke, "that it isn't the money I should trouble about. Why, I could give you some, if need be."

She made a gesture of surprise.

"Ah!" he said quickly and in a low voice, "I shouldn't have to go far to find you some, rely on that."

And he began asking after Père Tellier, the owner of the "Café Français," who was being treated by Monsieur Bovary at the time.

"What's the matter with Père Tellier? He makes the whole house shake with his coughing, and I'm afraid he'll soon need a pine coat rather than a flannel jacket. He certainly lived it up when he was young! These people, madame, they never know when to stop! He burned himself up with brandy. Still it's sad, all the same, to see an acquaintance go."

And while he fastened up his box he discoursed about the doctor's patients.

"It's the weather, no doubt," he said, looking frowningly at the floor, "that causes these illnesses. I myself don't feel just right. One of these days I shall even have to consult the doctor for a pain I have in my back. Well, good-bye, Madame Bovary. At your service; your very humble servant."

And he gently closed the door behind him.

Emma had her dinner served in her bedroom on a tray by the fireside; she took a long time eating; everything seemed wonderful.

"How good I was!" she said to herself, thinking of the scarves.

She heard steps on the stairs. It was Léon. She got up and took from the chest of drawers the first pile of dusters to be hemmed. When he came in she seemed very busy.

The conversation languished; Madame Bovary let it drop every few minutes, while he himself seemed quite embarrassed. Seated on a low chair near the fire, he kept turning the ivory thimble case with his fingers. She stitched on, or from time to time turned down the hem of the cloth with her nail. She did not speak; he was silent, captivated by her silence, as he would have been by her speech.

"Poor fellow!" she thought.

"How have I displeased her?" he asked himself.

At last, however, Léon said that one of these days, he had to go to Rouen on business.

"Your music subscription has expired; shall I renew it?"

"No," she replied.

"Why?"

"Because . . ."

And pursing her lips she slowly drew a long stitch of grey thread.

This work irritated Léon. It seemed to roughen the ends of her fingers. A gallant phrase came into his head, but he did not risk it.

"Then you are giving it up?" he went on.

"What?" she asked hurriedly. "Music? Ah! yes! Have I not my house to look after, my husband to attend to, a thousand things, in fact, many duties that must be considered first?"

She looked at the clock. Charles was late. Then she affected anxiety. Two or three times she even repeated, "He is so good!"

The clerk was fond of Monsieur Bovary. But this tenderness on his behalf came as an unpleasant surprise; still, he sang his praise: everyone did, he said, especially the pharmacist.

"Ah! he is a good man," continued Emma.

"Certainly," replied the clerk.

And he began talking of Madame Homais, whose very untidy appearance generally made them laugh.

"What does it matter?" interrupted Emma. "A good housewife does not trouble about her appearance."

Then she relapsed into silence.

It was the same on the following days; her talks, her manners, everything changed. She took interest in the housework, went to church regularly, and looked after her maid with more severity.

She took Berthe away from the nurse. When visitors called, Félicité brought her in, and Madame Bovary undressed her to show off her limbs. She claimed to love children; they were her consolation, her joy, her passion, and she accompanied her caresses with lyrical outbursts that would have reminded any one but the Yonvillians of Sachette in "Notre Dame de Paris."

When Charles came home he found his slippers put to warm near the fire. His waistcoat now never wanted lining, nor his shirt buttons, and it was quite a pleasure to see in the cupboard the nightcaps arranged in piles of the same height. She no longer grumbled as before when asked to take a walk in the garden; what he proposed was always done, although she never anticipated the wishes to which she submitted without a murmur; and when Léon saw him sit by his fireside after dinner, his two hands on his stomach, his two feet on the fender, his cheeks flushed with wine, his eyes moist with happiness, the child crawling along the carpet, and this woman with the slender waist who came behind his armchair to kiss his forehead:

"What madness!" he said to himself. "How could I ever hope to reach her?"

She seemed so virtuous and inaccessible to him that he lost all hope, even the faintest. But, by thus renouncing her, he made her ascend to extraordinary heights. She transcended, in his eyes, those sensuous attributes which were forever out of his reach; and in his heart she rose forever, soaring away from him like a winged apotheosis. It was one of those pure feelings that do not interfere with life, that are cultivated for their rarity, and whose loss would afflict more than their fulfilment rejoices.

Emma grew thinner, her cheeks paler, her face longer. With her black hair, her large eyes, her straight nose, her birdlike walk, and always silent now, did she not seem to be passing through life scarcely touching it, bearing on her brow the slight mark of a sublime destiny? She was so sad and so calm, at once so gentle and so reserved, that near her one came under the spell of an icy charm, as we shudder in churches at the perfume of the flowers mingling with the cold of the marble. Even others could not fail to be impressed. The pharmacist said:

"She is a real lady! She would not be out of place in a sous-préfecture!"

The housewives admired her thrift, the patients her politeness, the poor her charity.

But she was eaten up with desires, with rage, with hate. The rigid folds of her dress covered a tormented heart of which her chaste lips never spoke. She was in love with Léon, and sought solitude that she might more easily delight in his image. His physical presence troubled the voluptuousness of this meditation. Emma thrilled at the sound of his step; then in his presence the emotion subsided, and afterwards there remained in her only an immense astonishment that ended in sorrow.

Léon did not know that when he left her in despair she rose after he had gone to see him in the street. She concerned herself about his comings and goings; she watched his face; she invented quite a story to find an excuse for going to his room. She envied the pharmacist's wife for sleeping under the same roof, and her thoughts constantly centered upon this house, like the Lion d'Or pigeons who alighted there to dip their pink feet and white wings in the rainpipes. But the more Emma grew conscious of her love, the more she repressed it, hoping thus to hide and to stifle her true feeling. She would have liked Léon to know, and she imagined circumstances, catastrophes that would make this possible. What restrained her was, no doubt, idleness and fear, as well as a sense of shame. She thought she had repulsed him too much, that the time was past, that all was lost. Then, pride, the joy of being able to say to herself, "I am virtuous," and to look at herself in the mirror striking resigned poses, consoled her a little for the sacrifice she thought she was making.

Then the desires of the flesh, the longing for money, and the melancholy of passion all blended into one suffering, and instead of putting it out of her mind, she made her thoughts cling to it, urging herself to pain and seeking everywhere the opportunity to revive it. A poorly served dish, a half open door would aggravate her; she bewailed the clothes she did not have, the happiness she had missed, her overexalted dreams, her too cramped home.

What exasperated her was that Charles did not seem to be aware of her torment. His conviction that he was making her happy looked to her a stupid insult, and his self-assurance on this point sheer ingratitude. For whom, then, was she being virtuous? Was it not for him, the obstacle to all happiness, the cause of all misery, and, as it were, the sharp clasp of that complex strap that buckled her in al all sides?

Thus he became the butt of all the hatred resulting from her frustrations; but all efforts to conquer them augmented her suffering— for this useless humiliation still added to her despair and widened the gap between them. His very gentleness would drive her at times to rebellion. Domestic mediocrity urged her on to wild extravagance, matrimonial tenderness to adulterous desires. She would have liked

Charles to beat her, that she might have a better right to hate him, to revenge herself upon him. She was surprised sometimes at the shocking thoughts that came into her head, and she had to go on smiling, to hear repeated to her at all hours that she was happy, to pretend to be happy and let it be believed.

Yet, at moments, she loathed this hypocrisy. She was tempted to flee somewhere with Léon and try a new life; but at once a dark, shapeless chasm would open within her soul.

"Besides, he no longer loves me," she thought. "What is to become of me? What help can I hope for, what consolation, what relief?"

Such thoughts would leave her shattered, exhausted, frozen, sobbing silently, with flowing tears.

"Why don't you tell monsieur?" the maid asked her when she came in during these crises.

"It is nerves," said Emma. "Don't mention it to him, he would worry."

"Ah! yes," Félicité went on, "you are just like La Guérine, the daughter of Père Guérin, the fisherman at le Pollet[6], that I used to know at Dieppe before I came to see you. She was so sad, so sad, that to see her standing on the threshold of her house, she looked like a winding-sheet spread out before the door. Her illness, it appears, was a kind of fog that she had in the head, and the doctors could do nothing about it, neither could the priest. When she had a bad spell, she went off by herself to the sea-shore, so that the customs officer, going his rounds, often found her flat on her face, crying on the pebbles. Then, after her marriage, it stopped, they say."

"But with me," replied Emma, "it was after marriage that it began."

VI

One evening when she was sitting by the open window, watching Lestiboudois, the sexton, trim the boxwood, she suddenly heard the Angelus ringing.

It was the beginning of April, when the primroses are in bloom, and a warm wind blows over the newly-turned flower beds, and the gardens, like women, seem to be getting ready for the summer dances. Through the bars of the arbour and away beyond, the river could be seen in the fields, meandering through the grass in sinuous curves. The evening vapors rose between the leafless poplars, touching their outlines with a violet tint, paler and more transparent than a subtle gauze caught amidst their branches. Cattle moved around in the distance; neither their steps nor their lowing could be heard; and the bell, still ringing through the air, kept up its peaceful lamentation.

6. Suburb of Dieppe, where the fishermen live.

This repeated tinkling stirred in the young woman distant memories of her youth and school-days. She remembered the great candle-sticks that rose above the vases full of flowers on the altar, and the tabernacle with its small columns. She would have liked to be once more lost in the long line of white veils, marked off here and there by the stiff black hoods of the good sisters bending over their praying-chairs. At mass on Sundays, when she looked up, she saw the gentle face of the Virgin amid the blue smoke of the rising incense. The image awoke a tender emotion in her; she felt limp and helpless, like the down of a bird whirled by the tempest, and it was unconsciously that she went towards the church, ready for any kind of devotion, provided she could humble her soul and lose all sense of selfhood.

On the Square she met Lestiboudois on his way back, for, in order not to lose out on a full day's wages, he preferred to interrupt his gardening-work and go ring the Angelus when it suited him best. Besides, the earlier ringing warned the boys that catechism time had come.

Already a few who had arrived were playing marbles on the stones of the cemetery. Others, astride the wall, swung their legs, trampling with their wooden shoes the large nettles that grew between the little enclosure and the newest graves. This was the only green spot. All the rest was but stones, always covered with a fine dust, in spite of Lestiboudois' broom.

The children played around in their socks, as if they were on their own ground. The shouts of their voices could be heard through the humming of the bell. The noise subsided with the swinging of the great rope that, hanging from the top of the belfry, dragged its end on the ground. Swallows flitted to and fro uttering little cries, cutting the air with the edge of their wings, and swiftly returned to their yellow nests under the eave-tiles of the coping. At the end of the church a lamp was burning, the wick of a night-light hung up in a glass. Seen from a distance, it looked like a white stain trembling in the oil. A long ray of the sun fell across the nave and seemed to darken the lower sides and the corners.

"Where is the priest?" Madame Bovary asked one of the boys, who was entertaining himself by shaking the turnstile in its too loose socket.

"He is coming," he answered.

Indeed, the door of the rectory creaked and the Abbé Bournisien appeared; the children fled in a heap into the church.

"The little brats!" muttered the priest, "always the same!" Then, picking up a ragged catechism on which he had stepped:

"They have respect for nothing!"

But, as soon as he caught sight of Madame Bovary:

"Excuse me," he said; "I did not recognise you."

He thrust the catechism into his pocket, and stopped, balancing the heavy key of the sacristy between his two fingers.

The full light of the setting sun upon his face made the cloth of his cassock, shiny at the elbows and frayed at the hem, seem paler. Grease and tobacco stains ran along his broad chest, following the line of his buttons, growing sparser in the vicinity of his neckcloth, in which rested the massive folds of his red chin; it was dotted with yellow spots that disappeared beneath the coarse hair of his greyish beard. He had just eaten his dinner, and was breathing noisily.

"And how are you?" he added.

"Not well," replied Emma; "I am suffering."

"So do I," answered the priest. "The first heat of the year is hard to bear, isn't it? But, after all, we are born to suffer, as St. Paul says. But, what does Monsieur Bovary think of it?"

"He!" she said with a gesture of contempt.

"What!" he replied, genuinely surprised, "doesn't he prescribe something for you?"

"Ah!" said Emma, "it is no earthly remedy I need."

But the curé time and again was looking into the church, where the kneeling boys were shouldering one another, and tumbling over like packs of cards.

"I should like to know . . ." she went on.

"You look out, Riboudet," the priest cried angrily, "I'll box your ears, you scoundrel!" Then turning to Emma. "He's Boudet the carpenter's son; his parents are well off, and let him do just as he pleases. Yet he could learn quickly if he would, for he is very sharp. And so sometimes for a joke I call him Riboudet (like the road one takes to go to Maromme), and I even say 'Mon Riboudet.' Ha! ha! 'Mont Riboudet.' The other day I repeated this little joke to the bishop, and he laughed. Can you imagine? He deigned to laugh. And how is Monsieur Bovary?"

She seemed not to hear him. And he went on . . .

"Always very busy, no doubt; for he and I are certainly the busiest people in the parish. But he is doctor of the body," he added with a thick laugh, "and I of the soul."

She fixed her pleading eyes upon the priest. "Yes," she said, "you solace all sorrows."

"Ah! don't tell me of it, Madame Bovary. This morning I had to go to Bas-Diauville for a cow was all swollen; they thought it was under a spell. All their cows, I don't know how it is . . . But pardon me! Longuemarre and Boudet! Bless me! Will you stop it?"

And he bounded into the church.

The boys were just then clustering round the large desk, climbing over the cantor's footstool, opening the missal; and others on tiptoe were just about to venture into the confessional. But the priest suddenly distributed a shower of blows among them. Seizing them by the collars of their coats, he lifted them from the ground, and deposited them on their knees on the stones of the choir, firmly, as if he meant to plant them there.

"Yes," said he, when he returned to Emma, unfolding his large cotton handkerchief, one corner of which he put between his teeth, "farmers are much to be pitied."

"Others, too," she replied.

"Certainly. Workingmen in the cities, for instance."

"I wasn't thinking of them . . ."

"Oh, but excuse me! I've known housewives there, virtuous women, I assure you, real saints, who didn't even have bread to eat."

"But those," replied Emma, and the corners of her mouth twitched as she spoke, "those, Monsieur le Curé, who have bread and have no . . ."

"Fire in the winter," said the priest.

"Oh, what does it matter?"

"What! What does it matter? It seems to me that when one has firing and food . . . for, after all . . ."

"My God! my God!" she sighed.

"Do you feel unwell?" he asked, approaching her anxiously. "It is indigestion, no doubt? You must get home, Madame Bovary; drink a little tea, that will strengthen you, or else a glass of fresh water with a little moist sugar."

"Why?"

And she looked like one awaking from a dream.

"Well, you see, you were putting your hand to your forehead. I thought you felt faint."

Then, bethinking himself: "But you were asking me something? What was it? I don't remember."

"I? Oh, nothing . . . nothing," Emma repeated.

And the glance she cast round her slowly fell upon the old man in the cassock. They looked at each other face to face without speaking.

"Well then, Madame Bovary," he said at last, "excuse me, but duty comes first as the saying goes; I must look after my brats. The first communion will soon be upon us, and I fear we shall be behind, as ever. So after Ascension Day I regularly keep them an extra hour every Wednesday. Poor children! One cannot lead them too soon into the path of the Lord . . . he himself advised us to do so, through the mouth of his Divine Son. Good health to you, madame; my respects to your husband."

And he went into the church making a genuflexion as soon as he reached the door.

Emma saw him disappear between the double row of benches, walking with heavy tread, his head a little bent over his shoulder, and with his two half-open hands stretched sidewards.

Then she turned on her heel all of one piece, like a statue on a pivot, and went homewards. But the loud voice of the priest, the clear voices of the boys still reached her ears, and pursued her:

"Are you a Christian?"

"Yes, I am a Christian."

"What is a Christian?"

"He who, being baptized . . . baptized . . . baptized . . ."

She climbed the steps of the staircase holding on to the banisters, and when she was in her room threw herself into an arm-chair.

The whitish light of the window-panes was softly wavering. The pieces of furniture seemed more frozen in their places, about to lose themselves in the shadow as in an ocean of darkness. The fire was out, the clock went on ticking, and Emma vaguely wondered at this calm of all things while within herself there was such tumult. But little Berthe was there, between the window and the work-table, tottering on her knitted shoes, and trying to reach the end of her mother's apron-strings.

"Leave me alone," Emma said, pushing her back with her hand.

The little girl soon came up closer against her knees, and leaning on them with her arms, she looked up with her large blue eyes, while a small thread of clear saliva drooled from her lips on to the silk of her apron.

"Leave me alone," repeated the young woman quite angrily.

Her expression frightened the child, who began to scream.

"Will you leave me alone?" she said, forcing her away with her elbow.

Berthe fell at the foot of the chest of drawers against the brass handle; she cut her cheek, blood appeared. Madame Bovary rushed to lift her up, broke the bell-rope, called for the maid with all her might, and she was just going to curse herself when Charles appeared. It was dinner time; he was coming home.

"Look, dear!" said Emma calmly, "the child fell down while she was playing, and she hurt herself."

Charles reassured her; it was only a slight cut, and he went for some adhesive plaster.

Madame Bovary did not go downstairs to the dining-room; she wished to remain alone to look after the child. Then watching her sleep, the little anxiety she still felt gradually wore off, and she seemed very stupid to herself, and very kind to have been so worried just now at so little. Berthe, in fact, no longer cried. Her breathing now imperceptibly raised the cotton covering. Big tears lay in the corner of the half-closed eyelids, through whose lashes one could see two pale sunken pupils; the adhesive plaster on her cheek pulled the skin aside.

"It is very strange," thought Emma, "how ugly this child is!"

When at eleven o'clock Charles came back from the pharmacist's shop, where he had gone after dinner to return the remainder of the plaster, he found his wife standing by the cradle.

"I assure you it's nothing," he said, kissing her on the forehead. "Don't worry, my poor darling; you will make yourself ill."

He had stayed a long time at the pharmacist's. Although he had not seemed much concerned, Homais, nevertheless, had exerted himself to buoy him up, to "raise his spirits." Then they had talked of the various dangers that threaten childhood, of the carelessness of servants. Madame Homais knew what he meant: she still carried on her chest the scars of a load of charcoal that a cook dropped on her when she was a child. Hence that her kind parents took all sorts of precautions. The knives were not sharpened, nor the floors waxed; there were iron gratings in front of the windows and strong bars across the fireplace. In spite of their spirit, the little Homais could not stir without some one watching them; at the slightest cold their father stuffed them with cough-syrups; and until they turned four they all were mercilessly forced to use padded headwear. This, it is true, was a fancy of Madame Homais'; her husband was secretly afflicted by it. Fearing the possible consequences of such compression to the intellectual organs, he even went so far as to say to her:

"Do you want to make them into Caribs or Botocudos?"

Charles, however, had several times tried to interrupt the conversation.

"I would like a word with you," he whispered, addressing the clerk who preceded him on the stairs.

"Can he suspect anything?" Léon asked himself. His heart beat faster, and all sorts of conjectures occured to him.

At last, Charles, having closed the door behind him, begged him to inquire at Rouen after the price of a fine daguerreotype. It was a sentimental surprise he intended for his wife, a delicate attention: his own portrait in black tail coat. But he wanted first to know how much it would cost. It wouldn't cause Monsieur Léon too much trouble to find out, since he went to town almost every week.

Why? Monsieur Homais suspected some love affair, an intrigue. But he was mistaken. Léon was carrying on no flirtations. He was sadder than ever, as Madame Lefrançois saw from the amount of food he left on his plate. To find out more about it she questioned the tax-collector. Binet answered roughly that he wasn't being paid to spy on him.

All the same, his companion's behavior seemed very strange to him, for Léon often threw himself back in his chair, and stretching out his arms, complained vaguely about life.

"It's because you have no distractions," said the collector.

"What distractions?"

"If I were you I'd have a lathe."

"But I don't know how to turn," answered the clerk.

"Ah! that's true," said the other, rubbing his chin with an air of mingled contempt and satisfaction.

Léon was weary of loving without success; moreover, he was beginning to feel that depression caused by the repetition of the same life, with no interest to inspire and no hope to sustain it. He was so bored with Yonville and the Yonvillers, that the sight of certain persons, of certain houses, irritated him beyond endurance; and the pharmacist, good companion though he was, was becoming absolutely unbearable to him. Yet the prospect of a new condition of life frightened as much as it seduced him.

This apprehension soon changed into impatience, and then Paris beckoned from afar with the music of its masked balls, the laughter of the grisettes. Since he was to go to law-school there anyway, why not set out at once? Who prevented him? And, inwardly, he began making preparations; he arranged his occupations beforehand. In his mind, he decorated an apartment. He would lead an artist's life there! He would take guitar lessons! He would have a dressing-gown, a Basque béret, blue velvet slippers! He already admired two crossed foils over his chimney-piece, with a skull on the guitar above them.

The main difficulty was to obtain his mother's consent, though nothing could seem more reasonable. Even his employer advised him to go to some other law office where he could learn more rapidly. Taking a middle course, then, Léon looked for some position as second clerk in Rouen; found none, and at last wrote his mother a long letter full of details, in which he set forth the reasons for going to live in Paris at once. She consented.

He did not hurry. Every day for a month Hivert carried boxes, valises, parcels for him from Yonville to Rouen and from Rouen to Yonville; and when Léon had rounded out his wardrobe, had his three armchairs restuffed, bought a supply of neckties, in a word, had made more preparations than for a trip round the world, he put it off from week to week, until he received a second letter from his mother urging him to leave, since he wanted to pass his examination before the vacation.

When the moment for the farewells had come, Madame Homais wept, Justin sobbed; Homais, as a strong man, concealed his emotion; he wished to carry his friend's overcoat himself as far as the gate of the notary, who was taking Léon to Rouen in his carriage. The latter had just time to bid farewell to Monsieur Bovary.

When he reached the head of the stairs he stopped, he was so out of breath. When he entered, Madame Bovary rose hurriedly.

"It is I again!" said Léon.

"I was sure of it!"

She bit her lips, and a rush of blood flowing under her skin made her red from the roots of her hair to the top of her collar. She remained standing, leaning with her shoulder against the wainscot.

"The doctor is not here?" he went on.

"He is out."

She repeated:

"He is out."

Then there was silence. They looked one at the other, and their thoughts, united in the same agony, clung together like two hearts in a passionate embrace.

"I would like to kiss little Berthe good-bye," said Léon.

Emma went down a few steps and called Félicité.

He threw one long look around him that took in the walls, the shelves, the fireplace, as if to appropriate everything, to carry it with him.

She returned, and the servant brought Berthe, who was swinging an upside down windmill at the end of a string. Léon kissed her several times on the neck.

"Good-bye poor child! good-bye, dear little one! good-bye!" And he gave her back to her mother.

"Take her away," she said.

They remained alone—Madame Bovary, her back turned, her face pressed against a window-pane; Léon held his cap in his hand, tapping it softly against his thigh.

"It is going to rain," said Emma.

"I have a coat," he answered.

"Ah!"

She turned round, her chin lowered, her forehead bent forward. The light covered it to the curve of the eyebrows, like a single piece of marble, without revealing what Emma was seeing on the horizon or what she was thinking within herself.

"Well, good-bye," he sighed.

She raised her head with a quick movement.

"Yes, good-bye . . . go!"

They faced each other; he held out his hand; she hesitated.

"In the English manner, then," she said, offering him her hand and forcing a laugh.

Léon felt it between his fingers, and the very substance of all his being seemed to pass into that moist palm.

He opened his hand; their eyes met again, and he disappeared. When he reached the market-place, he stopped and hid behind a pillar to look for the last time at this white house with the four green blinds. He thought he saw a shadow behind the window in the room; but the curtain, sliding along the rod as though no one were touching it, slowly opened its long oblique folds, that spread out all at once, and thus hung straight and motionless as a plaster wall. Léon ran away.

From afar he saw his employer's buggy in the road, and by it a man in a coarse apron holding the horse. Homais and Monsieur Guillaumin were talking. They were waiting for him.

"Embrace me," said the pharmacist with tears in his eyes. "Here is your coat, my good friend. Mind the cold; take care of yourself; don't overdo it!"

"Come, Léon, jump in," said the notary.

Homais bent over the splash-board, and in a voice broken by sobs uttered these three sad words:

"A pleasant journey!"

"Good-night," said Monsieur Guillaumin. "Go ahead!"

They departed and Homais went home.

Madame Bovary had opened her window that looked out over the garden and watched the clouds. They were gathering round the sunset in the direction of Rouen, and rolling back swiftly in black swirls, behind which the great rays of the sun looked out like the golden arrows of a suspended trophy, while the rest of the empty heavens was white as porcelain. But a gust of wind bowed the poplars, and suddenly the rain fell; it rattled against the green leaves. Then the sun reappeared, the hens clucked, sparrows shook their wings in the damp thickets, and the pools of water on the gravel as they flowed away carried off the pink flowers of an acacia.

"Ah! how far off he must be already!" she thought.

Monsieur Homais, as usual, came at half-past six during dinner.

"Well," said he, "so we've sent off our young friend!"

"So it seems," replied the doctor.

Then, turning on his chair: "Any news at home?"

"Nothing much. Only my wife was a little out of sorts this afternoon. You know women—a nothing upsets them, especially my wife. And we shouldn't object to that, since their nervous system is much more fragile than ours."

"Poor Léon!" said Charles. "How will he live at Paris? Will he get used to it?"

Madame Bovary sighed.

"Of course!" said the pharmacist, smacking his lips. "The late night suppers! the masked balls, the champagne—he won't be losing his time, I assure you."

"I don't think he'll go wrong," objected Bovary.

"Nor do I," said Monsieur Homais quickly; "although he'll have to do like the rest for fear of passing for a Jesuit. And you don't know what a life those jokers lead in the Latin quarter, actresses and the rest! Besides, students are thought a great deal of in Paris. Provided they have a few accomplishments, they are received in the best society; there are even ladies of the Faubourg Saint-Germain who fall in love with them, which later gives them opportunities for making very good matches."

"But," said the doctor, "I fear for him that . . . down there . . ."

"You are right," interrupted the pharmacist, "that is the other side of the coin. And you are constantly obliged to keep your hand in your pocket there. Let us say, for instance, you are in a public garden. A fellow appears, well dressed, even wearing a decoration, and whom one would take for a diplomat. He addresses you, you chat with him; he forces himself upon you; offers you a pinch of snuff, or picks up your hat. Then you become more intimate; he takes you to a café, invites you to his countryhouse, introduces you, between two drinks, to all sorts of people; and three-fourths of the time it's only to get hold of your money or involve you in some shady deal"

"That is true," said Charles; "but I was thinking specially of illnesses—of typhoid fever, for example, that attacks students from the provinces."

Emma shuddered.

"Because of the change of diet," continued the pharmacist, "and of the resulting upset for the whole system. And then the water at Paris, don't you know! The dishes at restaurants, all the spiced food, end by heating the blood, and are not worth, whatever people may say of them, a good hearty stew. As for me, I have always preferred home cooking; it is healthier. So when I was studying pharmacy at Rouen, I boarded in a boarding-house; and dined with the professors."

And thus he went on, expounding his general opinions and his personal preferences, until Justin came to fetch him for a mulled egg for a customer.

"Not a moment's peace!" he cried; "always at it! I can't go out for a minute! Like a plough-horse, I have always to be sweating blood and water! What drudgery!" Then, when he was at the door, "By the way, do you know the news?"

"What news?"

"It is very likely," Homais went on, raising his eyebrows and assuming one of his gravest expressions, "that the agricultural fair of the Seine-Inférieure will be held this year at Yonville-l'Abbaye."

The rumor, at all events, is going the round. This morning the paper alluded to it. It would be of the utmost importance for our district. But we'll talk it over later. I can see, thank you; Justin has the lantern."

VII

The next day was a dreary one for Emma. Everything seemed shrouded in an atmosphere of bleakness that hung darkly over the outward aspect of things, and sorrow blew into her soul with gentle moans, as the winter wind makes in ruined castles. Her reverie was that of things gone forever, the exhaustion that seizes you after everything is done; the pain, in short, caused by the interruption of a familiar motion, the sudden halting of a long drawn out vibration.

As on the return from Vaubyessard, when the quadrilles were running in her head, she was full of a gloomy melancholy, of a numb despair. Léon reappeared, taller, handsomer, more charming, more vague. Though separated from her, he had not left her; he was there, and the walls of the house seemed to hold his shadow. She could not detach her eyes from the carpet where he had walked, from those empty chairs where he had sat. The river still flowed on and slowly drove its ripples along the slippery banks. They had often walked there listening to the murmur of the waves over the moss-covered pebbles. How bright the sun had been! What happy afternoons they had known, alone, in the shade at the end of the garden! He read aloud, bare-headed, sitting on a footstool of dry sticks; the fresh wind of the meadow set trembling the leaves of the book and the nasturtiums of the arbour. Ah! he was gone, the only charm of her life, the only possible hope of joy. Why had she not seized this happiness when it came to her? Why did she not keep him from leaving, beg him on her knees, when he was about to flee from her? And she cursed herself for not having loved Léon. She thirsted for his lips. She wanted to run after him, to throw herself into his arms and say to him, "It is I; I am yours." But Emma recoiled beforehand at the difficulties of the enterprise, and her desires, increased by regret, became only the more acute.

Henceforth the memory of Léon was the center of her boredom; it burnt there more brightly than the fires left by travellers on the snow of a Russian steppe. She threw herself at his image, pressed herself against it; she stirred carefully the dying embers, sought all around her anything that could make it flare; and the most distant reminiscences, like the most immediate occasions, what she experienced as well as what she imagined, her wasted voluptuous desires that were unsatisfied, her projects of happiness that crackled in the wind like dead boughs, her sterile virtue, her lost hopes, the yoke of domesticity,—she gathered it all up, took everything, and made it all serve as fuel for her melancholy.

The flames, however, subsided, either because the supply had exhausted itself, or because it had been piled up too much. Love, little by little, was quelled by absence; regret stifled beneath habit; and the bright fire that had empurpled her pale sky was overspread and faded by degrees. In her slumbering conscience, she took her disgust for her husband for aspirations towards her lover, the burning of hate for the warmth of tenderness; but as the tempest still raged, and as passion burnt itself down to the very cinders, and no help came, no sun rose, there was night on all sides, and she was lost in the terrible cold that pierced her through.

Then the evil days of Tostes began again. She thought herself now far more unhappy; for she had the experience of grief, with the certainty that it would not end.

A woman who had consented to such sacrifices could well allow herself certain whims. She bought a gothic prie-Dieu, and in a month spent fourteen francs on lemons for polishing her nails; she wrote to Rouen for a blue cashmere gown; she chose one of Lheureux's finest scarves, and wore it knotted round her waist over her dressing-gown; thus dressed, she lay stretched out on the couch with closed blinds.

She often changed her hairdo; she did her hair *à la Chinoise*, in flowing curls, in plaited coils; she parted it on one side and rolled it under, like a man's.

She wanted to learn Italian; she bought dictionaries, a grammar, and a supply of white paper. She tried serious reading, history, and philosophy. Sometimes in the night Charles woke up with a start, thinking he was being called to a patient:

"I'm coming," he stammered.

It was the noise of a match Emma had struck to relight the lamp. But her reading fared like her pieces of embroidery, all of which, only just begun, filled her cupboard; she took it up, left it, passed on to other books.

She had attacks in which she could easily have been driven to commit any folly. She maintained one day, to contradict her husband, that she could drink off a large glass of brandy, and, as Charles was stupid enough to dare her to, she swallowed the brandy to the last drop.

In spite of her vaporish airs (as the housewives of Yonville called them), Emma, all the same, never seemed gay, and usually she had at the corners of her mouth that immobile contraction that puckers the faces of old maids, and those of men whose ambition has failed. She was pale all over, white as a sheet; the skin of her nose was drawn at the nostrils, her eyes had a vague look. After discovering three grey hairs on her temples, she talked much of her old age.

She often had spells. One day she even spat blood, and, as Charles fussed round her showing his anxiety . . .

"Bah!" she answered, "what does it matter?"

Charles fled to his study and wept there, both his elbows on the table, sitting in his office chair under the phrenological head.

Then he wrote to his mother to beg her to come, and they had many long consultations together on the subject of Emma.

What should they decide? What was to be done since she rejected all medical treatment?

"Do you know what you wife wants?" replied Madame Bovary senior. "She wants to be forced to occupy herself with some manual work. If she were obliged, like so many others, to earn her living, she wouldn't have these vapors, that come to her from a lot of ideas she stuffs into her head, and from the idleness in which she lives."

"Yet she is always busy," said Charles.

"Ah! always busy at what? Reading novels, bad books, works against religion, and in which they mock at priests in speeches taken from Voltaire. But all that leads you far astray, my poor child. A person who has no religion is bound to go astray."

So it was decided to keep Emma from reading novels. The enterprise did not seem easy. The old lady took it upon herself: She was, when she passed through Rouen, to go herself to the lending library and represent that Emma had discontinued her subscription. Would they not have a right to call in the police if the bookseller persisted all the same in his poisonous trade?

The farewells of mother and daughter-in-law were cold. During the three weeks that they had been together they had not exchanged half-a-dozen words except for the usual questions and greetings when they met at table and in the evening before going to bed.

Madame Bovary left on a Wednesday, the market-day at Yonville.

Since morning, the Square had been crowded by end on end of carts, which, with their shafts in the air, spread all along the line of houses from the church to the inn. On the other side there were canvas booths for the sale of cotton goods, blankets, and woolen stockings, together with harness for horses, and packages of blue ribbon, whose ends fluttered in the wind. The coarse hardware was spread out on the ground between pyramids of eggs and hampers of cheeses showing pieces of sticky straw. Near the wheat threshers clucking hens passed their necks through the bars of flat cages. The crowds piled up in one place and refused to budge; they threatened at times to smash the window of the pharmacy. On

Wednesdays his shop was never empty, and the people pushed in less to buy drugs than for consultations, so great was Homais' reputation in the neighboring villages. His unshakable assurance deeply impresssed the country people. They considered him a greater doctor than all the doctors.

Emma was standing in the open window (she often did so: in the provinces, the window takes the place of the theatre and the promenade) and she amused herself with watching the rustic crowd, when she saw a gentleman in a green velvet coat. Although he was wearing heavy boots, he had on yellow gloves; he was coming towards the doctor's house, followed by a worried looking peasant with lowered head and quite a thoughtful air.

"Can I see the doctor?" he asked Justin, who was talking on the doorsteps with Félicité.

And, mistaking him for a servant of the house, he added,

"Tell him that M. Rodolphe Boulanger *de la* Huchette is here."

It was not out of affectation that the new arrival added *"de la* Huchette" to his name, but to make himself the better known. La Huchette, in fact, was an estate near Yonville, where he had just bought the château and two farms that he cultivated himself, without, however, taking too many pains. He lived as a bachelor, and was supposed to have an income of "at least fifteen thousand francs a year."

Charles came into the room. Monsieur Boulanger introduced his man, who wanted to be bled because he felt "as if ants were crawling all over him."

"It will clear me out," was his answer to all reasonable objections.

So Bovary brought a bandage and a basin, and asked Justin to hold it. Then addressing the peasant, who was already turning pale:

"Don't be scared, my friend."

"No, no, sir," said the other; "go ahead!"

And with an air of bravado he held out his heavy arm. At the prick of the lancet the blood spurted out, splashing against the looking-glass.

"Hold the basin nearer," exclaimed Charles.

"Look!" said the peasant, "one would swear it was a little fountain flowing. How red my blood is! That's a good sign, isn't it?"

"Sometimes," answered the officier de santé, "one feels nothing at first, and them they start fainting, especially when they're strong like this one."

At these words the peasant dropped the lancet-case he was holding back of his chair. A shudder of his shoulders made the chairback creak. His hat fell off.

"I thought as much," said Bovary, pressing his finger on the vein.

The basin was beginning to tremble in Justin's hands; his knees shook, he turned pale.

"My wife! get my wife!" called Charles.

With one bound she rushed down the staircase.

"Vinegar," he cried. "Lord, two at a time!"

And he was so upset he could hardly put on the compress.

"It is nothing," said Monsieur Boulanger quietly, taking Justin in his arms. He seated him on the table with his back resting against the wall.

Madame Bovary opened the collar of his shirt. The strings of his shirt had got into a knot, and she was for some minutes moving her light fingers about the young fellow's neck. Then she poured some vinegar on her cambric handkerchief; she moistened his temples with little dabs, and then blew delicately upon them.

The ploughman revived, but Justin remained unconscious. His eyeballs disappeared in their whites like blue flowers in milk.

"We must hide this from him," said Charles.

Madame Bovary took the basin to put it under the table. With the movement she made in bending down, her dress (it was a summer dress with four flounces, yellow, long in the waist and wide in the skirt) spread out around on the tiles; and as Emma, stooping, staggered a little in stretching out her arms, the pull of her dress made it hug more closely the line of her bosom. Then she went to fetch a bottle of water, and she was melting some pieces of sugar when the pharmacist arrived. The maid had gone for him at the height of the confusion; seeing his pupil with his eyes open he gave a sigh of relief; then going round him he looked at him from head to foot.

"You fool!" he said, "you're a real fool! A capital idiot! And all that for a little blood-letting! and coming from a fellow who isn't afraid of anything! a real squirrel, climbing to incredible heights in order to steal nuts! You can be proud of yourself! showing a fine talent for the pharmaceutical profession; for, later on, you may be called before the courts of justice in serious circumstances, to enlighten the consciences of the magistrates, and you would have to keep your head then, to reason, show yourself a man, or else pass for an imbecile."

Justin did not answer. The pharmacist went on:

"Who asked you to come? You are always pestering the doctor and madame. Anyway, on Wednesday, I need you in the shop. There are over 20 people there now waiting to be served. I left them just out of concern for you. Get going! hurry! Wait for me there and keep an eye on the jars."

When Justin, who was rearranging his clothes, had gone, they talked for a little while about fainting-fits. Madame Bovary had never fainted.

"That is most unusual for a lady," said Monsieur Boulanger; "but some people are very susceptible. Thus in a duel, I have seen a witness faint away at the mere sound of the loading of pistols."

"As for me," said the pharmacist, "the sight of other people's blood doesn't affect me in the least, but the mere thought of my own flowing would make me faint if I reflected upon it too much."

Monsieur Boulanger, however, dismissed his servant and told him to be quiet, now that his whim was satisfied.

"It gave me the opportunity of making your acquaintance," he added, and he looked at Emma as he said this.

Then he put three francs on the corner of the table, bowed casually, and went out.

He soon had crossed to the other bank of the river (this was his way back to La Huchette), and Emma saw him in the meadow, walking under the poplars, slackening his pace now and then as one who reflects.

"She is nice, very nice, that doctor's wife," he said to himself. "Fine teeth, black eyes, a dainty foot, a figure like a Parisienne's. Where the devil does she come from? Where did that boor ever pick her up?"

Monsieur Rodolphe Boulanger was thirty-four; he combined brutality of temperament with a shrewd judgment, having had much experience with women and being something of a connoisseur. This one had seemed pretty to him; so he kept dreaming about her and her husband.

"I think he is very stupid. She must be tired of him, no doubt. He has dirty nails, and hasn't shaven for three days. While he is trotting after his patients, she sits there mending socks. How bored she gets! How she'd want to be in the city and go dancing every night! Poor little woman! She is gaping after love like a carp on the kitchen table after water. Three gallant words and she'd adore me, I'm sure of it. She'd be tender, charming. Yes; but how get rid of her afterwards?"

The prospect of love's involvements brought to mind, by contrast, his present mistress. She was an actress in Rouen whom he kept, and when he had pondered over this image, even in memory he found himself satiated.

"Madame Bovary," he thought, "is much prettier, much fresher too. Virginie is decidedly beginning to grow fat. Her enthusiasms bore me to tears. And that habit of hers of eating prawns all the time . . . !"

The fields were empty; around him Rodolphe only heard the

noise of the grass as it rubbed against his boots, and the chirping of the cricket hidden away among the oats. He again saw Emma in her room, dressed as he had seen her, and he undressed her.

"Oh, I will have her," he cried, smashing, with a blow of his cane, a clod of earth before him.

At once, he began to consider the strategy. He wondered:

"Where shall we meet? And how? We shall always be having the brat on our hands, and the maid, the neighbors, the husband, all sorts of worries. Bah!" he concluded, "it would be too time-consuming!"

Then he started again:

"But she really has eyes that bore into your heart. And that pale complexion! And I, who love pale women!"

When he reached the top of the Argueil hills he had made up his mind.

"All that remains is to create the proper opportunity. Well, I will call in now and then, I'll send game and poultry; I'll have myself bled, if need be. We shall become friends; I'll invite them to my place. Of course!" he added, "the agricultural fair is coming on; she'll be there, I'll see her. We'll begin boldly, for that's the surest way."

VIII

At last it came, the much-awaited agricultural fair. Ever since the morning of the great day, the villagers, on their doorsteps, were discussing the preparations. The facade of the townhall had been hung with garlands of ivy; a tent had been erected in a meadow for the banquet; and in the middle of the Place, in front of the church, a kind of a small cannon was to announce the arrival of the prefect and the names of the fortunate farmers who had won prizes. The National Guard of Buchy (there was none at Yonville) had come to join the corps of firemen, of whom Binet was captain. On that day he wore a collar even higher than usual; and, tightly buttoned in his tunic, his figure was so stiff and motionless that all life seemed to be confined to his legs, which moved in time with the music, with a single motion. As there was some rivalry between the tax-collector and the colonel, both, to show off their talents, drilled their men separately. The red epaulettes and the black breastplates kept parading up and down, one after the other; there was no end to it, and it constantly began again. Never had there been such a display of pomp. Several citizens had washed down their houses the evening before; tricolor flags hung from half-open windows; all the cafés were full; and in the lovely weather the starched caps, the golden crosses, and the colored neckerchiefs seemed whiter than snow, shone in the sun, and relieved with their motley colors the somber monotony of the frock-coats and blue smocks. The neighboring farmers' wives, when they got off their horses, removed the long pin with which they had gathered their dresses tight around them for fear of getting them spattered; while their husbands protected their hats by covering them with handkerchiefs, of which they held one corner in their teeth.

The crowd came into the main street from both ends of the village. People poured in from the lanes, the alleys, the houses; and from time to time one heard the banging of doors closing behind ladies of the town in cotton gloves, who were going out to see the fête. Most admired of all were too long lamp-stands covered with lanterns, that flanked a platform on which the authorities were to sit. Aside from this, a kind of pole had been placed against the four columns of the townhall, each bearing a small standard of greenish cloth, embellished with inscriptions in gold letters. On one was written, "To Commerce"; on the other, "To Agriculture"; on the third, "To Industry"; and on the fourth, "To the Fine Arts".

But the jubilation that brightened all faces seemed to darken that of Madame Lefrançois, the innkeeper. Standing on her kitchen-steps she muttered to herself:

"How stupid! How stupid they are with their canvas booth! Do they think the prefect will be glad to dine down there under a tent like a gipsy? They call all this fussing for the good of the town! As if it helped the town to send to Neufchâtel for the keeper of a cookshop! And for whom? For cowheads! for tramps!"

The pharmacist passed by. He was wearing a frock-coat, nankeen trousers, beaver shoes, and, to everyone's surprise, a hat—a low crowned hat.

"Your servant," he said. "Excuse me, I am in a hurry."

And as the fat widow asked where he was going . . .

"It seems odd to you, doesn't it, I who am always more cooped up in my laboratory than the man's rat in his cheese."

"What cheese?" asked the landlady.

"Oh, nothing, never mind!" Homais continued. "I merely wished to convey to you, Madame Lefrançois, that I usually live at home like a recluse. To-day, however, considering the circumstances, it is necessary . . ."

"Oh, are you going down there?" she said contemptuously.

"Yes, I am going," replied the pharmacist, astonished. "Am I not a member of the Advisory committee?"

Mère Lefrançois looked at him for a few moments, and ended by saying with a smile:

"That's another matter! But is agriculture any of your business? Do you understand anything about it?"

"Certainly I understand it, since I am a pharmacist,—that is to say, a chemist. And the object of chemistry, Madame Lefrançois, being the knowledge of the reciprocal and molecular action of all natural bodies, it follows that agriculture is comprised within its domain. And, in fact, the composition of the manure, the fermentation of liquids, the analyses of gases, and the effects of miasmas, what, I ask you, is all this, if it isn't chemistry, pure and simple?"

The landlady did not answer. Homais went on:

"Do you think that to be an agriculturist it is necessary to have tilled the earth or fattened fowls oneself? It is much more important to know the composition of the substances in question—the geological strata, the atmospheric actions, the quality of the soil, the minerals, the waters, the density of the different bodies, their capillarity, and what not. And one must be master of all the principles of hygiene in order to direct, criticise the construction of buildings, the feeding of animals; the diet of the servants. And, moreover, Madame Lefrançois, one must know botany, be able to distinguish between plants, you understand, which are the wholesome and those that are deleterious, which are unproductive and which nutritive, if it is well to pull them up here and re-sow them there, to propagate some, destroy others; in brief, one must keep pace with science by reading publications and papers, be always on the alert to detect improvements."

The landlady never took her eyes off the "Café Français" and the pharmacist went on:

"Would to God our agriculturists were chemists, or that at least they would pay more attention to the counsels of science. Thus lately I myself wrote a substantial paper, a memoir of over seventy-two pages, entitled, 'Cider, its Manufacture and its Effects, together with some New Reflections on this Subject,' that I sent to the Agricultural Society in Rouen, and which even procured me the honor of being received among its members—Section, Agriculture; Class, Pomology. Well, if my work had been given to the public . . ."

But the pharmacist stopped, so distracted did Madame Lefrançois seem.

"Just look at them!" she said. "It's past comprehension! Such a hash-house!" And with a shrug of the shoulders that stretched out the stitches of her sweater, she pointed with both hands at the rival establishment, from where singing erupted. "Well, it won't last long," she added, "It'll be over before a week."

Homais drew back in surprise. She came down three steps and whispered in his ear:

"What! you didn't know it? They'll foreclose this week. It's Lheureux who does the selling; he killed them off with his notes."

"What a dreadful catastrophe!" exclaimed the pharmacist, who always found expressions that filled all imaginable circumstances.

Then the landlady began telling him this story, that she had heard from Theodore, Monsieur Guillaumin's servant, and although she detested Tellier, she blamed Lheureux. He was "a wheedler, a fawner."

"There!" she said. "Look at him! There he goes down the square; he is greeting Madame Bovary, who's wearing a green hat. And she is on Monsieur Boulanger's arm."

"Madame Bovary!" exclaimed Homais. "I must go at once and pay her my respects. Perhaps she'll be pleased to have a seat in the enclosure under the peristyle." And, without heeding Madame Lefrançois, who was calling him back for more gossip, the pharmacist walked off rapidly with a smile on his face and his walk jauntier than ever, bowing copiously to right and left, and taking up much room with the large tails of his frock-coat that fluttered behind him in the wind.

Rodolphe having caught sight of him from afar, quickened his pace, but Madame Bovary couldn't keep up; so he walked more slowly, and, smiling at her, said roughly:

"It's only to get away from that fat fellow, you know, the pharmacist."

She nudged him with her elbow.

"How shall I understand that?" he asked himself.

And, walking on, he looked at her out of the corner of his eyes.

Her profile was so calm that it revealed nothing.

It stood out in the light from the oval of her hat that was tied with pale ribbons like waving rushes. Her eyes with their long curved lashes looked straight before her, and though wide open, they seemed slightly slanted at the cheek-bones, because of the blood pulsing gently under the delicate skin. A rosy light shone through the partition between her nostrils. Her head was bent upon her shoulder, and the tips of her teeth shone through her lips like pearls.

"Is she making fun of me?" thought Rodolphe.

Emma's gesture, however, had only been meant for a warning; for Monsieur Lheureux was accompanying them, and spoke now and again as if to enter into the conversation.

"What a beautiful day! Everybody is outside! The wind is from the east!"

Neither Madame Bovary nor Rodolphe answered him, but their slightest movement made him draw near saying, "I beg your pardon!" and raising his hat.

When they reached the blacksmith's house, instead of following the road up to the fence, Rodolphe suddenly turned down a path, drawing Madame Bovary with him. He called out:

"Good evening, Monsieur Lheureux! We'll see you soon!"

"How you got rid of him!" she said, laughing.

"Why," he went on, "allow oneself to be intruded upon by others? And as to-day I have the happiness of being with you . . ."

Emma blushed. He did not finish his sentence. Then he talked of the fine weather and of the pleasure of walking on the grass. A few daisies had sprung up again.

"Here are some pretty Easter daisies," he said, "and enough to provide oracles for all the lovers in the vicinity."

He added,

"Shall I pick some? What do you think?"

"Are you in love?" she asked, coughing a little.

"H'm, h'm! who knows?" answered Rodolphe.

The meadow was beginning to fill up, and the housewives were hustling about with their great umbrellas, their baskets, and their babies. One often had to make way for a long file of country girls, servant-maids with blue stockings, flat shoes and silver rings, who smelt of milk when one passed close to them. They walked along holding one another by the hand, and thus they spread over the whole field from the row of open trees to the banquet tent. But this was the judging time, and the farmers one after the other entered a kind of enclosure formed by ropes supported on sticks.

The beasts were there, their noses turned toward the rope, and making a confused line with their unequal rumps. Drowsy pigs were burrowing in the earth with their snouts, calves were lowing and bleating; the cows, one leg folded under them stretched their bellies on the grass, slowly chewing their cud, and blinking their heavy eyelids at the gnats that buzzed around them. Ploughmen with bare arms were holding by the halter prancing stallions that neighed with dilated nostrils looking in the direction of the mares. These stood quietly, stretching out their heads and flowing manes, while their foals rested in their shadow, or sucked them from time to time. And above the long undulation of these crowded bodies one saw some white mane rising in the wind like a wave, or some sharp horns sticking out, and the heads of men running about. Apart, outside the enclosure, a hundred paces off, was a large black bull, muzzled, with an iron ring in its nostrils, and who moved no more than if he had been in bronze. A child in rags was holding him by a rope.

Between the two lines the committee-men were walking with heavy steps, examining each animal, then consulting one another in a low voice. One who seemed of more importance now and then took notes in a book as he walked along. This was the president of the jury, Monsieur Derozerays de la Panville. As soon as he recognised Rodolphe he came forward quickly, and smiling amiably, said:

"What! Monsieur Boulanger, you are deserting us?"

Rodolphe protested that he would come. But when the president had disappeared:

"To tell the truth," he said, "I shall not go. Your company is better than his."

And while poking fun at the show, Rodolphe, to move about more easily, showed the gendarme his blue card, and even stopped now and then in front of some fine beast, which Madame Bovary did not at all admire. He noticed this, and began jeering at the Yonville ladies and their dresses; then he apologised for his own casual attire. It had the inconsistency of things at once commonplace and refined which enchants or exasperates the ordinary man because he suspects that it reveals an unconventional existence, a dubious morality, the affectations of the artist, and, above all, a certain contempt for established conventions. The wind, blowing up his batiste shirt with pleated cuffs revealed a waistcoat of grey linen, and his broad-striped trousers disclosed at the ankle nankeen boots with patent leather gaiters. These were so polished that they reflected the grass. He trampled on horse's dung, one hand in the pocket of his jacket and his straw hat tilted on one side.

"Anyway," he added, "when one lives in the country. . . . ."

"Nothing is worth while," said Emma.

"That is true," replied Rodolphe. "To think that not one of these people is capable of understanding even the cut of a coat!"

Then they talked about provincial mediocrity, of the lives it stifles, the lost illusions.

"No wonder," said Rodolphe, "that I am more and more sinking in gloom."

"You!" she said in astonishment; "I thought you very light-hearted."

"Oh, yes, it seems that way because I know how to wear a mask of mockery in society, and yet, how many a time at the sight of a cemetery by moonlight have I not asked myself whether it were not better to join those sleeping there!"

"Oh! and your friends?" she said. "How can you forget them."

"My friends! What friends? Have I any? Who cares about me?" And he followed up the last words with a kind of hissing whistle.

They were obliged to separate because of a great pile of chairs that a man was carrying behind them. He was so overladen that one could only see the tips of his wooden shoes and the ends of his two outstretched arms. It was Lestiboudois, the gravedigger, who was carrying the church chairs about amongst the people. Alive to all that concerned his interests, he had hit upon this means of turning the agricultural show to his advantage, and his idea was succeeding, for he no longer knew which way to turn. In fact, the villagers, who were tired and hot, quarrelled for these seats, whose straw smelt of incense, and they leant against the thick backs, stained with the wax of candles, with a certain veneration.

Madame Bovary again took Rodolphe's arm; he went on as if speaking to himself:

"Yes, I have missed so many things. Always alone! Ah! if I had some aim in life, if I had met some love, if I had found some one! Oh, how I would have spent all the energy of which I am capable, surmounted everything, overcome everything!"

"Yet it seems to me," said Emma, "that you are not to be pitied."

"Ah! you think so?" said Rodolphe.

"For, after all," she went on, "you are free . . ."

She hesitated,

"Rich . . ."

"Don't mock me," he replied.

And she protested that she was not mocking him, when the sound of a cannon was heard; immediately all began crowding one another towards the village.

It was a false alarm. The prefect seemed not to be coming, and the members of the jury felt much embarrassed, not knowing if they ought to begin the meeting or wait longer.

At last, at the end of the Place a large hired landau appeared, drawn by two thin horses, generously whipped by a coachman in a white hat. Binet had only just time to shout, "Present arms!" and the colonel to imitate him. There was a rush towards the guns; every one pushed forward. A few even forgot their collars.

But the prefectoral coach seemed to sense the trouble, for the two yoked nags, dawdling in their harness, came at a slow trot in front of the townhall at the very moment when the National Guard and firemen deployed, beating time with their boots.

"Present arms!" shouted Binet.

"Halt!" shouted the colonel. "By the left flank, march!"

And after presenting arms, during which the clang of the band, letting loose, rang out like a brass kettle rolling downstairs, all the guns were lowered.

Then was seen stepping down from the carriage a gentleman in a short coat with silver braiding, with bald brow, and wearing a tuft of hair at the back of his head, of a sallow complexion and the most benign of aspects. His eyes, very large and covered by heavy lids, were half-closed to look at the crowd, while at the same time he raised his sharp nose, and forced a smile upon his sunken mouth. He recognised the mayor by his scarf, and explained to him that the prefect was not able to come. He himself was a councillor at the prefecture; then he added a few apologies. Monsieur Tuvache reciprocated with polite compliments, humbly acknowledged by the other; and they remained thus, face to face, their foreheads almost touching, surrounded by members of the jury, the municipal council, the notable personages, the National Guard and the crowd. The councillor pressing his little cocked hat to his breast repeated his greetings, while Tuvache, bent like a bow, also smiled, stammered, tried to say something, protested his devotion to the monarchy and the honor that was being done to Yonville.

Hippolyte, the groom from the inn, took the head of the horses from the coachman, and, limping along with his clubfoot, led them to the door of the "Lion d'Or" where a number of peasants collected to look at the carriage. The drum beat, the howitzer thundered, and the gentlemen one by one mounted the platform, where they sat down in red utrecht velvet arm-chairs that had been lent by Madame Tuvache.

All these people looked alike. Their fair flabby faces, somewhat tanned by the sun, were the color of sweet cider, and their puffy whiskers emerged from stiff collars, kept up by white cravats with broad bows. All the waistcoats were of velvet, double-breasted; all the watches had, at the end of a long ribbon, an oval seal; all rested their two hands on their thighs, carefully stretching the stride of their trousers, whose unspunged glossy cloth shone more brilliantly than the leather of their heavy boots.

The ladies of the company stood at the back under the porch between the pillars, while the common herd was opposite, standing up or sitting on chairs. Lestiboudois had brought there all the chairs that he had moved from the field, and he even kept running back every minute to fetch others from the church. He caused such confusion with this piece of business that one had great difficulty in getting to the small steps of the platform.

"I think," said Monsieur Lheureux to the pharmacist who was heading for his seat, "that they ought to have put up two Venetian masts with something rather severe and rich for ornaments; it would have been a very pretty sight."

"Certainly," replied Homais; "but what can you expect? The mayor took everything on his own shoulders. He hasn't much taste. Poor Tuvache! he is completely devoid of what is called the genius of art."

Meanwhile, Rodolphe and Madame Bovary had ascended to the first floor of the townhall, to the "council-room," and, as it was empty, he suggested that they could enjoy the sight there more comfortably. He fetched three chairs from the round table under the bust of the monarch, and having carried them to one of the windows, they sat down together.

There was commotion on the platform, long whisperings, much parleying. At last the councillor got up. It was known by now that his name was Lieuvain, and in the crowd the name was now passing from lip to lip. After he had reshuffled a few pages, and bent over them to see better, he began:

"Gentlemen! May I be permitted first of all (before addressing you on the object of our meeting to-day, and this sentiment will, I am sure, be shared by you all), may I be permitted, I say, to pay a tribute to the higher administration, to the government, to the monarch, gentlemen, our sovereign, to that beloved king, to whom no branch of public or private prosperity is a matter of indifference, and who directs with a hand at once so firm and wise the chariot of the state amid the incessant perils of a stormy sea, knowing, moreover, how to make peace respected as well as war, industry, commerce, agriculture, and the fine arts."

"I ought," said Rodolphe, "to get back a little further."

"Why?" said Emma.

But at this moment the voice of the councillor rose to an extraordinary pitch. He declaimed—

"This is no longer the time, gentlemen, when civil discord made blood flow in our market squares, when the landowner, the businessman, the working-man himself, lying down to peaceful sleep, trembled lest he should be awakened suddenly by the noise of alarming tocsins, when the most subversive doctrines audaciously sapped foundations . . ."

"Well, some one down there might see me," Rodolphe resumed, "then I should have to invent excuses for a fortnight; and with my bad reputation . . ."

"Oh, you are slandering yourself," said Emma.

"No! It is dreadful, I assure you."

"But, gentlemen," continued the councillor, "if, banishing from my memory the remembrance of these sad pictures, I carry my eyes back to the present situation of our dear country, what do I see there? Everywhere commerce and the arts are flourishing; everywhere new means of communication, like so many new arteries in the body politic, establish within it new relations. Our great industrial centers have recovered all their activity; religion, more consolidated, smiles in all hearts; our ports are full, confidence is born again, and France breathes once more! . . . ."

"Besides," added Rodolphe, "perhaps from the world's point of view they are right."

"How so?" she asked.

"What!" said he. "Don't you know that there are souls constantly tormented? They need by turns to dream and to act, the purest passions and the most turbulent joys, and thus they fling themselves into all sorts of fantasies, of follies."

Then she looked at him as one looks at a traveler who has voyaged over strange lands, and went on:

"We have not even this distraction, we poor women!"

"A sad distraction, for happiness isn't found in it."

"But is it ever found?" she asked.

"Yes; one day it comes," he answered.

"And this is what you have understood," said the councillor. "You, farmers, agricultural laborers! you pacific pioneers of a work that belongs wholly to civilisation! you, men of progress and morality, you have understood, I say, that political storms are even more redoubtable than atmospheric disturbances!"

"A day comes," repeated Rodolphe, "one is near despair. Then the horizon expands; it is as if a voice cried, 'It is here!' You feel the need of confiding the whole of your life, of giving everything, sacrificing everything to this person. There is no need for explanations; one understands each other, having met before in dreams!" (And he looked at her.) "At last, here it is, this treasure so sought after, here before you. It glitters, it flashes; yet one still doubts, one does not believe it; one remains dazzled, as if one went out from darkness into light."

And as he ended Rodolphe suited the action to the word. He passed his hand over his face, like a man about to faint. Then he let it fall on Emma's. She drew hers back. But the councillor was still reading.

"And who would be surprised at it, gentlemen? He only who was so blind, so imprisoned (I do not fear to say it), so imprisoned by the prejudices of another age as still to misunderstand the spirit of our rural populations. Where, indeed, is more patriotism to be found than in the country, greater devotion to the public welfare, in a word, more intelligence? And, gentlemen, I do not mean that superficial intelligence, vain ornament of idle minds, but rather that profound and balanced intelligence that applies itself above all else to useful objects, thus contributing to the good of all, to the common amelioration and to the support of the state, born of respect for law and the practice of duty . . ."

"Ah! again!" said Rodolphe. "Always 'duty.' I am sick of the word. They are a lot of old jackasses in woolen vests and old bigots with foot-warmers and rosaries who constantly drone into our ears

Romance vs. practical

'Duty, duty!' Ah! by Jove! as if one's real duty were not to feel what is great, cherish the beautiful, and not accept all the conventions of society with the hypocrisy it forces upon us."

"Yet . . . yet . . ." objected Madame Bovary.

"No, no! Why cry out against the passions? Are they not the one beautiful thing on earth, the source of heroism, of enthusiasm, of poetry, music, the arts, in a word, of everything?"

"But one must," said Emma, "to some extent bow to the opinion of the world and accept its morality."

"Ah, but there are two moralities," he replied, "the petty one, the morality of small men that constantly keeps changing, but yells itself hoarse; crude and loud like the crowd of imbeciles that you see down there. But the other, the eternal, that is about us and above, like the landscape that surrounds us, and the blue heavens that give us light."

morality

Monsieur Lieuvain had just wiped his mouth with a pocket-handkerchief. He continued:

"It would be presumptuous of me, gentlemen, to point out to you the uses of agriculture. Who supplies our wants, who provides our means of subsistence, if not the farmer? It is the farmer, gentlemen, who sows with laborious hand the fertile furrows of the country, brings forth the wheat, which, being ground, is made into a powder by means of ingenious machinery, issues from there under the name of flour, and is then transported to our cities, soon delivered to the baker, who makes it into food for poor and rich alike. Again, is it not the farmer who fattens his flocks in the pastures in order to provide us with warm clothing? For how should we clothe or nourish ourselves without his labor? And, gentlemen, is it even necessary to go so far for examples? Who has not frequently reflected on all the momentous things that we get out of that modest animal, the ornament of poultry-yards, that provides us at once with a soft pillow for our bed, with succulent flesh for our tables, and eggs? But I should never end if I were to enumerate one after the other all the different products which the earth, well cultivated, like a generous mother, lavishes upon her children. Here it is the vine; elsewhere apple trees for cider; there colza; further, cheeses; and flax; gentlemen, let us not forget flax, which has made such great strides forward these last years and to which I call your special attention!"

He had no need to call it, for all the mouths of the multitude were wide open, as if to drink in his words. Tuvache by his side listened to him with staring eyes. Monsieur Derozerays from time to time softly closed his eyelids, and farther on the pharmacist, with his son Napoleon between his knees, put his hand behind his ear in order not to lose a syllable. The chins of the other members of the jury nodded slowly up and down in their waistcoats in sign of approval. The firemen at the foot of the platform rested on their bayonets; and Binet, motionless, stood with out-turned elbows, the point of his sabre in the air. Perhaps he could hear, but he certainly couldn't see a thing, for the visor of his helmet fell down on his nose. His lieutenant, the youngest son of Monsieur Tuvache, had an even bigger one; it was so large that he could hardly keep it on, in spite of the cotton scarf that peeped out from underneath. He wore a smile of childlike innocence, and his thin pale face, dripping with sweat, expressed satisfaction, some exhaustion and sleepiness.

The square was crowded up to the houses. People were leaning on their elbows at all the windows, others were standing on their doorsteps, and Justin, in front of the pharmacy, seemed fascinated by the spectacle. In spite of the silence Monsieur Lieuvain's voice was lost in the air. It reached you in fragments of phrases, interrupted here and there by the creaking of chairs in the crowd; then, the long bellowing of an ox would suddenly burst forth from behind, or else the bleating of the lambs, who answered one another from street to street. Even the cowherds and shepherds had driven their beasts this far, and one could hear their lowing from time to time, while with their tongues they tore down some scrap of foliage that hung over their muzzles.

Rodolphe had drawn nearer to Emma, and was whispering hurriedly in her ear:

"Doesn't this conspiracy of society revolt you? Is there a single sentiment it does not condemn? The noblest instincts, the purest feelings are persecuted, slandered; and if at length two poor souls do meet, all is organized in such a way as to keep them from becoming one. Yet they will try, they will call to each other. Not in vain, for sooner or later, be it in six or ten years, they will come together in love; for fate has decreed it, and they are born for each other."

His arms were folded across his knees, and thus lifting his face at her from close by, he looked fixedly at her. She noticed in his eyes small golden lines radiating from the black pupils; she even smelt the perfume of the pomade that made his hair glossy. Then something gave way in her; she recalled the Viscount who had waltzed with her at Vaubyessard, and whose beard exhaled a similar scent of vanilla and lemon, and mechanically she half-closed her eyes the better to breathe it in. But in making this movement, as she leant back in her chair, she saw in the distance, right on the line of the horizon, the old diligence the "Hirondelle," that was slowly descending the hill of Leux, dragging after it a long trail of dust. It was in this yellow carriage that Léon had so often come back to her, and by this route down there that he had gone for ever. She fancied she saw him opposite at his window; then all grew confused; clouds gathered; it seemed to her that she was again turning in the waltz under the light of the lustres on the arm of the Viscount, and that Léon was not far away, that he was coming . . . and yet all the time she was conscious of Rodolphe's head by her side. The sweetness of this sensation revived her past desires, and like grains of sand under a gust of wind, they swirled around in the subtle breath of the perfume that diffused over her soul. She breathed deeply several times to drink in the freshness of the ivy round the columns. She took off her gloves and wiped her hands; then she fanned her face with her handkerchief while she kept hearing, through the throbbing of her temples, the murmur of the crowd and the voice of the councillor intoning his phrases.

He was saying:

"Persevere! listen neither to the suggestions of routine, nor to the over-hasty councils of a rash empiricism. Apply yourselves, above all, to the amelioration of the soil, to good manures, to the development of the breeds, whether equine, bovine, ovine, or porcine. May these shows be to you pacific arenas, where the victor in leaving will hold forth a hand to the vanquished, and will fraternise with him in the hope of even greater success. And you, aged servants! humble helpers, whose hard labor no Government up to this day has taken into consideration, receive the reward of your silent virtues, and be assured that the state henceforward has its eye upon you; that it encourages you, protects you; that it will accede to your just demands, and alleviate as much as possible the heavy burden of your painful sacrifices."

Monsieur Lieuvain sat down; Monsieur Derozerays got up, beginning another speech. His was not perhaps so florid as that of the councillor, but it stood out by a more direct style, that is to say, by more specific knowledge and more elevated considerations. Thus the praise of the Government took up less space; religion and agriculture more. He showed the relation between both, and how they had always contributed to civilisation. Rodolphe was talking dreams, forebodings, magnetism with Madame Bovary. Going back to the cradle of society, the orator painted those fierce times when men lived on acorns in the heart of woods. Then they had left off the skins of beasts, had put on cloth, tilled the soil, planted the vine. Was this a good, or wasn't there more harm than good in this discovery? That was the problem to which Monsieur Derozerays addressed himself. From magnetism little by little Rodolphe had come to affinities, and while the president was citing Cincinnatus and his plough, Diocletian planting his cabbages, and the Emperors of China inaugurating the year by the sowing of seed, the young man was explaining to the young woman that these irresistible attractions find their cause in some previous state of existence.

"Take us, for instance," he said, "how did we happen to meet? What chance willed it? It was because across infinite distances, like two streams uniting, our particular inclinations pushed us toward one another."

And he seized her hand; she did not withdraw it.

"First prize for general farming!" announced the president.

"—Just now, for example, when I went to your home . . ."

"To Mr. Bizat of Quincampoix."

"—Did I know I would accompany you?"

"Seventy francs!"

"—A hundred times I tried to leave; yet I followed you and stayed . . ."

"For manures!"

"—As I would stay to-night, to-morrow, all other days, all my life!"

"To Monsieur Caron of Argueil, a gold medal!"

"—For I have never enjoyed anyone's company so much."

"To Monsieur Bain of Givry-Saint-Martin."

"—And I will never forget you."

"For a merino ram . . ."

"—Whereas you will forget me; I'll pass through your life as a mere shadow . . ."

"To Monsieur Belot of Notre-Dame."

"—But no, tell me there can be a place for me in your thoughts, in your life, can't there?"

"Hog! first prize equally divided between Messrs. Lehérissé and Cullembourg, sixty francs!"

Rodolphe was holding her hand on his; it was warm and quivering like a captive dove that wants to fly away; perhaps she was trying to take it away or perhaps she was answering his pressure, at any rate, she moved her fingers; he exclaimed

"Oh, thank you! You do not repulse me! You are kind! You understand that I am yours! Let me see you, let me look at you!"

A gust of wind that blew in at the window ruffled the cloth on the table, and in the square below all the large bonnets rose up like the fluttering wings of white butterflies.

"Use of oil-cakes!" continued the president.

He was hurrying now: "Flemish manure, flax-growing, drainage, long term leases . . . domestic service."

Rodolphe was no longer speaking. They looked at each other. As their desire increased, their dry lips trembled and languidly, effortlessly, their fingers intertwined.

"Catherine Nicaise Elizabeth Leroux, of Sassetot-la-Guerrière, for fifty-four years of service at the same farm, a silver medal—value, twenty-five francs!"

"Where is Catherine Leroux?" repeated the councillor.

She did not appear, and one could hear whispering voices:

"Go ahead!"

"No."

"To the left!"

"Don't be afraid!"

"Oh, how stupid she is!"

"Well, is she there?" cried Tuvache.

"Yes; here she is."

"Then what's she waiting for?"

There came forward on the platform a frightened-looking little old lady who seemed to shrink within her poor clothes. On her feet she wore heavy wooden shoes, and from her hips hung a large blue apron. Her pale face framed in a borderless cap was more wrinkled than a withered russet apple, and from the sleeves of her red jacket looked out two large hands with gnarled joints. The dust from the barns, washing soda and grease from the wool had so encrusted, roughened, hardened them that they seemed dirty, although they had been rinsed in clear water; and by dint of long service they remained half open, as if to bear humble witness of so much suffering endured. Something of monastic rigidity dignified her. No trace of sadness or tenderness weakened her pale face. Having lived so long among animals, she had taken on their silent and tranquil ways. It was the first time that she found herself in the midst of so large a company; and inwardly scared by the flags, the drums, the gentlemen in frock-coats, and the decorations of the councillor, she stood motionless, not knowing whether she should advance or run away, nor why the crowd was cheering and the jury smiling at her. Thus, a half century of servitude confronted these beaming bourgeois.

"Step forward, venerable Catherine Nicaise Elizabeth Leroux!" said the councillor, who had taken the list of prize-winners from the president; and, looking at the piece of paper and the old woman by turns, he repeated in a fatherly tone:

"Step forward, step forward!"

"Are you deaf?" said Tuvache, who was jumping around in his arm-chair; and he began shouting in her ear, "Fifty-four years of service. A silver medal! Twenty-five francs! For you!"

Then, when she had her medal, she looked at it, and a smile of beatitude spread over her face; and as she walked away they could hear her muttering:

"I'll give it to our curé at home, to say some masses for me!"

"What fanaticism!" exclaimed the pharmacist, leaning across to the notary.

The meeting was over, the crowd dispersed, and now that the speeches had been read, everything fell back into place again, and everything into the old grooves; the masters bullied the servants, the servants beat the animals, indolent victors returning to their stables with a green wreath between their horns.

The National Guards, however, had climbed up to the second floor of the townhall; brioches were stuck on their bayonets, and the drummer of the battalion carried a basket with bottles. Madame Bovary took Rodolphe's arm; he saw her home; they separated at her door; then he walked about alone in the meadow while waiting for the banquet to start.

The feast was long, noisy, ill served; the guests were so crowded that they could hardly move their elbows; and the narrow planks that served as benches almost broke under their weight. They ate huge amounts. Each one stuffed himself with all he could lay hands on. Sweat stood on every brow, and a whitish steam, like the vapour of a stream on an autumn morning, floated above the table between the hanging lamps. Rodolphe, leaning against the canvas of the tent, was thinking so intently of Emma that he heard nothing. Behind him on the grass the servants were piling up the dirty plates, his neighbors were talking; he did not answer them; they filled his glass, and there was silence in his thoughts in spite of the noise around him. He was dreaming of what she had said, of the line of her lips; her face, as in a magic mirror, shone on the plates of the shakos, the folds of her gown fell along the walls, and endless days of love unrolled before him in the future.

He saw her again in the evening during the fireworks, but she was with her husband, Madame Homais, and the pharmacist, who was worrying about the danger of stray rockets. Time and again he left the company to give some advice to Binet.

The fireworks sent to Monsieur Tuvache had, through an excess of caution, been locked in his cellar; so the damp powder would not light, and the main piece, that was to represent a dragon biting his tail, failed completely. From time to time, a meagre Roman-candle went off; then the gaping crowd sent up a roar that mingled with the giggling of the women who were being tickled in the darkness. Emma silently nestled against Charles's shoulder; then, raising her chin, she watched the luminous rays of the rockets against the dark sky. Rodolphe gazed at her in the light of the burning lanterns.

One by one, they went out. Stars appeared. A few drops of rain began to fall. She tied her scarf over her bare head.

At this moment the councillor's carriage came out from the inn. His coachman, who was drunk, suddenly fell asleep, and one could see the mass of his body from afar above the hood, framed by the two lanterns, swaying from right to left with the motion of the springs.

"Truly," said the pharmacist, "severe measures should be taken against drunkenness! I should like to see written up weekly at the door of the townhall on a board *ad hoc* the names of all those who during the week got intoxicated on alcohol. Besides, with regard to statistics, one would thus have, as it were, public records that one could refer to if needed . . . But excuse me!"

And he once more ran off to the captain. The latter was returning to see his lathe.

"You might do well," said Homais to him, "to send one of your men, or to go yourself . . ."

"Oh, leave me alone!" answered the tax-collector. "I'm telling you everything is taken care of."

"There is nothing for you to worry about," said the pharmacist, when he returned to his friends. "Monsieur Binet has assured me that all precautions have been taken. No sparks have fallen; the pumps are full. Let's go to bed."

"I can certainly use some sleep," said Madame Homais with a huge yawn. "But never mind; we've had a beautiful day for our fete."

Rodolphe repeated in a low voice, and with a tender look, "Oh, yes! very beautiful!"

And after a final good night, they parted ways.

Two days later, in the "Fanal de Rouen," there was a long article on the show. Homais had composed it on the spur of the moment, the very morning after the banquet.

"Why these festoons, these flowers, these garlands? Whereto was the crowd hurrying, like the waves of a furious sea under the torrents of a tropical sun pouring its heat upon our meadows?"

Then he spoke of the condition of the peasants. Certainly the Government was doing much, but not enough. "Be bold!" he told them; "a thousand reforms are needed; let us carry them out! Then, reporting on the entry of the councillor, he did not forget "the martial spirit of our militia," nor "our dazzling village maidens," nor the "bald-headed elders like patriarchs, some of whom, left over from our immortal phalanxes, still felt their hearts beat at the manly sound of the drums." He cited himself among the first of the members of the jury, and he even called attention in a note to the fact that Monsieur Homais, pharmacist, had sent a memoir on cider to the agricultural society. When he came to the distribution of the prizes, he painted the joy of the prize-winners in dithyrambic strophes. "The father embraced the son, the brother the brother, the husband his wife. More than one showed his humble medal with pride; and no doubt when he got home to his good housewife, he hung it up weeping on the modest walls of his cottage.

"About six o'clock a banquet prepared in the meadow of Monsieur Leigeard brought together the main participants in the festivities. The utmost merriment reigned throughout. Several toasts were proposed: Monsieur Lieuvain, To the king! Monsieur Tuvache, To the prefect! Monsieur Derozerays, To Agriculture! Monsieur Homais, To the twin sisters, Industry and Fine Arts! Monsieur Leplichey, To Improvements! At night some brilliant fireworks suddenly lit up the sky. It was a real kaleidoscope, an operatic scene; and for a moment our little locality might have thought itself transported into the midst of a dream from the 'Thousand and One Nights.'

"Let us state that no untoward event disturbed this family meeting."

And he added: "Only the absence of the clergy was noted. No doubt the priests do not understand progress in the same way. Just as you please, *messieurs de Loyola!*"

IX

Six weeks passed. Rodolphe did not come again. At last one evening he appeared.

The day after the fair he told himself:

"Let's not go back too soon; that would be a mistake."

And at the end of a week he had gone off hunting. After the hunting he first feared that too much time had passed, and then he reasoned thus:

"If she loved me from the first day, impatience must make her love me even more. Let's persist!"

And he knew that his calculation had been right when, on entering the room, he saw Emma turn pale.

She was alone. Night was falling. The small muslin curtain along the windows deepened the twilight, and the gilding of the barometer, on which the rays of the sun fell, shone in the looking-glass between the meshes of the coral.

Rodolphe remained standing, and Emma hardly answered his first conventional phrases.

"I have been busy," he said, "I have been ill."

"Nothing serious?" she cried.

"Well," said Rodolphe, sitting down at her side on a footstool, "no . . . It was because I did not want to come back."

"Why?"

"Can't you guess?"

He looked at her again, but so hard that she lowered her head, blushing. He pursued:

"Emma . . ."

"Monsieur!" she exclaimed, drawing back a little.

"Ah! you see," he replied in a melancholy voice, "that I was right not to come back; for this name, this name that fills my whole soul, and that escaped me, you forbid me its use! Madame Bovary! . . . why, the whole world calls you thus! Moreover, it is not your name; it is the name of another!"

He repeated,

"Of another!"

And he hid his face in his hands.

"Yes, I think of you constantly! . . . The thought of you drives me to despair. Ah! forgive me! . . . I'll go . . . Adieu . . . I'll go far away, so far that you will never hear of me again; yet . . . today . . . I don't know what force made me come here. For one does not struggle against Heaven; it is impossible to resist the smile of angels; one is carried away by the beautiful, the lovely, the adorable."

It was the first time that Emma had heard such words addressed to her, and her pride unfolded languidly in the warmth of this language, like someone stretching in a hot bath.

"But if I didn't come," he continued, "if I couldn't see you, at least I have gazed long on all that surrounds you. At night, every night, I arose; I came here; I watched your house, the roof glimmering in the moon, the trees in the garden swaying before your window, and the little lamp, a gleam shining through the window-panes in the darkness. Ah! you never knew that there, so near you, so far from you, was a poor wretch . . ."

She turned towards him with a sob.

"Oh, you are kind!" she said.

"No, I love you, that is all! You do not doubt that! Tell me; one word, one single word!"

And Rodolphe imperceptibly glided from the footstool to the ground; but a sound of wooden shoes was heard in the kitchen, and he noticed that the door of the room was not closed.

"You would do an act of charity," he went on, rising, "if you accepted to gratify a whim!" It was to visit her home, he wished to see it, and since Madame Bovary could see no objection to this, they both rose just when Charles came in.

"Good morning, doctor," Rodolphe said to him.

Flattered by this unexpected title, Charles launched into elaborate displays of politeness. Of this the other took advantage to pull himself together.

"Madame was speaking to me," he then said, "about her health."

Charles interrupted; she was indeed giving him thousands of worries; her palpitations were beginning again. Then Rodolphe asked if riding would not be helpful.

"Certainly! excellent, just the thing! What a good idea! You ought to try it."

And as she objected that she had no horse, Monsieur Rodolphe offered one. She refused his offer; he did not insist. Then to explain his visit he said that his ploughman, the man of the blood-letting, still suffered from dizziness.

"I'll drop by," said Bovary.

"No, no! I'll send him to you; we'll come; that will be more convenient for you."

"Ah! very good! I thank you."

And as soon as they were alone, "Why don't you accept Monsieur Boulanger's offer? It was so gracious of him."

She seemed to pout, invented a thousand excuses, and finally declared that perhaps it would look odd.

"That's the least of my worries!" said Charles, turning on his heel. "Health first! You are making a mistake."

"Could I go riding without proper clothes?"

"You must order a riding outfit," he answered.

The riding-habit decided her.

When it was ready, Charles wrote to Monsieur Boulanger that his wife was able to accept his invitation and thanked him in advance for his kindness.

The next day at noon Rodolphe appeared at Charles's door with two saddle-horses. One had pink rosettes at his ears and a deerskin side-saddle.

Rodolphe had put on high soft boots, assuming that she had never seen the likes of them. In fact, Emma was charmed with his appearance as he stood on the landing in his great velvet coat and white corduroy breeches. She was ready; she was waiting for him.

Justin escaped from the store to watch her depart, and the pharmacist himself also came out. He was giving Monsieur Boulanger some good advice.

"An accident happens so easily. Be careful! Your horses may be skittish!"

She heard a noise above her; it was Félicité drumming on the window-panes to amuse little Berthe. The child blew her a kiss; her mother answered with a wave of her whip.

"Have a pleasant ride!" cried Monsieur Homais. "Be careful! above all, be careful!"

And he flourished his newspaper as he saw them disappear.

As soon as he felt the ground, Emma's horse set off at a gallop. Rodolphe galloped by her side. Now and then they exchanged a word. With slightly bent head, her hand well up, and her right arm stretched out, she gave herself up to the cadence of the movement that rocked her in her saddle.

At the bottom of the hill Rodolphe gave his horse its head; they set off together at a bound, then at the top suddenly the horses stopped, and her large blue veil fell about her.

It was early in October. There was fog over the land. Hazy clouds hovered on the horizon between the outlines of the hills; others, rent asunder, floated up and disappeared. Sometimes through a rift in the clouds, beneath a ray of sunshine, gleamed from afar the roofs of Yonville, with the gardens at the water's edge, the yards, the walls and the church steeple. Emma half closed her eyes to pick out her house, and never had this poor village where she lived appeared so small. From the height on which they were the whole valley seemed an immense pale lake sending off its vapour into the air. Clumps of trees here and there stood out like black rocks, and the tall lines of the poplars that rose above the mist were like a beach stirred by the wind.

By the side, on the grass between the pines, a brown light shimmered in the warm atmosphere. The earth, ruddy like the powder of tobacco, deadened the noise of their steps, and as they walked, the horses kicked up fallen pine cones before them.

Rodolphe and Emma thus skirted the woods. She turned away from time to time to avoid his look, and then she saw only the line of pine trunks, whose monotonous succession made her a little giddy. The horses were panting; the leather of the saddles creaked.

Just as they were entering the forest the sun came out.

"God is with us!" said Rodolphe.

"Do you think so?" she said.

"Forward! forward!" he continued.

He clucked with his tongue. The horses set off at a trot.

Long ferns by the roadside caught in Emma's stirrup. Rodolphe leant forward and removed them as they rode along. At other times, to turn aside the branches, he passed close to her, and Emma felt his knee brushing against her leg. The sky was blue now. The leaves no longer stirred. There were spaces full of heather in flower, and patches of purple alternated with the confused tangle of the trees, grey, fawn, or golden colored, according to the nature of their leaves. Often in the thicket one could hear the fluttering of wings, or else the hoarse, soft cry of the ravens flying off amidst the oaks.

They dismounted. Rodolphe fastened up the horses. She walked on in front on the moss between the paths.

But her long dress got in her way, although she held it up by the skirt; and Rodolphe, walking behind her, saw between the black cloth and the black shoe the delicacy of her white stocking, that seemed to him as if it were a part of her nakedness.

She stopped.

"I am tired," she said.

"Come, try some more," he went on. "Courage!"

Some hundred paces further on she stopped again, and through her veil, that fell sideways from her man's hat over her hips, her face appeared in a bluish transparency as if she were floating under azure waves.

"But where are we going?"

He did not answer. She was breathing irregularly. Rodolphe looked round him biting his moustache.

They came to a larger space which had been cleared of undergrowth. They sat down on the trunk of a fallen tree, and Rodolphe began speaking to her of his love.

He did not frighten her at first with compliments. He was calm, serious, melancholy.

Emma listened to him with bowed head, and stirred the bits of wood on the ground with the tip of her foot.

But at the words, "Are not our destinies now forever united?"

"Oh, no!" she replied. "You know they aren't. It is impossible!"

She rose to go. He seized her by the wrist. She stopped. Then, having gazed at him for a few moments with an amorous and moist look, she said hurriedly:

"Well let's not speak of it again! Where are the horses? Let's go back."

He made a gesture of anger and annoyance. She repeated:

"Where are the horses? Where are the horses?"

Then smiling a strange smile, looking straight at her, his teeth set, he advanced with outstretched arms. She recoiled trembling. She stammered:

"Oh, you frighten me! You hurt me! Take me back!"

"If it must be," he went on, his face changing; and he again became respectful, caressing, timid. She gave him her arm. They went back. He said:

"What was the matter with you? Why? I do not understand. You were mistaken, no doubt. In my soul you are as a Madonna on a pedestal, in a place lofty, secure, immaculate. But I cannot live without you! I need your eyes, your voice, your thought! Be my friend, my sister, my angel!"

And he stretched out his arm and caught her by the waist. Gently she tried to disengage herself. He supported her thus as they walked along.

They heard the two horses browsing on the leaves.

"Not quite yet!" said Rodolphe. "Stay a minute longer! Please stay!"

He drew her farther on to a small pool where duckweeds made a greenness on the water. Faded waterlilies lay motionless between the reeds. At the noise of their steps in the grass, frogs jumped away to hide themselves.

"I shouldn't, I shouldn't!" she said. "I am out of my mind listening to you!"

"Why? . . . Emma! Emma!"

"Oh, Rodolphe! . . ." she said slowly and she pressed against his shoulder.

The cloth of her dress clung to the velvet of his coat. She threw back her white neck which swelled in a sigh, and, faltering, weeping, and hiding her face in her hands, with one long shudder, she abandoned herself to him.

The shades of night were falling; the horizontal sun passing between the branches dazzled the eyes. Here and there around her, in the leaves or on the ground, trembled luminous patches, as if humming-birds flying about had scattered their feathers. Silence was everywhere; something sweet seemed to come forth from the trees. She felt her heartbeat return, and the blood coursing through her flesh like a river of milk. Then far away, beyond the wood, on the other hills, she heard a vague prolonged cry, a voice which lingered, and in silence she heard it mingling like music with the last pulsations of her throbbing nerves. Rodolphe, a cigar between his lips, was mending with his penknife one of the two broken bridles.

They returned to Yonville by the same road. On the mud they saw again the traces of their horses side by side, the same thickets, the same stones in the grass; nothing around them seemed changed; and yet for her something had happened more stupendous than if the mountains had moved in their places. Rodolphe now and again bent forward and took her hand to kiss it.

She was charming on horseback—upright, with her slender waist, her knee bent on the mane of her horse, her face somewhat flushed by the fresh air in the red of the evening.

On entering Yonville she made her horse prance in the road.

People looked at her from the windows.

At dinner her husband thought she looked well, but she pretended not to hear him when he inquired about her ride, and she remained sitting there with her elbow at the side of her plate between the two lighted candles.

"Emma!" he said.

"What?"

"Well, I spent the afternoon at Monsieur Alexandre's. He has an old filly, still very fine, just a little broken in the knees, and that could be bought, I am sure, for a hundred crowns." He added, "And thinking it might please you, I have reserved her . . . I bought her . . . Have I done right? Do tell me!"

She nodded her head in assent; then a quarter of an hour later:

"Are you going out to-night?" she asked.

"Yes. Why?"

"Oh, nothing, nothing, dear!"

And as soon as she had got rid of Charles she went and shut herself up in her room.

At first she felt stunned; she saw the trees, the paths, the ditches, Rodolphe, and she again felt the pressure of his arms, while the leaves rustled and the reeds whistled.

But when she saw herself in the mirror she wondered at her face. Never had her eyes been so large, so black, nor so deep. Something subtle about her being transfigured her.

She repeated: "I have a lover! a lover!" delighting at the idea as if a second puberty had come to her. So at last she was to know those joys of love, that fever of happiness of which she had despaired! She was entering upon a marvelous world where all would be passion, ecstasy, delirium. She felt herself surrounded by an endless rapture. A blue space surrounded her and ordinary existence appeared only intermittently between these heights, dark and far away beneath her.

Then she recalled the heroines of the books that she had read, and the lyric legion of these adulterous women began to sing in her memory with the voice of sisters that charmed her. She became herself, as it were, an actual part of these lyrical imaginings; at long last, as she saw herself among those lovers she had so envied, she fulfilled the love-dream of her youth. Besides, Emma felt a satisfaction of revenge. How she had suffered! But she had won out at last, and the love so long pent up erupted in joyous outbursts. She tasted it without remorse, without anxiety, without concern.

The next day brought a new-discovered sweetness. They exchanged vows. She told him of her sorrows. Rodolphe interrupted her with kisses; and she, looking at him through half-closed eyes, asked him to call her again by her name and to say that he loved her. They were in the forest, as yesterday, this time in the hut of some *sabot* makers. The walls were of straw, and the roof so low they had to stoop. They were seated side by side on a bed of dry leaves.

From that day on they wrote to one another regularly every evening. Emma placed her letter at the end of the garden, by the river, in a crack of the wall. Rodolphe came to fetch it, and put another in its place that she always accused of being too short.

One morning, when Charles had gone out before daybreak, she felt the urge to see Rodolphe at once. She would go quickly to La Huchette, stay there an hour, and be back again at Yonville while every one was still asleep. The idea made her breathless with desire, and she soon found herself in the middle of the field, walking with rapid steps, without looking behind her.

Day was just breaking. Emma recognised her lover's house from a distance. Its two dove-tailed weathercocks stood out black against the pale dawn.

Beyond the farmyard there was a separate building that she assumed must be the château. She entered it as if the doors at her approach had opened wide of their own accord. A large straight staircase led up to the corridor. Emma raised the latch of a door, and suddenly at the end of the room she saw a man sleeping. It was Rodolphe. She uttered a cry.

"You here? You here?" he repeated. "How did you manage to come? Ah! your dress is wet."

"I love you!" she answered, winding her arm around his neck.

This first bold attempt having been successful, now every time Charles went out early Emma dressed quickly and slipped on tiptoe down the steps that led to the waterside.

But when the cow plank was taken up, she had to follow the walls alongside the river; the bank was slippery; to keep from falling, she had to catch hold of the tufts of faded wall-flowers. Then she went across ploughed fields, stumbling, her thin shoes sinking in the heavy mud. Her scarf, knotted round her head, fluttered to the wind in the meadows. She was afraid of the oxen; she began to run; she arrived out of breath, with rosy cheeks, and breathing out from her whole person a fresh perfume of sap, of verdure, of the open air. At this hour Rodolphe was still asleep. It was like a spring morning bursting into his room.

The golden curtains along the windows let a heavy, whitish light filter into the room. Emma would find her way gropingly, with blinking eyes, the drops of dew hanging from her hair, making a topaz halo around her face. Rodolphe, laughing, would draw her to him and press her to his breast.

Then she inspected the room, opened the drawers of the tables, combed her hair with his comb, and looked at herself in his shaving mirror. Often she put between her teeth the big pipe that lay on the bedtable, amongst lemons and pieces of sugar near the water bottle.

It took them a good quarter of an hour to say good-bye. Then Emma cried: she would have wished never to leave Rodolphe. Something stronger than herself drew her to him; until, one day, when she arrived unexpectedly, he frowned as one put out.

"What is wrong?" she said. "Are you ill? tell me!"

He ended up declaring earnestly that her visits were too dangerous and that she was compromising herself.

X

Gradually Rodolphe's fears took possession of her. At first, love had intoxicated her, and she had thought of nothing beyond. But now that he was indispensable to her life, she feared losing the smallest part of his love or upsetting him in the least. When she came back from his house, she looked all about her, anxiously watching every form that passed in the horizon, and every village window from which she could be seen. She listened for steps, cries, the noise of the ploughs, and she stopped short, white, and trembling more than the aspen leaves swaying overhead.

One morning as she was thus returning, she suddenly thought she saw the long barrel of a carbine that seemed to be aimed at her. It stuck out sideways from the end of a small barrel half-buried in the grass on the edge of a ditch. Emma, half-fainting with terror, nevertheless walked on, and a man stepped out of the barrel like a Jack-in-the-box jumping out of his cage. He had gaiters buckled up to the knees, his cap pulled down over his eyes; his lips shivered in the cold and his nose was red. It was Captain Binet lying in ambush for wild ducks.

"You ought to have called out long ago!" he exclaimed. "When one sees a gun, one should always give warning."

The tax-collector was thus trying to hide his own fright, for a prefectorial order prohibited duck-hunting except in boats, Monsieur Binet, despite his respect for the laws, was breaking the law and he expected to see the garde champêtre turn up any moment. But this anxiety whetted his pleasure, and, all alone in his barrel, he congratulated himself on his luck and his cleverness.

The sight of Emma seemed to relieve him of a great weight, and he at once opened the conversation.

"Pretty cold, isn't it; it's nippy!"

Emma didn't answer. He pursued:

"You're certainly off to an early start today."

"Yes," she stammered; "I am just coming from the nurse who is keeping my child."

"Ah, yes indeed, yes indeed. As for myself, I am here, just as you see me, since break of day; but the weather is so muggy, that unless one had the bird at the mouth of the gun . . ."

"Good day, Monsieur Binet," she interrupted, turning her back on him.

"Your servant, madame," he replied drily.

And he went back into his barrel.

Emma regretted having left the tax-collector so abruptly. No doubt he would jump to the worst conclusions. The story about the nurse was the weakest possible excuse, for every one at Yonville knew that the Bovary baby had been at home with her parents for a year. Besides, no one was living in this direction; this path led only to La Huchette. Binet, then, could not fail to guess where she came from, and he would not remain silent; he would talk, that was certain. She remained until evening racking her brain with every lie she could think up, but the image of that idiot with his game bag would not leave her.

Seeing her so gloomy, Charles proposed after dinner to take her to the pharmacist by way of distraction, and the first person she caught sight of in the shop was him again, the tax-collector! He was standing in front of the counter, lit up by the gleams of the red jar, saying:

"Could I have half an ounce of vitriol, please?"

"Justin," cried the pharmacist, "bring us the sulphuric acid."

Then to Emma, who was going up to Madame Homais' room, "Don't go up, it's not worth the trouble, she is just coming down. Why not warm yourself by the fire . . . Excuse me . . . Good-day, doctor" (for the pharmacist much enjoyed pronouncing the word "doctor," as if addressing another by it reflected on himself some of the grandeur of the title). "Justin, take care not to upset the mortars! You'd better fetch some chairs from the little room; you know very well that the arm-chairs are not to be taken out of the drawing-room."

And he was just about to put his arm-chair back in its place when Binet asked him for half an ounce of sugar acid.

"Sugar acid!" said the pharmacist contemptuously, "never heard of it! There is no such thing. Perhaps it is Oxalic acid you want. It is Oxalic, isn't it?"

Binet explained that he wanted a corrosive to make himself some copper-water with which to remove rust from his hunting things. Emma shuddered. The pharmacist was saying:

"Indeed, the dampness we're having is certainly not propitious."

"Nevertheless," replied the tax-collector, with a sly look, "some people seem to like it." She was stifling.

"And give me . . ."

"Will he never go?" she thought.

"Half an ounce of resin and turpentine, four ounces of beeswax, and three half ounces of animal charcoal, if you please, to clean the leather of my togs."

The druggist was beginning to cut the wax when Madame Homais appeared with Irma in her arms, Napoleon by her side, and Athalie following. She sat down on the velvet seat by the window, and the boy squatted down on a footstool, while his eldest sister hovered round the jujube box near her papa. The latter was filling funnels and corking phials, sticking on labels, making up parcels. Around him all were silent; only from time to time could one hear the weights jingling in the scales, and a few words of advice from the pharmacist to his apprentice.

"And how is your little girl?" Madame Homais asked suddenly.

"Silence!" exclaimed her husband, who was writing down some

figures on a scratch pad.

"Why didn't you bring her?" she went on in a low voice.

"Hush! hush!" said Emma, pointing a finger at the pharmacist.

But Binet, quite absorbed in checking over his bill, had probably heard nothing. At last he went out. Then Emma, relieved, uttered a deep sigh.

"How heavily you are breathing!" said Madame Homais.

"It is so hot in here," she replied.

So the next day they agreed to arrange their rendezvous. Emma wanted to bribe her servant with a present, but it would be better to find some safe house at Yonville. Rodolphe promised to look for one.

All through the winter, three or four times a week, in the dead of night he came to the garden. Emma had on purpose taken away the key of the gate, letting Charles think it was lost.

To call her, Rodolphe threw a handful of sand at the shutters. She jumped up with a start; but sometimes he had to wait, for Charles had the habit of talking endlessly by the fireside.

She was wild with impatience; if her eyes could have done it, they would have hurled him out of the window. At last she would begin to undress, then take up a book, and go on reading very quietly as if the book amused her. But Charles, who was in bed, would call her to bed.

"Come, now, Emma," he said, "it is time."

"Yes, I am coming," she answered.

Then, as the candles shone in his eyes, he turned to the wall and fell asleep. She escaped, holding her breath, smiling, half undressed.

Rodolphe had a large cloak; he wrapped it around her, and putting his arm round her waist, he drew her without a word to the end of the garden.

It was in the arbour, on the same bench of half rotten sticks where formerly Léon had stared at her so amorously on the summer evenings. She never thought of him now.

The stars shone through the leafless jasmine branches. Behind them they heard the river flowing, and now and again on the bank the rustling of the dry reeds. Masses of deeper darkness stood out here and there in the night and sometimes, shaken with one single motion, they would rise up and sway like immense black waves pressing forward to engulf them. The cold of the nights made them clasp each other more tightly; the sighs of their lips seemed to them deeper; their eyes, that they could hardly see, larger; and in the midst of the silence words softly spoken would fall on their souls with a crystalline sound, that echoed in endless reverberations.

When the night was rainy, they took refuge in the consulting-room between the cart-shed and the stable. She would light one of the kitchen candles that she had hidden behind the books. Rodolphe settled down there as if at home. The sight of the library, of the desk, of the entire room, in fine, would arouse his mirth; and he could not refrain from making jokes at Charles' expense despite Emma's embarrassment. She would have liked to see him more serious, and even on occasions more dramatic; as, for example, when she thought she heard a noise of approaching steps in the alley.

"Some one is coming!" she said.

He blew out the light.

"Have you your pistols?"

"Why?"

"Why, to defend yourself," replied Emma.

"From your husband? Oh, the poor fellow!" And Rodolphe finished his sentence with a gesture that said, "I could crush him with a flip of my finger."

She was awed at his bravery, although she felt in it a sort of indecency and a naïve coarseness that scandalised her.

Rodolphe reflected a good deal on the pistol incident. If she had spoken in earnest, he thought it most ridiculous, even odious; for he had no reason whatever to hate the good Charles, not exactly being devoured by jealousy; and in this same connection, Emma had made him a solemn promise that he did not think in the best of taste.

Besides, she was becoming dreadfully sentimental. She had insisted on exchanging miniatures; handfuls of hair had been cut off, and now she was asking for a ring—a real wedding-ring, in token of eternal union. She often spoke to him of the evening chimes, of the "voices of nature." Then she talked to him of their respective mothers. Rodolphe's had died twenty years ago. Emma none the less consoled him with conventional phrases, like those one would use with a bereaved child; sometimes she even said to him, gazing at the moon:

"I am sure that, from up there, both approve our love."

But she was so pretty! He had possessed so few women of similar ingenuousness. This love without debauchery was a new experience for him, and, drawing him out of his lazy habits, caressed at once his pride and his sensuality. Although his bourgeois common sense disapproved of it, Emma's exaltations, deep down in his heart, enchanted him, since they were directed his way. Then, sure of her love, he no longer made an effort, and insensibly his manner changed.

No longer, did he, as before, find words so tender that they made her cry, nor passionate caresses that drove her into ecstasy; their great love, in which she had lived immersed, seemed to run out beneath her, like the water of a river absorbed by its own bed; and she could see the bottom. She would not believe it; she redoubled in tenderness, and Rodolphe concealed his indifference less and less.

She did not know if she regretted having yielded to him, or whether she did not wish, on the contrary, to love him even more. The humiliation of having given in turned into resentment, tempered by their voluptuous pleasures. It was not tenderness; it was like a continual seduction. He held her fully in his power; she almost feared him.

On the surface, however, things seemed calm enough, Rodolphe having carried out his adultery just as he had wanted; and at the end of six months, when the spring-time came, they were to one another like a married couple, tranquilly keeping up a domestic flame.

It was the time of year when old Rouault sent his turkey in rememberance of the setting of his leg. The present always arrived with a letter. Emma cut the string that tied it to the basket, and read the following lines:

My Dear Children,—I hope this will find you in good health, and that it will be as good as the others, for it seems to me a little more tender, if I may venture to say so, and heavier. But next time, for a change, I'll give you a turkeycock, unless you would prefer a capon; and send me back the hamper, if you please, with the two old ones. I have had an accident with sheds; the coverings flew off one windy night among the trees. The harvest has not been over-good either. Finally, I don't know when I shall come to see you. It is so difficult now to leave the house since I am alone, my poor Emma.

Here there was a break in the lines as if the old fellow had dropped his pen to dream a little while.

"As for myself, I am very well, except for a cold I caught the other day at Yvetot, where I had gone to hire a shepherd, having got rid of mine because no cooking was good enough for his taste. We are to be pitied with rascals like him! Moreover, he was dishonest.

I heard from a peddler who had a tooth pulled out when he passed through your part of the country this winter, that Bovary was as usual working hard. That doesn't surprise me; and he showed me his tooth; we had some coffee together. I asked him if he had seen you, and he said no, but that he had seen two horses in the stables, from which I conclude that business is looking up. So much the better, my dear children, and may God send you every imaginable happiness!

It grieves me not yet to have seen my dear little grand-daughter, Berthe Bovary. I have planted an Orleans plum-tree for her in the garden under your room, and I won't have it touched until we can make jam from it, that I will keep in the cupboard for her when she comes.

Good-bye, my dear children. I kiss you, my girl, you too, my son-in-law, and the little one on both cheeks. I am, with best compliments, your loving father.

THEODORE ROUAULT

She held the coarse paper in her fingers for some minutes. A continuous stream of spelling mistakes ran through the letter, and Emma followed the kindly thought that cackled right through it like a hen half hidden in a hedge of thorns. The writing had been dried with ashes from the hearth, for a little grey powder slipped from the letter on her dress, and she almost thought she saw her father bending over the hearth to take up the tongs. How long since she had been with him, sitting on the footstool in the chimney-corner, where she used to burn the end of a stick in the crackling flame of the sea-sedges! She remembered the summer evenings all full of sunshine. The colts whinnied when one passed by, and galloped, galloped . . . Under her window there was a beehive and at times, the bees wheeling round in the light, struck against her window like rebounding balls of gold. What happiness she had known at that time, what freedom, what hope! What a wealth of illusions! It was all gone now. She had lost them one by one, at every stage in the growth of her soul, in the succession of her conditions; maidenhood, marriage and love—shedding them along her path like a traveller who leaves something of his wealth at every inn along his road.

But who was it, then, who made her so unhappy? What extraordinary catastrophe had destroyed her life? And she raised her head, as if seeking around her for the cause of all that suffering.

An April sunray was dancing on the china in the shelves; the fire burned; beneath her slippers she felt the softness of the carpet; the day was bright, the air warm, and she heard her child shouting with laughter.

In fact, the little girl was just then rolling on the lawn in the new-mown grass. She was lying flat on her stomach at the top of a rick. The maid was holding her by her skirt. Lestiboudois was raking by her side, and every time he came near she bent forward, beating the air with both her arms.

"Bring her to me," said her mother, rushing over to kiss her. "How I love you, my poor child! How I love you!"

Then noticing that the tips of her ears were rather dirty, she rang at once for warm water, and washed her, changed her underwear, her stockings, her shoes, asked a thousand questions about her health, as if on the return from a long journey, and finally, kissing her again and crying a little, she gave her back to the maid, who was dumbfounded at this sudden outburst.

That evening Rodolphe found her more reserved than usual.

"It will blow over," he thought, "a passing whim . . ."

And he missed three successive rendezvous. When he did appear, her attitude was cold, almost contemptuous.

"Ah! you're wasting time, sweetheart!"

And he pretended not to notice her melancholy sighs, nor the handkerchief she pulled out.

Then Emma knew what it was to repent!

She even wondered why she hated Charles; wouldn't it have been better trying to love him? But he offered little hold for these re-awakened sentiments, so she remained rather embarrassed with her sacrificial intentions until the pharmacist provided her with a timely opportunity.

XI

He had recently read a paper praising a new method for curing club-foot, and since he was a partisan of progress, he conceived the patriotic idea that Yonville should show its pioneering spirit by having some club-foot operations performed there.

"Look here," he told Emma, "what do we risk?" and he ticked off on his fingers the advantages of the attempt, "success practically assured, relief and better appearance for the patient, quick fame for the surgeon. Why, for example, should not your husband relieve poor Hippolyte of the 'Lion d'Or'? He is bound to tell all passing travellers about his cure, and then" (Homais lowered his voice and looked round him) "who is to prevent me from sending a short piece on the subject to the paper? And! My God! an article gets around . . . people talk about it . . . it snowballs! And who knows? who knows?"

After all, Bovary might very well succeed. Emma had no reason to suppose he lacked skill, it would be a satisfaction for her to have urged him to a step by which his reputation and fortune would be increased! She only longed to lean on something more solid than love.

Pressed by her and the pharmacist, Charles allowed himself to be persuaded. He sent to Rouen for Dr. Duval's volume, and every evening, with his head between his hands, he embarked on his reading assignment.

While he struggled with the equinus, varus and valgus—that is to say, *katastrephopody, endostrephopody,* and *exostrephopody,* or in other words, the various deviations of the foot, to the inside, outside, or downwards, as well as with *hypostrephopody* and *anastrephopody* or torsion below and contraction above,—Monsieur Homais was trying out all possible arguments on the stable boy in order to persuade him to submit to the operation.

"At the very most you'll feel a slight pain, a small prick, like a little blood letting, less than the extraction of certain corns."

Hippolyte thought it over, rolling his stupid eyes.

"Anyway," continued the pharmacist, "it is none of my business. I am telling you this for your own sake! out of pure humanity! I would like to see you freed from that hideous caudication as well as that swaying in your lumbar region which, whatever you say, must considerably interfere with the proper performance of your work."

Then Homais represented to him how much more dashing and nimble he would feel afterwards, and even hinted that he would be more likely to please the women; and the stable boy broke into a stupid grin. Then he attacked him through his vanity:

"Come on, act like a man! Think what would have happened if you had been called into the army, and had to fight under our national banner! . . . Ah! Hippolyte!"

And Homais left him, declaring that he could not understand such blindness, such obstinacy, in refusing the benefits of science.

The poor wretch finally gave in, for it was like a conspiracy. Binet, who never interfered with other people's business, Madame Lefrançois, Artémise, the neighbors, even the mayor, Monsieur Tuvache—every one tried to convince him by lecture and reproof; but what finally won him over was that it would cost him nothing. Bovary even undertook to provide the machine for the operation. This generosity was an idea of Emma's, and Charles consented to it, thinking in his heart of hearts that his wife was an angel.

So with the advice of the pharmacist, and after three fresh starts, he had a kind of box made by the carpenter, with the assistance of the locksmith; it weighed about eight pounds, for iron, wood, sheet-iron, leather, screws, and nuts had not been spared.

Yet, to know which of Hippolyte's tendons had to be cut, it was necessary first of all to find out what kind of club-foot he had.

His foot almost formed a straight line with the leg, which, however, did not prevent it from being turned in, so that it was an equinus combined with something of a varus, or else a slight varus with a strong tendency to equinus. But on the equine foot, wide indeed as a horse's hoof, with its horny skin, and large toes, whose black nails resembled the nails of a horse shoe, the cripple ran about like a deer from morn till night. He was constantly to be seen on the Square, jumping round the carts, thrusting his limping foot forwards. He seemed even stronger on that leg than the other. By dint of hard service it had acquired, as it were, moral qualities of patience and energy; and when he was given some heavy work to do, he would support himself on it in preference to the sound one.

Now, as it was an equinus, it was necessary to cut the Achilles tendon first; if need be, the anterior tibial muscle could be seen to afterwards to take care of the varus. For the doctor did not dare to risk both operations at once; he was already sufficiently worried for fear of injuring some important region that he did not know.

Neither Ambroise Paré, applying a ligature to an artery, for the first time since Celsus did it fifteen centuries before; nor Dupuytren, cutting open abscesses through a thick layer of brain; nor Gensoul on first removing the superior maxilla, had hearts that trembled, hands that shook, minds that strained as Monsieur Bovary's when he approached Hippolyte, his tenotomy knife between his fingers. Just as in a hospital, near by on a table lay a heap of lint, with waxed thread, many bandages—a pyramid of bandages— every bandage to be found at the pharmacy. It was Monsieur Homais who since morning had been organising all these preparations, as much to dazzle the multitude as to keep up his illusions. Charles pierced the skin; a dry crackling was heard. The tendon was cut, the operation over. Hippolyte could not believe his eyes: he bent over Bovary's hands to cover them with kisses.

"Come, be calm," said the pharmacist; "later on you will show your gratitude to your benefactor."

And he went down to report the result to five or six bystanders who were waiting in the yard, and who fancied that Hippolyte would reappear walking straight up. Then Charles, having strapped his patient into the machine, went home, where Emma was anxiously waiting for him on the doorstep. She threw herself on his neck; they sat down at the table; he ate much, and at dessert he even wanted to take a cup of coffee, a luxury he only permitted himself on Sundays when there was company.

The evening was charming, full of shared conversation and common dreams. They talked about their future success, of the improvements to be made in their house; with his rising reputation, he saw his comforts increasing, his wife always loving him; and she was happy to refresh herself with a new sentiment, healthier and purer, and to feel at last some tenderness for this poor man who adored her. The thought of Rodolphe for one moment passed through her mind, but her eyes turned again to Charles; she even noticed with surprise that he had rather handsome teeth.

They were in bed when Monsieur Homais, sidestepping the cook, suddenly entered the room, holding in his hand a newly written sheet of paper. It was the article he intended for the "Fanal de Rouen." He brought it them to read.

"You read it," said Bovary.

He read:

" 'Braving the prejudices that still spread over the face of Europe like a net, the light nevertheless begins to penetrate into our country places. Thus on Tuesday our little town of Yonville found itself the scene of a surgical operation which was at the same time an act of loftiest philanthropy. Monsieur Bovary, one of our most distinguished practitioners . . ."

"Oh, that is too much! too much!" said Charles, choking with emotion.

—"But certainly not! far from it! . . . 'operated on a club-foot.' I have not used the scientific term, because you know in newspapers . . . not everyone would understand . . . the masses, after all, must . . ."

"Certainly," said Bovary; "please go on!"

"I proceed," said the pharmacist. " 'Monsieur Bovary, one of our most distinguished practitioners, performed an operation on a club-footed man, one Hippolyte Tautain, stable-man for the last twenty-five years at the hotel of the "Lion d'Or," kept by Widow Lefrancois, at the Place d'Armes. The novelty of the experiment and the general interest in the patient had attracted such a number of people that a crowd gathered on the threshold of the establishment. The operation, moverover, was performed as if by magic, and barely a few drops of blood appeared on the skin, as though to say that the rebellious tendon had at last given way under the efforts of the medical arts. The patient, strangely enough (we affirm it *de visu*) complained of no pain. His condition up to the present time leaves nothing to be desired. Everything tends to show that his convalescence will be brief; and who knows if, at our next village festivity we shall not see our good Hippolyte appear in the midst of a bacchic dance, surrounded by a group of gay companions, and thus bear witness to all assembled, by his spirit and his capers, of his total recovery? Honor, then, to those generous men of science! Honor to those tireless spirits who consecrate their vigils to the improvement and relief of their kind! Honor to them! Hasn't the time come to cry out that the blind shall see, the deaf hear, the lame walk? What fanaticism formerly promised to a few elect, science now accomplishes for all men. We shall keep our readers informed as to the subsequent progression of this remarkable cure.' "

All this did not prevent Mère Lefrançois from coming five days later, scared out of her wits and shouting:

"Help! he is dying! I am going out of my mind!"

Charles rushed to the "Lion d'Or," and the pharmacist, who caught sight of him passing along the Square without a hat, left his shop. He arrived himself breathless, flushed, anxious, and asked from every one who was going up the stairs:

"What can be the matter with our interesting patient?"

The interesting patient was writhing, in dreadful convulsions, so violent that the contraption in which his foot was locked almost beat down the wall.

With many precautions, in order not to disturb the position of the limb, the box was removed, and an awful spectacle came into view. The outlines of the foot disappeared in such a swelling that the entire skin seemed about to burst; moreover, the leg was covered with bruises caused by the famous machine. Hippolyte had abundantly complained, but nobody had paid any attention to him; now they admitted he might have some grounds for protest and he was freed for a few hours. But hardly had the oedema somewhat gone down, that the two specialists thought fit to put back the limb in the machine, strapping it even tighter to speed up matters. At last, three days after, when Hippolyte could not stand it any longer, they once more removed the machine, and were much surprised at the result they saw. A livid tumescence spread over the entire leg, and a black liquid oozed from several blisters. Things had taken a turn for the worse. Hippolyte was getting bored, and Mère Lefrançois had him installed in the little room near the kitchen, so that he might at least have some distraction.

But the tax-collector, who dined there every day, complained bitterly of such companionship. Then Hippolyte was removed to the billiard-room.

He lay there moaning under his heavy blankets, pale and unshaven, with sunken eyes; from time to time he rubbed his sweating head over the fly-covered pillow. Madame Bovary came to see him. She brought him linen for his poultices; she comforted, and encouraged him. Besides, he did not want for company, especially on market days, when farmers around him were hitting the billiard balls around and fencing with the cues while they drank, sang and brawled.

"How are things?" they would say, clapping him on the shoulder. "Ah! not so well from what we hear. But that's your fault. You should do this! do that!"

And then they told him stories of people who had all been cured by other means. Then by way of consolation they added:

"You pamper yourself too much! You should get up; you coddle yourself like a king. Just the same, old boy, you do smell pretty awful!"

Gangrene was indeed spreading higher and higher. It made Bovary ill to think of it. He came every hour, every moment. Hippolyte looked at him with terrified eyes and sobbed:

"When will I be cured?—Oh, please save me! . . . How unhappy I am! . . . How unhappy I am!"

And the doctor left him, prescribing a strict diet.

"Don't listen to him," said Mère Lefrançois. "Haven't they tortured you enough already? You'll grow still weaker. Here! swallow this."

And she gave him some strong broth, a slice of mutton, a piece of bacon, and sometimes small glasses of brandy, that he had not the strength to put to his lips.

The abbé Bournisien, hearing that he was growing worse, asked to see him. He began by pitying his sufferings, declaring at the same time that he ought to rejoice since it was the will of the Lord, and hasten to reconcile himself with Heaven.

"For," said the ecclesiastic in a paternal tone, "you rather neglected your duties; you were rarely seen at divine worship. How many years is it since you approached the holy table? I understand that your work, that the whirl of the world may have distracted you from your salvation. But now the time has come. Yet don't despair. I have known great sinners, who, about to appear before God (you are not yet at this point I know), had implored His mercy, and who certainly died in a truly repenting frame of mind. Let us hope that, like them, you will set us a good example! Thus, as a precaution, what is to prevent you from saying morning and evening a Hail Mary and an Our Father? Yes, do that, for my sake, to oblige me. That won't cost you anything. Will you promise me?"

The poor devil promised. The curé came back day after day. He chatted with the landlady, and even told anecdotes interspersed with jokes and puns that Hippolyte did not understand. Then, as soon as he could, he would return to religious considerations, putting on an appropriate expression.

His zeal seemed to bring results, for the club-foot soon manifested a desire to go on a pilgrimage to Bon-Secours if he were cured; to which Monsieur Bournisien replied that he saw no objection; two precautions were better than one; moreover, it certainly could do no harm.

The pharmacist was incensed by what he called the priest's machinations; they were prejudicial, he said, to Hippolyte's convalescence, and he kept repeating to Madame Lefrançois, "Leave him alone! leave him alone! You're ruining his morale with your mysticism."

But the good woman would no longer listen to him; she blamed him for being the cause of it all. In sheer rebellion, she hung near the patient's bedside a well-filled basin of holy water and a sprig of boxwood.

Religion, however, seemed no more able than surgery to bring relief and the irresistible putrefaction kept spreading from the foot to the groin. It was all very well to vary the potions and change the poultices; the muscles each day rotted more and more; Charles replied by an affirmative nod of the head when Mère Lefrançois asked him if she could not, as a last resort, send for Monsieur Canivet, a famous surgeon from Neufchâtel.

Charles' fifty-year old colleague, a doctor of medicine with a well established practice and a solid self confidence, did not refrain from laughing disdainfully when he had uncovered the leg, gangrened to the knee. Then having flatly declared that it must be amputated, he went off to the pharmacist's to rail at the asses who could have reduced a poor man to such a state. Shaking Monsieur Homais by his coat-button, he shouted for everyone to hear:

"That is what you get from listening to the fads from Paris! What will they come up with next, these gentlemen from the capital! It is like strabismus, chloroform, lithotrity, monstrosities the Government ought to prohibit. But they want to be clever and cram you full of remedies without troubling about the consequences. We are not so clever out here, not we! We are no specialists, no cure-alls, no fancy talkers! We are practitioners; we cure people, and we wouldn't dream of operating on someone who is in perfect health. Straighten club-feet! As if one could straighten club-feet indeed! It is as if one wished to make a hunchback straight!"

Homais suffered as he listened to this discourse, and he concealed his discomfort beneath a courtier's smile; for he needed to humour Monsieur Canivet, whose prescriptions sometimes came as far as Yonville. So he did not take up the defence of Bovary; he did not even make a single remark, and, renouncing his principles, he sacrificed his dignity to the more serious interests of his business.

This thigh amputation by Doctor Canivet was a great event in the village. On that day all the inhabitants got up earlier, and the Grande Rue, crowded as it was, had something lugubrious about it, as though one were preparing for an execution. At the grocers they discussed Hippolyte's illness; the shops did no business, and Madame Tuvache, the mayor's wife, did not stir from her window, such was her impatience to see the surgeon arrive.

He came in his gig, which he drove himself. The springs of the right side had all given way beneath his corpulence and the carriage tilted a little as it rolled along, revealing on the cushion near him a large case covered in red sheep-leather, whose three brass clasps shone grandly.

Like a whirlwind, the doctor entered the porch of the Lion d'Or and, shouting loudly, he ordered to unharness. Then he went into the stable to see that his horse was eating his oats all right; for on arriving at a patient's he first of all looked after his mare and his gig. The habit made people say, "Ah, that Monsieur Canivet, what a character!" but he was the more esteemed for his composure. The universe as a whole might have been blown apart, and he would not have changed the least of his habits.

Homais introduced himself.

"I count on you," said the doctor. "Are you ready? Come along!"

But the pharmacist blushingly confessed that he was too sensitive to witness such an operation.

"When one is a simple spectator," he said, "the imagination, you know, is easily impressed. And then, my nerves are so . . ."

"Bah!" interrupted Canivet; "on the contrary, you seem like the apoplectic type to me. But I am not surprised, for you gentlemen pharmacists are always poking about your kitchens, which must end by spoiling your constitutions. Now just look at me. I get up every day at four o'clock; I shave with cold water (and am never cold). I don't wear flannel underwear, and I never catch cold; my carcass is good enough! I take things in my stride, philosophically, as they come my way. That is why I am not squeamish like you, and it doesn't matter to me whether I carve up a Christian or the first fowl that comes my way. Habit, you'll say . . . mere habit! . . ."

Then, without any consideration for Hippolyte, who was sweating with agony between his sheets, these gentlemen began a conversation, in which the druggist compared the coolness of a surgeon to that of a general; and this comparison was pleasing to Canivet, who held forth on the demands of his art. He looked upon it as a sacred office, although the ordinary practitioners dishonored it. At last, coming back to the patient, he examined the bandages brought by Homais, the same that had appeared for the club-foot, and asked for some one to hold the limb for him. Lestiboudois was sent for, and Monsieur Canivet having turned up his sleeves, passed into the billiard-room, while the druggist stayed with Artémise and the landlady, both whiter than their aprons, and with ears strained towards the door.

Meanwhile, Bovary didn't dare to stir from his house.

He kept downstairs in the sitting-room by the side of the fireless chimney, his chin on his breast, his hands clasped, his eyes staring. "What a misfortune," he thought, "what a disappointment!" Yet, he had taken all possible precautions. Luck must have been against him. All the same, if Hippolyte died later on, he would be considered the murderer. And how would he defend himself against the questions his patients were bound to ask him during his calls? Maybe, after all, he had made some slip. He thought and thought, but nothing came. The most famous surgeons also made mistakes. But no one would ever believe that; on the contrary, people would laugh, jeer! The news would spread as far as Neufchâtel, as Rouen, everywhere! Who could say if his colleagues would not write against him? Polemics would ensue; he would have to answer in the papers. Hippolyte might even prosecute him. He saw himself dishonored, ruined, lost; and his imagination, assailed by numberless hypothe-

ses, tossed amongst them like an empty cask dragged out to sea
and pitched about by the waves.

Emma, opposite, watched him; she did not share his humiliation;
she felt another—that of having imagined that such a man could
have any worth, as if twenty times already she had not sufficiently
perceived his mediocrity.

Charles was pacing the room. His boots creaked on the floor.

"Sit down," she said; "you irritate me!"

He sat down again.

How was it that she—she, who was so intelligent—could have
allowed herself to be deceived again? Moreover, what madness had
driven her to ruin her life by continual sacrifices? She recalled all
her instincts of luxury, all the privations of her soul, the sordidness
of marriage, of the household, her dreams sinking into the mire like
wounded swallows; all that she had longed for, all that she had
denied herself, all that she might have had! And for what? for
what?

In the midst of the silence that hung over the village a heart-
rending cry pierced the air. Bovary turned white as a sheet. She knit
her brows with a nervous gesture, then returned to her thought.
And it was for him, for this creature, for this man, who understood
nothing, who felt nothing! For he sat there as if nothing had
happened, not even suspecting that the ridicule of his name would
henceforth sully hers as well as his. She had made efforts to love
him, and she had repented with tears for having yielded to another!

"But it was perhaps a valgus after all!" exclaimed Bovary suddenly, interrupting his meditations.

At the unexpected shock of this phrase falling on her thought
like a leaden bullet on a silver plate, Emma shuddered and raised
her head in an effort to find out what he meant to say; and they
gazed at one another in silence, almost amazed to see each other, so
far sundered were they by their respective states of consciousness.
Charles gazed at her with the dull look of a drunken man, while he
listened motionless to the last cries of the sufferer, following each
other in long-drawn modulations, broken by sharp spasms like the
far-off howling of some beast being slaughtered. Emma bit her w'n
lips, and rolling between her fingers a piece of wood she had peeled
from the coral-tree, fixed on Charles the burning glance of her eyes
like two arrows of fire about to dart forth. Everything in him
irritated her now; his face, his dress, all the things he did not say,
his whole person, in short, his existence. She repented of her past
virtue as of a crime, and what still remained of it crumbled away
beneath the furious blows of her pride. She revelled in all the evil
ironies of triumphant adultery. The memory of her lover came back
to her with irresistible, dizzying attractions; she threw her whole

soul towards this image, carried by renewed passion; and Charles seemed to her as removed from her life, as eternally absent, as incongruous and annihilated, as if he were dying under her very eyes.

There was a sound of steps on the pavement. Charles looked up, and through the lowered blinds he saw Dr. Canivet standing in broad sunshine at the corner of the market, wiping his brow with his handerchief. Homais, behind him, was carrying a large red bag in his hand, and both were going towards the pharmacy.

Then with a feeling of sudden tenderness and discouragement Charles turned to his wife and said:

"Oh, kiss me, my dear!"

"Don't touch me!" she cried, flushed with anger.

"What is it? what is it?" he repeated, in utter bewilderment. "Don't be upset! calm down! You know that I love you . . . come! . . ."

"Stop it!" she cried with a terrible look.

And rushing from the room, Emma closed the door so violently that the barometer fell from the wall and smashed on the floor.

Charles sank back into his arm-chair thoroughly shaken, wondering what could have come over her, imagining it might be some nervous disease, weeping, and vaguely feeling something fatal and incomprehensible was whirling around him.

When Rodolphe came to the garden that evening, he found his mistress waiting for him at the foot of the steps on the lowest stair. They threw their arms round one another, and all their rancor melted like snow beneath the warmth of that kiss.

XII

Their love resumed its course. Often in the middle of the day, Emma would suddenly write to him, then beckon Justin through the window; he quickly untied his apron and flew to La Huchette. Rodolphe would come; she had to tell him again how bored she was, that her husband was odious, her life dreadful.

"What do you expect me to do about it?" he asked one day impatiently.

"Ah, if only you wanted . . ."

She was sitting on the floor between his knees, her hair loosened, staring in a void.

"Wanted what?" said Rodolphe.

She sighed.

"We would go and live elsewhere . . . anywhere . . ."

"Are you out of your mind!" he said laughing. "How could we?"

She mentioned it again; he pretended not to understand, and changed the subject. What he did not understand was all this worry about so simple an affair as love. But she had a motive, a reason that gave added grounds to her attachment.

Her tenderness, in fact, grew daily as her repulsion toward her husband increased. The more she yielded to the one, the more she loathed the other. Never did Charles seem so unattractive, slow-witted, clumsy and vulgar as when she met him after her rendez-vous with Rodolphe. Then while playing the part of the virtuous wife, she would burn with passion at the thought of his head, the black curl falling over the sun-tanned brow; of his figure, both elegant and strong, of the man so experienced in his thought, so impetuous in his desires! It was for him that she filed her nails with a sculptor's care, that there was never enough cold-cream for her skin, nor patchouli for her handkerchiefs. She loaded herself with bracelets, rings, and necklaces. When she expected him, she filled her two large blue glass vases with roses, and prepared herself and her room like a courtesan receiving a prince. The servant was kept busy steadily laundering her linen, and all day Félicité did not stir from the kitchen, where little Justin, who often kept her company, watched her at work.

With his elbows on the long board on which she was ironing, he greedily watched all these women's garments spread out about him, the dimity petticoats, the fichus, the collars, and the drawers with running strings, wide at the hips and narrowing below.

"What is that for?" asked the young boy, passing his hand over the crinoline or the hooks and eyes.

"Why, haven't you ever seen anything?" Félicité answered laughing. "As if your mistress, Madame Homais, didn't wear the same."

"Oh, well, Madame Homais . . ."

And he added thoughtfully,

"Is she a lady like Madame?"

But Félicité grew impatient of seeing him hanging round her. She was six years older than he, and Theodore, Monsieur Guillau-min's servant, was beginning to pay court to her.

"Leave me alone," she said, moving her pot of starch. "You'd better be off and pound almonds; you are always snooping around women. Before you bother with such things, naughty boy, wait till you've got a beard to your chin."

"Oh, don't be cross! I'll go and clean her boots."

And he hurriedly took down Emma's boots from the shelf all coated with mud—the mud of the rendezvous—that crumbled into powder beneath his fingers, and that he watched as it gently rose in a ray of sunlight.

"How scared you are of spoiling them!" said the maid, who wasn't so particular when she cleaned them herself, because if the boots looked slightly worn Madame would give them to her.

Emma kept a number in her cupboard that she squandered one after the other, without Charles allowing himself the slightest observation.

He also spent three hundred francs for a wooden leg that she thought had to be given to Hippolyte. The top was covered with cork, and it had spring joints, a complicated mechanism, covered over by black trowsers ending in a patent-leather boot. But Hippolyte didn't dare use such a handsome leg every day, and he begged Madame Bovary to get him another more convenient one. The doctor, of course, had to pay for this purchase as well.

So little by little the stable-boy returned to work. One saw him running about the village as before, and when Charles heard from afar the tap of the wooden leg on the pavement, he quickly went in another direction.

It was Monsieur Lheureux, the shopkeeper, who had ordered the wooden leg. This provided him with an excuse for visiting Emma. He chatted with her about the new goods from Paris, about a thousand feminine trifles, made himself very obliging and never asked for his money. Emma yielded to this lazy mode of satisfying all her caprices. When she wanted to give Rodolphe a handsome riding-crop from an umbrella store in Rouen, Monsieur Lheureux placed it on her table the very next week.

But the next day he called on her with a bill for two hundred and seventy francs, not counting the centimes. Emma was much embarrassed; all the drawers of the writing-table were empty; they owed over a fortnight's wages to Lestiboudois, six months to the maid, and there were several other bills. Bovary was impatiently waiting to hear from Monsieur Derozeray who was in the habit of settling every year about Midsummer.

She succeeded at first in putting off Lheureux. At last he lost patience; he was being sued; he was short of capital and unless he could collect on some of his accounts, he would be forced to take back all the goods she had received.

"Oh, very well, take them!" said Emma.

"I was only joking," he replied; "the only thing I regret is the riding crop. Well, I'll have to ask Monsieur to return it to me."

"No, no!" she said.

"Ah! I've got you!" thought Lheureux.

And, certain of his discovery, he went out muttering to himself and with his usual low whistle . . .

"Good! we shall see! we shall see!"

She was wondering how to handle the situation when the maid entered and put on the mantelpiece a small roll of blue paper "with the compliments of Monsieur Derozerays'." Emma grasped it, tore it open. It contained fifteen napoleons: the account paid in full. Hearing Charles on the stairs, she threw the money to the back of her drawer, and took out the key.

Three days later, Lheureux returned.

"I have a suggestion to make," he said. "If, instead of the sum, agreed on, you would take. . . ."

"Here it is," she said handing him fourteen napoleons.

The shopkeeper was taken aback. Then, to conceal his disappointment, he was profuse in apologies and offers of service, all of which Emma declined; she remained a few moments fingering in the pocket of her apron the two five-franc pieces of change he had returned to her. She told herself she would economise in order to pay back later . . . "Bah!", she thought, "he'll forget all about it."

Besides the riding-crop with its silver-gilt top, Rodolphe had received a signet with the motto *Amor nel cor*,[7] furthermore, a scarf for a muffler, and, finally, a cigar-case exactly like the Viscount's, that Charles had formerly picked up in the road, and that Emma had kept. These presents, however, humiliated him; he refused several; she insisted, and he ended by obeying, thinking her tyrannical and over-exacting.

Then she had strange ideas.

"When midnight strikes," she said, "you must think of me."

And if he confessed that he had not thought of her, there were floods of reproaches that always ended with the eternal question:

"Do you love me?"

"Why, of course I love you," he answered.

"A great deal?"

"Certainly!"

"You haven't loved any others?"

"Did you think you'd got a virgin?" he exclaimed laughing.

Emma cried, and he tried to console her, adorning his protestations with puns.

"Oh," she went on, "I love you! I love you so that I could not live without you, do you see? There are times when I long to see you again, when I am torn by all the anger of love. I ask myself, where is he? Perhaps he is talking to other women. They smile upon him; he approaches. Oh no; no one else pleases you. There are some more beautiful, but I love you best. I know how to love best. I am your servant, your concubine! You are my king, my idol!

7. Louise Colet, whom Flaubert used to call his "muse" and to whom many of the letters dealing with the composition of *Madame Bovary* are addressed, gave him a stamp bearing this motto. Flaubert later quarrelled with her, and the autobiographical allusion is somewhat ungallantly ironical. It enraged the lady in question, who avenged herself by a bad poem that appeared in *Le monde illustré* of January 29, 1859.

You are good, you are beautiful, you are clever, you are strong!"

He had so often heard these things said that they did not strike him as original. Emma was like all his mistresses; and the charm of novelty, gradually falling away like a garment, laid bare the eternal monotony of passion, that has always the same shape and the same language. He was unable to see, this man so full of experience, the variety of feelings hidden within the same expressions. Since libertine or venal lips had murmured similar phrases, he only faintly believed in the candor of Emma's; he thought one should beware of exaggerated declarations which only serve to cloak a tepid love; as though the abundance of one's soul did not sometimes overflow with empty metaphors, since no one ever has been able to give the exact measure of his needs, his concepts, or his sorrows. The human tongue is like a cracked cauldron on which we beat out tunes to set a bear dancing when we would make the stars weep with our melodies.

But with the superiority of critical insight of the person who holds back his emotions in any engagement, Rodolphe perceived that there were other pleasures to be exploited in this love. He discarded all modesty as inconvenient. He treated her without consideration. And he made her into something at once malleable and corrupt. It was an idiotic sort of attachment, full of admiration on his side and voluptuousness on hers, a beatitude which left her numb; and her soul sunk deep into this intoxication and drowned in it, all shrivelled up, like the duke of Clarence in his butt of malmsey.

Solely as a result of her amorous practices, Madame Bovary began to change in appearance. Her glances were bolder, her speech freer; she even went as far as to go out walking with Rodolphe, a cigarette in her mouth, "just to scandalize the town"; finally, those who had doubted doubted no longer when they saw her descend one day from the Hirondelle wearing a tight-fitting waistcoat cut like a man's. And Madame Bovary senior who, after a frightful scene with her husband, had come to seek refuge with her son, was not the least scandalized lady in town. Many other things displeased her too: first of all, Charles had not followed her advice in banning novels from the house; then, the "tone" of the house upset her; she allowed herself to make observations, and there were arguments, especially, on one occasion, concerning Felicité.

The previous evening, while crossing the corridor, Madame Bovary senior had come upon her in the company of a man of about forty wearing a brown collar, who on hearing footsteps, had quickly fled from the kitchen. Emma had burst out laughing; but the good woman was furious, declaring that anyone who took morality seriously ought to keep an eye on their servant's behavior.

"What kind of society do you come from?" asked the daughter-in-law, with so impertinent a look that Madame Bovary asked her if she were not perhaps defending her own case.

"Get out!" said the young woman, rising in fury.

"Emma! . . . Mother! . . ." cried Charles, trying to reconcile them.

But both had fled in their exasperation. Emma was stamping her feet as she repeated:

"Oh! what manners! What a peasant!"

He ran to his mother; she was beside herself She stammered:

"How insolent she is! and how flighty! worse perhaps!"

And she was ready to leave at once if the other did not apologise. So Charles went back again to his wife and implored her to give way; he threw himself at her feet; finally, she said:

"Very well! I'll go to her."

And she actually held out her hand to her mother-in-law with the dignity of a marquise as she said:

"Excuse me, madame."

Then, having returned to her room, she threw herself flat on her bed and cried there like a child, her face buried in the pillow.

She and Rodolphe had agreed that in the event of anything extraordinary occurring, she should fasten a small piece of white paper to the blind, so that if by chance he happened to be in Yonville, he could hurry to the lane behind the house. Emma made the signal; she had been waiting three-quarters of an hour when she suddenly caught sight of Rodolphe at the corner of the square. She felt tempted to open the window and call him, but he had already disappeared. She fell back in despair.

Soon, however, it seemed to her that someone was walking on the pavement. It was he, no doubt. She went downstairs, crossed the yard. He was there outside. She threw herself into his arms.

"Watch out!" he said.

"Ah! if only you knew!" she replied.

And she began telling him everything, hurriedly, disjointedly, exaggerating the facts, inventing many, and with so many digressions that he understood nothing at all.

"Come now, my poor angel, be brave, console yourself, be patient!"

"But I have been patient; I have suffered for four years. A love like ours ought to show itself in the face of heaven. They torture me! I can bear it no longer! Save me!"

She clung to Rodolphe. Her eyes, full of tears, flashed like flames beneath a wave; her panting made her breast rise and fall; never had she seemed more lovely, so much so that he lost his head and said:

"What do you want me to do?"

"Take me away," she cried, "carry me off! . . . I beg you!"

She pressed her lips against his mouth, as if to capture the unhoped for consent the moment it was breathed forth in a kiss.

"But . . ." Rodolphe began.

"What?"

"Your little girl!"

She reflected a few moments, then replied:

"We'll take her with us, there is no other way!"

"What a woman!" he said to himself, watching her as she went. For she had run into the garden. Some one was calling her.

On the following days the elder Madame Bovary was much surprised at the change in her daughter-in-law. Emma, in fact, was showing herself more docile, and even carried her deference to the point of asking for a recipe for pickles.

Was it the better to deceive them both? Or did she wish by a sort of voluptuous stoicism to feel the more profoundly the bitterness of the things she was about to leave? But she paid no heed to them; on the contrary, she lived as lost in the anticipated delight of her coming happiness. It was an eternal subject for conversation with Rodolphe. She leant on his shoulder murmuring:

"Think, we will soon be in the mail-coach! Can you imagine? Is it possible? It seems to me that the moment the carriage will start, it will be as if we were rising in a balloon, as if we were setting out for the clouds. Do you know that I count the hours? . . . Don't you?"

Never had Madame Bovary been so beautiful as at this period; she had that indefinable beauty that results from joy, from enthusiasm, from success, and that expresses the harmony between temperament and circumstances. Her cravings, her sorrows, her sensuous pleasures and her ever-young illusions had slowly brought her to full maturity, and she blossomed forth in the fulness of her being, like a flower feeding on manure, on rain, wind and sunshine. Her half-closed eyelids seemed perfectly shaped for the long languid glances that escaped from them; her breathing dilated the fine nostrils and raised the fleshy corners of her mouth, shaded in the light by a slight black down. Some artist skilled in corruption seemed to have devised the shape of her hair as it fell on her neck, coiled in a heavy mass, casually reassembled after being loosened daily in adultery. Her voice now took more mellow inflections, her figure also; something subtle and penetrating escaped even from the folds of her gown and from the line of her foot. Charles thought her exquisite and altogether irresistible, as when they were first married.

When he came home in the middle of the night, he did not dare to wake her. The porcelain night-light threw a round trembling gleam upon the ceiling, and the drawn curtains of the little cot formed as it were a white hut standing out in the shade by the bedside. Charles looked at them. He seemed to hear the light breathing of his child. She would grow big now; every season would bring rapid progress. He already saw her coming from school as the day drew in, laughing, with ink-stains on her jacket, and carrying her basket on her arm. Then she would have to be sent to a boarding-school; that would cost much; how was it to be done? He kept thinking about it. He thought of hiring a small farm in the neighborhood, that he would supervise every morning on his way to his patients. He would not spend what he brought in; he would put it in the savings-bank. Then he would invest in some stocks, he didn't know which; besides, his practice would increase; he counted on it, for he wanted Berthe to be well-educated, to be accomplished, to learn to play the piano. Ah! how pretty she would be later on when she was fifteen, when, resembling her mother, she would, like her, wear large straw hats in the summer-time; from a distance they would be taken for two sisters. He pictured her to himself working in the evening by their side beneath the light of the lamp; she would embroider him slippers; she would look after the house; she would fill all the home with her charm and her gaiety. At last, they would think of her marriage; they would find her some good young fellow with a steady business; he would make her happy; this would last for ever.

Emma was not asleep; she pretended to be; and while he dozed off by her side she awakened to other dreams.

To the gallop of four horses she was carried away for a week towards a new land, from where they would never return. They went on and on, their arms entwined, without speaking a word. Often from the top of a mountain there suddenly appeared some splendid city with domes, and bridges, and ships, forests of citron trees, and cathedrals of white marble, their pointed steeples crowned with storks' nests. The horses slowed down to a walk because of the wide pavement, and on the ground there were bouquets of flowers, offered by women dressed in red. They heard the chiming of bells, the neighing of mules, together with the murmur of guitars and the noise of fountains, whose rising spray refreshed heaps of fruit arranged like a pyramid at the foot of pale statues that smiled beneath playing waters. And then, one night they came to a fishing village, where brown nets were drying in the wind along the cliffs and in front of the huts. It was there that they would stay; they would live in a low, flat-roofed house, shaded by a palm-tree, in the heart of a gulf, by the sea. They would row in gondolas, swing in hammocks, and their existence would be easy and free as their wide silk gowns, warm and star-spangled as the nights they would contemplate. However, in the immensity of this future that she conjured up, nothing specific stood out; the days, all magnificent, resembled each other like waves; and the vision swayed in the horizon, infinite, harmonised, azure, and bathed in sunshine. But the child began to cough in her cot or Bovary snored more loudly, and Emma did not fall asleep till morning, when the dawn whitened the windows, and when little Justin was already in the square taking down the shutters of the pharmacy.

She had sent for Monsieur Lheureux, and had said to him:

"I want a cloak—a large lined cloak with a deep collar."

"You are going on a journey?" he asked.

"No; but . . . never mind. I count on you to get it in a hurry."

He bowed.

"Besides, I shall want," she went on, "a trunk . . . not too heavy . . . a handy size."

"Yes, yes, I understand. About three feet by a foot and a half, as they are being made just now."

"And a travelling bag."

"No question about it," thought Lheureux, "she is up to something."

"And," said Madame Bovary, taking her watch from her belt, "take this; you can pay yourself out of it."

But the shopkeeper protested that it was not necessary; as if he didn't know and trust her. She was being childish!

She insisted, however, on his taking at least the chain, and Lheureux had already put it in his pocket and was going, when she called him back.

"You will leave everything at your place. As to the cloak"—she seemed to be reflecting—"do not bring it either; you can give me the maker's address, and tell him to have it ready for me."

It was the next month that they were to run away. She was to leave Yonville as if she was going on some business to Rouen. Rodolphe would have booked the seats, obtained the passports, and even have written to Paris in order to have the whole mail-coach reserved for them as far as Marseilles, where they would buy a carriage, and go on from there straight by the Genoa road. She would have sent her luggage to Lheureux, from where it would be taken directly to the "Hirondelle," so that no one would have any suspicion. And in all this there never was any allusion to the child. Rodolphe avoided the subject; it may be that he had forgotten about it.

He wished to have two more weeks before him to arrange some affairs; then at the end of a week he wanted two more; then he said he as ill; next he went on a journey. The month of August passed, and, after all these delays, they decided that it was to be irrevocably fixed for the 4th September—a Monday.

At last the Saturday before arrived.

Rodolphe came in the evening earlier than usual.

"Is everything ready?" she asked him.

"Yes."

Then they walked round a garden-bed, and sat down near the terrace on the kerb-stone of the wall.

"You are sad," said Emma.

"No; why?"

And yet he looked at her strangely, though with tenderness.

"Is it because you are going away?" she went on; "because you are leaving behind what is dear to you, your own life? I can understand that . . . But I have nothing in the world! You are everything I have, and I'll be everything to you. I'll be your family, your country; I'll look after you, I'll love you."

"How sweet you are!" he said, taking her in his arms.

"Am I really?" she said with a voluptuous laugh. "Do you love me? Swear it then!"

"Do I love you? Do I? But I adore you, my love!"

The moon, full and purple-colored, was rising right out of the earth at the end of the meadow. It rose quickly between the branches of the poplar trees, partly hidden as by a tattered black curtain. Then it appeared dazzling white, lighting up the empty sky; slowing down, it let fall upon the river a great stain that broke up into an infinity of stars; and the silver sheen seemed to writhe through the very depths like a headless serpent covered with luminous scales; it also resembled some monster candelabra from which sparkling diamonds fell like molten drops. The soft night was about them; masses of shadow filled the branches. Emma, her eyes half closed, breathed in with deep sighs the fresh wind that was blowing. They did not speak, caught as they were in their dream. The tenderness of the old days came back to their hearts, full and silent as the flowing river, with the soft perfume of the syringas, and threw across their memories shadows more immense and more sombre than those of the still willows that lengthened out over the grass. Often some night-animal, hedgehog or weasel, setting out on the hunt, disturbed the lovers, or sometimes they heard a ripe peach fall by itself from the tree.

"Ah! what a lovely night!" said Rodolphe.

"We shall have others," replied Emma.

Then, as if speaking to herself:

"Yes, it will be good to travel. And yet, why should my heart be so heavy? Is it dread of the unknown? The weight of old habits? . . . Or else? No, it is the excess of happiness. How weak I am! You must forgive me!"

"There is still time!" he cried. "Think! You may regret it later!"

"Never!" she cried impetuously.

And, drawing closer to him:

"What ill could come to me? There is no desert, no precipice, no ocean I would not traverse with you. The longer we live together the more it will be like an embrace, every day closer, more complete. There will be nothing to trouble us, no cares, no obstacle. We shall be alone, all to ourselves forever . . . Say something, answer me!"

At regular intervals he answered, "Yes . . . Yes . . ." She had passed her hands through his hair, and she repeated in a childlike voice through her tears:

"Rodolphe! Rodolphe! . . . Sweet little Rodolphe!"

Midnight struck.

"Midnight!" she said. "Come, it is to-morrow. One more day!"

He rose to go; and as if the movement he made had been the signal for their flight, Emma suddenly seemed gay:

"You have the passports?"

"Yes."

"You are forgetting nothing?"

"No."

"Are you sure?"

"Absolutely."

"You'll be waiting for me at the Hotel de Provence, won't you? . . . at noon?"

He nodded.

"Till to-morrow then!" said Emma in a last caress; and she watched him go.

He did not turn round. She ran after him, and, leaning over the water's edge between the bushes:

"Till to-morrow!" she cried.

He was already on the other side of the river and walking fast across the meadow.

After a few moments Rodolphe stopped; and when he saw her with her white gown gradually fade away in the shade like a ghost, his heart beat so wildly that he had to support himself against a tree.

"What a fool I am!" he said, swearing a dreadful oath. "All the same, she was the prettiest mistress ever."

And immediately Emma's beauty, with all the pleasures of their love, came back to him. For a moment he weakened, but then he rebelled against her.

"For, after all," he exclaimed, gesticulating, "I can't exile myself, and with a child on my hands to boot!"

He was saying these things to strengthen his determination.

"And besides, the worries, the cost! No, no, a thousand times no! It would have been too stupid."

XIII

No sooner was Rodolphe at home than he sat down quickly at his desk under the stag's head that hung as a trophy on the wall. But when he had the pen between his fingers, he could think of nothing, so that, resting on his elbows, he began to reflect. Emma seemed to him to have receded into a far-off past, as if the resolution he had taken had suddenly placed an immeasurable distance between them.

In order to recapture something of her presence, he fetched from the cupboard at the bedside an old Rheims cookie-box, in which he usually kept his love letters. An odour of dry dust and withered roses emanated from it. First he saw a handkerchief stained with pale drops. It was a handkerchief of hers. Once when they were walking her nose had bled; he had forgotten it. Near it, almost too large for the box, was Emma's miniature: her dress seemed pretentious to him, and her languishing look in the worst possible taste. Then, from looking at this image and recalling the memory of the original, Emma's features little by little grew confused in his remembrance, as if the living and the painted face, rubbing one against the other, had erased each other. Finally, he read some of her letters; they were full of explanations relating to their journey, short, technical, and urgent, like business notes. He wanted to see the long ones again, those of old times. In order to find them at the bottom of the box, Rodolphe disturbed all the others, and mechanically began rummaging among this mass of papers and things, finding pell-mell bouquets, garters, a black mask, pins, and hair . . . lots of hair! Some dark, some fair, some, catching in the hinges of the box, even broke when he opened it.

Following his memories, he examined the writing and the style of the letters, as varied as their spelling. They were tender or jovial, facetious, melancholy; there were some that asked for love, others that asked for money. A word recalled faces to him, certain gestures, the sound of a voice; sometimes, however, he remembered nothing at all.

All these women, crowding into his consciousness, rather shrank in size, levelled down by the uniformity of his feeling. Seizing the letters at random, he amused himself for a while by letting them cascade from his right into his left hand. At last, bored and weary, Rodolphe took back the box to the cupboard, saying to himself:

"What a lot of nonsense!"

Which summed up his opinion; for pleasures, like schoolboys in a school courtyard, had so trampled upon his heart that no green thing was left; whatever entered there, more heedless than children, did not even, like them, leave a name carved upon the wall.

"Come," he said, "let's go."

He wrote:

> Courage, Emma! you must be brave! I don't want to be the one to ruin your life . . .

"After all, that's true," thought Rodolphe. "I am acting in her interest; I am honest."

> Have you carefully weighed your resolution? Do you know to what an abyss I was dragging you, poor angel? No, you don't, I assure you. You were coming confident and fearless, believing in a future happiness . . . Ah! the wretched creatures we are! We nearly lost our minds!

Rodolphe paused to think of some good excuse.

"If I told her that I lost all my money? No! Besides, that would stop nothing. It would all start again later on. As if one could make women like that listen to reason!"

He thought for a moment, then added:

> I shall not forget you, believe me; and I shall forever have a profound devotion for you; but some day, sooner or later, this ardour (such is the fate of human things) would doubtlessly have diminished. Weariness would have been unavoidable, and who knows if I would not even have had the atrocious pain of witnessing your remorse, of sharing it myself, since I would have been its cause? The mere idea of the grief that would come to you tortures me, Emma. Forget me! Why did I ever know you? Why were you so beautiful? Is it my fault? God, no! only fate is to blame!

"That's a word that always helps," he said to himself.

> Ah, if you had been one of those shallow women of which there are so many, I might, out of selfishness, have tried an experiment, in that case without danger for you. But your exquisite sensitivity, at once your charm and your torment, has prevented you from understanding, adorable woman that you are, the falseness of our future position. I myself had not fully realized this till now; I was living in the bliss of this ideal happiness as under the shade of a poisonous tree, without forseeing the consequences.

"She may suspect that it is out of stinginess that I am giving her up . . . But never mind, let's get this over with!"

> This is a cruel world, Emma. Wherever we might have gone, it would have persecuted us. You would have had to put up with indiscreet questions, calumny, contempt, insult perhaps. Imagine you being insulted! It is unbearable! . . . I who would place you on a throne! I who bear with me your memory as a talisman! For I am going to punish myself by exile for all the ill I have done you. I am going away. I don't know where, I am too close to madness to think. Farewell! Continue to be good! Remember the unfortu-

nate man who caused your undoing. Teach my name to your child; let her repeat it in her prayers.

The wicks of the candles flickered. Rodolphe got up to close the window, and when he sat down again:

"I think that covers it. Ah, let me add this for fear she might pursue me here."

I shall be far away when you read these sad lines, for I have wished to flee as quickly as possible to shun the temptation of seeing you again. No weakness! I shall return, and perhaps later on we shall be able to talk coldly of our past love. Adieu!

And there was a last "adieu" divided into two words: "A Dieu!" which he thought in very excellent taste.

"Now how am I to sign?" he asked himself. " 'Yours devotedly?' No! 'Your friend?' Yes, that's it."

YOUR FRIEND.

He re-read his letter and thought it quite good.

"Poor little woman!" he thought tenderly. "She'll think me harder than a rock. There ought to have been some tears on this; but I can't cry; it isn't my fault." Then, having emptied some water into a glass, Rodolphe dipped his finger into it, and let a big drop fall on the paper, making a pale stain on the ink. Then looking for a seal, he came upon the one "*Amor nel cor.*"

"Hardly the right thing under the circumstances . . . But who cares?"

Whereupon he smoked three pipes and went to bed.

Upon arising the next morning—around two o'clock in the afternoon, for he had slept late—Rodolphe had a basket of apricots picked. He put his letter at the bottom under some vine leaves, and at once ordered Girard, his ploughman, to take it with care to Madame Bovary. They used to correspond this way before and he would send her fruit or game according to season.

"If she asks about me," he said, "tell her that I have gone on a journey. You must give the basket to her herself, into her own hands. Get going now, and be careful!"

Girard put on his new smock, knotted his handkerchief round the apricots, and, walking heavily in his hobnailed boots, quietly made his way to Yonville.

When he got to the house, Madame Bovary was arranging a bundle of linen on the kitchen-table with Félicité.

"Here," said the ploughboy, "is something for you from my master."

She was seized with apprehension, and as she sought in her pocket for some small change, she looked at the peasant with haggard eyes, while he himself stared at her with amazement, not understanding how such a small present could stir up such violent emotions. Finally he left. Félicité stayed. She could bear it no longer; she ran into the sitting room as if to take the apricots there, overturned the basket, tore away the leaves, found the letter, opened it, and, as if pursued by some fearful fire, Emma flew in terror to her room.

Charles was there; she saw him; he spoke to her; she heard nothing, and she ran quickly up the stairs, breathless, distraught, crazed, and ever holding this horrible piece of paper, that crackled between her fingers like a plate of sheet-iron. On the second floor she stopped before the closed attic-door.

Then she tried to calm herself; she recalled the letter; she must finish it but she didn't dare. Where and how was she to read it? She would be seen!

"Here," she thought, "I'll be safe here."

Emma pushed open the door and went in.

The slates projected a heavy heat that gripped her temples, stifled her; she dragged herself to the closed window, drew back the bolt, and the dazzling sunlight burst in.

Opposite, beyond the roofs, the open country stretched as far as the eye could reach. Down below, underneath her, the village square was empty; the stones of the pavement glittered, the weathercocks on the houses stood motionless. At the corner of the street, from a lower story, rose a kind of humming with strident modulations. It was Binet turning.

She leant against the window-frame, and re-read the letter with angry sneers. But the more she concentrated on it, the more confused she grew. She could see him, hear him, feel his embrace; the throbbing of her heart, beating irregularly in her breast like the blows of a battering ram, grew faster and faster. She looked about her wishing that the earth might crumble. Why not end it all? What restrained her? She was free. She advanced, looked at the paving-stones, saying to herself, "Jump! jump!"

The ray of light reflected straight from below drew the weight of her body towards the abyss. The ground of the village square seemed to tilt over and climb up the walls, the floor to pitch forward like in a tossing boat. She was right at the edge, almost hanging, surrounded by vast space. The blue of the sky invaded her, the air was whirling in her hollow head; she had but to yield, to let herself be taken; and the humming of the lathe never ceased, like an angry voice calling her.

"My wife! my wife!" cried Charles.

She stopped.

"Where have you gone? Come here!"

The thought that she had just escaped from death almost made her faint with terror. She closed her eyes; then she started at the touch of a hand on her sleeve; it was Félicité.

"Monsieur is waiting for you, madame; the soup is on the table."

And she had to go down! and sit at the table!

She tried to eat. The food choked her. Then she unfolded her napkin as if to examine the darns, and really tried to concentrate on this work, counting the stitches in the linen. Suddenly she remembered the letter. How had she lost it? Where could it be found? But she felt such weariness of spirit that she could not even invent a pretext for leaving the table. Then she became a coward; she was afraid of Charles; he knew all, that was certain! Just then, he said, in an odd tone:

"We are not likely to see Monsieur Rodolphe soon again, it seems."

"Who told you?" she said, shuddering.

"Who told me!" he replied, rather astonished at her abrupt tone. "Why, Girard, whom I met just now at the door of the Café Français. He has gone on a journey, or is about to go."

She could not suppress a sob.

"What is so surprising about that? He goes away like that from time to time for a change, and I certainly can't blame him. A bachelor, and rich as he is! And from what I hear, he isn't exactly starved for pleasures, our friend! he enjoys life. Monsieur Langlois told me . . ."

He stopped for propriety's sake because the maid had just come in.

She collected the apricots that were strewn over the sideboard and put them back in the basket. Charles, unaware that his wife had turned scarlet, had them brought to him, took one, and bit into it.

"Perfect!" he said; "have a taste!"

And he handed her the basket, which she gently put away from her.

"Smell them! Such perfume!" he insisted, moving it back and forth under her nose.

"I am choking," she exclaimed, leaping up.

By sheer willpower, she succeeded in forcing back the spasm.

"It is nothing," she said, "it is nothing! Just nerves. Sit down and eat."

For she dreaded most of all that he would question her, try to help and not leave her to herself.

Charles, to obey her, sat down again, and he spat the stones of the apricots into his hands, afterwards putting them on his plate.

Suddenly a blue tilbury passed across the square at a rapid trot. Emma uttered a cry and fell back rigid on the floor.

After many hesitations, Rodolphe had finally decided to set out for Rouen. Now, as from La Huchette to Buchy there is no other way than by Yonville, he had to go through the village, and Emma had recognised him by the rays of the lanterns, which like lightning flashed through the twilight.

The general commotion which broke out in the house brought the pharmacist over in a hurry. The table, with all the plates, had been knocked over; sauce, meat, knives, the salt, and cruet-stand were strewn over the room; Charles was calling for help; Berthe, scared, was crying; and Félicité, whose hands trembled, was unlacing her mistress, whose whole body shivered convulsively.

"I'll run to my laboratory for some aromatic vinegar," said the pharmacist.

Then as she opened her eyes on smelling the bottle:

"I thought so," he said, "this thing would resuscitate a corpse!"

"Speak to us," said Charles "try to recover! It is Charles, who loves you . . . Do you know me? Look, here is your little girl; kiss her, darling!"

The child stretched out her arms to cling to her mother's neck. But turning away her head, Emma said in a broken voice:

"No, no . . . I want no one!"

She fainted again. They carried her to her bed.

She lay there stretched at full length, her lips apart, her eyelids closed, her hands open, motionless, and white as a waxen image. Two streams of tears flowed from her eyes and fell slowly upon the pillow.

Charles stood at the back of the alcove, and the pharmacist, near him, maintained the meditative silence that is fitting on the serious occasions of life.

"Don't worry," he said, touching his elbow; "I think the paroxysm is past."

"Yes, she is resting a little now," answered Charles, watching her sleep. "Poor girl! poor girl! She has dropped off now!"

Then Homais asked how the accident had occurred. Charles answered that she had been taken ill suddenly while she was eating some apricots.

"Extraordinary!" continued the pharmacist. "It is quite possible that the apricots caused the syncope. Some natures are so sensitive to certain smells; it would even be a very fine question to study both from a pathological and physiological point of view. The priests know all about it; that's why they use aromatics in all their ceremonies. It is to stupefy the senses and to bring on ecstasies,—a thing, moreover, very easy in persons of the weaker sex, who are more sensitive than we are. Some are reported fainting at the smell of burnt horn, or fresh bread . . ."

"Be careful not to wake her!" warned Bovary.

But the pharmacist was not to be stopped. "Not only," he resumed, "are human beings subject to such anomalies, but animals also. You are of course not ignorant of the singularly aphrodisiac effect produced by the *Nepeta cataria,* vulgarly called catnip, on the feline race; and, on the other hand, to quote an example whose authenticity I can vouch for, Bridaux (one of my old schoolmates, at present established in the Rue Malpalu) owns a dog that falls into convulsions as soon as you hold out a snuff-box to him. He often performs the experiment before his friends at his summer-house in Bois-Guillaume. Could you believe that a simple sternutative could cause such damage to a quadrupedal organism? Wouldn't you agree that it is extremely curious?"

"Yes," said Charles, who was not listening.

"It just goes to show," pursued the pharmacist, smiling with benign self-satisfaction, "the numberless irregularities of the nervous system. With regard to madame, I must say that she has always seemed extremely susceptible to me. And so I should by no means recommend to you, my dear friend, any of those so-called remedies that, under the pretence of attacking the symptoms, attack the constitution. No, no gratuitous medications! Diet, that is all; sedatives, emollients, dulcifiers. And then, don't you think we ought to stimulate the imagination?"

"In what way? How?" said Bovary.

"Ah, that is the problem. 'That is the question' (he said it in English) as I lately read in a newspaper."

But Emma, awaking, cried out:

"The letter! Where is the letter?"

They thought she was delirious; and she was by midnight. Brain-fever had set in.

For forty-three days Charles did not leave her. He gave up all his patients; he no longer went to bed; he was constantly feeling her pulse, applying mustard plasters and cold-water compresses. He sent Justin as far as Neufchâtel for ice; the ice melted on the way; he sent him back again. He called Monsieur Canivet into consultation; he sent for Dr. Larivière, his old master, from Rouen; he was in despair. What alarmed him most was Emma's prostration, for she did not speak, did not listen, did not even seem to suffer—as if both her body and her soul were resting after all their tribulations.

About the middle of October she could sit up in bed supported by pillows. Charles wept when he saw her eat her first piece of bread and jam. Her strength returned; she got up for a few hours of an afternoon, and one day, when she felt better, he tried to take her, leaning on his arm, for a walk round the garden. The sand of the paths was disappearing beneath the dead leaves; she walked slowly, dragging her slippers, and leaning against Charles's shoulder. She smiled all the time.

They went thus to the end of the garden near the terrace. She drew herself up slowly, shading her eyes with her hand. She looked far off, as far as she could, but on the horizon were only great bonfires of grass smoking on the hills.

"You will tire yourself, darling!" said Bovary.

And, pushing her gently to make her enter the arbour: "Sit down on this seat; you'll be comfortable."

"Oh! no; not there!" she said in a faltering voice.

She was seized with giddiness, and that evening, she suffered a relapse, less specific in character, it is true, and with more complex symptoms. At times it was her heart that troubled her, then her head or her limbs; she had vomitings, in which Charles thought he detected the first signs of cancer.

And, on top of all this, the poor fellow had money troubles!

XIV

To begin with, he did not know how to reimburse Monsieur Homais for all the drugs he had supplied and although, as a doctor, he could have forgone paying for them, he blushed at the thought of such an obligation. Then the expenses of the household, now that the maid was in charge, became staggering. Bills flooded the house; the tradesmen grumbled; Monsieur Lheureux especially harassed him. At the height of Emma's illness, he had taken advantage of the situation to increase his bill; he hurriedly brought the cloak, the travelling-bag, two trunks instead of one, and a number of other things. Charles protested in vain; the shopkeeper rudely replied that the merchandise had been ordered and that he had no intention of taking it back. Besides, it would interfere with madame's convalescence; the doctor had better think it over; in short, he was resolved to sue him rather than give up his rights and take it off his hands. Charles subsequently ordered them sent back to the shop. Félicité forgot and, having other things on his mind, Charles thought no more about it. Monsieur Lheureux did not desist and, alternating threats with whines, he finally forced Bovary into signing him a six months' promissory note. But hardly had he signed the note that a bold idea occurred to him: he meant to borrow a thousand francs from Lheureux. So, with an embarrassed air, he asked if he could get them, adding that it would be for a year, at any interest. Lheureux ran off to his shop, brought back the money, and dictated another note, by which Bovary undertook to pay to his order on the 1st of September next the sum of one thousand and seventy francs, which, with the hundred and eighty already agreed to, made just twelve hundred and fifty. He was thus lending at six per cent in addition to one-fourth for commission; and since the merchandise brought him a good third profit at least, he stood to make one hundred and thirty francs in twelve months. He hoped that the business would not stop there; that the notes would not be paid on time and would have to be renewed, and that his puny little investment, thriving in the doctor's care like a patient in a rest home, would return to him one day considerably plumper, fat enough to burst the bag.

All of Lheureux's enterprises were thriving. He got the franchise for supplying the Neufchâtel hospital with cider; Monsieur Guillaumin promised him some shares in the turf-bogs of Gaumesnil, and he dreamt of establishing a new coach service between Argueil and Rouen, which no doubt would not be long in putting the ramshackle van of the "Lion d'Or" out of business. Travelling faster, at a cheaper rate, and carrying more luggage, it would concentrate into his hands all of Yonville's business.

Charles often wondered how he would ever be able to pay back so much money next year. He tried to think of solutions, such as applying to his father or selling something. But his father would be deaf, and he—he had nothing to sell. He foresaw such difficulties that he quickly dismissed so disagreeable a subject of meditation from his mind. He reproached himself with forgetting Emma, as if, all his thoughts belonging to this woman, it was robbing her of something not to be constantly thinking of her.

It was a severe winter. Madame Bovary's convalescence was slow. On good days they wheeled her arm-chair to the window that overlooked the square, for she now disliked the garden, and the blinds on that side were always down. She wanted her horse to be sold; what she formerly liked now displeased her. The limit of her concerns seemed to be her own health. She stayed in bed taking light meals, rang for the maid to inquire about her tea or merely to chat. The snow on the market-roof threw a white, still light into the room; then the rain began to fall; and every day Emma would wait with a kind of anxiety for the inevitable return of some trifling event that was of little or no concern to her. The most important was the arrival of the "Hirondelle" in the evening. Then the inn-keeper would shout and other voices answered, while Hippolyte's lantern, as he took down the luggage from the roof, was like a star in the darkness. At noontime, Charles came home; then he left again; next she took some broth, and towards five o'clock, as night fell, the children coming back from school, dragging their wooden shoes along the pavement, beat with their rulers against the clapper of the shutters.

Around this time of day, Monsieur Bournisien came to see her. He inquired after her health, gave her news, exhorted her to religion in a playful, gossipy tone that was not without charm. The mere sight of his cassock comforted her.

Once, at the height of her illness, she thought she was about to die and asked for communion; and while they were making the preparations in her room for the sacrament, while they were clearing the night table of its medicine bottles and turning it into an altar, and while Félicité was strewing dahlia flowers on the floor, Emma felt some power passing over her that freed her from her pains, from all perception, from all feeling. Her body, relieved, no longer thought; another life was beginning; it seemed to her that her being, mounting toward God, would be annihilated in that love like a burning incense that melts into vapour. The bed-clothes were sprinkled with holy water, the priest drew the white host from the holy pyx and she fainted with celestial joy as she advanced her lips to accept the body of the Saviour presented to her. The curtains of the alcove floated gently round her like clouds, and the rays of the two tapers burning on the night table seemed to shine like dazzling halos. Then she let her head fall back, fancying she heard in space the music of seraphic harps, and perceived in an azure sky, on a golden throne in the midst of saints holding green palms, God the Father, resplendent with majesty, who ordered to earth angels with wings of fire to carry her away in their arms.

This splendid vision dwelt in her memory as the most beautiful thing that it was possible to dream, so that now she strove to recall her sensation; it was still with her, albeit in a less overpowering manner, but with the same profound sweetness. Her soul, tortured by pride, at length found rest in Christian humility, and, tasting the joy of weakness, she saw within herself the destruction of her will opening wide the gates for heavenly grace to conquer her. She realised the existence of a bliss that could replace happiness, another love beyond all loves, without pause and without end, that would grow forever! Amid the illusions of her hope, she saw a state of purity floating above the earth, mingling with heaven. She wanted to become a saint. She bought rosaries and wore holy medals; she wished to have in her room, by the side of her bed, a reliquary set in emeralds that she might kiss it every evening.

The priest was delighted with her new state of mind, although he couldn't help worrying that Emma's excessive fervor might lead to heresy, to extravagance. But not being much versed in these matters once they went beyond a certain point he wrote to Monsieur Boulard, the bishop's bookseller, to send him "something first rate for a lady with a very distinguished mind." With as much concern as if he were shipping kitchen ware to savages, the bookseller made a random package of whatever happened to be current in the religious booktrade at the time. It contained little question and answer manuals, pamphlets written in the brusque tone of Joseph de Maistre, pseudo-novels in rose-coloured bindings and a sugary style, manufactured by sentimental seminarists or penitent blue-stockings. There were titles such as "Consider carefully: the Man of the World at the Feet of the Virgin Mary, by Monsieur de * * * , decorated with many Orders"; "The Errors of Voltaire, for the Use of the Young," &c.

Madame Bovary's mind was not yet sufficiently clear to apply herself seriously to anything; moreover, she began this reading in too great a hurry. She grew provoked at the doctrines of religion; the arrogance of the polemic writings displeased her by their ferocious attacks on people she did not know; and the secular stories, sprinkled with religious seasoning, seemed to her written in such ignorance of the world, that they rather led her away from the truths she wanted to see confirmed. Nevertheless, she persevered; and when the volume slipped from her hands, she fancied herself seized with the finest Catholic melancholy ever conceived by an ethereal soul.

As for the memory of Rodolphe, she had locked it away in the deepest recesses of her heart, and it remained there solemn and motionless as a pharaoh's mummy in a catacomb. A fragance escaped from this embalmed love, that, penetrating through everything, perfumed with tenderness the immaculate atmosphere in which she longed to live. When she knelt on her Gothic prie-Dieu, she addressed to the Lord the same suave words that she had murmured formerly to her lover in the outpourings of adultery. She was searching for faith; but no delights descended from the heavens, and she arose with aching limbs and the vague feeling that she was being cheated.

Yet she thought this search all the more admirable, and in the pride of her devoutness Emma compared herself to those grand ladies of long ago whose glory she had dreamed of over a portrait of La Vallière, and who, trailing with so much majesty the lace-trimmed trains of their long gowns, retired into solitude to shed at the feet of Christ the tears of hearts that life had wounded.

Then she indulged in excessive charity. She sewed clothes for the poor, she sent wood to women in childbirth; and on coming home one day, Charles found three tramps eating soup in the kitchen. Her little girl, whom her husband had sent back to the nurse during her illness, returned home. She wanted to teach her to read; even Berthe's crying no longer irritated her. She was resigned, universally tolerant. Her speech was full of elevated expressions. She would say:

"Is your stomach-ache any better, my angel?"

The elder Madame Bovary couldn't find fault with anything

except perhaps this mania of knitting jackets for orphans instead of mending her own dishtowels; but, harassed with domestic quarrels, the good woman took pleasure in this quiet house, and she even stayed there till after Easter, to escape the sarcasms of old Bovary, who never failed to order a big pork sausage on Good Friday.

Besides the companionship of her mother-in-law, who strengthened her resolutions somewhat by the rigor of her judgment and her stern appearance, Emma almost every day had other visitors: Madame Langlois, Madame Caron, Madame Dubreuil, Madame Tuvache, and regularly from two to five o'clock the sterling Madame Homais who, for her part, had never believed any of the gossip about her neighbor. The Homais children also came to see her, accompanied by Justin. He went up with them to her bedroom, and remained standing near the door without daring to move or to utter a word. Often enough Madame Bovary, taking no heed of him, would start dressing. She began by taking out her comb and tossing her head, in a brusk gesture, and when for the first time the poor boy saw this mass of hair fall in ringlets to her knees, it was as if he entered suddenly into a new and strange world, whose splendour terrified him.

Emma probably did not notice his silent attentions or his timidity. She had no inkling that love, which presumably had left her life forever, was pulsating right there, under that coarse shirt, in that adolescent heart open to the emanations of her beauty. Besides, she now wrapped all things in the same mood of indifference, she combined gentleness of speech with such haughty looks, affected such contradictory ways, that one could no longer distinguish selfishness from charity, or corruption from virtue. One evening, for example, she first got angry with the maid, who had asked to go out, and stammered as she tried to find some pretext; then suddenly:

"So you love him, don't you?" she said.

And without waiting for an answer from Félicité, who was blushing, she added sadly:

"All right! run along, and have a good time!"

In early spring she had the garden all changed around, over Bovary's objections; yet he was pleased to see her at last express some will of her own. She did so more and more as her strength returned. First, she found occasion to expel Mère Rollet, the nurse, who during her convalescence had taken to visiting the kitchen in the company of her two nurslings and her young boarder, whose appetite surpassed that of a cannibal. She cut down on the visits of the Homais family, gradually freed herself from the other visitors, and even went to church less assiduously, to the great approval of the pharmacist, who remarked to her:

"I suspect you were beginning to fall for the priest's sales talk!"

As before, Monsieur Bournisien would drop in every day after catechism class. He preferred to take the air in the "grove," as he called the arbour. This was the time when Charles came home. They were hot; some sweet cider was brought out, and they drank together to madame's complete recovery.

Binet was often there, that is to say, a little lower down against the terrace wall, fishing for crayfish. Bovary invited him to have a drink, and he proved to be a real expert on the uncorking of the stone bottles.

Looking around with utter self-satisfaction, first at his companions, then at the furthest confines of the landscape, he would say:

"You must first hold the bottle perpendicularly on the table, and after the strings are cut, press the cork upwards inch by inch, gently, very gently—the way they handle soda water in restaurants."

But during his demonstration the cider often spurted right into their faces, and the priest, laughing his thick laugh, would never fail to make his little joke:

"Its excellence certainly strikes the eye!"

He was undoubtedly a kindly fellow and one day he was not even scandalised at the pharmacist, who advised Charles to give madame some distraction by taking her to the theatre at Rouen to hear the illustrious tenor, Lagardy. Homais, surprised at this silence, wanted to know his opinion, and the priest declared that he considered music less dangerous for morals than literature.

But the pharmacist took up the defence of letters. The theatre, he contended, served to decry prejudices and, while pretending to amuse, it taught virtue.

"*Castigat ridendo mores*, Monsieur Bournisien! Look at most of Voltaire's tragedies: they contain a wealth of philosophical considerations that make them into a real school of morals and diplomacy for the people."

"I," said Binet, "once saw a play called the 'Gamin de Paris,' in which there is a really fine part of an old general. He settles the account of a rich young fellow who has seduced a working girl, and at the end . . ."

"Of course," pursued Homais, "there is bad literature as there is bad pharmacy, but to condemn in a lump the most important of the fine arts seems to me a stupidity, a Gothic aberration worthy of the abominable times that imprisoned Galileo."

"I know very well," objected the curé, "that there are good works, good authors. Still, the very fact of crowding people of different sexes into the same room, made to look enticing by displays of worldly pomp, these pagan disguises, the makeup, the lights, the effeminate voices, all this must, in the long-run, engender a certain mental libertinage, give rise to immodest thoughts and impure temptations. Such, at any rate, is the opinion of all the church fathers. Moreover," he added, suddenly assuming a mystic tone of voice while he rolled a pinch of snuff between his fingers, "if the Church has condemned the theatre, she must be right; we must bow to her decrees."

"Why," asked the druggist, "should she excommunicate actors when formerly they used to take part openly in religious ceremonies? They would play right in the middle of the choir and perform a kind of farce called "mystery plays" that frequently offended against the laws of decency."

The curé merely groaned and the pharmacist persisted:

"It's like in the Bible; you know . . . there are things in it . . . certain details . . . I'd call them downright daring . . . bordering on obscenity!"

And as Monsieur Bournisien signaled his annoyance:

"Ah! you'll admit that it is not a book to place in the hands of a young girl, and I wouldn't at all like it if Athalie . . ."

"But it is the Protestants, and not we," protested the other impatiently, "who recommend the Bible."

"All the same," said Homais. "I am surprised that in our days, in this century of enlightenment, any one should still persist in proscribing an intellectual relaxation that is inoffensive, morally uplifting, and sometimes even good for the health—isn't that right, doctor?"

"Quite," the doctor replied in a non-committal tone, either because, sharing the same ideas, he wished to offend no one, or else because he simply had no ideas on the subject.

The conversation seemed at an end when the pharmacist thought fit to try a parting shot.

"I've known priests who put on civilian clothes to go watch burlesque shows."

"Come, come!" said the curé.

"Ah yes, I've known some!"

And, separating the words, he repeated:

"I—have—known—some!"

"Well, they did wrong," said Bournisien, prepared to listen to anything with resignation.

"And they didn't stop at that, either!" persisted the pharmacist.

"That's enough! . . ." exclaimed the priest, looking so fierce that the other thought safe to retreat.

"I only mean to say," he replied in a much less aggressive tone, "that tolerance is the surest way to draw people to religion."

"That is true! that is true!" conceded the priest, sitting down again.

But he stayed only a few minutes. Hardly had he left that Monsieur Homais said to the doctor:

"That's what I call a good fight! See how I found his weak spot? I didn't give him much of a chance . . . Now take my advice. Take madame to the theatre, if only to get for once the better of one of these rooks! If someone could keep the store in my absence, I'd go with you. But hurry! Lagardy is only going to give one performance; he's going to play in England for a tremendous fee. From what I hear, he's quite a character. He's simply loaded with money! He travels with three mistresses and a cook. All these great artists burn the candle at both ends; they need to lead a dissolute life to stir the imagination of the public. But they die at the poorhouse, because they don't have the sense to save their money when it comes in. Well, enjoy your dinner! See you to-morrow."

This theatre idea quickly grew in Bovary's mind; he at once communicated it to his wife, who at first refused, alleging the fatigue, the worry, the expense; but, for once, Charles did not give in, so sure was he that this occasion would do her good. He saw nothing to prevent it: his mother had sent three hundred francs he no longer counted on, the current bills were far from staggering and Lheureux's notes were not due for such a long time that he could dismiss them from his mind. Besides, imagining that she was refusing out of consideration for him, he insisted all the more, until she finally consented. The next day at eight o'clock they set out in the "Hirondelle."

The pharmacist, who had nothing whatever to keep him at Yonville but fancied himself to be indispensable, sighed with envy as he saw them go.

"Well, a pleasant journey!" he said to them; "happy mortals that you are!"

Then addressing himself to Emma, who was wearing a blue silk gown with four flounces:

"You are prettier than ever. You'll make quite an impression in Rouen."

The diligence stopped at the "Croix-Rouge" on the Place Beauvoisine. It was a typical provincial inn, with large stables and small bedrooms and chickens in the courtyard, picking at the oats under the muddy gigs of travelling salesmen;—a fine old place, with worm-eaten balconies that creak in the wind on winter nights, always crowded, noisy and full of food, its black tables stained with coffee and brandy, the thick windows yellowed by flies, the napkins spotted with cheap red wine. Like farmboys dressed in Sunday-clothes, the place still reeks of the country; it has a café on the street and a vegetable-garden on the back. Charles at once set out on his errands. He confused stage-boxes and gallery, orchestra seats and regular boxes, asked for explanations which he did not understand, was sent from the box-office to the manager, came back to the inn, returned to the theatre and ended up by crossing the full length of the town, from theatre to outer boulevard, several times.

Madame bought herself a hat, gloves, and a bouquet. Monsieur worried greatly about missing the beginning, and, without having had time to swallow a plate of soup, they arrived at the gates of the theatre well before opening time.

XV

The crowd was lined up against the wall, evenly distributed on both sides of the entrance rails. At the corner of the neighbouring streets huge bills, printed in Gothic letters, announced "Lucie de Lammermoor-Lagardy-Opera &c." The weather was fine, the people hot; sweat trickled among fancy coiffures and pocket handkerchiefs were mopping red foreheads; now and then a warm wind that blew from the river gently stirred the edges of the canvass awnings hanging from the doors of the cafés. A little lower down, however, one was refreshed by a current of icy air that smelt of tallow, leather, and oil, breathed forth from the Rue des Charrettes with its huge, dark warehouses resounding with the noise of rolling barrels.

For fear of seeming ridiculous, Emma first wanted to take a little stroll in the harbor, and Bovary carefully kept clutching the tickets in his trouser pockets, pressed against his stomach.

Her heart began to beat as soon as she reached the entrance hall. She involuntarily smiled with vanity on seeing the crowd rushing to the right by the other corridor while she went up the staircase to the reserved seats. She was as pleased as a child to push the large tapestried door open with her finger; she breathed deeply the dusty smell of the lobbies, and when she was seated in her box she drew herself up with the self-assurance of a duchess.

The theatre was beginning to fill; opera-glasses were taken from their cases, and the subscribers greeted and bowed as they spotted each other at a distance. They sought relief from the pressures of commerce in the arts, but, unable to take their minds off business matters, they still talked about cotton, spirits of wine, or indigo. The placid and meek heads of the old men, with their pale whitish hair and complexion, resembled silver medals tarnished by lead fumes. The young beaux were strutting about in the orchestra, exhibiting their pink or apple-green cravats under their gaping waistcoats; sitting above them, Madame Bovary admired how they leant the tight-drawn palm of their yellow gloves on the golden knobs of their canes.

Now the lights of the orchestra were lit; the chandelier, let down from the ceiling, threw the sudden gaiety of its sparkling crystals over the theatre; then the musicians began to file in; and first there was the protracted hubbub of roaring cellos, squeaking violins, blaring trumpets and piping flutes. But three knocks were heard on the stage, a rolling of drums began, the brass instruments played some chords, and the curtain rose, discovering a country-scene.

It was the cross-roads of a wood, with a fountain on the left, shaded by an oak tree. Peasants and lords with tartans over their shoulders were singing a hunting-song in chorus; a captain suddenly appeared, who evoked the spirit of evil by lifting both his arms to heaven. Another followed; they departed, and the hunters started afresh.

She felt herself carried back to the reading of her youth, into the midst of Walter Scott. She seemed to hear through the mist the sound of the Scotch bagpipes re-echoing over the moors. Her remembrance of the novel helping her to understand the libretto, she followed the story phrase by phrase, while the burst of music dispersed the fleeting thoughts that came back to her. She gave herself up to the flow of the melodies, and felt all her being vibrate as if the violin bows were being drawn over her nerves. Her eyes could hardly take in all the costumes, the scenery, the actors, the painted trees that shook whenever someone walked, and the velvet caps, cloaks, swords—all those imaginary things that vibrated in the music as in the atmosphere of another world. But a young woman stepped forward, throwing a purse to a squire in green. She was left alone on the stage, and the flute was heard like the murmur of a fountain or the warbling of birds. Lucie bravely attacked her cavatina in G major. She begged for love, longed for wings. Emma, too, would have liked to flee away from life, locked in a passionate embrace. Suddenly Edgar Lagardy appeared.

He had that splendid pallor that gives something of the majesty of marble to the ardent races of the South. His vigourous form was tightly clad in a brown-coloured doublet; a small chiselled dagger swung against his left thigh, and he rolled languid eyes while flashing his white teeth. They said that a Polish princess having heard him sing one night on the beach at Biarritz, where he used to be a boatsman, had fallen in love with him. She had lost her entire fortune for his sake. He had deserted her for other women, and this sentimental fame did not fail to enhance his artistic reputation. A skilled ham actor, he never forgot to have a phrase on his seductiveness and his sensitive soul inserted in the accounts about him. He had a fine voice, colossal aplomb, more temperament than intelligence, more pathos than lyric feeling; all this made for an admirable charlatan type, in which there was something of the hairdresser as well as of the bullfighter.

From the first scene he brought down the house. He pressed

Lucie in his arms, he left her, he came back, he seemed desperate; he had outbursts of rage, then elegiac gurglings of infinite sweetness, and tones like sobs and kisses escaped from his bare throat. Emma bent forward to see him, scratching the velvet of the box with her nails. Her heart filled with these melodious lamentations that were accompanied by the lugubrious moanings of the double-basses, like the cries of the drowning in the tumult of a tempest. She recognised all the intoxication and the anguish that had brought her close to death. The voice of the prima donna seemed to echo her own conscience, and the whole fictional story seemed to capture something of her own life. But no one on earth had loved her with such love. He had not wept like Edgar that last moonlit night when they had said "Till tomorrow! Till tomorrow! . . ." The theatre rang with cheers; they repeated the entire stretto; the lovers spoke of the flowers on their tomb, of vows, exile, fate, hopes; and when they uttered the final farewell, Emma gave a sharp cry that mingled with the vibrations of the last chords.

"But why," asked Bovary, "is that lord torturing her like that?"

"No, no!" she answered; "he is her lover!"

"Yet he vows vengeance on her family, while the other one who came on before said, 'I love Lucie and she loves me!' Besides, he went off with her father arm in arm. For he certainly is her father, isn't he—the ugly little man with a cock's feather in his hat?"

Despite Emma's explanations, as soon as the recitative duet began in which Gilbert lays bare his abominable machinations to his master Ashton, Charles, seeing the false engagement ring that is to deceive Lucie, thought it was a love-gift sent by Edgar. He confessed, moreover, that he did not understand the story because of the music, which interfered very much with the words.

"What does it matter?" said Emma. "Do be quiet!"

"Yes, but you know," he went on, leaning against her shoulder, "I like to understand things."

"Be quiet! be quiet!" she cried impatiently.

Lucie came on, half supported by her women, a wreath of orange blossoms in her hair, and paler than the white satin of her gown. Emma dreamed of her marriage day; she saw herself at home again among the fields in the little path as they walked to the church. Why didn't she, like this woman, resist and implore? Instead, she had walked joyously and unwittingly towards the abyss . . . Ah! if in the freshness of her beauty, before the degradation of marriage and the disillusions of adultery, she could have anchored her life upon some great, strong heart! Virtue, affection, sensuous pleasure and duty would have combined to give her eternal bliss. But such happiness, she realized, was a lie, a mockery to taunt desire. She knew now how small the passions were that art magnified. So, striving for detachment, Emma resolved to see in this reproduction of her sorrows a mere formal fiction for the entertainment of the eye, and she smiled inwardly in scornful pity when from behind the velvet curtains at the back of the stage a man appeared in a black cloak.

His large Spanish hat fell at a gesture he made, and immediately the instruments and the singers began the sextet. Edgar, flashing with fury, dominated all the others with his clearer voice; Ashton hurled homicidal provocations at him in deep notes; Lucie uttered her shrill lament; Arthur sang modulated asides in a middle register and the deep basso of the minister pealed forth like an organ, while the female voices re-echoed his words in a delightful chorus. They were lined up in one single gesticulating row, breathing forth anger, vengeance, jealousy, terror, mercy and surprise all at once from their open mouths. The outraged lover brandished his naked sword; his lace ruff rose and fell jerkily with the movements of his chest, and he walked from right to left with long strides, clanking against the boards the silver-gilt spurs of his soft, flaring boots. She thought that he must have inexhaustible supplies of love in him to lavish it upon the crowd with such effusion. All her attempts at critical detachment were swept away by the poetic power of the acting, and, drawn to the man by the illusion of the part, she tried to imagine his life—extraordinary, magnificent, notorious, the life that could have been hers if fate had willed it. If only they had met! He would have loved her, they would have travelled together through all the kingdoms of Europe from capital to capital, sharing in his success and in his hardships, picking up the flowers thrown to him, mending his clothes. Every night, hidden behind the golden lattice of her box, she would have drunk in eagerly the expansions of this soul that would have sung for her alone; from the stage, even as he acted, he would have looked at her. A mad idea took possession of her: he was looking at her right now! She longed to run to his arms, to take refuge in his strength, as in the incarnation of love itself, and to say to him, to cry out, "Take me away! carry me with you! let us leave! All my passion and all my dreams are yours!"

The curtain fell.

The smell of gas mingled with the people's breath and the waving fans made the air even more suffocating. Emma wanted to go out; the crowd filled the corridors, and she fell back in her armchair with palpitations that choked her. Charles, fearing that she would faint, ran to the refreshment-room to get a glass of orgeat.

He had great difficulty in getting back to his seat, for as he was holding the glass in his hands, his elbows bumped into someone at every step; he even spilt three-fourths on the shoulders of a Rouen lady in short sleeves, who feeling the cold liquid running down her

back, started to scream like a peacock, as if she were being mur-
dered. Her mill-owner husband lashed out at his clumsiness, and
while she used her handkerchief to wipe off the stains from her
handsome cherry-coloured taffeta gown, he angrily muttered about
indemnity, costs, reimbursement. Charles was quite out of breath
when he finally reached his wife:

"I thought I'd never make it. What a crowd! . . . What a
crowd!"

And he added:

"Just guess whom I met up there! Monsieur Léon!"

"Léon?"

"Himself! He's coming along to pay his respects."

And as he finished these words the ex-clerk of Yonville entered
the box.

He held out his hand with the casual ease of a gentleman; and
Madame Bovary extended hers, yielding no doubt to the pressure of
a stronger will. She had not felt it since that spring evening when
the rain fell upon the green leaves, and they had said good-bye
while standing near the window. But soon recalling herself to the
necessities of the situation, she managed to shake off the torpor of
her memories, and began stammering a few hurried words.

"Ah! good evening . . . What, you here?"

"Silence!" cried a voice from the orchestra, for the third act was
beginning.

"So you are at Rouen?"

"Yes."

"And since when?"

"Be quiet! Throw them out!"

People were looking at them; they fell silent.

But from that moment she listened no more; and the chorus of
the guests, the scene between Ashton and his servant, the grand
duet in D major, all became more distant, as if the instruments had
grown less sonorous and the characters more remote. She remembered the card games at the pharmacist, the walk to the nurse, the
poetry readings in the arbour, the tête-à-têtes by the fireside—all
the sadness of their love, so calm and so protracted, so discreet, so
tender, and that she had nevertheless forgotten. And why had he
come back? What combination of circumstances had brought him
back into her life? He was standing behind her, leaning with his
shoulder against the wall of the box; now and again she felt herself
shudder as she felt the warmth of his breath on her hair.

"Do you find this amusing?" he said, bending over her so closely
that the end of his moustache brushed her cheek.

She replied flippantly:

"Heavens, no! not particularly."

Then he suggested that they leave the theatre and have an ice somewhere.

"Oh, not yet; let us stay," said Bovary. "Her hair's undone; this is going to be tragic."

But the madness scene did not interest Emma, and she thought the singer was overacting.

"She screams too loud," she said, turning to Charles who was listening.

"Yes . . . perhaps . . . a little," he replied, torn between his genuine enjoyment and his respect for his wife's opinion.

Then Léon sighed:

"Don't you find it hot . . ."

"Unbearably so! Yes!"

"Don't you feel well?" Bovary inquired.

"Yes, I am stifling; let's go."

Monsieur Léon draped her long lace shawl carefully about her shoulders, and the three of them left and sat down near the harbor, on the terrace of a café. First they spoke of her illness, although Emma interrupted Charles from time to time, for fear, she said, of boring Monsieur Léon; and the latter told them that he had come to spend two years in a big Rouen law firm, in order to gain some experience of how business is conducted in Normandy—so different from Paris. Then he inquired after Berthe, the Homais, Mère Lefrançois, and as they had, in the husband's presence, nothing more to say to one another, the conversation soon came to an end.

People coming out of the theatre walked along the pavement, humming or shouting at the top of their voices, "O *bel ange, ma Lucie!*" Then Léon, playing the dilettante, began to talk music. He had seen Tamburini, Rubini, Persiani, Grisi, and, compared with them, Lagardy, despite his grand outbursts, was nowhere.

"Yet," interrupted Charles, who was slowly sipping his rum-sherbet, "they say that he is quite admirable in the last act. I regret leaving before the end, just when I was beginning to enjoy myself."

"Why," said the clerk, "he will soon give another performance."

But Charles replied that they had to leave the next day. "Unless," he added, turning to his wife, "you'd like to stay by yourself, my darling?"

And changing his tactics at the unexpected opportunity that presented itself to his hopes, the young man sang the praises of Lagardy in the last aria. It was really superb, sublime. Then Charles insisted:

"You'll come back on Sunday. Come, make up your mind. If you feel that this is doing you the least bit of good, you shouldn't hesitate to stay."

The adjoining tables, however, were emptying; a waiter came and stood discreetly near them. Charles, who understood, took out his purse; the clerk held back his arm, and made a point of leaving two extra pieces of silver that he made chink on the marble.

"I am really sorry," said Bovary," for all the money you are . . ."

The other silenced him with a gesture of affable disdain and, taking his hat, said:

"So, we are agreed, to-morrow at six o'clock?"

Charles explained once more that he could not absent himself longer, but that nothing prevented Emma . . .

"But," she stammered, with a strange smile, "I don't know if I ought . . ."

"Well, you must think it over. Sleep over it and we'll see in the morning."

Then, to Léon, who was walking along with them:

"Now that you are in our part of the world, I hope you'll come and have dinner with us from time to time."

The clerk declared he would not fail to do so, being obliged, moreover, to go to Yonville on some business for his office. And they parted before the passage Saint-Herbland just as the cathedral struck half-past eleven.

Part Three

I

Monsieur Léon, while studying law, had been a fairly assiduous customer at the Chaumière, a dance-hall where he was particularly successful with the grisettes who thought him distinguished looking. He was the best-mannered of the students; he wore his hair neither too long nor too short, didn't spend all his quarter's money on the first day of the month, and kept on good terms with his professors. As for excesses, he had always abstained from them, as much from cowardice as from refinement.

Often when he stayed in his room to read, or else when sitting in the evening under the linden-trees of the Luxembourg, he let his law-code fall to the ground, and the memory of Emma came back to him. But gradually this feeling grew weaker, and other desires took the upperhand, although the original passion still acted through them. For Léon did not lose all hope; there was for him, as it were, a vague promise floating in the future, like a golden fruit suspended from some fantastic tree.

Then, seeing her again after three years of absence, his passion reawakened. He must, he thought, finally make up his mind to possess her. Moreover, his timidity had worn off in the gay company of his student days, and he returned to the provinces in utter contempt of whoever had not set foot on the asphalt of the boulevards. In the presence of a genuine Parisienne, in the house of some famous physician surrounded by honors and luxury, the poor clerk would no doubt have trembled like a child; but here, on the quais of Rouen, with the wife of a small country-doctor, he felt at his ease, sure to shine. Self-confidence depends on environment: one does not speak in the same tone in the drawing room than in the kitchen; and the wealthy woman seems to have about her, to guard her virtue, all her bank-notes, like an armour, in the lining of her corset.

On leaving the Bovarys the night before, Léon had followed them through the streets at a distance; when he saw them enter the Croix-Rouge, he returned home and spent the night planning his strategy.

So the next afternoon about five o'clock he walked into the kitchen of the inn, pale and apprehensive, driven by a coward's resolution that stops at nothing.

"Monsieur isn't in," a servant told him.

This seemed to him a good omen. He went upstairs.

She didn't seem surprised at his arrival; on the contrary, she apologized for having failed to tell him where they were staying.

"Oh, I guessed it!" said Léon.

He pretended he had found her by chance, guided by instinct. When he saw her smile, he tried to repair his blunder by telling her he had spent the morning looking for her in all the hotels in the town.

"So you have made up your mind to stay?" he added.

"Yes," she said, "and I shouldn't have. One should avoid getting used to inaccessible pleasures when one is burdened by so many responsibilities . . ."

"Oh, I can imagine . . ."

"No, you can't, you are not a woman."

But men too had their trials, and the conversation started off by some philosphical considerations. Emma expatiated on the frailty of earthly affections, and the eternal isolation that stifles the human heart.

To show off, or in a naive imitation of this melancholy which stirred his own, the young man declared that he had been dreadfully despondent. He was bored by the law, attracted by other vocations and his mother had never ceased to harrass him in all her letters. As they talked, they stated the reasons for their respective unhappiness with more precision and they felt a shared exaltation in this growing confidence. But they sometimes stopped short of revealing their thought in full, and then sought to invent a phrase that might nevertheless express it. She did not confess her passion for another; he did not say that he had forgotten her.

Perhaps he no longer remembered the suppers with girls after masked balls; and no doubt she did not recollect the rendezvous of old when she ran across the fields in the morning to her lover's house. The noises of the town hardly reached them, and the room seemed small, as if to bring them even closer together in their solitude. Emma, in a dimity dressing gown, leant her chignon against the back of the old arm-chair; the yellow wall-paper formed, as it were, a golden background behind her, and her bare head was reflected in the mirror with the white parting in the middle, the tip of her ears peeping out from the folds of her hair.

"How bad of me!" she said, "you must forgive me for boring you with my eternal complaints."

"No, never, never!"

"If only you knew," she went on, raising to the ceiling her beautiful eyes, in which a tear was trembling, "if only you knew all I dreamed!"

"So did I! Oh, I too have suffered! Often I went out; I went away. I left, dragging myself along the quays, seeking distraction amid the din of the crowd without being able to banish the heaviness that weighed upon me. In an engraver's shop on the boulevard I found an Italian print of one of the Muses. She is draped in a tunic, and she is looking at the moon, with forget-me-nots in her flowing hair. Something continually drove me there, I would stay for hour after hour."

Then, in a trembling voice:

"She looked a little like you."

Madame Bovary turned away her head that he might not see the irrepressible smile she felt rising to her lips.

"Often," he went on, "I wrote you letters that I tore up."

She did not answer. He continued;

"I sometimes fancied that some chance would bring you. I thought I recognised you at street-corners, and I ran after carriages when I saw a shawl or a veil like yours flutter in the window . . ."

She seemed resolved to let him speak without interruption. With arms crossed and her head lowered, she stared at the rosettes on her slippers, and from time to time moved her toes under the satin.

At last she sighed.

"But what I find worst of all is to drag out, as I do, a useless existence. If our pains could be of use to some one, we should find consolation in the thought of the sacrifice."

He started off in praise of virtue, duty, and silent immolation, having himself an incredible longing for self-sacrifice that he could not satisfy.

"What I would like," she said "is to work in a hospital as a nursing Sister."

"Unfortunately," he replied, "no such holy vocations are open to men, and I can think of no profession . . . except perhaps a doctor's . . ."

With a slight shrug of the shoulders, Emma interrupted him to speak of her illness, which had almost killed her. How she regretted her cure! if she had died, she would not now be suffering. Léon was quick to express his own longing for "the quiet of the tomb"; one night, he had even made his will, asking to be buried in that beautiful coverlet with velvet stripes he had received from her. For this was how they would have wished to be, each setting up an ideal to which they were now trying to adapt their past life. Besides, speech is like a rolling machine that always stretches the sentiment it expresses.

But this made-up story of the coverlet made her ask:

"Why?"

"Why?" He hesitated.

"Because I loved you so!"

And congratulating himself at having surmounted the obstacle, Léon watched her face out of the corner of his eye.

It was like the sky when a gust of wind sweeps the clouds away. The mass of darkening sad thoughts lifted from her blue eyes; her whole face shone.

He waited. At last she replied:

"I always suspected it."

Then they went over all the trifling events of that far-off existence, of which the joys and sorrows had just been conjured up by that one word. He remembered the clematis arbour, the dresses she had worn, the furniture of her room, the entire house.

"And our poor cactuses, where are they?"

"The cold killed them this winter."

"How often did I think of them! I see them again as they looked when on summer mornings the sun shone on your blinds, and I saw your two bare arms among the flowers.

"Poor friend!" she said, holding out her hand.

Léon swiftly pressed his lips to it. Then, when he had taken a deep breath:

"In those days, you were like an incomprehensible power to me which held me captive. Once, for instance, I came to see you, but you probably don't remember."

"I do," she said; "go on."

"You were downstairs in the hall, ready to go out, standing on the last stair; you were wearing a hat with small blue flowers; and without being invited, in spite of myself, I went with you. But I grew more and more conscious of my folly every moment, and I kept walking by your side, not daring to follow you completely but unable to leave. When you went into a shop, I waited in the street, and I watched you through the window taking off your gloves and counting the change on the counter. Then you rang at Madame Tuvache's; you were let in, and I stood like an idiot in front of the great heavy door that had closed after you."

Madame Bovary, as she listened to him, wondered that she was so old. All these things reappearing before her seemed to expand her existence; it was like some sentimental immensity to which she returned; and from time to time she said in a low voice, her eyes half closed:

"Yes, it is true . . . it is true . . ."

They heard eight o'clock strike on the different towers that surround the Place Beauvoisine, a neighborhood of schools, churches, and large empty private dwellings. They no longer spoke, but as they looked upon each other, they felt their heads whirl, as if waves of sound had escaped from their fixed glances. They were hand in hand now, and the past, the future, reminiscences and dreams, all were confounded in the sweetness of this ecstasy. Night was darkening over the walls, leaving visible only, half hidden in the shade, the coarse colours of four bills representing scenes from *La Tour de Nesle*,[1] with Spanish and French captions underneath. Through the sash-window they could see a patch of sky between the pointed roofs.

She rose to light two wax-candles on the chest of drawers, then she sat down again.

"Well . . . ?" said Léon.

"Well . . . ?" she replied.

He was wondering how to resume the interrupted conversation, when she said to him:

"How is it that no one until now has ever expressed such sentiments to me?"

The clerk retorted that idealistic natures rarely found understanding. But he had loved her from the very first moment; the thought of their possible happiness filled him with despair. If only they had met earlier, by some stroke of chance, they would have been forever bound together.

"I have sometimes thought of it," she went on.

"What a dream!" murmured Léon.

And fingering gently the blue border of her long white belt, he

1. A melodrama by Alexandre Dumas the elder and Gaillardet (1832) in which Marie de Bourgogne, famous for her crimes, is the main heroine. Almost all literary allusions connected with Emma have to do with violent or adulterous women.

added,

"Who prevents us from starting all over again?"

"No, my friend," she replied; "I am too old . . . You are too young . . . forget me! Others will love you . . . you will love them."

"Not as I love you!"

"What a child you are! Come, let us be sensible, I want it."

She told him again that their love was impossible, that they must remain, as before, like brother and sister to each other.

Was she speaking seriously? No doubt Emma did not herself know, absorbed as she was by the charm of the seduction and the necessity of defending herself; looking tenderly at the young man, she gently repulsed the timid caresses that his trembling hands attempted.

"Ah! forgive me!" he cried, drawing back.

Emma was seized with a vague fear at this shyness, more dangerous to her than the boldness of Rodolphe when he advanced to her open-armed. No man had ever seemed to her so beautiful. His demeanor suggested an exquisite candor. He lowered his long curling eyelashes. The soft skin of his cheek was flushed, she thought, with desire for her, and Emma felt an invincible longing to press her lips to it. Then, leaning towards the clock as if to see the time:

"How late it is!" she exclaimed. "How we have been chattering!"

He understood the hint and took up his hat.

"You made me forget about the opera! And poor Bovary who left me here especially for that! Monsieur Lormeaux, of the Rue Grand-Pont, was to take me and his wife."

And there would be no other opportunity, as she was to leave the next day.

"Really?" said Léon.

"Yes."

"But I must see you again," he went on. "I had something to tell you . . ."

"What?"

"Something . . . important, serious. I cannot possibly let you go like this. If only you knew . . . Listen to me . . . Haven't you understood? Can't you guess?"

"You made yourself very clear" said Emma.

"Ah! you can jest! But you shouldn't. Have mercy, and allow me to see you again . . . only once . . . one single time."

"Well . . ."

She stopped; then, as if changing her mind:

"But not here!"

"Wherever you say."

"Will you . . ."

She seemed to think; then suddenly:

"To-morrow at eleven o'clock in the cathedral."

"I shall be there," he cried, seizing her hands, which she withdrew.

And as they were both standing up, he behind and Emma with lowered head, he stooped over her and pressed long kisses on her neck.

"You are crazy, you are crazy!" she cried between bursts of laughter, as the kisses multiplied.

Then bending his head over her shoulder, he seemed to beg the consent of her eyes, but when they met his, they seemed icy and distant.

Léon took three paces backwards. He stopped on the threshold; then he whispered in a trembling voice:

"Till to-morrow."

She answered with a nod, and vanished like a bird into the next room.

In the evening Emma wrote the clerk an interminable letter, in which she cancelled the rendezvous; all was over between them; they must not, for the sake of their happiness, meet again. But when the letter was finished, as she did not know Léon's address, she was puzzled.

"I'll give it to him myself," she said; "he'll come."

The next morning, humming a tune while he stood on his balcony by the open window, Léon polished his shoes with special care. He put on white trousers, silken socks, a green coat, emptied all the scent he had into his handkerchief, then having had his hair curled, he uncurled it again, in order to give it a more natural elegance.

"It is still too early," he thought, looking at the barber's cuckoo-clock, that pointed to the hour of nine.

He read an old fashion journal, went out, smoked a cigar, walked up three streets, thought the time had come and walked slowly towards the porch of Notre Dame.

It was a beautiful summer morning. Silver sparkled in the window of the jeweler's store and the light, falling obliquely on the cathedral, threw shimmering reflections on the edges of the grey stones; a flock of birds fluttered in the grey sky round the trefoiled turrets; the square, resounding with cries, was fragrant with the flowers that bordered the pavement, roses, jasmines, carnations, narcissus, and tuberoses, unevenly spaced out between moist grasses, catnip, and chickweed for the birds; the fountains gurgled in the center, and under large umbrellas, amidst heaps of piled up mellons, bare-headed flower vendors wrapped bunches of violets in pieces of paper.

The young man took one. It was the first time that he had bought flowers for a woman, and his breast, as he smelt them, swelled with pride, as if this homage that he meant for another had been reflected upon himself.

But he was afraid of being seen and resolutely entered the church.

The verger was just then standing on the threshold in the middle of the left doorway, under the figure of Salomé dancing, known in Rouen as the "dancing Marianne". He wore a feather cap, a rapier dangled against his leg and he looked more majestic than a cardinal, as shining as a pyx.

He came towards Léon, and, with the bland benign smile of a priest when questioning a child, asked:

"I gather that Monsieur is a visitor in this town? Would Monsieur care to be shown the church?"

"No!" said Léon.

And he first went round the lower aisles. Then he went out to look at the Place. Emma was not coming yet, so he returned as far as the choir.

The nave was reflected in the full fonts together with the base of the arches and some fragments of the stained glass windows. But the reflections of the painted glass, broken by the marble rim, were continued farther on upon the pavement, like a many-coloured carpet. The broad daylight from outside entered the church in three enormous rays through the three opened portals. From time to time a sacristan crossed the far end of the church, making the sidewise genuflection of a hurried worshipper in the direction of the altar. The crystal lustres hung motionless. In the choir a silver lamp was burning, and from the side chapels and dark places of the church sounds like sighs arose, together with the clang of a closing grating that echoed under the lofty vaults.

Léon walked solemnly alongside the walls. Life had never seemed so good to him. She would soon appear, charming and agitated, looking back to see if anyone was watching her—with her flounced dress, her gold eyeglass, her delicate shoes, with all sorts of elegant trifles that he had never been allowed to taste, and with the ineffable seduction of yielding virtue. The church was set around her like a huge boudoir; the arches bent down to shelter in their darkness the avowal of her love; the windows shone resplendent to light up her face, and the censers would burn that she might appear like an angel amid sweet-smelling clouds.

Meanwhile, she did not come. He sat down on a chair, and his eyes fell upon a blue stained window representing boatmen carrying baskets. He looked at it long, attentively, and he counted the scales of the fishes and the button-holes of the doublets, while his thoughts wandered off in search of Emma.

The verger, left to himself, resented the presence of someone who dared to admire the cathedral without his assistance. He considered this a shocking way to behave, robbing him of his due, close to committing sacrilege.

There was a rustle of silk on the pavement, the edge of a hat, a hooded cape—it was she! Léon rose and ran to meet her.

Emma was pale. She walked hurriedly.

"Read this!" she said, holding out a piece of paper to him. "Oh, no!"

And she abruptly withdrew her hand to enter the chapel of the Virgin, where, kneeling on a chair, she began to pray.

The young man was irritated by this display of piety; then he nevertheless felt a certain charm in seeing her thus lost in devotions in the middle of a rendezvous, like an Andalusian marquise; then he grew bored, for she seemed to go on for ever.

Emma prayed, or rather tried to pray, hoping that some sudden resolution might descend to her from heaven; and to draw down divine aid she filled her eyes with the splendors of the tabernacle. She breathed in the perfumes of the full-blown flowers in the large vases, and listened to the stillness of the church—a stillness that only heightened the tumult in her own heart.

She rose, and they were about to leave, when the verger quickly approached:

"Madame is perhaps a stranger here? Madame would like to visit the church?"

"Oh, no!" the clerk cried.

"Why not?" she said.

For, with her expiring virtue, she clung to the Virgin, the sculptures, the tombs—to anything.

Then, in order to do things right, the verger took them to the entrance near the square, where, pointing out with his cane a large circle of black stones, without inscription or carving:

"This," he said majestically, "is the circumference of the beautiful bell of Ambroise. It weighed forty thousand pounds. There was not its equal in all Europe. The workman who cast it died of joy . . ."

"Let's go," said Léon.

The old man started off again; then, having got back to the chapel of the Virgin, he waved his arm in a theatrical gesture of demonstration, and, prouder than a country squire showing his orchard, he announced:

"This simple stone covers Pierre de Brézé, lord of Varenne and of Brissac, grand marshal of Poitou, and governor of Normandy, who died at the battle of Montlhéry on the 16th of July, 1465."

Léon was furiously biting his lips of impatience.

"And on the right, this gentleman in full armour, on the prancing horse, is his grandson, Louis de Brézé, lord of Breval and of Montchauvet, Count de Maulevrier, Baron de Mauny, chamberlain to the king, Knight of the Order, and also governor of Normandy; he died on the 23rd of July, 1531—a Sunday, as the inscription specifies; and below, this figure, about to descend into the tomb, portrays the same person. How could one conceive of a better way to depict the void of human destiny?"

Madame Bovary lifted her eyeglass. Motionless, Léon watched her without even trying to protest, to make a gesture, so discouraged was he by this double display of idle talk and indifference.

Nothing could stop the guide:

"Near him, this kneeling woman who weeps is his spouse, Diane de Poitiers, comtesse de Brézé, duchesse de Valentinois, born in 1499, died in 1566, and to the left, the one with the child is the Holy Virgin. Now if you turn to this side, you will see the tombs of the Ambroise. They were both cardinals and archbishops of Rouen. That one was minister under Louis XII. He did a great deal for the cathedral. In his will he left thirty thousand gold crowns for the poor."

And without ceasing to talk, he pushed them into a chapel crowded with wooden railings; he pushed some aside and discovered a kind of wooden block that looked vaguely like a poorly carved statue.

"It seems hard to believe," he sighed sadly, "but this used to adorn the tomb of Richard Coeur de Lion, King of England and Duke of Normandy. It was the Calvinists, Monsieur, who reduced it to this condition. They were mean enough to bury it in the earth, under the episcopal throne of Monseigneur the bishop. You can see from here the door by which Monseigneur passes to his house. Let's move on to the gargoyle windows."

But Léon hastily extracted some silver coins from his pocket and seized Emma's arm. The verger stood dumbfounded, not able to understand this untimely munificence when there were still so many things for the stranger to see. He called after him:

"Monsieur! The steeple! the steeple!"

"No, thank you!" said Léon.

"You are missing the best! It is four hundred and forty feet high, nine less than the great pyramid of Egypt. It is all cast iron, it . . ."

Léon was fleeing, for it seemed to him that his love, that for nearly two hours had been frozen in the church like the stones, would now vanish like a vapor through that sort of truncated fun-nel, rectangular cage or open chimney that rises so grotesquely from the cathedral like the extravagant brainchild of some fantastic roofer.

"But where are we going?" she said.

He pushed on without answering, and Madame Bovary was already dipping her finger in the holy water when behind them they heard a panting breath interrupted by the regular sound of a tapping cane. Léon turned around.

"Monsieur!"

"What is it?"

And he recognised the verger, holding under his arms and bracing against his stomach some twenty large volumes, all of them works on the cathedral.

"Idiot!" muttered Léon, rushing out of the church.

A boy was playing on the sidewalk:

"Go and get me a cab!"

The child bounded off like a ball by the rue des Quatre-Vents; then they were alone a few minutes, face to face, and a little embarrassed.

"Oh Léon! Truly . . . I don't know . . . if I should . . ."

She simpered. Then, in a serious tone:

"It's very improper, you know, it isn't done."

"Everybody does it in Paris!" replied the clerk.

This, like a decisive argument, entirely convinced her. She had made up her mind.

But no cab arrived. Léon shuddered at the thought that she might return into the church. At last the cab appeared.

"At least, you should go out by the northern gate," cried the verger, who was left alone on the threshold, "and look at the Ressurection, the Last Judgment, Paradise, King David, and the damned burning in the flames of Hell!"

"Where to, sir?" asked the coachman.

"Anywhere!" said Léon, pushing Emma into the cab.

And the lumbering machine set out.

It went down the Rue Grand-Pont, crossed the Place des Arts, the Quai Napoleon, the Pont Neuf, and stopped short before the statue of Pierre Corneille.

"Go on," cried a voice that came from within.

The cab went on again, and as soon as it reached the Carrefour Lafayette, set off down-hill, and entered the railroad station at a gallop.

"No, straight on!" cried the same voice.

The cab came out by the gate, and soon having reached the Mall, trotted quietly beneath the elm-trees. The coachman wiped his brow, put his leather hat between his knees, and drove his carriage beyond the side alley by the meadow to the margin of the waters.

It went along by the river, along the towing-path paved with sharp pebbles, and for a long while in the direction of Oyssel, beyond the islands.

But suddenly it turned sideways across Quatremares, Sotteville, La Grande-Chaussée, the Rue d'Elbeuf, and made its third halt in front of the Jardin des Plantes.

"Get on, will you?" cried the voice more furiously.

And at once resuming its course, it passed by Saint Sever, by the Quai des Curandiers, the Quai aux Meules, once more over the bridge, by the Place du Champ de Mars, and behind the hospital gardens, where old men in black coats were walking in the sun along the ivy-covered terraces. It went up the Boulevard Bouvreuil, along the Boulevard Cauchoise, then the whole of Mont-Riboudet to the Deville hills.

It came back; and then, without any fixed plan or direction, wandered about at random. The cab was seen at Saint-Pol, at Lescure, at Mont Gargan, at La Rougue-Marc and Place du Gail-lardbois; in the Rue Maladrerie, Rue Dinanderie, before Saint-Romain, Saint-Vivien, Saint-Maclou, Saint-Nicaise—in front of the Customs, at the Basse-Vieille-Tour, the "Trois Pipes," and the Cimetière monumental. From time to time the coachman on his seat cast despairing glances at the passing cafés. He could not understand what furious locomotive urge prevented these people from ever coming to a stop. Time and again he would try, but exclamations of anger would at once burst forth behind him. Then he would whip his two sweating nags, but he no longer bothered dodging bumps in the road; the cab would hook on to things on all sides but he couldn't have cared less, demoralised as he was, almost weeping with thirst, fatigue and despair.

Near the harbor, among the trucks and the barrels, and along the street corners and the sidewalks, bourgeois stared in wonder at this thing unheard of in the provinces: a cab with all blinds drawn that reappeared incessantly, more tightly sealed than a tomb and tossed around like a ship on the waves.

One time, around noon, in the open country, just as the sun beat most fiercely against the old plated lanterns, a bare hand appeared under the yellow canvass curtain, and threw out some scraps of paper that scattered in the wind, alighting further off like white butterflies on a field of red clover all in bloom.

Then, at about six o'clock the carriage stopped in a back street of the Beauvoisine Quarter, and a woman got out, walking with her veil down and without looking back.

II

On reaching the inn, Madame Bovary was surprised not to see

the stage coach. Hivert had waited for her fifty-three minutes, but finally left without her.

Nothing forced her to go, but she had promised to return that same evening. Moreover, Charles expected her, and in her heart she felt already that cowardly docility that is for some women at once the chastisement and atonement of adultery.

She packed her bag quickly, paid her bill, took a cab in the yard, hurrying on the driver, urging him on, every moment inquiring about time and distance traversed. He succeeded in catching up with the Hirondelle as it neared the first houses of Quincampoix.

Hardly was she seated in her corner that she closed her eyes, and opened them at the foot of the hill, when from afar she recognised Félicité, who was on the look-out in front of the blacksmith's. Hivert pulled up his horses, and the maid, reaching up to the window, said in a tone of mystery:

"Madame, you must go at once to Monsieur Homais. It's for something urgent."

The village was silent as usual. At the corner of the streets little pink mounds lay smoking in the air, for this was the time for jam-making, and every one at Yonville prepared his supply on the same day. But in front of the pharmacist's shop one might admire a far larger heap; it surpassed the others with the superiority that a laboratory must have over domestic ovens, a general need over individual fancy.

She went in. The big arm chair had fallen over and even the "Fanal de Rouen" lay on the ground, outspread between two pestles. She pushed open the door of the hall, and in the middle of the kitchen, amid brown jars full of picked currants, powdered and lump sugar, scales on the table and pans on the fire, she saw assembled all the Homais, big and little, with aprons reaching to their chins, and holding forks in their hands. Justin was standing with bowed head, and the pharmacist was screaming:

"Who told you to go fetch it in the *Capharnaum?*"

"What is it? What is the matter?"

"What is it?" replied the pharmacist. "We are making jelly; it is cooking; but it threatens to boil over because there is too much juice, and I ask for another pan. Then this one here, out of laziness, goes to my laboratory, and dares to take the key to the capharnaum from the nail!"

This name had been given to a small room under the eaves, crammed with the tools and the goods of his trade. He often spent long hours there alone, labelling, decanting, and packaging. He looked upon it not as a simple store-room, but as a veritable sanctuary from where the creations of his own hands were to set forth: pills, lotions and potions that would spread far and wide his rising fame. No one in the world was allowed to set foot there, and he revered it to the point of sweeping it himself. If the pharmacy, open to all comers, was the stage where he displayed his pride, the Capharnaum was the refuge where in selfish concentration, Homais indulged in his most relished pursuits. Therefore, Justin's thoughtlessness seemed to him a monstrous piece of irreverence, and, his face redder than the currants, he continued:

"Yes, the key to the Capharnaum! The key that locks up the acids and caustic alkalis! To go and get a spare pan! a pan with a lid! and that I shall perhaps never use! Everything is of importance in the delicate operations of our art! One must maintain the proper distinctions, and not employ for nearly domestic purposes what is destined for pharmaceutical science! It is as if one were to carve a fowl with a scalpel; as if a magistrate . . ."

"Quiet down," Madame Homais was saying.

And Athalie, pulling at his coat, cried:

"Papa! papa!"

"No, leave me alone!" the pharmacist cried, "leave me alone! I tell you, I might as well be running a grocery store. Just keep at it, don't mind me and break everything to pieces! Smash the testtubes, let the leeches loose, burn the marshmallows, put pickles in the medical jars, tear up the bandages!"

"I thought you wanted to . . ."

"In a moment . . . Do you know what risks you took? Didn't you see something in the corner, on the left, on the third shelf? Speak! Answer me! Say something!"

"I . . . don't . . . know . . ." stammered the boy.

"Ah! you don't know! Well, *I* do! You saw a bottle of blue glass sealed with yellow wax, that contains a white powder carefully marked *Dangerous!* And do you know what is in it? Arsenic! And you go and touch it! You take a pan that stands right next to it!"

"Right next to it!" cried Madame Homais, clasping her hands. "Arsenic! You might have poisoned us all."

And the children began to scream as if they already felt dreadful stomach pains.

"Or poison a patient!" continued the pharmacist. "Do you want to see me dragged into court like a common criminal? or taken to the scaffold? As if you didn't know how careful one has to be in handling chemicals, even I who spent my life doing nothing else. Often I am horrified when I think of my responsibility; the Government persecutes us, and the absurd legislation that rules us is a veritable Damocles' sword suspended over our heads."

Emma gave up trying to find out what they wanted her for, and the pharmacist continued without pausing for breath:

"That is how you thank us for the many kindnesses we have shown you! That is how you reward me for the truly paternal care that I lavish on you! Where would you be if I hadn't taken you in hand? What would you be doing? Who provides you with food, education, clothes, and all the means to rise to a respectable level in society? But if you want to get there, you'll have to learn to pull hard at the oars—get callouses on your hands, as they saying goes. *Fabricando fit faber, age quod agis.*"

He was so exasperated he quoted Latin. He would have used Chinese or Greenlandic had he known them, for he was rocked by one of these crises in which the soul reveals all it contains, just as the storm lays bare the ocean from the seaweed on the shore down to the sand on its deepest bottom.

And he went on:

"I am beginning to regret that I ever took you in charge! I would have done a lot better if I'd let you wallow in poverty and filth, where you were born. The best you can hope for is to be a cowhand. You are not fit to be a scientist! You hardly know how to stick on a label! And there you are, dwelling with me snug as a parson, living in clover, taking your ease!"

Emma turned in despair to Madame Homais:

"I was told to come . . . "

"Heavens!" the lady exclaimed in a mournful tone "How am I to tell you? . . . Such a misfortune!"

She could not finish. The pharmacist was thundering:

"Empty it! Clean it! Take it back! And hurry!"

And seizing Justin by the collar of his apron, he shook him so vigorously that a book fell out of his pocket. The boy stooped, but Homais was the quicker, and, having picked up the volume, he stared at it with bulging eyes and open mouth.

"Conjugal . . . love!" he said, slowly separating the two words. "Ah! very good! very good! very pretty! And with illustrations! . . . Truly, this is too much!"

Madame Homais drew near.

"No, don't touch it!"

The children wanted to look at the pictures.

"Leave the room," he said imperiously.

They went out.

First he walked up and down, with the open book in his hand, rolling his eyes, choking, fuming, apoplectic. Then he came straight to his apprentice, and, planting himself in front of him with folded arms:

"So you are blessed with all the vices under the sun, you little wretch? Watch out! you are following a dangerous path! . . . Did it never occur to you that this infamous book might fall into the hands of my children, kindle a spark in their minds, tarnish the purity of Athalie, corrupt Napoleon! He is close to being a man. Are you quite sure, at least, that they have not read it? Can you certify to me . . ."

"But, Monsieur," said Emma, "you wished to tell me . . ."

"Oh yes, madame . . . you father-in-law is dead."

Indeed, the elder Bovary had suddenly died from a stroke the evening before, as he got up from the table; overanxious to spare Emma's sensitive nerves, Charles had asked Monsieur Homais to break the horrible news to her as carefully as possible.

Homais had meditated at length over his speech; he had rounded, polished it, given it the proper cadence; it was a master-piece of prudence and transitions, of subtle turns and delicacy; but anger had got the better of rhetoric.

Emma, abandoning all hope to learn any further details, left the pharmacy; for Monsieur Homais had resumed his vituperations. He was growing calmer, however, and was now grumbling in a paternal tone whilst he fanned himself with his skull-cap.

"It is not that I entirely disapprove of the book. The author was a doctor! It contains scientific information that a man might well want to know; I'd go as far as saying that he ought to know. But later . . . later! You should at least wait till you are yourself full-grown, and your character formed.

When Emma knocked at the door, Charles, who was waiting for her, came forward with open arms and said in a tearful voice:

"Ah! my dear wife. . . ."

And he leant over gently to kiss her. But at the contact of his lips the memory of the other returned; she passed her hand over her face and shuddered.

Yet, she answered:

"Yes, I know . . . I know . . ."

He showed her the letter in which his mother told the event without any sentimental hypocrisy. Her only regret was that her husband had not received the consolation of religion; he had died at Doudeville, in the street, at the door of a café after a patriotic dinner with some ex-officers.

Emma gave him back the letter; then at dinner, for appearance's sake, she affected a lack of appetite. But as he urged her to try, she resolutely began eating, while Charles opposite her sat motionless and dejected.

Now and then he raised his head and gave her a long, distressed look. Once he sighed:

"I'd have liked to see him again!"

She was silent. At last, realizing that she must say something:

"How old was your father?" she asked.

"Fifty-eight."

"Ah!"

And that was all.

A quarter of an hour later, he added: "My poor mother! what will become of her now?"

She made a gesture of ignorance.

Seeing her so taciturn, Charles imagined her much affected, and forced himself to say nothing, not to reawaken this sorrow which moved him. And, shaking off his own:

"Did you enjoy yourself yesterday?" he asked.

"Yes."

When the cloth was removed, Bovary did not rise, nor did Emma; and as she looked at him, the monotony of the spectacle drove little by little all pity from her heart. He seemed to her paltry, weak, a nonentity—a sorry creature in every way. How to get rid of him? What an interminable evening! She felt a stupor invading her, as if from opium fumes.

They heard the sharp noise of a wooden leg on the boards of the entrance hall. It was Hippolyte bringing back Emma's luggage.

To put them down, he had to bring around his wooden stump painfully in a quarter circle.

"He doesn't even seem to remember" she thought, looking at the poor devil, whose coarse red hair was wet with perspiration.

Bovary was searching for a coin at the bottom of his purse; he did not seem to realize how humiliating the man's presence was for him, standing there as the living embodiment of his hopeless ineptitude.

"Oh, you have a pretty bouquet," he said, noticing Léon's violets on the mantlepiece.

"Yes," she replied indifferently; "it's a bouquet I bought just now . . . from a beggar-woman."

Charles picked up the flowers and, bathing his tear-stained eyes in their freshness, he delicately sniffed their perfume. She took them quickly from his hand and put them in a glass of water.

The next day the elder Madame Bovary arrived. She and her son spent much time weeping. Pretending to be busy in the house, Emma managed to stay by herself.

The following day, they had to discuss together the arrangements for the period of mourning. They went and sat down with their workboxes by the waterside under the arbor.

Charles was thinking of his father, and was surprised to feel so much affection for this man, whom up till now he thought he cared little about. The older Madame Bovary was thinking of her husband. The worst days of the past seemed enviable to her. All was forgotten beneath the instinctive regret of such a long habit, and from time to time, while sewing, a big tear rolled down her nose and hung suspened there a moment.

Emma was thinking that it was scarcely forty-eight hours since they had been together, far from the world, lost in ecstasy, and not having eyes enough to gaze upon each other. She tried to recall the slightest details of that past day. But the presence of her husband and mother-in-law bothered her. She would have liked to stop hearing and seeing, in order to keep intact the stillness of her love; but, try as she would, the memory would vanish under the impact of outer sensations.

She was removing the lining of a dress, and the strips were scattered around her. Mother Bovary, without looking up, kept her scissors busy, and Charles, in his felt slippers and his old brown coat that he used as a dressing gown, sat in silence with both hands in his pockets; near them Berthe, in a little white apron, was raking the sandwalks with her spade.

Suddenly they saw Monsieur Lheureux, the storekeeper, come in through the gate.

He came to offer his services "on this sad occasion." Emma replied that none were needed, but the shopkeeper wouldn't take no for an answer.

"I beg your pardon," he said, "but I should like to have a word in private."

Then, in a low voice, he added:

"It is about this little matter . . . you know . . ." Charles turned crimson.

"Oh yes . . . of course."

And, in his confusion, he turned to his wife:

"Darling, could you perhaps . . . ?"

She seemed to understand him, for she rose; and Charles said to his mother:

"Nothing important. Some household trifle, I suppose."

Fearing her reproaches, he didn't want her to know about the note.

As soon as they were alone, Monsieur Lheureux began by congratulating Emma outspokenly on the inheritance, then talked of this and that, the fruit trees, the harvest, his own health which had endless ups and downs. He had to work like a devil and, regardless of what people thought, didn't make enough to buy butter for his bread.

Emma let him talk. She had been so dreadfully bored, these last two days!

"And so you're quite well again?" he went on. "Believe me, your husband was in quite a state. He's a good fellow, though we did have a little misunderstanding."

She asked what the misunderstanding was about, for Charles had told her nothing of the dispute about the goods supplied to her.

"As if you didn't know!" exclaimed Lheureux. "It was about your little caprice . . . the trunks."

He had drawn his hat over his eyes, and, with his hands behind his back, smiling and whistling, he looked straight at her in an unbearable manner. Did he suspect anything? She was lost in all kinds of apprehensions. Finally he said:

"We made it up, and I've come to propose still another arrangement."

He offered to renew the note Bovary had signed. The doctor, of course, would do as he pleased; he was not to trouble himself, especially just now, when he would have a lot to attend to.

"It seems to me he'd do well to turn it all over to some one else, —to you for example. With a power of attorney it could be easily managed, and then the two of us could have our little business transactions together . . ."

She did not understand. He did not insist, and brought the conversation back to his trade; it was impossible that Madame didn't need anything. He would send her a black barège, twelve yards, just enough to make a dress.

"The one you've on is good enough for the house, but you want another for calls. I saw that the very moment that I came in. I've got a quick eye for these things!"

He did not send the material, he brought it. Then he came again to take her measurements; he came again on other pretexts, always trying to make himself agreeable, useful, like a vassal serving his master, as Homais might have put it, and never failing to drop a hint about the power of attorney. He never mentioned the note. She didn't think of it; although Charles doubtlessly had mentioned something at the beginning of her convalescence, so many emotions had passed through her head that she no longer remembered it. Besides, she made it a point never to bring up any money questions. Charles' mother seemed surprised at this, and attributed the change in her ways to the religious sentiments she had contracted during her illness.

But as soon as she left, Emma greatly astounded Bovary by her practical good sense. They would have to make inquiries, look into the mortgages, decide whether it would be more advantageous to sell by auction or by other means.

She quoted legal jargon at random, and grand words such as "order", "the future", "foresight". She constantly exaggerated the difficulties of settling his father's affairs; at last, one day she showed him the rough draft of a power of attorney to manage and administer his business, arrange all notes, sign and endorse all bills, pay all sums, etc. She had profited by Lheureux's lessons.

Charles naively asked her where this paper came from.

"From Master Guillaumin."

And with the utmost coolness she added:

"I don't trust him overmuch. Notaries have such a bad reputation. Perhaps we ought to consult . . . But the only person we know . . . There is no one."

"Unless perhaps Léon . . ." replied Charles, who was thinking.

But it was difficult to explain matters by letter. Then she offered to make the journey. He refused. She insisted. It was quite a contest of mutual consideration. At last she exclaimed, in a childish tone of mock-rebellion:

"No, enough, I will!"

"How good you are!" he said, kissing her on the forehead.

The next morning she set out in the "Hirondelle" for Rouen to consult Monsieur Léon, and she stayed there three days.

III

They were three full, exquisite, magnificent days—a true honeymoon. They stayed at the Hôtel-de-Boulogne, on the harbor; and they lived there behind drawn blinds and closed doors, with flowers on the floor, and iced fruit syrups that were brought them early in the morning.

Towards evening they took a covered boat and went to dine on one of the islands.

At this time of the day, one could hear the caulking irons sound against the hulls in the dockyard. Tar smoke rose up between the trees and large oily patches floated on the water, undulating unevenly in the purple sunlight like surfaces of Florentine bronze.

They drifted down among moored ships whose long slanting cables grazed lightly the top of their boat.

The sounds of the city gradually fainted in the distance, the rattling of carriages, the tumult of voices, the yelping of dogs on the decks of barges. She loosened her hat and they landed on their island.

They sat down in the low-ceilinged room of a tavern with black fishing-nets hanging across the door. They ate fried smelts, cream and cherries. They lay down upon the grass, kissed behind the poplar trees; like two Robinson Crusoes, they would gladly have lived forever in this spot; in their bliss, it seemed to them the most magnificent place on earth. It was not the first time that they had seen trees, a blue sky, meadows; or heard the water flow and the wind blow in the branches. But they had never really felt any of this; it was as if nature had not existed before, or had only begun to be beautiful since the gratification of their desires.

At nightfall they returned. The boat glided along the shores of the islands. They stayed below, hidden in darkness, without saying a word. The square-tipped oars sounded against the iron oar-locks; in the stillness, they seemed to mark time like the beat of a metronome, while the rope that trailed behind never ceased its gentle splash against the water.

One night the moon rose, and they did not fail to make fine phrases about how melancholical and poetic it appeared to them. She even began to sing:

> One night, do you remember,
> We were sailing . . .

Her thin musical voice died away over the water; Léon could hear the wind-borne trills pass by him like a fluttering of wings.

She faced him, leaning against the wall of the cabin while the moon shone through the open blinds. Her black dress, falling around her like a fan, made her seem more slender, taller. Her head was raised, her hands clapsed, her eyes turned towards heaven. At times the shadow of the willows hid her completely; then she reappeared suddenly, like a vision in the moonlight.

Léon, on the floor by her side, found under his hand a ribbon of scarlet silk.

The boatman looked at it, and said at last:

"Perhaps it belongs to the party I took out the other day. They were a jolly bunch of ladies and gentlemen, with cakes, champagne, trumpets—everything in style! There was one especially, a tall handsome man with small moustaches, who was the life of the party. They kept asking him 'Come on, Adolphe—or Dodolphe, or something like that—tell us a story . . .'"

She shuddered.

"Don't you feel well?" Léon inquired, coming closer.

"Oh, it's nothing! Just a chill from the cold night air."

"He's another one who seems to have no trouble finding women," the old sailor added softly, intending to pay Léon a compliment.

Then, spitting on his hands, he took the oars again.

Yet the time to part had come. The farewells were sad. He was to send his letters to Mère Rollet, and she gave him such precise instructions about a double envelope that he was much impressed with her shrewdness in love matters.

"So you can guarantee me that everything is in order?" she said with her last kiss.

"Yes, certainly."

"But why," he thought afterwards as he came back through the streets alone, "is she so very anxious to get this power of attorney?"

IV

Léon soon put on superior airs with his friends, avoided their company, and completely neglected his work.

He waited for her letters, read and re-read them. He wrote to her. He called her to mind with all the strength of his desires and of his memories. Instead of lessening with absence, his longing to see her kept growing to the point where, one Saturday morning he escaped from his office.

When, from the summit of the hill, he saw in the valley below the church-spire with its metal flag swinging in the wind, he felt that delight mingled with triumphant vanity and selfish benevolence that millionaires must experience when they come back to their native village.

He went prowling around round her house. A light was burning in the kitchen. He watched for her shadow behind the curtains, but nothing appeared.

Mére Lefrançois, on seeing him, uttered many exclamations. She thought he had grown taller and thinner, while Artémise, on the contrary, thought him stouter and darker.

He ate in the little dining-room, as in the past, but alone, without the tax collector; for Binet, tired of waiting for the "Hirondelle," had definitely moved his meal an hour earlier. Now he dined punctually at five, which didn't keep him from complaining that the rickety old carriage was late.

Léon finally made up his mind, and knocked at the doctor's door. Madame was in her room, and did not come down for a quarter of an hour. The doctor seemed delighted to see him, but he never left the house that evening, nor the next day.

He saw her alone in the evening, very late, behind the garden in the lane;—in the lane, as with the other one! It was a stormy night, and they talked under an umbrella by lightning flashes.

They couldn't bear the thought of parting.

"I'd rather die!" said Emma.

She seized his arm convulsively, and wept.

"Good bye! When shall I see you again?"

They came back again to embrace once more, and it was then that she promised him to find soon, no matter how, some assured way of meeting in freedom at least once a week. Emma was certain to find a way. She was generally in a hopeful frame of mind: the inheritance money was bound to come in soon.

On the strength of it she bought a pair of yellow curtains with large stripes for her room; Monsieur Lheureux had recommended them as a particularly good buy. She dreamt of getting a carpet, and Lheureux, declaring that it wasn't that much of an investment after all, politely undertook to supply her with one. She could no longer do without his services. Twenty times a day she sent for him, and he at once interrupted whatever he was doing, without a murmur. Neither could people understand why Mére Rollet ate at her house every day, and even paid her private visits.

It was about this time, in the early part of the Winter, that a sudden urge to make music seemed to come over her.

One evening when Charles was listening to her, she began the same piece four times over, each time with much vexation, while he, totally oblivious to her mistakes, exclaimed:

"Bravo! . . . Very good! . . . Don't stop. Keep going!"

"Oh, no. It's awful! My fingers are much too rusty!"

The next day he begged her to play for him again.

"Very well, if you wish."

And Charles had to confess that she had slipped a little. She played wrong notes and blundered; then, stopping short:

"Ah! it's no use. I ought to take some lessons, but . . ."

Biting her lip, she added:

"Twenty francs a lesson, that's too expensive!"

"Maybe it is . . . a little," said Charles with a stupid giggle. "But it seems to me that one might be able to do it for less; for there are artists of little reputation, who are often better than the celebrities."

"Find them!" said Emma.

The next day on coming home, he gave her a sly look, and finally could no longer repress what he had to say:

"How stubborn you can be at times! I went to Barfuchéres to-day. Well, Madame Liégard assured me that her three daughters, who go to school at Miséricorde, take lessons at fifty sous apiece, and that from an excellent teacher!"

She shrugged her shoulders and did not open her piano again.

But whenever she passed in front of it (provided Bovary was present), she sighed:

"Ah! my poor piano!"

And whenever someone came to call, she did not fail to inform them that she had given up music, and could not begin again now for important reasons. People would commiserate. What a pity! She had so much talent! They even spoke to Bovary about it. They put him to shame, especially the pharmacist.

"You are wrong. One should never let any natural faculties lie fallow. Besides, just think, my good friend, that by inducing madame to study, you are economising on the subsequent musical education of your child. For my own part, I think that mothers ought themselves to instruct their children. It's an idea of Rousseau's, still rather new perhaps, but bound to win out sooner or later, like vaccination and breast-feeding."

So Charles returned once more to this question of the piano. Emma replied bitterly that it would be better to sell it. Poor piano!

it had given his vanity so many satisfactions that to see it go was for Bovary, in an undefinable manner, like Emma's partial suicide.

"If you really want it . . ." he said, "a lesson from time to time wouldn't ruin us after all."

"But lessons," she replied, "are only of use if one persists."

And this is how she managed to obtain her husband's permission to go to town once a week to see her lover. At the end of a month she was even considered to have made considerable progress.

V

She went on Thursdays. She got up and dressed silently, in order not to awaken Charles, who would have reproached her for getting ready too early. Then she walked up and down, stood at the windows, and looked out over the Square. The early dawn was broadening between the pillars of the market, and the pharmacy, still boarded up, showed in the pale light of the dawn the large letters of the signboard.

When the clock pointed to a quarter past seven, she went to the "Lion d'Or," where a yawning Artémise unlocked the door for her. She would poke the fire in Madame's honor, and Emma remained alone in the kitchen. Now and again she went out. Hivert was leisurely harnessing his horses while listening to the Mére Lefrançois who, sticking her head and night cap through a window, was instructing him on his errands and giving him explanations that would have bewildered any one else. Emma tapped her boots on the cobblestones of the yard.

At last, when he had eaten his soup, put on his cloak, lighted his pipe, and grasped his whip, he calmly took his place on the seat.

The "Hirondelle" started at a slow trot, and for about a mile stopped time and again to pick up waiting passengers along the roadside, before their house-gates. Those who had booked seats the night before kept it waiting; some even were still in bed in their houses. Hivert called, shouted, swore; then he got down from his seat and knocked loudly at the doors. The wind blew through the cracked windows.

Gradually, the four benches filled up. The carriage rolled off; rows of apple-trees followed one upon another, and the road between its two long ditches, full of yellow water, rose, constantly narrowing towards the horizon.

Emma knew every inch of the road: after a certain meadow there was a sign post, then a barn or roadmender's hut. Sometimes, in hope of being surprised, she would close her eyes, but she never lost a clear sense of the distance still to be covered.

At last the brick houses began to follow one another more closely, the earth resounded beneath the wheels, the "Hirondelle" glided between the gardens, revealing through an occasional opening, statues, a summer pavillion, trimmed yew trees, a swing. Then all at once, the city came into sight.

Sloping down like an amphitheatre, and drowned in the fog, it overflowed unevenly beyond its bridges. Then the open country mounted again in a monotonous sweep until it touched in the distance the elusive line of the pale sky. Seen thus from above, the whole landscape seemed frozen, like a picture; the anchored ships were massed in one corner, the river curved round the foot of the green hills, and the oblong islands looked like giant fishes lying motionless on the water. The factory chimneys belched forth immense plumes of brown smoke, their tips carried off in the wind. One heard the rumbling of the foundries, mingled with the clear chimes of the churches, dimly outlined in the fog. The leafless trees on the boulevards seemed violet thickets in the midst of the houses, and the roofs, shining from the rain, threw back unequal reflections, according to the heights of the various districts. From time to time a gust of wind would drive the clouds towards the slopes of Saint Catherine, like aerial waves breaking silently against a cliff.

Something seemed to emanate from this mass of human lives that left her dizzy; her heart swelled as though the hundred and twenty thousand souls palpitating there had all at once wafted to her the passions with which her imagination had endowed them. Her love grew in the presence of this vastness, and filled with the tumult of the vague murmuring which rose from below. She poured it out, onto the squares, the avenues, the streets; and the old Norman city spread out before her like some incredible capital, a Babylon into which she was about to enter. She lifted the window with both hands to lean out, drinking in the breeze; the three horses galloped, the stones grated in the mud, the diligence rocked, and Hivert, from afar, hailed the carts on the road, while the well-to-do residents of Bois Guillaume sedately descended the hill to town in their little family carriages.

The coach made a stop at the city gates; Emma undid her overshoes, put on other gloves, rearranged her shawl, and some twenty paces farther she descended from the "Hirondelle."

The town was beginning to awake. Shop-boys in caps were polishing the front windows of the stores, and women, with baskets balanced on their hips, would stand on the street corners calling out from time to time some sonorous cry. She walked with downcast eyes, close to the walls, and smiling with pleasure beneath her lowered black veil.

For fear of being seen, she did not usually take the most direct road. She would plunge into dark alleys, and emerge, all in a sweat, near the little fountain at the beginning of the Rue Nationale. This was the quarter of the theaters, cabarets, and prostitutes. Often, a cart loaded with shaking scenery passed close by her. Waiters in aprons were sprinkling sand on the flagstones between green shrubs. There was a smell of absinthe, cigars and oysters.

She turned a corner; she recognised him by his curling hair that escaped from beneath his hat.

Léon kept on walking ahead of her along the sidewalk. She followed him into the hotel. He went up, opened the door, entered — What an embrace!

Then, after the kisses, the words rushed forth. They told each other the sorrows of the week, the forebodings, the anxiety for the letters; but now everything was forgotten; they gazed at each other with voluptuous laughs, and tender names.

The bed was a large one, made of mahogany and shaped like a boat. The red silk curtains which hung from the ceiling, were gathered together too low, close to the lyre-shaped headboards;—and nothing in the world was so lovely as her brown hair and white skin set off against that deep crimson color, when with a gesture of modesty, she closed her arms and hid her face in her hands.

The warm room, with its subdued carpet, its frivolous ornaments and its soft light, seemed made for the intimacies of passion. The curtain-rods, ending in arrows, the brass pegs and the great balls of the andirons would suddenly light up if a ray of sunlight entered. On the chimney, between the candelabra there were two of those pink shells in which one hears the murmur of the sea when one holds them against one's ear.

How they loved that room, so full of gaiety, despite its somewhat faded splendour! They always found the furniture arranged the same way, and sometimes hairpins, that she had forgotten the Thursday before, under the pedestal of the clock. They lunched by the fireside on a little round table, inlaid with rosewood. Emma carved, put bits on his plate while playing all sorts of coquettish tricks; she would laugh a ringing libertine laugh when the froth from the champagne overflowed the fragile glass onto the rings of her fingers. They were so completely lost in the possession of each other that they thought themselves in their own house, that they would go on living there until separated by death, like an eternally young married couple. They said "our room," "our carpet," she even said "my slippers," referring to the gift Léon had bought to satisfy a whim of hers. They were rose-colored satin, bordered with swansdown. When she sat on his lap, her leg, which was then too short, hung in the air, and the dainty shoe having no back, was held on only by the toes of her bare foot.

He savoured for the first time the inexpressible delights of feminine refinement. He had never encountered this grace of language, this direction in dress, these poses of a weary dove. He admired the exaltation of her soul and the lace on her petticoat. Besides, was she not a "woman of the world", and a married woman! in short a real mistress!

According to her changing moods, in turn meditative and gay, talkative and silent, passionate and langorous, she awakened in him a thousand desires, called up instincts or memories. She was the mistress of all the novels, the heroine of all the dramas, the vague "she" of all the volumes of verse. On her shoulders, he rediscovered the amber color of the "Odalisque au Bain";[2] her waist was long like the feudal chatelaines; she resembled Musset's "Femme Pâle de Barcelone".[3] Above all, she was his Angel.

It often seemed to him that his soul, fleeing toward her, broke like a wave against the contours of her head, and was drawn irrisistibly down into the whiteness of her breast.

He knelt on the ground before her; and resting his elbows on her lap, he would gaze at her smilingly, his face uplifted.

She bent over him, and murmured, as if choking with intoxication:

"Oh! don't move! don't speak! Look at me! There is something so tender that comes from your eyes. It does me so much good!"

She called him child.

"Do you love me, child?"

And she never heard his reply, his lips always rose so fast to find her mouth.

There was a little bronze cupid on the clock, who simpered as he held up his arms under a golden garland. They had laughed at it many a time, but when they had to part everything seemed serious.

Motionless, they looked at each other and kept repeating:

"Till Thursday! . . . Till Thursday! . . ."

Suddenly she would take his head between her hands and kiss him quickly on the forehead while crying "Adieu" and rush down the stairs.

She went next to a hairdresser in the Rue de la Comédie to have her hair arranged. Night would be falling; they lit the gas in the shop.

She heard the bell in the theatre calling the actors to the performance; and she saw white-faced men and women in faded dresses pass by on the other side of the street and enter in at the stage door.

It was hot in the little low-ceilinged room with its stove humming amidst the wigs and pommades. The smell of the tongs together with the oily hands that were manipulating her hair, would soon stupefy her and she would begin to doze a bit in her dressing gown.

2. Famous painting by Jean Auguste Dominique Ingres.
3. Alfred de Musset frequently incar-nates, for Flaubert, the type of stilted romantic sentimentality he despises.

Often, as he did her hair, the man offered her tickets for a masked ball.

Then she left! She remounted the streets; reached the Croix Rouge, retrieved her overshoes which she had hidden under the bench that morning, and settled into her place among the impatient passengers. The other passengers got out at the foot of the hill in order to spare the horses. She remained alone in the carriage.

At every turn, they could see more and more of the city below, forming a luminous mist above the mass of houses. Emma knelt on the cushions, and let her eyes wander over the dazzling light. She sobbed, called to Léon, sent him tender words and kisses which were lost in the wind.

There was a wretched creature on the hillside, who would wander about with his stick right in the midst of the carriages. A mass of rags covered his shoulders, and an old staved-in beaver hat, shaped like a basin, hid his face; but when he took it off he revealed two gaping bloody orbits in the place of eyelids. The flesh hung in red strips; and from them flowed a liquid which congealed into green scales reaching down to his nose with its black nostrils, which kept sniffing convulsively. To speak to you he threw back his head with an idiotic laugh;—then his blueish eyeballs, rolling round and round, would rub against the open wound near the temples.

He sang a little song as he followed the carriages:

> Often the warmth of a summer day
> Makes a young girl dream her heart away.

And all the rest was about birds and sunshine and green leaves.

Sometimes he would appear behind Emma, his head bare. She would draw back with a cry. Hivert liked to tease him. He would advise him to get a booth at the Saint Romain fair, or else ask him, laughing, how his girl friend was.

Often the coach was already in motion when his hat would be thrust violently in at the window, while he clung with his other arm to the footboard, between the spattering of the wheels. His voice, at first weak and quavering, would grow sharp. It lingered into the night like an inarticulate lament of some vague despair; and, heard through the jingling of the horses' bells, the murmuring of the trees, and the rumble of the empty coach, it had something so distant and sad that it filled Emma with dread. It went to the very depths of her soul, like a whirlwind in an abyss, and carried her away to a boundless realm of melancholy. But Hivert, noticing a weight behind, would lash out savagely at the blind man with his whip. The thong lashed his wounds and he fell back into the mud with a shriek.

The passengers in the Hirondelle would all finally drop off to sleep, some with their mouths open, others their chins pressed against their chests, leaning on their neighbor's shoulder, or with their arm passed through the strap, all the time swaying regularly with the jolting of the carriage; and the sight of the lantern, that was swinging back and forth outside and reflecting on the rumps of the shaft horses, penetrated into the coach through the chocolate-colored curtains, throwing blood-red shadows over all those motionless beings within. Emma, drunk with grief, shivered under her coat and felt her feet grow colder and colder, with death in her soul.

Charles at home would be waiting for her; the "Hirondelle" was always late on Thursdays. Madame arrived at last! She scarcely kissed the child. The dinner was not ready, no matter! She excused the cook. The girl now seemed allowed to do just as she liked.

Often her husband, noting her pallor, asked if she were unwell.

"No," said Emma.

"But," he replied, "you seem so strange this evening."

"Oh, it's nothing! nothing!"

There were even days when she had no sooner come in than she went up to her room; and Justin, who would happen to be there, moved about noiselessly, more adroit at helping her than the best of maids. He put the matches ready, the candlestick, a book, arranged her nightgown, turned back the bedclothes.

"All right," she'd say "that's fine, get going!"

For he stood there, his hands hanging down and his eyes wide open, as if enmeshed in the innumerable threads of a sudden reverie.

The following day was frightful, and those that came after still more unbearable, because of her impatience to once again seize her happiness,—this fierce lust, enflamed by recent memories, which on the seventh day would erupt freely within Léon's embraces. His own passion was manifested by continual expressions of wonder and gratitude. Emma tasted this love discretely, and with all her being, nourished it by every tender device she knew, and trembled a little that some day it might be lost.

She often said to him, with a sweet melancholy in her voice:

"Ah! you too, you will leave me! You will marry! You will be like all the others."

He asked:

"What others?"

"Why, like all men," she replied.

Then added, repulsing him with a languid movement:

"You are all of you wretches!"

One day, as they were talking philosophically of earthly disillusions she happened to mention (in order to provoke his jealousy, or perhaps through some irrisistible urge to confide in him) that in the past, before she knew him, she had loved someone else. "Not like you," she went on quickly, swearing on the head of her child "that nothing had happened."

The young man believed her, but none the less questioned her to find out what kind of a man *He* was.

"He was a ship's captain, my dear."

Was this not preventing any inquiry, and, at the same time, assuming a higher ground because of the aura of fascination which is supposed to surround a man who must have been of warlike nature and accustomed to receive homage?

The clerk then felt the lowliness of his position; he longed for epaulettes, crosses, titles. These things would please her; he suspected as much from her extravagant habits.

However, Emma never mentioned a number of her most extravagant ideas, such as her desire to have a blue tilbury to drive into Rouen, drawn by an English horse and driven by a groom in turned down boots. It was Justin who had inspired her with this whim, by begging her to take him into service as footman; and if the privation of it did not lessen the pleasure of her arrival at each of their weekly rendez-vous, it certainly augmented the bitterness of the return.

Often, when they were talking together of Paris, she would end by murmuring,

"Ah, how happy we could be living there."

"Are we not happy?" the young man would gently ask, passing his hands over her hair.

"Yes, that is true," she said. "I am mad: kiss me!"

To her husband she was more charming than ever. She made him pistachio-creams and played him waltzes after dinner. He thought himself the most fortunate of men, and Emma was without uneasiness, when, suddenly one evening:

"It is Mademoiselle Lempereur, isn't it, who gives you lessons?"

"Yes."

"Well, I saw her just now," Charles went on, "at Madame Liégard's. I spoke to her about you; and she doesn't know you."

This was like a thunderbolt. However, she replied quite naturally:

"She must have forgotten my name."

"But perhaps," said the doctor, "there are several Demoiselles Lempereur at Rouen who are music teachers."

"Possibly!"

Then she added quickly:

"Nevertheless, I have her receipts, here! Look."

And she went to the writing-table, ransacked all the drawers, mixed up the papers, and at last lost her head so completely that Charles earnestly begged her not to take so much trouble about those wretched receipts.

"Oh! I will find them," she said.

And, in fact, on the following Friday, as Charles was putting on one of his boots in the dark closet where his clothes were kept, he felt a piece of paper between the leather and his sock. He took it out and read:

"Received, for three months' lessons and several pieces of music, the sum of sixty-three francs.—FELICIE LEMPEREUR, professor of music."

"How the devil did it get into my boots?"

"It must," she replied, "have fallen from the old box of bills that is on the edge of the shelf."

From that moment on, her existence was one long tissue of lies, in which she wrapped her love as under a veil in order to hide it. It became a need, an obsession, a delight, to such a point that, if she claimed to have walked on the right side of the street the previous day, one could be sure she had walked on the left.

One morning, when she had gone, as usual, rather lightly clothed, it suddenly began to snow, and as Charles was watching the weather from the window, he caught sight of Monsieur Bournisien in the chaise of Monsieur Tuvache, who was driving him to Rouen. Then he went down to give the priest a thick shawl that he was to hand over to Emma as soon as he reached the Croix-Rouge. When he got to the inn, Monsieur Bournisien asked for the wife of the Yonville doctor. The landlady replied that she very rarely came to her establishment. So that evening, when he recognised Madame Bovary in the "Hirondelle," the curé told her his dilemma, without, however, appearing to attach much importance to it, for he began praising a preacher who was doing wonders at the Cathedral, and whom all the ladies were rushing to hear.

Still, even if he had not asked for any explanations, others, later on, might prove less discreet. So she thought it would be a good idea to get out of the coach at the Croix Rouge each time she came so that the good folk of her village seeing her on the stairs would not become suspicious.

One day, however, Monsieur Lheureux met her coming out of the Hôtel de Boulogne on Léon's arm; and she was frightened, thinking he would gossip. He was not such a fool.

But three days after he came to her room, shut the door, and said:

"I must have some money."

She declared she could not give him any. Lheureux began to moan, reminding her of all the favors he had done her.

In fact, of the two bills signed by Charles, Emma up to the present had paid only one. As to the second, the shopkeeper, at her request, had consented to replace it by another, which again had been renewed for a long date. Then he drew from his pocket a list of goods not paid for; to wit, the curtains, the carpet, the material for the arm-chairs, several dresses, and diverse articles of dress, totalling in all a sum of about two thousand francs.

She hung her head; he continued:

"But if you haven't any ready money, you do have some property."

And he called to her attention a miserable little shack situated at Barneville, near Aumale, that brought in almost nothing. It had formerly been part of a small farm sold by Monsieur Bovary senior; for Lheureux knew everything, even down to the number of acres and the names of the neighbors.

"If I were in your place," he said, "I'd get it off my hands, and have some money left over."

She pointed out the difficulty of finding a buyer; he said he thought he could find one; but she asked him how she should manage to sell it.

"Haven't you your power of attorney?" he replied.

The phrase came to her like a breath of fresh air. "Leave me the bill," said Emma.

"Oh, it isn't worth while," answered Lheureux.

He came back the following week boasting that after having gone to a great deal of trouble, he had finally tracked down a certain man named Langlois, who had had his eye on the property for a long time but had never mentioned a price.

"Never mind the price!" she cried.

On the contrary, he said, they must take their time and sound the fellow out. The affair was certainly worth the trouble of a trip, and, as she could not undertake it, he offered to go to the place and bargain with Langlois. On his return he announced that the purchaser proposed four thousand francs.

Emma's heart rose at this news.

"Frankly," he added, "that's a good price."

She drew half the sum at once, and when she was about to pay her account the shopkeeper said:

"It grieves me, it really does, to see you give up such a considerable sum of money as that all at once." She stared at the bank notes and began to dream of the countless rendez-vous with Léon that those two thousand francs represented.

"What! What do you mean!" she stammered.

"Oh!" he went on, laughing good-naturedly, "one puts anything one likes on receipts. Don't you think I know what household affairs are?"

And he looked at her fixedly, while in his hand he held two long papers which he kept sliding between his nails. At last, opening his billfold, he spread out on the table four bills to order, each for a thousand francs.

"Sign these," he said, "and keep it all!"

She cried out, scandalised.

"But if I give you the balance," replied Monsieur Lheureux impudently, "isn't that doing you a service?"

And taking a pen he wrote at the bottom of the account, "Received from Madame Bovary four thousand francs."

"What is there to worry about, since in six months you'll draw the arrears for your cottage, and I don't make the last bill due till after you've been paid?"

Emma was becoming somewhat confused in her calculations and her ears rang as though gold pieces were bursting out of their bags and tinkling onto the floor all around her. At last Lheureux explained that he had a very good friend named Vinçart, a banker in Rouen, who would discount these four bills. Then he himself would hand over to madame the remainder after the actual debt was paid.

But instead of two thousand francs he brought her only eighteen hundred, for his friend Vinçart (which was "only fair") had deducted two hundred francs for commission and discount.

Then he carelessly asked for a receipt.

"You understand . . . in business . . . sometimes . . . And with the date, please don't forget the date."

A whole horizon of new possibilities now opened up before Emma. She was wise enough to set aside three thousand francs, with which the first three bills were paid when they fell due; but the fourth happened to arrive at the house on a Thursday, and a stunned Charles patiently awaited his wife's return for an explanation.

If she had not told him about this note, it was only to spare him such domestic worries; she sat on his lap, caressed him, cooed at him, gave a long enumeration of all the indispensable things that had been got on credit.

"Really, you must confess, considering the number of things, it isn't too expensive."

Charles, at his wit's end, soon had recourse to the eternal Lheureux, who promised to arrange everything if Charles would sign two more notes, one of which was for seven hundred francs and would be payable in three months. To take care of this he wrote his mother a pathetic letter. Instead of sending a reply she came herself; and when Emma wanted to know whether he had got anything out of her:

"Yes," he replied; "but she wants to see the account."

The next morning at daybreak Emma ran to Lheureux to beg him to make out another account for not more than a thousand francs: for to show the one for four thousand it would be necessary to say that she had paid two-thirds, and confess, consequently, the sale of the property, for the transaction had been well handled by the shopkeeper and only came to light later on.

Despite the low price of each article, Madame Bovary senior of course thought the expenditure extravagant.

"Couldn't you do without a carpet? Why did you re-cover the arm-chairs? In my time there was a single arm-chair in a house, for elderly persons,—at any rate it was so at my mother's, who was a respectable woman, I assure you.—Everybody can't be rich! No fortune can hold out against waste! I should be ashamed to pamper myself as you do! And yet I am old. I need looking after . . . and look at this! Look at this! alterations! frills and finery! What is that! silk for lining at two francs; . . . when you get jaconet for ten sous, or even for eight which does just as well!"

Emma lying on a lounge, replied as calmly as she could "Ah! Madame, enough! enough! . . ."

The other went on lecturing her, predicting they would end in the workhouse. But it was Bovary's fault. Luckily he had promised to destroy that power of attorney.

"What?"

"Ah! he swore he would," went on the good woman.

Emma opened the window, called Charles, and the poor fellow was obliged to confess the promise torn from him by his mother.

Emma disappeared, then came back quickly, and majestically handed her a large sheet of paper.

"Thank you," said the old woman. And she threw the power of attorney into the fire.

Emma began to laugh, a strident, piercing, continuous laugh; she had an attack of hysterics.

"Oh! my God!" cried Charles. "Ah! You are in the wrong too! You come here and make scenes with her! . . ."

His mother, shrugging her shoulders, declared it was "all put on."

But Charles, rebelling for the first time, took his wife's part, so that Madame Bovary senior said she would leave. She went the very next day, and on the threshold, as he was trying to detain her, she replied:

"No, no! You love her better than me, and you a·e right. It is natural. Take care of yourself! . . . for I'm not likely to be back again soon to 'make scenes' as you say."

Charles nevertheless was very crestfallen before Emma, who did not hide the resentment she still felt at his want of confidence, and it needed many prayers before she would consent to another power of attorney. He even accompanied her to Monsieur Guillaumin to have a second one, just like the other, drawn up.

"I know how it is," said the notary; "a man of science can't be worried with the practical details of life."

And Charles felt relieved by this comfortable reflection, which gave his weakness the flattering appearance of higher preoccupation.

How exhalted she was the following Thursday at the hotel in their room with Léon! She laughed, cried, sang, sent for sherbets, wanted to smoke cigarettes, seemed to him wild and extravagant, but adorable, superb.

He did not know what combination of forces within her was driving her to throw herself so recklessly after the pleasures of life. She became irritable, greedy, voluptuous. She walked boldly through the streets with him, her head high, unconcerned, she said, about being compromised. At times, however, Emma shuddered at the sudden thought of meeting Rodolphe, for it seemed to her that, although they were separated forever, she was not completely free from the power he held over her.

One night she did not return to Yonville at all. Charles lost his head with anxiety, and little Berthe refusing to go to bed without her mamma, sobbed as though her heart would break. Justin had gone out searching the road at random. Monsieur Homais even had left his pharmacy.

At last, at eleven o'clock, able to bear it no longer, Charles harnessed his chaise, jumped in, whipped up his horse, and reached the Croix-Rouge about two o'clock in the morning. No one there! He thought that the clerk had perhaps seen her; but where did he live? Happily, Charles remembered his employer's address, and rushed off there.

Day was breaking, and he could make out some letters over the door; he knocked. Some one, without opening the door, shouted out the required information and added a generous number of insults concerning people who disturb others in the middle of the night.

The house inhabited by the clerk had neither bell, knocker, nor porter. Charles beat on the shutters with his fists. A policeman happened to pass by; he felt nervous and left.

"What a fool I am" he said. "M. Lormeaux must have asked her to stay to dinner."

The Lormeaux no longer lived in Rouen.

"She probably stayed to look after Madame Dubreuil. Oh, but Madame Dubreuil has been dead these ten months . . . Then where can she be?"

An idea occurred to him. At a café he asked for a Directory, and hurriedly looked for the name of Mademoiselle Lempereur, who turned out to live at No. 74 Rue de la Renelle-des-Maroquiniers.

As he was turning into the street, Emma herself appeared at the other end of it; he threw himself upon her rather than embraced her, crying:

"What kept you yesterday?"

"I was not well."

"What! . . . Where! . . . How! . . ."

She passed her hand over her forehead and answered,

"At Mme. Lempereur's."

"I was sure of it! I was just on my way there."

"Oh!" said Emma. "It's not worth while now. She just stepped out a minute ago; don't get so excited. I will never feel free, you understand, if the slightest delay is going to make you lose your head like this."

This was a sort of permission that she gave herself, so as to get perfect freedom in her escapades. And she took full and free advantage of it. Whenever she was seized with the desire to see Léon, she would set out upon any pretext whatever, and if he were not expecting her that day, she would go to fetch him at his office.

It was a great delight at first, but soon he no longer concealed the truth, which was, that his master complained very much about these interruptions.

"Oh, who cares!" she said, "come along."

And he slipped out.

She wanted him to dress all in black, and grow a pointed beard, to look like the portraits of Louis XIII. She asked to see his rooms and found them lacking in taste. This embarrassed him but she paid no attention; she then advised him to buy curtains like hers, and when he objected to the expense:

"Ah! ah! you hold onto your pennies!" she said laughing.

Each time Léon had to tell her everything that he had done since their last meeting. She asked him for some verses—some verses "for herself," a "love poem" in honor of her. But he never succeeded in getting a rhyme for the second verse; and at last ended by copying a sonnet from a Keepsake.

He did this less from vanity, than simply out of a desire to please her. He never questioned her ideas; he accepted all her tastes; he was becoming her mistress rather than she his. She had tender words and kisses that thrilled his soul. Where could she have learnt this corruption so deep and well masked as to be almost unseizable?

VI

On his trips to see her, Léon often dined at the pharmacist's, and he felt obliged out of politeness to invite him in turn.

"With pleasure!" Monsieur Homais had replied; "besides, I must recharge my mind a bit, for I am getting rusty here. We'll go to the theatre, to the restaurant. We'll do the town."

"Oh, my dear!" tenderly murmured Madame Homais, alarmed at the vague perils he was preparing to brave.

"Well, what? Do you think I'm not sufficiently ruining my health living here amid the continual emanations of the pharmacy? But there! That's just like a woman! They are jealous of science, and then are opposed to our taking the most legitimate distractions. No matter! Count upon me. One of these days I shall turn up at Rouen, and we'll paint the town together."

The pharmacist would formerly have taken good care not to use such an expression, but he was cultivating a flippant Parisian manner which he thought very stylish; and, like his neighbor, Madame Bovary, he questioned the clerk avidly about life in the capital; he even used slang in order to impress . . . the "bourgeois", saying "flip", "cool", "sweet", "neat-o", and "I must break it up", for "I must leave."

So one Thursday Emma was surprised to meet Monsieur Homais in the kitchen of the "Lion d'Or," wearing a traveller's costume, that is to say, wrapped in an old cloak which no one knew he had, while he carried a valise in one hand and the foot-warmer of his establishment in the other. He had confided his intentions to no one, for fear of causing the public anxiety by his absence.

The prospect of seeing again the scenes of his youth no doubt excited him for he never stopped talking during the whole trip; the coach had barely stopped when he leaped out in search of Léon; and in vain the clerk struggled to free himself. M. Homais dragged him off to the flashy Cafe de la Normandie, where he entered majestically, without taking off his hat, for he thought it highly provincial to uncover in any public place.

Emma waited for Léon three quarters of an hour. At last she ran to his office, and, lost in all sorts of conjectures, accusing him of indifference, and reproaching herself for her weakness, she spent the afternoon, her face pressed against the window-panes.

At two o'clock they were still at table opposite each other. The large room was emptying; the stove-pipe, in the shape of a palm-tree, spread its gilt leaves over the white ceiling; and near them, just outside the window, in the full sun, a little fountain gurgled into a white basin, where, among the watercress and asparagus, sluggish lobsters stretched out their claws towards a heap of quail lying on their sides.

Homais relished it all. He was more intoxicated by the luxury than by the fine food and drink, but nevertheless, the Pommard wine began to go to his head, and by the time the "omelette au rhum" appeared, he began expounding scandalous theories on women. What attracted him above all else, was "chic." He adored an elegant outfit and hairdo in a well-furnished apartment, and when it came to their physical proportions, he didn't mind them on the plump side.

Léon watched the clock in despair. The pharmacist went on drinking, eating, and talking.

"You must be completely deprived here in Rouen," he said suddenly. "But then the object of your affections doesn't live far away."

And, when the other blushed:

"Come now, be frank. Can you deny that at Yonville . . ."

The young man began to stammer.

"At Madame Bovary's, can you deny that you were courting . . ."

"Whom do you mean?"

"The maid!"

He was not joking; but vanity getting the better of his judgement, Léon protested indignantly in spite of himself. Besides, he only liked dark women.

"I approve of your taste," said the pharmacist; "they have more temperament."

And whispering into his friend's ear, he pointed out the symptoms by which one could detect temperament in a woman. He even launched into an ethnographic digression: the German was romantic, the French woman licentious, the Italian passionate.

"And negresses?" asked the clerk.

"They are for artistic tastes!" said Homais. "Waiter! Two demi-tasses!"

"Shall we go?" asked Léon, at last reaching the end of his patience.

"Yes" said Homais in English.

But before leaving he wanted to see the proprietor of the establishment and made him a few compliments. Then the young man, to be alone, alleged he had some business engagement.

"Ah! I will escort you," said Homais.

And all the while he was walking through the streets with him he talked of his wife, his children, of their future, and of his business; told him in what a dilapidated condition he had found it, and to what a state of perfection he had now raised it.

When they arrived in front of the Hôtel de Boulogne, Léon left him abruptly, ran up the stairs, and found his mistress almost hysterical.

On hearing the name of the pharmacist, she flew into a passion. Nevertheless, he kept overwhelming her with good reasons; it wasn't his fault; didn't she know Homais? Could she believe that he would prefer his company? But she turned away; he held her back, and falling on his knees, he encircled her waist with his arm, in a pose at once langorous, passionate, and imploring.

She stood there looking at him, her large flashing eyes were serious, almost terrible. Then her tears clouded them over, her pink eyelids lowered, and she gave him her hands. Léon was just pressing them to his lips when a servant appeared to say that someone wanted to see the gentleman.

"You will come back?" she said.

"Yes."

"But when?"

"Immediately."

"It's a trick," said the pharmacist, when he saw Léon. "I wanted to interrupt this visit, that seemed to me to annoy you. Let's go and have a glass of *garus*⁴ at Bridoux'."

Léon swore that he must get back to his office. Then the pharmacist began making jokes about legal papers and procedure.

"Forget about Cujas and Barthole a bit, what the Devil! Who's going to stop you? Be a man! Let's go to Bridoux'. You'll see his dog. It's very interesting."

And as the clerk still insisted:

"I'll go with you. I'll read a paper while I wait for you, or thumb through a code."

Léon, bewildered by Emma's anger, Monsieur Homais' chatter, and perhaps, by the heaviness of the luncheon, was undecided, and, as though he were under the spell of the pharmacist who kept repeating:

"Let's go to Bridoux'. It's just by here, in the Rue Malpalu."

Then, out of cowardice, out of stupidity, out of that undefinable necessity that leads us towards those actions we are most set against, he allowed himself to be led off to Bridoux'; they found him in his small courtyard overseeing three workmen who panted as they turned the huge wheel of a selza water machine. Homais gave them some advice; he embraced Bridoux; they drank some garus. Twenty times Léon tried to escape, but the other seized him by the arm saying:

"Wait a minute! I'm coming! We'll go to the Fanal de Rouen' to see the fellows there. I'll introduce you to Thomassin."

He finally got rid of him, however, and flew to the hotel. Emma was gone.

She had just left in exasperation. She detested him now. His failure to come as he had promised she took as an insult, and she looked for other reasons for separating from him: he was incapable of heroism, weak, banal, more spiritless than a woman, avaricious,

4. A liqueur named after its inventor, Garus.

and timorous as well.

Later when she was calmer, she realized that she had doubtless been unjust to him. But the picking apart of those we love always alienates us from them. One must not touch one's idols, a little of the gilt always comes off on one's fingers.

They gradually began to talk more frequently of matters outside their love, and in the letters that Emma wrote him she spoke of flowers, poetry, the moon and the stars, naïve resources of a waning passion striving to keep itself alive by all external aids. She was constantly promising herself a profound happiness on her next trip; then she confessed to herself that she had felt nothing extraordinary. This disappointment quickly gave way to a new hope, and Emma returned to him more avid and inflamed than before. She undressed brutally, ripping off the thin laces of her corset so violently that they would whistle round her hips like a gliding snake. She went on tiptoe, barefooted, to see once more that the door was locked, then with one movement, she would let her clothes fall at once to the ground;—then, pale and serious, without a word, she would throw herself against his breast with a long shudder.

Yet there was upon that brow covered with cold drops, on those stammering lips, in those wild eyes, in the grip of those arms, something strange, vague and sinister that seemed to Léon to be subtly gliding between them to force them apart.

He did not dare to question her; but finding how experienced she was, he told himself that she must have passed through all the extremes of both pleasure and pain. What had once charmed now frightened him a little. Furthermore, he revolted against the daily increased absorption of his personality into hers. He resented her, because of this constant victory. He even strove not to love her; then, when he heard the creaking of her boots, he felt his courage desert him, like drunkards at the sight of strong liquor.

It is true, she showered him with every sort of attention, from exotic foods, to little coquettish refinements in her dress and languishing glances. She used to bring roses from Yonville hidden in her bosom which she would toss up into his face; she was worried about his health, advised him how he should behave; and in order to bind him closer to her, hoping perhaps that heaven would take her part, she hung a medal of the Virgin round his neck. She inquired like a virtuous mother about his companions. She said to him:

"Don't see them; don't go out; only think of us; love me!"

She would have liked to be able to watch over his life, and the idea occurred to her of having him followed in the streets. Near the hotel there was always a kind of vagabond who accosted travellers, and who would surely not refuse . . . But her pride revolted at this.

"Ah! So what! What does it matter if he betrays me! What do I care?"

One day, when they had parted early and she was returning alone along the boulevard, she saw the walls of her convent; she sat down on a bench in the shade of the elms. How calm her life had been in those days! How she envied her first undefinable sentiments of love which she had tried to construct from the books she read.

The first months of her marriage, her rides in the forest, the viscount who had waltzed with her, and Lagardy singing, all repassed before her eyes . . . And Léon suddenly appeared to her as far off as the others.

"I do love him!" she said to herself.

No matter! She was not happy, she never had been. Why was her life so unsatisfactory, why did everything she leaned on instantly rot and give way? . . . But suppose there existed somewhere some one strong and beautiful, a man of valor, passionate yet refined, the heart of a poet in the form of an angel, a bronze stringed lyre, playing elegaic epithalamia to the heavens, why might she not someday happen on him? What a vain thought! Besides, nothing was worth the trouble of seeking it; everything was a lie. Every smile concealed a yawn of boredom, every joy a curse, every pleasure its own disgust, and the sweetest kisses left upon your lips only the unattainable desire for a greater delight.

A coarse metallic rattle sounded around her, and the convent bell struck four. And it seemed to her that she had been sitting on that bench since the beginning of time. But an infinity of time can be compressed into a minute like a crowd of people into a small space.

Emma lived all absorbed in her passions and worried no more about money matters than an archduchess.

There came a day, however, when a seedy looking man with a red face and a bald head came to her house, saying he had been sent by Monsieur Vinçart of Rouen. He took out the pins that held together the side-pockets of his long green overcoat, stuck them into his sleeve, and politely handed her a paper.

It was a bill for seven hundred francs, signed by her, and which Lheureux, in spite of all his promises had endorsed to Vinçart.

She sent her servant for him. He could not come.

Then the stranger who had remained standing, casting around him to the right and left curious glances which were hidden behind his blond eyebrows, asked with an innocent air:

"What answer am I to take Vinçart?"

"Well!" said Emma, "tell him . . . that I haven't got it . . . I'll pay him next week . . . He must wait . . . yes, next week."

And the fellow went without another word.

But the next day at twelve o'clock she received a summons, and the sight of the stamped paper, on which appeared several times in large letters, "Maître Hereng, bailiff at Buchy," so frightened her that she rushed in all haste to Lheureux. She found him in his shop, tying up a parcel.

"At your service," he said. "What can I do for you?"

But Lheureux continued what he was doing, aided by a young girl of about thirteen, somewhat hunchbacked, who was both his clerk and his servant.

Then, his sabots clattering on the wooden planks of the shop, he mounted in front of Madame Bovary to the second floor and showed her into a narrow closet, where, in a large pine wood desk, lay some ledgers, protected by an iron bar laid horizontally across them and padlocked down. Against the wall, under some remnants of calico, one caught sight of a safe, but of such dimensions that it must contain something besides promisory notes and cash. Monsieur Lheureux, in fact, went in for pawnbroking, and it was there that he had put Madame Bovary's gold chain, together with the earrings of poor old Tellier, who had been forced, at last, to sell his café, and had bought a small grocery store in Quincampoix, where he was dying of catarrh amongst his candles, that were less yellow than his face.

Lheureux sat down in a large cane arm-chair, saying:

"What's new?"

"Look here!"

"Well, what do you want me to do about it?"

Then she lost her temper, reminding him that he had promised not to endorse her notes away. He admitted it.

"But I was pressed myself; they were holding a knife against my throat too."

"And what will happen now?" she went on.

"Oh, it's very simple; a judgment and then a seizure . . . that's about it!"

Emma kept down a desire to strike him, and asked gently if there was no way of quieting Monsieur Vinçart.

"Oh, sure! appease Vinçart, indeed! You don't know him; he's fiercer than an Arab!"

Nevertheless, Monsieur Lheureux had to help her.

"All right then, listen, it seems to me that I've been pretty good to you so far."

And opening one of his ledgers:

"Look!" he said.

Then moving his finger up the page:

"Let's see . . . let's see . . . ! August 3d, two hundred francs . . . June 17th, a hundred and fifty . . . March 23d, forty-six . . . In April . . ."

He stopped, as if afraid of making some mistake.

"I won't even mention the bills signed by Monsieur Bovary, one for seven hundred francs, and another for three hundred. As to the little payments on your account and the interest, I'd never get to the end of the list, I can't figure that high. I'll have nothing more to do with it."

She wept; she even called him "her good Monsieur Lheureux." But he always fell back upon "that rascal Vinçart." Besides, he hadn't a penny, no one was paying him these days, they were eating his coat off his back, a poor shopkeeper like himself couldn't advance money.

Emma was silent, and Monsieur Lheureux, who was biting the feathers of a quil, no doubt became uneasy at her silence, for he went on:

"Perhaps, if something were paid on this, one of these days . . . I might . . ."

"Well," she said, "as soon as the balance on the Barneville property . . ."

"What? . . ."

And on hearing that Langlois had not yet paid he seemed much surprised. Then in a honied voice:

"Then we'll agree, what do you say to . . . ?"

"Oh! Whatever you say!"

On this he closed his eyes to reflect, wrote down a few figures, and saying that this was really going to hurt him, it was a risky affair, that he was "bleeding" himself for her, he wrote out four bills for two hundred and fifty francs each, to fall due month by month.

"Provided that Vinçart will listen to me! However, it's settled. I don't back down on my word. I'm as square as a brick."

Next he carelessly showed her several new goods; not one of which, however, was in his opinion worthy of madame.

"When I think that there's a dress that costs seven cents a yard and guaranteed color-fast! And they actually swallow it all down! Of course you understand one doesn't tell them what it really is!" He hoped by this confession of chicanery towards others to convince her of his honesty with her.

Then he called her back to show her three yards of guipure that he had lately picked up "at a sale."

"Isn't it lovely?" said Lheureux. "It is very much used now for the backs of arm-chairs. It's quite the rage."

And, quicker than a juggler, he wrapped up the guipure in some blue paper and put it in Emma's hands.

"But at least let me know . . ."

"Yes, some other time," he replied, turning on his heel.

That same evening she urged Bovary to write to his mother, to ask her to send at once the whole of the balance due from the father's estate. The mother-in-law replied that she had nothing more: that the liquidation was complete, and, aside from Barne-ville, there remained for them an income of six hundred francs, that she would pay them punctually.

Madame Bovary then sent bills to two or three patients, and was soon making great use of this method which turned out to be very successful. She was always careful to add a postscript: "Do not mention this to my husband; you know how proud he is . . . forgive my having to . . . your humble servant. . . ." There were a few complaints; she intercepted them.

To get money she began selling her old gloves, her old hats, all sorts of old odds and ends, and she bargained rapaciously, her peasant blood standing her in good stead. Then on her trips to town she searched the second hand stores for nick-nacks which she was sure, if no one else, Monsieur Lheureux would certainly take off her hands. She bought ostrich feathers, Chinese porcelain, and trunks; she borrowed form Félicité, from Madame Lefrançois, from the landlady at the "Croix Rouge," from everybody, no matter where. With the money she at last received from Barneville she paid two bills; the other fifteen hundred francs fell due. She renewed the notes, and then renewed them again!

Sometimes, it is true, she tried to add up her accounts, but the results were always so staggering, she couldn't believe they were possible. Then she would begin over again, soon get confused, leave everything where it was and forget about it.

The house was a dreary place now! Tradesmen were seen leaving it with angry faces. Handkerchiefs hung drying on the stoves, and little Berthe, to the great scandal of Madame Homais, wore stockings with holes in them. If Charles timidly ventured a remark, she would snap back at him savagely that it certainly wasn't her fault!

What was the meaning of all these fits of temper? He explained everything by her old nervous illness, and reproaching himself with having taken her infirmities for faults, accused himself of egotism, and longed to go and take her in his arms.

"Ah, no!" he said to himself; "I would only annoy her."

And he stayed where he was.

After dinner he would walk about alone in the garden; he took little Berthe on his lap and unfolding his medical journal, tried to teach her to read. But the child, who had never had any schooling at all, would soon open wide her large eyes in bewilderment and begin to cry. Then he would comfort her; he fetched water in her watering can to make rivers on the sand path, or broke off branches from the privet hedges to plant trees in the flower beds. This did not spoil the garden much, which was now overgrown with long weeds. They owed Lestiboudois for so many day's wages. Then the child would grow cold and ask for her mother.

"Go call your nurse," said Charles. "You know, my darling, that mama does not like to be disturbed!"

Autumn was setting in, and the leaves were already falling—as they had two years ago when she was ill!—Where would it all end! . . . And he would continue to pace up and down, his hands behind his back.

Madame was in her room. No one was allowed to enter. There she stayed from morning to night, listless and hardly dressed, from time to time lighting a tablet of Turkish incense she had bought at the shop of an Algerian in Rouen. In order to get rid of this sleeping man stretched out beside her at night, she finally managed by continual badgering to relegate him to a room on the third floor; then she would read until morning, lurid novels where there would be scenes of orgies, violence and bloodshed. Often she would be seized by a sudden terror and cry out. Charles would come running.

"Oh! Leave me alone!" she would say.

Or at other times, when she was burnt more fiercely by that inner flame which her adultery kept feeding, panting and overcome with desire, she would throw open the window breathing in the chill air and letting the wind blow back her hair which hung too heavy on her neck, and, looking up at the stars, she would long for the love of a prince. She thought of him, of Léon. She would then have given anything for a single one of those meetings which would appease her.

These were her gala days. She was determined that they should be magnificent! When he could not pay all the expenses himself, she made up the deficit liberally, which happened pretty well every time. He tried to convince her that they would be just as well off somewhere else, in a more modest hotel, but she always found some objection.

One day she drew six small silver-gilt spoons from her bag (they were old Rouault's wedding present), begging him to pawn them at once for her; Léon obeyed, although the errand annoyed him. He was afraid of compromising himself.

Then, on reflection, he began to think that his mistress was beginning to behave rather strangely, and perhaps they were not wrong in wishing to separate him from her.

In fact, some one had sent his mother a long anonymous letter to warn her that he was "ruining himself with a married woman"; and immediately the good woman had visions of the eternal bug-a-boo of every family, that is to say, that vague and terrible creature, the siren, the fantastic monster which makes its home in the treacherous depths of love. She wrote to Maître Dubocage, his employer, who behaved perfectly in the affair. He kept him for three quarters of an hour trying to open his eyes, to warn him of the abyss into which he was falling. Such an intrigue would damage him later on in his career. He implored him to break with her, and, if he would not make this sacrifice in his own interest, to do it at least for his, Dubocage's sake.

Léon finally swore he would not see Emma again; and he reproached himself with not having kept his word, considering all the trouble and reproaches she was likely to bring down on him, not counting the jokes made by his fellow clerks as they sat around the stove in the morning. Besides, he was soon to be head clerk; it was time to settle down. So he gave up his flute, his exalted sentiments, his poetic imagination; for every bourgeois in the flush of his youth, were it but for a day, a moment, has believed himself capable of immense passions, of lofty enterprises. The most mediocre libertine has dreamed of sultanas; every notary bears within him the débris of a poet.

He was bored now when Emma suddenly began to sob on his breast; and his heart, like the people who can only stand a certain amount of music, became drowsy through indifference to the vibrations of a love whose subtleties he could no longer distinguish.

They knew one another too well to experience any of those sudden surprises which multiply the enjoyment of a possession a hundredfold. She was as sick of him as he was weary of her. Emma found again in adultery all the platitudes of marriage.

But how to get rid of him? Then, though she felt humiliated by the sordidity of such a happiness, she clung to it out of habit, or out of degeneration; she pursued it more desperately than ever, destroying every pleasure by always wishing for it to be too great. She blamed Léon for her disappointed hopes, as if he had betrayed her; and she even longed for some catastrophe that would bring about their separation, since she had not the courage to do it herself.

She none the less went on writing him love letters, in keeping with the notion that a woman must write to her lover.

But while writing to him, it was another man she saw, a phantom fashioned out of her most ardent memories, of her favorite books, her strongest desires, and at last he became so real, so tangible, that her heart beat wildly in awe and admiration, though unable to see him distinctly, for, like a god, he was hidden beneath the abundance of his attributes. He dwelt in that azure land where silken ladders swung from balconies in the moonlight, beneath a flower-scented breeze. She felt him near her; he was coming and would ravish her entire being in a kiss. Then she would fall back to earth again shattered; for these vague ecstasies of imaginary love, would exhaust her more than the wildest orgies.

She now felt a constant pain throughout her body. Often she even received summonses, stamped paper that she barely looked at. She would have liked not to be alive, or to be always asleep.

On the day of Mid-Lent she did not return to Yonville; that evening she went to a masked ball. She wore velvet breeches, red stockings, a peruke, and a three-cornered hat cocked over one ear. She danced all night to the wild sounds of the trombones; people gathered around her, and in the morning she found herself on the steps of the theatre together with five or six other masked dancers, dressed as stevadores or sailors, friends of Léon's who were talking about going out to find some supper.

The neighboring cafés were full. They found a dreadful looking restaurant at the harbor, where the proprietor showed them to a little room on the fifth floor.

The men were whispering in a corner, no doubt consulting about expenses. There were a clerk, two medical students, and a shop assistant: what company for her! As to the women, Emma soon perceived from the tone of their voices that most of them probably came from the lowest class. This frightened her, she drew back her chair and lowered her eyes.

The others began to eat; she ate nothing. Her head was on fire, her eyes smarted, and her skin was ice-cold. In her head she seemed to feel the floor of the ball-room rebounding again beneath the rhythmical pulsation of thousands of dancing feet. The smell of punch and cigar smoke made her dizzy. She fainted: they carried her to the window.

Day was breaking, and a large purple stain was spreading across the pale sky in the direction of the St. Catherine hills. The ashen river was shivering in the wind; there was no one on the bridges; the street lamps were going out.

She came to herself, however, and began to think of Berthe asleep at home in the maid's room. But just then a cart loaded with long strips of iron passed by, and made a deafening metallic vibration against the walls of the house.

She abruptly slipped out of the room; removed her costume; told Léon she had to return; and found herself alone at last in the Hôtel de Boulogne. Everything, herself included, was now unbearable to her. She would have liked to take wing like a bird, and fly off far away to become young again in the realms of immaculate purity.

She left the hotel, crossed the Boulevard, the Place Cauchoise, and the Faubourg, as far as an open street that overlooked the park. She walked rapidly, the fresh air calmed her; and, little by little, the faces of the crowd, the masks, the quadrilles, the lights, the supper, those women, all, disappeared like rising mists. Then, reaching the "Croix-Rouge," she threw herself on the bed in her little room on the second floor, where there were pictures of the "Tour de Nesle." At four o'clock Hivert awoke her.

When she got home, Félicité showed her a grey paper stuck behind the clock. She read:

"In virtue of the seizure in execution of a judgment."

What judgment . . . ? As a matter of fact, the evening before another paper had been brought that she had not yet seen, and she was stunned by these words:

"By power of the king, the law, and the courts, Mme. Bovary is hereby ordered . . ."

Then, skipping several lines, she read:

"Within twenty-four hours, at the latest . . ." But what? "To pay the sum of eight thousand francs." There was even written at the bottom of the page, "She will be constrained thereto by every form of law, and notably by a writ of distraint on her furniture and effects."

What should she do? . . . In twenty-four hours; tomorrow! Lheureux, she thought, probably wanted to frighten her again, for, all at once, she saw through his manoeuvres, the reason for his favors. The only thing that reassured her was the extraordinary amount of the figure.

Nevertheless, as a result of buying and not paying, of borrowing, signing notes, and renewing these notes which grew ever larger each time they fell due, she had ended by preparing a capital for Monsieur Lheureux which he was impatiently waiting to collect to use in his own financial speculations.

She went over to his place, assuming an air of indifference.

"Do you know what has happened to me? It's a joke, I'm sure!"

"No."

"What do you mean?"

He slowly turned around, and, folding his arms, said to her:

"Did you think, my dear lady, that I was going to go on to the end of time providing you with merchandise and cash, just for the love of God? I certainly have to get back what I laid out, let's be fair."

She objected to the amount of the debt.

"Ah! Too bad! The court has recognised it! There's a judgment. You've been notified. Besides, it isn't my fault. It's Vinçart's."

"But couldn't you . . . ?"

"No! Not a single thing!"

"But . . . Still . . . let's talk it over."

And she began beating about the bush; she had known nothing about it . . . it was a surprise . . .

"Whose fault is that?" said Lheureux, bowing ironically. "While I'm slaving like a nigger, you go gallivanting about."

"Ah! Don't preach to me!"

"It never does any harm," he replied.

She turned coward; she implored him; she even pressed her pretty white and slender hand against the shopkeeper's knee.

"There, that'll do! Any one'd think you wanted to seduce me!"

"You are a wretch!" she cried.

"Oh, oh! What a fuss you are making!"

"I will show you up. I'll tell my husband . . ."

"All right! I too, I'll show your husband something!"

And Lheureux drew from his strong box the receipt for eighteen hundred francs that she had given him when Vinçart had discounted the bills.

"Do you think," he added, "that he won't catch on to your little theft, the poor dear man?"

She collapsed, more overcome than if felled by the blow of a club. He was walking up and down from the window to the bureau, repeating all the while:

"I'll show him all right . . . I'll show him all right . . . "

Then he approached her, and said in a soft voice:

"It's no fun, I know; but after all it hasn't killed anyone, and, since that is the only way that is left for you paying back my money . . ."

"But where am I to get any?" said Emma, wringing her hands.

"Bah! when one has friends like you!"

And he looked at her with such a knowing and terrible stare, that she shuddered to the very core of her heart.

"I promise you," she said, "I'll sign . . ."

"I've enough of your signatures!"

"I will sell something else . . ."

"Oh come!" he said, shrugging his shoulders. "You've nothing left to sell."

And he called through the peep-hole that looked down into the shop:

"Annette, don't forget the three coupons of No. 14."

The servant appeared; Emma caught the hint and asked how much money would be needed to put a stop to the proceedings.

"It is too late."

"But if I were to bring you several thousand francs, a quarter of the sum, a third, almost all?"

"No; it's no use!"

And he pushed her gently towards the staircase.

"I implore you, Monsieur Lheureux, just a few days more!"

She was sobbing.

"Ah that's good! let's have some tears!"

"You'll drive me to do something desperate!"

"Don't make me laugh!" said he, shutting the door.

VII

She was stoical the next day when Maître Hareng, the bailiff, with two assistants arrived at her house to draw up inventory for the seizure.

They began with Bovary's consulting-room, and did not write down the phrenological head, which was considered an "instument of his profession"; but in the kitchen they counted the plates, the saucepans, the chairs, the candlesticks, and in the bedroom all the nick-nacks on the wall-shelf. They examined her dresses, the linen, the dressing-room; and her whole existence, to its most intimate details, was stretched out like a cadavre in an autopsy before the eyes of these three men.

Maître Hareng, buttoned up in his thin black coat, wearing a white choker and very tight foot-straps, repeated from time to time:

"Allow me madame? Allow me?"

Often he uttered exclamations:

"Charming! very pretty."

Then he began writing again, dipping his pen into the horn inkstand he carried in his left hand.

When they had done with the rooms they went up to the attic,

She kept a desk there in which Rodolphe's letters were locked. It had to be opened.

"Ah! a correspondence!" said Maître Hareng, with a discreet smile. "But allow me! for I must make sure the box contains nothing else." And he tipped up the papers lightly, as if to let the napoleons fall out. This made her furious to see this coarse hand, with red moist fingers like slugs, touching these pages against which her heart had beaten.

They went at last! Félicité came back. Emma had sent her out to watch for Bovary in order to keep him away, and they hastily installed the man set to guard the seizure, in the attic, where he swore he would not stir.

During the evening Charles seemed to her careworn. Emma watched him with a look of anguish, fancying she saw an accusation in every line of his face. Then, when her eyes wandered over the chimney-piece ornamented with Chinese screens, over the large curtains, the arm-chairs, all those things that had softened the bitterness of her life, remorse seized her, or rather an immense regret, that, far from destroying her passion, rather irritated it. Charles placidly poked the fire, both his feet on the andirons.

Once the man, no doubt bored in his hiding-place, made a slight noise.

"Is any one walking upstairs?" said Charles.

"No," she replied; "it is a window that has been left open, and is banging in the wind."

The next day which was Sunday, she went to Rouen to call on all the brokers whose names she knew. They were either in the country, or away on a trip. She was not discouraged; and those whom she did manage to see she asked for money, insisting that she absolutely had to have it, that she would pay it back. Some laughed in her face; all refused.

At two o'clock she ran to Léon's apartment, and knocked at the door. No one answered. At length he appeared.

"What brings you here?"

"Am I disturbing you?"

"No . . . but . . ." And he admitted that his landlord didn't like his having "women" there.

"I must speak to you," she went on.

Then he took down the key, but she stopped him.

"No, no! Over there, in our home!"

And they went to their room at the Hôtel de Boulogne.

On arriving she drank off a large glass of water. She was very pale. She said to him:

"Léon, I have a favor to ask you."

And, shaking him by both hands which she held tightly in hers, she added:

"Listen, I must have eight thousand francs."

"But you are mad!"

"Not yet."

And thereupon, telling him the story of the seizure, she explained her distress to him; for Charles knew nothing of it; her mother-in-law detested her; old Rouault could do nothing; but he, Léon, he would set about finding this indispensable sum . . .

"But what do you want me . . . ?"

"What a coward you are!" she cried.

Then he said stupidly, "You're making things out to be worse than they are. Your fellow there could probably be quieted with three thousand francs."

All the more reason to try and do something; it was inconceivable that they couldn't find three thousand francs. Besides, Léon could sign the notes instead of her.

"Go! try! you must! run! . . . Oh! Try! try! I will love you so!"

He went out, and came back at the end of an hour, saying, with a solemn face:

"I have been to three people . . . with no success!"

Then they sat there facing each other on either side of the

fireplace, motionless, without speaking. Emma shrugged her shoulders as she tapped her foot impatiently. He heard her murmur:

"If I were in your place I'd certainly find some!"

"Where?"

"At your office."

And she looked at him.

A diabolical determination showed in her burning eyes which were half closed in a lascivious and encouraging manner;—so that the young man felt himself growing weak beneath the mute will of this woman who was urging him to commit a crime. Then he was afraid, and to avoid any explanation he smote his forehead crying:

"Morel is coming back tonight! He will not refuse me, I hope" (this was one of his friends, the son of a very rich merchant); "and I will bring it you to-morrow," he added.

Emma did not seem to welcome this new hope with all the joy he had expected. Did she suspect the lie? He went on, blushing:

"However, if you don't see me by three o'clock, do not wait for me, my darling. I must leave now, forgive me. Good-bye!"

He pressed her hand, but it felt quite lifeless. Emma had no strength left for any sentiment whatever.

Four o'clock struck; and she rose to return to Yonville, mechanically obeying the force of old habits.

The weather was beautiful; it was one of those March days, clear and sharp, when the sun shines in a perfectly white sky. The people of Rouen, dressed in their Sunday-clothes, seemed happy as they strolled by. She reached the Place du Parvis. People were coming out of the cathedral after vespers; the crowd flowed out through the three portals like a river through the three arches of a bridge, and in the middle, more immobile than a rock, stood the verger.

Then she remembered the day when, eager and full of hope, she had entered beneath this large nave, that had opened out before her, less profound than her love; and she walked on weeping beneath her veil, dazed, staggering, almost fainting.

"Look out!" cried a voice issuing from behind a carriage gate which was swinging open.

She stopped to let pass a black horse, prancing between the shafts of a tilbury, driven by a gentleman dressed in sables. Who was it? She knew him . . . The carriage sprang forward and disappeared.

Why, it was he, the Viscount! She turned away; the street was empty. She was so crushed, so sad, that she had to lean against a wall to keep herself from falling.

Then she thought she had been mistaken.

How could she tell? Everything, within herself and without, was abandoning her. She felt that she was lost, that she was wandering about at random within undefinable abysses, and she was almost happy, on reaching the "Croix Rouge," to see the good Homais, who was watching a large box full of pharmaceutical stores being hoisted on to the "Hirondelle"; holding in his hand a silk handkerchief containing six "cheminots" for his wife.

Madame Homais was very fond of these small, heavy rolls shaped like turbans which are eaten during Lent with salt butter: a last relic of Gothic fare, going back, perhaps, to the Crusades, and with which the hardy Normans would stuff themselves in times gone-by, thinking that they saw, illuminated in the golden light of the torches, between the tankards of Hippocras and the gigantic slabs of meat, the heads of Saracens to be devoured. The druggist's wife crunched them up as they had done, heroically, in spite of her wretched teeth; so whenever Homais made a trip to town, he never failed to bring her home some which he bought at the great baker's in the Rue Massacre.

"Charmed to see you," he said, offering Emma a hand to help her into the "Hirondelle."

Then he tied his "cheminots" to the baggage net and remained with his head bare and his arms folded in an attitude pensive and Napoleonic.

But when the blind man appeared as usual at the foot of the hill he exclaimed indignantly:

"I can't understand why the authorities continue to tolerate such criminal occupations! These unfortunate people should be locked up, forced to do some work. I give you my word, Progress marches at a snail's pace! We are paddling about in a state of total barbarism!"

The blind man held out his hat which flapped about in the window as though it were a pocket in the upholstery which had come loose.

"This," said the pharmacist, "is a scrofulous disease."

And though he knew the poor devil, he pretended to see him for the first time, muttering such words as "cornea," "opaque cornea," "sclerotic," "facies," then asked him in a paternal tone:

"My friend, have you suffered long from this dreadful affliction? Instead of getting drunk in the café you would do better to follow a diet."

He advised him to drink good wine, good beer and to eat good roasts of meat. The blind man went on with his song. He actually seemed almost insane. At last Monsieur Homais opened his purse.

"Now there's a sou; give me back two liards: don't forget what I told you, you'll find it does you good."

Hivert openly cast some doubt on its efficacy. But the druggist said that he would cure the man himself with an antiphlogistic salve of his own composition, and he gave his address: "Monsieur

Homais, near the market, everyone knows me."

"All right!" said Hivert, "in payment, you can 'put on your act' for us."

The blind man squatted down on his haunches with his head thrown back, and rolling his greenish eyes and sticking out his tongue, he rubbed his stomach with both hands while uttering a sort of low howl like a famished dog. Emma, overcome with disgust, threw him a five franc piece over her shoulder. It was all her fortune. It seemed like a grand thing to her to throw it away like this.

The coach had already started again when Monsieur Homais suddenly leaned out of the window and shouted:

"No farinacious foods or dairy products, wear woolen clothing next to the skin, and expose the diseased areas to the smoke of juniper berries."

The sight of the familiar things that passed before her eyes gradually diverted Emma from her present suffering. An intolerable fatigue overwhelmed her, and she reached home stupefied, discouraged, almost asleep.

"Let come what may!" she told herself.

Besides, anything could happen. Couldn't some extraordinary event occur at any moment? Lheureux might even die.

At nine o'clock in the morning she was awakened by the sound of voices in the square. A crowd around the market was reading a large bill fixed to one of the posts, and she saw Justin climb on a milepost and tear down the bill. The local policeman had just seized him by the collar. Monsieur Homais came out of his shop, and Mère Lefrançois, in the midst of the crowd, was talking the loudest of all.

"Madame! madame!" cried Félicité, running in, "it's an outrage!"

And the poor girl, all in tears, handed her a yellow paper that she had just torn off the door. Emma read with a glance that her furniture was for sale.

Then they looked at one another in silence. Servant and master had no secrets from each other. At last Félicité whispered:

"If I were you, madame, I'd go see Monsieur Guillaumin."

"You think so?"

The question meant:

"You who know all about the house from the butler, has the master sometimes spoken of me?"

"Yes, you'd do well to go there."

She dressed, put on her black gown, and her cape with jet beads, and that she might not be seen (there was still a crowd on the Square), she took the path by the river, outside the village.

She was out of breath when she reached the notary's gate. The sky was sombre, and a little snow was falling.

At the sound of the bell, Theodore in a red waistcoat appeared on the steps; he came to open the door with a casual air, as if she were an old acquaintance, and showed her into the dining-room.

A large porcelain stove crackled beneath a cactus that filled up the niche in the wall, and in black wood frames against the oak-stained paper hung Steuben's "Esmeralda" and Schopin's "Put-iphar." The ready-laid table, the two silver chafing-dishes, the crystal door-knobs, the parquet and the furniture, all shone with a scrupulous, English cleanliness; the windows were ornamented at each corner with stained glass.

"Now this," thought Emma, "is the kind of dining-room I ought to have."

The notary came in. With his left hand, he pressed his palm-embroidered dressing gown against his body, while with his other hand he quickly took off and replaced his brown velvet skullcap, which he wore jauntily cocked to the right. After circling around his bald cranium, the end of three strains of blond hair stuck out from underneath the cap.

After he had offered her a seat he sat down to breakfast, apologising profusely for his rudeness.

"I have come," she said, "to beg you, sir . . ."

"What, madame? I am listening."

And she began telling him about her situation.

Monsieur Guillaumin knew all about it. He was working in secret partnership with the shopkeeper, who always provided him with the capital for the mortgage loans he was asked to arrange.

So he knew (and better than she herself) the long story of these notes, small at first, bearing the names of several endorsers, made out for long terms and constantly renewed up to the day when, gathering together all the protested notes, the shopkeeper had asked his friend Vinçart to take in his own name all the necessary legal steps to collect the money, not wishing to appear as a shark in the eyes of his fellow-citizens.

She mingled her story with recriminations against Lheureux, to which the notary from time to time gave meaningless replies. Eating his cutlet and drinking his tea, he buried his chin in his sky-blue cravat, into which were thrust two diamond pins, held together by a small gold chain; and he smiled a singular smile, in a sugary, ambiguous fashion. Noticing that her feet were damp:

"Do get closer to the stove," he said, "put your feet up against the porcelain."

She was afraid of dirtying it but the notary replied gallantly:

"Pretty things never spoil anything."

Then she tried to appeal to his better feelings and, growing moved herself, she began telling him about the tightness of her household, her worries, her wants. He could understand that—such an elegant woman!—and, without interrupting his lunch, he turned completely round towards her, so that his knee brushed against her boot; the sole was beginning to curl in the heat of the stove.

But when she asked for three thousand francs, his lips drew tight and he said how sorry he was not to have had the management of her capital before, for there were hundreds of ways very convenient, even for a lady, of turning her money to account. In the turf-pits of Gaumesnil or in Le Havre real estate, they could have ventured, with hardly any risk, on some excellent speculations; and he let her consume herself with rage at the thought of the fabulous sums that she would certainly have made.

"How was it," he went on, "that you didn't come to me?"

"I don't know," she said.

"Why not? Did I frighten you so much? It is I, on the contrary, who ought to complain. We hardly know one another; yet I am very devoted to you. You do not doubt that any longer, I hope?"

He held out his hand, took hers, kissed it greedily, then held it on his knee; and he played delicately with her fingers, while muttering thousands of compliments.

His bland voice rustled like a running brook; a light shone in his eyes through the glimmering of his spectacles, and his hand was advancing up Emma's sleeve to press her arm. She felt against her cheek his panting breath. This man was intolerable.

She sprang to her feet and told him:

"Sir, I am waiting."

"For what?" said the notary, who suddenly became very pale.

"This money."

"But . . ."

Then, yielding to an irresistible wave of desire:

"Well then, . . . yes!"

He dragged himself towards her on his knees, regardless of his dressing gown.

"I beg you, stay! I love you!"

He seized her by the waist. Madame Bovary's face flushed purple. She recoiled with a terrible look, exclaiming:

"You shamelessly take advantage of my distress, sir! I am to be pitied—not to be sold."

And she went out.

The notary remained dumbfounded, his eyes fixed on his fine embroidered slippers. They were a love gift, and their sight finally consoled him. Besides, he reflected that such an adventure might have carried him too far.

"The wretch! the scoundrel! . . . what an infamy!" she said to herself, as she fled with nervous steps under the aspens that lined the road. The disappointment of her failure increased the indignation of her outraged modesty; it seemed to her that Providence pursued her implacably, and, strengthening herself in her pride, she had never felt so much esteem for herself nor so much contempt for others. A spirit of warfare transformed her. She would have liked to strike all men, to spit in their faces, to crush them; she kept walking straight on, as quickly as she could, pale, shaking and furious, searching the empty horizon with tear-dimmed eyes, almost rejoicing in the hatred that was choking her.

When she saw her house a numbness came over her. She could not go on; yet she had to. Besides, what escape was there for her?

Félicité was waiting for her at the door.

"Well?"

"No!" said Emma.

And for a quarter of an hour the two of them went over the various persons in Yonville who might perhaps be inclined to help her. But each time that Félicité named some one Emma replied:

"Out of the question! they won't!"

"And the master'll soon be in."

"I know that well enough . . . Now leave me alone."

She had tried everything; there was nothing more to be done now; and when Charles came in she would have to tell him:

"Step aside! This rug on which you are walking is no longer ours. In your own house you don't own a chair, a pin, a straw, and it is I, poor man, who have ruined you."

Then there would be a great sob; next he would weep abundantly, and at last, the surprise past, he would forgive her.

"Yes," she murmured, grinding her teeth, "*he* will forgive me, the man I could never forgive for having known me, even if he had a million to spare! . . . Never! never!"

The thought of Bovary's magnanimity exasperated her. He was bound to find out the catastrophe, whether she confessed or not, now, soon, or to-morrow; so there was no escape from the horrible scene and she would have to bear the weight of his generosity. She wanted to return to Lheureux, but what good would it do? To write to her father—it was too late; and perhaps she began to repent now that she had not yielded to the notary, when she heard the trot of a horse in the alley. It was he; he was opening the gate; he was whiter than the plaster wall. Rushing to the stairs, she fled to the Square; and the wife of the mayor, who was talking to Lestiboudois in front of the church, saw her enter the house of the tax-collector.

She hurried off to tell Madame Caron, and the two ladies went up to the attic; hidden behind a sheet strung up on two poles, they stationed themselves comfortably in full command of Binet's room.

He was alone in his garret, busily copying in wood one of those indescribable bits of ivory, composed of crescents, of spheres hollowed out one within the other, the whole as straight as an obelisk, and of no use whatever; and he was beginning on the last piece—he was nearing his goal! In the twilight of the workshop the white dust was flying from his tools like a shower of sparks under the hoofs of a galloping horse; the two wheels were turning, droning; Binet smiled, his chin lowered, his nostrils distended. He seemed lost in the state of complete bliss that only the most menial tasks can offer: distracting the mind by easily overcome obstacles, they satisfy it completely, leading to a fulfilled achievement that leaves no room for dreams beyond.

"Ah! there she is!" exclaimed Madame Tuvache.

But the noise of the lathe made it impossible to hear what she was saying.

At last the two ladies thought they made out the word "francs," and Madame Tuvache whispered in a low voice:

"She's asking for extra time to pay her taxes."

"Apparently!" replied the other.

They saw her walking up and down, examining the napkin-rings, the candlesticks, the banister rails against the walls, while Binet stroked his beard with satisfaction.

"Do you think she wants to order something from him?" said Madame Tuvache.

"Why, he never sells anything," objected her neighbor.

The tax-collector seemed to be listening with wide-open eyes, as if he did not understand. She went on in a tender, suppliant manner. She came nearer to him, her breast heaving; they no longer spoke.

"Is she making advances to him?" said Madame Tuvache.

Binet was scarlet to his very ears. She took hold of his hands.

"Oh, it's too much!"

And no doubt she was suggesting something abominable to him; for the tax-collector—yet he was brave, had fought at Bautzen and at Lutzen, had been through the French campaign, and had even been proposed for the Croix de Guerre—suddenly, as at the sight of a serpent, recoiled as far as he could from her, exclaiming:

"Madame! How dare you? . . ."

"Women like that ought to be whipped," said Madame Tuvache.

"But where did she go?" Madame Caron asked. For while they talked, she had vanished out of sight, till they discovered her running up the Grande Rue and turning right as if making for the graveyard, leaving them lost in wonder.

"Mère Rollet," she cried on reaching the nurse's home, "I am choking; unlace me!" She fell sobbing on the bed. Nurse Rollet covered her with a petticoat and remained standing by her side. Then, as she did not answer, the woman withdrew, took her wheel and began spinning flax.

"Please, stop that!" she murmured, fancying she heard Binet's lathe.

"What's bothering her?" said the nurse to herself. "Why has she come here?"

She had come, impelled by a kind of horror that drove her from her home.

Lying on her back, motionless, and with staring eyes, she saw things but vaguely, although she tried with idiotic persistence to focus her attention on them. She looked at the scaling walls, two logs smoking end to end in the fireplace, and a long spider crawling over her head in a cracked beam. At last she began to collect her thoughts. She remembered—one day, with Léon . . . Oh! how long ago that was—the sun was shining on the river, and the air full of the scent from the clematis . . . Then, carried by her memories as by a rushing torrent, she soon remembered what had happened the day before.

"What time is it?" she asked.

Mère Rollet went out, raised the fingers of her right hand to that side of the sky that was brightest, and came back slowly, saying:

"Nearly three."

"Ah! thank you, thank you!"

For he would come, he was bound to. He would have found the money. But he would, perhaps, go down to her house, not guessing where she was, and she told the nurse to run and fetch him.

"Be quick!"

"I'm going, my dear lady, I'm going!"

She wondered now why she had not thought of him from the first. Yesterday he had given his word; he would not break it. And she already saw herself at Lheureux's spreading out her three banknotes on his desk. Then she would have to invent some story to explain matters to Bovary. What would she tell him?

The nurse, however, was a long time returning. But, as there was no clock in the cot, Emma feared she was perhaps exaggerating the length of time. She began walking round the garden, step by step; she went into the path by the hedge, and returned quickly, hoping that the woman would have come back by another road. At last, weary of waiting, assailed by fears that she thrust from her, no longer conscious whether she had been here a century or a moment, she sat down in a corner, closed her eyes, and stopped her ears. The gate grated; she sprang up. Before she could speak, Mère Rollet told her:

"There is no one at your house!"

"What?"

"He isn't there. And Monsieur is crying. He is calling for you. Everybody is looking for you."

Emma did not answer. She gasped with wild, rolling eyes, while the peasant woman, frightened at her face drew back instinctively, thinking her mad. Suddenly she struck her brow and uttered a cry; for the thought of Rodolphe, like a flash of lightning in a dark night, had struck into her soul. He was so good, so tender, so generous! And besides, should he hesitate to come to her assistance, she would know well enough how one single glance would reawaken their lost love. So she set out towards La Huchette, unaware that she was hastening to offer what had so angered her a while ago, not in the least conscious of her prostitution.

VIII

She asked herself as she walked along, "What am I going to say? How shall I begin?" And as she went on she recognised the thickets, the trees, the sea-rushes on the hill, the château beyond. All the sensations of her first love came back to her, and her poor oppressed heart expanded in the warmth of this tenderness. A warm wind blew in her face; melting snow fell drop by drop from the leave-buds onto the grass.

She entered, as in the past, through the small park-gate, reached the main courtyard, planted with a double row of lindens, their long whispering branches swaying in the wind. The dogs in their kennels barked, but their resounding voices brought no one out.

She went up the large straight staircase with wooden banisters that led to the hallway paved with dusty flagstones, into which a row of doors opened, as in a monastery or an inn. He was at the top, right at the end, on the left. When she placed her fingers on the lock her strength suddenly deserted her. She was afraid, almost wished he would not be there, though this was her only hope, her last chance of salvation. She collected her thoughts for one moment, and, strengthening herself by the feeling of present necessity, went in.

He was sitting in front of the fire, both his feet propped against the mantelpiece, smoking a pipe.

"Oh, it's you!" he said, getting up hurriedly.

"Yes, it is I . . . I have come, Rodolphe, to ask your advice."

And, despite all her efforts, it was impossible for her to open her lips.

"You have not changed; you're as charming as ever!"

"Oh," she replied bitterly, "they are poor charms since you disdained them."

Then he began a long justification of his conduct, excusing himself in vague terms, since he was unable to invent better.

She yielded to his words, still more to his voice and the sight of him, so that she pretended to believe, or perhaps believed, in the pretext he gave for their break; it was a secret on which depended the honor, the very life of a third person.

"Never mind," she said, looking at him sadly. "I have suffered much."

He replied philosophically:

"Life is that way!"

"Has life," Emma went on, "been kind to you at least since our separation?"

"Oh, neither good . . . nor bad."

"Perhaps it would have been better never to have parted."

"Yes, perhaps."

"You think so?" she said, drawing nearer.

Then, with a sigh:

"Oh, Rodolphe! if only you knew! . . . I loved you so!"

It was then that she took his hand, and they remained some time, their fingers intertwined, like that first day at the Agricultural Fair. With a gesture of pride he struggled against this emotion. But sinking upon his breast she told him:

"How did you think I could live without you? One cannot lose the habit of happiness. I was desperate, I thought I was going to die! I'll tell you about it . . . But you, you fled from me!"

With the natural cowardice that characterizes the stronger sex, he had carefully avoided her for the last three years; now Emma persisted, with coaxing little motions of the head, playful and feline:

"I know you love others, you may as well admit it. Oh! I don't blame them, I understand! You seduced them just as you seduced me. You're a man, a real man! you have all it takes to make yourself loved. But we'll start all over, won't we? We'll love each other as before! Look, I am laughing, I am happy! . . . Say something!"

She was irresistible, with a tear trembling in her eye, like a raindrop in a blue flower-cup, after the storm.

He had drawn her upon his knees, and with the back of his hand was caressing her smooth hair; a last ray of the sun was mirrored there, like a golden arrow. She lowered her head; at last he kissed her on the eyelids quite gently with the tips of his lips.

"Why, you have been crying! Why?"

She burst into tears. Rodolphe thought this was an outburst of her love. As she did not speak, he took this silence to be a last remnant of resistance, so he exclaimed:

"Oh, forgive me! You are the only one who really pleases me. I was a fool, a wicked fool! I love you, I'll always love you! What is the matter? Tell me . . ."

He knelt before her.

"Well, Rodolphe . . . I am ruined! You must lend me three thousand francs."

"But . . ." he said, as he slowly rose to his feet, "but . . ." His face assumed a grave expression.

"You know," she went on quickly, "that my husband had entrusted his money to a notary to invest, and he absconded. So we borrowed; the patients don't pay us. Moreover, the estate isn't settled yet; we shall have the money later on. But to-day, for want of three thousand francs, we are to be sold out, right now, this very minute. Counting on your friendship, I have come to you for help."

"Ah!" thought Rodolphe, turning very pale, "so that's what she came for."

At last he said, very calmly:

"My dear lady, I haven't got them."

He did not lie. If he had had it, he would probably have given the money, although it is generally unpleasant to do such fine things: a demand for money being, of all the winds that blow upon love, the coldest and most destructive.

She stared at him in silence for minutes.

"You haven't got them!"

She repeated several times:

"You haven't got them! . . . I ought to have spared myself this last shame. You never loved me. You are no better than the others."

She was losing her head, giving herself away.

Rodolphe interrupted her, declaring he was himself "hard up."

"Oh! I feel sorry for you!" said Emma, "exceedingly sorry!"

And fixing her eyes upon an embossed rifle that shone against its panoply:

"But when one is so poor one doesn't have silver on the butt of one's gun. One doesn't buy a clock inlaid with tortoiseshell," she went on, pointing to the Boulle clock, "nor silver-gilt whistles for one's whips," and she touched them, "nor charms for one's watch. Oh, he has all he needs! even a liqueur-stand in his bedroom; for you pamper yourself, you live well. You have a château, farms, woods; you go hunting; you travel to Paris. Why, if it were but that," she cried, taking up two cuff-links from the mantlepiece, "even for the least of these trifles, one could get money . . . Oh, I don't want anything from you; you can keep them!"

And she flung the links away with such force that their gold chain broke as it struck against the wall.

"But I! I would have given you everything. I would have sold all, worked for you with my hands, I would have begged on the highroads for a smile, for a look, to hear you say 'Thank you!' And you sit there quietly in your arm-chair, as if you had not made me suffer enough already! But for you, and you know it, I might have lived happily. What made you do it? Was it a bet? Yet you loved me . . . you said so. And but a moment ago . . . Ah! it would have been better to have driven me away. My hands are hot with your kisses, and there is the spot on the carpet where at my knees you swore an eternity of love! You made me believe you; for two years you held me in the most magnificent, the sweetest dream! . . . Our plans for the journey, do you remember? Oh, your letter! your letter! it tore my heart! And then when I come back to him— to him, rich, happy, free—to implore the help the first stranger would give, a suppliant, and bringing back to him all my tenderness, he repulses me because it could cost him three thousand francs!"

"I haven't got them," replied Rodolphe, with that perfect calm with which resigned rage covers itself as with a shield.

She went out. The walls trembled, the ceiling was crushing her, and she passed back through the long alley, stumbling against the heaps of dead leaves scattered by the wind. At last she reached the low hedge in front of the gate; she broke her nails against the lock in her haste to open it. Then a hundred paces beyond, breathless, almost falling, she stopped. And now turning round, she once more saw the impassive château, with the park, the gardens, the three courts, and all the windows of the façade.

She remained lost in stupor, and only conscious of herself through the beating of her arteries, that seemed to burst forth like a deafening music filling all the fields. The earth beneath her feet was more yielding than the sea, and the furrows seemed to her immense brown waves breaking into foam. All the memories and ideas that crowded her head seemed to explode at once like a thousand pieces of fireworks. She saw her father, Lheureux's closet, their room at home, another landscape. Madness was coming upon her; she grew afraid, and managed to recover herself, in a confused way, it is true, for she did not remember the cause of her dreadful confusion, namely the money. She suffered only in her love, and felt her soul escaping from her in this memory, as wounded men, dying, feel their life ebb from their bleeding wounds.

Night was falling, crows were flying about.

Suddenly it seemed to her that fiery spheres were exploding in the air like bullets when they strike, and were whirling, whirling, to melt at last upon the snow between the branches of the trees. In the midst of each of them appeared the face of Rodolphe. They multiplied and drew near, they penetrated her. It all disappeared; she recognised the lights of the houses that shone through the fog.

Now her plight, like an abyss, loomed before her. She was panting as if her heart would burst. Then in an ecstasy of heroism, that
made her almost joyous, she ran down the hill, crossed the cow-
plank, the footpath, the alley, the market, and reached the pharmacy. She was about to enter, but at the sound of the bell some one
might come, and slipping in by the gate, holding her breath, feeling
her way along the walls, she went as far as the door of the kitchen,
where a candle was burning on the stove. Justin in his shirt-sleeves
was carrying out a dish.

"Ah! they're eating; let's wait."

He returned; she tapped at the window. He came out.

"The key! the one for upstairs where he keeps the . . ."

"What?"

And he looked at her, astonished at the pallor of her face, that
stood out white against the black background of the night. She
seemed to him extraordinarily beautiful and majestic as a phantom.
Without understanding what she wanted, he had the presentiment
of something terrible.

But she went on quickly in a low voice that was sweet and
melting:

"I want it; give it to me."

As the partition wall was thin, they could hear the clatter of the
forks on the plates in the dining-room.

She pretended that she wanted to kill the rats that kept her from
sleeping.

"I must go ask Monsieur."

"No, stay!"

Then with a casual air:

"Oh, it's not worth bothering him about, I'll tell him myself
later. Come, hold the light for me."

She entered the corridor into which the laboratory door opened.
Against the wall was a key labelled *Capharnaüm*.

"Justin!" called the pharmacist, growing impatient.

"Let's go up."

And he followed her. The key turned in the lock, and she went
straight to the third shelf, so well did her memory guide her, seized
the blue jar, tore out the cork, plunged in her hand, and withdraw-
ing it full of white powder, she ate it greedily.

"Stop!" he cried, throwing himself upon her.

"Quiet! They might hear us . . ."

He was in despair, ready to call out.

"Say nothing, or all the blame will fall on your master."

Then she went home, suddenly calmed, with something of the
serenity of one that has done his duty.

When Charles, thunderstruck at the news of the execution, rushed home, Emma had just gone out. He cried aloud, wept, fainted, but she did not return. Where could she be? He sent Félicité to Homais, to Monsieur Tuvache, to Lheureux, to the "Lion d'Or," everywhere, and in between the waves of his anxiety he saw his reputation destroyed, their fortune lost, Berthe's future ruined. By what?—Not a word! He waited till six in the evening. At last, unable to bear it any longer, and fancying she had gone to Rouen, he set out along the highroad, walked a mile, met no one, again waited, and returned home.

She had come back.

"What happened? . . . Why did you? . . . Tell me . . ."

She sat down at her writing-table and wrote a letter, which she sealed slowly, adding the date and the hour.

Then she said in a solemn tone:

"You are to read it to-morrow; till then, I beg you, don't ask me a single question. No, not one!"

"But . . ."

"Oh, leave me!"

She lay down full length on her bed.

A bitter taste in her mouth awakened her. She saw Charles, and again closed her eyes.

She was studying herself curiously, to detect the first signs of suffering. But no! nothing as yet. She heard the ticking of the clock, the crackling of the fire, and Charles breathing as he stood upright by her bed.

"Ah! it is but a little thing, death!" she thought. "I shall fall asleep and all will be over."

She drank a mouthful of water and turned her face to the wall. The frightful taste of ink persisted.

"I am thirsty; oh! so thirsty," she sighed.

"What is the matter?" said Charles, who was handing her a glass.

"It's nothing . . . Open the window, I'm choking."

She was seized with a sickness so sudden that she had hardly time to draw out her handkerchief from under the pillow.

"Take it away," she said quickly; "throw it away."

He spoke to her; she did not answer. She lay motionless, afraid that the slightest movement might make her vomit. But she felt an icy cold creeping from her feet to her heart.

"Ah! It's beginning," she murmured.

"What did you say?"

She gently rocked her head to and fro in anguish, opening her jaws as if something very heavy were weighing upon her tongue. At eight o'clock the vomiting began again.

Charles noticed that at the bottom of the basin there was a trace of white sediment sticking to the sides of the porcelain.

"This is extraordinary, very strange!" he repeated.

"No!" she loudly replied, "you are mistaken."

Then gently, almost caressingly, he passed his hand over her stomach. She uttered a sharp cry. He recoiled in terror.

Then she began to moan, faintly at first. Her shoulders were shaken by a strong shudder, and she was growing paler than the sheets in which she buried her clenched fists. Her unequal pulse was now almost imperceptible.

Drops of sweat oozed from her face, that had turned blue and rigid as under the effect of a metallic vapor. Her teeth chattered, her dilated eyes looked vaguely about her, and to all questions she replied only with a shake of the head; she even smiled once or twice. Gradually, her moaning grew louder; she couldn't repress a muffled scream; she pretended she felt better and that she'd soon get up. But she was seized with convulsions and cried out:

"God! It's horrible!"

He threw himself on his knees by her bed.

"Tell me! what have you eaten? Answer, for heaven's sake!"

And he looked at her with a tenderness in his eyes such as she had never seen.

"Well, there . . . there . . ." she said in a faltering voice.

He flew to the writing-table, tore open the seal, and read aloud: "Let no one be blamed . . ." He stopped, passed his hands over his eyes, and read it over again.

"What! . . . Help! Help!"

He could only keep repeating the word: "Poisoned! poisoned!" Félicité ran to Homais, who proclaimed it in the market-place; Madame Lefrançois heard it at the "Lion d'Or;" some got up to go and tell their neighbors, and all night the village was on the alert.

Distracted, stammering, reeling, Charles wandered about the room. He knocked against the furniture, tore his hair, and the pharmacist had never believed that there could be so terrible a sight.

He went home to write to Monsieur Canivet and to Doctor Larivière. His mind kept wandering, he had to start over fifteen times. Hippolyte went to Neufchâtel, and Justin so spurred Bovary's horse that he left it foundered and three parts dead by the hill at Bois-Guillaume.

Charles tried to look up his medical dictionary, but could not read it; the lines were jumping before his eyes.

"Be calm," said the pharmacist; "we must administer a powerful antidote. What is the poison?"

Charles showed him the letter. It was arsenic.

"Very well," said Homais, "we must make an analysis."

For he knew that in cases of poisoning an analysis must be made; and the other, who did not understand, answered:

"Oh, do it! Do anything! Save her . . ."

Then going back to her, he sank upon the carpet, and lay there with his head leaning against the edge of her bed, sobbing.

"Don't cry," she said to him. "Soon I won't trouble you any longer."

"Why did you do it? Who made you?"

She replied:

"There was no other way!"

"Weren't you happy? Is it my fault? But I did the best I could!"

"Yes, that's true . . . you're good, not like the others."

And she slowly passed her hand over his hair. The sweetness of this sensation deepened his sadness; he felt his whole being dissolving in despair at the thought that he must lose her, just when she was confessing more love for him than she ever did. He didn't know what to do, felt paralyzed by fear; the need for an immediate decision took away his last bit of self-control.

Emma thought that, at last, she was through with lying, cheating and with the numberless desires that had tortured her. She hated no one now; a twilight dimness was settling upon her thoughts, and, of all earthly noises, Emma heard none but the intermittent lamentations of this poor heart, sweet and remote like the echo of a symphony dying away.

"Bring me the child," she said, raising herself on her elbow.

"You're not feeling worse, are you?" asked Charles.

"No, no!"

The child, serious, and still half-asleep, was carried in on the maid's arm in her long white nightgown, from which her bare feet peeped out. She looked wonderingly at the disordered room, and half-closed her eyes, dazzled by the burning candles on the table. They reminded her, no doubt, of the morning of New Year's day and Mid-Lent, when thus awakened early by candlelight she came to her mother's bed to fetch her presents.

"But where is it, mamma?" she asked.

And as everybody was silent, "But I can't see my little stocking."

Félicité held her over the bed while she still kept looking towards the mantelpiece.

"Did nurse take it away?" she asked.

At the mention of this name, that carried her back to the memory of her adulteries and her calamities, Madame Bovary turned away her head, as at the loathing of another bitterer poison that rose to her mouth. But Berthe remained perched on the bed.

"Oh, how big your eyes are, mamma! How pale you are! how you sweat!"

Her mother looked at her.

"I'm frightened!" cried the child, recoiling.

Emma took her hand to kiss it; the child struggled.

"Enough! Take her away!" cried Charles, who was sobbing at the foot of the bed.

Then the symptoms ceased for a moment; she seemed less agitated; and at every insignificant word she spoke, every time she drew breath a little easier, his hopes revived. At last, when Canivet came in, he threw himself into his arms.

"Ah; it's you. Thank you! How good of you to come. But she's better. See! look at her."

His colleague was by no means of this opinion, and "never beating about the bush"—as he put it—he prescribed an emetic in order to empty the stomach completely.

She soon began vomiting blood. Her lips became drawn. Her limbs were convulsed, her whole body covered with brown spots, and her pulse slipped beneath the fingers like a stretched thread, like a harp-string about to break.

After this she began to scream horribly. She cursed the poison, railed at it, and implored it to be quick, and thrust away with her stiffened arms everything that Charles, in more agony than herself, tried to make her drink. He stood up, his handkerchief to his lips, moaning, weeping, and choked by sobs that shook his whole body. Félicité was running up and down the room. Homais, motionless, uttered great sighs; and Monsieur Canivet, always retaining his self-command, nevertheless began to feel uneasy.

"The devil! yet she has been purged, and since the cause has been removed . . ."

"The effect must cease," said Homais, "that's obvious."

"Oh, save her!" cried Bovary.

And, without listening to the pharmacist, who was still venturing the hypothesis. "It is perhaps a salutary paroxysm," Canivet was about to administer theriaca, when they heard the cracking of a whip; all the windows rattled, and a postchaise drawn by three horses abreast, up to their ears in mud, drove at a gallop round the corner of market. It was Doctor Larivière.

The apparition of a god would not have caused more commotion. Bovary raised his hands; Canivet stopped short; and Homais pulled off his cap long before the doctor had come in.

He belonged to that great school of surgeons created by Bichat, to 'that generation, now extinct, of philosophical practitioners, who, cherishing their art with a fanatical love, exercised it with enthusiasm and wisdom. Every one in his hospital trembled when he was angry: and his students so revered him that they tried, as soon as they were themselves in practice, to imitate him as much as possible. They could be found in all the neighboring towns wearing exactly the same merino overcoat and black frock. The doctor's buttoned cuffs slightly covered his fleshy hands—very beautiful hands, never covered by gloves, as though to be more ready to plunge into suffering. Disdainful of honors, of titles, and of academies, hospitable, generous, fatherly to the poor, and practising virtue without believing in it, he would almost have passed for a saint if the keenness of his intellect had not caused him to be feared as a demon. His glance, more penetrating than his scalpels, looked straight into your soul, and would detect any lie, regardless how well hidden. He went through life with the benign dignity that goes with the assurance of talent and wealth, with forty years of a hard-working, blameless life.

He frowned as soon as he had passed the door when he saw the cadaverous face of Emma stretched out on her back with her mouth open. Then, while apparently listening to Canivet, he rubbed his fingers up and down beneath his nostrils, repeating:

"I see, yes, yes . . ."

But he slowly shrugged his shoulders. Bovary watched him; they looked at one another; and this man, accustomed as he was to the sight of pain, could not keep back a tear that fell on his shirt front.

He tried to take Canivet into the next room. Charles followed him.

"She is sinking, isn't she? If we put on poultices? Anything! Oh, think of something, you who have saved so many!"

Charles put both arms around him, and looked at him in anxious supplication, half-fainting against his breast.

"Come, my poor boy, courage! There is nothing more to be done."

And Doctor Larivière turned away.

"You are leaving?"

"I'll be back."

He went out as if to give an order to the coachman, followed by Canivet, who was equally glad to escape from the spectacle of Emma dying.

The pharmacist caught up with them on the Square. He could not by temperament keep away from celebrities, so he begged Monsieur Larivière to do him the signal honor of staying for lunch.

He sent quickly to the "Lion d'Or" for some pigeons; to the butcher's for all the cutlets that could be found; to Tuvache for cream; and to Lestiboudois for eggs; and Homais himself aided in the preparations, while Madame Homais was saying as she tightened her apron-strings:

"I hope you'll forgive us, sir, for in this village, if one is caught unawares . . ."

"Stemmed glasses!" whispered Homais.

"If only we were in the city, I'd be able to find stuffed pig's feet . . ."

"Be quiet . . . Please doctor, à table!"

He thought fit, after the first few mouthfuls, to supply some details about the catastrophe.

"We first had a feeling of siccity in the pharynx, then intolerable pains at the epigastrium, super-purgation, coma."

"But how did she poison herself?"

"I don't know, doctor, and I don't even know where she can have procured the arsenious acid."

Justin, who was just bringing in a pile of plates, began to tremble.

"What's the matter?" said the pharmacist.

At this question the young man dropped the whole lot on the floor with a dreadful crash.

"Imbecile!" cried Homais, "clumsy lout! blockhead! confounded ass!"

But suddenly controlling himself:

"I wished, doctor, to make an analysis, and *primo* I delicately introduced a tube . . ."

"You would have done better," said the physician, "to introduce your fingers into her throat."

His colleague was silent, having just before privately received a severe lecture about his emetic, so that this good Canivet, so arrogant and so verbose at the time of the club-foot, was to-day very modest. He smiled an incessantly approving smile.

Homais dilated in Amphytrionic pride, and the affecting thought of Bovary vaguely contributed to his pleasure by a kind of selfish comparison with his own lot. Moreover, the presence of the surgeon exalted him. He displayed his erudition, spoke effusively about cantharides, upas, the manchineel, adder bites.

"I have even read that various persons have found themselves under toxicological symptoms, and, as it were, paralyzed by blood sausage that had been too strongly smoked. At least, this was stated in a very fine paper prepared by one of our pharmaceutical authorities, one of our masters, the illustrious Cadet de Gassicourt!"

Madame Homais reappeared, carrying one of those shaky machines that are heated with spirits of wine; for Homais liked to make his coffee at the table, having, moreover, torrefied it, pulverised it, and mixed it himself.

"*Saccharum*, doctor?" he said, offering sugar.

Then he had all his children brought down, anxious to have the physician's opinion on their constitutions.

At last Monsieur Larivière was about to leave, when Madame Homais asked for a consultation about her husband. He was making his blood too thick by falling asleep every evening after dinner.

"Oh, it isn't his blood I'd call too thick," said the physician.

And, smiling a little at his unnoticed joke, the doctor opened the door. But the shop was full of people; he had the greatest difficulty in getting rid of Monsieur Tuvache, who feared his wife would get pneumonia because she was in the habit of spitting on the ashes; then of Monseiur Binet, who sometimes experienced sudden attacks of great hunger; and of Madame Caron, who suffered from prickling sensations; of Lheureux, who had dizzy spells; of Lestiboudois, who had rheumatism; and of Madame Lefrançois, who had heartburn. At last the three horses started; and it was the general opinion that he had not shown himself at all obliging.

Public attention was distracted by the appearance of Monsieur Bournisien, who was going across the square carrying the holy oil.

Homais, as was due to his principles, compared priests to ravens attracted by the smell of death. The sight of an ecclesiastic was personally disagreeable to him, for the cassock made him think of the shroud, and his dislike of the one matched his fear of the other.

Nevertheless, not shrinking from what he called his "Mission," he returned to Bovary's house with Canivet, who had been strongly urged by Dr. Larivière to make this call; and he would, but for his wife's objections, have taken his two sons with him, in order to accustom them to great occasions; that this might be a lesson, an example, a solemn picture, that should remain in their heads later on.

The room when they went in was full of mournful solemnity. On the work-table, covered over with a white cloth, there were five or six small balls of cotton in a silver dish, near a large crucifix between two lighted candles.

Emma, her chin sunken upon her breast, had her eyes inordinately wide open, and her poor hands wandered over the sheets with that hideous and gentle movement of the dying, that seems as if they already wanted to cover themselves with the shroud. Pale as a statue and with eyes red as fire, Charles, beyond weeping, stood opposite her at the foot of the bed, while the priest, bending one knee, was muttering in a low voice.

She turned her face slowly, and seemed filled with joy on suddenly seeing the violet stole. She was doubtlessly reminded, in this moment of sudden serenity, of the lost bliss of her first mystical flights, mingling with the visions of eternal beatitude that were beginning.

The priest rose to take the crucifix; then she stretched forward her neck like one suffering from thirst, and glueing her lips to the body of the Man-God, she pressed upon it with all her expiring strength the fullest kiss of love that she had ever given. Then he recited the *Misereatur* and the *Indulgentiam*, dipped his right thumb in the oil, and began to give extreme unction. First, upon the eyes, that had so coveted all wordly goods; then upon the nostrils, that had been so greedy of the warm breeze and the scents of love; then upon the mouth, that had spoken lies, moaned in pride and cried out in lust; then upon the hands that had taken delight in the texture of sensuality; and finally upon the soles of the feet, so swift when she had hastened to satisfy her desires, and that would now walk no more.

The curé wiped his fingers, threw the bit of oil-stained cotton into the fire, and came and sat down by the dying woman, to tell her that she must now blend her sufferings with those of Jesus Christ and abandon herself to the divine mercy.

Finishing his exhortations, he tried to place in her hand a blessed candle, symbol of the celestial glory with which she was soon to be surrounded. Emma, too weak, could not close her fingers, and if it hadn't been for Monsieur Bournisien, the taper would have fallen to the ground.

Yet she was no longer quite so pale, and her face had an expression of serenity as if the sacrament had cured her.

The priest did not fail to point this out; he even explained to Bovary that the Lord sometimes prolonged the life of persons when he thought it useful for their salvation; and Charles remembered the day when, so near death, she had received communion. Perhaps there was no need to despair, he thought.

In fact, she looked around her slowly, as one awakening from a dream; then in a distinct voice she asked for her mirror, and remained bent over it for some time, until big tears fell from her eyes. Then she turned away her head with a sigh and fell back upon the pillows.

Her chest soon began heaving rapidly; the whole of her tongue protruded from her mouth; her eyes, as they rolled, grew paler, like the two globes of a lamp that is going out, so that one might have thought her already dead but for the fearful labouring of her ribs, shaken by violent breathing, as if the soul were struggling to free itself. Félicité knelt down before the crucifix, and the pharmacist himself slightly bent his knees, while Monsieur Canivet looked out vaguely at the Square. Bournisien had resumed his praying, his face bowed against the edge of the bed, his long black cassock trailing behind him in the room. Charles was on the other side, on his knees, his arms outstretched towards Emma. He had taken her hands and pressed them, shuddering at every heartbeat, as at the tremors of a falling ruin. As the death-rattle became stronger the priest prayed faster; his prayers mingled with Bovary's stifled sobs, and sometimes all seemed lost in the muffled murmur of the Latin syllables that sounded like a tolling bell.

Suddenly from the pavement outside came the loud noise of wooden shoes and the clattering of a stick; and a voice rose—a raucous voice—that sang

> Often the heat of a summer's day
> Makes a young girl dream her heart away.

Emma raised herself like a galvanised corpse, her hair streaming, her eyes fixed, staring.

> To gather up all the new-cut stalks
> Of wheat left by the scythe's cold swing,
> Nanette bends over as she walks
> Toward the furrows from where they spring.

"The blind man!" she cried.

And Emma began to laugh, an atrocious, frantic, desperate laugh, thinking she saw the hideous face of the poor wretch loom out of the eternal darkness like a menace.

> The wind blew very hard that day
> It blew her petticoat away.

A final spasm threw her back upon the mattress. They all drew near. She had ceased to exist.

IX

Someone's death always causes a kind of stupefaction; so difficult it is to grasp this advent of nothingness and to resign ourselves to the fact that it has actually taken place. But still, when he saw that she did not move, Charles flung himself upon her, crying:

"Farewell! farewell!"

Homais and Canivet dragged him from the room.

"Control yourself!"

"Yes," he said, struggling, "I'll be quiet. I won't do anything. But let me stay. I want to see her. She is my wife!"

And he wept.

"Cry," said the pharmacist; "let nature take its course; that will relieve you."

Weaker than a child, Charles let himself be led downstairs into the sitting-room, and Monsieur Homais soon went home. On the Square he was accosted by the blind man, who, having dragged himself as far as Yonville in the hope of getting the antiphlogistic salve, was asking every passer-by where the pharmacist lived.

"Good heavens, man, as if I didn't have other fish to fry! I can't help it, but you'll have to come back later."

And he hurried into the shop.

He had to write two letters, to prepare a soothing potion for Bovary, to invent some lie that would conceal the poisoning, and work it up into an article for the "Fanal," without counting the people who were waiting to get the news from him; and when the Yonvillers had all heard his story of the arsenic that she had mistaken for sugar in making a vanilla cream, Homais once more returned to Bovary's.

He found him alone (Monsieur Canivet had left), sitting in an arm-chair near the window, staring with a vacant look at the stone floor.

"Well," Homais said, "you ought yourself to fix the hour for the ceremony."

"Why? What ceremony?"

Then, in a stammering, frightened voice:

"Oh, no! not that. No! I want to keep her here."

Homais, to save face, took up a pitcher from the whatnot to water the geraniums.

"Ah! thank you," said Charles; "how kind of you!"

But he did not finish, choked by the flow of memories that Homais' action had released in him.

Then to distract him, Homais thought fit to talk a little about horticulture: plants wanted moisture. Charles bowed his head in approval.

"Besides, we'll soon be having fine weather again."

"Ah!" said Bovary.

The pharmacist, at his wit's end, gently drew aside the small window-curtain.

"Look! there's Monsieur Tuvache passing by."

Charles repeated mechanically:

"Monsieur Tuvache passing by!"

Homais did not dare to bring up the funeral arrangements again; it was the priest who finally convinced him of the necessity to bury Emma.

He shut himself up in his consulting-room, took a pen, and after sobbing for some time, wrote:

"I wish her to be buried in her wedding dress, with white shoes, and a wreath. Her hair is to be spread out over her shoulders. Three coffins, one oak, one mahogany, one of lead. Let no one try to overrule me; I shall have the strength to resist him. She is to be covered with a large piece of green velvet. This is my wish; see that it is done."

The two men were much taken aback by Bovary's romantic ideas. The pharmacist was first to remonstrate with him:

"This velvet seems excessive to me. Besides, think of the expense . . ."

"What's that to you?" cried Charles. "Leave me alone! You didn't love her. Go away!"

The priest took him by the arm for a walk in the garden. He discoursed on the vanity of earthly things. God was very great, very good: one must submit to his decrees without a murmur, even learn to be grateful for one's suffering.

Charles burst into blasphemy:

"I hate your God!"

"The spirit of rebellion is still upon you," sighed the priest.

Bovary was far away. He was striding along by the wall, near the espalier, and he ground his teeth; he raised to heaven looks of malediction, but not so much as a leaf stirred.

A fine rain was falling: Charles, whose chest was bare, at last began to shiver; he went in and sat down in the kitchen.

At six o'clock a noise like a clatter of old iron was heard on the square; it was the "Hirondelle" coming in, and he remained with his forehead pressed against the window-pane, watching all the passengers get out, one after the other. Félicité put down a mattress for him in the drawing-room. He threw himself upon it and fell asleep.

Although a philosopher, Monsieur Homais respected the dead. So bearing poor Charles no grudge, he returned in the evening to sit up with the body, bringing with him three books and a writing-pad for taking notes.

Monsieur Bournisien was there, and two large candles were burning at the head of the bed, which had been taken out of the alcove.

The pharmacist, unable to keep silent, soon began to express some regrets about this "unfortunate young woman," and the priest replied that there was nothing to do now but pray for her.

"Still," Homais insisted, "it is one of two things; either she died in a state of grace (as the Church calls it), and then she doesn't need our prayers; or else she died unrepentant (that is, I believe, the correct technical term), and then . . ."

Bournisien interrupted him, replying testily that it was none the less necessary to pray.

"But," the pharmacist objected, "since God knows all our needs, what can be the good of prayer?"

"What!" the priest exclaimed, "of prayer? Why, aren't you a Christian?"

"I beg your pardon," said Homais; "I admire Christianity. It freed the slaves, brought morality into the world . . ."

"That isn't the point. Look at the texts . . ."

"Oh! oh! As to texts, look at history; everybody knows that the Jesuits have falsified all the texts!"

Charles came in, and advancing towards the bed, slowly drew the curtains.

Emma's head was turned towards her right shoulder, the corner of her mouth, which was open, seemed like a black hole at the lower part of her face; her two thumbs were bent into the palms of her hands; a kind of white dust besprinkled her lashes, and her eyes were beginning to disappear in a viscous pallor, as if covered by a spiderweb. The sheet sunk in from her breast to her knees, and then rose at the tips of her toes, and it seemed to Charles that infinite masses, an enormous load, were weighing upon her.

The church clock struck two. They could hear the loud murmur of the river flowing in the darkness at the foot of the terrace. Monsieur Bournisien noisily blew his nose from time to time, and Homais' pen was scratching over the paper.

"Come, my good friend," he said, "don't stay here; the sight is too much for you."

When Charles had left, the pharmacist and the priest resumed their argument.

"Read Voltaire," said the one, "read D'Holbach, read the *Encyclopédie!*"[8]

"Read the 'Letters of some Portuguese Jews,'" said the other; "read 'The Meaning of Christianity,' by the former magistrate Nicolas."

They grew warm, they grew red, they both talked at once without listening to each other. Bournisien was scandalised at such audacity; Homais marvelled at such stupidity; and they were about to come to blows when Charles suddenly reappeared. He couldn't resist coming upstairs as though he were spellbound.

He stood at the foot of the bed to see her better, and he lost himself in a contemplation so deep that it was no longer painful.

He recalled stories of catalepsy, the marvels of magnetism, and he said to himself that by willing it with all his force he might perhaps succeed in reviving her. Once he even bent towards her, and cried in a low voice, "Emma! Emma!" His strong breathing made the flames of the candles tremble against the wall.

At daybreak the elder Madame Bovary arrived. As he embraced her, Charles burst into another flood of tears. She tried, as the pharmacist had done, to remonstrate with him on the expenses for the funeral. He became so angry that she was silent, and he even

5. Paul-Henri Dietrich, baron d' Holbach (1723–89), friend and disciple of Diderot, was one of the most outspoken opponents of religion in the French Enlightenment. The *Encyclopedie*, a dictionary of the sciences, arts and letters, edited by Diderot and d'Alembert (1751–72) is the intellectual monument of the French Enlightenment, a fountainhead of later secular and agnostic thought.

commissioned her to go to town at once and buy what was necessary.

Charles remained alone the whole afternoon; they had taken Berthe to Madame Homais'; Félicité was in the room upstairs with Madame Lefrançois.

In the evening he had some visitors. He rose and shook hands with them, unable to speak. Then they sat down together, and formed a large semicircle in front of the fire. With lowered head, they crossed and uncrossed their legs, and uttered from time to time a deep sigh. They were bored to tears, yet none would be the first to go.

Homais, when he returned at nine o'clock (for the last two days Homais seemed to have made the public Square his residence), was laden with a supply of camphor, benzoin and aromatic herbs. He also carried a large jar full of chlorine water, to keep off the miasma. Just then the servant, Madame Lefrançois and the elder Madame Bovary were busy getting Emma dressed, and they were drawing down the long stiff veil that covered her to her satin shoes.

Félicité was sobbing:

"Oh, my poor mistress! my poor mistress!"

"Look at her," said the innkeeper, sighing; "how pretty she still is! Now, couldn't you swear she was going to get up in a minute?"

Then they bent over her to put on her wreath. They had to raise the head a little, and a rush of black liquid poured from her mouth, as if she were vomiting.

"Heavens! Watch out for her dress!" cried Madame Lefrançois. "Now, just come and help us," she said to the pharmacist, "or are you afraid?"

"Afraid?" he replied, "I? As if I hadn't seen a lot worse when I was a student at the Hotel-Dieu. We used to make punch in the dissecting room! Nothingness does not frighten a philosopher; I have often said that I intend to leave my body to the hospitals, to serve the cause of science."

On arriving, the curé inquired after Monsieur Bovary and, at Homais' reply, he said:

"Of course, the blow is still too recent."

Then Homais congratulated him on not being exposed, like other people, to the loss of a beloved companion; this lead to a discussion on the celibacy of priests.

"You must admit," said the pharmacist, "that it is against nature for a man to do without women. There have been crimes . . ."

"For Heaven's sake!" exclaimed the priest, "how do you expect an individual who is married to keep the secrets of the confessional, for example?"

Homais attacked confession. Bournisien defended it; he discoursed on the acts of restitution that it brought about. He cited various anecdotes about thieves who had suddenly become honest. Military men on approaching the tribunal of penitence had finally seen the light. At Fribourg there was a minister . . .

His companion had fallen asleep. Then he felt somewhat stifled by the over-heavy atmosphere of the room; he opened the window; this awoke the pharmacist.

"Come, take a pinch of snuff," he told him. "Take it, it'll do you good."

A continual barking was heard in the distance.

"Do you hear that dog howling?" said the pharmacist.

"They smell the dead," replied the priest. "It's like bees; they leave their hives when there is a death in the neighborhood."

Homais failed to object to these prejudices, for he had again dropped asleep. Monsieur Bournisien, stronger than he, went on moving his lips and muttering for some time, then insensibly his chin sank down, he dropped his big black book, and began to snore.

They sat opposite one another, with bulging stomachs, puffed-up faces, and frowning looks, after so much disagreement uniting at last in the same human weakness, and they moved no more than the corpse by their side, that also seemed to be sleeping.

Charles coming in did not wake them. It was the last time; he came to bid her farewell.

The aromatic herbs were still smoking, and spirals of bluish vapour blended at the window with the entering fog. There were few stars, and the night was warm.

The wax of the candles fell in great drops upon the sheets of the bed. Charles watched them burn, straining his eyes in the glare of their yellow flame.

The watered satin of her gown shimmered white as moonlight. Emma was lost beneath it; and it seemed to him that, spreading beyond her own self, she blended confusedly with everything around her—the silence, the night, the passing wind, the damp odors rising from the ground.

Then suddenly he saw her in the garden at Tostes, on a bench against the thorn hedge, or else at Rouen in the streets, on the threshold of their house, in the yard at Bertaux. He again heard the laughter of the happy boys dancing under the appletrees: the room was filled with the perfume of her hair; and her dress rustled in his arms with a crackling noise. It was the same dress she was wearing now!

For a long while he thus recalled all his lost joys, her attitudes, her movements, the sound of her voice. Wave upon wave of despair came over him, like the tides of an overflowing sea.

He was seized by a terrible curiosity. Slowly, with the tips of his fingers, his heart pounding, he lifted her veil. But he uttered a cry of horror that awoke the other two.

They dragged him down into the sitting-room. Then Félicité came up to say that he wanted some of her hair.

"Cut some off," replied the pharmacist.

And as she did not dare to, he himself stepped forward, scissors in hand. He trembled so that he nicked the skin of the temple in several places. At last, stiffening himself against emotion, Homais gave two or three great cuts at random that left white patches amongst that beautiful black hair.

The pharmacist and the curé resumed their original occupations, not without time and again falling asleep—something of which they accused each other whenever they awoke. Monsieur Bournisien sprinkled the room with holy water and Homais threw a little chlorine on the floor.

Félicité had been so considerate as to put on the chest of drawers, for each of them, a bottle of brandy, some cheese, and a large brioche, and about four o'clock in the morning, unable to restrain himself any longer, the pharmacist sighed:

"I must say that I wouldn't mind taking some sustenance."

The priest did not need any persuading; he left to say mass and, upon his return, they ate and drank, chuckling a little without knowing why, stimulated by that vague gaiety that comes upon us after times of sadness. At the last glass the priest said to the pharmacist, as he clapped him on the shoulder:

"We'll end up good friends, you and I."

In the passage downstairs they met the undertaker's men, who were coming in. Then for two hours Charles had to suffer the torture of hearing the hammer resound against the wood. Next day they lowered her into her oak coffin, that was fitted into the other two; but as the bier was too large, they had to fill up the gaps with the wool of a mattress. At last, when the three lids had been planed down, nailed, soldered, it was placed outside in front of the door; the house was thrown open, and the people of Yonville began to flock round.

Old Rouault arrived, and fainted on the square at the sight of the black cloth.

X

He had only received Homais' letter thirty-six hours after the event; and, to cushion the blow, he had worded it in such a manner that it was impossible to make out just what had happened.

First, the old man had been shaken as if struck by apoplexy. Next, he understood that she was not dead, but she might be . . . At last, he had put on his smock, taken his hat, fastened his spurs to his boots, and set out at full speed; and the whole of the way old Rouault, panting, had been devoured by anxiety. He felt so dizzy that he was forced to dismount. He fancied he heard voices around him and thought he was losing his mind.

Day broke. He saw three black hens asleep in a tree. He shuddered, horrified at this omen. Then he promised the Holy Virgin three chasubles for the church, and vowed that he would go barefooted from the cemetery at Bertaux to the chapel of Vassonville.

He entered Maromme calling out ahead at the people of the inn, burst open the door with a thrust of his shoulder, made for a sack of oats and emptied a bottle of sweet cider into the manger; then he remounted his nag, whose feet struck sparks as it galloped along.

He told himself that they would certainly save her; the doctors were bound to discover a remedy. He remembered all the miraculous cures he had been told about.

Then she appeared to him dead: She was there, before his eyes, lying on her back in the middle of the road. He reined in his horse, and the hallucination disappeared.

At Quincampoix, to give himself heart, he drank three cups of coffee one after the other.

He imagined that they had written the wrong name on the letter. He looked for the letter in his pocket, felt it there, but did not dare to open it.

At last he began to think it was all a bad joke, a spiteful farce, somebody's idea of a fine prank; besides, if she were dead, he would have known. It couldn't be! the countryside looked as usual: the sky was blue, the trees swayed; a flock of sheep passed by. He reached the village; they saw him coming, hunched over his horse, whipping it savagely till its saddle-girths dripped with blood.

When he recovered consciousness, he fell, weeping, into Bovary's arms:

"My daughter! Emma! my child! tell me . . ."

The other replied between sobs:

"I don't know! I don't know! It's a curse!"

The pharmacist pulled them apart.

"Spare him the horrible details. I'll tell monsieur all about it. People are coming, show some dignity, for heaven's sake! Let's behave like philosophers."

Poor Charles tried as hard as he could, and repeated several times:

"Yes, be brave . . ."

"Damn it, I'll be brave," cried the old man, "I'll stay with her till the end!"

The bell was tolling. All was ready; they had to start.

Seated together in a stall of the choir, they saw the three chanting choristers continually pass and repass in front of them. The serpent-player was blowing with all his might. Monsieur Bournisien, in full regalia, was singing in a shrill voice. He bowed before the tabernacle, raising his hands, stretched out his arms. Lestiboudois went about the church with his verger's staff. The bier stood near the lectern, between four rows of candles. Charles felt an urge to get up and put them out.

Yet he tried to stir into himself the proper devotional feelings, to throw himself into the hope of a future life in which he would see her again. He tried to convince himself that she had gone on a long journey, far away, for a long time. But when he thought of her lying there, and that it was all over and that they would put her in the earth, he was seized with a fierce, gloomy, desperate rage. It seemed at times that he felt nothing, and he welcomed this lull in his pain, while blaming himself bitterly for being such a scoundrel.

The sharp noise of an iron-tipped stick was heard on the stones, striking them at irregular intervals. It came from the end of the church, and stopped short at the lower aisles. A man in a coarse brown jacket knelt down painfully. It was Hippolyte, the stable-boy at the "Lion d'Or." He had put on his new leg.

One of the choir boys came round the nave taking collection, and the coppers chinked one after the other on the silver plate.

"Oh hurry up!" cried Bovary, angrily throwing him a five-franc piece. "I can't stand it any longer."

The singer thanked him with a deep bow.

They sang, they knelt, they stood up; it was endless! He remembered how once, in the early days of their marriage, they had been to mass together, and they had sat down on the other side, on the right, by the wall. The bell began again. There was a great shuffling of chairs; the pall bearers slipped their three poles under the coffin, and every one left the church.

Then Justin appeared in the doorway of the pharmacy, but retreated suddenly, pale and staggering.

People stood at the windows to see the procession pass by. Charles walked first, as straight as he could. He tried to look brave and nodded to those who joined the crowd, coming from the side streets or from the open doors. The six men, three on either side, walked slowly, panting a little. The priests, the choristers, and the two choir-boys recited the *De profundis*, and their voices echoed over the fields, rising and falling with the shape of the hills. Sometimes they disappeared in the windings of the path; but the great silver cross always remained visible among the trees.

The women followed, wearing black coats with turned-down hoods; each of them carried a large lighted candle, and Charles felt himself grow faint at this continual repetition of prayers and torchlights, oppressed by the sweetish smell of wax and of cassocks. A fresh breeze was blowing; the rye and colza were turning green and along the roadside, dewdrops hung from the hawthorn hedges. All sorts of joyous sounds filled the air; the jolting of a cart rolling way off in the ruts, the crowing of a cock, repeated again and again, or the gamboling of a foal under the apple-trees. The pure sky was dappled with rosy clouds; a blueish haze hung over the iris-covered cottages. Charles recognized each courtyard as he passed. He remembered mornings like this, when, after visiting a patient, he left one of those houses to return home, to his wife.

The black cloth decorated with silver tears, flapped from time to time in the wind, baring the coffin underneath. The tired bearers walked more slowly, and the bier advanced jerkily, like a boat that pitches with every wave.

They reached the cemetery.

The men went right down to a place in the grass where a grave had been dug. They grouped themselves all round; and while the priest spoke, the red soil thrown up at the sides kept noiselessly slipping down at the corners.

Then, when the four ropes were laid out, the coffin was pushed onto them. He watched it go down; it seemed to go down forever.

At last a thud was heard; the ropes creaked and were drawn up. Then Bournisien took the spade handed to him by Lestiboudois; while his right hand kept sprinkling holy water, he vigorously threw in a spadeful of earth with the left; and the wood of the coffin, struck by the pebbles, gave forth that dread sound that seems to us the reverberation of eternity.

The priest passed the holy water sprinkler to his neighbor, Monsieur Homais. The pharmacist swung it gravely, then handed it to Charles, who sank to his knees and threw in handfuls of earth, crying, "Adieu!" He sent her kisses; he dragged himself towards the grave, as if to engulf himself with her.

They led him away, and he soon grew calmer, feeling perhaps, like the others, a vague satisfaction that it was all over.

Old Rouault on his way back began quietly smoking a pipe, to Homais' silent disapproval. He also noticed that Monsieur Binet had not come, that Tuvache had disappeared after mass, and that Theodore, the notary's servant, wore a blue coat—"as if he couldn't respect customs, and wear a black coat, for Heaven's sake!" And to share his observations with others he went from group to group. They were deploring Emma's death, especially Lheureux, who had not failed to come to the funeral.

"Poor little lady! What a blow for her husband!"

"Can you imagine," the pharmacist replied, "that he would have done away with himself if I hadn't intervened?"

"Such a fine person! To think that I saw her only last Saturday in my store."

"I haven't had leisure," said Homais, "to prepare a few words that I would cast over her tomb."

On getting home, Charles undressed, and old Rouault put on his blue smock. It was new, and as he had repeatedly wiped his eyes on the sleeves during his journey, the dye had stained his face, and traces of tears lined the layer of dust that covered it.

Mother Bovary joined them. All three were silent. At last the old man sighed:

"Do you remember, my friend, I came to Tostes once when you had just lost your first deceased? I consoled you that time. I could think of something to say then, but now . . ."

Then, with a loud groan that shook his whole chest,

"Ah! this is the end for me! I saw my wife go . . . then my son . . . and now today my daughter!"

He wanted to go back at once to Bertaux, saying that he couldn't sleep in this house. He even refused to see his grand-daughter.

"No, no! It would grieve me too much. You'll kiss her many times for me. Good bye . . . You're a good man! And I'll never forget this," he said, slapping his thigh. "Never fear, you shall always have your turkey."

But when he reached the top of the hill he turned back, as he had turned once before on the road of Saint-Victor when he had parted from her. The windows of the village were all ablaze in the slanting rays of the sun that was setting behind the meadow. He put his hand over his eyes, and saw at the horizon a walled enclosure, with black clusters of trees among the white stones; then he went on his way at a gentle trot, for his nag was limping.

Despite their fatigue, Charles and his mother stayed up talking very long that evening. They spoke of the days of the past and of the future. She would come to live at Yonville; she would keep house for him; they would never part again. She was subtly affectionate, rejoicing in her heart at regaining some of the tenderness that had wandered from her for so many years. Midnight struck. The village was silent as usual, and Charles lay awake, never ceasing to think of her.

Rodolphe, who, to distract himself, had been roaming in the woods all day, was quietly asleep in his château; and Léon, away in the city, also slept.

There was another who at that hour was not asleep.

On the grave between the pine-trees a child was on his knees weeping, and his heart, rent by sobs, was panting in the dark under the weight of an immense sorrow, tender as the moon and unfathomable as the night.

The gate suddenly grated. It was Lestiboudois coming to fetch the spade he had forgotten. He recognised Justin climbing over the wall, and knew at last who had been stealing his potatoes.

XI

The next day Charles had the child brought back. She asked for her mamma. They told her she was away; that she would bring her back some toys. Berthe mentioned her again several times, then finally forgot her. The child's gaiety broke Bovary's heart, and he had to put up besides with the intolerable consolations of the pharmacist.

Before long, money troubles started again. Monsieur Lheureux was putting his friend Vinçart back on the warpath, and before long Charles was signing notes for exorbitant amounts. For he would never consent to let the smallest of the things that had belonged to *her* be sold. His mother was exasperated with him; he grew even more angry than she did. He was a changed man. She left the house.

Then every one began to collect what they could. Mademoiselle Lempereur presented a bill for six months' teaching, although Emma had never taken a lesson (despite the receipted bill she had shown Bovary); it was an arrangement between the two women. The lending library demanded three years' subscriptions; Mère Rollet claimed postage for some twenty letters, and when Charles asked for an explanation, she was tactful enough to reply:

"Oh, I know nothing about it. It was her business."

With every debt he paid Charles thought he had reached the end. But others followed ceaselessly.

He tried to collect accounts due him from patients. He was shown the letters his wife had written. Then he had to apologise.

Félicité now wore Madame Bovary's dresses; not all, for he had kept some, and he locked himself up in Emma's room to look at them. Félicité was about her former mistress's height and often, on seeing her from behind, Charles thought she had come back and cried out:

"Oh, stay, don't go away!"

But at Pentecost she ran away from Yonville, carried off by Theodore, stealing all that was left of the wardrobe.

It was about this time that the widow Dupuis had the honor to inform him of the "marriage of Monsieur Léon Dupuis her son, notary at Yvetot, to Mademoiselle Léocadié Lebœuf Bondeville." Charles, among the other congratulations he sent him, wrote this sentence:

"How happy this would have made my poor wife!"

One day when, wandering aimlessly about the house, he had gone up to the attic, he felt a crumpled piece of paper under his slipper. He opened it and read: "Courage, Emma, courage. I would not bring misery into your life." It was Rodolphe's letter, fallen to the ground between the boxes, where it had remained till now, when the wind from the open dormer had blown it toward the door. And Charles stood, motionless and staring, in the very same place where, long ago, Emma, in despair, and paler even than he had thought of dying. At last he discovered a small R at the bottom of the second page. What did this mean? He remembered Rodolphe's attentions, his sudden disappearance, his embarrassed air on two or three subsequent occasions. But the respectful tone of the letter deceived him.

"Perhaps they loved one another platonically," he told himself.

Besides, Charles was not of those who go to the root of things; he shrank from the proofs, and his vague jealousy was lost in the immensity of his sorrow.

Every one, he thought, must have adored her; all men inevitably must have coveted her. This made her seem even more beautiful, and it awoke in him a fierce and persistent desire, which inflamed his despair and grew boundless, since it could never be assuaged.

To please her, as if she were still living, he adopted her taste, her ideas; he bought patent leather boots and took to wearing white cravats. He waxed his moustache and, just like her, signed promissory notes. She corrupted him from beyond the grave.

He was obliged to sell his silver piece by piece; next he sold the drawing-room furniture. All the rooms were stripped; but the bedroom, her own room, remained as before. After his dinner Charles went up there. He pushed the round table in front of the fire, and drew up *her* arm-chair. He sat down facing it. A candle burnt in one of the gilt candlesticks. Berthe, at his side, colored pictures.

He suffered, poor man, at seeing her so badly dressed, with laceless boots, and the arm-holes of her pinafore torn down to the hips; for the cleaning woman took no care of her. But she was so sweet, so pretty, and her little head bent forward so gracefully, letting her fair hair fall over her rosy cheeks, that an infinite joy came upon him, a happiness mingled with bitterness, like those ill-made wines that taste of resin. He mended her toys, made her puppets from cardboard, or sewed up half-torn dolls. Then, if his eyes fell upon the sewing kit, a ribbon lying about, or even a pin left in a crack of the table, he began to dream, and looked so sad that she became as sad as he.

No one now came to see them, for Justin had run away to Rouen, where he worked in a grocery, and the pharmacist's children saw less and less of the child. In view of the difference in their social positions, Monsieur Homais had chosen to discontinue the former intimacy.

The blind man, whom his salve had not cured, had gone back to the hill of Bois-Guillaume, where he told the travellers of his fail-ure, to such an extent, that Homais when he went to town hid him-self behind the curtains of the "Hirondelle" to avoid meeting him. He detested him, and wishing, in the interests of his own reputa-tion, to get rid of him at all costs, he directed against him a secret campaign, that betrayed the depth of his intellect and the baseness of his vanity. Thus, for six consecutive months, one could read in the "Fanal de Rouen" editorials such as these:

"Anyone who has ever wended his way towards the fertile plains of Picardy has, no doubt, remarked, by the Bois-Guillaume hill, an unfortunate wretch suffering from a horrible facial wound. He bothers the passers by, pursues them and levies a regular tax on all travellers. Are we still living in the monstrous times of the Middle Ages, when vagabonds were permitted to display in our public places leprosy and scrofulas they had brought back from the Cru-sades?"

Or:

"In spite of the laws against vagrancy, the approaches to our great towns continue to be infected by bands of beggars. Some are seen going about alone, and these are, by no means, the least dangerous. Why don't our City Authorities intervene?"

Then Homais invented incidents:

"Yesterday, by the Bois-Guillaume hill, a skittish horse . . ." And then followed the story of an accident caused by the presence of the blind man.

He managed so well that the fellow was locked up. But he was released. He began again, and so did Homais. It was a struggle. Homais won out, for his foe was condemned to lifelong confine-ment in an asylum.

This success emboldened him, and henceforth there was no longer a dog run over, a barn burnt down, a woman beaten in the parish, of which he did not immediately inform the public, guided always by the love of progress and the hate of priests. He instituted comparisons between the public and parochial schools to the detri-ment of the latter; called to mind the massacre of St. Bartholomew *à propos* of a grant of one hundred francs to the church; de-nounced abuses and kept people on their toes. That was his phrase. Homais was digging and delving; he was becoming dangerous.

However, he was stifling in the narrow limits of journalism, and soon a book, a major work, became a necessity. Then he composed "General Statistics of the Canton of Yonville, followed by Climato-logical Remarks." The statistics drove him to philosophy. He busied himself with great questions: the social problem, the moral plight of the poorer classes, pisciculture, rubber, railways, &c. He even began to blush at being a bourgeois. He affected bohemian manners, he smoked. He bought two *chic* Pompadour statuettes to adorn his drawing-room.

He by no means gave up his store. On the contrary, he kept well abreast of new discoveries. He followed the great trend towards chocolates; he was the first to introduce *Cho-ca* and *Revalenta* into the Seine-Inférieure. He was enthusiastic about the hydro-electric Pulvermacher health-belts; he wore one himself, and when at night he took off his flannel undershirt, Madame Homais was dazzled by the golden spiral that almost hid him from view. Her ardor would redouble for that man, swaddled more than a Scythian and as resplendent as one of the Magi.

He had fine ideas about Emma's tomb. First he proposed a broken column surmounted by a drapery, next a pyramid, then a Temple of Vesta, a sort of rotunda . . . or else a large pile of ruins. And in all his plans Homais always stuck to the weeping willow, which he looked upon as the indispensable symbol of sorrow.

Charles and he made a journey to Rouen together to look at some tombs, accompanied by an artist, one Vaufrylard, a friend of Bridoux's, who never ceased to make puns. At last, after having examined some hundred drawings, having ordered an estimate and made another journey to Rouen, Charles decided in favor of a mausoleum, whose two principal sides were to be decorated with "a spirit bearing an extinguished torch."

As to the inscription, Homais could think of nothing finer than *Sta viator*, and he got no further; he racked his brain in vain; all that he could come up with was *Sta viator*. At last he hit upon *Amabilem conjugem calcas*, which was adopted.

A strange thing was happening to Bovary: while continually thinking of Emma, he was nevertheless forgetting her. He grew desperate as he felt this image fading from his memory in spite of all efforts to retain it. Yet every night he dreamt of her; it was always the same dream. He approached her, but when he was about to embrace her she fell into decay in his arms.

For a week he was seen going to church in the evening. Monsieur Bournisien even paid him two or three visits, then gave him up. Moreover, the old man was growing bigoted and fanatic, according to Homais. He thundered against the spirit of the age, and never failed, every other week, in his sermon, to recount the death agony of Voltaire, who died devouring his excrements, as every one knows.

In spite of Bovary's thrifty life, he was far from being able to pay off his old debts. Lheureux refused to renew any more notes. Execution became imminent. Then he appealed to his mother, who consented to let him take a mortgage on her property, but with a great many recriminations against Emma; and in return for her sacrifice she asked for a shawl that had escaped from Félicité's raids. Charles refused to give it to her; they quarrelled.

She made the first peace overtures by offering to let the little girl, who could help her in the house, live with her. Charles consented to this, but when the time for parting came, all his courage failed him. Then there was a final, complete break between them.

As his affections vanished, he clung more closely to the love of his child. She worried him, however, for she coughed sometimes, and had red patches on her cheeks.

Across the square, facing his house, the prospering family of the pharmacist was more flourishing and thriving than ever. Napoleon helped him in the laboratory, Athalie embroidered him a skullcap, Irma cut out rounds of paper to cover the preserves, and Franklin recited the tables of Pythagoras by rote, without the slightest hesitation. He was the happiest of fathers, the most fortunate of men.

Not quite, however! A secret ambition devoured him. Homais hankered after the cross of the Legion of Honour. He had plenty of claims to it.

"First, having at the time of the cholera distinguished myself by a boundless devotion; second, by having published, at my expense, various works of public usefulness, such as" (and he recalled his pamphlet entitled, *On Cider, its Manufacture and Effects*, besides observations on the wooly aphis that he had sent to the Academy; his volume of statistics, and down to his pharmaceutical thesis); "without counting that I am a member of several learned societies" (he was member of a single one).

"And if this won't do," he said, turning on his heels, "there always is the assistance I give at fires!"

Homais' next step was trying to win over the Government to his cause. He secretly did the prefect several favors during the elections. He sold, in a word, prostituted himself. He even addressed a petition to the sovereign in which he implored him to "do him justice;" he called him "our good king," and compared him to Henri IV.

And every morning the pharmacist rushed for the paper to see if his nomination appeared. It was never there. At last, unable to bear it any longer, he had a grass plot in his garden designed to represent the Star of the Cross of Honour, with two little strips of grass running from the top to imitate the ribbon. He walked round it with folded arms, meditating on the folly of the Government and the ingratitude of men.

Out of respect, or because he took an almost sensuous pleasure in dragging out his investigations, Charles had not yet opened the secret drawer of Emma's rosewood desk. One day, however, he sat down before it, turned the key, and pressed the spring. All Léon's letters were there. There could be no doubt this time. He devoured them to the very last, ransacked every corner, all the furniture, all the drawers, behind the walls, sobbing and shouting in mad distress. He discovered a box and kicked it open. Rodolphe's portrait flew out at him, from among the pile of love-letters.

People wondered at his despondency. He never went out, saw no one, refused even to visit his patients. Then they said "he shut himself up to drink."

At times, however, someone would climb on the garden hedge, moved by curiosity. They would stare in amazement at this long-bearded, shabbily clothed, wild figure of a man, who wept aloud as he walked up and down.

On summer evenings, he would take his little girl with him to visit the cemetery. They came back at nightfall, when the only light left in the village was that in Binet's window.

He was unable, however, to savor his grief to the full, for he had no one to share it with. He paid visits to Madame Lefrançois to be able to speak of *her*. But the innkeeper only listened with half an ear, having troubles of her own. For Monsieur Lheureux had finally set up his own business, *les Favorites du Commerce*, and Hivert, every one's favorite messenger, threatened to go to work for the competition unless he received higher wages.

One day when he had gone to the market at Argueil to sell his horse—his last resource—he met Rodolphe.

They both turned pale when they caught sight of one another. Rodolphe, who had only sent his card for the funeral, first stammered some apologies, then grew bolder, and even invited Charles (it was in the month of August and very hot) to share a bottle of beer with him at the terrace of a café.

Leaning his elbows on the table, he chewed his cigar as he talked, and Charles was lost in reverie at the sight of the face she had loved. He seemed to find back something of her there. It was quite a shock to him. He would have liked to have been this man.

The other went on talking of agriculture, cattle and fertilizers, filling with banalities all the gaps where an allusion might slip in. Charles was not listening to him; Rodolphe noticed it, and he could follow the sequence of memories that crossed his face. This face gradually reddened; Charles's nostrils fluttered, his lips quivered. For a moment, Charles stared at him in somber fury and Rodolphe, startled and terrified, stopped talking. But soon the same look of mournful weariness returned to his face.

"I can't blame you for it," he said.

Rodolphe remained silent. And Charles, his head in his hands, went on in a broken voice, with the resigned accent of infinite grief:

"No, I can't blame you any longer."

He even made a phrase, the only one he'd ever made:

"Fate willed it this way."

Rodolphe, who had been the agent of this fate, thought him very meek for a man in his situation, comic even and slightly despicable.

The next day Charles sat down on the garden seat under the arbor. Rays of light were straying through the trellis, the vine leaves threw their shadows on the sand, jasmines perfumed the blue air, Spanish flies buzzed round the lilies in bloom, and Charles was panting like an adolescent under the vague desires of love that filled his aching heart.

At seven o'clock little Berthe who had not seen him all afternoon, came to fetch him for dinner.

His head was leaning against the wall, with closed eyes and open mouth, and in his hand was a long tress of black hair.

"Papa, come!"

And thinking he wanted to play, she gave him a gentle push. He fell to the ground. He was dead.

Thirty-six hours later, at the pharmacist's request, Monsieur Canivet arrived. He performed an autopsy, but found nothing.

When everything had been sold, there remained twelve francs and seventy-five centimes, just enough to send Mademoiselle Bovary off to her grandmother. The woman died the same year; and since Rouault was paralyzed, it was an aunt who took charge of her. She is poor, and sends her to a cotton-mill to earn a living.

Since Bovary's death three doctors have succeeded one another in Yonville without any success, so effectively did Homais hasten to eradicate them. He has more customers than there are sinners in hell; the authorities treat him kindly and he has the public on his side.

He has just been given the cross of the Legion of Honor.

Backgrounds
and
Sources

Earlier Versions of
Madame Bovary

GUSTAVE FLAUBERT

Scenarios and Scenes†

[The article by Albert Béguin "On Rereading *Madame Bovary*" (p. 292)
summarizes the importance of the "new version" established by Jean Pommier and Gabrielle Leleu. By collating Flaubert's numerous early drafts,
the editors have compiled a 511-page continuous text covering the action of the entire novel, preceded by 103 pages of scenarios, plans for
specific scenes, sketches for certain episodes, etc. From this mass of material,
we have selected a few passages hoping to give a representative sampling of
Flaubert's spontaneous writing, so ruthlessly eliminated from the final version. A deliberate attempt has been made to preserve something of the tone
of the original in translation; the syntax is often faulty or indefinite, and
certain uses of language are exceedingly odd. The reader should remember,
however, that none of this material was destined to be published.

The first three passages are scenarios, outlines, and notes that seem
almost incoherent at first sight. At closer examination, they reveal how
complete and definitive Flaubert's conception of his novel was from the
very beginning. The first passage is the earliest known outline for the
entire novel. Some of the smaller details of the final version are already present and the general sequence of events will in fact change very little between
this outline and the final version. The names are different; certain episodes
(such as Emma's trip to Paris, or her giving in to her first lover) will disappear altogether; the first sketch of Charles Bovary is interestingly different from the final character. Yet, on the whole, the original outline is
remarkably close to the final text of *Madame Bovary*.]

[*The Earliest Known Outline*]

Charles Bovary officier de santé 33 years when the story begins
already left a widower by a wife older than he / marries him out of
cupidity or rather stupidity of which he is the dupe—his childhood

† From *Madame Bovary, Nouvelle version précédée de scénarios inédits*
("New Version preceded by Unpublished Scenarios"), edited by Jean Pommier and Gabrielle Leleu (Paris: Li-
brarie José Corti, 1949); reprinted by
permission of the publisher. Translated
by Paul de Man.

in the country until he is 15—(tramps through the countryside—period of unrest) three or four years away at school—then a laborious med. student—pointless poverty of which he is not aware (his lodgings over the Eau de Robec in Rouen) gentle and sensitive disposition, correct, just and obtuse, no imagination one or two mistresses who introduce him to love he graduates—his mother with him / visits him from time to time spends a week or two at Charles' lodgings / (ambitious and manipulating—his father drunken and brash)—then his first wife

Mme. Bovary Marie (she signs Maria, Marianne or Marietta) daughter of a well to do farmer raised at a convent in Rouen (remembrance of her dreams when she passes again before her convent)—aristocratic friends—her dress the piano. At the show at the Saint-Romain fairs when her father a good fellow pious in the fashion of the Pays de Caux = (father Desnoyers) takes her there.

Loves her husband at first who is not bad looking—well built and somewhat conceited—but without much passion. His senses are still dormant. She introduces (little by little) more luxuries into the household than they can afford—her solitary life when her husband is away on calls—his homecomings in the evening, wet, just as she is beginning to read a romantic novel—usually about life in Paris. (Fashion magazines. Journal des Demoiselles) (a ball given at a chateau). the awakening of love without result. / long wait for a passionate stirring of the soul or an event which does not take place—the following year the ball is not given at the same period. / she ends by coming to detest the region and forces her husband to move.

They move elsewhere / it is still worse—the chief clerk of the attorney across the way / walks everyday under her window on his way to his office—he has a room in the house of the pharmacist across the street / the same sort of man as her husband but (by nature) superior though similar.—she resists her inclinations for a long time—then gives herself to him / calm—it is just the same as with her husband—lassitude with the soft character of this first lover.

a second lover 33 years old—a man of experience—dark—brutal —witty (flashy playboy type but mostly on the surface) jokingly grabs her and vigorously stirs up her passions—underneath his apparent gaiety he is archly conservative a hunter in corduroys / rough—swarthy—energetic and active—he is slowly ruining himself / practical bored sensual he demoralizes her by making her see life a little the way it is—

a trip to Paris

her return home—life is empty—she grows calmer—the head-clerk returns—(he is made chief-clerk at Rouen)—trip to Rouen on

Thursdays—the Hotel d'Angleterre—fulfillment—passion—

despair of unassuagable sensual comfort (satisfied love creates the need for a general well being—disinterest in material things exists only at the beginning of love affairs) to which is added the poetic need of luxury—life of sin

reading of novels (from the point of imaginative sensuality) expenses—bills presented by local merchant!—

emptiness (of passion) for her lover increasing as her senses develop. revulsion—however she still cannot love her husband.

re-try with the captain—(he kicks her out)

(she tries to return to her husband—she respects him and perceives her approaching destruction)

last orgy with Leopold—Suicide

(illness.—)

her death.

eve of her death—rainy afternoon the coach passes under her open window—

funeral—

empty solitude of Charles with his little girl—evening. he becomes aware day by day of his wife's debts. The chief-clerk marries—

one day Charles while walking in the garden suddenly dies—his little girl in an orphanage.

[*The Dance at Vaubyessard—First Outline*][1]

arrival at night. appearance of Vaubyessard.

porch—

vestibule (—windowed gallery—) billiard room sound of the balls—reserved dress of the players—pictures partially in the shadow.

drawing room

dinner. butler dressed in black (looking more like a magistrate than a servant) dishes under glass, crystal, fruits served with meats —puddings—iced champagne—truffles—the duke.

dressing. she fixes her hair—(little) conjugal dialogue.

(she arrives just as they are beginning to dance) (description of the salon—scramble on the dance floor)—mantelpiece—magnolia in Chinese vases—)

the ball—the young people—general characterization of the "lions": hands complexion—air at once brutal and effeminate, through handling horses and actresses. supple outfits, starched shirts, (—waistcoats—) pants that hug the thigh, some buttoned below.—stockings—odors batiste handkerchieves—(women in-

1. Cf. Norton Critical Edition, pp. 30–40.

cluded)

dance.—delight in the measure—glissade—tray of steaming punch.

groups.—Rouen types: politicians—a reporter from a legitimist newspaper 1832

(peasants looking on)

the supper was served on—¼ of an hour—Rhine wine. cold meats in aspic—bisque.

resumes—the musicians.

cotillon—the viscount of *. yellow waistcoat—"try" to Emma—at the doorway they collide passes her hand under his waistcoat. sensation of his body through his shirt—returns to her place dizzy watches him dance—people begin to leave little by little (stinging eyes—burning cheeks. cold feet)

return to her room—morning rain—goes out—mountain-ash berry lantern in the grass—Chinese pavillion. colored glass—(falls asleep. concentrated sun) (sight of the closed windows of the chateau—they are asleep—) servants who are grooming the horses —water.

after breakfast (saddle room) / Charles and the businessman visit the vegetable gardens and the farm / swans on the bridge. hothouse—departure.

return silence—countryside—encounter with the gentlemen—red sky movement of the carriage—pretends to sleep.

house—dismisses Nastasie—drunken sleep—immense tomorrow.

[Projected Epilogue][2]

The day he received it (his decoration) he couldn't believe it. Mr. X, a deputy, had sent him a bit of ribbon—tries it on looks at himself in the mirror dazzled.—

He shared in this ray of glory which beginning with the sub-prefect (a knight) went through the prefect (an officer) the general (a commander)—the ministers high dignitaries up to the king who held the grand-cross what am I saying up to the emperor Napoleon who had created it—Homais absorbed into the sun of Austerlitz.

All aspects of the cross. The Academy—diplomat—warrior—the thought was enough to kill one.—and it is one of the *greatest* proofs of his character that it did not kill him.)

Self-doubts—looks at his bocals—doubts his existence. (delirium.

2. Of this projected epilogue, developing considerably the figure of Homais, almost nothing remains in the final version. It throws a great deal of light on the symbolic significance of the pharmacist in the novel. Although the last lines of *Madame Bovary* indeed deal with Homais and his decoration (p. 255), we are never allowed such intimate glimpses into his inner self as we find in this outline.

fantastic effects. The cross reflected in bottles, rain thunder of red ribbon)—"am I not a character in a novel, the fruit of an imagination in delirium, the invention of some little beggar whom I have seen being born / and who invented me in order to prove that I do not exist / —Oh that is impossible. There are my foetuses. (there are my children there. there.)"

And picking up his discourse he finishes with that great phrase of modern rationalism Cogito, ergo sum.

[The following passages, numbered 1 to 15, are all taken from the "new version" established by Professor Pommier and Mademoiselle Leleu. With two exceptions (passages 4 and 15) they have been chosen to indicate what Albert Béguin has called Flaubert's talent for "following as closely as possible the hidden movements of the inner life." Themes such as memory, material sensation, subjective vision, *rêverie*, etc. are much in evidence in all the passages. The richness of the elaborate metaphorical language is particularly striking. It should be noted that passages of this kind, in which the stress is altogether on the inner life of the character, are by no means confined to Emma, as will be the case, generally speaking, in the final version. Some of the most lyrical fragments, containing the most original metaphors, refer to Charles (as in passages 1, 2, and 14), Léon (passages 6 and 7), or even Homais (Epilogue).

Passage 4 is altogether different. It is an instance of the heavily ironic imitation of realistic speech that appears in great abundance in the early drafts and that Flaubert often cut from the final version. The scene is taken from the dance at Vaubyessard; similar developments occurred in other scenes, especially in Homais's speeches. Passage 15 gives the final encounter between Charles and Rodolphe near the end of the book (p. 254); it contains the memorable sentence on Charles's love for Emma "almost reaching the proportions of a pure idea through generosity and impersonality," a sentence of crucial importance for an interpretation of the novel.

The titles of the passages are given for easier identification and do not appear in the text.]

[1. *Charles's Youth in Rouen*][3]

On summer evenings, when the close streets are empty and when the servants after dinner are playing shuttle-cock at the doors, he would stand at the window looking out at the passers by. Beneath him, down below, the river, which makes this quarter of Rouen into a bargain basement Venise, flowed by, saffron or indigo, underneath the little bridges that covered it. Drying in the hot air, the strips of dyed cotton suspended from the attic windows swung back and forth from their long racks, and working men, squatting by the edge of the water, washed their arms and necks. Across from him, beyond the tile roofs, he could see the sky, immense and pure, and the

---

3. Pommier and Leleu edition, p. 145; Norton Critical Edition, p. 7.

setting sun. How beautiful it must be there now! He remembered the long evenings, when he would come home at this hour with his companions, riding on the croups of their work horses, the hoofs of their mounts striking sparks as they walked along the cart roads. He could see from there the huge wagons returning, loaded with hay that brushed against the doors of the farmhouses as they passed. In earlier times, he had ridden on these wagons, and he could see again the stars shining on the barn. They were shining on the barn now. A cock crows in the distance, the watchdogs are being released. The shepherd alone in the fields will soon be closing the gates of the paddock. He whistles for his dog. The crickets in the wheat fields are singing with little repetitive cries. And he closed his window again.

He became sad. He lost weight, his body grew long, and his face, which had always been gentle, took on an expression of quiet suffering, making him look even more distinguished.

[2. *Charles on His Way to the Bertaux Farm*][4]

So at about three in the morning Charles, wrapped in his overcoat and with his cap pulled down over his eyes, set out for the Bertaux farm. The rain had stopped, the moon was rising and here and there the sky was clearing. Still congealed in the warmth of his first sleep, he let himself slump on the back of his horse. . . . Half asleep, still clinging to the warmth of his bed, and pursuing his dream, he would remember on awakening that he was about to be concerned with a broken leg and try to call to mind all the fractures he had seen and how they were treated. Through his half sleep, he saw pass before him re-knit femurs, splints, and bandages. Then, as his mind became weary from trying to remember and his horse walked slower, sleep overtook him of its own accord and he would fall again into a tepid drowsiness, where his most recent sensation came back to him. He saw himself simultaneously, both husband and student, lying on his own bed beside his wife, as he had just left it, and, at the same time, walking busily about in an operating room. He felt under his elbow the sensation of a desk in an amphitheater, which was also his pillow at home. He smelled the odor of cataplasms and his wife's hair . . . And it all mingled into one whole, seeking for something with an uneasy longing, unable to lift its lead-weighted wings, while the confused memory turned round and round in place below. The wind came up, it was cold.

4. Pommier and Leleu, p. 151; Norton Critical Edition, p. 9; see also J. P. Richard's comment on this scene on p. 433.

[3. *Emma at Tostes*][5]

Usually she would walk as far as the clump of beeches outside of
Banneville, to the abandoned pavilion built on the town walls,
just on the other side of the moat. In this moat, among the other
grasses, there grows a reed with sharp cutting leaves. She would sit
by the edge. It is a deserted spot. No one walks that way. The trees
are very high.

She would arrive there out of breath from her walk, and begin to
look about her for familiar landmarks to see if anything had
changed since she had last come. She would recognize the marks in
the grass where she had sat before, the same weeds growing among
the loose stones in the wall, clumps of moss reddened by the sun
sticking to the frames of the windows whose closed blinds were
falling apart on their rusty iron hinges. Her thoughts, like her little
greyhound, wandered to right and left, without aim, object or direction. Her eye followed the handsome animal with his delicate paws
as he traced great circles in the ploughed furrows, in pursuit of
some rat or field mouse, shaking his head in the patches of wheat
and poppies which tickled his nose.

When her gaze had wandered at random over the whole surrounding horizon, her attention hardly brushing against the
thoughts which followed each other in her head, like two concentric
circles turning one within the other and contracting simultaneously
their circumferences, her thought would return to herself and her
gaze would turn inward. Seated on the ground, digging up small
handfuls of earth with the tip of her umbrella, she always came
back to the same question.

"Why in heaven's name did I marry?"

She asked herself if it wouldn't have been possible by some other
combination of fate to have met another man; and like a poet who
combines, she tried to discover in her head those adventures which
had not happened, that life which wasn't hers, that husband whom
she didn't know.

[4. *Conversations at Vaubyessard*][6]

A few, who had dressed with the intention of dancing, wore tight
fitting pants which were fastened above the calf by three buttons.
Emma watched their feet shod in open-work stockings advancing
toward her, revealing from time to time, by a movement of the toe,

---

5. Pommier and Leleu, pp. 200–01;
Norton Critical Edition, p. 31.
6. Pommier and Leleu, pp. 209–12;
the passage, dropped from the final version, was inserted on p. 37.

the interior of their dancing slippers lined with blue satin.

It was not difficult to see that they were only moderately enjoying themselves; the marquise even had to seek out two or three to entreat them to dance with some of the ladies.

It is true that the society at the ball that evening was not really altogether their set. In addition to a few close friends who were from the neighborhood or were taking the baths at Dieppe, and the guests at the château who had come there to spend the hunting season, the marquis had invited for reasons of politics some of the local dignitaries from Rouen. The mayor, the commander of the local regiment, the judge of the small claims court, a few magistrates and some of the more notable businessmen of the region were there with their wives. The marquis strolled from one group to another, and mixed amiably in the various conversations, receiving a compliment, returning three, and then moving on toward another group.

He approached three voluble gentlemen wearing velvet waistcoats.

"Ah, M. le Marquis," said one of them, who was holding a half-finished glass of punch in one hand, "what a delightful party you have got up for us!"

"Nothing at all!" answered the marquis bowing. "Just a little country occasion, a simple family affair."

"What, M. le Marquis, a little country occasion! Why it's a banquet from the Chaussée d'Antin! A symposium of ministers! A real Tuileries ball!"

The marquis, who resided in the aristocratic quarter of Paris, utterly despised the ministers, and detested the Tuileries, blushed to the roots of his hair at this triple insult.

The guest thought he had made a good hit and continued:

"The dinner, I assure you, was of a magnificence . . ."

The marquis moved off as though to speak with someone who was passing by.

"Yes, a very nice dinner," continued the notary turning toward his neighbor.

"What I like best in a dinner," added the other with a serious expression, "is luxury, sensational dishes. Did you notice the salmon, M. Belami?"

"Yes, you're right, a real beauty."

"Last year," put in the third gentleman, "we gave a dinner honoring the colonel of the National Guard. I was invited in my capacity as officer. We had a fine salmon there, but it didn't compare with this one."

"I like very much this way of changing the silverware after each course," said the man who liked luxury.

"That's called 'English service,' " said the notary.

Then they began to talk about the silverware they had seen.

"It must have cost a good thirty thousand francs," said the first man.

"I should say so," answered the second, "from thirty to thirty-five thousand!"

"If you count the coffee spoons, it might easily reach forty thousand!" added the third.

"Shh! Speak lower. The marquis is coming back."

The marquis stopped at the entrance to the game room where Charles was standing silently watching a game of whist of which he understood nothing.

"Aren't you playing, Councilor?", he asked a bald–headed gentleman whose nose supported a pair of silver–rimmed spectacles.

"I am sorry, M. le Marquis, but the groups have already been made up. I am stretching my legs a bit to get the stiffness out. I am so much in my office that it is a real pleasure for me to stand up. Besides, the sight of these lively dancers is worth getting up to see. What a charming picture! It is truly a basket of flowers! A basket of flowers, truly, M. le Marquis!"

"Not all the flowers are in the bud," said the marquis lowering his voice.

"Oh! Very good, M. le Marquis, very good! Ha ha! Indeed, women are not perpetual."

"Ah! Charming!" said the marquis, "not perpetual. The word is perfect. I'll remember it to use myself when the occasion arises. Something which has always astonished me," he added, assuming a serious expression, "is the way serious men manage to preserve their sense of humor when they are out on a social occasion and leave on the threshold of their offices the important concerns which fill their heads."

"To the contrary, M. le Marquis, to the contrary! The more the imagination is held in check during the day, the more it releases of its own accord during the evening, like a bow. It brings about, in my case at least, a sort of revulsion, a nervous reaction, if I may use the expression, which relaxes me and leaves me the better disposed for my work the next day. During the second session this year, I presided over the Criminal Court. I didn't arrive home until very late. Well, I ate like a horse, I was gay as a colt, and I never felt better!"

Then, he added bowing:

"Your district, moreover, is one of the ones which gives us the least trouble."

"Yes, our country-spirit is on the whole pretty good," said the marquis. "However, the morals of the rural population are becom-

ing worse every day due to the proximity of the factories. The example of quickly–acquired wealth is handed down from the capital-
ist to the petty bourgeois, strikes the artisan, wins over the worker
himself, and thus establishes a firm hold among the lower classes,
causing much deplorable moral unrest. The book-traffic is also
doing a great deal of harm to our young farmgirls. Instead of going
to Vespers, they spend their Sundays reading all matter of corrupt
little books which are ruining them, and on which the government
ought to keep an eye."

Having divided five minutes between the dangers of education,
the encroachment of industry and the immorality of the poorer
classes, the marquis entered the gameroom and the magistrate went
over to pay his court to the marquise. She was chatting with a lean
young man whose elbow rested on the mantelpiece near to a flowering magnolia planted in a Chinese vase. He had long blond hair, a
golden watchchain attached to his straight-buttoned waistcoat, and
a somewhat worn black suit. He took no refreshments, did not
dance, and was holding forth to the marquise on a grand project of
his to set up retreats for young girls in all the towns within the five
departments. He was a reporter for a legitimist newspaper in Le
Havre; a former proctor in a private academy; then an insurance
salesman and the author of a book of Christian elegies dedicated to
the Bishop of Bayeux. A man of art and imagination, he closed his
letters with a seal showing a half-opened heart stuck with a pen
and bearing this inscription: "This well is her source."

[5. *Emma and the Colored Window Panes at Vaubyessard*][7]

"Did you eat any of those little things made out of two slices of
bread with meat in the middle?"

"Sandwiches?"

"I can never remember that name though it certainly fits them
just right."

And he fell asleep.

But she never slept that night. She took off her dress, wrapped a
shawl around her shoulders and looked out.

The night was dark. A few drops of rain were falling. One after
the other the lights in the château went out. She listened to the
sound of the stream flowing far off among the trees; the cold air
soothed her eyes; her face was burning, and to warm her feet, she
would walk up and down from time to time striking the tip of her
fingers against the ground. She waited for day to break.

At dawn, when the big door below was opened, she went down

7. Pommier and Leleu, pp. 215–17; the passage, dropped from the final version,
was inserted on p. 38.

and walked in the garden. The rest of the household were still asleep. She looked at the château with its closed blinds, trying to guess which rooms might by chance belong to the various persons she had noticed the evening before. But were they still there? Not one of them would be thinking of her; how did it happen that she was still thinking of them and longing to see them again?

There was mud on the sand along the little paths; she walked slowly crushing the berries from the mountain-ash trees which the wind had blown down. On turning into one lane, something round rolled under her foot. It was one of the lanterns from the ball; the extinguished wick was damp, lying in its cracked cup surrounded by dirty white wax. She stood before it a few minutes, rolling it over with her foot as though it were the corpse of some animal. A valet in a red vest appeared in the distance at the top of the stair landing, pushing before him some armchairs which he started to brush off. There began to be some movement now in the direction of the stables. A peasant girl who was passing by with a bundle of hay on her head bowed low in greeting.

Wandering at random, she reached a small wood, where she stopped in amazement before a little low house whose bell-shaped roof was turned up at the four corners and covered with tiles painted to look like fishscales and decorated on all sides by a row of wooden bells. The river here overflowed onto the grass forming a bay of sleeping water, where two canoes waited motionless beside a green cabin built for the swans among the water lilies. Looking in from without, one could see nothing of the interior. The door looked closed but opened under her touch, and she found herself in a room covered with blue wallpaper, with painted leaves and caged parakeets. The furniture consisted of a circular couch of gray percale, some bamboo chairs and a table of round green marble resting on a wicker base. It was a retreat for summer days, a place for meetings, where, hidden from all eyes, but viewing the horizon through a break in the trees, lovers must have come many times in the still hours to pass the melancholy moments of love against the murmuring of the water. The walls, behind the portraits, seemed to be thinking of things they did not wish to tell. In the middle of the river, rounding his wings to the wind, a swan was gliding, leaving on the still water a long furrow which fanned out behind him.

Diamond–shaped panes had been set into one of the two windows. She looked out at the countryside through the colored glass.

Through the blue pane everything seemed sad. A motionless azure haze diffused through the air, lengthened the meadows and pushed back the hills. The tips of the trees were velveted with a pale brown dust, dotted irregularly here and there as though there had been a snowfall, and far off in a distant field, a fire of dry leaves someone was burning seemed to have flames of wine alcohol.

Seen through the yellow glass, the leaves on the trees became smaller, the grass lighter, and the whole landscape as though it had been cut out of metal. The detached clouds looked like eiderdown quilts of golden dust ready to fall apart; the atmosphere seemed on fire. It was joyous and warm in this immense topaz color mixed with azure.

She put her eye to the green pane. Everything was green, the sand, the water, the flowers, the earth itself became indistinguishable from the lawns. The shadows were all black, the leaden water seemed frozen to its banks.

But she remained longest in front of the red glass. In a reflection of purple that overspread the landscape in all directions, robbing everything of its own color, the trees and grass became almost gray, and even red itself disappeared. The enlarged stream flowed like a rose–colored river, the peat–covered flower beds seemed to be seas of coagulated blood, the immense sky blazed with innumerable fires. She became frightened.

She turned away her eyes, and through the window with transparent panes, suddenly, ordinary daylight reappeared, all pale with little patches of skycolored mist.

The morning dew was rising in the meadow; a flock of sheep were grazing on the park lawns as they trooped by; in a turret window of the château, a woman in a nightgown was cleaning out her comb in the wind; and, all at once, the white sunlight leapt into the closed room, where the walls as they warmed gave off a tepid odor that seemed to drain her of her strength. Exhausted, she sank down on a cushion. Emma felt a pain at the back of her head and, although she didn't sleep, she began to dream.

She was suddenly startled awake by a flock of rooks who grazed the top of the trees and settled in a grove of pines beyond.

She was frightened that someone would find her there; she hurried back.

Charles had gone off with the businessman to visit the farm and the gardens. He admired the fields, felt the brick walls of the wine press, and asked about the Marquis' income.

[6. *Léon after His First Encounter with Emma*][8]

There was no doubt that the dinner on the previous evening had been a big event in his life, for his life up to that time had had very few events. The only son of a widow of no great wealth, who had sent him to school in a seminary at Yvetot, and later, for reasons of economy, to do his apprenticeship in a law office in Yonville, he had

8. Pommier and Leleu, pp. 260–61; Norton Critical Edition, p. 61.

never before found himself in an intimate conversation with a lady for two full hours. But how had he suddenly been able to express, and with such eloquence, all those confused matters which the evening before he would have had difficulty even formulating for himself! Is it that our hearts, like small pebbles, wait motionless in the spot where Providence has placed them, for the precise shock which will strike a spark? Or is it with them as with a broker's safe, that there exists between their mysterious hinges and certain words which one must know, a connecting spring which releases when it is touched so that the doors instantly open wide and the cash-filled drawers roll out of their own accord? He was reserved in his speech and usually maintained that silence about his own affairs appropriate to feminine natures, combining modesty with deceit. It was generally agreed at Yonville that his manners were distinguished, for he listened respectfully to the advice of his elders and did not seem too hot-headed in politics something remarkable in a young man. However, he had been a little revolutionized during the last vacation by a cousin of his, an artist who lived in Paris, a Phalansterian and a disciple of Saint-Simon,[9] a romantic who was in bad grace with his grandparents because of his beard. He had given Léon a great many things to read and had taught him a number of others. It was since that time that he had hung portraits of George Sand and Lamartine in his room, giving him, in the eyes of any who penetrated that far, a certain air of eccentric melancholy which went well with his long hair and dreamy expression.

[7. *Léon and Emma During the Evenings at Homais's House*][1]

At that time, she used to wear those hats called "la Paysanne" which revealed her ears. They reminded Léon of ones he had seen at the opera. And while he gazed at Emma's braids, where the lamp light made ripples on the ebony strands, there would come slowly over his soul a reminiscence of similar emanations and forgotten sentiments. His feelings for other women in other times, the languors of adolescence, the wonder at his awakening manhood, the melancholy of his first desires, a thousand scattered yearnings were reunited in this new excitement which absorbed them all. In order to make his expectations more concrete, he would search his memory for familiar objects. In the sensuousness of remembrance, both felt and dreamt, the young man's thought would gently dissolve and it seemed sometimes that Emma almost disappeared in the very il-

9. Phalansterians are disciples of Charles Fourier who, with Saint-Simon, represent the French, pre-Marxian trend of utopian socialism [*Editor*].

1. Pommier and Leleu, p. 279; the passage, dropped from the final version, was inserted on p. 70.

luminations which radiated from her. But suddenly, when she would turn her face toward him and he would see her black eyes flashing, her moist lips speaking, her white teeth shining, it changed to a desire at once biting, precise and urgent. Something sharp would run all through him and he wanted to touch her on the shoulders that he might know her through some other sense than that of the eyes.

[8. *Emma after the Departure of Léon*][2]

The next day was for Emma a day of mourning. It seemed to her that everything around her was enveloped in a black fog which floated vaguely over the surface of things, pushing them back so that they receded into the distance. Inert, as though she were paralyzed, she remained until evening with this new feeling of a terrible desertion. A somber melancholy blew into her heart, uttering soft moans, like the wind in winter when it blows in abandoned castles. And again she felt, as she had on her return from Vaubyessard, an infinite regret, an aimless despair. It was that sadness which follows the accomplishment of all that will never return, that bottomless fatigue which any completed action leaves behind. It was the sorrow brought to the heart or soul by any irrevocable deed, by separations, deaths, departures, certain arrivals, broken habits or fulfilled pleasures, the interruption of any accustomed movement or the sudden breaking off of a prolonged vibration. The silence which follows becomes the very measure of its sonority, while its length can be gaged by the intoxication which results.

Emma, as on her return from Vaubyessard, when quadrilles still whirled in her head and her eyes still smarted from the glare of the candles, suffered a boundless regret, a numbing despair. And within the remembrance of Léon, at once so near and so distant, confused things came back to her; details returned and her whole past was rekindled in the reflexion of this sorrow. This simple young man seemed to her the handsomest of men, the purest of souls. Former conversations and sudden glances came back to her in puffs of recollections, more melodious and lyrical than vóices singing in harmony; his eyes out-sparkled the reflection of chandeliers on crystal plates and the odor of his hair which smelled of lemon, seemed sweeter and more penetrating than the perfume of a hothouse. There had been days she had not noticed at the time, that had lain dormant since and which now reappeared in their entirety. Long and pale like the ghosts of virgins who have died of love, they clustered around her, saying: "It is we! It is we! You should have taken us while we still lived!"

2. Pommier and Leleu, pp. 319–21; Norton Critical Edition, p. 88.

And wherever her eyes wandered or her ears strayed, there was a remembrance of Léon: the flowering stream along whose banks they had strolled together, the nasturtium–covered arbor in the garden where he used to read to her, her workbasket beside her on the bench, the places on the parquet where his feet had rested, the furniture he had sat on, the pharmacist's house, with his window between the inscriptions. The pot of basil was still drying in the sun. She thought she could see him leaning out. And she thirsted for his lips, she longed for his love and cursed herself for having allowed him to leave. She could not comprehend through what weakness or virtue she had deprived herself of such a happiness. But he was gone, the only hope of her life! He would never return! It was useless for her to hope any longer. She wanted to run after him, to say to him: "Here I am!" Then she gave way before the difficulties of carrying out such a plan and turned all her fury on her own mistake.

She clung to this memory; it was the center of her lassitude, all her thoughts converged upon it and nourished it. It was the intimate creation of her idleness. In her life, abandoned, cold, naked and monotonous, it stood alone like a fire of dead twigs left in the middle of the Russian Steppes by departing travelers. She threw herself upon the remembered image, crushed herself against it, joyously, jealously, and with a trembling hand stirred up the embers which were about to go out. To make it burn brighter and flame higher, that she might re–light her sadness by this love–flame which was flickering in the night, she looked around her for things with which to feed it; the most insignificant details of the past or the future, reminiscences of simple words, whims, comparisons, dislikes, all these she threw in and warmed herself before this hearth with the full length of her soul.

For a long time, she watched over this fire to keep it going. Bending over it she nourished the flame. But the flame no longer burned so brightly, perhaps because her provision of fuel was exhausted, or else she had smothered it by piling her fuel on too high. Little by little, through absence, her love too went out, and even her reveries diminished in routine. From this hearth, there now came more smoke than flame, more despair than desire, and the purple light which had reddened her pale sky grew lesser by degrees. The pricks of her daily existence, which fell on her like sharp hailstones, disappeared more slowly. She mistook her hatred for Charles for a longing for Léon, the searing smart of hate for the warmth of love; but, while her torment increased and its cause receded, her hope departed, blowing out the cold embers of her consumed passion. Then she remained alone, and all was total night, an immense wasteland.

Emma then, in spite of all she could do, thought less and less of

Léon and more and more of Charles. The one had abandoned her, the other obsessed her continually. Her illusions were gone, her sorrows remained. But what she did preserve, deep down within her, was the concept of an extraordinary happiness whose realization she imagined possible under conditions no longer there. And although her dream changed in time, becoming more embellished as the distance increased, the aftertaste nevertheless persisted. The comparison between her life as it was and her life as it should be made her detest her present state with more fury than ever.

[9. *Emma's Happiness with Rodolphe*][3]

Then she would take the letter to the end of the garden, near the river, and slip it into a crevice in the wall. Rodolphe would come and pick it up, leaving in its place another which she always reproached for being too short.

She wrote hers breathlessly, without stopping, her heart pounding, her cheeks on fire, and the paper filled with the volubility of her love that overflowed into the very margins of the page. She reminded him of their joys of the evening before and was already chafing impatiently in anticipation of the next day. Between these recent memories and her secure anticipations, love burned as between two concentric chimneys and its sensations were reawakened by her effort to translate them. In this way, Emma drew out her passion by passing it through the laminating presses of style. Yet it lost nothing of its solidity since the satisfaction of her desires added each day something new.

Literary reminiscences, mystical impulses, carnal ecstasies and ephemeral caresses, all were confused in the immensity of this passion. A heap of experiences, great and small, some ordinary some exotic, some insipid some succulent, reappeared there, giving the passion variety, like those Spanish salads where one finds fruits and vegetables, chunks of goat meat and slices of citron floating about in pale-blond oil.

As the days followed one another, a more complete happiness took possession of her. Something of the happiness of her soul seemed to vibrate in the slightest fibers of her nerves. She felt a myriad green buds begin to swell within her, as under a constant warm rain, and she breathed more easily. Her renewed senses blossomed out more fully; she saw further into the distance, around her there was more sun, more air, more good odors. She understood better many human mysteries which had formerly perplexed her. And the whole of her life seemed to her to be at once both tranquil

3. Pommier and Leleu, pp. 383–84; the passage, dropped from the final version, was inserted on p. 117.

and beautiful. All the planes of her horizon having come within closer reach, she could touch her dreams with the palms of her hands, satisfied with her own personality and enchanted with her lover; desiring nothing more, without envy, without dreams, but not without memory, she gave herself to him.

When Charles would come home late at night, he did not dare to awaken her. But Emma had heard his footstep on the stairs and she awoke in the middle of an amorous dream, while Charles fell asleep at her side, lost in similar imaginings. In order to recapture something of what had charmed her a moment ago, she tried to think of Rodolphe so strongly that the image came closer and closer, appearing to her as clearly as in reality. Then it seemed to Emma that she had escaped out of herself and that she circled about him like an impalpable breath of wind. So much was the consciousness of her own being lost in that contemplation, that she no longer seemed to exist. The memories of the joys of the evening before made her more impatient for the delights of the morrow, and she would feast herself for a long time on the imagined spectacle of those two eyes which shone on her like black suns. Sometimes, half numbed among the shadows, and because of that man lying there beside her, she would be struck by a momentary illusion, but she would immediately return to the thought of her lover. Was he dreaming of her now while the wind was whipping against the windows and, no doubt, making the weathervanes on his château cry out? If only she could live there! and she saw herself living with him in his house and accompanying him on voyages, having become his concubine, his wife! But that would surely come about! They would not be separated until death! And something would eventually happen to make their love more free. Without knowing how, she was somehow certain! A succession of days, numberless and beautiful, unrolled against the splendid horizon like a chorus of dancing fairies gliding over a rainbow. But the child would suddenly begin to cough in its cradle or Charles would snore louder, and Emma, sighing, would listen to the striking of the hours. She would not fall asleep until morning when daylight whitened the window panes and one already heard Justin on the square opening the pharmacist's shutters.

[10. *Emma and Rodolphe*][4]

She felt herself totally possessed by his caprice, like a violin which vibrates under the fingers of a master. By turns, it would play a gay and sensuous air, like an Italian cavatina, or again, a melody per-

4. Pommier and Leleu, p. 417 (note); dropped from the final version, inserted on p. 118.

fectly attuned to those pauses in happiness, the intervals of silence which sing as loudly as the music itself. Then love would descend the scale to a lower register; reveries without cause would hover softly and then disappear, swept away by a whirlwind of confused ideas. This too would break off, and a supreme ecstasy would mount, break off and mount again, rising to the outermost extreme, like a little note, fragile and serious, which mounts, sliding over the E string, and throbbing with a sound so pure, so full, so delicate it seems that nothing beyond that point could exist.

[11. Emma's Mystical Visions During Her Illness][5]

One day she thought she was dying and asked for communion. Bournisien hastened to the house, placing her under a canopy which was carried by Lestiboudois and a choir boy; then, as the preparations for the sacrament proceeded, the commode encumbered with medicine bottles was pushed aside, and the candelabras were brought in while Félicité began to scatter dahlias about. Emma felt her pain cease. Her body became ethereal, her thoughts cleared, as though her soul which had strayed so long the meandering paths of delirium had returned to her and she had reclaimed it. Her thoughts seemed to come like rushes of wind from within, propelling her forward, now unencumbered by the weight of sin. A new life would begin, either here below or there on high, it didn't matter! How she was refreshed by the drops of holy water, falling like celestial dew from above! And it was with a movement of joy that she advanced to unite herself with the body of Jesus Christ who was offering himself to her lips. Lost in ecstasy, she listened to the murmur of the Latin words with long endings like the sound of mystical waves passing through the air; the rays of the candles came to her like visions of paradise; and over her head, the white bed curtains billowed softly around her like the clouds to which her thoughts were flying. Fainting from joy and weakness, she let her head fall back on her pillows, hearing in the beating of her heart the harps of the seraphim. She thought she saw before her fever-dazzled eyes God the father surrounded by virgins and martyrs who stretched out their arms toward her. And for a long time, her fingers wandered over the rosary with the gentle gesture of a dying person clinging to something that pulls him upward. It was as though she were feeling something in her unconsciousness which helped her to mount.

This mystical vision remained in her memory as the most beautiful, the most voluptuous thing she had ever dreamed possible. And afterward she kept trying to recapture the sensation. This feeling

5. Pommier and Leleu, p. 453; Norton Critical Edition, p. 154.

continued, but in another form, less violent and less exclusive. It seemed as if a constant flow of hope and tranquility were pouring over her soul. And mixed with this serenity were memories of her convent, the sweet aftertaste of her first ideal loves, which, in her weakened state, erasing somewhat the interval between, brought her back unawares to the days of her childhood when she knew nothing but limpidity, innocence and quietude. Her passion-worn soul would find rest at last in humility; for the first time, she savored the delights of weakness and watched with joy the defeat of her will which would make way for an even greater penetration of grace. So there still existed for her on earth, in place of the human joys which had deceived her, an unmixed happiness, a love transcending all loves, that fed upon itself, that would never cease, that would constantly grow! Amidst the ardors or prayer and under the illusions of her desire, she perceived a state of sanctity, composed of resignation and whitened with tears, a cold splendor, flashing like an aurora borealis, which colored her life to its outermost boundaries with a crimson reflection of heaven, fusing the two into one. She was seized by a longing to be there. She really wished to become a saint.

[12. *Léon in the Cathedral*][6]

Confusing his love with the setting which gave it life, Léon came at last to believe that he was almost the god of the temple, the center of this cult whose priestess he awaited. His hands broke into a lascivious sweat and his soul filled with a mystical ecstasy. Something soft and liquid soothed him, propelled him, lifted him off the ground. He was all desire, all anxiety and joy, all vibration, and if the organ which hung under the great rose–window, like a silver forest beneath a fantastic sun, had suddenly begun to sing, it would certainly not have exhaled toward heaven melodies more sonorous, halleluiahs more joyous, an hosanna more triumphant than the amorous canticle which overflowed from his expectations. Like that immense instrument filled with hushed music, he felt that there reposed deep down within himself an infinity of love, which only awaited the contact of a breath or the pressure of a hand to break into fanfares and ecstasies.

[13. *Emma's Final Reminiscences*][7]

One day when they had separated early and she was returning along the boulevard, she suddenly noticed the walls of her old con-

6. Pommier and Leleu, p. 491; the passage, dropped from the final version, was inserted on p. 173.

7. Pommier and Leleu, p. 558; Norton Critical Edition, p. 206.

vent. She recognized the dormitory, the laundry, the class rooms. Overcome by a depression, she sank down on a bench in the shade of the great elms which were swaying in the wind.

They had not grown. They still made the same murmuring sound she had so loved in those days when, on summer mornings, still half asleep, she had arrived with the others in the great study hall with its opened windows. The lilies in the garden, already warmed by the sun, were releasing their lovely scent. She could hear the little birds. She sat down at her desk.

How calm those times had been! What dreams! How she envied now all those indescribable sentiments of love which serve no purpose but to fill books. She had felt them, however, and she examined them now, the way one holds up broken shells to the light. Formerly, they had sparkled with marvelous colors, and were filled with a limpid purity, wherein pearls were forming, perhaps, worthy to be set upon the forehead of a king. Then they had disappeared; he heart was filled only with the dust of their debris; she thought she could hear them far off, murmuring indistinctly as under some terrible oscillation. It was her dreadful lassitude which was rolling them back and forth like the tides.

[14. *Charles at Emma's Deathbed*][8]

And each time he would gently wipe off her skin with bits of cotton which he then placed on the tray. She allowed herself to be manipulated without making a motion and never ceasing to smile.

But he had not finished yet, and moving to the far end of the alcove he lifted up the spread which covered the mattress and revealed her feet. They were white as alabaster with blue nails somewhat turned up at the ends. Charles kept following with an idiotic stare all the movements of the priest who was preparing them for the last journey where no one walks. The first time he had seen them had been one evening when, on his knees, he had untied the narrow ribbons of her white shoes. And the whole house around him was singing with joy in harmony with his intoxicated heart. He had shuddered, dazzled by the proximity of possession and felt as though he were suffocating under the overflow of a limitless desire, even sweeter than the perfume of her braids, deeper than her eyes, fuller than her dress which crackled like electric sparks in his arms. And amidst their silence, they heard the wedding carriages disappear one by one, gliding over the grass.

8. Pommier and Leleu, p. 611; the passage, dropped from the final version, was inserted on p. 237.

[15. *The Final Meeting Between Charles and Rodolphe*][9]

Charles followed him, and while Rodolphe in a corner across from him, his elbows resting on the table, chewed on his cigar and talked of this and that, Charles studied him, lost in reverie at the sight of the face which she had loved. He seemed to find back something of her there, to be brought closer to her; it was astonishing! He would have liked to have been this man and he exclaimed:

"How did you do it?"

Rodolphe understood vaguely. Nevertheless, in order to avoid giving himself away he went on talking about the probable outcome of the harvest.

"Go ahead, talk about her! Speak since she loved you!" cried Charles, breaking into sobs, his head between his hands.

Then he raised his head and stared at him as though in a daze, with a sad and gentle expression.

"No, I don't blame you for it."

Then he made a phrase, a grand phrase, the only one he'd ever made:

"Fate willed it this way."

Rodolphe, however, who had been somewhat the agent of this fate, was extremely surprised. He found him all too good-natured for a man in his situation, too accommodating, even comic and slightly despicable.

For he understood nothing of that voracious love which throws itself upon things at random to assuage its hunger, that passion empty of pride, without human respect or conscience, plunging entire into the being which is loved, taking possession of his sentiments, palpitating with them and almost reaching the proportions of a pure idea through generosity and impersonality.

The following day, at about one o'clock in the afternoon, Charles went to sit on the bench beneath the arbor. Rays of light were straying through the trellis in the spaces between the green. The shadows of the grape leaves made patterns on the sand. The murmuring stream washed with quiet waves against the terrace, jasmin perfumed the air, the katy–dids droned among the flowering lilies, and an immense lassitude fell from the blue heaven.

He was stifled, like an adolescent, under the amorous waves which swelled in his aching heart. And all the sorrows of his life returned to him, the joys of his marriage from the first day to the last. It had already been eighteen months now!

At seven o'clock in the evening, Berthe came to fetch him for dinner . . .

9. Pommier and Leleu, p. 641; Norton Critical Edition, p. 254.

D. L. DEMOREST

[Structures of Imagery in *Madame Bovary*]†

Flaubert's images are chosen to convey a precise impression of a character, a situation, a moment, or a mood. As the serpent is the symbol of Eve the lost woman, so, for Flaubert, water is the symbol of Venus the delectable. And these illustrate admirably Emma's soul as it evokes, at every instant, lakes, torrents and oceans, these same oceans whose waves evoke all that is disastrous in love. Therefore images of fluidity appear so frequently in the novel, interpreting both sensations and sentiments.

In his correspondence, Flaubert tells us that in writing the reveries in *Madame Bovary*, he will be "navigating upon those blue lakes" (II, 38) like the pale blue lakes of *Graziella*[1] (II, 397) and the milky oceans of château literature (II, 371). As for torrents and raging seas, they are old acquaintances of all who know Flaubert's youthful works.

Putting aside, for the moment, the symbolism of the stream which flows behind the house at Yonville, many of the basic images associated with the psychological analyses of the characters are not original: days resemble one another like waves, love is unquenchable, happiness dries up, Emma's love diminishes beneath her "like the water of a river which is absorbed by its bed." Others are somewhat unpleasant, such as this one which nevertheless shows the subjective value which Flaubert attached to these images: when he looks at Emma, Léon feels that his soul "fleeing toward her, broke like a wave against the contours of her head, and was drawn irresistibly down into the whiteness of her breast."

Among the images of the objective world, we see Emma's glance drowned in lassitude; or again, as she goes toward her downfall in the forest: "through her veil . . . her face appeared in a bluish transparency as if she were swimming through azure waves." The author obviously gave particular attention to this image since the early drafts contain several versions where the veil falls "like black waves," where there are "bluish undulations," or "an ultramarine

---

† The essay is taken from Chapter XII of Professor D. L. Demorest's thesis entitled *L'expression figurée dans l'œuvre de Flaubert* ("Figurative Language in the Work of Flaubert") (Paris: Louis Conard, 1931), pp. 454–74, and is reprinted by permission of the author. Translated by Paul de Man. A few paragraphs have been omitted and copious notes, containing additional evidence, have not been included.
1. *Graziella* (1849) is a pseudo-autobiographical prose narrative text by Lamartine, describing a sentimental episode of youthful love. With Musset, Lamartine is the main target of Flaubert's attacks on false sentimentality [Editor].

cloud," "the transparent water of a few azure waves." They include no less than four variants on the idea of "swimming." When she gives herself to Rodolphe she feels "her blood flow through her flesh like a river of milk" and "love so long pent up, erupted in joyous outbursts." As she rides toward the forest, her imagination transforms the mist in the valley into one of those Lamartinian lakes of which she dreams:

> From the height on which they were the whole valley seemed an immense pale lake sending off its vapor into the air. Clumps of trees here and there stood out like black rocks, and the tall lines of poplars that rose above the mist were like a beach stirred by the wind.

Emma's reactions to nature as seen in the last two examples appear in many other passages such as her panoramic view of Rouen on her way to and from her meetings with Léon, where she imagines herself surrounded by the "passions of one hundred and twenty thousand souls"; or again, when she perceives the shadows of the trees in the garden, that night when our romantic heroine asks Rodolphe whether he has brought his pistols to defend her against Charles should he appear:

> The city appeared . . . drowned in the fog . . . The islands looked like giant fishes lying motionless on the water . . . From time to time a gust of wind would drive off the clouds towards the slopes of Saint Catherine, like aerial waves breaking silently against a cliff.

> All the lights of the city . . . forming a luminous mist.
> Masses of deeper darkness stood out here and there in the night . . . and would sway like immense black waves pressing forward to engulf them.

This last passage represents, in images of the objective world, everything which threatens to engulf this precarious love, while many other passages carry out the theme of masses of water in movement. In his sketches for her promenade with Léon, Flaubert writes: "fields . . . furrows following one another, . . . white waves of a motionless ocean"; and in the scene of the horseback ride, just before she gives herself to Rodolphe, "the ground trembled beneath her feet as on the bridge of a ship." When Rodolphe abandons her, she thinks of throwing herself out of the attic window, and "the ground of the village Square seemed to tilt over and climb up the walls, the floor to pitch forward like in a tossing boat." Later after the first visit to the cathedral, Emma's liaison with Léon is sealed in a coach. And in one of those double images where the antithesis contains the synthesis, and which are obviously symbolic, the idea of a ship of love is fused with that of death: "a cab with all blinds drawn that reappeared incessantly, more tightly sealed than a tomb and tossed around like a ship on the waves." The bed on which Emma and Léon drift unconsciously toward shipwreck is a "large mahogany bed shaped like a boat."

Shipwreck comes, and as Emma leaves Rouen for the last time she passes in front of the cathedral just as people are leaving after the Vespers service. The majestic verger, who had appeared to her at the beginning of her affair with Léon (among the statues and the tombs in the chapels) like a sort of life-preserver to which her honor should have clung, now appears to her again at the end of her career like a rock of retribution upon which all her hopes have shattered:

> People were coming out after vespers; the crowd flowed out through the three portals like a river through the three arches of a bridge, and in the middle, more immobile than a rock, stood the verger.

Desperate, and "swept away in her memories as in a raging tempest" she suddenly thinks of Rodolphe. She runs to him. "She was irresistible, with a tear trembling in her eye, like a raindrop in a blue flower-cup, after the storm." After her supreme effort with him fails, Emma, stunned, crosses the fields and "the earth seemed to her more yielding than the sea, and the furrows seemed to her immense brown waves breaking into foam." These lines bring to mind the image of the pitching ship with huge black waves cited above, and already prefigures the following image of her last terrestrial voyage: "The black cloth decorated with silver tears, flapped from time to time in the wind, revealing the coffin underneath. The tired bearers walked more slowly, and the bier advanced jerkily, like a boat that pitches with every wave."

We can see more clearly now why "her journey to Vaubyessard had made a gap in her life, like the huge crevasses that a thunderstorm will sometimes carve in the mountains, in the course of a single night," and why love is spoken of as overflowing in a raging torrent, or falling on life like a tempest from heaven. Peace is said to be more vague than the ocean, Emma's room becomes a dark ocean. Finally there is the passage describing Emma's life after Vaubyessard, ironically fusing the present and future in showing her scanning the solitude of her life with desperate eyes like a sailor in distress.

The infrequent images borrowed from the insect world in *Madame Bovary* play a clearly symbolic role. The two following examples which illustrate beautifully Flaubert's classical need for symmetry, were used by him as transition-images uniting two periods in Emma's life. The first symbolizes the end of any feeling of duty or affection toward Charles, at the moment of their departure from Tostes; the second marks the end of all vestiges of conjugal fidelity as she embarks on her ultimate love affair with Léon. After having written him that her duty stands between them, she listens to another voice, and goes off with him in the closed carriage:

> One day when, in view of her departure, she was tidying a drawer, something pricked her finger. It was a wire of her wedding bouquet. The orange blossoms were yellow with dust and the silver-bordered satin ribbons frayed at the edges. She threw it into the fire. It flared up more quickly than dry straw. Then it was like a red bush in the cinders, slowly shrinking away. She watched it burn. The little pasteboard berries burst, the wire twisted, the gold lace melted and the shrivelled paper petals, fluttering like black butterflies at the back of the stove, at last flew up the chimney.

> One time . . . in the open country . . . , a bare hand appeared under the yellow canvas curtain, and threw out some scraps of paper that scattered in the wind, alighting further off like white butterflies on a field of red clover all in bloom.

If we study these two passages, especially the first, we can appreciate Flaubert's skill at valorizing even purely realistic, non-metaphorical details, so that the slightest notation becomes charged with significance and suggestion.

In the following pages, I will try to point out the symbolic significance of several passages which contain no images, keeping in mind that in these matters it is easy to be led astray. When we become aware of how often Flaubert gives his words a more than literal meaning, we are tempted to see symbols in everything. But all the better for the reader if he can add to what has already been put there consciously by an author. At any rate, this sort of exploration is surer to bring true discoveries in the case of a writer like Flaubert who deliberately and instinctively charges every page with suggestion, contrary to the technique of many writers who cannot master this medium or who reject it as too artificial or too obscure.

I will try to limit myself to those passages which seem the most obvious, and which make up a series of themes, or leitmotifs which characterize Flaubert's talent for tight composition.

The first example is interesting because it has several precedents in Flaubert's youthful works, and comes directly from the romantic tradition of Victor Hugo and even Dumas. For the first time Charles is approaching the Bertaux farm where Emma lives with her father: ". . . the horse slipped on the wet grass; Charles had to stoop to pass under the branches. The watchdogs in their kennels barked, dragging at their chain. As he entered, the horse took fright and stumbled." This same theme appears elsewhere. On returning with Léon along the river bank from the house of the go–between nurse, Emma totters on the green stepping stones which tremble under her foot; after Léon's departure, she dreams of him when she looks at the little river with its "slippery banks. They had often walked there to the murmur of the waves over the moss-covered pebbles." When she returns from visiting Rodolphe, she must fol- low the river "with its slippery banks." This theme has been care- fully chosen and preserved by Flaubert who put it in several scenarios. In one he says: "In returning from her meetings, she is forced to return . . . between the tree and the river, by a narrow stone wall." And in the second scenario, printed by M. Conard: ". . . obliged to walk between the trees and the river along a narrow stone wall covered with mud at the risk of falling into the water."

The dress in which Emma is buried is her wedding gown, and Flaubert who once said that he could never look at a beautiful well-dressed woman without thinking of her skeleton, was certainly bound to conceive of this irony. When we also take into account that a woman's wedding gown represents her chastity, and that dresses in general, in this work as well as in other Flaubert novels, represent purity and inaccessibility, we can see why in speaking of the wedding procession he writes: "Emma's dress, which was too long, trailed a little on the ground; from time to time she stopped to pull it up, and then delicately, with her gloved hand, she picked off the coarse grass and thistles, while Charles, empty-handed, waited until she had finished." Flaubert added in one of his sketches, that when Emma tried to pull off a thistle, "the silk lining crackled." Again on returning from the wetnurse, while Emma and Léon are walking together for the first time, they walk along the river bank and "long, thin grasses huddled together in it as the current drove them, and spread themselves upon the limpid water like streaming hair." Further on, "the walls of the gardens . . . , were heated like the glass roof of a hothouse. Wall flowers had sprung up between the bricks, and with the tip of her open parasol, Madame Bovary, as she passed, made some of their faded flowers crumble into yellow dust, or else a spray of overhanging honeysuckle and clematis would catch in the fringe of the parasol and scrape for a moment over the silk."

As Emma and Rodolphe approach the fatal woods, "Long ferns by the roadside caught in Emma's stirrups, Rodolphe leant forward and removed them as they rode along." In several of the drafts, her veil catches on brambles or twigs as they walk. As on the day of her marriage, "her long dress got in her way, although she held it up by the skirt" at the very moment of her surrender, "the cloth of her dress clung to the velvet of his coat".

Emma has the audacity to go in broad daylight across the fields to Rodolphe's house: "But when the cow plank was taken up, she had to follow the stone wall alongside the river: the bank was slippery and to keep from falling, she had to catch hold of the tufts of faded wallflowers. Then she went across the ploughed fields, stumbling, her thin shoes sinking in the heavy mud."

In the two passages, we find the same faded wallflowers.

Finally, on fleeing from Rodolphe the day she poisons herself, "she passed back through the long alley, stumbling against the heaps of dead leaves scattered by the wind." And this time the cow plank is lowered, as though to aid her in her fatal flight to the pharmacist's house where she takes arsenic.

Léon and Emma go to the house of the wetnurse who will later become Emma's go-between. "To get to her house, it was necessary to turn to the left on leaving the street, as if heading for the cemetery," and, on the day of the poisoning, the village matrons seeing her leave Binet's house "and, turning right as making for the cemetery . . . were lost in wonder." The coach which encloses the lovers "like a tomb," also passes by the Rouen cemetery.

We have seen how Emma's dancing slippers, soiled by wax and dust after the ball at Vaubyessard, become a symbol; how, before her fall, she was afraid to dirty them in the pools of water left in the hoofprints of the cattle. Later on we find Justin dreaming as he wipes off the mud left from her meetings with Léon.

These same little shoes and dresses which Emma passes on casually to Félicité are exact parallels to the maid's clandestine love affair with Theodore, for which Emma has set the example, and which she protects and encourages. After Emma's death, Félicité inherits part of her mistress's wardrobe and steals the rest when she elopes with Theodore. It is another example of Emma's posthumous influence.

There are a certain number of actions or attitudes which could be cited here. For example, Rodolphe crushes a clod of earth with his stick, crying: "Oh, I will have her!"; at the moment when he is about to abandon Emma, he opens an old box in which he keeps his love letters from various ladies, and as he does so, "an odor of dry dust and withered roses emanated from it" and the tangled hair of women he had loved "caught in the hinges of the box, and broke when he opened it." Then there is the day when Charles "discovered a box and kicked it open . . . Rodolphe's portrait flew out at him, from among the pile of love letters."

* * *

Another hidden symbol, which will reappear later on in *The Sentimental Education*, is the cactus which Léon brings Emma in the course of their first idyll. It causes her to prick her finger, just as her wedding bouquet of orange blossoms does when she is about to leave Tostes. Mme. Bovary tells Léon about these plants when she finds him again after their long period of separation and oblivion: "The cold killed them last winter." When Rodolphe comes into the room to set in motion his plan of seduction: "the gilding of the barometer, on which the rays of the sun fell, shone in the looking–glass." But after the disastrous conclusion of the operation on the club–footed boy, Charles is disheartened and asks his wife to kiss him: " 'Stop it!' she cried with a terrible look. And rushing from the room, Emma closed the door so violently that the barometer fell from the wall and smashed on the floor."

We have pointed out several passages which reflect the states of mind of various characters in the book, and others which are pre-figured symbols of doom. Many passages, both with and without images, combine the two. There are comparisons of waves and ships, which we have already examined. There is also the description of the desolate garden at Tostes, as seen by Emma on a handsome winter day; the grapevine "like a great sick serpent under the coping of the wall, along which, on drawing near, one saw the many-footed woodlick crawling. Under the spruce by the hedgerow, the curé in the three-cornered hat reading his breviary had lost his right foot, and the very plaster, scaling off with the frost, had left white scabs on his face." During the move from Tostes to Yonville, "the plaster curé . . . , thrown out of the carriage by a particularly severe joust, had broken into a thousand pieces on the pavement of Quincampoix!" In the outskirts of Tostes, where Emma walks to assuage her lassitude, the great empty plains become symbols of her life: "occasionally there came gusts of wind, breezes from the sea rolling in one sweep over the whole plateau of the Caux country, which brought to these fields a salt freshness." The same is true of the sky after Léon's departure, which is empty except in the direction of the setting sun. A symmetrical parallel to the breaking of the little plaster curé is the escape of Emma's little greyhound, Djali, who accompanies her on her monotonous walks across the sterile plateau. Often "noting the melancholy face of the graceful animal, who yawned slowly, she softened, and comparing her to herself, spoke to her aloud as to somebody in pain whom one is con-soling"; "her thoughts . . . wandered at random, like her grey-hound, who ran round and round in the fields, yelping after the yel-low butterflies, chasing the field mice or nibbling the poppies on the edge of a wheatfield." Then the same fate which overtakes the plaster curé catches the romantically named greyhound: it leaps out of the coach and flees across the fields. Emma is furious and weeps; they search for the dog everywhere, but he is gone forever. Something like this would hardly be probable in real life, and would certainly not have been included by Flaubert if, like in the long passage on the phantom dog in the first *Sentimental Education*, he had not wished to give it a symbolic value. The plaster curé doubtlessly represents Emma's virtue, and the greyhound, the monotonous but nevertheless free, foot-loose and relatively happy period of her life at Tostes.

There is a kind of counter symbolism in several passages which have an ironic function: some statement by one of the characters has an altogether different meaning for the reader than the sense in which it was intended by the speaker. For instance, the inscription on Emma's tomb, chosen by Homais: "Amabilem conjugem calcas!", or his admonition to Emma and Rodolphe when they are setting out on their horseback ride: "An accident happens so easily. Be careful! . . . Be careful! Above all, be careful!" When Emma's riding outfit is ready, "Charles wrote to M. Boulanger that his wife was at his disposition and that they counted on his good will." Similarly, when Emma is looking for an excuse to go to Rouen to see Léon, she suggests to Charles that she is seeking advice on a legal matter; "How good you are!" he said, kissing her on the forehead. Finally, on receiving an announcement of Léon's marriage, Charles, then a widower, writes to the clerk saying: "How happy my poor wife would have been." Rodolphe hides his letter to Emma in which he announces the end of their love-affair in the bottom of a basket of apricots. On taking a bite of one of them, Charles says:

"Perfect! . . . taste it!"
And he handed her the basket which she gently put away from her.
"Smell them! Such perfume!" he insisted, moving it back and forth under her nose.
Charles, to obey her, sat down again, and he spat the stones of the apricots into his hand, afterwards putting them on his plate.

The symmetrical arrangement of the book requires a parallel to this passage. After Rodolphe comes Léon. And on Emma's return from her first love-meeting with the clerk, Charles, whose father has just died, takes the bouquet of violets which Léon has given her and which she pretends to have bought herself: "Charles picked up the flowers and, bathing his tear-stained eyes in their freshness, he delicately sniffed their perfume. She took them quickly from his hand and put them in a glass of water."

Certain characters become symbols. Hippolyte, the poor club-foot, appears at significant moments with the wooden leg which Emma has given him, obsessing Charles for whom he is "the living embodiment of his hopeless ineptitude." Again, in the church during Emma's funeral, "The sharp noise of an iron-tipped stick was heard on the stones, striking them at irregular intervals . . . It was

Hippolyte . . . He had put on his new leg." Binet also is a symbol. He is the bourgeois human equivalent of "that mongrel land without character" which he inhabits; he functions, in a way, like the personification of Emma's conscience ever since the day when he pops like a devil out of his barrel, gun in hand, and discovers Emma's secret as she returns from Rodolphe's house. After this, she naturally avoids him as much as possible. The day that she is abandoned by Rodolphe and is about to throw herself out of the attic window, she hears Binet making his napkin rings "and the humming of the lathe never ceased, like an angry voice calling her." Finally, on the day of the poisoning, she goes to his workshop, where he turns his lathe, and he recoils from her as at the sight of a snake, and propells her toward her suicide. Faint from despair, at the house of the nurse, she hears the spinning wheel, and: " 'Oh, make it stop!' she murmured, fancying she heard Binet's lathe." The day of her funeral, he "abstained from coming."

But it is above all the blind man who becomes the incarnation of Emma's Nemesis. The use of this blind man, which Flaubert spells with a capital B after the scene of Emma's death, is certainly a romantic device of the purest nature. * * *

It is clear, almost too clear, from Emma's first encounter with the blind man, just what role he will play in the drama. But we must remember that if he is a symbol for us, he is above all a symbol for Emma herself; taking this into account, his apparitions become natural: "He sang a little song while following the coaches: 'Often the warmth of a summer's day / Makes a young girl dream her heart away.' And the rest of the song was all about birds, the sun and the leaves". In other words, here is exactly the scene of the forest, which finds another precise and terrible echo in this description of the blind man's voice:

> His voice, at first weak and quavering, would grow sharp. It lingered in the night like an inarticulate lament of some vague despairs, . . . it had something so distant and sad that it filled Emma with dread. It went to the very depth of her soul, like a whirlwind in an abyss, and carried her away to a boundless realm of melancholy. But Hivert . . . would lash out savagely at the blind man with his whip . . . and he fell back into the mud with a shriek.

Then "Emma, drunk with grief . . . felt . . . death in her soul." According to several first sketches, this voice "hummed in her ears like a hornet's nest. He jumped onto the footboard; then that hideous face would appear framed in the coach window like a head from a guillotine."

On the fateful day when Emma is returning from Rouen for the last time, she encounters the hideous specter "who uttered a sort of low howl like a famished dog. Emma, overcome with disgust, threw him a five franc piece over her shoulder. It was all her fortune. It seemed like a grand thing to her to throw it away like this."

Finally, in the death scene, the song's every word is a symbol of Emma's life and death. Emma hears the song of the blind man through the open window:

> "To gather up all the new-cut stalks
> Of wheat left by the scythe's cold swing,
> Nanette bends over as she walks
> Toward the furrows from where they spring."

"The blind man!" she cried.
And Emma began to laugh, . . . thinking she saw the hideous face of the poor wretch loom out of the eternal darkness like a menace.

> "The wind blew very hard that day
> It blew her petticoat away."

A final spasm threw her back upon the mattress. They all drew near. She had ceased to exist.

The sordid nurse who acts as go-between, also becomes, in Emma's eyes, an incarnation of punishment. When little Berthe mentions the nurse's name to her dying mother, "the mention of this name carried her back to the memory of her adulteries and her calamities. Madame Bovary turned away her head, as at the loathing of another more bitter poison that rose to her mouth."

Finally, there are three other characters who serve as parallel leitmotifs. Their intermingled memories return to Emma's mind and keep accumulating throughout her career. Like Flaubert, Emma lives entirely in memory and by dreams. The viscount ceases to be a person and becomes a center of love-dreams. The same is true of the cigar box, for to Emma, objects and men soon become symbols, in the same way that lovers only exist for each other as incarnations of love. This binds the heroine even more tightly to the author. * * * In a passage suppressed by Flaubert after the first printing in the *Revue de Paris*, Léon's teeth, voice, glances, hair, and breath are compared to the silver plates, the orchestra, the lights from the crystal chandeliers, the hothouse air and the perfume of the magnolias at Vaubyessard. In the scene at the fair, the memory of the viscount and that of Léon intermingle in Emma's mind while Rodolphe is paying court to her. When Emma and Léon take a boat excursion, the boatman speaks to them of a certain "Dodolphe," a ladies's man he has often taken out in his boat with a very gay crowd. Emma shudders. Finally, without going back over Emma's attempts to get money from Léon and Rodolphe, we should mention her memory of the viscount mingled with that of Léon at the beginning of their love–affair, the day when she sees the verger standing like a rock before the cathedral of Rouen:

Then she remembered the day when, eager and full of hope, she had entered beneath this large nave, that had opened out before her, less profound than her love; and she walked on weeping beneath her veil, dazed, staggering, almost fainting.

"Look out!" cried a voice issuing from behind a carriage gate which was swinging open.

She stopped to let pass a black horse, prancing between the shafts of a tilbury, driven by a gentleman . . . it was he, the vicomte! She turned away; the street was empty. And she was . . . crushed. . . . Everything within herself and without was abandoning her. She felt lost, that she was wandering about at random within undefinable abysses. . . .

* * *

The symbolism of some of the names which Flaubert chose so carefully for his characters deserves study. The name Bovary admirably describes the man whom we find ruminating or "chewing the cud of his happiness," and whose life, like his first name, rolls gently toward his destiny. His family name makes a pair with that of Léon's wife, Mlle. Lebeuf. Indeed, the most significant and most frequently repeated symbols in the novel are bovine—cattle, either in herds or alone, their hoofprints stamped in the mud, their apparition unwelcome to Emma in moments of reverie or discouragement. Lheureux certainly merits his name as the happy or fortunate one, for he and Homais are the ones who triumph in the book. Homais is a pejorative form of Homme or man, as is well indicated in one of the early sketches where Flaubert writes "Homais comes from *homo* = homme." There is also a rather obvious counter-symbol in the name of Virginia given to Rodolphe's mistress, and it is not difficult to see the imitative harmony in such names as the Abbé Bournisien, or Lestiboudois, the enterprising and ever-complaining sacristan, or in Hippolyte, the clubfoot who hops like his name when he walks.

Flaubert, who appears to have suffered from hallucinations, attributes them to his characters. Consequently, everything for them becomes symbol. We have seen many examples of this. Emma's last days are one continual hallucination, especially after her unfruitful visit to Rodolphe. The first time she came there, she entered the château "as if the doors at her approach had opened wide of their own accord," on leaving the "impassive château" for the last time, it seems to her that "the ceiling was crushing her"; the earth becomes a sea of immense waves, her ideas and memories "like a thousand pieces of fireworks . . . were coming upon her . . ." and:

> She suffered only in her love, and felt her soul escaping from her in this memory, as wounded men, dying, feel their life ebb from their bleeding wounds.
> Night was falling, crows were flying about.
> Suddenly it seemed to her that fiery spheres were exploding in the air like bullets when they strike, and were whirling, whirling, to melt at last upon the snow between the branches of the trees. In the midst of each of them appeared the face of Rodolphe. They multiplied and drew near, they penetrated her. It all disappeared; she recognized the lights of the houses that shone through the fog.

She is ready for the apparition of the blind man.

In the scenes of Emma's agony and death, with a few important exceptions, such as the apparition of the blind man and the comparisons drawn from her former music lessons, the images no longer reflect Emma's hallucinations. Flaubert, the father of the impressionists, and Flaubert, the son of the surgeon, observe together the transformations to which the body of the poor heroine is subjected:

> She was growing paler than the sheets in which she buried her clenched fists. . . . Drops of sweat oozed from her face that had turned blue and rigid as under the effect of a metallic vapor. . . . her poor hands wandered over the sheets with that hideous and gentle movement of the dying, that seems as if they already wanted to cover themselves with the shroud. . . . her eyes, as they rolled, grew paler, like the two globes of a lamp that is going out . . . , her ribs [were] shaken by violent breathing, as if the soul were struggling to free itself. Emma raised herself like a galvanized corpse . . . The corner of her mouth . . . seemed like a black hole at the lower part of her face; . . . and her eyes were beginning to disappear in a viscous pallor, like a thin web, as though spiders had been spinning over it . . . it seemed to Charles that infinite masses, an enormous load, were weighing upon her.

Since Flaubert, during his trip to Egypt, had trained himself in the art of seeing things as they are, without subjective distortions, it is not surprising that *Madame Bovary* contains several passages which aim only at precise description. Indeed we may rather wonder why there are so few in this book in which the descriptions are otherwise so admirably clear. This is because Flaubert's use of figurative language, while clearly defining a shape or movement, is aimed primarily at evoking the striking and suggestive image, though never at the expense of objective precision. Flaubert preferred not to divert the attention of the reader with purely descriptive metaphors in a work whose main objective was to attain that profound and complex reality which only the combined talents of a writer who was an artist as well as a physiologist, a psychologist as well as a historian of moral customs, could reveal.

ALBERT BÉGUIN

On Rereading *Madame Bovary*†

There are certain books one can not reread without being seduced again by the effect they made upon us when we first read them. *Madame Bovary* is surrounded by just such a protective halo. Even after one has lost one's taste for Flaubert's rhetoric, or learned to prefer by far the bitter sadness of *The Sentimental Education* to the firm structure of *Madame Bovary*, the novel nevertheless retains its power; perhaps we should call it the power of an irresistible boredom. The book is closer to truth than to life; it is too tightly written, built on the obsessive continuity of successive paragraphs patterned on the same few rhythmical designs. Each new reading leaves one more disappointed. Something seems to be lacking that one hoped to find again. Certain suggestions, physical sensations, and inward states of being lingered on in one's memory, and one looks in vain for them in the text. One of Flaubert's main qualities is that he suggests more than he says; this talent is not without danger, when it turns out that the book, at a few years' distance, seems much less rich than one remembered.

It has long since been known that Flaubert's exhausting labor consisted mostly of cutting down and that, from his earliest version to the final text, he made a systematic effort to prune away anything that seemed superfluous. We can now compare the original text of the novel with the final printed version. Some fifteen years ago, Mlle. Gabrielle Leleu had already published part of the manuscripts that were kept at Rouen.[1] But the typographical arrangement of this publication was such that it could only be destined for specialists. With the collaboration of M. Jean Pommier, the same author now gives us a "new version" of *Madame Bovary*.[2] The term "new version" is misleading; it actually is the very first version which, in fact, never existed in this form. The editors reconstructed

† *"En relisant* Madame Bovary," *La Table Ronde* (March 27, 1950), pp. 160–64. Reprinted by permission of Plon. Translated by Paul de Man.
1. *Madame Bovary: Sketches and un-* *published fragments* (Louis Conard, 1936).
2. *Madame Bovary: A New Version, preceded by unpublished Scenarios* (José Corti, 1949).

an imaginary first draft, by selecting, from the mass of manuscripts, those seeming closest to an original draft. The method is avowedly arbitrary, but it offers the considerable advantage of allowing a continuous reading which reveals what Flaubert could have been . . . if he had not been Flaubert—that is to say, a writer who never ceased wasting some of his most precious gifts in order to satisfy the tyrannical demands of an aesthetic prejudice.

In rereading *Madame Bovary* in this early form, predating the version that took Flaubert so many years of patient labor, one has the real impression of meeting a different work. The style has not yet been polished; it is uneven and frequently faulty, though amazingly free in invention. The human content, however, is infinitely richer than in the printed version. And yet, Flaubert has made few changes in the organization of his narrative; the different scenes follow each other in the same order, no important episodes have been suppressed, the characters remain the same. If the book is almost twice as long, it is because Flaubert ruthlessly eliminated from every paragraph, from every sentence, whatever could not be fitted to the movement of language which he wanted to obtain. He succeeded in this at the expense of numerous psychological insights and of admirable beauties of expression, often of exceptional originality.

This is not the place to reopen the old debate between Proust and Thibaudet[3] on whether Flaubert was a born writer, or a writer devoid of original talent. One might say that, while he was the first to perceive, with the perspicacity of a great innovator, certain undiscovered aspects of the human soul, he had to keep most of them hidden because their expression would have required a freedom in the handling of language for which he was not yet ready. Obsessed by the *idée fixe* of a perfect form (an idea which may very well not apply to the novel and to the expression of a temporal experience that is infinitely complex), Flaubert wrote by nature a shapeless language about which he had serious misgivings. This language was marvelously suited for experimentation and discovery; it could alternate sudden explorations in depth with the suggestive flights of an extraordinarily fertile lyricism of images. It reads with difficulty, because it has been awkwardly composed, but it leads from surprise to surprise.

The passages most affected by Flaubert's pruning are of three kinds. Flaubert first tones down the passages in which physical life is too boldly described. Then, he mercilessly sacrifices thousands of psychological shades in the description of the characters, of their daydreams, their moments of reminiscence which make of his entire work an early "remembrance of things past." Finally, he eliminates

3. Allusion to the polemic in the *Nouvelle Revue française* referred to in the Preface [*Editor*].

often very beautiful metaphors that occur spontaneously, and give to the first version a poetic quality entirely lacking in the edited text. A few examples are necessary at this point.

Flaubert was certainly not being prudish when he cut the passages that reveal his very keen interest in the movements of sensuous life. True, he is no doubt acting out of concern for general decorum when he erases the four-letter words that frequently occur in his first drafts. But these are emendations of the same order as the suppression of many terms that stem from Norman dialect. However, when he tones down certain erotic passages, he is not merely acting out of fear of being considered crude. "Emma, left by herself and unable to sleep, felt such a violent desire for Rodolphe that she fancied she had to see him at once, without delay" becomes "She fancied she had to see Rodolphe at once." Elsewhere, referring to the meetings between Emma and Léon, one reads: ". . . Then they faced each other; they looked at each other, touching with their hands, their faces, their breasts, as if they didn't have senses enough with which to savor the joys of love, burning with desire, stamping their feet while staring at each other with lascivious laughs, until they could no longer wait for the moment of possession." In the printed version, this becomes the colorless lines: ". . . they faced each other, with voluptuous laughs and tender words." A little further on, Flaubert eliminates a long passage on the pleasures of love which ended like this: ". . . the pleasures of the senses did not invalidate this ideal image; to the contrary, they made it stronger. Emma reconquered happiness in this blonde-colored passion and, knowing how uncertain it was, tried to increase it by means of all the artifices of her tenderness, savoring it with the craving of the poor, the thirst of the sick, the avarice of the elderly." No prudery is involved in the elimination of such passages, nor is prudery the main consideration in the suppression of rather strange scenes, such as the moment in which the officiating priest anoints the feet of the dying Mme. Bovary and awakens in her husband the memory of their wedding night, or the macabre scene in which Charles presses his lips on the forehead of her dead body in a "horrible kiss, of which the sensation remains forever on his lips, as a foretaste of the final putrefaction." In all these emendations, Flaubert obviously defeats himself as a writer; the original sentence, because of its violence and truthfulness, does not lend itself to reorganization: it grows awkward and confused. In order to safeguard the uniformity of rhythm and in obedience to the accepted principle of style, sacrifices become necessary. One should add an obvious lack of boldness on Flaubert's behalf in the face of certain verbal inventions that seem too unusual—such as, for instance, the "blonde-colored passion" which would have delighted a contemporary writer but which Flaubert doesn't dare to keep.

The same scruples, in a man who is held captive by his conception of style, lead him to eschew the majority of the psychological observations which gave the first version its pre–Proustian character. Something of this undoubtedly subsists in the novel as we know it; part of its suggestive power stems precisely from the recurring theme of involuntary recollection. This resurrection of the past (coupled with a prefiguration of the future) occurs in all the characters without exception and at all times; it constitutes the main ingredient of what has been called "bovarysme." The examples in the first draft however are both more frequent and more striking. Instead of Emma Bovary, it is her clod of a husband who experiences "intermittences of the heart" upon returning to the Bertaux farm after the death of his first wife: "Interrupted for a moment by this forgotten episode, his distant feeling was recovered, the past became the present and his memory a renewed emotion." He sees Emma again, and "the poor branches of his heart, nailed down by his restricted existence as on a flat wall beyond which they were not allowed to spread, upon receiving the glow that emanated from the young girl, blossomed in thousands of buds, of little flowers." One could find innumerable instances of similar quotations, in which the reverie leads to a strange awareness of subjective time. After the evening at the Vaubyessard castle, Emma loses the sense of passing time: "What was it that set so far asunder the morning of the day before yesterday and the evening of today, so that both now seemed like two different existences put end to end?" (Final version: "What was it that set thus far asunder the morning of the day before yesterday and the evening of today?"). Much later, after the sinister orgy with Léon and his friends, Emma wanders through Rouen at dawn "her head full of noise, colors and sadness"; it seems to her that she is reliving an earlier moment of her life, although she is unable to remember "the place, the cause, or the time" at which it took place. At last she realizes that she is remembering the dance that she has only just left: "It seemed way behind her in a distant past, and already so far gone that she regretted no longer being there." Nothing of this observation remains in the revised text, with an unquestionable loss of depth and originality. Much less intimately linked with such metamorphoses of time, Emma's ennui becomes much more banal as it loses its metaphysical component.

Still for the same reason, Flaubert dispenses with the images that arise spontaneously in his first writing. When the memory of Rodolphe, buried away in Emma's heart, begins to fade away, the first version alone has a lyrical passage: "She had sung over him the funeral dirge of her lost youth . . . Between him and herself now stretched a long gallery of unknown pains, full of darkness, dust, and gold." The musical and color metaphors that recur in the early drafts gave them a particularly intense poetic quality to which, again, Flaubert refuses to abandon himself. The tyrannical law of the verbal cadence once more stifles the deeper rhythm, the multiple rhythm of the flesh, the image and time, which Flaubert perceived better than anyone but to which he seems to have refused to listen when he prepared his final manuscript.

I know of no other equally pathetic case in which a literary success could be achieved only at the cost of a secret undoing. In the course of his labors, Flaubert goes through two very different stages. In the first stage, which is that of invention, he listens as to an inner dictation and tries to follow as closely as possible the hidden movements of the inner life—something of which he has an astoundingly subtle knowledge. He is particularly astute at exploring the confines where the psychological and the physiological merge; these mysterious border regions are first to claim his attention. Like a clairvoyant blind man, he seeks his way to the discovery of an almost inexpressible reality. One can recognize this stage in a passage from the earlier version, when he speaks of the long daily letters that Emma writes to Rodolphe: ". . . Her sensations were reawakened by her efforts to translate them. In this way, Emma drew out her passion by passing it through the laminating presses of style. Yet it lost nothing of its solidity since the satisfaction of her desires added each day something new."

However, in the next stage, when Flaubert reconsidered his text for an infinite number of further revisions, his writing ceased to be this magical and Proustian device to resurrect the past. The rescuing act of memory no longer occurs and the expression "laminating presses of style" takes on an altogether different meaning. Detached henceforth from the deeper realities which he had begun to discover, the novelist's only concern is to perfect what he now merely considers as a mass of sound that demands to be ordered. He no longer needs to record, as he did before, thousands of sensations in order to re-create one imaginary instant and, by means of this artificial reconstruction, put himself exactly in the same situation as the character he is describing. At first he had to identify himself as closely as possible with his creation, reliving his emotions, sharing his dreams; but now the author has to create a distance between himself and the character. Hence Flaubert's constant complaints about his labors, which were apparently an endless ordeal. All the flights of the imagination have died down; what remains on the page is a heavy and shapeless mass that demands to be modeled into shape in order to represent, not life itself, but an ideal model, an aesthetic canon of perfection.

The extent of the sacrifices Flaubert had to make, as well as the damage caused by his excessive pusillanimity, are nowhere more apparent than in the final encounter between the widowed Charles Bovary and his wife's former lover Rodolphe. Why did Flaubert not, at the very least, rescue the full depth of the statement he attributes to Charles when, on meeting his rival, he suddenly asks him: *"How did you do it?"* It is true that Flaubert rather disappointingly pursues: "Rodolphe vaguely understood. . . ."[4]

If it were not a vain game, one would like to dream of a Flaubert born fifty or seventy years later, who could have accepted without further ado the gift of a style beyond rules and of a way of writing capable of recapturing exactly the inner movement it was expressing. Writing at the time of Proust, he would perhaps have known a happiness that was refused to him as long as he worshipped the idol of Art, to which he sacrificed his soul and his blood. But, in that case, we would not now have that irreplaceable great book *Madame Bovary*, the book of the impossible escape, the heavy-hearted poem of eternal *ennui*.

4. The passage from an early draft is given on p. 279 [*Editor*].

Biographical Sources

RENÉ DUMESNIL

[The Real Source of *Madame Bovary*]†

Nothing demonstrates the continuity of Flaubert's effort better than the writing of *Madame Bovary*. We have come to accept as true Maxime DuCamp's account: when Flaubert read his first version of *The Vision of Saint Anthony* to Bouilhet and DuCamp,[1] *Madame Bovary* came into being from Bouilhet's suggestion: "Why don't you write the Delaunay story?" Flaubert is supposed to have thrown back his head and exclaimed: "What an idea!" Delaunay was really called Delamare, but that makes little difference. If this punishing task was indeed imposed on a horrified Flaubert by his judges with the verdict: "It is our opinion that the manuscript of *Saint Anthony* must be thrown into the fire and the subject never brought up again," then it seems highly dubious that he would have accepted with enthusiasm "putting his Muse on bread and water." His letters bear this out well enough. Actually, his trip to the Far East was often poisoned by the prospect awaiting him on his return: of spending months—he did not foresee at that time that it would be more than five years—in the company of the people he detested most in the world, the bourgeois inhabitants of a county seat, a pharmacist named Homais, a curé called Bournisien, a tax collector whose horizon was limited to the wheel of his lathe hollowing out napkin rings. . . .

There is a whole archive of exegetic works on the *real*(?) Emma Bovary. Extraordinary importance is attached to irrelevant and useless details, as though their publication might somehow illuminate the impenetrable mystery of a work of art. The very day after the book appeared, people demanded to know the identity of Madame Bovary. When Flaubert, feeling persecuted, answered with a statement that was in effect the simple truth—"*I am Madame Bovary!*"—everyone assumed he was joking.

Yet, could anything be more true, more certain?

† From *La Vocation Litteraire de G. Flaubert* ("The Vocation of Gustave Flaubert") by René Dumesnil (Paris: Gallimard, 1961), pp. 221–25 and 230– 33; reprinted by permission of the publisher. Translated by Paul de Man.
1. See p. 312 and p. 408 for notes on Bouilhet and DuCamp.

The only authentic "source" of the novel published in 1856 comes from Flaubert himself, then a schoolboy going on seventeen. It is the manuscript of his "Philosophical Tale: *Passion and Virtue*," dated by him December 10, 1837.

All the articles and books that have been written on Emma Rouault, Charles Bovary, and Yonville-l'Abbaye, in real life supposedly Delphine Couturier, the wife of an *officier de Santé* named Delamare who practiced medicine at a place called Ry—all these sources which have been much disputed and are often dubious, offer little but anecdotal interest. They are of less importance to the real critic seeking to penetrate the psychological motivations of the writer than other details without which the novel would have neither color nor resonance. The subject is extremely banal, so banal that Flaubert had imagined that, by using it as a point of departure, he could write a book with no subject at all.

All the details drawn from reality, though they are of no importance in themselves, nevertheless constitute the material of a work of art, because of the irrefutable logic that has guided their selection and assemblage. But the author himself is the sole source; not one of these characters is a portrait in the literal sense of the word, not one of the pictures is a photograph, not one of the landscapes can be traced in the Registry of Deeds. Nothing that makes up the living substance and marrow of the book has any existence but in Flaubert himself. Certainly, every detail is true and has, no doubt, been observed and perhaps even measured by Flaubert. Yet, it is all these documents together, taken from various times and various places and patiently assembled by a novelist of genius in the silence of the house at Croisset, which made a novel whose life came only from himself.

A long process of maturation took place in the mind of the writer. It took twenty years and was carried out in silence. In this process, the subconscious played a part at least equal to that of the conscious mind. Memory records many observations which only precipitate when they are mixed together. . . . This is where the hand of the novelist can be seen: it regulates the operation of that strange alchemy which transforms life into a work of art. But in order to succeed, one needs a little magic and much, much patience. The magic is provided by talent which has been constantly cultivated since the first call to the vocation.

* * *

Passion and Virtue is the story of a young woman named Mazza. She already embodies everything that Emma Bovary will be; from the very first lines, we find her dreaming of a man she has seen only two times: "the first time was at a dance given at the ministry, the second time at the Comédie Française, and although he was neither a man of extraordinary talents nor very handsome, she had often thought of him. In the evening, after the lamp had been blown out, she would remain a few instants dreaming, her heavy hair covering her bare breasts, her head turned toward the window where the night threw forth a pale light, her arms hanging over the edge of the couch, and her soul floating between emotions at once vague and repellent, like those confused sounds which rise from the fields on autumn evenings." Here, in the space of ten lines, we can clearly see both the analogies and differences between *Passion and Virtue* and *Madame Bovary*. Mazza's portrait is very similar to Emma's: they both have the same dreamy character combined with the same thirst to possess the absolute. The setting, however, is entirely different. Here the scene is Paris, in that elegant and fortune-blessed society where everything is possible—at least to those who only know it from literature or from hearsay. But it must be said in Flaubert's defense, that if he wrote about things which he knew hardly if at all, he was simply following the example set by the majority of the novelists of his time. Sainte-Beuve said that Stendhal in *Armance* talks about the "salons" of the Faubourg Saint-Germain as though they were "an unknown country peopled with strange monsters; the people whom he depicts there have not the slightest resemblance to reality, and this enigmatic novel is false in its detail." Accuracy of detail and plausibility will come soon enough; *Madame Bovary* will not be lacking in either. But already in *Passion and Virtue*, though it lacks the experience which a sixteen-year-old author could not yet have acquired, one can see the seeds of those qualities which will be most admired in the later works. And the structure itself, despite some awkward moments, is already well established.

Just as Charles is by nature the exact opposite of Emma, M. Willer, a financier totally absorbed in the fluctuations of the stock market, knows nothing of Mazza's reveries. Evil fortune brings it about that she encounters her Rodolphe, a certain Ernest: "Far from being one of those men of exceptional feeling whom one meets in books and plays, he was a man with a dry heart, a precise mind, and on top of all that, a chemical engineer. But he was an expert seducer: he knew by heart the devices, the tricks, the *chic* (to use a vulgar word) by which an adroit man arrives at his ends." And page by page, the parallels and analogies between the novel of the sixteen–year–old and the masterpiece of the mature man become more numerous and apparent. The one is already the other, only in an embryonic state; it will take a gestation period of fifteen years for this subject, reluctantly reconsidered and laboriously executed, like a schoolboy's exercise, to grow into the masterpiece we know. The shock of seeing his *Temptation of Saint Anthony* so severely condemned by his friends, just before he was about to leave for the Orient, no doubt helped to speed up the process.

Ernest is adroit. He introduces himself into Mazza's household, "he lends her novels, takes her to the theater, making sure always to do something startling and different; and then, day by day, he is freer in his visits to her house and manages to become a friend of the family, of her husband, of the servants. . . ." Rodolphe will act in exactly the same way; he will manage diabolically to have her husband suggest, even insist, that for reasons of health, she should go out riding in the forest with the very man who has only been waiting for this opportunity to make her his mistress.

So Mazza gives herself to Ernest. She give herself body and soul, just as Emma will to Rodolphe. And like Rodolphe, Ernest "begins to love her a little more than a little shop-girl or a bit-part actress" and becomes frightened of this love, "like children who run away from the sea saying it is too large." Ernest, like Rodolphe, will invent pretexts for the separation he wants. The letter he writes to her is almost identical to the one Rodolphe will send to Emma: "Farewell, Mazza! I will never see you again. I have been sent by the Minister of the Interior on an important mission to analyze the products and the soil of Mexico. Farewell! I embark at Le Havre. If you wish to be happy, cease to love me. Love Virtue and Duty instead. This is my final word to you. Farewell again! I embrace you. Ernest."

Rodolphe will add a bit more polish. But we must not forget that the author of *Passion and Virtue* was a boy of sixteen. Mazza runs all the way to Le Havre, arriving only in time to see "a white sail sinking beneath the horizon."

She returns stunned, wounded. "She sees life as one long cry of pain"; she "writhes in agony in the embrace of her husband, weeping at a memory." She becomes a widow. After a long wait, she finally receives a cold and indifferent letter in which Ernest announces his marriage to the only daughter of his superior. Mazza drinks poison and dies.

There is no point in emphasizing how many elements of the 1857 work are lacking in the 1837 sketch; Emma's degeneration, the slow fatal progress which leads her implacably from fall to fall till she finally takes the poison, the sureness of touch which made Sainte-Beuve exclaim: "The son and brother of distinguished physicians, M. Gustave Flaubert handles his pen the way other men use the scalpel: anatomists and physiologists, I recognize you throughout!" This does not prevent *Passion and Virtue* from being of considerable interest to the critic who will see in it the confirmation and development of a compelling vocation.

JEAN-PAUL SARTRE

[Flaubert and *Madame Bovary:* Outline of a New Method]†

Let us suppose that I wish to make a study of Flaubert—who is presented in histories of literature as the father of realism. I learn that he said: "I myself am Madame Bovary." I discover that his more subtle contemporaries—in particular Baudelaire, with his "feminine" temperament—had surmised this identification. I learn that the "father of realism" during his trip through the Orient dreamed of writing the story of a mystic virgin, living in the Netherlands, consumed by dreams, a woman who would have been the symbol of Flaubert's own cult of art. Finally, going back to his biography, I discover his dependence, his obedience, his "relative being," in short all the qualities which at that period were commonly called "feminine." At last I find out, a little late, that his physicians dubbed him a nervous old woman and that he felt vaguely flattered. Yet it is certain that he was *not to any degree at all* an invert. Our problem then—without leaving the work itself (that is, the literary significations)—is to ask ourselves why the author (that is, the pure synthetic activity which creates Madame Bovary) was able to metamorphose himself into a woman, what signification the metamorphosis possesses *in itself* (which presupposes a phenomenological study of Emma Bovary in the book), just what this woman is (of whom Baudelaire said that she possesses at once the folly and the will of a man), what the artistic transformation of male into female means in the nineteenth century (we must study the context of *Mlle. de Maupin*,[1] etc.), and finally, just who Gustave Flaubert *must have been* in order to have within the field of his possibles the possibility of portraying himself as a woman. The reply is independent of all biography, since this problem could be posed in Kantian terms: "Under what conditions is the feminization of experience possible?" In order to answer it, we must never forget that the author's style is directly bound up with a conception of the world; the sentence and paragraph structure, the use and po-

† From Jean-Paul Sartre, *Search for a Method*, translated by Hazel Barnes, pp. 140–50. Copyright © 1963 by Alfred A. Knopf, Inc.; reprinted by permission of the publishers, Alfred A. Knopf, Inc.

Search for a Method is the prefatory essay to Sartre's philosophical treatise *Critique de la Raison dialectique* (Paris: Gallimard, 1961). The passage is a methodological blueprint for a projected study of Flaubert which Sartre is preparing.
1. *Mademoiselle de Maupin;* a novel by Théophile Gautier (1811–72), is the story of a woman singer who dresses like a man [*Editor*].

sition of the substantive, the verb, etc., the arrangement of the paragraphs, and the qualities of the narrative—to refer to only a few specific points—all express hidden presuppositions which can be determined *differentially* without as yet resorting to biography. Nevertheless, we shall never arrive at anything but *problems*. It is true that the statements of Flaubert's contemporaries will help us. Baudelaire asserted that the profound meaning of *The Temptation of St. Anthony*, a furiously "artistic" work which Bouilhet [2] called "a diarrhea of pearls" and which in a completely confused fashion deals with the great metaphysical themes of the period (the destiny of man, life, death, God, religion, nothingness, etc.), is fundamentally identical with that of *Madame Bovary*, a work which is (on the surface) dry and objective. What kind of person, then, can Flaubert be, must he be, to express his own reality in the form of a frenzied idealism and of a realism more spiteful than detached? Who can he, must he, be in order to objectify himself in his work first as a mystic monk and then some years later as a resolute, "slightly masculine" woman?

At this point it is necessary to resort to biography—that is, to the facts *collected* by Flaubert's contemporaries and *verified* by historians. The work poses questions to the life. But we must understand in what sense; the work as the objectification of the person is, in fact, *more complete, more total* than the life. It has its roots in the life, to be sure; it illuminates the life, but it does not find its total explanation in the life alone. But it is too soon as yet for this total explanation to become apparent to us. The life is illuminated by the work as a reality whose total determination is found outside of it—both in the conditions which produce it and in the artistic creation which fulfills it and *completes it by expressing it*. Thus the work—when one has examined it—becomes a hypothesis and a research tool to clarify the biography. It questions and holds on to concrete episodes as replies to its questions.[3] But these answers *are not complete*. They are insufficient and limited insofar as the objectification in art is irreducible to the objectification in everyday behavior. There is a hiatus between the work and the life. Nevertheless, the

2. See note on p. 312 [*Editor*].
3. I do not recall that anyone has been surprised that the Norman giant projected himself in his work as a woman. But I do not recall either that anyone has studied Flaubert's femininity (his truculent, "loudmouthed" side has misled critics; but this is only a bit of camouflage—Flaubert has confirmed it a hundred times). Yet the order is discernible: the *logical scandal* is Madame Bovary, a masculine woman and feminized man, a lyric and realistic work. It is this scandal with its peculiar contradictions which must draw our attention to the life of Flaubert and to his lived femininity. We must detect it in his behavior—and first of all, in his sexual behavior. Now his letters to Louise Colet are sexual behavior; they are each one moments in the diplomacy of Flaubert with regard to this pertinacious poetess. We shall not find an embryonic *Madame Bovary* in the correspondence, but we shall greatly clarify the correspondence by means of *Madame Bovary* (and, of course, by the other works).

man, with his human relations thus clarified, appears to us in turn as a synthetic collection of questions. The work has revealed Flaubert's narcissism, his onanism, his idealism, his solitude, his dependence, his femininity, his passivity. But these qualities in turn are problems for us. They lead us to suspect at once both social structures (Flaubert is a property owner, he lives on unearned income, etc.) and a *unique* childhood drama. In short, these regressive questions provide us with the means to question his family group as a reality lived and denied by the child Flaubert. Our questions are based on two sorts of information: objective testimonies about the family (class characteristics, family type, individual aspect) and furiously subjective statements by Flaubert about his parents, his brother, his sister, etc. At this level we must be able constantly to refer back to the work and to know whether it contains a biographical truth such as the correspondence itself (falsified by its author) cannot contain. But we must know also that the work *never* reveals the secrets of the biography; the book can at most serve as a schema or conducting thread allowing us to discover the secrets in the life itself.

At this level, we study the early childhood as a way of living general conditions without clearly understanding or reflecting on them; consequently, we may find the meaning of the lived experience in the intellectual petite bourgeoisie, formed under the Empire, and in its way of living the evolution of French society. Here we pass over into the pure objective; that is, into the historical totalization. It is History itself which we must question—the halted advance of family capitalism, the return of the landed proprietors, the contradictions in the government, the misery of a still insufficiently developed Proletariat. But these interrogations are *constituting* in the sense in which the Kantian concepts are called "constitutive"; for they permit us to realize concrete syntheses there where we had as yet only abstract, general conditions. Beginning with an obscurely lived childhood, we can reconstruct the true character of petit bourgeois families. We compare Flaubert's with the family of Baudelaire (at a more "elevated" social level), with that of the Goncourt brothers (a petit bourgeois family which entered into the nobility about the end of the eighteenth century by the simple acquisition of "noble" property), with that of Louis Bouilhet, etc. In this connection we study the real relations between scientists and practitioners (the father Flaubert) and industrialists (the father of his friend, Le Poittevin). In this sense the study of the child Flaubert, as a universality lived in particularity, enriches the general study of the petite bourgeoisie in 1830. By means of the structures presiding over the particular family group, we enrich and make concrete the always too general characteristics of the class considered; in discontinuous "collectives," for example, we apprehend the complex relation between a petite bourgeoisie of civil servants and intellectuals, on the one hand, and the "elite" of industrialists and landed proprietors on the others, or, again, the *roots* of this petite bourgeoisie, its peasant origin, etc., its relations with fallen aristocrats.[4] It is on this level that we are going to discover the major contradiction which the child, Gustave Flaubert, lived in his own way: the opposition between the bourgeois analytic mind and the synthetic myths of religion. Here again a systematic cross-reference is established between the particular anecdotes which clarify these vague contradictions (because the stories gather them together into a single exploding whole) and the general determination of living conditions which allows us to reconstruct *progressively* (because they have already been studied) the material existence of the groups considered.

The sum total of these procedures—regression and cross-reference—has revealed what I shall call the profundity of the lived. Recently an essayist, thinking to refute existentialism, wrote: "It is not man who is profound; it is the world." He was perfectly right, and we agree with him without reservation. Only we should add that the world is human, the profundity of man is the world; therefore profundity comes to the world through man. The exploration of this profundity is a descent from the absolute concrete (*Madame Bovary* in the hands of a reader contemporary with Flaubert—whether it be Baudelaire or the Empress or the Prosecuting Attorney) to its most abstract conditioning (material conditions, the conflict of productive forces and of the relations of production insofar as these conditions appear in their universality and are given as lived by all the members of an undefined group[5]—that is, practically, by *abstract* subjects). Across *Madame Bovary* we can and must catch sight of the movement of landowners and capitalists, the evolution of the rising classes, the slow maturation of the Proletariat: everything is there. But the most concrete significations are radically irreducible to the most abstract significations. The "differential" at each signifying plane reflects the differential of the higher plane by impoverishing it and by contracting it; it clarifies the differential of the lower plane and serves as a rubric for the synthetic unification of our most abstract knowing. This *cross-reference* contributes to enrich the object with all the profundity of History; it determines,

4. Flaubert's father, the son of a village veterinarian (a royalist), "distinguished" by the imperial administration, marries a girl whose family is connected with the nobility through marriage. He associates with rich industrialists; he buys land.
5. In reality the petite bourgeoisie in 1830 is a numerically defined group (although there obviously exist unclassifiable intermediaries who unite it with the peasant, the bourgeois, the landowners). But *methodologically* this concrete universal will always remain indeterminate because the statistics are incomplete.

within the historical totalization, the still empty location for the object.

At this point in our research we have still not succeeded in revealing anything more than a hierarchy of heterogeneous significations: *Madame Bovary,* Flaubert's "femininity," his childhood in a hospital building, existing contradictions in the contemporary petite bourgeoisie, the evolution of the family, of property, etc.[6] Each signification clarifies the other, but their irreducibility creates a veritable discontinuity between them. Each serves as an encompassing framework for the preceding, but the included signification is richer than the including signification. In a word, we have only the outline for the dialectical movement, not the movement itself.

It is then and only then that we must employ the progressive method. The problem is to recover the totalizing movement of enrichment which engenders each moment in terms of the prior moment, the impulse which starts from lived obscurities in order to arrive at the final objectification—in short, the *project* by which Flaubert, in order to escape from the petite bourgeoisie, will launch himself across the various fields of possibles toward the alienated objectification of himself and will constitute himself inevitably and indissolubly as the author of *Madame Bovary* and as that petit bourgeois which he refused to be. This project has *a meaning,* it is not the simple negativity of flight; by it a man aims at the production of himself in the world as a certain objective totality. It is not the pure and simple abstract decision to write which makes up the peculiar quality of Flaubert, but the decision to write in a certain manner in order to manifest himself in the world in a particular way; in a word, it is the particular signification—within the framework of the contemporary ideology—which he gives to literature as the negation of his original condition and as the objective solution to his contradictions. To rediscover the meaning of this "wrenching away from toward . . ." we shall be aided by our knowing all the signifying planes which he has traversed, which we have interpreted as his footprints, and which have brought him to the final objectification. We have the series: as we move back and forth between material and social conditioning and the work, the problem is to find the *tension* extending from objectivity to objectivity, to discover the law of expansion which surpasses one signification *by means* of the following one and which maintains the second in the first. In truth the problem is to invent a movement, to re-create it, but the hypothesis is

6. Flaubert's wealth consisted exclusively of real estate: this hereditary landlord will be ruined by industry; at the end of his life he will sell his lands in order to save his son-in-law, who was involved in foreign trade and had connections with Scandinavian industry. Meanwhile we shall see him often complaining that his rental income is less than what the same investments would bring in if his father had put it into industry.

immediately verifiable; the only valid one is that which will realize within a creative movement the transverse unity of *all* the heterogeneous structures.

Nevertheless, the project is in danger of being deviated—by the collective instruments; thus the terminal objectification perhaps does not correspond exactly to the original choice. We must take up the regressive analysis again, making a still closer study of the instrumental field so as to determine the possible deviations; we must employ all that we have learned about the contemporary techniques of Knowledge as we look again at the unfolding life so as to examine the evolution of the choices and actions, their coherence or their apparent incoherence. *St. Anthony* expresses the whole Flaubert in his purity and in all the contradictions of his original project, but *St. Anthony* is a failure. Bouilhet and Maxime du Camp condemn it completely, they demand that it "tell a story." *There* is the deviation. Flaubert tells an anecdote, but he makes it support everything —the sky, hell, himself, St. Anthony, etc. The monstrous, splendid work which results from it, that in which he is objectified and alienated, is *Madame Bovary*. Thus the return to the biography shows us the hiatuses, the fissures, the accidents, at the same time that it confirms the hypothesis (the hypothesis of the original project) by revealing the direction and continuity of the life. We shall define the method of the existentialist approach as a regressive-progressive and analytic-synthetic method. It is at the same time an enriching cross-reference between the object (which contains the whole period as hierarchized significations) and the period (which contains the object in its totalization). In fact, when the object is *rediscovered* in its profundity and in its particularity, then instead of remaining external to the totalization (as it was up until the time when the Marxists undertook to integrate it into history), it enters immediately into contradiction with it. In short, the simple inert juxtaposition of the epoch and the object gives way abruptly to a living conflict.

If one has lazily defined Flaubert as a realist and if one has decided that realism suited the public in the Second Empire (which will permit us to develop a brilliant, completely false theory about the evolution of realism between 1857 and 1957), one will never succeed in comprehending either that strange monster which is *Madame Bovary* or the author or the public. Once more one will be playing with shadows. But if one has taken the trouble, in a study which is going to be long and difficult, to demonstrate within this novel the objectification of the subjective and its alienation—in short, if one grasps it in the concrete sense which it still holds at the moment when it escapes from its author and *at the same time* from the outside as an object which is allowed to develop freely, then the book abruptly comes to oppose the objective reality which it will hold for public opinion, for the magistrates, for contemporary writers. This is the moment to return to the period and to ask ourselves, for example, this very simple question: There was at that time a realist school—Courbet in painting and Duranty[7] in literature were its representatives. Duranty had frequently presented his credo and drafted his manifestos. Flaubert despised realism and said so over and over throughout his life; he loved only the absolute purity of art. *Why* did the public decide at the outset that Flaubert was the realist, and why did it love in him *that particular realism;* that is, that admirable faked confession, that disguised lyricism, that implicit metaphysic? Why did it so value as an admirable character portrayal of a woman (or as a pitiless description of woman) what was at bottom only a poor disguised man? Then we must ask ourselves *what kind of realism* this public demanded or, if you prefer, what kind of literature it demanded under that name and why. This last moment is of primary importance; it is quite simply the moment of alienation. Flaubert sees his work stolen away from him by the very success which the period bestows on it; he no longer recognizes his book, it is foreign to him. Suddenly he loses his own objective existence. But at the same time his work throws a new light upon the period; it enables us to pose a new question to History: Just what must that period have been in order that it should demand *this* book and mendaciously find there its own image? Here we are at the veritable moment of historical action or of what I shall willingly call the misunderstanding. But this is not the place to develop this new point. It is enough to say by way of conclusion that the man and his time will be integrated into the dialectical totalization when we have shown how History surpasses this contradiction.

7. Gustave Courbet (1819–77) was the militant leader of the realistic school of French painters; Louis-Edmond Duranty (1833–80) played for a moment a similar part on the literary scene but, unlike Courbet's, his work is now entirely forgotten [*Editor*].

GUSTAVE FLAUBERT

Letters about *Madame Bovary*†

To Louise Colet[1]

[*Croisset, January 12 or 14, 1852*]

I am hideously worried, mortally depressed. My accursed Bovary is harrying me and driving me mad. Last Sunday Bouilhet criticized one of my characters and the outline. I can do nothing about it: there is some truth in what he says, but I feel that the opposite is true also. Ah, I am tired and discouraged! You call me Master. What a wretched Master!

No—it is possible that the whole thing hasn't had enough spade-work, for distinctions between thought and style are a sophism. Everything depends on the conception. So much the worse! I am going to continue, and as quickly as I can, in order to have a complete picture. There are moments when all this makes me wish I were dead. Ah! No one will be able to say that I haven't experienced the agonies of Art!

Friday night [*Croisset, January 16, 1852*]

There are in me, literally speaking, two distinct persons: one who is infatuated with bombast, lyricism, eagle flights, sonorities of phrase and the high points of ideas; and another who digs and burrows into the truth as deeply as he can, who likes to treat a humble fact as respectfully as a big one, who would like to make you feel almost *physically* the things he reproduces; this latter person likes to laugh, and enjoys the animal sides of man. . . .

What seems beautiful to me, what I should like to write, is a book about nothing, a book dependent on nothing external, which would be held together by the strength of its style, just as the earth, suspended in the void, depends on nothing external for its support;

† From *The Selected Letters of Gustave Flaubert*, translated and edited by Francis Steegmuller (New York: Farrar, Straus, and Giroux, Inc., 1953). Copyright © 1953 by Francis Steegmuller; reprinted by permission of the publishers. The passages here reprinted are those immediately relevant to *Madame Bovary;* Steegmuller himself made a selection from the very numerous letters that touch on the novel.
1. Louise Colet (1810–76), born Revoil, wife of an obscure professor of music at the Conservatory, is hardly remembered for the poetry she wrote. But she played an important part in the literary life of the French Second Empire, as mistress and close *confidante* of several famous men of letters, including Alfred de Musset and Flaubert. The letters about *Madame Bovary* stem from the happiest period in her relationship with Flaubert; after the publication of the novel, in 1854, the two became bitter enemies [*Editor*].

a book which would have almost no subject, or at least in which the subject would be almost invisible, if such a thing is possible. The finest works are those that contain the least matter; the closer expression comes to thought, the closer language comes to coinciding and merging with it, the finer the result. I believe that the future of Art lies in this direction. I see it, as it has developed from its beginnings, growing progressively more ethereal, from the Egyptian pylons to Gothic lancets, from the 20,000-line Hindu poems to the effusions of Byron. Form, as it is mastered, becomes attenuated; it becomes dissociated from any liturgy, rule, yardstick; the epic is discarded in favor of the novel, verse in favor of prose; there is no longer any orthodoxy, and form is as free as the will of its creator. This emancipation from matter can be observed everywhere: governments have gone through similar evolution, from the oriental despotisms to the socialisms of the future.

It is for this reason that there are no noble subjects or ignoble subjects; from the standpoint of pure Art one might almost establish the axiom that there is no such thing as subject, style in itself being an absolute manner of seeing things.

[*Croisset,*] *Saturday night, February 1, 1852*

Bad week. Work didn't go; I had reached a point where I didn't know what to say. It was all shadings and refinements; I was completely in the dark: it is very difficult to clarify by means of words what is still obscure in your thoughts. I made outlines, spoiled a lot of paper, floundered and fumbled. Now I shall perhaps find my way again. Oh, what a rascally thing style is! I think you have no idea of what kind of a book I am writing. In my other books I was slovenly; in this one I am trying to be impeccable, and to follow a geometrically straight line. No lyricism, no comments, the author's personality absent. It will make sad reading; there will be atrociously wretched and sordid things. Bouilhet, who arrived last Sunday at three just after I had written you, thinks the tone is right and hopes the book will be good. May God grant it! But it promises to take up an enormous amount of time. I shall certainly not be through by the beginning of next winter. I am doing no more than five or six pages a week.

[*Croisset,*] *February 8,* [1852]

So you are decidedly enthusiastic about *Saint Antoine!* Well, that makes one, at least! That's something. Though I don't accept everything you say about it, I think my friends refused to see what there was in it. Their judgment was superficial; I don't say unfair, but superficial. . . .

Now I am in an entirely different world, a world of attentive ob-

servations of the most humdrum details. I am delving into the
damp and moldy corners of the soul. It is a far cry from the mythological and theological fireworks of *Saint Antoine*. And, just as the
subject is different, so I am writing in an entirely different manner.
Nowhere in my book must the author express his emotions or his
opinions.

I think that it will be less lofty than *Saint Antoine* as regards
ideas (a fact that I consider of little importance), but perhaps it
will be more intense and unusual, without being obviously so.

Wednesday, 1 A.M. [*Croisset, March 3, 1852*]

Thank you, thank you, my darling, for all the affection you send
me. It makes me proud that you should feel happy about me; how I
will embrace you next week!

I have just reread several children's books for my novel. I am half
crazy tonight, after all the things I looked at today—from old keepsakes to tales of shipwrecks and buccaneers. I came upon old engravings that I had colored when I was seven or eight and that I
hadn't seen since. There are rocks painted blue and trees painted
green. At the sight of some of them (for instance a scene showing
people stranded on ice floes) I re-experienced feelings of terror that
I had as a child. I should like something that would put it out of
my mind; I am almost afraid to go to bed. There is a story of Dutch
sailors in ice-bound waters, with bears attacking them in their hut
(this picture used to keep me awake), and one about Chinese pi-
rates sacking a temple full of golden idols. My travels and my childhood memories color off from each other, fuse, whirl dazzlingly before my eyes, and rise up in a spiral. . . .

For two days now I have been trying to live the dreams of young
girls, and for this purpose I have been navigating in milky oceans of
books about castles and troubadours in white-plumed velvet caps.
Remind me to speak to you about this. You can give me exact details that I need.

Saturday, 1 A.M. [*Croisset, March 20–21, 1852*]

The entire value of my book, if it has any, will consist of my having known how to walk straight ahead on a hair, balanced above the
two abysses of lyricism and vulgarity (which I seek to fuse in analytical narrative). When I think of what it can be I am dazzled. But
then, when I reflect that so much beauty has been entrusted to me,
I am so terrified that I am seized with cramps and long to rush off
and hide—anywhere. I have been working like a mule for fifteen
long years. All my life I have lived with a maniacal stubbornness,
keeping all my other passions locked up in cages and visiting them
only now and then, for diversion. Oh, if ever I produce a good book

I'll have worked for it! Would to God that Buffon's blasphemous words were true.[2] I should certainly be among the foremost.

Saturday, 12:30 A.M. [Croisset, March 27, 1852]

Tonight I finished scribbling the first draft of my young girl's dreams. I'll spend another fortnight sailing on these blue lakes, after which I'll go to a ball and then spend a rainy winter, which I'll end with a pregnancy. And about a third of my book will be done.

Saturday night [Croisset, April 24, 1852]

If I haven't written sooner in reply to your sorrowful and discouraged-sounding letter, it is because I have been in a great fit of work. The day before yesterday I went to bed at five in the morning and yesterday at three. Since last Monday I have put everything else aside, and have done nothing all week but sweat over my *Bovary*, disgruntled at making such slow progress. I have now reached my ball, which I will begin Monday. I hope that may go better. Since you last saw me I have written 25 pages in all (25 pages in six weeks). They were tough. Tomorrow I shall read them to Bouilhet. As for myself, I have gone over them so much, recopied them, changed them, handled them, that for the time being I can't make head or tail of them. But I think they will stand up. You speak of your discouragements: if you could see mine! Sometimes I don't understand why my arms don't drop from my body with fatigue, why my brains don't melt away. I am leading a stern existence, stripped of all external pleasure, and am sustained only by a kind of permanent rage, which sometimes makes me weep tears of impotence but which never abates. I love my work with a love that is frenzied and perverted, as an ascetic loves the hair shirt that scratches his belly. Sometimes, when I am empty, when words don't come, when I find I haven't written a single sentence after scribbling whole pages, I collapse on my couch and lie there dazed, bogged in a swamp of despair, hating myself and blaming myself for this demented pride * * *

Thursday, 4 A.M. [Croisset, July 22, 1852]

I am in the process of copying and correcting the entire first part of *Bovary*. My eyes are smarting. I should like to be able to read these 158 pages at a single glance and grasp them with all their details in a single thought. A week from Sunday I shall read the whole thing to Bouilhet,[3] and a day or two later you will see me. What a

2. The quotation from Buffon is *"Le génie est une longue patience"* ("genius is a matter of endless patience") [*Editor*].

3. Louis Bouilhet (1822–69), himself a poet of some distinction, had known Flaubert ever since they both were pupils at the Lycée in Rouen. He later became his closest friend and literary counselor, editing his works with a thoroughness that was frequently, but not always, judicious [*Editor*].

bitch of a thing prose is! It is never finished; there is always something to be done over. Still, I think it is possible to give it the consistency of verse. A good prose sentence should be like a good line of poetry—*unchangeable*, just as rhythmic, just as sonorous. Such, at least, is my ambition (I am sure of one thing: no one has ever conceived a more perfect type of prose than I; but as to the execution, how weak, how weak, oh God!). Nor does it seem to me impossible to give psychological analysis the swiftness, clarity, and impetus of a strictly dramatic narrative. That has never been attempted, and it would be beautiful. Have I succeeded a little in this? I have no idea. At this moment I have no definite opinion about my work.

Sunday, 11 P.M. [Croisset, September 19, 1852]

What trouble my *Bovary* is giving me! Still, I am beginning to see my way a little. Never in my life have I written anything more difficult than what I am doing now—trivial dialogue. . . . I have to portray, simultaneously and in the same conversation, five or six characters who speak, several others who are spoken about, the scene, and the whole town, giving physical descriptions of people and objects; and in the midst of all that I have to show a man and a woman who are beginning (through a similarity in tastes) to fall in love with each other. If only I had space! But the whole thing has to be swift without being dry, and well worked out without taking up too much room; and many details which would be more striking here I have to keep in reserve for use elsewhere. I am going to put the whole thing down quickly, and then proceed by a series of increasingly drastic revisions; by going over and over it I can perhaps pull it together. The language itself is a great stumbling-block. My characters are completely commonplace, but they have to speak in a literary style, and politeness of language takes away so much picturesqueness from any speech!

Saturday night, 3 o'clock [Croisset, January 15, 1853]

The beginning of the week was frightful, but things have been going better since Thursday. I still have six to eight pages to do before reaching a break, and then I'll come to see you. I think that will be in a fortnight. Bouilhet will probably come with me. His reason for not writing you more often is that he has nothing to report or has no time. Do you realize that the poor devil has to give eight hours of lessons a day? . . .

Last week I spent *five days writing one page*, and I dropped everything else for it—my Greek, my English; I gave myself up to it entirely. What worries me in my book is the element of *entertainment*. That side is weak; there is not enough action. I maintain, however, that *ideas* are action. It is more difficult to hold the reader's interest with them, I know, but this is a problem for style to solve. I now have fifty pages in a row without a single event. It is an uninterrupted portrayal of a bourgeois existence and of a love that remains inactive—a love all the more difficult to depict because it is timid and deep, but alas! lacking in inner turbulence, because my gentleman has a sober nature. I had something similar in the first part: the husband loves his wife in somewhat the same fashion as her lover. Here are two mediocrities in the same milieu, and I must differentiate between them. If I bring it off it will be a great achievement, I think, for it will be like painting in monotone without contrasts—not easy. But I fear that all these subtleties will be wearisome, and that the reader will long for more movement. But one must be loyal to one's conception. If I tried to insert action I should be following a rule and would spoil everything. One must sing with one's own voice: and mine will never be dramatic or attractive. Besides, I am convinced that everything is a question of style, or rather of form, of presentation.

* * *

Wednesday night, midnight [Croisset, April 6, 1853]
What is making me go so slowly is that nothing in this book is derived from myself; never has my personality been of less use to me. Later I may be able to produce things that are better (I certainly hope so); it is difficult for me to imagine that I will ever write anything more carefully calculated. Everything is deliberate. If it's a failure, it will at least have been good practice. What is natural for me is unnatural for others—I am at home in the realm of the extraordinary and the fantastic, in flights of metaphysics and mythology. *Saint Antoine* didn't demand a quarter of the mental tension that *Bovary* is causing me. It was an outlet for my feelings; I had only pleasure in writing it, and the eighteen months spent writing its five hundred pages were the most deeply voluptuous of my entire life. Think of me now: having constantly to be in the skins of people for whom I feel aversion. For six months I have been a platonic lover, and at this very moment the sound of church bells is causing me Catholic raptures and I feel like going to confession!

Saturday night, 1 A.M. [Croisset, June 25–26, 1853]
At last I have finished the first section of my second part. I have now reached the point I should have reached before our last meeting at Mantes—you see how far behind I am. I shall spend another week reading it over and copying it, and a week from tomorrow shall spew it all out to Bouilhet. If it is all right it will be a great worry off my mind and a considerable accomplishment, I assure

you, for I had very little to go on. But I think that this book will have a great defect: namely, a want of proportion between its various parts. I have so far 260 pages containing only preparations for action—more or less disguised expositions of character (some of them, it is true, more developed than others), of landscapes and of places. My conclusion, which will be the account of my little lady's death and funeral and of her husband's grief, will be sixty pages long at least. That leaves, for the body of the action itself, 120 to 160 pages at the most. Isn't this a real defect? What reassures me (though not completely) is that the book is a biography rather than a fully developed story. It is not essentially dramatic; and if the dramatic element is well submerged in the general tone of the book the lack of proportion in the development of the various parts may pass unnoticed. But then isn't life a little like this? An act of coition lasts a minute, and it has been anticipated for months on end. Our passions are like volcanoes; they are continually rumbling, but they erupt only from time to time.

* * *

Tuesday, 1 A.M. [Croisset, June 28–29, 1853]

I have been in excellent form this week. I have written eight pages, all of which I think can stand pretty much as they are. Tonight I have just outlined the entire big scene of the Agricultural Show. It will be colossal—thirty pages at least. Against the background of this rustico-municipal celebration, with all its details (all my secondary characters will be shown in action), there will be continuous dialogue between a gentleman and the lady he is doing his best to seduce. Moreover, somewhere in the middle I have a solemn speech by a counselor of the prefecture, and at the end (this I have already finished) a newspaper article written by my pharmacist, who gives an account of the celebration in fine philosophical, poetical, progressive style. You see it is no small chore. I am sure of my local color and of many of my effects; but it's a hideous job to keep it from getting too long—especially since this sort of thing shouldn't be skimpy. Once this is behind me I shall soon reach my scene of the lovers in the autumn woods, with their horses cropping the leaves beside them; and then I think I'll have clear sailing—I'll have passed Charybdis, at least, even though Scylla still remains to be negotiated.

Sunday, 4 o'clock [Trouville, August 14, 1853]

I spent an hour yesterday watching the ladies bathe. What a sight! What a hideous sight! The two sexes used to bathe together here. But now they are kept separate by means of signposts, preventive nets, and a uniformed inspector—nothing more depressingly grotesque can be imagined. However, yesterday, from the place where I was standing in the sun, with my spectacles on my nose, I could contemplate the bathing beauties at my leisure. The human race must indeed have become absolutely moronic to have lost its sense of elegance to this degree. Nothing is more pitiful than these bags in which women encase their bodies, and these oilcloth caps! What faces! What figures! And what feet! Red, scrawny, covered with corns and bunions, deformed by shoes, long as shuttles or wide as washerwomen's paddles. And in the midst of everything, scrofulous brats screaming and crying. Further off, grandmas knitting and respectable old gentlemen with gold-rimmed spectacles reading newspapers, looking up from time to time between lines to savor the vastness of the horizon with an air of approval. The whole thing made me long all afternoon to escape from Europe and go live in the Sandwich Islands or the forests of Brazil. There, at least, the beaches are not polluted by such ugly feet, by such foul-looking specimens of humanity.

The day before yesterday, in the woods of Touques, in a charming spot beside a spring, I found old cigar butts and scraps of paté. People had been picnicking. I described such a scene in *Novembre*, eleven years ago; it was entirely imagined, and the other day it came true. Everything one invents is true, you may be sure. Poetry is as precise as geometry. Induction is as accurate as deduction; and besides, after reaching a certain point one no longer makes any mistake about the things of the soul. My poor Bovary, without a doubt, is suffering and weeping at this very instant in twenty villages of France.

Friday night, 2 A.M. [Croisset, December 23, 1853]

I must love you to write you tonight, for I am *exhausted*. My head feels as though it were being squeezed in an iron vise. Since two o'clock yesterday afternoon (except for about twenty-five minutes for dinner), I have been writing *Bovary*. I am in the midst of love-making; I am sweating and my throat is tight. This has been one of the rare days of my life passed completely in illusion from beginning to end. At six o'clock this evening, as I was writing the word "hysterics," I was so swept away, was bellowing so loudly and feeling so deeply what my little Bovary was going through, that I was afraid of having hysterics myself. I got up from my table and opened the window to calm myself. My head was spinning. Now I have great pains in my knees, in my back, and in my head. I feel like a man who has ——ed too much (forgive me for the expression)—a kind of rapturous lassitude. And since I am in the midst of love it is only proper that I should not fall asleep before sending you a caress, a kiss, and whatever thoughts are left in me. Will what I write be good? I have no idea—I am hurrying a little, to be able to show Bouilhet a complete section when he comes to see me. What is certain is that my book has been going at a lively rate for the past week. May it continue so, for I am weary of my usual snail's pace. But I fear the awakening, the disillusion that may come from the recopied pages. No matter; it is a delicious thing to write, whether well or badly—to be no longer yourself but to move in an entire universe of your own creating. Today, for instance, man and woman, lover and beloved, I rode in a forest on an autumn afternoon under the yellow leaves, and I was also the horse, the leaves, the wind, the words my people spoke, even the red sun that made them half-shut their love-drowned eyes. Is this pride or piety? Is it a silly overflow of exaggerated self-satisfaction, or is it really a vague and noble religious instinct? But when I think of these marvelous pleasures I have enjoyed I am tempted to offer God a prayer of thanks—if only I knew he could hear me! Praised be the Lord for not creating me a cotton merchant, a vaudevillian, a wit, etc.! Let us sing to Apollo like the ancient bards, and breathe deeply of the cold air of Parnassus; let us strum our guitars and clash our cymbals, and whirl like dervishes in the eternal pageant of Forms and Ideas.

Monday night, 1 o'clock [Croisset, January 2, 1854]

[Bouilhet] was satisfied with my love scene. However, before said passage I have a transition of eight lines which took me three days; it doesn't contain a superfluous word, yet I must do it over once again because it is too slow. It is a piece of direct discourse which has to be changed into indirect, and in which I haven't room to say everything that should be said. It all has to be swift and casual, since it must remain inconspicuous in the ensemble. After this I shall still have three or four other infinitesimal corrections, which will take me one more entire week. How slow I am! No matter; I am getting ahead. I have taken a great step forward, and feel an inner relief that gives me new vigor, even though tonight I literally sweated with effort. It is so difficult to undo what is done, and well done, in order to put something new in its place, and yet hide all traces of the patch. . . .

How true it is that concern with morality makes every work of the imagination false and stupid! I am becoming quite a critic. The novel I am writing sharpens this faculty, for it is essentially a work of criticism, or rather of anatomy. The reader will not notice, I hope, all the psychological work hidden under the form, but he will sense its effect. At the same time I am also tempted to write big, sumptuous things—battles, sieges, descriptions of the fabulous ancient East. Thursday night I spent two wonderful hours, my head in my hands, dreaming of the bright walls of Ecbatana. Nothing has been written about all that. How many things still hover in the limbo of human thought! There is no shortage of subjects, but only of men.

* * *

Friday night, midnight [*Croisset, April 7, 1854*]

I have just made a fresh copy of what I have written since New Year, or rather since the middle of February, for on my return from Paris I burned all my January work. It amounts to thirteen pages, no more, no less, thirteen pages in seven weeks. However, they are in shape, I think, and as perfect as I can make them. There are only two or three repetitions of the same word which must be removed, and two turns of phrase that are still too much alike. At last something is completed. It was a difficult transition: the reader had to be led gradually and imperceptibly from psychology to action. Now I am about to begin the dramatic, eventful part. Two or three more big pushes and the end will be in sight. By July or August I hope to tackle the denouement. What a struggle it has been! My God, what a struggle! Such drudgery! Such discouragement! I spent all last evening frantically poring over surgical texts. I am studying the theory of clubfeet. In three hours I devoured an entire volume on this interesting subject and took notes. I came upon some really fine sentences. "The maternal breast is an impenetrable and mysterious sanctuary, where . . . etc." An excellent treatise, incidentally. Why am I not young? How I should work! One ought to know everything, to write. All of us scribblers are monstrously ignorant. If only we weren't so lacking in stamina, what a rich field of ideas and similes we could tap! Books that have been the source of entire literatures, like Homer and Rabelais, contain the sum of all the knowledge of their times. They knew everything, those fellows, and we know nothing. Ronsard's poetics contains a curious precept: he advises the poet to become well versed in the arts and crafts—to frequent blacksmiths, goldsmiths, locksmiths, etc.—in order to enrich his stock of metaphors. And indeed that is the sort of thing that makes for rich and varied language. The sentences in a book must quiver like the leaves in a forest, all dissimilar in their similarity.

Saturday night, 1 o'clock [*Croisset, April 22, 1854*]

I am still struggling with clubfeet. My dear brother failed to keep two appointments with me this week, and unless he comes tomorrow I shall be forced to make another trip to Rouen. No matter; my work progresses. I have had a good deal of trouble these last few days over a religious speech. From my point of view, what I have written is completely impious. How different it would have been in a different period! If I had been born a hundred years earlier how much rhetoric I'd have put into it! Instead, I have written a mere, almost literal description of what must have taken place. The leading characteristic of our century is its historical sense. This is why we have to confine ourselves to relating the facts—but *all* the facts, the *heart* of the facts. No one will ever say about me what is said about you in the sublime prospectus of the *Librairie Nouvelle*: "All her writings converge on this lofty goal" (the ideal of a better future). No, we must sing merely for the sake of singing. Why is the ocean never still? What is the *goal* of nature? Well, I think the goal of mankind exactly the same. Things exist because they exist, and you can't do anything about it, my good people. We are always turning in the same circle, always rolling the same stone. Weren't men freer and more intelligent in the time of Pericles than they are under Napoleon III? On what do you base your statement that I am losing "the understanding of certain feelings" that I do not experience? First of all, please note that I *do* experience them. My heart is "human," and if I do not want a child "of my own" it is because I feel that if I had one my heart would become too "paternal." I love my little niece as though she were my daughter, and my "active" concern for her is enough to prove that those are not mere words. But I should rather be skinned alive than "exploit" this in my writing. I refuse to consider Art a drain-pipe for passion, a kind of chamberpot, a slightly more elegant substitute for gossip and confidences. No, no! Genuine poetry is not the scum of the heart. * * *

I am expressing myself badly, but well enough, I think, for you to understand the general trend of my resistance to your criticism, judicious as they may be. You were asking me to turn it into another book. You were asking me to violate the inner poetics that determined the pattern (as a philosopher would say) after which it was conceived. Finally, I should have failed in my duty to myself and to you, in acting out of deference and not out of conviction.

Art requires neither complaisance nor politeness; nothing but faith—faith and freedom.

To Léon Laurent-Pichat[4]

[Croisset, between December 1 and 15, 1856]

Dear Friend

First, thank you for pointing out the difference between your personal and your editorial attitudes concerning my book; I therefore

---

4. Léon Laurent-Pichat (1823–86) was co-director, with Maxime DuCamp, of the *Revue de Paris*, in which *Madame Bovary* first appeared [*Editor*].

now address not the poet Laurent-Pichat, but the *Revue*, an abstract personality whose interests you represent. This is my reply to the *Revue de Paris*:

1. You kept the manuscript of *Madame Bovary* for three months, and thus you had every opportunity, before beginning to print the work, to know your own mind regarding it. The alternatives were to take it or leave it. You took it, and you must abide by the consequences.

2. Once the agreement was concluded, I consented to the elimination of a passage which I consider very important, because you claimed that to print it might involve you in difficulties. I complied gracefully, but I will not conceal from you (and now I am speaking to my friend Pichat) that I at once began to regret bitterly ever having had the idea of publishing. Let us speak our minds fully or not at all.

3. I consider that I have already done a great deal, and you consider that I should do still more. *I will do nothing*; I will not make a correction, not a cut; I will not suppress a comma; nothing, nothing! But if you consider that I am embarrassing you, if you are afraid, the simple thing to do is to stop publication of *Madame Bovary*. This would not disturb me in the slightest.

Now that I have finished addressing the *Revue*, let me point out one thing to my friend:

By eliminating the passage about the cab you have not made the story a whit less shocking; and you will accomplish no more by the cuts you ask for in the sixth installment.

You are objecting to details, whereas actually you should object to the whole. The brutal element is basic, not incidental. Negroes cannot be made white, and you cannot change a book's blood. All you can do is to weaken it.

I need scarcely say that if I break with the *Revue de Paris* I shall nevertheless retain friendly feelings for its editors.

I know how to distinguish between literature and literary business.

To Madame Maurice Schlesinger[5]

Paris, January 14, 1857

How touched I was by your kind letter, dear Madame! I can give you full answers to the questions you ask concerning the author and the book. Here is the whole story:

The *Revue de Paris*, in which I published my novel (in install-

5. Madame Maurice Schlesinger (1810–88) was, more than Louise Colet, the most important woman in Flaubert's life, although their relationship was always a frustrated one. She is the model for Madame Arnoux in the *Sentimental Education* [*Editor*].

ments from October 1 to December 15), had previously received two warnings—being an anti-government organ. The authorities thought that it would be a clever move to suppress it entirely, on the grounds of immorality and atheism; and quite at random they picked out some passages from my book which they called licentious and blasphemous. I was summoned before the investigating magistrate and the proceedings began. But friends made strenuous efforts on my behalf, sloshing about for me in the most exalted filth of the capital. Now I am assured that everything has been stopped, though I have heard nothing official. I have no doubts of my success; the whole thing has been too stupid. Consequently, I shall be able to publish my novel in book form. You will receive it in about six weeks, I think, and for your amusement I will mark the incriminated passages. One of them, a description of Extreme Unction, is nothing but a page from the *Rituel de Paris*, put into decent French; but the noble guardians of our religion are not very well versed in catechism.

Still, I might very well have been convicted and despite everything sentenced to a year of imprisonment, not to mention a fine of a thousand francs. In addition, each new volume by your friend would have been severely scrutinized by the gentlemen of the police, and a second offense would have put me in a dungeon for five years: in short, I'd have been unable to print a line. Thus, I have learned: (1) that it is extremely unpleasant to be involved in a political affair; (2) that social hypocrisy is a serious matter. But this time it was so stupid that it grew ashamed of itself, loosened its grip, and crawled back into its hole.

As for the book itself, which is moral, ultra-moral, and which might well be awarded the Montyon prize were it a little less frank (an honor which I covet but little), it has had as much success as a novel can have in a magazine.

The literary world has paid me some pretty compliments—whether sincere or not I do not know. I am even told that Monsieur de Lamartine is loudly singing my praises—which surprises me very much, for everything in my book must annoy him! The *Presse* and the *Moniteur* have made me some very substantial offers. I have been asked to write a comic(!) opera and my *Bovary* has been discussed in various publications large and small. And that, dear Madame, with no modesty whatever, is the balance sheet of my fame. Have no worry about the critics—they will treat me kindly, for they well know that I have no desire to compete with them in any way; on the contrary, they will be charming—it is so pleasant to have new idols with which to overturn the old.

Essays in Criticism

Contemporary Reactions

CHARLES AUGUSTIN SAINTE-BEUVE

Madame Bovary, by Gustave Flaubert†

Monday, May 4th, 1857

I have not forgotten that this work has recently been the object of a nowise literary debate; what stands out foremost in my memory, however, are the conclusions and the wisdom of the judges. Henceforth, this work belongs to the realm of art and of art alone; it is accountable to literary critics only and critics can deal with it in full independence.

They can and they should. Often enough, we labor hard at resuscitating things of the past, older writers, works no longer read to which we restore a flash of interest, a semblance of life; but when genuine and live works pass within our grasp, with full canvas flying and banners floating in the breeze as if taunting with the question: *What do you think of us?*—a true critic, in whose veins flows a drop of the blood of Pope, Boileau, Johnson, Jeffrey,[1] Hazlitt or simply M. de la Harpe,[2] will burn with impatience, frustrated at having to remain silent, eager to speak up, to herald and salute the work as it passes by. Long ago, Pindar said about poetry: I hail old wine and youthful songs!—youthful songs: this means last night's new play, the novel of the day, all what is being discussed by the young the very moment it appears.

I had not read the first version of *Madame Bovary* when it appeared in serial form in a periodical. Striking as some parts may have been, the general idea and structure must have suffered from this mode of publication. Startled by some daring episode, the reader must have wondered if worse was still to come: he might well have assumed that the work was heading for perilous regions and that the author intended something which, in fact, he did not intend at all. Reading the book as one continuous unit, one finds each

† The article first appeared as Sainte-Beuve's weekly book review (always published on Monday) on May 4, 1857. It was later included in his *Causeries du Lundi* ("*Monday Talks*"), XIII. Translated by Paul de Man.
1. Francis Jeffrey (1773–1850); Scotch critic and essayist, one of the founders of the *Edinburgh Review* [*Editor*].
2. J. F. de la Harpe (1724–1805) was a French neo-classic critic for whose views Sainte-Beuve would only have a limited sympathy [*Editor*].

scene falling back into place. *Madame Bovary* is first and foremost a book, a carefully composed book, amply premeditated and totally coherent, in which nothing is left to chance and in which the author or, better, the painter does exactly what he intends to do from beginning to end.

The writer has obviously lived a great deal in the country, in the region of Normandy which he describes so truthfully. Generally, those who stay in the country and respond to nature with enough sensitivity to describe it well, tend to love it or, at least, to stress its beauty, especially after they have moved away; they are tempted to make it into an idyllic setting, an idealized world of nostalgically remembered happiness and well-being. As long as he lived there, Bernardin de Saint-Pierre was bored to tears by the Isle de France but, once he had left the region he fondly remembered the beauty of the landscapes, the peaceful serenity of the valleys; he made it the dwelling place of his chosen creatures and wrote *Paul and Virginia*. Without going as far as Bernardin de Sainte-Pierre, Georges Sand probably thought her Berry was pretty dull; later, however, she chose to show only the attractive aspects of the place and certainly did not try to disenchant her readers with the Creuse Valley. Even when she peopled it with passion-driven and theorizing characters, she preserved a rural, pastoral element, poetic in the Hellenic sense of the term. But here, in the case of the author of *Madame Bovary*, we come upon an altogether different manner, another kind of inspiration and, in truth, upon a different generation. The ideal is gone, the lyrical has died out; it can no longer hold us. Stern and implacable truth has entered art as the last word of experience. The author of *Madame Bovary* stayed in the provinces and in the country, in villages and small towns; he did not merely cross the region on a spring day, like the traveller mentioned by la Bruyère who, standing on a hill, composes his dream as a painter would, along the slope of the hillside—he actually lived there. And what did he see? Pettiness, poverty, conceit, stupidity, routine, monotony and boredom—and so he tells us. Those genuine and faithfully rendered landscapes inhabited by the rural spirit of the region become the setting for boorish lovers, for vulgar, prosaic, foolishly pretentious, totally ignorant or half-educated beings. One single creature capable of the nobility of dreams and aspiring to a better world is thrown into this milieu; she feels alien and oppressed; she suffers so much in solitude that she is altered and degraded. In pursuing her false dream and absent beauty she gradually reaches ruin and depravation. Is this moral? Is it consoling? The question does not seem to have occurred to the writer; his only concern was: is this true? I presume that he himself witnessed something similar, or that, at any rate, he chose to condense on a tightly composed canvas the outcome of various observations, against a background of bitterness and irony.

Another equally surprising anomaly: among all those very real and alive characters, not a single one seems to be the kind of person the author himself would have wanted to be; the care he lavishes on them is only aimed at relentless precision; none are treated with the consideration one would show towards a friend. The novelist entirely refrains from taking sides; he is present only in order to watch, to reveal and to say everything, but not even his profile appears in a single corner of the novel. The work is entirely impersonal. This, in itself, demonstrates remarkable strength.

Next to Madame Bovary, the most important character is Monsieur Bovary. We meet the young Charles Bovary (for his father, too, is very accurately portrayed) from his very first days in school: he is a docile and well-behaved but awkward boy, a hopelessly mediocre nonentity, rather stupid, thoroughly undistinguished, tame, passive, submissively destined to follow step by step a previously mapped out path or to walk in the footsteps of his guides. Son of a somewhat rakish army surgeon, he shows none of his father's dash or vices. His mother's savings enable him to undertake rather pale studies in Rouen, leading to a painfully earned medical degree. Having to decide in which town to set up practice. he selects Tostes, a smallish place not far from Dieppe. He is married off to a much older widow rumored to have a small yearly income. He allows himself to be pushed into such arrangements without even seeming to realize how remote he remains from happiness.

One night, he finds himself summoned to les Bertaux, a farm located at a good six miles' distance from his home. He is to set the broken leg of a wealthy farmer, widowed father of a single daughter. This sequence of episodes, the trip through the night on horseback, the arrival at the large farm, his first encounter with the young girl who has nothing of the farmer's daughter, having instead been raised as a well-bred young lady in a convent, the attitude of the rich man—all this is admirably rendered in minute detail, as if we were present at the scene: it is like a Dutch or Flemish painting of Normandy. Bovary gets into the habit of returning to the Bertaux farm, more often than his attendance upon his patient requires, and he keeps going there even after Rouault is cured. Unnoticed even to himself, his frequent visits to the farm gradually grow into a habit, a delightful distraction from his painful routine.

On these days he rose early, set off at a gallop, urging on his horse, then got down to wipe his boots in the grass and put on black gloves before entering. He liked the courtyard, seeing himself enter and noticing the gate turn against his shoulder, the cock crow on the wall, the farmboys run to meet him. He liked the granary and the stables; he liked old Rouault, who pressed his hand and called him his savior; he liked the small wooden shoes of Mademoiselle Emma on the scoured flags of the kitchen—her high heels made her a little taller; and when she walked in front of him, the wooden soles springing up quickly struck with a sharp sound against the leather of her boots.

She always reconducted him to the first step of the porch. When his horse had not yet been brought round she stayed there. They had said "Good-bye"; there was no more talking. The open air wrapped her round, playing with the soft down on the back of her neck, or blew to and fro on her hips her apron–strings, that fluttered like streamers. Once, during a thaw, the bark of the trees in the yard was oozing, the snow melted on the roofs of the buildings; she stood on the threshold, went to fetch her sunshade and opened it. The parasol, made of an iridescent silk that let the sunlight sift through, colored the white skin of her face with shifting reflections. Beneath it, she smiled at the gentle warmth; drops of water fell one by one on the taut silk.

It would be hard to imagine a picture of greater freshness and precision, so well composed and delicately lighted, in which the memory of the classical is so well disguised to appear modern. The noise of the melting snow dripping down on the umbrella reminds me of a similar noise: the tinkle of ice drops as they fall from the branches on the dry leaves of the path in William Cowper's "Winter walk at noon."[3] One invaluable quality distinguishes M. Flaubert from many other more or less talented observers who nowadays lay claim, at times legitimately, to the faithful portrayal of mere reality: he possesses style. At times, he even has too much style, and his pen may then indulge in oddities and minutiae of continued description that sometimes interfere with the general effect. His objects and his faces, even those that seem best suited to catch our eye, are somewhat flattened and overshadowed by the excessive relief of surrounding accessories. Madame Bovary herself, the Mademoiselle Emma who seemed so charming on our first encounter with her, is so often described in minute detail that I fail to visualize her physical appearance clearly in its totality, or in a distinct and decisive manner.

The first Madame Bovary soon dies and Emma becomes the second and only Madame Bovary. The chapter of the wedding at Bertaux is pictorially perfect, particularly rich in truthful details, combining spontaneity with stiff formality, at times ugly and awkward, but ribald and graceful as well, ranging from delicacy to sheer gluttony. The scene is balanced by the dance at the La Vaubyessard

3. Cowper's lines are as follows: "The redbreast warbles still, but is content / * * * and flitting light / From spray to spray, where'er he rests he shakes / From many a twig the pendent drops of ice, / That tinkle in the wither'd leaves below" [*Editor*].

castle and, with the later chapter on the Agricultural Fair, the three episodes are like so many pictures which, if they had been painted on canvas, would belong in a gallery with the best works of this kind.

Emma becomes Madame Bovary, settles in the little home in Tostes, with its crammed rooms, a small garden longer than it is wide looking out over the fields. She immediately creates order, cleanliness, and an atmosphere of elegance around her. Her husband, eager to please her, buys her a secondhand carriage that will allow her to travel on the neighboring roads whenever she wishes. For the first time in his life, Charles Bovary is happy and he knows it; after looking after his patients all day, he finds joy and contentment on his return home. He is in love with his wife and only wishes this bourgeois and tranquil happiness to last forever. She, however, has known headier dreams. As a young girl, she has often wondered how to achieve happiness, and she soon realizes, even during her honeymoon, that this is not the way.

Here begins a profound, sensitive, and tightly knit analysis, a cruel dissection that will only end with the book. We enter into the heart of Madame Bovary. How to describe it?—she is woman; at first she is merely romantically inclined, by no means corrupt. Her portrayer, M. Flaubert, does not spare her. He denounces without pity the overrefined tastes of her childhood, the coquettish little girl, the dreamy schoolgirl overindulging her fancies. Shall I confess it? one often feels more tolerant towards her than the author himself. Thrust in a situation to which she ought to adjust, she always has a quality too much and a virtue too little: all her errors and her undoing stem from there. The quality she has in excess consists not only in being a romantic nature, but of having needs of heart and mind as well as ambition, aspirations towards a higher, more refined and more ornate existence than what befell her. The virtue she lacks stems from her failure to learn that the necessary condition to make life possible is the ability to tolerate *ennui*, the shapeless frustration resulting from the absence of a pleasant life better suited to our own tastes. She cannot silently and discreetly resign herself to the impossibility of finding a purpose, a meaningful course of action, in being useful to others or in the love for her child. She does not relent easily, she struggles to remain in the path of virtue; it will take her years of unsuccessful attempts before she gives in to evil. She comes closer every day, and at last she is uncontrollably lost. But I am rationalizing, whereas the author of *Madame Bovary* merely wants to show us, day by day, minute by minute, the thoughts and actions of this heroine.

The long and melancholy days spent in loneliness as Emma is left by herself during the first months of her married life, her walks to the beechgroves of Banneville in the company of her faithful little greyhound Djali, the endless questioning of her own destiny as she asks herself *what might have been*—all this is unravelled and argued with the same delicacy and analytical subtlety we meet with in the most intimate and dream-inducing of the older novels. As in the days of René or Oberman,[4] nature mingles at times its unpredictable and irregular movements with the longings and vague desires of the soul:

> Occasionally there came gusts of wind, breezes from the sea rolling in one sweep over the whole plateau of the Caux country, which brought to these fields a salt freshness. The rushes, close to the ground, whistled; the branches of the birch trees trembled in a swift rustling, while their crowns, ceaselessly swaying, kept up a deep murmur. Emma drew her shawl round her shoulders and rose.
>
> In the avenue a green light dimmed by the leaves lit up the short moss that crackled softly beneath her feet. The sun was setting; the sky showed red between the branches, and the trunks of the trees, uniform, and planted in a straight line, seemed a brown colonnade standing out against a background of cold. A fear took hold of her; she called Djali, and hurriedly returned to Tostes by the highroad, threw herself into an armchair, and for the rest of the evening did not speak.

It is around this time that the marquis of Andervilliers, a neighbor aspiring to political office, invites all people of note or influence in the region to a dance at the castle. He met the doctor by chance when, for lack of another surgeon, Bovary cured him of a mouth infection; on one of his visits to Tostes, he caught a glimpse of Madame Bovary and judged her sufficiently acceptable to be invited. Hence the visit of M. and Madame Bovary to the Vaubyessard castle, one of the crucial scenes of the book, and masterfully handled.

Emma is received with the politeness that a young and attractive woman is bound to encounter. On entering, she breathes the perfume of elegance and aristocracy, the chimera for which she has always been longing and which she considers her proper destiny. She waltzes without ever having been taught, guesses all there is to guess and succeeds beyond expectations in making an impression. All this will contribute to her downfall. She is poisoned by the air she has breathed there: the poison will act slowly but it has penetrated into her blood and will never leave her. All the details, even the most trivial, of this memorable evening are locked forever in her heart and will start their relentless action. "Her journey to Vaubyessard

4. Novel in letter form by Sénancour (1770–1846), distinguished, among other things, by the subtle sense of landscape and natural setting [*Editor*].

had made a gap in her life, like the huge crevasses that a thunderstorm will sometimes carve in the mountains, in the course of a single night." The morning after the dance, having left Vaubyessard in
the early hours of the day, M. and Madame Bovary find themselves
seated again in their small home, before their humble dinner table,
with the smell of onion soup and veal stew rising from the plates;
when Charles, happily rubbing his hands, exclaims, "How glad I
am to be back home!" she stares at him with utter contempt. Her
mind has come a long way since last night, and it has travelled in
the opposite direction. When they left together, driving their carriage to the party, they were at most two very different human
beings, but now, after their return, a boundless gap keeps them
apart.

I summarize briefly what takes many pages and will stretch over
years. It must be said in Emma's favor that her downfall is by no
means speedy. She casts around for help in her effort at constraint:
she looks for it in herself and in others. In herself:—she has a serious shortcoming: she lacks all capacity for sympathy as if, at an
early date, the imagination has consumed all other faculties and
sentiments. In others:—another misfortune! the hapless Charles,
who loves her and whom she, at moments, tries to love, entirely
fails to understand her. If, at least, he were an ambitious man, concerned with earning a reputation in his profession, forcing himself
through study or hard work, to make his name an honored one—
but he is nothing of the sort: he has neither drive, nor curiosity,
none of the inner powers that propel a man beyond the circle of his
daily existence, help him to move ahead and make his wife proud to
bear his name. "He is not a man," she exclaims in anger. "What a
sorry creature he is!" She will never forgive him for having humiliated her.

At last, she is seized by a kind of disease; they call it a nervous
condition, but it is like a nostalgia, a homesickness for an *unknown
country*. Always as blind as he is eager to help, Charles tries everything to cure her and can think of nothing better than a change of
residence; as a result, he abandons the practice he was acquiring at
Tostes for another far corner of Normandy, the town of Yonville-
l'Abbaye in the county of Neufchâtel. Until now the entire novel
has been a prelude; the real action only begins with the move to
Yonville, and except for the continued careful analysis, it now
proceeds at a somewhat faster pace.

At the moment of the move, Madame Bovary is pregnant with
her first and only child, a girl. The child will bring a slight counter-
weight into her life; sudden and capricious outbursts of tenderness
slow down the progress of evil. However, Emma's motherly feelings
have been poorly prepared: her heart is already too deeply ravaged

by barren passions and sterile ambitions to allow happy, natural, and self-sacrificing instincts to develop fully.

The new region where the Bovarys are settling down, bordering on the Picardie, "a mongrel area where the language is devoid of intonation, as the landscape is devoid of character," is described with pitiless truthfulness; the town and its main inhabitants, the priest, the innkeeper, the sacristan, the lawyer, etc. are taken from reality and haunt one's memory. Among those who will henceforth occupy the front of the stage and remain there till the end, filling it with their busy emptiness, we must single out M. Homais, a creation which M. Flaubert raises to the level of a type. We have all known and met M. Homais, though perhaps never in such a towering and triumphant incarnation: he is the weighty, self-important man-about-town, with a ready phrase for every situation, boastful of his own enlightenment, insistently commonplace, but devious and tricky, managing to enlist stupidity itself in the service of his interests. M. Homais is the M. Prudhomme of pseudo-science.

M. and Madame Bovary meet some of the main villagers upon their arrival at the Lion d'Or inn. One of the regular customers, M. Léon Dupuis, a lawyer's clerk, engages Madame Bovary in conversation. In a tightly handled, very natural sounding but deeply ironic dialogue, the author shows them outdoing each other in false sentiments, their taste for vague poetry and fake romanticism covering up for their real designs; it is only a beginning, but a damaging passage for those who believe in a poetry of the heart and have tried their hand at sentimental elegies: their devices are revealed, imitated and parodied, leaving one disgusted with love conversations that take themselves seriously.

Things do not quite work out as one would expect after this first encounter: the insignificant M. Léon will make headway in Madame Bovary's heart, but not so soon or so far, and not yet. For a while, Madame Bovary remains in fact an honest woman, although her secret name, as one would read it imprinted in her inner self, would already spell "betrayal" and "adultery." M. Léon, in fact, is a very small personage, but he is young, amiable, and he thinks that he is in love. At times, she thinks that she, too, loves him. All this is stimulated as well as hampered by their closely watched existences, by the difficulty of seeing each other, by their respective shyness. She wages inner battles, with no one present to appreciate the honor of her victories: "What exasperated her more than anything was that her husband seemed totally oblivious of her torture." One day, she tries to confide in the well-meaning priest, M. Bournisien, a vulgar and crude man who has no inkling of the moral distress that confronts him. Fortunately, M. Léon leaves town to pursue his studies in Paris. The embarrassed farewells, the stifled regrets, later magnified for her by memory and inflamed by the workings of her imagination, the uneven shades of feeling which they assume to be despair, all lend themselves to perfectly consistent and clearly constructed analysis. The underlying foundation is always one of irony.

The great day at Yonville-l'Abbaye comes with the agricultural fair of the Seine-Inférieure. The description of this momentous event constitutes the third large group scene in the book, and it is richly successful in its genre. Madame Bovary fulfills her destiny on this occasion. A reputedly handsome gentleman of the vicinity, the pseudo-aristocratic M. Rodolphe Boulanger de la Huchette, had noticed her at home a few days earlier, while bringing over one of his farmers to see the doctor. He is thirty-four years old, crude but with a veneer of elegance, a great chaser of women preoccupied by little else in life; her handsome eyes make him wish to add her to the list of his conquests. Although he is one of the judges, he sacrifices his official position to her company and never leaves her side on the day of the fair. This leads to a well-constructed and piquant scene: while the presiding official is delivering the inaugural address, solemnly propounding the political, economic and moral platitudes which the occasion calls for, Rodolphe, looking in from a window in the town hall, whispers in Emma's ears the eternal phrases that have so often led to the downfall of daughters of Eve. The pompous official speech, properly filled with pathos, counterpointed in a minor key by the equally banal and shopworn sentimentality of Rodolphe's cooings, make for a particularly effective and ironic scene. Convincingly enough, Madame Bovary, who withstood Léon but whose heart is shaken by the secret regret that she perhaps withstood him too well, now gives in from the very first day to this stranger—while Rodolphe is enough of a lout to think of himself as her sole conqueror. Such quirks and inconsistencies of Emma's feminine nature are excellently observed.

Once the decisive step had been taken, Madame Bovary will make up for lost time. She is hopelessly in love with Rodolphe, she pursues him and does not hesitate to compromise her reputation for his sake. From now on, we will no longer follow her so closely. The episode of the clubfoot, an inept operation undertaken and bungled by her husband, destroys once and forever whatever love or esteem she might have preserved towards him. Completely possessed by her passion, she reaches the point where she cannot stand to be away for a day from Rodolphe; she demands an elopement, begs for a cabin hidden in the woods or by the seashore. We come upon a touching and poignant scene: the unsuspecting Bovary, returning late at night from calling on his patients, dreams before the cradle of his daughter of all the happiness he foresees in her future, while next to him his wife, pretending to be asleep, dreams only of fanciful elopement in horse-drawn carriages, of romantic bliss, imaginary voyages, the Orient, Granada, Alhambra, etc. This double dream, treated as an extended juxtaposition, the abused father whose only thought is of sweet and joyful domesticity, side by side with the beautiful and determinedly destructive adulteress, is the work of an artist who, when he gets hold of a theme, extracts from it the maximum effect.

Many particularly true-to-nature phrases and expressions deserve to be singled out. One night, Rodolphe has come to visit Madame Bovary and is sitting in the empty consulting room; when a noise is heard, Emma asks him: "Have you got your gun?" The question makes him laugh. Against whom would he have to use his weapon if not against Bovary—and this is certainly the least of his intentions. All the same, the word has been said. Madame Bovary said it without thinking, but it reveals her to be the kind of woman who, in the grip of passion, would stop at nothing. She shows it again later, after Rodolphe, who was willing enough to make love to a pretty neighbor but never even considered eloping, has abandoned her. During a trip to Rouen she meets Léon again; his former shyness has now completely disappeared and his corruption hastens Emma's. She ruins her household and goes into debt without her husband's knowledge; one day, pursued by her creditors, she urges Léon to find her 3000 francs at once: "If I were in your place, I'd know where to find them.—Where?—At your office." Madame Bovary is ready to demand murder and theft, the ultimate degradation, from her lovers, if they were willing to heed her. But Flaubert is right in merely suggesting such possibilities by means of violent utterances of this kind.

The last half of the work is not less carefully or less precisely expressed than the first, yet I must mention an all too apparent weakness: although it was certainly not the author's deliberate intention, his very method, describing everything and leaving nothing out, leads him to include many too vividly suggestive details, which come close to appealing to the reader's erotic sensuality. He should definitely not have gone so far. After all, a book is not and could never be reality itself. At certain points, description can overreach the aim, not of the moralist, but of the discriminating artist. I know that even at the most daring moments, M. Flaubert's feeling remains thoroughly critical and ironic; his tone is never seductive or tender; nothing, in fact, could be less tempting than his descriptions of sin. But he is dealing with a French reader all too eager to look for licentiousness and likely to discover it at the slightest provocation.

Madame Bovary's terrifying death, which could well be called her punishment, is presented in relentless detail. The author here dares to sound dark chords that verge on dissonance. M. Bovary's death, which follows immediately, is a touching episode and revives our sympathy for this good and unhappy man. I have mentioned earlier the presence of strikingly apt and natural phrases: in his grief at the death of his wife, Bovary, who has done the utmost not to learn of her guilt, continues to refer all events back to her person; on receiving the announcement of Léon's wedding, he exclaims, "How happy this would have made my poor wife!" Later, he finds both Léon's and Rodolphe's letters but forgives everything and never ceases to love the deceitful creature he has lost; he finally dies brokenhearted.

Frequently, in the course of the narrative, the author has the opportunity to make a character fulfill and, so to speak, redeem himself and thus to add the ideal to the real. It would have taken very little. Charles Bovary near the end, for instance: with one slight pressure of the hand, leaving a mark in the clay he was moulding into shape, the artist could have made this vulgar face into a noble and touching figure. The reader would have consented; he almost demands it. But the writer never relents; he has chosen not to.

When the old Rouault comes to the burial of his daughter, in the midst of his desperate grief, he is given a line both grotesque and sublime in its veracity: every year, he used to send Charles Bovary a turkey in memory of his cured leg; upon leaving him, with tears in his eyes, his last heartfelt words are: "Don't worry, I will keep sending you your turkey!"

Although I am fully aware of the particular bias which constitutes the method and *ars poetica* of the author, I have one reproach to make: virtue is too absent from this book; no one represents it. The little Justin, who loves Emma in silence, is the only devoted, disinterested character, but he goes by almost unnoticed. Why did Flaubert not include a single character who, by the spectacle of his virtue, would have offered some comfort, some repose to the reader and become a friendly presence? He deserves to be told: "Moralist, you know everything but you are cruel." The book is certainly not without a moral; the author has not spelled out the lesson, but the reader can reach his own frightening conclusions. Yet, is it the true function of art to refuse all consolation, to reject all clemency and gentleness for the sake of total truth? Moreover, even if truth were the only aim, can it be said that truth resides entirely with evil, with human stupidity and perverseness? Even in the provinces, full as life is of wranglings, persecutions, petty frustrations and meddling hostility, there also remain good and beautiful souls who have preserved their innocence, perhaps better and more deeply than elsewhere; instances of modesty, resignation, helpfulness extending over many years—we all know some of them. Even in your so-truthful characters, you cannot deny that you artfully collect and assemble ridiculous and evil traits; why not gather with equal art traits of virtue on at least one head, one charming or beloved brow? Hidden in the provinces, in the center of France, I have known a young woman of superior intelligence and feeling: married but childless, with no one to love or to care for, she could easily have succumbed to boredom. Instead, she adopted other children, and became the benefactor of the neighborhood, a civilizing influence in the somewhat backward region where destiny had led her. She taught the village children to read and initiated them to the principles of morality. She would walk for miles on foot accompanied by one of her pupils, and would teach him under a tree, on a footpath, in the heath. Such souls exist in the provinces and in the country: why should they not also be shown? Their presence elevates and consoles while broadening our view of humanity.

On the whole, this book bears the imprint of the times. I am told that it was begun several years ago, but it appears at the right moment. It is the right kind of book to read after hearing the precise and caustic dialogue of an Alexandre Dumas comedy, after applauding *The Fake Gentlemen*, or between two articles by Taine. In many places and under many different forms, I detect symptoms of a new literary manner: scientific, experimental, adult, powerful, a little harsh. Such are the outstanding characteristics of the leaders of the new generation. Son and brother of distinguished surgeons, M. Flaubert handles the pen like others the scalpel. Anatomists and physiologists, I meet you at every turn!

CHARLES BAUDELAIRE

Madame Bovary, by Gustave Flaubert†

I

In the field of criticism, the writer who comes after everybody else is not without possessing certain advantages over the prophetic reviewer who predicts, ordains and, one might say, creates success with the authority born from his courage and his loyalty.

M. Gustave Flaubert is no longer in need of loyalty, if ever he was. Some of the subtlest and most authoritative critics have added

† The article first appeared in *L'artiste* on October 18, 1857. It can now be found in editions of Baudelaire's complete works, such as, for instance, *Oeuvres*, edited by Y. G. Le Dantec (Paris: Bibliothèque de la Plèiade, 1951), pp. 995–1005. Translated by Paul de Man.

luster and distinction to his excellent book. All that remains to be done is perhaps to point out some aspects that have remained unnoticed and to emphasize certain traits and insights which, in my opinion, have not been sufficiently praised and commented upon. Moreover, as I was suggesting, the situation of the latecomer who follows in the wake of established opinion, possesses a paradoxical charm. Being alone and in no hurry, he enjoys more freedom than his predecessors; he seems to be summarizing an earlier debate; consequently, he must avoid the excesses of the prosecution as well as of the defense and seek for a new approach, with no other incitement than his love for Beauty and for Justice.

II

I have just pronounced the splendid and frightening word: Justice; may I be allowed—as it is my pleasure—to thank the magistrates of France for the splendid example of fairness and good taste which they have displayed in this circumstance. On the one hand, they confronted a blind and violent moral zeal, misguidedly acting on the wrong terrain; on the other, a novel by an as yet unknown writer—and what a novel!—the most loyal, the most objective of novels, comparable in its banality to a field in the country, soaked and lashed like nature itself by endless storms and winds. Between the two, the judges chose to be as loyal and unpartial as the book that had been offered them as a scapegoat. Better still, if we may be allowed to conjecture on the basis of the written opinions that accompanied the judgment, it now seems that even if they had discovered something truly objectionable in the book they would nevertheless have absolved it in recognition of the *Beauty* that clothes it. This striking concern for Beauty, coming from men whose faculties are primarily called upon to serve the Rightful and True, is a very moving symptom, especially if one compares it with the burning appetites of a society that has entirely forsworn all spiritual love and, forgetting its ancient entrails, now only cares for its visceral organs. It can be said, because of its highly poetic tendency, that this decision is a definitive one; the Muse has won her case in court and all writers worthy of that name have been exonerated once and forever in the person of M. Gustave Flaubert.

I do not agree with those who claim, perhaps with a slight and unconscious envy, that the book owes its popular success to the trial and subsequent acquittal. Left unmolested, it would have created the same turmoil, awakened the same curiosity and amazement. Enlightened readers had long since given it their praise. Even when an earlier version appeared in the *Revue de Paris,* marred by harmful excisions that destroyed the inner balance, it had created quite a stir. Gustave Flaubert grew famous overnight and found himself in a situation both favorable and harmful; his exceptional and genuine talent was able to overcome this equivocal predicament, caused by circumstances which I will try to analyze as well as I can.

III

Flaubert's situation can be called favorable because, ever since the death of Balzac—this prodigious meteor whose passage covered our country with a cloud of glory, like a bizarre and unusual sunlight, a polar dawn throwing its magic light over a frozen desert—all curiosity about the novel had been appeased and dormant. Some amazing experiments, it must be admitted, had been tried.[1]

* * *

I would be the last to reproach these writers, some of them inspired by Dickens, others molded after Byron or Bulwer, because their pride or an excess of talent prevented them from equaling even a Paul de Kock[2] in stepping upon the unsteady threshold of popular success—this indecent slut asking only to be violated. Nor will I praise them for their failure, as little as I praise M. Gustave Flaubert for succeeding at once where others have tried for a lifetime. I see there, at most, an additional proof of strength and I will try to determine the reasons which lead the author in that particular direction rather than another.

But I also stated that the situation of the newcomer-novelist is a dangerous one due, alas, to a dismally simple reason. For many years, the interest which the public is willing to devote to matters of the spirit has considerably diminished and the allotment of its available enthusiasm has steadily decreased. The last years of Louis-Philippe's reign saw the final outbursts of a spirit still willing to be stimulated by the display of imaginative powers; the new novelist, however, is confronted with a completely worn-out public or, worse even, a stupefied and greedy audience, whose only hatred is for fiction, and only love for material possession.

In these circumstances, the reaction of a cultured mind, devoted to beauty but trained to fight in its defense, must have been to evaluate the good as well as the bad of the situation and to reason as follows:

"How can I most effectively stir up all these decrepit souls? They do not know what they would like; they only know that they positively hate greatness and consider the naïveté, the ardor of passion and the spontaneity of poetry embarrassing and insulting. Therefore, since the nineteenth century reader considers the choice of great subject-matter to be in poor taste, let us resolve to be vulgar. Let us

1. Baudelaire then mentions a group of novelists, most of them (except for Barbey D'Aurevilly) now forgotten, who enjoyed popular success in his day [*Editor*].

2. Paul de Kock (1793–1871) was an immensely successful author of popular fiction [*Editor*].

beware above all of giving away our real feelings and of speaking in our own name. In narrating passions and adventures which would tend to kindle sympathetic fires in the ordinary reader, we will remain icily detached. We will remain objective and impersonal as the realists tell us.

"Moreover, since of late our ears have been assaulted by infantile chatter of a group of theory-makers and since we have heard of a certain literary device called *realism*—a degrading insult flung in the face of all analytical writers, a vague and overflexible term applied by indiscriminate minds to the minute description of detail rather than to a new method of literary creation—we shall take advantage of the general ignorance and confusion. We shall apply a nervous, picturesque, subtle and precise style to a banal canvas. We shall make the most trivial of plots express the most ebullient and ardent feelings. Solemn and definitive words will be uttered by the silliest of voices.

"And where we can find the breeding-ground of stupidity, the setting that produces inane absurdities and is inhabited by the most intolerant imbeciles?

"In the provinces.

"What characters, in the provinces, are particularly insufferable?

"Petty people in petty positions, with minds distorted by their actions.

"What is the tritest theme of all, worn out by repetition, by being played over and over again like a tired barrel-organ?

"Adultery.

"Neither do I have to make my 'heroine' heroic. Provided she be sufficiently handsome, daring, ambitious, irresistibly drawn to a higher world, she cannot fail to awaken interest. This will make the *tour de force* even nobler and give our sinful heroine the—comparatively speaking—rare distinction of differing entirely from the self-complacent gossips to which previous writers had accustomed us.

"I do not have to concern myself any longer with the style, the picturesque backgrounds, the description of the setting; I can do all this with almost excessive skill. I will proceed instead by fine logic and analysis, and thus demonstrate that all subjects are equally good or bad depending on how they are treated, and that the most vulgar ones can become the best of all."

Madame Bovary was born from these resolutions as the impossible task, the true *gageure*, the wager which all works of art must be.

In order to complete his exploit to the full, it remained for the author to relinquish, so to speak, his actual sex and make himself into a woman. The result is miraculous, for in spite of his zeal at wearing masks he could not help but infuse some male blood into the veins of his creation; the most energetic and ambitious, but also the most imaginative part of Madame Bovary's personality have definitely remained masculine in kind. Like weapon-bearing Pallas issuing forth from the forehead of Zeus, this bizarre and androgynous creature houses the seductiveness of a virile soul within the body of a beautiful woman.

IV

Several critics who called the book beautiful because of the precision and liveliness of its descriptions, have claimed that it lacks the central character who acts as a moral judge and expresses the author's conscience. Where can we find the proverbial and legendary figure whose task it is to explain the fable and to guide the reader's judgment? In other words, where is the lesson, the cause?

What an absurdity! The eternal and incorrigible confusion of genres and of purposes is not yet overcome! A true work of art does not need to make moral pleas. The inner logic of the work suffices for all moral implications and it is the reader's task to draw the right conclusions from its outcome.

As for the intimate, deeper center of the book, there is no doubt that it resides in the adulterous woman; she alone possesses all the attributes of a worthy hero, albeit in the guise of a disgraced victim. I have just stated that she is almost masculine and that, perhaps unconsciously, the author had bestowed upon her all the qualities of manliness.

Let the reader carefully consider the following characteristics:

1. The imagination, the highest and most tyrannical of faculties, takes the place of the heart or what is called the heart: that from which reason is generally excluded; most of the time, women, like animals, are dominated by the heart.

2. Sudden forcefulness and quickness of decision, a mystical fusion of reason and passion typical of men created for action.

3. An unlimited urge to seduce and to dominate, including a willingness to stoop to the lowest means of seduction, such as the vulgar appeal of dress, perfume and make-up—all summarized in two words: dandyism, exclusive love of domination.

And yet, Madame Bovary gives in to her lovers; carried away by the sophistry of her imagination, she gives herself with magnificent generosity, in an entirely masculine manner, to fools who don't begin to measure up to her, exactly as poets will put themselves at the mercy of foolish women.

As another proof of the masculine qualities which she carries in her arteries, one should notice that she is much less incensed by the obvious physical shortcomings of her husband or by his glaring provincialism, than by this total absence of genius, his intellectual ineptness forcefully brought home by the stupid operation of the clubfoot.

One should reread the pages that deal with this episode; some are shortsighted enough to consider it superfluous but it serves precisely to bring the central character fully into light. Her fierce anger, pent up for years, suddenly bursts into the open; doors slam; the awed husband, who was never able to give his romantically inclined wife the slightest spiritual satisfaction, is relegated to his room; he is locked up in punishment for his guilty ignorance while Madame Bovary, in despair, cries out like a smaller Lady Macbeth mismated with an inadequate captain: "Ah! if *only* I were the wife of one of those balding and stooping scholars whose eyes, sheltered by dark glasses, are forever fixed on the archives of science! I would be proud to be seen at his arm; I would be the companion of a prince of the spirit—but to be chained forever, like a convict, to a fool who is not even capable of mending a crippled foot, bah!" Caught in her petty surroundings, stifled by a narrow horizon, this woman is a truly sublime example of her kind.

I find proof of Madame Bovary's ambiguous temperament even in her convent education.

The nuns have observed that the young girl is endowed with an amazing power to enjoy life, to anticipate all the pleasures she will be able to extract from it. This characterizes the man of action.

Meanwhile, she becomes intoxicated with the color of the stained-glass windows, with the Oriental shades that the ornate windows cast on her schoolgirl prayer book; she gorges herself on the solemn music of Vespers and obeying the impulse of her nerves rather than of her mind, she substitutes in her soul for the real God a God of pure fantasy, a God of the future and of chance, a picture-God wearing spurs and mustaches. This is characteristic of the hysterical poet.

The Academy of Medicine has not as yet been able to explain the mysterious condition of hysteria. In women, it acts like a stifling ball rising in the body (I mention only the main symptom), while in nervous men it can be the cause of many forms of impotence as well as of a limitless ability at excess. Why could this physiological mystery not serve as the central subject, the true core, of a literary work?

V

When all is said, this woman has real greatness, and she provokes our pity. In spite of the author's systematic tough-mindedness, in spite of his efforts to retreat entirely from the stage and manipulate his characters rather like a puppeteer handles his puppets, all *intellectual* women owe him a debt of gratitude. By endowing them with a talent for dreaming as well as for calculating—a combination that constitutes the perfect human being—he has elevated the female species to new heights, far above the realm of the purely animal and close to the ideal realm of men.

Madame Bovary has been called ridiculous by some. Indeed, we meet her at times mistaking some species of gentleman—could he even be called a country squire?—dressed in hunting vests and contrasting dress for a hero out of Walter Scott! At another moment, she is enamored of an insignificant little clerk who is not even capable of performing a dangerous action for his mistress. Trapped finally within the narrow confines of a village, this bizarre Pasiphae, now a poor exhausted creature, still pursues the ideal in the county bars and taverns. But does it matter? Even then, we must admit, she is, like Caesar at Carpentras, in pursuit of the ideal!

I will not echo the Lycanthrope,[3] remembered for a subversiveness which no longer prevails, when he said: "Confronted with all that is vulgar and inept in the present time, can we not take refuge in cigarettes and adultery?" But I assert that our world, even when it is weighed on precision scales, turns out to be exceedingly harsh considering it was engendered by Christ; it could hardly be entitled to throw the first stone at adultery. A few cuckolds more or less are not likely to increase the rotating speed of the spheres and to hasten by a second the final destruction of the universe. The time has come to put a stop to an increasingly contagious hypocrisy; we should expose the ridicule of men and women, themselves perverted to a point of utter triviality, who dare to attack a defenseless writer after he has deigned, with the chastity of an ancient teacher of rhetoric, to cast a mantle of glory over a bedroom-farce subject that would be repulsive and grotesque if it had not been touched by the opalescent light of poetry.

If I allowed myself to pursue this analytical bent any further, I would never finish; the book is so suggestive that one could fill a volume with one's observations. For the moment, I merely wish to indicate that the critics have overlooked or even attacked several of the most important passages in the novel. This is the case, for instance, of the section dealing with the bungled clubfoot operation. And nothing could be more authentically *modern* than the desolate and remarkable scene in which the future adulteress—for the poor woman, at that point, is still in the earliest stages of her downfall —calls on the Church for assistance. We expect the Church to be like the divine Mother, ready at all times to extend a helping hand, like a pharmacist who always has to be available. Yet Emma finds the attention of Father Bournisien, the parish priest, primarily

3. Pétrus Borel, alias Le Lycanthrope ("the Wolf–man") (1809–1859), was a friend of Gautier and Nerval, author of *Madame Putiphar*, a novel much admired by Baudelaire, who described him as "one of the stars in the somber sky of romanticism" [*Editor*].

taken up by the gymnastics of catechism pupils scattered among the stalls and chairs of the church; his candid reply to Emma is, "If you are unwell, madame, and since M. Bovary is a doctor, why don't you speak to your husband?"

Thus absolved by the ineptness of the priest, what woman would not wish to immerse herself in the swirling waters of adultery—and which one of us, in a more naïve age and in troubled cricumstances, did not find himself confronted with similarly incompetent priests?

VI

Since I happen to have at hand two books by this same author (*Madame Bovary* and the as yet still uncollected fragments of the *Temptation of Saint Anthony*), my original intent had been to establish a kind of parallel between both. I meant to point out identities and correspondences. It would have been easy enough to uncover beneath the tight texture of *Madame Bovary*, the elements of high lyricism and irony that abound in the *Temptation of Saint Anthony*. Here the author appears without disguise; his Saint Anthony is Madame Bovary tempted by all the demons of illusion and heresy, by all the obscenities of matter that encompass her; harassed by all the aberrations that lead to our downfall, Saint Anthony thus becomes a stronger apologist than his smaller and fictional bourgeois equivalent. This work, which unfortunately exists only in fragments, contains dazzling passages. I am not only referring to the prodigious feast given by Nebuchadnezzar, the marvelous apparition of a frivolous Queen of Sheba dancing in miniature shape on the retina of an ascete, or the conspicuously overdone setting in which Apollonius of Tyana appears, escorted by his keeper, the idiotic millionaire whom he is dragging after him around the world. I mostly want to direct the reader's mind toward the *subcurrent* that runs through the entire book, the subterranean, rebellious painful level, the darker strain that serves as a guide in traversing this pandemonic capharnaüm of solitude.

As I said before, I could easily have shown that in *Madame Bovary* M. Flaubert deliberately muted the high ironic and lyrical faculties which he gave full rein in the *Temptation*; the latter work, truly the secret chamber of his mind, evidently remains the most interesting of the two for poets and philosophers.

Maybe I will some day have the pleasure of performing this task.

Stylistic Studies

HENRY JAMES

[Style and Morality in *Madame Bovary*]†

Flaubert's imagination was great and splendid; in spite of which, strangely enough, his masterpiece is not his most imaginative work. *Madame Bovary*, beyond question, holds that first place, and *Madame Bovary* is concerned with the career of a country doctor's wife in a petty Norman town. The elements of the picture are of the fewest, the situation of the heroine almost of the meanest, the material for interest, considering the interest yielded, of the most unpromising; but these facts only throw into relief one of those incalculable incidents that attend the proceedings of genius. *Madame Bovary* was doomed by circumstances and causes—the freshness of comparative youth and good faith on the author's part being perhaps the chief—definitely to take its position, even though its subject was fundamentally a negation of the remote, the splendid and the strange, the stuff of his fondest and most cultivated dreams. It would have seemed very nearly to exclude the free play of the imagination, and the way this faculty on the author's part nevertheless presides is one of those accidents, manœuvres, inspirations, we hardly know what to call them, by which masterpieces grow. He of course knew more or less what he was doing for his book in making Emma Bovary a victim of the imaginative habit, but he must have been far from designing or measuring the total effect which renders the work so general, so complete an expression of himself. His separate idiosyncrasies, his irritated sensibility to the life about him, with the power to catch it in the fact and hold it hard, and his hunger for style and history and poetry, for the rich and the rare, great reverberations, great adumbrations, are here represented together as they are not in his later writings. There is nothing of the near, of the directly observed, though there may be much of the directly perceived and the minutely detailed, either in *Salammbo* or in *Saint Anthony*, and little enough of the extravagance of illusion in that indefinable last word of restrained evocation and cold execu-

† Reprinted with the permission of Charles Scribner's Sons from *Notes on Novelists With Some Other Notes* by Henry James, pp. 59–66. Copyright 1914 Charles Scribner's Sons; renewal copyright 1942 Henry James.

tion the *Sentimental Education*. M. Faguet has of course excellently noted this—that the fortune and felicity of the book were assured by the stroke that made the central figure an embodiment of helpless romanticism. Flaubert himself but narrowly escaped being such an embodiment after all, and he is thus able to express the romantic mind with extraordinary truth. As to the rest of the matter he had the luck of having been in possession from the first, having begun so early to nurse and work up his plan that, familiarity and the native air, the native soil, aiding, he had finally made out to the last lurking shade the small sordid sunny dusty village picture, its emptiness constituted and peopled. It is in the background and the accessories that the real, the real of his theme, abides; and the romantic, the romantic of his theme, accordingly occupies the front. Emma Bovary's poor adventures are a tragedy for the very reason that in a world unsuspecting, unassisting, unconsoling, she has herself to distil the rich and the rare. Ignorant, unguided, undiverted, ridden by the very nature and mixture of her consciousness, she makes of the business an inordinate failure, a failure which in its turn makes for Flaubert the most pointed, the most *told* of anecdotes.

There are many things to say about *Madame Bovary*, but an old admirer of the book would be but half-hearted—so far as they represent reserves or puzzlements—were he not to note first of all the circumstances by which it is most endeared to him. To remember it from far back is to have been present all along at a process of singular interest to a literary mind, a case indeed full of comfort and cheer. The finest of Flaubert's novels is today, on the French shelf of fiction, one of the first of the classics; it has attained that position, slowly but steadily, before our eyes; and we seem so to follow the evolution of the fate of a classic. We see how the thing takes place; which we rarely can, for we mostly miss either the beginning or the end, especially in the case of a consecration as complete as this. The consecrations of the past are too far behind and those of the future too far in front. That the production before us *should* have come in for the heavenly crown may be a fact to offer English and American readers a mystifying side; but it is exactly our ground and a part moreover of the total interest. The author of these remarks remembers, as with a sense of the way such things happen, that when a very young person in Paris he took up from the parental table the latest number of the periodical in which Flaubert's then duly unrecognized masterpiece was in course of publication. The moment is not historic, but it was to become in the light of history, as may be said, so unforgettable that every small feature of it yet again lives for him: it rests there like the backward end of the span. The cover of the old Revue de Paris was yellow, if I mistake not, like that of the new, and *Madame Bovary: Moeurs de Province*, on the inside of it, was already, on the spot, as a title, mysteriously arresting, inscrutably charged. I was ignorant of what had preceded and was not to know till much later what followed; but present to me still is the act of standing there before the fire, my back against the low beplushed and begarnished French chimneypiece and taking in what I might of that instalment, taking it in with so surprised an interest, and perhaps as well such a stir of faint foreknowledge, that the sunny little salon, the autumn day, the window ajar and the cheerful outside clatter of the Rue Montaigne are all now for me more or less in the story and the story more or less in them. The story, however, was at that moment having a difficult life; its fortune was all to make; its merit was so far from suspected that, as Maxime Du Camp—though verily with no excess of contrition—relates, its cloth of gold barely escaped the editorial shears. This, with much more, contributes for us to the course of things to come. The book, on its appearance as a volume, proved a shock to the high propriety of the guardians of public morals under the second Empire, and Flaubert was prosecuted as author of a work indecent to scandal. The prosecution in the event fell to the ground, but I should perhaps have mentioned this agitation as one of the very few, of any public order, in his short list. *The Candidate* fell at the Vaudeville Theatre, several years later, with a violence indicated by its withdrawal after a performance of but two nights, the first of these marked by a deafening uproar; only if the comedy was not to recover from this accident the misprised lustre of the novel was entirely to reassert itself. It is strange enough at present—so far have we travelled since then—that *Madame Bovary* should in so comparatively recent a past have been to that extent a cause of reprobation; and suggestive above all, in such connections, as to the large unconsciousness of superior minds. The desire of the superior mind of the day—that is the governmental, official, legal—to distinguish a book with such a destiny before it is a case conceivable, but conception breaks down before its design of making the distinction purely invidious. We can imagine its knowing so little, however face to face with the object, what it had got hold of; but for it to have been so urged on by a blind inward spring to publish to posterity the extent of its ignorance, that would have been beyond imagination, beyond everything but pity.

And yet it is not after all that the place the book has taken is so overwhelmingly explained by its inherent dignity; for here comes in the curiosity of the matter. Here comes in especially its fund of admonition for alien readers. The dignity of its substance is the dignity of Madame Bovary herself as a vessel of experience—a question as to which, unmistakably, I judge, we can only depart from the consensus of French critical opinion. M. Faguet for example commends the character of the heroine as one of the most living and discriminated figures of women in all literature, praises it as a field for the display of the romantic spirit that leaves nothing to be desired. Subject to an observation I shall presently make and that bears heavily in general, I think, on Flaubert as a painter of life, subject to this restriction he is right; which is a proof that a work of art may be markedly open to objection and at the same time be rare in its kind, and that when it is perfect to this point nothing else particularly matters. *Madame Bovary* has a perfection that not only stamps it, but that makes it stand almost alone; it holds itself with such a supreme unapproachable assurance as both excites and defies judgment. For it deals not in the least, as to unapproachability, with things exalted or refined; it only confers on its sufficiently vulgar elements of exhibition a final unsurpassable form. The form is in *itself* as interesting, as active, as much of the essence of the subject as the idea, and yet so close is its fit and so inseparable its life that we catch it at no moment on any errand of its own. That verily is to *be* interesting—all round; that is to be genuine and whole. The work is a classic because the thing, such as it is, is ideally *done*, and because it shows that in such doing eternal beauty may dwell. A pretty young woman who lives, socially and morally speaking, in a hole, and who is ignorant, foolish, flimsy, unhappy, takes a pair of lovers by whom she is successively deserted; in the midst of the bewilderment of which, giving up her husband and her child, letting everything go, she sinks deeper into duplicity, debt, despair, and arrives on the spot, on the small scene itself of her poor depravities, at a pitiful tragic end. In especial she does these things while remaining absorbed in romantic intention and vision, and she remains absorbed in romantic intention and vision while fairly rolling in the dust. That is the triumph of the book as the triumph stands, that Emma interests us by the nature of her consciousness and the play of her mind, thanks to the reality and beauty with which those sources are invested. It is not only that they represent *her* state; they are so true, so observed and felt, and especially so shown, that they represent the state, actual or potential, of all persons like her, persons romantically determined. Then her setting, the medium in which she struggles, becomes in its way as important, becomes eminent with the eminence of art; the tiny world in which she revolves, the contracted cage in which she flutters, is hung out in space for her, and her companions in captivity there are as true as herself.

I have said enough to show what I mean by Flaubert's having in this picture expressed something of his intimate self, given his heroine something of his own imagination: a point precisely that brings me back to the restriction at which I just now hinted, in which M. Faguet fails to indulge and yet which is immediate for the alien reader. Our complaint is that Emma Bovary, in spite of the nature of her consciousness and in spite of her reflecting so much that of her creator, is really too small an affair. This, critically speaking, is in view both of the value and the fortune of her history, a wonderful circumstance. She associates herself with Frédéric Moreau in the *Education* to suggest for us a question that can be answered, I hold, only to Flaubert's detriment. Emma taken alone would possibly not so directly press it, but in her company the hero of our author's second study of the "real" drives it home. Why did Flaubert choose, as special conduits of the life he proposed to depict, such inferior and in the case of Frédéric such abject human specimens? I insist only in respect to the latter, the perfection of Madame Bovary scarce leaving one much warrant for wishing anything other. Even here, however, the general scale and size of Emma, who is small even of her sort, should be a warning to hyperbole. If I say that in the matter of Frédéric at all events the answer is inevitably detrimental I mean that it weighs heavily on our author's general credit. He wished in each case to make a picture of experience—middling experience, it is true—and of the world close to him; but if he imagined nothing better for his purpose than such a heroine and such a hero, both such limited reflectors and registers, we are forced to believe it to have been by a defect of his mind. And that sign of weakness remains even if it be objected that the images in question were addressed to his purpose better than others would have been: the purpose itself then shows as inferior. The *Sentimental Education* is a strange, an indescribable work, about which there would be many more things to say than I have space for, and all of them of the deepest interest. It is moreover, to simplify my statement, very much less satisfying a thing, less pleasing whether in its unity or its variety, than its specific predecessor. But take it as we will, for a success or a failure—M. Faguet indeed ranks it, by the measure of its quantity of intention, a failure, and I on the whole agree with him—the personage offered us as bearing the weight of the drama, and in whom we are invited to that extent to interest ourselves, leaves us mainly wondering what our entertainer could have been thinking of. He takes Frédéric Moreau on the threshold of life and conducts him to the extreme of maturity without apparently suspecting for a moment either our wonder or our protest—"Why, why *him*?" Frédéric is positively too poor for his part, too scant for his charge; and we feel with a kind of embarrassment, certainly with a kind of compassion, that it is somehow the business of a protagonist to prevent in his designer an excessive waste of faith. When I speak of the faith in Emma Bovary as proportionately wasted I reflect on M. Faguet's judgment that she is from the point of view of deep interest richly or at least roundedly representative. Representative of what? he makes us ask even while granting all the grounds of misery and tragedy involved. The plea for her is the plea made for all the figures that live without evaporation under the painter's hand—that they are not only particular persons but types of their kind, and as valid in one light as in the other. It is Emma's "kind" that I question for this responsibility, even if it be inquired of me why I then fail to question that of Charles Bovary, in its perfection, or that of the inimitable, the immortal Homais. If we express Emma's deficiency as the poverty of her consciousness for the typical function, it is certainly not, one must admit, that she is surpassed in this respect either by her platitudinous husband or by his friend the pretentious apothecary. The difference is none the less somehow in the fact that they are respectively studies but of their character and office, which function in each expresses adequately *all* they are. It may be, I concede, because Emma is the only woman in the book that she is taken by M. Faguet as *femininely* typical, typical in the larger illustrative way, whereas the others pass with him for images specifically conditioned. Emma is this same for myself, I plead; she is conditioned to such an excess of the specific, and the specific in her case leaves out so many even of the commoner elements of conceivable life in a woman when we are invited to see that life as pathetic, as dramatic agitation, that we challenge both the author's and the critic's scale of importances. The book is a picture of the middling as much as they like, but does Emma attain even to *that?* Hers is a narrow middling even for a little imaginative person whose "social" significance is small. It is greater on the whole than her capacity of consciousness, taking this all round; and so, in a word, we feel her less illustrational than she might have been not only if the world had offered her more points of contact, but if she had had more of these to give it.

PERCY LUBBOCK

[The Craft of Fiction in *Madame Bovary*]†

If Flaubert allows himself the liberty of telling his story in various ways—with a method, that is to say, which is often modified as he

† From *The Craft of Fiction* by Percy Lubbock, pp. 77–87, 88–92. All rights reserved; reprinted by permission of The Viking Press, Inc. and Jonathan Cape Ltd.

proceeds—it is likely that he has good cause to do so. Weighing every word and calculating every effect so patiently, he could not have been casual and careless over his method; he would not take one way rather than another because it saved him trouble, or because he failed to notice that there were other ways, or because they all seemed to him much the same. And yet at first sight it does seem that his manner of arriving at his subject—if his subject is Emma Bovary—is considerably casual. He begins with Charles, of all people—Charles, her husband, the stupid soul who falls heavily in love with her prettiness and never has the glimmer of an understanding of what she is; and he begins with the early history of Charles, and his upbringing, and the irrelevant first marriage that his mother forces upon him, and his widowhood; and then it happens that Charles has a professional visit to pay to a certain farm, the farmer's daughter happens to be Emma, and so we finally stumble upon the subject of the book. Is that the neatest possible mode of striking it? But Flaubert seems to be very sure of himself, and it is not uninteresting to ask exactly what he means.

As for his subject, it is of course Emma Bovary in the first place; the book is the portrait of a foolish woman, romantically inclined, in small and prosaic conditions. She is in the center of it all, certainly; there is no doubt of her position in the book. But *why* is she there? The true subject of the novel is not given, as we saw, by a mere summary of the course which is taken by the story. She may be there for her own sake, simply, or for the sake of the predicament in which she stands; she may be presented as a curious scrap of character, fit to be studied; or Flaubert may have been struck by her as the instrument, the victim, the occasion, of a particular train of events. Perhaps she is a creature portrayed because he thinks her typical and picturesque; perhaps she is a disturbing little force let loose among the lives that surround her; perhaps, on the other hand, she is a hapless sufferer in the clash between her aspirations and her fate. Given Emma and what she is by nature, given her environment and the facts of her story, there are dozens of different subjects, I dare say, latent in the case. The woman, the men, all they say and do, the whole scene behind them—none of it gives any clue to the right manner of treating them. The one irreducible idea out of which the book, as Flaubert wrote it, unfolds—this it is that must be sought.

Now if Emma was devised for her own sake, solely because a nature and a temper like hers seemed to Flaubert an amusing study—if his one aim was to make the portrait of a woman of that kind—then the rest of the matter falls into line, we shall know how to regard it. These conditions in which Emma finds herself will have been chosen by the author because they appeared to throw light on

her, to call out her natural qualities, to give her the best opportunity of disclosing what she is. Her stupid husband and her fascinating lovers will enter the scene in order that she may become
whatever she has it in her to be. Flaubert elects to place her in a
certain provincial town, full of odd characters; he gives the town
and its folk an extraordinary actuality; it is not a town *quelconque*,
not a generalized town, but as individual and recognizable as he can
make it. None the less—always supposing that Emma by herself is
the whole of his subject—he must have lit on this particular town
simply because it seemed to explain and expound her better than
another. If he had thought that a woman of her sort, rather meanly
ambitious, rather fatuously romantic, would have revealed her quality more intensely in a different world—in success, freedom, wealth
—he would have placed her otherwise; Charles and Rodolphe and
Homais and the rest of them would have vanished, the more illuminating set of circumstances (whatever they might be) would
have appeared instead. Emma's world as it is at present, in the
book that Flaubert wrote, would have to be regarded, accordingly,
as all a *consequence* of Emma, invented to do her a service, described in order that they may make the description of *her*. Her
world, that is to say, would belong to the treatment of the story;
none of it, not her husband, not the life of the market–town,
would be a part of the author's postulate, the groundwork of his
fable; it would be possible to imagine a different setting, better, it
might be, than that which Flaubert has chosen. All this—*if* the
subject of the book is nothing but the portrait of such a woman.

But of course it is not so; one glance at our remembrance of the
book is enough to show it. Emma's world could not be other than it
is, she could not be shifted into richer and larger conditions, without destroying the whole point and purpose of Flaubert's novel. She
by herself is not the subject of his book. What he proposes to ex-
hibit is the history of a woman like her in just such a world as hers,
a foolish woman in narrow circumstances; so that the provincial
scene, acting upon her, making her what she becomes, is as essential
as she is herself. Not a portrait, therefore, not a study of character
for its own sake, but something in the nature of a drama, where the
two chief players are a woman on one side and her whole environment on the other—that is *Madame Bovary*. There is a conflict, a
trial of strength, and a doubtful issue. Emma is not much of a
force, no doubt; her impulses are wild, her emotions are thin and
poor, she has no power of passion with which to fight the world. All
she has is her romantic dream and her plain, primitive appetite; but
these can be effective arms, after all, and she may yet succeed in
getting her way and making her own terms. On the other hand the
limitations of her life are very blank and uncompromising indeed;

they close all round her, hampering her flights, restricting her opportunities. The drama is set, at any rate, whatever may come of it; Emma marries her husband, is established at Yonville and faced with the poverty of her situation. Something will result, the issue will announce itself. It is the mark of a dramatic case that it contains an opposition of some kind, a pair of wills that collide, an action that pulls in two directions; and so far *Madame Bovary* has the look of a drama. Flaubert might work on the book from that point of view and throw the emphasis on the issue. The middle of his subject would then be found in the struggle between Emma and all that constitutes her life, between her romantic dreams and her besetting facts. The question is what will happen.

But then again—that is not exactly the question in this book. Obviously the emphasis is not upon the commonplace little events of Emma's career. They might, no doubt, be the steps in a dramatic tale, but they are nothing of the kind as Flaubert handles them. He makes it perfectly clear that his view is not centered upon the actual outcome of Emma's predicament, whether it will issue this way or that; *what* she does or fails to do is of very small moment. Her passages with Rodolphe and with Léon are pictures that pass; they solve nothing, they lead to no climax. Rodolphe's final rejection of her, for example, is no scene of drama, deciding a question that has been held in suspense; it is one of Emma's various mischances, with its own marked effect upon *her*, but it does not stand out in the book as a turning-point in the action. She goes her way and acts out her history; but of whatever suspense, whatever dramatic value, there might be in it Flaubert makes nothing, he evidently considers it of no account. Who, in recalling the book, thinks of the chain of incident that runs through it, compared with the long and living impression of a few of the people in it and of the place in which they are set? None of the events really matter for their own sake; they might have happened differently, not one of them is indispensable as it is. Emma must certainly have made what she could of her opportunities of romance, but they need not necessarily have appeared in the shape of Léon or Rodolphe; she would have found others if these had not been at hand. The *events*, therefore, Emma's excursions to Rouen, her forest-rides, her one or two memorable adventures in the world, all these are only Flaubert's way of telling his subject, of making it count to the eye. They are not in themselves what he has to say, they simply illustrate it.

What it comes to, I take it, is that though *Madame Bovary*, the novel, is a kind of drama—since there is the interaction of this woman confronted by these facts—it is a drama chosen for the sake of the picture in it, for the impression it gives of the manner in which certain lives are lived. It might have another force of its own;

it might be a strife of characters and wills, in which the men and women would take the matter into their own hands and make all the interest by their action; it might be a drama, say, as *Jane Eyre* is a drama, where another obscure little woman has a part to play, but where the question is how she plays it, what she achieves or misses in particular. To Flaubert the situation out of which he made his novel appeared in another light. It was not as dramatic as it was pictorial; there was not the stuff in Emma, more especially, that could make her the main figure of a drama; she is small and futile, she could not well uphold an interest that would depend directly on her behaviour. But for a picture, where the interest depends only on what she *is*—that is quite different. Her futility is then a real value; it can be made amusing and vivid to the last degree, so long as no other weight is thrown on it; she can make a perfect impression of life, though she cannot create much of a story. Let Emma and her plight, therefore, appear as a picture; let her be shown in the act of living her life, entangled as it is with her past and her present; that is how the final fact at the heart of Flaubert's subject will be best displayed.

Here is the clue, it seems, to his treatment of the theme. It is pictorial, and its object is to make Emma's existence as intelligible and visible as may be. We who read the book are to share her sense of life, till no uncertainty is left in it; we are to see and understand her experience, and to see *her* while she enjoys or endures it; we are to be placed within her world, to get the immediate taste of it, and outside her world as well, to get the full effect, more of it than she herself could see. Flaubert's subject demands no less, if the picture is to be complete. She herself must be known thoroughly—that is his first care; the movement of her mind is to be watched at work in all the ardour and the poverty of her imagination. How she creates her makeshift romances, how she feeds on them, how they fail her —it is all part of the picture. And then there is the dull and limited world in which her appetite is somehow to be satisfied, the small town that shuts her in and cuts her off; this, too, is to be rendered, and in order to make it clearly tell beside the figure of Emma it must be as distinct and individual, as thoroughly characterized as she is. It is more than a setting for Emma and her intrigue; it belongs to the book integrally, much more so than the accidental lovers who fall in Emma's way. They are mere occasions and attractions for her fancy; the town and the *curé* and the apothecary and the other indigenous gossips need a sharper definition. And accordingly Flaubert treats the scenery of his book, Yonville and its odd types, as intensely as he treats his heroine; he broods over it with concentration and gives it all the salience he can. The town with its life is not behind his heroine, subdued in tone to make a background; it is *with* her, no less fully to the front; its value in the picture is as strong as her own.

Such is the picture that Flaubert's book is to present. And what, then, of the point of view towards which it is to be directed? If it is to have that unity which it needs to produce its right effect there can be no uncertainty here, no arbitrary shifting of the place from which an onlooker faces it. And in the tale of *Madame Bovary* the question of the right point of view might be considerably perplexing. Where is Flaubert to find his center of vision?—from what point, within the book or without, will the unfolding of the subject be commanded most effectively? The difficulty is this—that while one aspect of his matter can only be seen from within, through the eyes of the woman, another must inevitably be seen from without, through nobody's eyes but the author's own. Part of his subject is Emma's sense of her world; we must see how it impresses her and what she makes of it, how it thwarts her and her imagination contrives to get a kind of sustenance out of it. The book is not really written at all unless it shows her view of things, as the woman she was, in that place, in those conditions. For this reason it is essential to pass into her consciousness, to make her *subjective*; and Flaubert takes care to do so and to make her so, as soon as she enters the book. But it is also enjoined by the story, as we found, that her place and conditions should be seen for what they are and known as intimately as herself. For this matter Emma's capacity fails.

Her intelligence is much too feeble and fitful to give a sufficient account of her world. The town of Yonville would be very poorly revealed to us if Flaubert had to keep within the measure of *her* perceptions: it would be thin and blank, it would be barely more than a dull background for the beautiful apparition of the men she desires. What were her neighbors to her? They existed in her consciousness only as tiresome interruptions and drawbacks, except now and then when she had occasion to make use of them. But to us, to the onlooker, they belong to her portrait, they represent the dead weight of provincial life which is the outstanding fact in her case. Emma's rudimentary idea of them is entirely inadequate; she has not a vestige of the humour and irony that is needed to give them shape. Moreover they affect her far more forcibly and more variously than she could even suspect; a sharper wit than hers must evidently intervene, helping out the primitive workings of her mind. Her pair of eyes is not enough; the picture beheld through them is a poor thing in itself, for she can see no more than her mind can grasp; and it does her no justice either, since she herself is so largely the creation of her surroundings.

It is a dilemma that appears in any story, wherever the matter to be represented is the experience of a simple soul or a dull intelligence. If it is the experience and the actual taste of it that is to be imparted, the story must be viewed as the poor creature saw it; and yet the poor creature cannot tell the story in full. A shift of the vision is necessary. And in *Madame Bovary*, it is to be noted, there is no one else within the book who is in a position to take up the tale when Emma fails. There is no other personage upon the scene who sees and understands any more than she; perception and discrimination are not to be found in Yonville at all—it is an essential point. The author's wit, therefore, and none other, must supply what is wanting. This necessity, to a writer of Flaubert's acute sense of effect, is one that demands a good deal of caution. The transition must be made without awkwardness, without calling attention to it. Flaubert is not the kind of storyteller who will leave it undisguised; he will not begin by "going behind" Emma, giving her view, and then openly, confessedly, revert to his own character and use his own standards. There is nothing more disconcerting in a novel than to *see* the writer changing his part in this way—throwing off the character into which he has been projecting himself and taking a new stand outside and away from the story.

* * *

Flaubert's way of disguising the inconsistency is not a peculiar art of his own, I dare say. Even in him it was probably quite unconscious, well as he was aware of most of the refinements of his craft; and perhaps it is only a sleight of hand that might come naturally to any good story teller. But it is interesting to follow Flaubert's method to the very end, for it holds out so consummately; and I think it is possible to define it here. I should say, then, that he deals with the difficulty I have described by keeping Emma always at a certain distance, even when he appears to be entering her mind most freely. He makes her subjective, places us so that we see through her eyes—yes; but he does so with an air of aloofness that forbids us ever to become entirely identified with her. This is how she thought and felt, he seems to say; look and you will understand; such is the soul of this foolish woman. A hint of irony is always perceptible, and it is enough to prevent us from being lost in her consciousness, immersed in it beyond easy recall. The woman's life is very real, perfectly felt; but the reader is made to accept his participation in it as a pleasing experiment, the kind of thing that appeals to a fastidious curiosity—there is no question of its ever being more than this. The *fact* of Emma is taken with entire seriousness, of course; she is there to be studied and explored, and no means of understanding her point of view will be neglected. But her value is another matter; as to that Flaubert never has an instant's illusion, he always knows her to be worthless.

He knows it without asserting it, needless to say; his valuation of her is only implied; it is in his tone—never in his words, which invariably respect her own estimate of herself. His irony, none the less, is close at hand and indispensable; he has a definite use for this resource and he could not forego it. His irony gives him perfect freedom to supersede Emma's limited vision whenever he pleases, to abandon her manner of looking at the world, and to pass immediately to his own more enlightened, more commanding height. Her manner was utterly convincing while she exhibited it; but we always knew that a finer mind was watching her display with a touch of disdain. From time to time it leaves her and begins to create the world of Homais and Binet and Lheureux and the rest, in a fashion far beyond any possible conception of hers. Yet there is no dislocation here, no awkward substitution of one set of values for another; very discreetly the same standard has reigned throughout. That is the way in which Flaubert's impersonality, so called, artfully operates.

And now another difficulty: there is still more that is needed and that is not yet provided for. Emma must be placed in her world and fitted into it securely. Some glimpse of her appearance in the sight of those about her—this, too, we look for, to make the whole account of her compact and complete. Her relation to her husband, for instance, is from her side expressed very clearly in her view of him, which we possess; but there are advantages in seeing it from his side too. What did *he* really think of her, how did she appear to him? Light on this question not only makes a more solid figure of her for the reader, but it also brings her once for all into the company of the people round her, establishes her in the circle of their experience. Emma from within we have seen, and Yonville from the author's point of vantage; and now here is Emma from a point by her very side, when the seeing eye becomes that of her husband. Flaubert manages this ingeniously, making his procedure serve a further purpose at the same time. For he has to remember that his story does not end with the death of Emma; it is rounded off, not by her death, but by her husband's discovery of her long faithlessness, when in the first days of his mourning he lights upon the packet of letters that betrays her. The end of the story is in the final stroke of irony which gives the man this far-reaching glance into the past, and reveals thereby the mental and emotional confusion of his being—since his only response is a sort of stupefied perplexity. Charles must be held in readiness, so to speak, for these last pages; his inner mind, and his point of view, must be created in advance and kept in reserve, so that the force of the climax, when it is reached, may be instantly felt. And so we have the early episodes of

Charles's youth and his first marriage, all his history up to the time when he falls in Emma's way; and Flaubert's questionable manner of working round to his subject is explained. Charles will be needed at the end, and Charles is here firmly set on his feet; the impression of Emma on those who encounter her is also needed, and here it is; and the whole book, mainly the affair of Emma herself, is effectively framed in this other affair, that of Charles, in which it opens and closes. *Madame Bovary* is a well-made book—so we have always been told, and so we find it to be, pulling it to pieces and putting it together again. It never is unrepaying to do so once more.

And it is a book that with its variety of method, and with its careful restriction of that variety to its bare needs, and with its scrupulous use of its resources—it is a book, altogether, that gives a good point of departure for an examination of the methods of fiction. The leading notions that are to be followed are clearly laid down in it, and I shall have nothing more to say that is not in some sense an extension and an amplification of hints to be found in *Madame Bovary*. For that reason I have lingered in detail over the treatment of the story about which, in other connections, a critic might draw different conclusions. I remember again how Flaubert vilified his subject while he was at work on it; his love of strong colours and flavours was disgusted by the drab prose of such a story— so he thought and said. But as the years went by and he fought his way from one chapter to another, did he begin to feel that it was not much of a subject after all, even of its kind? It is not clear; but after yet another re-reading of the book one wonders afresh. It is not a fertile subject—it is not; it does not strain and struggle for development, it only submits to it. But that aspect is not *my* subject, and *Madame Bovary*, a beautifully finished piece of work, is for my purpose singularly fertile.

W. VON WARTBURG

[Flaubert's Language]†

In their vocabulary as well as in their style, the realists seem to be the direct successors of the romantics. Yet Flaubert's use of language is very different from Balzac's. It is true that the Norman master has the pharmacist Homais use a mixture of scientific and collo-

† From W. von Wartburg, *Evolution et Structure de la Langue Française* ("Evolution and Structure of the French Language") (Bern: Francke Verlag Bern, 4th edition, 1946), pp. 243–45.

Reprinted by permission of the publisher. Translated by Paul de Man. Other references to Flaubert's style, too technical to be included here, appear on pp. 258 ff. of the same treatise.

quial speech that fully reveals his shortcomings and the evil caused by an incomplete semi-education. The village priest Bournisien speaks in commonplaces whose presumably elevated tone clashes with his lowly character. But whereas in Balzac every sentence is like a spontaneous, uncontrolled outburst originating in the fire of composition, Flaubert's every expression, phrase, or sentence has been most carefully tested. Realism removed many social, moral, and puristic barriers that stood in the way of numberless words. While making considerable use of this new-gained freedom, Flaubert curtails it by a set of new restrictions. He doesn't want the freedom to become lawlessness; such a relaxation of rules would take language away from its spiritual origins. Flaubert cannot tolerate the distance which, as a result of the development of civilization and of language, now separates the inner feeling from its expression, the thing from the word. "No one ever has been able to give the exact measure of his needs or his concepts or his sorrows. The human tongue is like a cracked cauldron on which we beat out tunes to set a bear dancing when we would make the stars weep with our melodies" [*Madame Bovary*, p. 138]. His entire life-work was aimed at bridging this distance. Flaubert demands a new discipline, which he first of all forces upon himself. He wishes to create a style unlike any other known before.

The huge vocabulary now available will allow him to find the right expression for every shade of meaning; on the other hand, every sentence must make use of the full esthetic, rhythmical, descriptive, and auditive resources of the language. Flaubert's own definition of style has often been quoted: "I think of a style that would be beautiful . . . rhythmical like poetry, precise like the language of science, capable of the sustained melody of a violincello and scintillating like fire. A style that would enter the mind like a stiletto and on which our thought could travel as over smooth water, like a boat with a favorable breeze. We must realize that prose has only just begun to discover its possibilities." Others considered words merely as symbols pointing toward the objects they designate; they thought them adequate when they were able to perform this service. But Flaubert is aware of a mysterious unity between the word and the object. "Style," he writes, "is by itself an absolute way of perceiving things" (*Correspondence* II, 86). The realists among the scholastic philosophers had contested the assertion of the nominalists, who thought of names as universals: *Universalia sunt nomina*. The realists considered them to be mere *realia*. Without being aware of it, Flaubert renewed in his way this ancient debate, transferring it to the level of language. He is aware of an inner unity between word, thing, and concept, between sentence and thought. This intimate union between the word and the thing it names finds its equivalence in the relationship between the sentence and its enunciatory function. The choice and the order of words reveal the state of mind of the characters.

In one of his letters, Flaubert himself stated: "Those fellows still stick to the old notion that form is like a garment. But no! form is the very flesh of thought, as thought is the soul of life" (*Correspondence* II, 216). Flaubert was to devote his life's work to the inner unity between words and things. Before him, the best authors had used some of the resources of language, but they had done so unconsciously. They worked by instinct, rather than with a full knowledge of the expressive power of words. Flaubert was able to cast the light of human consciousness on what had remained in darkness. He did for language what Descartes did for the Self when he made it the foundation of human consciousness.

Flaubert knew how to vary the structure of his sentences, the choice of words, the semantic shades of meaning. His language throws a sudden light on the inner life of his characters. We soon discover that Mr. Homais' style is double-faced: his writing style is altogether different from his speech, and nothing could be more revealing for the character of this pseudo-literate pharmacist.

Thematic Studies

CHARLES DU BOS

On the "Inner Environment" in the Work of Flaubert[†]

* * * Flaubert's work and doctrine remain one of the foremost literary achievements of all times; the best minds have to keep returning to it. If such a thing as artistic morality exists—and we know that, for some, it represents the only form of religion they can wholeheartedly accept—then Flaubert remains the most complete and conscious representative, in France, of this morality and this religion. This explains why he has been attacked so vigorously, but also why he has found such loyal admirers. My intention, in this essay, is not to take sides in recent polemics.[1] Rather, after many others, I would like to return to the concept of *milieu intérieur,* as Claude Bernard[2] so aptly called it—the "inner environment" or landscape where Flaubert's work originates. His genius found expression in the constant labor that allowed him, first to control and later to organize this inner world. In art, it is true, only solutions count; but when a problem has actually been solved and the solution is called *Madame Bovary, The Sentimental Education, The Temptation of Saint Anthony,* or *The Legend of Saint Julian the Hospitaler,* then one is entitled to move back in the opposite direction and proceed from the solution to the elements that were involved in the problem. It would be inadequate to say that Flaubert never dodged difficulties; he took pride in inventing, in accumulating as many obstacles as possible. For this reason he commands not only our admiration but the deepest respect as well.

All I ask is to be able to go on admiring the masters with that intimate passion for which I would give everything, everything.

[†] *"Sur le milieu intérieur dans Flaubert"* from *Approximations I* (Paris: Plon, 1922); reprinted by permission of the publisher. This essay was written in 1921, on the occasion of the centennial of Flaubert's birth, and appears in the volume of collected essays entitled *Approximations I.* Translated here, with some very minor deletions, by Paul de Man.

1. Du Bos is referring, in all likelihood, to the debate between Proust and Thibaudet in the *Nouvelle Revue Française* (see the Introduction). [*Editor*].
2. The influence of the physiologist Claude Bernard (1813–78) on "environment" theories in French realism is well-known [*Editor*].

But as for becoming one of them . . . never; that I know for certain. I lack too much, first of all the original gift, the inner depth.[3]

I wanted to put Flaubert's own statement at the outset of such a delicate inquiry. It is obvious that, had he indeed been lacking in original gifts, we would not now have his works and still be concerned with them. But the gift alluded to here, in this text from the *Correspondence*, indicates a prerequisite for mastery, and we know the very demanding and precise meaning of that word "mastery" for Flaubert. What, then, was his own starting-point?

I am in fact, by nature, a man of vague mists, and it is by dint of patience and study that I have rid myself of all the superfluous fat that weighed down my muscles. The books I want to write most of all are precisely those for which I am least gifted.[4]

One could not think of a better description for the "inner environment" from which Flaubert sets out; it is like a huge mass, impressive in its size, but uniform and only semi–conscious, as if it were asleep. A closer look reveals thousands of infinitesimal movements, all of which react on the whole compact mass: it is a stretched–out animal, on which can be observed the blind agitation of all the smaller animal cells that compound it. *Mens agitat molem;*[5] but in this case, only the *moles* appears at first glance; the *mens* is still hidden inside, diffused among the clammy innards of the original matter. One perceives no trace of the features that will become evident later. More than that: the mass itself is surrounded, for Flaubert, by the thickest possible mist. A steady effort is needed to penetrate this fog, a display of strength utterly out of proportion with the resulting effect.[6]

You know how I am a man of impulses and depressions. If only you knew the invisible nets of inaction that imprison my body, the mists that float in my mind! Often, the smallest task to be performed fills me with the deadly fatigue of utter boredom, and I must take infinite pains to get hold of a clear idea. During my youth, I must have been immersed in some stifling opiate that stayed with me all life long.[7]

3. *Correspondence*, I, 213 (Conard ed.). The letter is from August 15, 1846. I realize that Flaubert's statements about himself that appeared in the letters should not always be taken at face value, but I will not quote a single passage from the letters that is not corroborated by my own judgment, derived from the study of the work itself. Whenever this is the case, I prefer to quote from the original document in all its beauty, rather than to offer a pale copy. Moreover, Flaubert is a special case in that his self-knowledge is almost scientifically precise and therefore altogether reliable. This is not the least attractive aspect of his widely heralded impersonality.

4. *Ibid.*, II, 132–33, August, 1852.

5. "Spirit moves matter." Virgil, *Aeneid*, VI, 727.

6. "It is by dint of study that I cleared away all my northern mists." *Correspondence*, II, 292. See also his letter to Louise Colet of August, 1846, I, 198–99.

7. *Ibid.*, II, 72, October 21, 1851.

In the beginnings, Flaubert thus seems closer to the Nordic temperament of a Jean Paul or a Jacobsen[8] than to any French or classical writer. He lives immersed in dreams as in a boundless sea.[9] Yet he cannot abide there forever: for his reverie to grow into a complete and adequate world, it must acquire a special kind of transparency and gain the unequaled strength that can only be found in such clarity. Flaubert knew this well enough, as the following sentence from *November* indicates: "I was neither pure nor strong enough to perform my duty." Close to Jean Paul as he is, he does not quite belong to the same race; and certainly not to that of De Quincey or Maurice de Guérin.[1] Reverie for Flaubert is an inner state which he passively endures rather than provokes. Although in this state one's muscular strength is temporarily subdued, it nonetheless continues to exist, longing to assert itself. What the young Flaubert mostly experiences in his dreams are not so much escapes as a certain form of torpor alternating with flashes of insight.

"Mists that float in the mind" do not make up the whole of his world: all feelings with him tend to acquire the fluidity of sensations, and every sensation in turn freezes back into a kind of stupor. Flaubert's stupor is of extraordinary intensity. In general, one might say that in him all so-called negative states reach the highest possible pitch of intensity. The sheer weight of sensation, and the ensuing immersion into matter, seem to be the recurring characteristics of Flaubert's world. The degree and the persistence of this immersion finally restore to sensation the dignity of a sentiment. In relation to women, for instance, Flaubert's attitude is very close to that of Ingres; I am not thinking, of course, of the clarity of outline, but rather of the Turkish Bath atmosphere that in Ingres' work surrounds so many figures, and not only in the painting by that name. The Mme. Renaud of the first *Sentimental Education*[2] is what comes perhaps closest in literature to some of Ingres' ladies. The "servile lover" that Baudelaire had discovered in Ingres is here too. A voluptuous torpor, a concentration of all the senses in the sense of touch, reduces the woman primarily to the status of a

8. Du Bos links together the Danish author of *Niels Lyhne*, J. P. Jacobsen (1847–85), and the German romantic Jean Paul Richter (1763–1825) as examples of Nordic indetermination [*Editor*].

9. "Beware most of all of dreams. They are dangerously attractive monsters that have already destroyed many of my things. They are the sirens of the soul; they sing and call: one heeds their call and is forever lost." *Correspondence*, I, 184, April, 1846.

1. It can be said of the French poet Maurice de Guérin (1810–39) that, like De Quincey and, for that matter,

Baudelaire or Rimbaud, he willfully created dreamlike conditions in his mind as a means to achieve poetic vision [*Editor*].

2. Flaubert's novel *The Sentimental Education* exists in two versions. The final version, which is the novel as it is generally known, dates from 1869. It was preceded by a much earlier version under the same title that Flaubert wrote in 1845; in this version, the hero Henry escapes to America with a woman older than himself, a woman called Mme. Renaud. Her equivalent in the final version is Mme. Arnoux [*Editor*].

thing, of something ready to hand. There is something close to gluttony in the way the smallest detail in her dress and her jewelry becomes the succulent object of a greedy reverie. The unquestionably vulgar overtones of this atmosphere come from the secretive, self–fondling manner in which the sensation caresses itself. Only the strength of outline that Ingres possessed and that Flaubert will acquire can overcome this initial vulgarity in an artist.

"To penetrate every atom, to descend into the depths of matter, to be matter itself!" The immortal last page of *The Temptation* does not only express Flaubert's deepest need and nostalgia; it also defines, by the same token, his most original power, his true gift.

> Being perhaps not quite so much of a dreamer as one might think, I am actually blessed with a pretty good power of observation; but I see into the pores of things, like near-sighted people who have to press them against their noses in order to see. My literary self consists of two distinct individuals: the first relishes lyrical outbursts, cries of passion, eagle's flights, full-sounding phrases, and sublime thoughts; the other digs and works away at truth with all his power; he gives as much importance to the little fact as to the large one, and he would like to give an almost material feeling of the things he creates.[3]

We do not have to concern ourselves here with the first of these two individuals. . . . When Flaubert wrote this letter to Louise Colet, *Madame Bovary* had been started four months earlier; the composition would take him three and a half years. Yet nowhere in his writings is a better anticipatory judgment of such concentrated richness to be found: "To give an almost material feeling of the thing he creates"; only the "almost" could be deleted, for Flaubert is a genius of materiality; nothing surpasses the continuity and the power of his material thought.

Yet, at the outset, this power to identify himself with matter is precisely what subdues him; instead of being useful, it merely overpowers him. The young Flaubert always seems on the verge of melting away. . . . "I feel my heart weaker and softer than a peach as it melts on the tongue." In this case, the weakness is caused by a feminine scent, but it constantly reappears in the young Flaubert, not necessarily associated with love or erotic desire. His heart is all pulp, without a core, without resistance—an overpowering languor that borders on fainting.[4]

On the other hand, this immersive power to which I alluded ear-

3. *Correspondence*, II, 84–85, January 16, 1852.
4. The story *November*, which contains the entire young Flaubert, was finished in October, 1842, and it is not until October, 1843, that Flaubert's first symptoms of nervous illness occurred, in Pont Audemer. It may be that early symptoms were present, but on the strength of these dates I leave aside the suggestion of a pathological condition. Besides, no style could be less "nervous" than Flaubert's; one could call it "anti-nervous," to the point that, at times, one longs for its very opposite.

lier unfortunately leads to a certain lack of discrimination. "Everything becomes interesting, provided one looks at it long enough";[5] Flaubert will always remain faithful to this principle. Novalis[6] already had said: "Every object is the center of a paradise." However, Novalis' eyes were so oriented that things for him could become the centers of genuine paradises . . . whereas from his earliest youth Flaubert is primarily fascinated by the spectacle of human stupidity. One can hardly regret it, in view of what we owe to this fascination, especially in *Madame Bovary*. The classic statement "stupidity attracts me" is indeed, as has often been observed, a fundamental assertion of Flaubert's nature; he tracked down stupidity in all current phrases, in all the natural reflexes of language:

> Such a wide gap separates me now from the rest of the world that I am often surprised at hearing the simplest and most natural-sounding of statements. The most ordinary word fills me at times with boundless admiration. Certain gestures, certain inflections of voice fill me with wonder, and certain types of ineptness almost make me dizzy.[7]

Anyone who lives close to words knows with an almost painful intensity this sensation which, in Flaubert, must have reached its highest possible pitch. But now that Flaubert's position is well enough secured for posterity, we may feel free to go one step further. If Flaubert spent so much energy in tracking down the kind of stupidity that reveals itself in certain idiosyncrasies of language, it is because he had, to no small extent, to fight the same tendency within himself. When he let himself go, certain expressions occurred to him that he must have eschewed with particular satisfaction, not however without adding the final insult of first recording them in print. His original self contained an element of coarse, dark vulgarity, that came to the surface especially in his pranks, but not only there. It would not be at all surprising to discover that he actually lived, in his way, a drama very similar to Gogol's, who confided to a friend that he wrote *Dead Souls* to rid himself of the vices he felt within himself. He objectified them by making them into the characters of his novel "because," he added, "I never liked my own vices." The same is true of Flaubert.

This ability to absorb himself in all things is certainly also the cause of Flaubert's lack of proportion. All sensitive readers of Flaubert have been struck by this. But we should not regret this seeming weakness either, for his tendency to overdo things, which is apparent even in his efforts to combat it, is such an inherent part of

5. *Correspondence,* I, 174.
6. The German romantic poet Novalis (1772–1801) is frequently referred to by critics such as Du Bos and Béguin, who reawakened French interest in the German romantics [*Editor*].
7. *Correspondence,* I, 174.

his genius that if he had succeeded in overcoming it altogether something very distinctive would have been lost. The manner in which his excesses occur is most interesting and deserves close study. It could not be said that individual words are, in themselves, too overpowering; the expression is almost always perfectly right, singularly strong in its aptness. The disproportion does not stem from the expression itself, but from all the agonies that have had to be endured in order to reach it. Once "put in the right place" every word undoubtedly reveals its full power: it always seems effective and rich, at times magnificent, of a somewhat dark magnificence. But it always seems to overflow into the neighboring space, if only by the determination with which it occupies its hard-earned place. Consequently, we do not find in Flaubert those traces of divine inspiration that make for continuity of style. Let me not be misunderstood: the continuity of Flaubert's style can not be denied; it is even, to quote Marcel Proust's perfect expression, a "hermetically tight" continuity.[8] But the tightness is such that the blanks that separate the words become indeed just that: blanks between which there can be no play. He lacks the supreme achievement of the great musical performers, the gift for melodious inflection, for *legato*, that most ineffable of qualities which is like the air in which the style breathes. I know of no other great writer in whose style there is as little air as in Flaubert's; he must be very great indeed for us not to regret it more often than we do. That we can even come to like this lack of proportion is the measure of his exceptional greatness.

At the beginning, we find in Flaubert this rich, seemingly inexhaustible supply of matter; as soon, however, as we try to give it shape, we lose ourselves in it as if trapped in quicksand. Flaubert's only asset, as it were, was land, but he was not given the tools with which to till his soil. He belongs among those artists who lack the convenience of talent, and thus are forced to deploy their genius to the full. He is spared the false security that stems from the possession of one or several specific gifts; because of these gifts, we will never know what certain engaging minds would really have been capable of achieving. Flaubert, on the contrary, has to be admirably persistent in order to develop to the utmost whatever problem he chooses to attack. Bergson[9] has mentioned this "self-creation which seems to be the very purpose of human existence"; Flaubert is the best and most inspiring example of self-creation to be found in

8. There are no holes in Flaubert's style. He prefers an awkward, clumsy expression to a discontinuity. I am speaking here, needless to say, of Flaubert's style, and not of his language; I consider the definition of language as the "raw material of style," which seems of late to be gaining ground, as both helpful and proven. * * *

9. The French philosopher Henri Bergson (1859–1941) is the author of *Creative Evolution;* no reference is given by du Bos for this quotation [*Editor*].

literature.

The lateness of Flaubert's first publications should not make us forget his amazing precocity. In four years, between 1838 and 1842, his personal life completes a full circle: he consumes his youth until nothing remains of it. After that, he makes a clean sweep of his recent past:

> In the first period of his life, the artist should get rid of everything intimate, original, and personal that he carries within him.[1]

He had himself tested the validity of this piece of advice * * * His first work, *November*, is a masterpiece of confessional writing, the very type of book that could never be repeated. It was followed by the first *Sentimental Education*, of which he was later to say:

> It will always be deficient, for too many things are lacking and a book is always weak by its omissions.[2]

Still, as a spiritual autobiography, the work is far from worthless. Then, in 1846, when Flaubert was not yet twenty-five years old, we come upon the following statement:

> My life of action and feeling, of contradictory impulses and numberless sensations, came to a stop at the age of twenty-two. At that time, I suddenly made considerable progress, and a substantial change took place within me. Henceforth I divided myself and the world into an inner and an outer part. To please me, the outer part could not be varied, many-colored, harmonious, and spacious enough, and I intended to enjoy it as one enjoys a spectacle; as for the inner part, I wanted to make it as concentrated as possible and allow the purest rays of the spirit to flow through the open windows of the mind.[3]

> It now seems to me that I have reached a stage beyond change; this is probably an illusion, but if so, it is the only illusion that I still maintain. I can think of nothing that could change me, I mean change my life, my daily routine. I have adopted working habits that are a real blessing to me. I read or write regularly for eight to ten hours daily, and it literally makes me ill to be disturbed. Many days go by when I don't even go as far as the terrace, and the little boat hasn't even been put afloat. I thirst for endless study and harsh work. The inner life that I always wanted finally begins to reveal itself.[4]

The inner life? Flaubert has understood that, for him, the inner life implies a definitive, radical renunciation of everything one associates in youth with a personal life. Obeying a strong instinct of

1. *Correspondence*, I, 160, May 13, 1845.
2. *Ibid.*, II, 85, January 16, 1852.
3. *Ibid.*, I, 225, August 27, 1846.
4. *Ibid.*, I, 185, April, 1846.

self-preservation he separates himself once and forever from a past in which he can only lose himself.

> The tranquility that Jules's selfishness had created around him, and the barren heights on which, in his pride, he had chosen to dwell, had so suddenly separated him from his youth and demanded such a harsh and sustained effort of will power, that he was now immune to tenderness, his heart become a stone.[5]

What actually took place, rather than this hardening of feelings, is a transfer from the heart to the head. In this new environment —a particularly stable one in Flaubert's case—the heart reveals itself capable of new manifestations, this time stable rather than diffuse. In turn, they react upon the mind:

> These ideas were so bold and so fiery that they seemed to issue from the heart.[6]

The inner life gives Flaubert the very rhythm of continuity, the power to eliminate all that is accidental, the monotony of a long and difficult task, together with the warmth and satisfaction of accomplishment. The "endless studies" precede the "harsh work": from 1846 to 1849, Flaubert reads the masters, not just with the earlier intoxication, but in order to deepen his understanding.[7] In this encounter with the highest and most diverse models, his first conception of style takes shape. When he starts putting it into practice, he is still too influenced by an over–lyrical conception of style, which leads him to put an excessive emphasis on the "canon" of the single sentence. Still, from then on, Flaubert has found his way. When Bouilhet and Maxime du Camp reject the first version of *The Temptation*, he will not only continue in the same direction, but do so with even more deliberation; his conception of style becomes all the more rigorous and tight. From the day he begins *Madame Bovary* the period of "harsh work" has started.

This "harshness" is, for Flaubert, of capital importance. In speaking of an incident of his youth, he says: "I miss here what I miss in everything except art, namely harshness."[8]

But this harshness is not merely confined to the experience of the

---

5. *Sentimental Education* (version of 1845), *Unpublished Works of Flaubert's Youth*, III, p. 242 (Conard ed.). "Unjust toward his own past, hard on himself, his superhuman stoicism had led him to forget his own passions and made him unable to understand those he had known." *Ibid.*, p. 243.
6. *Ibid.*, p. 268.
7. Flaubert is the prime example of how admiration can help to create what was originally lacking, provided this admiration goes hand in hand with a heroic will power and a flawless moral conscience, and remains entirely disinterested. Flaubert always, up to the very end, put the masters far above himself. The only way in which he tried to measure up to them was by tackling harder and more numerous problems than the greatest prose writers, in their prudent wisdom, had ever chosen to confront.
8. *Correspondence*, I, 153, end of April, 1845.

artist. Flaubert's world is fully revealed in the juxtaposition of two of his most profound statements, the first one referring to Musset— "No one can live without religion"—and the other—"I am a mystic at heart and I believe in nothing." For Flaubert to be able to believe in art (and he needed this belief for fear of finding himself like Musset, aimlessly adrift, without a compass to chart his way), art had to make demands upon him as stern as those of the strictest religion, as stern even as the most ardent form of mysticism. Only then will art be a complete religion for him, intimate, mystical in an almost Platonic sense, since the exhilaration he derives from the masterpieces fulfills his desire for the absolute. Art and mysticism concur in forming the central concern of the mature Flaubert: the imperative necessity to confront difficulty in general and all individual difficulties in particular. This concern will remain as strong as a passion and as persistent as a law.

> I don't share Turgenev's severity towards *Jack*, nor his immense admiration for *Rougon*.[9] The former has charm, the latter strength. But none is *primarily* concerned with what, in my eyes, makes up the true purpose of art, namely beauty. I remember how my heart beat and what pleasure I felt in looking at the wall of the Acropolis, a naked wall (the one on the left when one ascends to the Propylaea). I wonder whether a book, regardless of what it has to say, could not produce a similar impression? Is there not an intrinsic quality, a kind of divine power, in the precision of the construction, the economy of the means, the polish of the surface, the harmony of the whole? (I am speaking as a Platonist.)[1]

This letter to George Sand is dated 1876, but many similar passages can be found in the letters written between 1851 and 1856, while Flaubert is at work on *Madame Bovary*; I have chosen this one, because it is the most explicit and the most complete. It states Flaubert's outlook on art at a time of his maturity, an outlook that will never change. Notice his attitude towards the specificity of the personal gift, towards quality considered by itself; this individual element that we call originality and tend to emphasize more and more as the main factor in art, plays a relatively subordinate part for Flaubert as compared to the general construction. We are far removed from the early days of the first *Temptation of Saint Anthony*, where all the stress fell on pure lyrical impulse and on the sonorous beauty of the isolated sentence. By now, everything exists in terms of the book, considered on the one hand as a living being, an autonomous organism and, on the other hand, a perfect work of art existing only for the sake of its own beauty. Some very great

9. The allusion is to two famous works from the French naturalist period: the novel *Jack* by Alphonse Daudet and the voluminous *Rougon-Macquart* series by Emile Zola [*Editor*].

1. *Correspondence*, IV, 252–53.

artists remain haunted by this idea of the intrinsic quality of the Book, quite apart from what it has to say. It represents the *telos xindunos*, the extreme horizon, an almost magical impossibility. The rare efforts to reach this half-mythical entity—the Book itself —are as heroic as they are exhausting. For Dante, or Milton, or Keats—poets who never miss their mark—richness and brilliance of expression always seem to contain "something as eternal as a principle"; a maximum of beauty goes together, in their case, with a maximum of precision. By pushing the creation of beauty to its utmost limit, they also reach truth; lower forms of truth, on the level of "live experience," have very little direct claim on them. In his more modest sphere Flaubert shares similar ambitions, and this forces him to face three very distinct sets of obligations. Flaubert's moving prayer—for a prayer it is, in the full sense of the word—on his return from Africa, before embarking on the writing of *Salammbo*, deserves rereading:

> I have spent three days almost continuously asleep. My trip has faded way in the distance, almost forgotten; my head is full of confusion. I feel as if I were emerging from a two-month-long masked ball. Shall I work? Or shall I fall back into lethargy?
> Let all the forces of nature that I have gathered within me issue forth in my book. Come to my rescue, ye powers that give shape to emotions and that resurrect the past! As we *aim for beauty, we must also respect life and truth*. God of souls, have pity on my will! Give me strength and give me hope . . .[2]

"As we aim for beauty, we must also respect life and truth . . ." These are the three crushing problems that Flaubert confronted all his life, without ever sacrificing one to the other. We should not think that all writers or, in this case, all novelists, are confronted every day with the same triple task; we know very well that this is not so. Most novelists will concentrate on one of the three possibilities, chosing the one for which they are particularly gifted; if their gift is such that it allows them to achieve a masterful solution of one of the problems, their success will carry over, not without justice, into the other two realms. But Flaubert's total and emphatic honesty will not tolerate the slightest confusion between the conflicting demands of life, truth, and beauty. Repelled by the usual compromises, he keeps the problems rigorously apart and treats each of them in its own right, as if it existed by itself, convinced that, in this respect, no degree of rigor can be excessive.

No virtue can ever become a weakness, whatever the excess—but if one virtue destroys another, does it still remain one?[3]

2. *Notes de Voyage*, II, 347 (Conard ed.).
3. *Correspondence*, II, 85.

In other words, Flaubert's task consists first of all of grouping to-gether the categories of beauty, truth, and life, and then of develop-ing each of them to the utmost. They are a terrible troika for any writer to control, all the more in the case of the novelist, working in a genre that Paul Bourget rightly describes as hybrid. Each of the three horses pulls with all its strength in one direction, and Flaubert might well feel he was being torn apart in trying to keep them abreast.

He receives his reward, however, in the impression of unassail-able strength that his books deliberately produce. This strength is present in the general framework as well as in the texture of the edifice, and it lightens the surface with the grace of final stability. The end product is like a piece of cloth that will never wear out. When, as in *Salammbo*, he does not have to bother with contempo-rary life, his concern with truth can confine itself to draping the material in all its splendor—in paragraphs of a beauty akin to a superbly ordered pageant, having a dignity like that of rich brocade. *Madame Bovary* is not only *the* classical novel; it is also the only novel that can be called a work of art in the strict, precise, and one might say, narrow sense of the term.

> The true writer is one who can, while staying with the same sub-ject, give a narrative, a description, an analysis, and a dialogue, in ten volumes as well as in three pages.[4]

In this respect, *Madame Bovary* is like the museum that all aspir-ing novelists committed to art can never cease to visit. But, in my opinion, Flaubert's masterpiece is *The Sentimental Education*, be-cause the subject is such that it allows him to carry out fully his dogma of impersonality. The first reading is necessarily unsatisfac-tory, but once fallen under the spell, one can never shake it off. There is nothing to hold onto, everything oozes. One may experi-ence the flow of time itself while watching the unfolding of this frieze, in which the figures seem to be sinking into the stone rather than to stand out from it, and over which hangs a sort of a secret whitish haze. The feeling of time that emanates from *The Senti-mental Education* pervades us like a deep vibration, a kind of *vertige*. It is further increased by the subtle distance that separates the time of Flaubert's actual experience, in the ordinary sense of the term, from that of literary creation, when he recovers the sediments life has left in him. Meanwhile, these experiences have been chemically transformed by an endless series of manipulations; there-fore the book renders at first a dry, wooden sound, without timbre or accent. This is due to the fact that life has entirely been trans-muted into "truth," into the truth of the most intimate of experi-

4. *Notes de Voyage*, II, 363 (Conard ed.).

ences, an experience that knows so much about the innermost nature of things that it lies far beyond any kind of tonal or expressive effect. The weight of sensation that we found in the early Flaubert has become this incalculable, inexhaustible weight of cumulative reflections. Life is still present, but it has been preserved and absorbed for so long that it may seem buried among its own ashes. But then, at times, an unforgettable phrase, like a glowing ember, will reach us with its muted warmth, like the glow a dying fire casts upon a passerby.

ALBERT THIBAUDET

Madame Bovary†

I leave aside the question of Madame Bovary's "real" origins. It is an established fact that an authentic Mme. Bovary existed; her name was Mme. Delamarre, born Couturier, and she died on March 7th, 1848, at Ry. Certain traits of other characters in the book have also been borrowed from life models. Local pride, however, has vastly exaggerated these facts. Fantastic details have been added, a legend has been invented, and the entire background of *Madame Bovary* can now be bought on postcards in the town of Ry, just as the baobab house might be offered for sale in Tasascon.[1] Flaubert was overstating the case when he claimed that *Madame Bovary* was pure invention and that no such place as Yonville-l'Abbaye ever existed. But the opposite assertion is equally false. What matters for us is the truth of his statement in a letter in 1853: "My poor Emma Bovary doubtlessly is suffering and crying at this very moment in at least twenty French villages."[2] This is one end of the chain; let us consider the other end. Descharmes wrote: A person who knew Mlle. Amelie Bosquet to whom Flaubert addressed many letters, recently told me that, when Mlle. Bosquet asked the novelist who had been the model for Mme. Bovary, he reportedly replied, emphatically repeating his statement: "I myself am Mme. Bovary! at least, I think so."[3] One should beware of hearsay stories, but we can be certain that this one could hardly have been invented by an elderly spinster.

In 1850, while traveling in Constantinople, Flaubert hears of

† From Chapter 5 of *Gustave Flaubert* by Albert Thibaudet (Paris: Gallimard, 1935); reprinted by permission of the publisher. Translated by Paul de Man.
1. In Alphonse Daudet's famous spoof on the vivid imagination of the inhabitants of the South of France entitled *Tartarin de Tarascon* (1872), the hero keeps a small cactus plant which he refers to as the giant-tree baobab [*Editor*].
2. *Correspondence*, III, 291.
3. René Descharmes, *Flaubert before 1857*, p. 103.

Balzac's death and he expresses his feelings in a letter to Bouilhet. I do not know whether Flaubert consciously saw himself as Balzac's successor. However, it is undeniable that in the years around 1850, so decisive in the history of the novel, an inner logic was developed within the novel, from Balzac to Flaubert, just as an inner logic took form in French tragedy from Corneille to Racine. The novels of Balzac are constructed novels, sometimes excessively so; his imagination always remained lit, like the fire in the Cyclops'[4] smithies. Balzac was a novelist endowed with the same natural power that inspired Corneille as a dramatist. But Flaubert set out from the antipodes of the Balzacian novel when he wrote the following sentence, one which would certainly have been endorsed by the author of *Berenice:*[5] "I would like to write books in which I have only to write sentences, if I may say so, just as I have only to breathe in order to remain alive; I am bored by the subtleties of composition, by combinations aimed at effect, by all the calculations involved in the design, but which, nevertheless, are art, for style depends on these and on these alone." Spontaneity of conception remains for him the highest value. This spontaneity, which is that of Racine, not that of Corneille or Balzac, does not prevent him from carrying out all the demands of his art with consummate skill. With cold detachment, he performs the technical machinations which bore him to tears; for Balzac, they would have been an inherent part of the work from its very beginning, a part of the original organic idea. The technique of *Madame Bovary* has become a model for all novels, as that of *Andromache*[6] is considered the model for all tragedies. Today, any discussion on the art of fiction among critics and novelists will inevitably turn to *Madame Bovary;* the book will be used to illustrate all new theories and will provide the main basis for the discussion.

And yet, Flaubert himself had serious misgivings about the organization of his novel. It pleases him as little as the organization of *Salammbo* and of the second *Sentimental Education.* With *Bouvard and Pécuchet,* he will abandon forever all idea of organization, in the usual sense of the term.

> I think that the book will have a serious weakness, namely the relative length of the parts. I already have 260 pages that contain only preparatory action . . . The conclusion, which will narrate the death of my heroine, her burial and the ensuing distress of the husband, will take at least 260 pages. This leaves only 120 to 160 pages for the action properly speaking.

4. The Cyclopses are mythological one-eyed giants said to assist Hephaistos (the Roman Vulcan) in his forge under Mount Etna [*Editor*].

5. *Berenice* is a famous tragedy by Racine, dating from 1670.
6. *Andromaque,* also by Racine, dates from 1657.

In his own defense, he states that the book is

> a biography, rather than a developed dramatic situation. It contains little action: if the dramatic element remains thoroughly immersed in the general tone of the work, the lack of proportion between the different episodes and their development is likely to remain unnoticed. Moreover, it seems to me that life itself is a litle like that.

Flaubert's choice of vocabulary is quite revealing here. "Action" and "dramatic element" are used as closely synonymous with composition or organization; it seems that the novel can do without them precisely because it is unlike the theater. The theater abstracts and retains privileged moments, moments of crisis; as such, it is forced to compose and to organize: it must group the moments in such a way that a maximum of useful effort is contained in a minimum of time and space. The dramatist is governed by time, whereas the novelist controls it; he can cut an entire life out of the cloth of time, and do so at his own will. Flaubert's novel is not a "human comedy" like Balzac's, but a pure novel. It is even less a *romanesque* novel of adventure; this is a false and superficial label applied to a bastard mixture of narrative and of stage effects which has never produced a perfect work: Balzac's *Colonel Chabert* is probably the masterpiece of the genre and it could never rank with his *Father Goriot* or *The Search for the Absolute*, precisely because it is a hybrid genre.

Like *David Copperfield* or George Eliot's *The Mill on the Floss*, *Madame Bovary* can be called a biography. But rather than the biography of one individual, it is a sequence of interrelated life histories. From a certain point of view, the individual biography which delimits the novel's dimension in time, is that of Charles Bovary, not Emma's. The book opens with his entrance into college—and with his cap—and it ends with his death.

To be more accurate, *Madame Bovary* seems to be a biography of human life in general rather than of a particular person (in its most extreme form, a novel would, in theory, consist of a pure scheme of life, whereas the most extreme form of drama would be a pure scheme of motion). To be human is to feel oneself as a conglomeration of possibilities, a multiplicity of potential personalities; the artist is the one who makes this potential real. It would take some effort to apply so general a truth to all characters in Flaubert's novel—such as, for instance, Charles Bovary. The first pages of the novel consist of memories from school-life. They are a first introduction into this complex world. They create a mood and allow Flaubert to put himself in the right frame of mind to embark on his task. Up till now, he had primarily represented himself in all his writings. But now, after what appears on the surface as a kind of literary conversion, he returns to the very beginnings of his life to find a human being who is the exact opposite of himself—or, rather, a non-being opposed to his own self. "It would now be impossible for any of us to remember anything about him. He was a youth of even temperament." Yet, *Madame Bovary* came into being because from the school scene on, which is like a summary of existence, Charles's entire life is prefigured. Without realizing it, Charles had already been selected as a mate by the Emma Flaubert who was going to drag him into the light of notoriety and make him part of an inseparable couple. This same Emma Flaubert had written in the early *Memoirs of a Madman*:[7] "I shall see myself seated at my desk in the classroom, absorbed in my dreams of the future, thinking the most sublime thoughts that the imagination of a child can conjure up, while the schoolmaster was making fun of my Latin verses, and my schoolmates looked at me in derision. The fools! They make fun of me! those cowardly, vulgar, narrow-minded simpletons; me whose spirit was swept to the outermost limits of creation and lost itself in all the worlds of poetry, me, who felt myself superior to them all, who was blessed with infinite joys and knew celestial ecstacies in contemplating the intimate revelations of my soul!" Fortunate mockery! It awakened Flaubert's consciousness and taught him self-mockery, bringing about the self-cure which would allow him to write *Madame Bovary*, thus repaying for the good they had done him, the dullards who had mocked him while he was raising them to a literary existence.

Flaubert's novel is entirely contained between Charles Bovary's cap and his profound statement at the end, the only one he will ever pronounce, after which nothing is left for him to do but drop to the ground like a ripe apple: "Fate willed it this way!" Such is Charles's beginning and his end. In a page of his early travel impressions entitled *Along Fields and Sea Shores*[8] Flaubert had already revealed his intention of writing the chapter on hats that is still missing in literature; the passage on Breton hats is a prelude to Charles's famous cap. With its "dumb ugliness that had depths of expression like an imbecile's face," the whole of Yonville-l'Abbaye is already contained in the cap. A miserable life, but a life just the same; the novel of a miserable life, but nevertheless a life, is being prepared to crown the forehead of the same child, whose name is not Charles but Legion. And by an ironic play of fate it is placed there before the eyes of the schoolboy whose Latin verses amused

7. *Mémoires d'un Fou*, a short narrative of approximately 75 pages, was written by Flaubert when he was 17 years old.

8. On *Par les Champs et par les Grèves*, see note 8 on p. 450.

his teacher and the class. In a certain literary perspective, this cap is related to the white plume of Henry IV and of Cyrano de Bergerac, as well as to the little white feather and dot in *Un Coup de Dés*.[9]

This type of lyricism or, rather, of counterlyricism is very typical of Flaubert. It demands some preparation to be appreciated and many a reader approves it with misgivings. The detail of the hat is as essential as it is gratuitous—a proper definition, be it said in passing, of pure lyricism and of spontaneous symbolism as well. Three times Flaubert has introduced into his novel this touch worthy of a great poet, similar to the rooster in Rembrandt's *Nightwatch*: the cap, the wedding cake and the toy of Homais' children. We know the latter only from Maxime du Camp's description: "Flaubert had planned to give the description of a toy he had seen. He had been struck by its odd features and wanted to use it in his novel as a plaything for Homais' sons. It took him all of ten pages to describe the complicated machine which represented, I believe, the court of the King of Siam. The battle between Bouilhet and Flaubert lasted for more than a week, but common sense finally won out and the toy disappeared from the book because it slowed down the action all too much." The text survives perhaps in Flaubert's papers. One day, it may reappear in new editions of *Madame Bovary* like the invocation to the Muses in Montesquieu's *Spirit of Laws*,[1] which the author suppressed for similar reasons but which now reappears in the form of notes in all recent editions.

The development of the action, in *Madame Bovary*, does not occur by a simple succession of events but by the concentric expansion of a theme, first encountered in its simplest form, then gradually gaining in richness and complexity. The process reflects the very motion of fate. We call "fated" a development that was already contained in a previous situation but without being apparent. We have a feeling of fatality when we feel that life was not worth living, because we have come back to exactly the same point from which we started, and discovered that the road which was to be one of discovery turns out to be the circular path of our prison walls.

And yet, this novel of fate is a novel of life and of hope.

When we consider these creatures as completed and unified destinies, their lives are indeed heart-rending failures; but all of them have known the sacred moments after which there can only be de-

---

9. King Henry IV invited the French to "rally around his white plume." Cyrano de Bergerac, himself the author of a famous seventeenth-century utopian narrative, wears a cocky hat in the heroic comedy that Edmond Rostand derived from his life in 1897. An element of defiant cockiness is also present in the feathered hat worn by the poet–hero of Mallarmé's late and obscure text *Un Coup de Dés;* Thibaudet is the author of a book on Mallarmé [*Editor*].

1. Montesquieu's famous treatise on the origins of law appeared in 1748 [*Editor*].

cline and preparation for the grave. Charles experiences it when, hidden in a cartload, he sees the signal announcing from the window of Rouault's farmhouse that he has been accepted. Emma experiences it in the early phases of her love for Rodolphe. Seen as a whole, the novel is not one–sidedly pessimistic; dark and light are evenly marked. Flaubert has not reached the total desolation of *Bouvard and Pécuchet*. Tostes and Yonville are like two concentric circles. Tostes is a more empty and cursory image than Yonville. The transition from one town to another, from one form of existence in the Bovary household to another which is yet the same, is a masterpiece of subtle progression. Tostes resembles Yonville as a sketch resembles the final picture. Flaubert takes pains not to fill in the details of his earlier outline, yet all the earlier characteristics of Yonville are already there, albeit in the general and abstract outline, without proper names, like an architectural model. "Every day at the same time the schoolmaster in a black skullcap opened the shutters of his house, and the village policeman, wearing his sword over his blouse, passed by." The two nameless figures suffice here to express the routine of a small town. But a small town is not just like one of those clocks on which the hours are struck by automatons; it also has a human content, people who want to be elsewhere, who are a prey to "Bovarysme." The hairdresser represents this urge, the artistic element: "He . . . lamented his wasted calling, his hopeless future, and dreaming of some shop in a big town—at Rouen, for example, overlooking the harbor, near the theater—he walked up and down all day from the town hall to the church, somber and waiting for customers." The barrel organ that plays under her window provides the proper musical accompaniment to the first sketch of the novel that will narrate these lives.

The end of the story at Tostes also ends the actual marital life of Madame Bovary. Since all the attention is concentrated on Emma and Charles's joint existence, no other characters are needed; Flaubert introduces none, except for the servant. Tostes is no stage on which things are happening; Flaubert uses it to show how Charles lives, sleeps, dresses, and eats, how he gets on his wife's nerves and depresses her. The first part closes when she throws her bridal bouquet in the fire. "She watched it burn . . . the little pasteboard berries burst . . ."

This sketch is followed by the completed picture, the stage on which characters and events will appear. Tostes was the small town; Yonville too is the small town but it is Yonville as well. Tostes lost itself to become the typical small town, but now the small town mingles with the reality of Yonville and becomes this reality; it is the usual transubstantiation of art. This is why the second part begins with a detailed description of Yonville, in the manner of

Balzac. The purpose is to create a genuine setting, to set the stage, not for a human comedy but for the comedy of human stupidity and suffering. Flaubert goes about this task with a quiet and merciless thoroughness: the notary's house, the church, the townhall, and facing the Golden Lion Hotel, M. Homais' pharmacy with its red and green bocals, which shine in the evening like Bengal fires. The dinner at the Golden Lion follows the typical, perhaps all too typical, technique of exposition, as in Racine's *Bajazet:* all the inhabitants of Yonville are successively described from the point of view that reveals them most clearly, and Homais is allowed to dominate the scene. This is the chosen setting in which all the characters, and especially Emma, will come to light and their destinies unfold.

Emma passes with good reason for one of the most masterful portraits of a woman in fiction; the most living and the truest to life. "A masterpiece," Dupanloup told Dumas, "yes, a true masterpiece, for those who have been confessors in the provinces." [2] Flaubert substituted his artistic intuition for the confessor's experience; he would not have created this masterpiece if he hadn't identified with his heroine and shared her existence. He created her, not only out of the recollections of his own soul, but out of the recollections of his own flesh. She is never seen from the same distant and ironic viewpoint as the other characters in the book. Women are well aware of this and recognize in her their inner beauty and their inner suffering, as a man endowed with a noble imagination is bound to recognize himself in Don Quixote. During his lawsuit, the wife of Emperor Napoleon III is said to have been on Flaubert's side.

Emma is a true heroine—unlike Sancho and Homais, who are counterheroes—because she has senses. In trying to explain the superiority of *Madame Bovary* over the *Sentimental Education,* Brunetière[3] said that Emma's character represents something "stronger and more refined than the commonplace" without which there can not be a truly great novel. "In the nature of this woman, commonplace as she is, there is something extreme and, for that reason, rare. It is the refinement of her senses." There is nothing extreme or rare in any of the characters in the *Education.* But Faguet writes: "Mme. Bovary is not exactly a sensuous person; she is above all a 'romantic,' a mental type, as the psychologists would call it; her first fault stems from an unbridled imagination rather than from a lack of control over the senses. The reason for the first

2. Dupanloup was a famous French prelate who lived from 1802 to 1878; Alexandre Dumas is the author of *The Three Musketeers.* The statement is quoted in the *Journal* of the Goncourt brothers, V, 230 [*Editor*].

3. The prominent critic and historian Ferdinand Brunetière (1849–1906) wrote on Flaubert in *The Naturalist Novel* [*Editor*].

downfall is her desire to know love; in her second downfall, she is moved by the desire to give herself to the man she loves."[4]

Brunetière is right, not Faguet. Emma is first and foremost a person of sensuous nature; she is like the artist in that she is endowed with an unusual degree of sensuality. This is why, as an artist, Flaubert can identify with her and assert: I myself am Mme. Bovary. Whenever Emma is seen in purely sensuous terms, he speaks of her with a delicate, almost religious feeling, the way Milton speaks of Eve. He relinquishes his cold and detached tone and shifts to a lyrical voice, indicating that the author is using the character as a substitute for himself. So, for instance, when she has first given herself to Rodolphe:

> The shades of night were falling: the horizontal sun passing between the branches dazzled the eyes. Here and there around her in the leaves or on the ground, trembled luminous patches, as if humming-birds flying about had scattered their feathers. Silence was everywhere; something sweet seemed to come forth from the trees. She felt her heartbeat return, and the blood coursing through her flesh like a river of milk. Then far away, beyond the wood, on the other hills, she heard a vague prolonged cry, a voice which lingered, and in silence she heard it mingling like music with the last pulsations of her throbbing nerves. Rodolphe, a cigar between his lips, was mending with his penknife one of the two broken bridles.

If the novel itself is like a substance in motion, then Emma is the one who is being carried by the flow of this stream. She is the stream, whereas Rodolphe is only another pebble among the stones deposited on the riverbanks.

Flaubert was able to forestall his own critics, and he rightly showed that "intelligent readers want their characters all of a piece and consistent, as they only appear in books." For him, to the contrary, "Ulysses is, perhaps, the strongest character–type in all ancient literature, and Hamlet in modern literature," because of their complexity. Mme. Bovary is not simple. Her sensuality is combined with a vulgar imagination and a considerable degree of naïveté—or, in other words, of stupidity. Flaubert needed a character of this kind to satisfy his poetical as well as his critical instinct, his sense of beauty as well as his taste for a sad, grotesque incongruity.

Emma, like Don Quixote, doesn't place her desire and the things she desires on the same plane. Emma's sensuous desire, like Don Quixote's generous fantasies, are in themselves magnificent realities in which Flaubert and Cervantes project the best part of themselves. They admire desire and abandonment, but they have

4. *The Naturalist Novel*, p. 181.

contempt for the things desired, the miserable bottle that comes out of a ridiculous pharmacy. Neither have any illusions about the value of the object desired by the imagination, and one half of their artistic nature—the realist half—mercilessly paints these mediocre and derisive objects.

Apart from her sensuous desire, everything else about Emma is mediocre. Flaubert marks her with this terrible trait: "She was incapable of understanding what she did not experience, or of believing anything that did not take on a conventional form." At heart, she is still the Norman peasant, "callous, not very responsive to the emotions of others, like most people of peasant stock whose souls always retain some of the coarseness of their father's hands."

She is more ardent than passionate. She loves life, pleasure, love itself much more than she loves a man; she is made to have lovers rather than a lover. It is true that she loves Rodolphe with all the fervor of her body, and with him she experiences the moment of her complete, perfect and brief fulfillment; her illness, however, after Rodolphe's desertion, is sufficient to cure her of this love. She does not die from love, but from weakness and a total inability to look ahead, a naïveté which makes her an easy prey to deceit in love as well as in business. She lives in the present and is unable to resist the slightest impulse. When she seems to be resisting temptation, during her first and silent love for Léon, this outward resistance is only a shell within which the *delectatio morosa* which Flaubert understood so well was allowed to expand freely. "The housewives admired her thrift, the patients her politeness, the poor her charity. But she was eaten up with desires, with rage, with hate. The rigid folds of her dress covered a tormented heart of which her chaste lips never spoke. She was in love with Léon, and sought solitude that she might more easily delight in his image. His physical presence troubled the voluptuousness of this meditation. Emma thrilled at the sound of his step; then in his presence the emotion subsided, and afterwards there remained in her only an immense astonishment that ended in sorrow." (Are these not memories from Flaubert's own adolescence, boldly transposed into a feminine character?) All this provides the real Emma with the necessary time to let her real self mature and appear in full daylight when the right moment comes. Later on, when the desire for her lover seizes upon her, she will simply go to find him in his own house. The final stages of her life that will lead her to her death are strictly personal, limited to the injustice and the criminality of the solitary self. Flaubert's novel is as Jansenist in spirit as Racine's *Phèdre*,[5] and he has treated

5. The somber atmosphere of guilt and contrition that pervades the tragedy *Phèdre* is often attributed to Racine's adhesion to the stern theology of the Jansenists, a dominant influence on French religious thought in the seventeenth century [*Editor*].

Emma's death as a damnation. He has made the devil present in the figure of the blind man, the grimacing monster she glimpsed during her adulterous trips to Rouen, the beggar to whom she throws her last piece of silver, as a lost soul is cast to the devil by the act of suicide. She dies with an atrocious laugh of horror and despair, as she hears him singing under her window, "thinking she saw the hideous face of the poor wretch loom out of the eternal darkness like a menace." This symbol of damnation was certainly present in Flaubert's mind; he wrote to Bouilhet that the blind man had to be present at Emma's death and that, for that reason, he needed to invent the episode of Homais' ointment. Lamartine, who was greatly disturbed by *Madame Bovary*, told Flaubert that he found the end of the book revolting: the punishment greatly surpassed the crime. It is true that we are here in a very different mood than in *Jocelyn*.[6]

The fact is that Lamartine, in *Jocelyn*, was delighting in himself, while Flaubert, in *Madame Bovary*, subjects himself to the most scathing self-criticism. Emma symbolizes the double illusion which he has only very recently overcome. First, the illusion that things change for the better in time, an illusion as necessary to life as water is to plants: "She did not believe that things could remain the same in different places, and since the portion of her life that lay behind her had been bad, no doubt that which remained to be lived would be better". Then, the same illusion in spatial terms: "The closer things were to her, the more her thoughts turned away from them. All her immediate surroundings, the boring countryside, the stupid petty bourgeois, the mediocrity of existence, seemed to her to be exceptions in the world, a particular fate of which she was the victim, while an immense domain of passion and happiness stretched out beyond, as far as the eye could reach." When she is in the convent, she dreams of the outside world; later, she will remember these schooldays as her only moments of true happiness, because at that time the entire world was still a blank page and her heart full of infinite possibilities. On returning home to her father, she can no longer cope with country life and she accepts Charles, the healthy doctor who rides around on horseback, merely because he represents the outside world. When she marries him, she dreams of other places. It is true then, after all, that she is Brunetière's sensuous woman as well as Faguet's woman of imagination. But she is still something else besides.

She is also the person without luck. From a certain point of view, *Madame Bovary* is the novel of failure and bad luck, of a particularly unfortunate concentration of circumstances. Is Emma really

6. *Jocelyn* is the title of a lengthy narrative poem by Lamartine written in 1836, full of pious sentiment [*Editor*].

altogether ridiculous and wrong when she believes that, in another setting and surrounded by different people, she might have been relatively happy? Don Quixote was bound to be disappointed, for he lives in a time and place when it is much easier to find windmills than knights-errant. His misadventures are not a matter of good or bad fortune; but, to a very considerable extent, Emma is a victim of circumstance. Considering how easily and thoroughly she is seduced by her lovers, it would seem that a certain kind of husband would conceivably have satisfied her heart and her senses. But Charles, one could say, has been systematically invented to be her undoer. She "made efforts to love him and repented in tears for having given in to another." It took the incident of the clubfoot to make her realize once and forever the incurable stupidity of her husband. In his failure, Charles becomes the cause and the symbol for all the failures in Emma's life. She could have experienced the great revenge and pride of women, to give birth to a man. "She hoped for a son; he would be strong and dark; she would call him Georges, and this idea of having a male child was like a revenge for all her impotence in the past." But it is a girl. In looking for religious help, she might have had better luck than with the unusually inept Bournisien, another character worthy of her bad luck. Her only acquaintance at Yonville is Mme. Homais who, by a refined irony of fate, is the female equivalent of Bovary himself. And Lheureux! with Homais, the one who ends up on top, as fortunate in life as his name suggests.[7] The walls against which she will finally dash herself to pieces have been erected around her as by an evil artist. When Charles says: Fate willed it that way! the reader acquiesces, and feels he has been reading the story of an ill-starred woman. *Madame Bovary*, like *Manon Lescaut*,[8] is a novel of love; like *Don Quixote*, it is a novel of the fictional imagination—but, aside from this, it is also, like Voltaire's *Candide*, a novel of fate.

A novel of fate, of destiny, can only exist in the absence of a strong will power. This is true in Emma's case. She is sustained by no will power, either from within herself, or from her husband. She is surrounded by the will of others, the will to seduce her in the person of Rodolphe, and the will to despoil her in Lheureux. In the absence of will power, she has enough passion, enough spontaneous excitement and somber selfishness to drive a man to criminal deeds. In her question: "Have you got your gun?" We see her willingness to make Rodolphe into a murderer; in her "At your office," that she would make Léon a thief; and by Binet's reply of "Madame, how dare you?" we surmise some suggestion

---

7. "Heureux" means happy in French; Lheureux is "the happy one" or, ironically, the one associated with happiness. [*Editor*].

8. *Manon Lescaut* (1713) by the Abbé Prévost tells the story of the ardent but ill-starred love affair between Manon and the chevalier Des Grieux [*Editor*].

on her part concerning the tax-collector's safe.

Though she is a creature of passion, she doesn't kill herself out of love but for money; she is not punished as an adulterous woman, but as an untidy housekeeper. This has surprised some, who consider that the two parts of the novel are not consistent with each other. But logical consistency, in fiction, is a certain road to disaster; there is no need for the two parts to be logically connected. In the flesh and the blood of a living creature, they are perfectly coherent. For women, beauty is first of all a matter of décor and, for the bourgeois daughter of a farmer, the substance of life is likely to consist of a rather showy kind of cheap silverware. It has been observed that in *Gil Blas*[9] much stress is put on eating and that Lesage is one of the first novelists to show his people at the dinner table. Similarly, Balzac had introduced in his novels lives shaped by the ups and downs of financial transactions, in which all feelings are colored and distorted by the power of money. In the nineteenth century, this was a fundamental theme of the realistic novel. In the bourgeois world (as well as the other), love and money go together just as closely as love goes together with ambition, pride, and the affairs of the king in classical tragedy. In the final part of the novel, Léon and Lheureux are the two extremities of the candle that Emma is burning at both ends.

All this aspect of the novel is prefigured in the evening at Vaubeyssard. The soles of Emma's satin shoes "were yellowed with the slippery wax of the dancing floor. Her heart resembled them; in its contact with wealth, something had rubbed off on it that could not be removed." At first, in her schoolgirl dreams, she had dreamt of love as an almost otherworldly experience. The ball at the château convinces her that the world of the keepsakes and the novels really exists, and she identifies it with the world of wealth. She is left with the empty cigar case which she has picked up and by means of which, as with an archeological document, she reconstructs a world of love and luxury, joined like body and soul in the dream of an ideal life. "In her desire, she would confuse the sensuous pleasures of wealth with the raptures of the heart, the refinement of manners with the delicacy of sentiments." Her life will follow a parallel course on the financial and on the sentimental plane. The disappointments of the one coincide with the troubles of the other. Rodolphe and Lheureux are placed on either side of her life to exploit and destroy her, not through malicious intent, but because they act in accordance with the law of nature and society. They act according to the "right" of the seducer, which in France is always backed by established custom, and by the "right" of the usurer which is mistaken for law. After Rodolphe's letter, Emma falls ill and almost dies; after Lheureux's distraint, she dies in fact. The two faces of

9. Lesage's novel of adventure appeared between 1715 and 1736 [*Editor*].

her destiny are symmetrical. This destiny is all of a piece. "The desires, the longing for money, and the melancholy of passion all blended into one suffering, and instead of putting it out of her mind, she made her thoughts cling to it, urging herself to pain and seeking everywhere the opportunity to revive it. A poorly served dish, a half open door would aggravate her; she bewailed the clothes she did not have, the happiness she had missed, her overexalted dreams, her too cramped home."

Like Sancho Panza and Molière's Tartuffe,[1] Mme. Bovary is so real that she transcends reality and has become a type. The victim of love and the victim of usury do not seem a harmonious combination in the eyes of certain critics, just as La Bruyère found it impossible to reconcile Tartuffe's hypocrisy with his lack of prudence in love.[2] Similarly, in his chapter on Stendhal in *Politicians and Moralists*, Faguet claims not to understand how Julien Sorel's ambition can be reconciled with his impetuous act of revenge in the shooting of Mme. de Rênal as the end of *The Red and the Black*. It seems, however, that a creature of fiction can only become a type when it exhibits such apparent anomalies of character; it seems that in this field also, as in the law of binocular vision, a perspective of real depth can only be achieved by the juxtaposition of two images. When Flaubert embarked on the gigantic *Temptation of Saint Anthony*, he had meant to write his *Faust*. He must have realized his mistake. It is striking, however, that it is precisely after his trip to the Orient, when he has given up his *Temptation* and embarked, at Bouilhet's advice, on the story of Delmarre and Delamarre's wife, that he succeeds in creating something close to a French *Faust*.

ERICH AUERBACH

[The Realism of Flaubert]†

In the generation which follows Balzac, there is a strong reaction: —In Flaubert realism becomes impartial, impersonal, and objective. In an earlier study, "Serious Imitation of Everyday Life," I ana-

1. In the play of that name Molière has described the typical hypocrite, as he describes the typical miser in the character Harpagon from *l'Avare* [*Editor*]. 2. Tartuffe's undoing is caused by his impetuous proposals to the wife of his too trusting protector [*Editor*].
† The passage is taken from Erich Auerbach's *Mimesis: The Representation of Reality in Western Literature*, translated from the German by W. R. Trask (Princeton University Press,

1953), pp. 425–33. Copyright © 1953, Princeton University Press; reprinted by permission of the publishers. The title of the chapter is "In the Hotel de la Mole," in reference to the extract from Stendhal's *The Red and the Black* with which it starts. The section on Stendhal is followed by a section on Balzac, using an example from *Father Goriot*, and the chapter ends with the section on *Madame Bovary* here reprinted.

lyzed a paragraph from *Madame Bovary* from this point of view, and will here, with slight changes and abridgements, reproduce the pages concerned, since they are in line with the present train of thought and since it is unlikely, in view of the time and place of their publication (Istanbul, 1937), that they have reached many readers. The paragraph concerned occurs in part 1, chapter 9, of *Madame Bovary*:

> Mais c'était surtout aux heures des repas qu'elle n'en pouvait plus, dans cette petite salle au rez-dechaussée, avec le poêle qui fumait, la porte qui criait, les murs qui suintaient, les pavés humides; toute l'amertume de l'existence lui semblait servie sur son assiette, et, à la fumée du bouilli, il montait du fond de son âme comme d'autres bouffées d'affadissement. Charles était long à manger; elle grignotait quelques noisettes, ou bien, appuyée du coude, s'amusait, avec la pointe de son couteau, de faire des raies sur la toile cirée.

> [But it was above all at mealtimes that she could bear it no longer, in that little room on the ground floor, with the smoking stove, the creaking door, the oozing walls, the damp floor-tiles; all the bitterness of life seemed to be served to her on her plate, and, with the steam from the boiled beef, there rose from the depths of her soul other exhalations as it were of disgust. Charles was a slow eater; she would nibble a few hazel-nuts, or else, leaning on her elbow, would amuse herself making marks on the oilcloth with the point of her table-knife.]

The paragraph forms the climax of a presentation whose subject is Emma Bovary's dissatisfaction with her life in Tostes. She has long hoped for a sudden event which would give a new turn to it—to her life without elegance, adventure, and love, in the depths of the provinces, beside a mediocre and boring husband; she has even made preparations for such an event, has lavished care on herself and her house, as if to earn that turn of fate, to be worthy of it; when it does not come, she is seized with unrest and despair. All this Flaubert describes in several pictures which portray Emma's world as it now appears to her; its cheerlessness, unvaryingness, grayness, staleness, airlessness, and inescapability now first become clearly apparent to her when she has no more hope of fleeing from it. Our paragraph is the climax of the portrayal of her despair. After it we are told how she lets everything in the house go, neglects herself, and begins to fall ill, so that her husband decides to leave Tostes, thinking that the climate does not agree with her.

The paragraph itself presents a picture—man and wife together at mealtime. But the picture is not presented in and for itself; it is subordinated to the dominant subject, Emma's despair. Hence it is not put before the reader directly: here the two sit at table—there the reader stands watching them. Instead, the reader first sees Emma, who has been much in evidence in the preceding pages, and he sees the picture first through her; directly, he sees only Emma's inner state; he sees what goes on at the meal indirectly, from within her state, in the light of her perception. The first words of the paragraph, *Mais c'était surtout aux heures des repas qu'elle n'en pouvait plus* . . . state the theme, and all that follows is but a development of it. Not only are the phrases dependent upon *dans* and *avec*, which define the physical scene, a commentary on *elle n'en pouvait plus* in their piling up of the individual elements of discomfort, but the following clause too, which tells of the distaste aroused in her by the food, accords with the principal purpose both in sense and rhythm. When we read further, *Charles était long à manger*, this, though grammatically a new sentence and rhythmically a new movement, is still only a resumption, a variation, of the principal theme; not until we come to the contrast between his leisurely eating and her disgust and to the nervous gestures of her despair, which are described immediately afterward, does the sentence acquire its true significance. The husband, unconcernedly eating, becomes ludicrous and almost ghastly; when Emma looks at him and sees him sitting there eating, he becomes the actual cause of the *elle n'en pouvait plus*; because everything else that arouses her desperation—the gloomy room, the commonplace food, the lack of a tablecloth, the hopelessness of it all—appears to her, and through her to the reader also, as something that is connected with him, that emanates from him, and that would be entirely different if he were different from what he is.

The situation, then, is not presented simply as a picture, but we are first given Emma and then the situation through her. It is not, however, a matter—as it is in many first-person novels and other later works of a similar type—of a simple representation of the content of Emma's consciousness, of *what* she feels *as* she feels it. Though the light which illuminates the picture proceeds from her, she is yet herself part of the picture, she is situated within it. In this she recalls the speaker in the scene from Petronius[1] discussed in our second chapter; but the means Flaubert employs are different. Here it is not Emma who speaks, but the writer. *Le poêle qui fumait, la porte qui criait, les murs qui suintaient, les pavés humides*—all this, of course, Emma sees and feels, but she would not be able to sum it all up in this way. *Toute l'amertume de l'existence lui semblait servie sur son assiette*—she doubtless has such a feeling; but if she wanted to express it, it would not come out like that; she has neither the intelligence nor the cold candor of self-accounting neces-

---

1. Auerbach used a passage from the Latin writer Petronius (1st century A.D.) in the second chapter of *Mimesis* [*Editor*].

sary for such a formulation. To be sure, there is nothing of Flaubert's life in these words, but only Emma's; Flaubert does nothing but bestow the power of mature expression upon the material which she affords, in its complete subjectivity. If Emma could do this herself, she would no longer be what she is, she would have outgrown herself and thereby saved herself. So she does not simply see, but is herself seen as one seeing, and is thus judged, simply through a plain description of her subjective life, out of her own feelings. Reading in a later passage (part 2, chapter 12): *jamais Charles ne lui paraissait aussi désagréable, avoir les doigts aussi carrés, l'esprit aussi lourd, les façons si communes. . .* , the reader perhaps thinks for a moment that this strange series is an emotional piling up of the causes that time and again bring Emma's aversion to her husband to the boiling point, and that she herself is, as it were, inwardly speaking these words; that this, then, is an example of *erlebte Rede*.[2] But this would be a mistake. We have here, to be sure, a number of paradigmatic causes of Emma's aversion, but they are put together deliberately by the writer, not emotionally by Emma. For Emma feels much more, and much more confusedly; she sees other things than these—in his body, his manners, his dress; memories mix in; meanwhile she perhaps hears him speak, perhaps feels his hand, his breath, sees him walk about, good-hearted, limited, unappetizing, and unaware; she has countless confused impressions. The only thing that is clearly defined is the result of all this, her aversion to him, which she must hide. Flaubert transfers the clearness to the impressions; he selects three, apparently quite at random, but which are paradigmatically taken from Bovary's physique, his mentality, and his behavior; and he arranges them as if they were three shocks which Emma felt one after the other. This is not at all a naturalistic representation of consciousness. Natural shocks occur quite differently. The ordering hand of the writer is present here, deliberately summing up the confusion of the psychological situation in the direction toward which it tends of itself—the direction of "aversion to Charles Bovary." This ordering of the psychological situation does not, to be sure, derive its standards from without, but from the material of the situation itself. It is the type of ordering which must be employed if the situation itself is to be translated into language without admixture.

In a comparison of this type of presentation with those of Stendhal and Balzac, it is to be observed by way of introduction that here too the two distinguishing characteristics of modern realism are to be found; here too real everyday occurrences in a low social stratum, the provincial petty bourgeoisie, are taken very seriously; here too everyday occurrences are accurately and profoundly set in a

2. Language as it is actually experienced and used by the speaker [*Editor*].

definite period of contemporary history (the period of the bourgeois monarchy)—less obviously than in Stendhal or Balzac, but unmistakably. In these two basic characteristics the three writers are at one, in contradistinction to all earlier realism; but Flaubert's attitude toward his subject is entirely different. In Stendhal and Balzac we frequently and indeed almost constantly hear what the writer thinks of his characters and events; sometimes Balzac accompanies his narrative with a running commentary—emotional or ironic or ethical or historical or economic. We also very frequently hear what the characters themselves think and feel, and often in such a manner that, in the passage concerned, the writer identifies himself with the character. Both these things are almost wholly absent from Flaubert's work. His opinion of his characters and events remains unspoken; and when the characters express themselves it is never in such a manner that the writer identifies himself with their opinion, or seeks to make the reader identify himself with it. We hear the writer speak; but he expresses no opinion and makes no comment. His role is limited to selecting the events and translating them into language; and this is done in the conviction that every event, if one is able to express it purely and completely, interprets itself and the persons involved in it far better and more completely than any opinion or judgment appended to it could do. Upon this conviction— that is, upon a profound faith in the truth of language responsibly, candidly, and carefully employed—Flaubert's artistic practice rests.

This is a very old, classic French tradition. There is already something of it in Boileau's line concerning the power of the rightly used word (on Malherbe: *D'un mot mis en sa place enseigna le pouvoir*)[3]; there are similar statements in La Bruyère.[4] Vauvenargues[5] said: *Il n'y aurait point d'erreurs qui ne périssent d'elles-mêmes, exprimées clairement*[6]. Flaubert's faith in language goes further than Vauvenargues's: he believes that the truth of the phenomenal world is also revealed in linguistic expression. Flaubert is a man who works extremely consciously and possesses a critical comprehension of art to a degree uncommon even in France; hence there occur in his letters, particularly of the years 1852–1854 during which he was writing *Madame Bovary* (*Troisième Série* in the *Nouvelle édition augmentée* of the *Correspondance*, 1927), many highly informative statements on the subject of his aim in art. They lead to a theory —mystical in the last analysis, but in practice, like all true mysti-

3. In his *Art of Poetry*, the seventeenth-century French critic Nicolas Boileau-Depréaux (1636–1711) greatly praises the poet Malherbe (1555–1628) for "using the right word in the right place" [*Editor*].
4. Like Boileau, La Bruyère (1645–96)
is a representative of French classicism [*Editor*].
5. Vauvenargues (1715–47) is an eighteenth-century moralist, author of *Maxims* [*Editor*].
6. There could be no errors that would not vanish by themselves, if they were clearly expressed.

cism, based upon reason, experience, and discipline—of a self-forgetful absorption in the subjects of reality which transforms them ("by a marvelous chemical process") and permits them to develop to mature expression. In this fashion subjects completely fill the writer; he forgets himself, his heart no longer serves him save to feel the hearts of others, and when, by fanatical patience, this condition is achieved, the perfect expression, which at once entirely comprehends the momentary subject and impartially judges it, comes of itself; subjects are seen as God sees them, in their true essence. With all this there goes a view of the mixture of styles which proceeds from the same mystical-realistic insight: there are no high and low subjects; the universe is a work of art produced without any taking of sides, the realistic artist must imitate the procedures of Creation, and every subject in its essence contains, before God's eyes, both the serious and the comic, both dignity and vulgarity; if it is rightly and surely reproduced, the level of style which is proper to it will be rightly and surely found; there is no need either for a general theory of levels, in which subjects are arranged according to their dignity, or for any analyses by the writer commenting upon the subject, after its presentation, with a view to better comprehension and more accurate classification; all this must result from the presentation of the subject itself.

It is illuminating to note the contrast between such a view and the grandiloquent and ostentatious parading of the writer's own feelings, and of the standards derived from them, of the type inaugurated by Rousseau and continued after him; a comparative interpretation of Flaubert's *Notre cœur ne doit être bon qu'à sentir celui des autres*,[7] and Rousseau's statement at the beginning of the Confessions, *Je sens mon cœur, et je connais les hommes*[8] could effectually represent the change in attitude which had taken place. But it also becomes clear from Flaubert's letters how laboriously and with what tensity of application he had attained to his convictions. Great subjects, and the free, irresponsible rule of the creative imagination, still have a great attraction for him; from this point of view he sees Shakespeare, Cervantes, and even Hugo wholly through the eyes of a romanticist, and he sometimes curses his own narrow petty-bourgeois subject which constrains him to tiresome stylistic meticulousness (*dire à la fois simplement et proprement des choses vulgaires*)[9]; this sometimes goes so far that he says things which contradict his basic views: . . . *et ce qu'il y a de désolant, c'est de penser que, même réussi dans la perfection, cela* [*Madame Bovary*] *ne peut être que passable et ne sera jamais*

---

7. Our heart is good only for feeling the heart of others.
8. I feel my own heart, and I know how men are.

9. To say vulgar things in a simple and decent way.

beau, à cause du fond même.[1] Withal, like so many important nineteenth-century artists, he hates his period; he sees its problems and the coming crises with great clarity; he sees the inner anarchy, the *manque de base theologique*,[2] the beginning menace of the mob, the lazy eclectic Historism, the domination of phrases, but he sees no solution and no issue; his fanatical mysticism of art is almost like a substitute religion, to which he clings convulsively, and his candor very often becomes sullen, petty, choleric, and neurotic. But this sometimes perturbs his impartiality and that love of his subjects which is comparable to the Creator's love. The paragraph which we have analyzed, however, is untouched by such deficiencies and weaknesses in his nature; it permits us to observe the working of his artistic purpose in its purity.

The scene shows a man and wife at table, the most everyday situation imaginable. Before Flaubert, it would have been conceivable as literature only as part of a comic tale, an idyl, or a satire. Here it is a picture of discomfort, and not a momentary and passing one, but a chronic discomfort, which completely rules an entire life, Emma Bovary's. To be sure, various things come later, among them love episodes; but no one could see the scene at table as part of the exposition for a love episode, just as no one would call *Madame Bovary* a love story in general. The novel is the representation of an entire human existence which has no issue; and our passage is a part of it, which, however, contains the whole. Nothing particular happens in the scene, nothing particular has happened just before it. It is a random moment from the regularly recurring hours at which the husband and wife eat together. They are not quarreling, there is no sort of tangible conflict. Emma is in complete despair, but her despair is not occasioned by any definite catastrophe; there is nothing purely concrete which she has lost or for which she has wished. Certainly she has many wishes, but they are entirely vague—elegance, love, a varied life; there must always have been such unconcrete despair, but no one ever thought of taking it seriously in literary works before; such formless tragedy, if it may be called tragedy, which is set in motion by the general situation itself, was first made conceivable as literature by romanticism; probably Flaubert was the first to have represented it in people of slight intellectual culture and fairly low social station; certainly he is the first who directly captures the chronic character of this psychological situation. Nothing happens, but that nothing has become a heavy, oppressive, threatening something. How he accomplishes this we have already seen; he organizes into compact and unequivocal discourse the con-

---

1. It pains me to think that, even if *Madame Bovary* is entirely successful, it could never be really beautiful but only passably so, because of the nature of the subject matter.
2. The lack of theological foundation.

fused impressions of discomfort which arise in Emma at sight of the room, the meal, her husband. Elsewhere too he seldom narrates events which carry the action quickly forward; in a series of pure pictures—pictures transforming the nothingness of listless and uniform days into an oppressive condition of repugnance, boredom, false hopes, paralyzing disappointments, and piteous fears—a gray and random human destiny moves toward its end.

The interpretation of the situation is contained in its description. The two are sitting at table together; the husband divines nothing of his wife's inner state; they have so little communion that things never even come to a quarrel, an argument, an open conflict. Each of them is so immersed in his own world—she in despair and vague wish-dreams, he in his stupid philistine self-complacency—that they are both entirely alone; they have nothing in common, and yet they have nothing of their own, for the sake of which it would be worthwhile to be lonely. For, privately, each of them has a silly, false world, which can not be reconciled with the reality of his situation, and so they both miss the possibilities life offers them. What is true of these two, applies to almost all the other characters in the novel; each of the many mediocre people who act in it has his own world of mediocre and silly stupidity, a world of illusions, habits, instincts, and slogans; each is alone, none can understand another, or help another to insight; there is no common world of men, because it could only come into existence if many should find their way to their own proper reality, the reality which is given to the individual—which then would be also the true common reality. Though men come together for business and pleasure, their coming together has no note of united activity; it becomes one-sided, ridiculous, painful, and it is charged with misunderstanding, vanity, futility, falsehood, and stupid hatred. But what the world would really be, the world of the "intelligent," Flaubert never tells us; in his book the world consists of pure stupidity, which completely misses true reality, so that the latter should properly not be discoverable in it at all; yet it is there; it is in the writer's language, which unmasks the stupidity by pure statement; language, then, has criteria for stupidity and thus also has a part in that reality of the "intelligent" which otherwise never appears in the book.

Emma Bovary, too, the principal personage of the novel, is completely submerged in that false reality, in human stupidity as is the "hero" of Flaubert's other realistic novel, Frédéric Moreau in the Sentimental Education. How does Flaubert's manner of representing such personages fit into the traditional categories "tragic" and "comic"? Certainly Emma's existence is apprehended to its depths, certainly the earlier intermediate categories, such as the "sentimental" or the "satiric" or the "didactic," are inapplicable, and very often the reader is moved by her fate in a way that appears very like tragic pity. But a real tragic heroine she is not. The way in which language here lays bare the silliness, immaturity, and disorder of her life, the very wretchedness of that life, in which she remains immersed (*toute l'amertume de l'existence lui semblait servie sur son assiette*), excludes the idea of true tragedy, and the author and the reader can never feel as at one with her as must be the case with the tragic hero; she is always being tried, judged, and, together with the entire world in which she is caught, condemned. But neither is she comic; surely not; for that, she is understood far too deeply from within her fateful entanglement—though Flaubert never practices any "psychological understanding" but simply lets the state of the facts speak for itself. He has found an attitude toward the reality of contemporary life which is entirely different from earlier attitudes and stylistic levels, including—and especially—Balzac's and Stendhal's. It could be called, quite simply, "objective seriousness." This sounds strange as a designation of the style of a literary work. Objective seriousness, which seeks to penetrate to the depths of the passions and entanglements of a human life, but without itself becoming moved, or at least without betraying that it is moved—this is an attitude which one expects from a priest, a teacher, or a psychologist rather than from an artist. But priest, teacher, and psychologist wish to accomplish something direct and practical—which is far from Flaubert's mind. He wishes, by his attitude—*pas de cris, pas de convulsion, rien que la fixit d'un regard pensif*[3]—to force language to render the truth concerning the subjects of his observation: "style itself and in its own right being an absolute manner of viewing things" (*Correspondence* 2, 346). Yet this leads in the end to a didactic purpose: criticism of the contemporary world; and we must not hesitate to say so, much as Flaubert may insist that he is an artist and nothing but an artist. The more one studies Flaubert, the clearer it becomes how much insight into the problematic nature and the hollowness of nineteenth–century bourgeois culture is contained in his realistic works; and many important passages from his letters confirm this. The demonification of everyday social intercourse which is to be found in Balzac is certainly entirely lacking in Flaubert; life no longer surges and foams, it flows viscously and sluggishly. The essence of the happenings of ordinary contemporary life seemed to Flaubert to consist not in tempestuous actions and passions, not in demonic men and forces, but in the prolonged chronic state whose surface movement is mere empty bustle, while underneath it there is another movement, almost imperceptible but universal and unceasing, so that the political, economic, and social subsoil appears comparatively stable and at the same time intolera-

---

3. No cries, no emotions, only the steadfastness of a thoughtful gaze.

bly charged with tension. Events seem to him hardly to change; but in the concretion of duration, which Flaubert is able to suggest both in the individual occurrence (as in our example) and in his total picture of the times, there appears something like a concealed threat: the period is charged with its stupid issuelessness as with an explosive.

GEORGES POULET

The Circle and the Center: Reality and *Madame Bovary*†

In his book *Mimesis*, for almost a decade the standard study of the concept of reality in Western literature and recently translated into English for the first time, Professor Erich Auerbach quotes the following passage from *Madame Bovary*:

> But it was above all at mealtimes that she could bear it no longer, in that little room on the ground floor, with the smoking stove, the creaking door, the oozing walls, the damp floor-tiles; all the bitterness of life seemed to be served to her on her plate, and, with the steam from the boiled beef, there rose from the depths of her soul other exhalations as it were of disgust. Charles was a slow eater; she would nibble a few hazel-nuts, or else, leaning on her elbow, would amuse herself making marks on the oilcloth with the point of her table-knife.

This passage, Auerbach declares, forms the climax of a presentation whose subject is Emma Bovary's dissatisfaction with her life at Tostes. In several cumulative pictures Flaubert describes the cheerlessness, drabness, unvaryingness, narrowness of Emma's world. This paragraph is therefore the climax of the portrayal of her despair. In itself it presents a picture: man and wife together at mealtime. But the picture is not represented in and for itself; it is subordinated to the dominant subject, Emma's despair. We are first given Emma, and then the situation through her. It is not, however, Mr. Auerbach continues, a matter of a simple representation of the content of Emma's consciousness, of what she feels, as she feels it. Though the light which illuminates the picture proceeds from her, she is yet herself part of the picture, she is situated within it.

It may be useful to reflect upon these enlightening, yet not completely satisfying remarks. No doubt, Flaubert's method consists in

† From *Western Review*, XIX (Summer 1955), 245–60; reprinted by permission of the author.

presenting, as an object for our contemplation, a subjective being which, in its stead, has for its own object of contemplation the surrounding reality of things. Emma, as Mr. Auerbach points out, "does not simply see, but is herself seen as one seeing." If Flaubert had simply decided to paint her from the outside, she would be merely an object among objects. With the room, the stove, the walls, the plate and the husband, she would be part and parcel of the plurality of things. If, on the other hand, Flaubert had wanted to make of her somebody like Bloom in *Ulysses,* or Clarissa Dalloway in *Mrs. Dalloway,* i.e., a purely subjective being, then there would have been no husband, plate, walls, stove, or room. Nothing would have been left, except the sensations and emotions caused in Emma by these objects; and there would have been no Emma, or at least in us no consciousness of her as a person standing against a background of things, since she would have been reduced to the status of a stream of thoughts and feelings. In both cases something essential in Flaubert's novel would have been lost, in one case the objective world, in the other the subjective mind, and in both, the extremely delicate relationship between objective and subjective, which is the very substance of the novel. It is this constant relation which not only links together the duel aspects of the novel, but which also keeps each of these two realities from fragmenting itself into a sheer multiplicity, here of thoughts and emotions, there of objects. There is in *Madame Bovary* an inner coherence, and this coherence is due to the fact that things, simultaneous or successive, are constantly fused together in the unity of a single perceptive mind, and that conversely this mind is kept from disappearing in the flux of its own consciousness by the objectivity of a world with which it is in constant touch. This essential interrelation is excellently commented upon by Mr. Auerbach in his examination of the paragraph of Madame Bovary quoted above. But it seems to me that there is still something to be done. For in this paragraph there is not only a theoretical representation of reality; there is also a concrete medium through which this representation has been achieved. It is the business of the critic to examine, within the text, by what action Flaubert accomplished his purpose, i.e., to show vividly the interrelation of a consciousness and its environment.

Let us therefore go back to the text. First we read: *Mais c'était surtout aux heures des repas. . . .* What is given to us at first, is time. This time is not a continuity. It is a moment which repeats itself again and again, but which is also, when it happens, the present moment of Emma's life; the moment, above all moments, when actually she cannot bear her existence any more. Thus what we have at first, is something purely and intensely subjective, an awareness of time, an awareness of despair. But as soon as this awareness is revealed, it is immediately located within a place, *la petite salle*, and surrounded with a long enumeration of details, all objective in themselves, but all endowed with affective powers: a stove that smokes, a door that creaks, walls oozing, floor-tiles which are damp. To these details there must be added all other particulars, which the author does not mention in this paragraph, but which were described at great length in the preceding pages, and which are present in the memory of the reader, as they are indeed in the memory of Emma herself. Thus what is given here is greatly swollen by what was given before. Details have an enormous cumulative power. This is the power of number, or, to use an Aristotelian distinction, this is a numbering and not a numbered number. This multiplicity—in itself meaningless—of all these details, takes force and meaning from the fact that they all affect in the same way the same person. Therefore, from their outside location around Emma, they combine their force and their weight, in order to come down and bring pressure upon her. To express this coming down and in, of the outside reality, crowding on consciousness, Flaubert writes this sentence: "All the bitterness of life seemed to be served to her on her plate, and with the steam from the boiled beef, there rose from the depths of her soul other exhalations as it were of disgust."

Let us consider successively the two balanced parts of this sentence. The first one is straight and to the point. One can feel in the directness with which it rushes toward its goal, the very motion by which the influx of despair, emanating from the surrounding objects, passes through a sort of tangible space, in order to reach the subject. To give this effect, Flaubert has purposely inverted the objective and the subjective. Instead of a room, a stove, a door, a tiled floor, there is now a "bitterness of life." The multiple objects have been transformed into their subjective equivalents; just as, conversely, the soul of Emma, which is the goal of the combined offensive carried out by things, has been symbolically represented by the narrow objective circumference of her plate. Thus a deliberate confusion has been created between the subjective and the objective; as if, by penetrating into Emma's soul, the images of things had lost their objectivity and been transformed into feelings, or as if Emma, by becoming affected by material things, had become also somehow material.

But there are still more discoveries to be made in this wonderful sentence. Its beauty consists in rendering exactly by the physical motion of the words, the psychic motion of the meaning. First the general expression, all the bitterness of life, substitutes to the manifold of things a subjective totality encompassing the whole of existence. Then, through the rapid flow of the following words, "seemed to be served to her on her plate," this peripheral reality shrinks down from all sides to lodge itself within the narrowest place, the plate of Emma. So the psychic motion, which in itself is invisible, has become a local and therefore a perceptible motion, through the figure of a space crossed over by the bitterness of existence finding its final home in the object on which is concentrated the attention of Emma. We are witnessing here an extraordinary narrowing of space, a rush of all causal forces, gathering from the depth of the past and from the three dimensions of external space, to converge on a central point, Emma's consciousness. But as soon as Flaubert has created this motion from the periphery to the center, he gives us a reverse motion from the center toward the periphery: "and, with the steam from the boiled beef, there rose from the depths of her soul other exhalations as it were of disgust." After the contraction the dilation. We do not doubt but that these exhalations go upward and outward, to join the outer regions wherefrom the condensed bitterness of existence came downward into Emma's plate. Thus, crossed over in both directions, the Flaubertian *milieu* appears as a vast surrounding space which spreads from Emma to an indeterminate circumference, and from the circumference to the consciousness of Emma.

This circular character of Flaubert's representation of reality is not a mere metaphor; or, if it is one, it is not one invented for the sake of the argument. On the contrary this metaphor occurs so often, and, when it occurs, fits so well and plays such an important part in the context, that we must consider it as the essential image by which Flaubert expresses the interrelation of objective world and subjective being. My purpose is to examine the different aspects and meanings presented by this metaphor in the work of Flaubert.

Let us take another passage from *Madame Bovary*. It can be found in a first draft of the novel, published in 1936 by Mlle. Leleu. The moment of Emma's life here described belongs to a period slightly antecedent to the passage examined previously. Here she is shown during a walk she takes with her dog, a little Italian greyhound, in the country near Tostes:

> She began by *looking round her mechanically* to see if nothing had changed, since last she had been there. She found the same wall flowers on the stones, on the slabs of the wall the same patches of dried up lichen, the same pebbles in the beds of nettles and the three windows, always closed, which were roting away. . . . Her thoughts, aimless at first, were wandering at random, like the handsome greyhound who, unleashed, was *running round and round in the field*, chasing a rat in a furrow, or bringing himself to a stop in order to nibble the poppies. . . . But when she had thus let her eyes roam over the horizon, whereas her *diffused* attention had barely skimmed a thousand

ideas following each other, than, *as two concentric circles at once contracting their circumferences,* her thoughts retired within herself, her wavering glances became transfixed, and sitting on the ground under the beeches, prodding the grass with the ivory tip of her sunshade, she was always coming back to this question: Why, oh dear, why did I marry?

Here, beyond question, the metaphor of the circle cannot be overlooked. It plays a conspicuous part. At first everything tends to become peripheral. Emma's thoughts wander at random, her eyes roam over the horizon, her attention is spread on a thousand ideas. The things that she perceives, the thoughts that she thinks, get farther and farther in the distance, and finally they distribute themselves in such a way that they form two concentric circles whose central point is Emma's consciousness. To give the right emphasis to this general impression of circularity, Flaubert has taken care to prefigure it by another circle, the one physically described by the dog running round and round in the field. But this is not all. Let us read again the beginning of the long sentence which constitutes the second half of the paragraph: "But when she had thus let her eyes roam over the horizon, whereas her diffused attention had barely skimmed a thousand ideas following each other. . . ." No doubt, these long undulating clauses, progressively opening, are shaped in this particular form, so as to give a physical impression of the corresponding widening of Emma's thoughts and feelings. But if we read the second part of the sentence, we detect a striking difference of rhythm. The clauses are shorter, straighter and faster; her thoughts retired within herself, her wavering glances became transfixed. . . . she was always coming back to this question. Here, manifestly, diffusion has been replaced by contraction. The circles are shrinking, the thoughts from all sides are coming back, the words are running, as if impatient to reach their goal and to come to a full stop. This final fixation of all motions is represented in two, or even in three distinct ways. Just as the dog, who was running round in the field, comes to a full stop in order to nibble the poppies, so Emma's mind, which was wandering far away in circles among her memories and dreams, comes back to an idea on which it concentrates. And, in a way, this idea is different from all preceding ones, since it is not diffuse, remote and infinitely varied, but precise, intimate and absolutely unique. It is not circumferential, it is central. However this one central thought is closely connected with the previous multiplicity. It is out of this multiplicity that it was issued. It was this very multiplicity which, by fusion, contraction and inward motion, produced finally the central thought, as the result and summing up. Thus the center contains the circumference. And this center is represented once more, symbolically, by a single dimensionless object, which has replaced in the picture the whole landscape: the pointed tip of a sunshade, digging the ground. The circular horizon has shrunk to a mere point.

This infinite contraction of the mental and external spaces is in no way mysterious, either in itself or in its occurrence. It is the most natural motion of the human mind. We know that it is because the diffused attention of Emma, wandering aimlessly, has touched many ideas, that these ideas have awakened, echoed in her mind, evoked the picture of her whole existence, and given expression finally to the question which was at the core of her consciousness. Nothing was more genuine than this moving inward from the circumference to the center. And, on the other hand, nothing was less instantaneous. From extreme eccentricity to extreme concentricity, it is step by step, by a slow and repeated process, that the thought goes back to the self. From the circumference to the center of the psychic circle, we see a gradual progress, we feel the time, we measure the distance.

We have seen space gradually contracting. Let us now see space completely contracted, space which cannot expand. All his life, Flaubert was intensely conscious of the narrowness of existence. Already in one of his earlier books, *Smarh*, he had spoken of "his sickly thought, *running in an iron circle.*" In *November* we find the following sentence: "Returning ceaselessly to my starting-point, I was *going round and round in an impassable circle.*" In August 1847, he wrote to Louise Colet: "I am attached to a patch of land, to a *circumscribed point* in the world, and the more I feel myself attached to it, the more I turn again and again furiously toward the sun and sky." Nor was this feeling in Flaubert confined to his youth. On April 6, 1858, in his full maturity, he wrote to Mlle. Leroyer de Chantepie:

> For the fourth time I am going to find myself again in Marseilles, and, this time, I shall be alone, absolutely alone. *The circle has shrunk.* The reflections I was making in 1849 when about to embark for Egypt, I am going to make again in a few days, when tramping the same streets. Thus our life *goes round continually* in the same train of miseries, like a squirrel in a cage, and each new step makes us gasp.

Similarly all the works of Flaubert's old age have for their main theme circumscribed existence. For instance in *A Simple Heart*, the story of Félicité, the maid-servant, from which I quote this passage:

> *The small circle of her ideas shrank even more,* and the chiming of bells, the bellowing of cattle did not exist any more. All living things now were moving as silently as ghosts. Only one sound still reached her ears: the voice of her parrot.

This parrot, first as a pet, then as a stuffed bird, becomes gradually the central object in the old maid's circle of existence. At the end there is no more circle. There is only the stuffed bird, which is the unique point on which the old maid's look is fixed at the moment of her death. Another story from that period is the legend of St. Julian the Hospitaller. Julian is a great hunter, pursuing his quarry in many countries, until, in a culminating scene, the animals at bay turn upon him, "*making around him a narrow circle.*" The same feeling of suffocation can be found in *Salammbo*, where a whole army is shut in, to perish by starvation, in a narrow mountain-pass. And the same picture of narrow activity, running blindly around in a small circle, is to be found in *Bouvard and Pécuchet*. Everywhere in the work of Flaubert there is the obsession of narrow, endless circularity. But nowhere does it appear more strikingly than in the story of Emma Bovary. Emma is essentially a person who feels herself enclosed and stifled within the bounds of the place where she lives and of the moment in which she thinks. Her whole existence at Tostes or at Yonville seems to her a shutting up within walls, a groping around inside narrow limits; limits so narrow that sometimes they seem to join each other, to condense into a point, the point of time and space where she is constrained to live. She is here, here only, in the dimensionless *here*; she is forbidden forever to escape outside, into the infinite *elsewhere*. Nevertheless this *elsewhere* exists, it exists everywhere else, it is spreading on every side, and it is toward that *elsewhere* that her longing irradiates incessantly. The extraordinary constriction of Emma's existence, reduced to a mere punctum, is described by Flaubert in this passage, taken from the first version of *Madame Bovary*:

> Then the train of the same days started again. They were going to follow each other in the same manner, in Indian file, always similar, innumerable, bringing nothing. And they were before her, hundreds and thousands of them, enough for ten or twenty years! It will never finish, it will last until her death. The other lives, constricted, flat, cramped as they were, had at least some chance of an adventure, of a broadening of *their limits*. Sometimes there dropped an accident which shook their surface. An unexpected happening could *create peripeties ad infinitum* . . . But, for her, nothing would happen.

First of all, the beauty of this passage is due to the intense feeling of duration which impregnates it: Then the train of the same days started again. Duration appears here as a mere prolongation of the past into the present. But it appears also as a prolongation of the present into the future: They were going to follow each other in the same manner, in Indian file. The three dimensions of time, past, present and future, identify themselves with one another, in such a way, that they become a uniform and continuous texture. As far as the eye can reach, duration extends, forward, backward, always the same, forming a homogeneous bulk of temporal matter. But by a process which, in his famous sonnet *The Swan*, Mallarmé will repeat, this vast extent of duration, spread uniformly on all sides, is also experienced by Emma as the narrowest possible span of time. The very uniformity of all past, present and future moments of existence, transforms and contracts all of them into a single moment; and this moment, incessantly rediscovered along the retrospective and prospective expanse of time, is never discovered but as the same narrow span infinitely repeated. So time is just an endless void of duration, in the middle of which life appears constricted, identical to itself, bringing nothing. However, this life is compared by Emma to others. These other lives, "constricted, flat, cramped as they were, had at least some chance of an adventure, of a broadening of their limits." Adventure considered as a widening of existence, is described by a symbol well-known since the Stoics: "Sometimes there dropped an accident which shook their surface. An unexpected happening could create peripeties ad infinitum." No doubt the image suggested here is the one of a stone dropped in a pool. From the point where it strikes the surface, concentric waves go out in all directions. The circles widen, multiply, get farther from the center. So an adventure, an accident, something unprovoked, uncalled for, may fall suddenly into the pool of life, burst into its stillness, produce circles of events going outward. The accident in itself is nothing; just a piece of gravel thrown in the water. But the small whirlpool it creates breaks the limits of the still narrow circle of existence, to replace them by an infinite circumference.[1] The most insignificant event may be the starting point of an immense future.

Everything, therefore, depends on these occurrences. But, thinks Emma, they only happen to other people, they will never happen to me. Now, in spite of Emma's forebodings, it is precisely Flaubert's purpose to make things happen to her. Not many happenings, just three or four. Emma's life is a pool in which, occasionally, stones are thrown. Or, more exactly, it is a series of pools, each one a little bigger than the preceding one, first the father's farm, then Tostes, then Yonville, finally Yonville plus Rouen. In the stillness of each of these pools, at a particular time, a stone is thrown. This throwing of the stone is invariably the appearance of a new lover. From the moment he comes out, there start waves of emotion, which for a time broaden Emma's life; up to the moment when, the lover having gone, the emotion being spent, Emma is brought back by a retrogressive process to her starting point.

1. See Marjorie Hope Nicolson, *The Breaking of the Circle*, Evanston, Ill., 1950.

Let us examine this starting point in the first and most fugitive of Emma's love affairs.

Invited with her husband to a ball in an aristocratic country house, *le château de la Vaubyessard*, Emma has been deeply moved by this incidental excursion in a *milieu* so different from hers. She has danced in the arms of a Parisian Viscount, whose elegance has made on her a profound expression: "All things turning around them, the lamps, the furniture, the wainscoting, the floor like a disc on a pivot." Let us keep in mind these physical gyrations in which we must see a prefiguration of the mental gyrations which, later on, will proceed in Emma's mind. The day after, Emma leaves the château and the Viscount, to come back to the narrow circle of her ordinary life. The only keepsake she has brought back from that memorable event is a cigar case which may, or may not, have belonged to the Viscount. Now this fortuitous dancing partner, whom Emma will not see any more, is a very small pebble in her life. Nevertheless we will see, starting from the point of its falling, waves and waves of dreams irradiating in Emma's imagination. To follow this phenomenon, we have not only the final version of the novel, but also some preliminary drafts, and even in the primitive scenario referring to Emma's life after her return, we find this sentence: "The Viscount is a center, he disappears, but the surroundings stay and widen." Another version, more elaborated, gives the explanation of this cryptic statement. First we are informed that sometimes Emma looks at the cigar case, which makes her dream of the Viscount. She wants to imagine his life in Paris, and she reads books about life in the capital. These books are mostly novels. Then comes the important passage:

> The memory of the Viscount was always passing, like a ghost, into what she was reading. She found his picture on every page. Examining the imaginary personages, she was always making parallels and comparisons with him. Thus he was enhanced by their poetry and he reflected his reality upon their fiction. Then *the circle of which he was the center, where all rays converged, gradually widened round him*, and, spreading equally in this expanse, the Viscount's personality became more and more diluted, like a drop of red wine that one lets fall in a glass of water.

The image of the drop of wine corresponds closely to the one of the pebble. In both instances a fallen object, by dilation or dilution, becomes the center and generating point of a circular motion. In the final version the image changes once again, but still represents the figure of a circle:

> The memory of the Viscount always returned as she read. Between him and the imaginary personages she made compari-

sons. But the circle of which he *was the center gradually widened round him,* and the *halo* that he bore, drawing away from his head, broadened out beyond, lighting up other dreams.

Here, instead of the pebble, or the drop of wine, we have the halo. The circle, narrow at first, becomes progressively so wide that it loses touch with the center, and, identifying itself with other dreams, irradiates confusedly in the distance toward a sort of peripheral happiness:

> *At the far end of life's vista, high above,* she thus saw happiness lying in a marvellous abode.

Here again we have a fundamental process of the Flaubertian mind, just the opposite of the one which makes the mind contract within narrow limits. It is the process of expansion, which generates innumerable reveries, leading from a central thought to a profusion of eddying images. As often as not, the starting point is a recollection. For instance, in a letter from Flaubert to Louise Colet, dated August 22, 1853, from Trouville, we find the following passage:

> All the memories of my youth are crying out under my feet, like shells on the beach. Each wave that I see breaking on the seashore awakens in me distant *resounding echoes.*

As in Proust, we can often find in Flaubert a whole world of reminiscences, "sortant d'une tasse de thé." But in Flaubert, contrarily to Proust, this springing forth of the past is never directed toward the recapture of any distinct reality. It is a spreading outward, a processus of indetermination. Thus, at the tinkling of a bell, stirring memories of Emma's youth, "Gentle vibrations made her thoughts quiver and *go widening in the infinite vagueness of retrospections.*" The distinctness of each recollection is thus progressively replaced by their multiplicity, their vibratility, and, finally, by the vastness of the place they have indistinctly filled up by their resonances. In *Smarh,* as in the three *Temptations,* we experience at a cosmic scale this feeling of expansion:

> How vast is creation! I see the planets rising and the stars running, carried away with their lights. *The dome of the sky* is *widening as I go upward with it,* the worlds are rolling around me. So I am *the center* of this moving creation.

And in the 1849 version of the *Temptation:*

> *The Devil:*—Diffuse, expand, spread out.
> *Anthony:*—I see the *circles widening,* I hear the rumbling sound of the spheres.

Or:

Thy joy will grow unceasingly, according to the increases of thy love, like the vibrations of seraphic harps, which, widening from sphere to sphere, unfold in the Infinite the praise of God.

Thus, independently of any religious or philosophical belief, by the essential trend of his imagination, Flaubert's soul, like the soul of St. Anthony, tends to become "diffuse, universal, stretched out." In a letter written by Flaubert to Louise Colet on the 3rd of March, 1852, we read:

I have come across some old drawings that I colored when I was seven or eight years old, and that I have not seen since. There are rocks painted in blue and trees in green. Looking at them (at a wintering in an ice-field especially) I relived some of the terrors I experienced when I was a child . . . My journeys, the recollections of my childhood, all these things reflect their colors on one another, they fall into line, dance in a prodigious blaze and *rise in a spiral*.

The theme of the spiral is frequent in Flaubert. It may have come from his friend Le Poittevin, whose novel, *Bélial*, is summed up in these words by Flaubert: "The general idea is the whirl, the *infinite spiral*." Already in the youthful *Memoirs of a Madman* Flaubert writes these curious words: "Oh! the infinite! the infinite! immense gulf, *spiral* which rises from the abyss to the higher regions of the unknown, old idea within which *we go round, taken with giddiness*." The first two *Temptations* are full of spirals. Thus the Ophits say, speaking of their snake-god: "His *spirals* are the *circles* of worlds spread out concentrically." And the Gnostics: "The mysterious Gnosis raises up endlessly its *spiral*, and, driven by us, thou shalt ascend ceaselessly toward the irradiating Syzygia, which will carry thee high above in the bosom of the perennial Bythos, in the immovable *circle* of the perfect Plerom." Moreover, we know that, on more than one occasion, Flaubert planned to write a novel precisely entitled *La Spirale*, which would have had for subject the transfiguration of reality through dream, and of which nothing remains except a few unprinted notes known through a German scholar, E. W. Fischer. Quoting from these notes the phrase "comme une spirale qui monte à l'infini," Mr. Fischer wonders about the meaning of the title: "Is it intended to mean that the thoughts of the hero are moving along circles which rise infinitely, fantastic circles around the reality, from which they fly, and to which, however, they are attached as to their starting-point?" It would be difficult to get closer to the spirit of the author. Very likely, through the symbol of an ever-rising spiral, Flaubert wanted once more to illustrate the circular widening of horizons, that we found already in *Madame Bovary*. If we want further proof, let us recall this other sentence from the *Correspondence:* "The heart in its affections, like mankind in its ideas, *spreads endlessly in widening circles."* Elsewhere Flaubert writes: "All feeling is an extension." But in the whole of the *Correspondence* there is nothing nearer *Madame Bovary* than the following passage: "My existence, like a stagnant swamp, is so still that *the least event dropping in it, causes innumerable circles. . . ."*

Yet in spreading outward the mind runs risks of which Flaubert was well aware. The first one, that we have already seen, is the risk of losing touch with the center of one's thoughts, and therefore with all order and precision. In their famous discussion with Flaubert after the reading of the *Temptation*, by the Heresies to Anthony: "We are the *diverging rays* which multiply the light, and all *converging* toward its base to increase its span." No doubt, in his desire of extending immensely the scope of his work, Flaubert, in the 1849 version, had developed divergency at the expense of convergency. But out of this multiplicity of directions and desegregation of all images in the void of space, a new danger appears, which is the danger of giddiness, madness, mental hemorrhage that nothing can stem. Flaubert writes: "I have often felt madness coming in for me. In my poor head there was a whirl of ideas and images, and it seemed to me that my consciousness, my very self, was sinking like a ship in the tempest." The ship sinks at the center of the whirl, while at the periphery there is a maddening circular motion. This is just such a psychic catastrophe as we witness in *Madame Bovary*, when Emma, rejected by Rodolphe, goes back through the fields. There is no center left in her, or, more exactly the mental center of her self is a bursting point, exploding and projecting itself in countless fragments in all directions:

> She remained lost in stupor, and having no more consciousness of herself than through the beating of her arteries, that she seemed to hear bursting forth like a deafening music filling all the fields. The earth beneath her feet was more yielding than the sea, and the furrows seemed to be immense brown waves breaking into foam. Everything in her head, of memories, ideas, went off at once like a thousand fireworks . . .
>
> Suddenly it seemed to her that fiery *spheres* were exploding in the air like detonating balls when they strike, and were whirling, whirling to melt at last upon the snow between the branches of the trees. In the midst of each of them appeared the face of Rodolphe. They multiplied and drew near her, penetrating her. Then all disappeared.

But at the opposite extreme of this ultimate state of mind, where there is no longer any circle, or center, or any existential coherence whatsoever, there are in *Madame Bovary* all the passages where the eccentric and concentric motions balance each other, and the circumference does not lose its relation to the center. In *Par les champs et par les grèves*, Flaubert writes: "A reverie can be great and give birth at least to fruitful melancholies, when, *starting from a fixed point and never losing touch with it*, the imagination hovers within its luminous *circle*." This hovering of the dreams within a luminous circle, to the center of which they are closely related, is expressed in the first *Sentimental Education*, at the moment when the hero discovers that he is loved:

> The universe appeared to him, through a luminous vista, full of glory and love, and his own life *surrounded by a halo,* like the face of a God; happiness spread over him; it was coming out of everything, it exuded even from the walls.

In a preceding passage, the halo, "drawing away from his head, broadened out beyond, lighting up other dreams." Here, instead of disappearing into the distance, the halo irradiated by love seems to reach a limit, from which its reflected light comes back toward the center of emanation. In our first example, we have seen all the surrounding bitterness of existence concentrate into Emma's plate. Here, through the same concentric approach, we see all the surrounding sweetness of the world reaching the soul.

The same process is repeated again and again in *Madame Bovary*. For instance, this description of the motion by which the image of Emma comes from the depths of the past into the center of Léon's consciousness:

> It seemed to him that the face of this woman was *sending from far away on his present life a kind of reverberation*, like these setting suns, which, close to the ground, cast out as far as us their luminous undulations.

Or this admirable passage, which unfortunately Flaubert did not retain in the final version, where through the happiness of her present love, Emma not only unfolds herself to the external reality, but also experiences in the apex of actual love the fulfillment of past desires, kept at the periphery of her mind:

> Besides, in loving him, not only did she fulfill her need of love, but she also satisfied all her old desires, which had been inhibited . . . All the feelings of her soul *converged in this love, as the spokes of a wheel around the axle which supports them.*

Thus, what Flaubert intended to show in *Madame Bovary* is a life which at one moment contracts and at another unfolds; a life which sometimes is reduced to a moment without duration and a point without dimension; and which sometimes, from that moment and from that point, extends to a circular consciousness of all its duration, of all the depths of its dreams, of all the spatiality of its environment:

> All these reminiscences were *widening her existence.* They seemed to form immensities of feelings, *to which she turned.*

The relation, here, is from a dimensionless present to the vastness of peripheral life. But it may also happen conversely that from the breadth of a present existence, now peripheral, all the activities of the soul converge on a single central object.

Thus in the *Correspondence:*

> It is to you that my thought flows back, when I have been through the circles of my reveries; *I cast myself on this thought at full length,* like a weary traveller on the grass alongside the road.

But, above all, this admirable passage of the first *Madame Bovary,* where we find the same image:

> She concentrated on this recollection; it became *the center* of her spleen; all her thoughts *converged upon it* . . . The humblest details, the past, the future, memories of simple words, fancies, comparisons, disgusts, she piled everything into this recollection, *her soul stretched at full length toward this center of heat.*

All these texts prove clearly that what Flaubert conceived and succeeded in devising, is a new way of presenting the relations between the mind and all surrounding reality, a more convincing way than the one used by his predecessors. While eighteenth century novelists, and Stendhal himself, were satisfied to go with the hero along the narrow track of successive time, and while Balzac constructed most of his plots as a line of force projected very straight in time and space, Flaubert is the first who builds his novels around a series of centers encompassed by their environments. For the first time in the history of the novel, human consciousness shows itself as it is, as a sort of core, around which sensations, thoughts and memories move in a perceptible space. Thus it becomes possible to discover and express the depth of the human mind; a depth which can be conceived as an expanse through which radiations diverge, or, conversely, as the convergence of all peripheral life upon the sentient being.

But there is yet a last form of circularity that must be examined. It is the *ordering* of all activities around an image which dwells permanently in the center of the soul. The whole novel becomes then the continuous reshaping of a reality in itself disordered, taking form, meaning and motion from the living center to which it is related. Such is, it seems to me, the true structure of the *Sentimental Education*. Critics often consider it as a formless novel, a novel which has precisely for its subject-matter the formlessness of existence. Charles Du Bos has written some beautiful pages on the "milieu intérieur" of this novel, in which, for him, "Nothing takes hold, everything is oozing, and it seems that we are inside the *flowing* motion of time." But in insisting on this flowing *away*, Du Bos failed to see that in the *Sentimental Education* there is also a constant flowing *in* and *around*. Here, clearly, there is no progression of water going down stream. As Flaubert told himself of his novel, "There is no progression of effect." Thus it would be more exact to compare its motion to the one of a *circular* river. Again and again, in the works of Flaubert, the word *circulation* appears, weighted with meaning. For instance, in the *Temptation*:

> The blood of man pulses in his heart and swells the veins of his feet. The breath of God *circulates* among the worlds and the contingencies of these worlds.
> Dost thou see, like blood in an enormous body, the universal Haensoph *circulating* in the hidden veins of all the worlds?

Thus, in the *Sentimental Education*, Frédéric Moreau is constantly perceiving, around him, currents of life quickening the circumambient world:

> He stayed to contemplate the quadrille, blinking his eyes to see better, breathing the soft perfumes of women, which were *circulating* like a kiss endlessly diffused.
> The ceiling, rounded in the form of a cupola, gave to the boudoir the shape of a basket; and a scented draught was *circulating* under the fluttering of fans.
> When he came up again to his study, he looked at the armchair where she had been seated and at all the objects she had touched. Something of her was *circulating around*. The caress of her presence was still enduring.

But this incessant motion of peripheral life would have no meaning, and the novel no form, if, at the center there were not a coordinating element. This element is the love of the hero. If Frédéric had not loved Madame Arnoux, the novel would have been formless and meaningless. But this is not the case. As Jean-Pierre Richard says in his study on *The Creation of Form in Flaubert*, in the *Sentimental Education*, "All objects are disposed around an oriented axle." Because, from the first page of the novel, Mme. Arnoux draws Frédéric's love, whatever amorphous elements exist in Frédéric's life, begin to gravitate around her image, taking light from her:

And as a traveller lost in the midst of a wood, whom all paths lead back to the same spot, continually, at the end of every idea, he was finding again the memory of Mme. Arnoux.

All the streets were leading toward her house; all carriages were standing in the squares to bring him there more quickly; Paris was related to her person, and the great city, with its thousand voices, was murmuring like an immense orchestra, *around her.*

Thus the main purpose of Flaubert's novel is to create relation and order. This order is formal. From the center to the circumference, from the circumference to the center, there are constant relations. These are the relations set by the sentient subject between each moment of its consciousness and its total environment. Flaubert's novel belongs to a region explored, in a famous article, by Professor Leo Spitzer: the region of *milieu* and *ambiance.* Sensible and emotive elements form a tangible circle, at the core of which there is, to quote the most perfect expression of Flaubert, "A *luminous center, toward which the entirety of things converge.*"

HARRY LEVIN

Madame Bovary: The Cathedral and the Hospital[†]

"One that we believed in, loved without criticism," Ernest Hemingway writes of Flaubert's bust in the Luxembourg gardens, "heavy now in stone as an idol should be." This is appropriate commemoration for a master who conceived his works as monuments and executed them in marmoreal fashion, whose masterpiece today attracts more sightseers than believers perhaps—like a shrine that has been turned into a museum. Lamenting the secularization of modern life, the neglect of old churches with its attendant loss of structures and symbols for common experience, Proust finds his best example in the liturgical echoes that harmonize the dying agonies of Madame Bovary. Sometimes Flaubert was fond of comparing himself to a cathedral, confessing that he habitually beheld the outer world through stained-glass windows. At other times his native habi-

† From *Essays in Criticism* (January, 1952), pp. 1–23; reprinted by permission of the author and *Essays in Criticism.* This article, in a revised version, forms part (pp. 246–69) of Professor Levin's book *The Gates of Horn: A Study of Five French Realists* (New York: Oxford University Press, 1963). In the book, the beginning of the essay is somewhat more developed than in the original article which is here reprinted, but the analysis of the actual novel is the same.

tat, the hospital, seemed a closer analogy: and then he would insist that disillusion was far more poetic than illusion. This quarrel between his two selves, the lyrical and the critical, which paralleled the romantic and realistic movements, found its archetype in the first of all novels: the book to which Flaubert traced his artistic origins, Don Quixote, with its "perpetual fusion of illusion and reality." By portraying—what, curiously enough, Kierkegaard had called for a few years previously—a female Quixote, Flaubert joined in the counter-attack that fiction is always launching against the fictitious. By a virile attempt to understand the femme incomprise, a bachelor's understanding of unhappy marriage, he challenged the ascendancy of the lady-novelists within their own domestic and sentimental sphere. He was rewarded when Emile Montégut announced that, just as Cervantes' novel had dealt a deathblow to chivalry, so Madame Bovary had killed romanticism. The latent romanticist within Flaubert had been suppressed when Maxime Du-Camp and Louis Bouilhet had advised him to burn the original draft of his Temptation of Saint Anthony. These friends had advised him to discipline himself by taking up a modern subject, something down to earth, such bourgeois stuff as Balzac had just been handling in The Poor Parents.

Bouilhet, who had studied medicine under Flaubert's father, proposed the local and recent case of another former student. In 1848 at the town of Ry, the second wife of a Dr. Delamare, after a series of adulteries and extravagances, had poisoned herself and precipitated her husband's suicide, leaving an orphan daughter. Flaubert acknowledged this suggestion, and the years of critical midwifery that supported it, when he dedicated Madame Bovary to Bouilhet. To DuCamp,[1] we are informed by the latter, Flaubert's acknowledgments were appropriately medical: "I was ridden by the cancer of lyricism, and you operated; it was just in time, but I cried out in pain." Part of the cure was their Mediterranean voyage, which left Flaubert bored with the exotic and homesick for the commonplace. From a French hotel-keeper in Cairo, a M. Bouvaret, he picked up a name for his bovine country doctor. Among his Notes of a Trip he jotted down an occasional reflection upon his future theme: "The poetry of the adulterous wife is only true to the extent that she is at liberty in the midst of fatality." To the heroine of George Sand,[2] resisting the prose of her environment, such poetry may be subjectively true. But to the extent that she is caught in the net-

---

1. Maxime DuCamp (1822–94), a writer now more remembered for his memoirs (Souvenirs littéraires) than his own works. He was a close friend of Flaubert and, as editor of the Revue de Paris, in part responsible for the cuts of Madame Bovary in serial form. On

Bouilhet, see note on p. 372 [Editor].
2. Alludes to the novel Lélia (first version 1833) by the woman novelist George Sand (1803–76), the melodramatic story of a woman divided between a spiritual vocation and amorous involvements [Editor].

work of objective circumstance, that free will is subjected to determining necessity, the truth about her is bound to be unpoetic: what seems beautiful must prove false. To the extent that her intimate fantasies are exposed by the light of external realities, that sense undercuts sensibility, Flaubert's treatment is like that of other realists. But where the fantasy of *Don Quixote* took the form of a vanishing heroism, which the heroine did not jeopardize with her presence, the feminine outlook of *Madame Bovary* is consistently belied by its masculine characters. Where romance, to Cervantes, signified knightly adventure, to Flaubert—more narrowly and intensively—it signifies passionate love. The means of exposure, which put Cervantes' realism on a solid and genial basis, was an appeal to the common sense of the bourgeoisie. That would have been, for Flaubert, almost as evanescent and fantastic as romanticism itself. Hence he often seems to have taken the realistic method and turned it inside out. "Realism seems to me with *Madame Bovary* to have said its last word," commented Henry James, with a sigh of somewhat premature relief.

The sharpest contradistinction to Don Quixote, whose vagaries were intellectual, Emma Bovary's are emotional. Hence they are counterweighted by no earthbound Sancho Panza, but by the intellectually pretentious M. Homais. The comic relief that he injects into Emma's tragedy is later to be elaborated into the unrelieved comedy of *Bouvard and Pécuchet*. Because it is herself that she misconceives, where Don Quixote's misconception of actuality could be corrected by reference to his fellow-men, she remains incorrigibly tragic. This narcissistic attitude of Emma's, this self-hallucination induced by over–reading, this "habit of conceiving ourselves otherwise than as we are," is so epidemic that Jules de Gaultier[3] could diagnose the weakness of the modern mind as *Bovarysme*. The vicarious lives that film–stars lead for shop–girls, the fictive euphoria that slogans promise and advertisements promote, the imaginary flourishes that supplement daily existence for all of us, are equally Bovaristic. If to Bovarize is simply to daydream, as everyone does to a greater or lesser extent, its criterion is not how much but whether our daydreams are egoistic like Emma's or altruistic like Don Quixote's. Every epoch depends upon some verbal medium for its conception of itself: on printed words and private fictions, if not on public rituals and collective myths. The trouble came when, instead of the imitation of Christ or the veneration of Mary, readers practised the emulation of Rastignac or the cult of Lélia.[4] Yet, whatever their models, they romanticized a real-

3. Jules de Gaultier, a French essayist born in 1858, coined the expression *Bovarysme* in a book by that name, first published in 1902.

4. Rastignac is one of the leading characters in Balzac's *Comédie humaine*. He is the central figure in *Le Père Goriot* and reappears, at various stages

ity which would otherwise have been formless and colorless; for
when nature has established norms of conduct, art is called upon to
publicize them. "There are people who would not fall in love if
they had never heard of love," said La Rochefoucauld. Denis de
Rougemont[5] has more recently tried to substantiate that epigram
by arguing that the erotic motive was superimposed upon the
West through medieval romance. And Paolo might never have loved
Francesca, in Dante's memorable episode, had not the book of
Galeotto acted as a go-between.

But the writer, unlike the reader, cannot afford to be swept off
his feet by emotions involved in his story. Thus Flaubert, in his first
Sentimental Education, describes the youthful reading of his poet,
Jules:

> He reread *René* and *Werther* and was disgusted with life; he
> reread Byron and dreamed of the solitude of his great-souled
> heroes; but too much of his admiration was based on personal
> sympathy, which has nothing in common with the disinterested
> admiration of the true artist. The last word in this kind of crit-
> icism, its most inane expression, is supplied to us every day by
> a number of worthy gentlemen and charming ladies interested
> in literature, who disapprove of this character because he is
> crude, of that situation because it is equivocal and rather
> smutty—discovering, in the last analysis, that in the place of
> such a person they would not have done the same thing, with-
> out understanding the necessary laws that preside over a work
> of art, or the logical deductions that follow from an idea.

It follows that Emma Bovary and her censors, though their ethics
differed, shared the same aesthetic approach. Jules on the other
hand would learn, as did Flaubert, to differentiate a work of art
from its subject-matter and the artist from his protagonist. The anecdote of Cervantes on his deathbed, identifying himself with his
hero, has its much quoted Flaubertian parallel: *Madame Bovary
c'est moi*. But this equivocal statement was not so much a confession as a cautious disclaimer of certain resemblances which Madame
Delamare's neighbors, without indulging in unwarranted gossip,
might have suspected. In so far as Flaubert lived the part, as any
novelist enters into his fully realized characterizations, it was a *tour
de force* of female impersonation. The identification was not nearly
so close as it had been with Saint Anthony or would become with
Frédéric Moreau. It is true that, on summer days, he worked in the
arbor where he stages trysts between Emma and Rodolphe; that the
cigar-case, the seal inscribed *Amor nel cor*, and other relics actually
commemorate his own affair with Louise Colet; that Louise may

of his spectacular career, in several
other volumes. On Lélia, see note
2 above [*Editor*].

5. The essay alluded to is translated
into English under the title *Love and
the Western World* [*Editor*].

well have suggested aspects of Emma, and Emma's husband and lovers may have embodied aspects of Gustave. But the very first premise of the book was the suppression of his own personality, and his later pronouncements adhere with stiffening conviction to the principle of *ne s'écrire*. Empathy is seasoned with antipathy whenever he writes about Emma to Louise; he repeatedly complains that the bourgeois vulgarity of his material disgusts and nauseates him. He would much prefer to write a book without a subject; or rather, he would like to abolish the transitions and obstacles between thought and expression; and he prophesies that literary convention, like the Marxian concept of the state, will some day wither away.

Flaubert had chosen the theme of the *Temptation of Saint Anthony* in accordance with his personal predilections. Baudelaire, who preferred the more imaginative work, explained *Madame Bovary* as a sort of wager. "The budding novelist found himself facing an absolutely worn-out society—worse than worn-out, brutal and greedy, fearing nothing but fiction and loving nothing but property." Deliberately choosing the drabbest setting, the pettiest characters, the most familiar plot, he undertook to create a masterpiece out of them: to turn their shapeless ugliness into formal beauty. He did not quite succeed in assimilating the psychology of his heroine, according to Baudelaire: "Madame Bovary has remained a man." Now it may be—it is, in fact, Dorothy Richardson's hypothesis— that no masculine novelist can ever quite penetrate the feminine mind. Nevertheless, as Matthew Arnold perceived, Tolstoy's portrayal of Anna Karenina could be more warmly sympathetic than the "petrified feeling" that went into Flaubert's portraiture. In attaching his narrative to his heroine, Flaubert was detaching himself from those whom she repudiated and from those who repudiated her. Thereby he ostensibly gave up, to the indignation of his critics, the moralistic prerogatives of the narrator. He replaced sentiment, so Brunetière[6] charged, with sensation. He developed the technical device that handbooks term "point of view" by adapting the rhythms of his style to the movement of his character's thoughts. By limiting what has more precisely been termed the "centre of consciousness" to the orbit of a single character—and, with Henry James, a peculiarly limited character—purists could intensify the focus of the novel still further. *Madame Bovary* begins, prologue-wise, in the first person; then it switches from an anonymous classmate to Charles Bovary; through his eyes we first glimpse Emma's fingernails and gradually experience his delayed reaction; thereafter the action is mainly, though by no means exclusively, circumscribed within her range of perception. But towards the end the perspective

6. The historian and critic Ferdinand Brunetière (1849–1906) wrote about Flaubert in *Le roman naturaliste* (1883) [*Editor*].

opens up and detaches itself from Emma more and more; her pan-
tomime interview with the tax-collector is reported as witnessed by a
chorus of townswomen; and Flaubert's account of her funeral ter-
minates with the various night-thoughts of the men that have loved
her.

And there are such moments as when, having escorted his lovers
into a curtained cab, Flaubert draws back a tactful distance and
projects a rapid sequence of long-range shots, so that—instead of
witnessing their embrace—we participate in a tour of the city of
Rouen, prolonged and accelerated to a metaphorical climax. The
invisible omnipresence that stagemanages these arrangements is
normally expressed by *on*, initially by *nous*, but never by *je*. The
author's commentary is to be inferred from his almost cinemato-
graphic manipulation of detail: the close-up of a religious statuette,
for example, which falls from the moving-wagon into fragments on
the road between Tostes and Yonville. This comment is transposed
to a scientific key when, after the unsuccessful operation, Emma
slams the door on Charles and breaks his barometer. Henceforth
the incongruous memento of his failure is the patentleather shoe attached to the artificial limb of his patient, the no longer club-footed
stableboy. A silly cap which characterizes Charles on his first appearance, a pocket-knife which betokens his coarseness in Emma's
eyes—nothing is mentioned that does not help to carry the total
burden of significance. Hence every object becomes, in its way, a
symbol; and the novelist seeks not merely the right word but the
right thing. Charles's first marriage is tellingly summed up by a
bouquet of withered orange blossoms in a glass jar, while the handsome cigar case retains the aroma of fashionable masculinity that
Emma has inhaled at the ball. Such effects are governed by a rigorous process of selection, far removed from the all-inclusiveness with
which Balzac accumulated background. The atmosphere, for Flaubert, is the story; the province is both his setting and his subject—
the colorlessness of local colour. The midland that he describes is a
bastard territory, somewhere along the borders of Normandy, Picardy, and Ile-de-France, where the speech has no accent, the landscape no character, the soil no richness. Even the cheese there-
abouts is lacking in savor. Everything seems, like Charles's conversation, "as flat as a sidewalk."

To render flatness flatly, however, is to risk the stalemate that
confronted Pope when he tried to excoriate dullness without being
dull. Flaubert, deploying his full stylistic resources, relieves the
ennui by colorful allusion and invidious comparison. What is literally boring he renders metaphorically interesting. The river quarter
of Rouen, at first sight, is "a small, ignoble Venice." The names of
famous surgeons are mock-heroically sounded in connection with

Charles's professional activities. Similes, ironically beautiful, frequently serve to underline ugly realities: thus the pimples on the face of his first wife had "budded like spring." Occasionally Flaubert seems to set thousands of miles between himself and the situation at hand, as when—with anthropological objectivity—he notes the similarity between a statue of the Virgin in the village church and an idol from the Sandwich Islands. Despite his more usual closeness to his *dramatis personae*, he austerely dissociates himself from their subjective opinions, and italicizes certain expressions which their lack of fastidiousness has forced him to use. He manages to approximate their points of view, while retaining the detachment of the third person and avoiding the formality of indirect discourse, through his mastery of *le style indirect libre*. Though this term seems to have no English equivalent, it denotes a kind of grammatical figuration, a modulation of tenses, and a dropping of pronominal antecedents which, thanks primarily to Flaubert, are now employed in most of our novels and short stories. "*Elle abandonna la musique, pourquoi jouer? qui l'entendrait?*" Diverging from Balzac, whose descriptions are like introductory stage-directions, Flaubert introduces objects as they swim into the ken of his personages. His personages, since they are the fluid receptacles of sense-impressions, are much less numerous and more complex than the clear-cut types from the facile Balzacian mint. His technique of characterization, as he formulated it to Taine, was "not to individualize a generality like Hugo or Schiller, but to generalize a particularity like Goethe or Shakespeare."

He forwarded this large intention by deciding to portray a particular individual who also happened to be a universal type. She had actually existed in the ill-fated Madame Delamare; and, as Zola remarked, her sisters went on existing throughout France. Even while Flaubert was writing his novel, her misadventures were being enacted by the wife of his friend, the sculptor Pradier. Strangely enough, her fate was later paralleled by that of the novel's English translator, Eleanor Marx-Aveling. American readers recognize Emma's kinship with Carol Kennicott, the capricious wife of Sinclair Lewis's country doctor in *Main Street*, and are struck by recurrent features of small-town existence which abridge the spatial and temporal intervals between Gopher Prairie and Yonville-l'Abbaye. Flaubert's preoccupation with his heroine's environment is emphasized by his sub-title, *Provincial Customs*. His social observation, which of course is more precise and analytic than Balzac's, concentrates upon a much smaller terrain and thoroughly exhausts it. His fiction starts from and returns to fact: when he read in a newspaper the very phrase that he had put into his imaginary orator's mouth, he congratulated himself that literature was being reduced to an exact science at last. When *Madame Bovary* appeared, it was blandly saluted by the critic Duranty as "a literary application of the calculus of probabilities." Though that is a far cry from any classical doctrine of probability, it looks beyond mere particularizing towards some meaningful pattern into which all the particulars must fit, a result which is predictable from the data, the logical deductions that follow from an idea. The concrete details that Flaubert selects, we have noticed, are always typical and often symbolic. We notice too his tendency to multiply the specific instance into a generalization. In his treatment of crowds, at the wedding or the exhibition, traits which were individually observed are collectively stated. Similarly, the plural is applied to immediate experiences which have become habitual, as in this summary of the doctor's routine:

> He ate omelets on farmhouse tables, poked his arm into damp beds, felt the warm spurts of blood-letting in his face, listened for death rattles, examined basins, turned over a good deal of dirty linen; but every evening he found a blazing fire, a laid–out table, comfortable chairs, and a well–dressed wife, so charming and sweet–smelling that it was hard to say whence the odor came, or whether her skin were not perfuming her chemise.

The second half of this highly Flaubertian sentence brings us home to Emma, balances the attractions of her day against the revulsions of Charles's, and registers the incompatibility of their respective ways of life. A sequence of vividly physical manifestations, ranging through the clinical towards the sensual, unfolds itself for us as it did for Charles. Strain is compensated by relaxation; pain and suffering give place to comfort and well-being; but, contrasted with the grim concreteness of his own sensations and the tangible solidity of his cases, there is something elusive and possibly deceptive in the person of Emma, which is vaguely hinted by her ambiguous perfume. More commonly we see the uxorious husband, from her vantage-point, as the thick-skinned personification of plodding mediocrity: the medical man well suited to the village of Tostes, whose competence is strained by the town of Yonville. From his earliest entrance into the schoolroom he falters between the comic and the pathetic; his solitary youth and loveless first marriage prepare him for the ungrateful role of the cuckold; on his visit to the château he seems indeed to be playing the bourgeois gentleman. His very schoolmates have found him too unromantic, yet his love is the most devoted that Emma finds—as Flaubert expressly states in his work-sheets, adding: "This must be made very clear." His own devotion to his motherless niece is doubtless reflected in Charles's tenderness towards his daughter, Berthe. In the final retrospect—the counter-part of that weary reunion which rounds out the *Sentimental Education*—Charles, over a bottle of beer with his wife's lover, Rodolphe, forgives him and blames the whole affair on "fatality." Rodolphe, though he has blamed fatality in his farewell letter to Emma, was scarcely a fatalist when he took the initiative; while Emma has enjoyed, as long as it lasted, the poetic illusion of liberty. Now that it has yielded to necessity, and the probable has become the inevitable, Charles is left to bear—and it kills him—the unpoetic truth.

The issue is poised between his materialistic plane, which is vulgar but real, and her ideal of refinement which is illusory. "Charles conjugal night: plans for his career. his child. Emma: dreams of travel. the lover. villa on the seashore. until dawn . . ." This bare notation was expanded by Flaubert into two of his most luminous pages—pages which reveal not only the nocturnal reveries of the doctor and his wife, her Italianate fancies and his Norman calculations, but the conflict within Flaubert's dual personality between lyricism and criticism—or, to use his synonym, "anatomy." To anatomize Emma's imagination is succinctly to recapitulate the romantic movement itself, moving from the primitive idyll of *Paul and Verginie* through the highly coloured mysticism of Chateaubriand's *Spirit of Christianity* towards the vicarious passions of George Sand and Balzac. Emma's sentimental education, accompanied by the excitations of music and perfumed by the incense of religiosity, is traced back to the convent where she has been schooled. From the drab milieu she has known as a farmer's daughter, her extracurricular reading conjures up the allurements of escape: steeds and guitars, balconies and fountains, medieval and oriental vistas. Dreaming between the lines, she loses her identity in the heroines of the novels she peruses, the mistresses to whom verses are inscribed, the models in the fashion magazines. The ball at the Château lends a touch of reality to her fictitious world, which Flaubert likened—in a discarded metaphor—to "a drop of wine in a glass of water." When she discovers a kindred soul in the young law clerk Léon, the only person in the community who seems comparably sensitive to boredom and yearning and the arts, their friendship is "a continual traffic in books and romances." And when a neighboring landowner, the sportsman-philanderer Rodolphe, assists her to fulfil her sexual desires, fantasy and actuality seem to merge in the realization: "I have a lover!"

But adultery ends by reasserting "the platitudes of marriage," and neither condition teaches Emma the meaning of "the words that looked so fine in books: felicity, passion, and intoxication." Here, more explicitly than in *Don Quixote* itself, language is of the essence; the basic misunderstanding, since it is verbal, is regulated by the flow and ebb of Flaubert's prose; and his rhetoric is con-

stantly expanding into purple passages which are trenchantly de-
flated by his irony. The resulting style, he feared, might read like
"Balzac *chateaubrianisé*." Yet if that compound means eloquent
banality rather than banal eloquence, it is not too inept a summary
of what Flaubert attempted and achieved; and those literary aus-
pices are not inappropriate for the incongruity between Emma's
high–flown sentiments and Charles's pedestrian bumblings. If we
ever forgot that the book was about an ill-matched pair, we should
be reminded by the way sentences double back upon themselves and
episodes are paired off against each other. The two turning points of
the first part, the fourth and eighth chapters, frame a significant
contrast between the peasantry and the aristocracy. The garish colors of the rustic wedding, the fresh haircuts of the farmers, the
lengthened communion dresses of the girls, the boisterous jokes and
substantial viands in the manner of Brueghel, are pointedly offset
by the grand entertainment at the Château de Vaubyessard, where
the stately dancers show "the complexion of wealth, that fair complexion which is enhanced by the pallor of porcelain, the shimmer
of satin, the veneer of fine furniture." In the second part a similar
pairing occurs which even more fatally brings out the variance between Charles and Emma: the operation versus the opera. On the
one hand his surgical incompetence, the gangrenescent cripple, and
the amputated foot are portents of Emma's relapse. On the other
the romantic libretto from Scott, the flamboyant tenor, and the
dazzling spectacle would corrupt purer souls than hers—notably
Natasha's in *War and Peace*.

The two antithetical strains are juxtaposed in the central chapters
of the book, where the agricultural exhibition takes place in the
public square while Rodolphe flirts with Emma in the privacy of
the deserted neo-Greek town hall. His amorous pleas are counterpointed by the official slogans of the political orators outside; a prize
for the highest quality of manure is awarded at the delicate moment
when he grasps her hand; the bifurcation is so thoroughgoing that
the national guard and the fire brigade refuse to march together;
and the series of anticlimaxes culminates when nightfall brings a
fizzle of dampened fireworks. Now Flaubert built up this scene by
writing out continuous speeches for both sets of characters, which
he thereupon broke down and rearranged within the larger framework of the situation. By such means he caught that interplay of
cross-purposes which is increasingly stressed through the third and
last part, above all in the cathedral and at the deathbed. He told
Louise Colet that the method of *Madame Bovary* would be biographical rather than dramatic; yet biography seems to branch out
into drama at all the crucial stages of Emma's career; and these in
turn furnish the novel with its six or eight major scenes—several of

which are overtly theatrical or, at any rate, ceremonial. Their relation to the rest of the book, and to his ambivalent purpose, may be gathered from his further remark that "dialogue should be written in the style of comedy, narrative in the style of epic." Mock-epic would probably be a more accurate classification of Flaubert's tone, as differentiated from the various inflections he reproduces, and softened by lyrical interludes when he is Emma. The many contrasting strands of discourse are so closely interwoven that the texture is uniformly rich, although it varies from one chapter to the next. Each of them advances the narrative a single step, scores a new point and captures another mood, much as a well-turned short story does in the hands of Flaubert's recent emulators.

The chapter, as Flaubert utilizes it, is in itself a distinctive literary genre. Its opening is ordinarily a clear-cut designation of time or place. Its conclusion habitually entails some striking effect: a pertinent image, an epigrammatic twist, a rhetorical question, a poignant afterthought. "She had loved him after all." The succession of episodes, like the articulation of a rosary, shapes the continuity of the work. The three-part structure allows the novelist, with a classicism seldom encountered in novels, to give his conception a beginning, a middle and an end: to study first the conditions of Emma's marriage, then her Platonic romance and her carnal affair, and finally the train of consequences that leads to her death. Different leading men play opposite her, so to speak, in these three successive parts: Charles in the first, Rodolphe in the second, Léon in the third. The setting broadens with her aspirations, starting from the narrowest horizon, Tostes, proceeding to the main locale, Yonville, and ultimately reaching the provincial capital, Rouen. Not that she wished to stop there. "She wanted simultaneously to die and to live in Paris," Flaubert reminds us in a characteristic zeugma, and he seems to have toyed with the notion of granting that two-edged wish. But he wisely decided to confine her to the province, reserving his study of the metropolis for the fortunes of Frédéric Moreau. The chronology of *Madame Bovary*, which spans the decade from 1837 to 1847, roughly corresponds with the period of the *Sentimental Education*, stopping just short of the mid-century crisis. Each of its subdivisions, conforming to a rough but Dantesque symmetry, covers slightly more than three years. The pivotal date for the story is 1843, the year in which Emma commits adultery with Rodolphe. Up to that stage, her illusions mount with manic fervor; after that, with steady disillusionment, she sinks towards her last depression. It will be recalled, for what it may be worth, that Flaubert's own career pivoted around his personal crisis in 1843.

Between the autumn of 1851 and the spring of 1856 his concentrated labor was the writing of *Madame Bovary*. For those who hold—with André Gide—that the gestation of art is more interesting than the finished product, no record could be more fascinating than Flaubert's correspondence during those four and a half years. The parallel lives of the author and the heroine, daily, weekly, monthly, yearly, charge the novel with their emotional tension. Imaginative effort was reinforced by documentation when Flaubert sought the proper shading for Emma's hallucinations by immersing himself in *Keepsakes* and other feminine periodicals. By plying his brother with queries about surgery and toxicology, he filled in the peculiar symptoms his outline required: "Agony precise medical details 'on the morning of the twenty-third she had vomiting spells again. . . .' " He familiarized himself with the children of his brain by drawing a map of Yonville and keeping files on its citizens. He controlled his plot—or should we say he calculated his probabilities?—by carefully drafting and firmly reworking scenarios. The embryonic material for his novel embodied 3600 pages of manuscript. The demiurgic function of reducing that mass to its present form might be likened to the cutting of a film, and—rather than speak of Flaubert's "composition" in the pictorial sense—we might refer, in kinetic terms, to montage. To watch him arranging his artful juxtapositions, or highlighting one detail and discarding another, is a lesson in artistic economy. To trace his revision of a single passage, sometimes through as many as twelve versions, is the hopeful stylist's *gradus ad Parnassum*. It is therefore a boon to students of literature that Flaubert's drafts and variants have been printed. But to reincorporate them into a composite text of *Madame Bovary*, interpolating what he excised, amplifying what he condensed, and thereby undoing much of what he did—as has latterly been done— is a doubtful service, to say the very least. Flaubert might have preferred Bowdlerization.

He did protest against expurgations when the novel was published serially in the *Revue de Paris*; but DuCamp and his fellow editors had not expurgated enough to appease the prudery of the imperial police; and Flaubert, together with the publisher and the printer, was prosecuted for outraging civic and religious morality. The outrage—so the prosecution alleged—was worse than pornography, it was blasphemy; Flaubert's offence was less a concern with sex than an attempt to link sex with religion. It mattered little that the linkage had been effected on the naive level of Emma's confused motivation; or that his analysis could be corroborated, by such sympathetic clerics as Bishop Dupanloup, from their first-hand remembrance of country confessionals. The ruse of citing passages out of context figured heavily in the trial, and the government staked much of its case on the passage where Emma receives extreme unction. It was a precarious example, since by definition this sacrament hovers ambiguously between the worlds of sense and spirit: shift the emphasis, as Joyce does in *Finnegans Wake,* and it becomes an apology for the flesh. Flaubert's defence, by warily refusing to admit the ambiguity, was able to claim the support of orthodox sanctions, along with the precedent of such diverse French writers as Bossuet and Sainte-Beuve. It argued that *Madame Bovary* as a whole, far from tempting its readers to sensualism, offered them an edifying object-lesson. Considerable stress was laid *ad hominem* on the bourgeois respectability of the Flaubert family. Won by such arguments, the judge acquitted Flaubert and his accomplices, with a parting disquisition on taste and a fatherly warning against "a realism which would be the negation of the beautiful and the good." Six months later, when *Flowers of Evil* was condemned, Flaubert must have wondered whether he or Baudelaire was the victim of judicial error. Meanwhile, in April 1857, when *Madame Bovary* came out as a book, its intrinsic ironies were enhanced by a preliminary dedication to Flaubert's lawyer and an appended transcript of the court proceedings.

Great books have their proverbial fates, among which banning and burning may not be the hardest, since they involve straight forward conflicts of principle. It may be harder for the series artist—be he Flaubert or Joyce—to emerge from the cloud of censorship into the glare of scandalous success. The public reception of Flaubert's first book, at all events, hardened those equivocal attitudes which had been poured into it. To avoid the accusation of immorality, he was pushed into the embarrassing position of a moralist. If the novel was not pornographic, it must be didactic—or had he stopped beating his wife? Taine spins an amusing anecdote of an English project to translate and circulate *Madame Bovary* as a Methodist tract, subtitled *The Consequences of Misbehaviour.* The respectable Lamartine, cited on Flaubert's behalf, declared that Emma's sins were too severely expiated. Why need Flaubert have been so much less merciful than Jesus was towards the woman taken in adultery? Partly because he was not exemplifying justice; partly because he may have been punishing himself; but mainly because her infractions of the seventh commandment were the incidental and ineffectual expression of an all-pervasive state of mind: Bovarism. Her nemesis, as Albert Thibaudet shrewdly perceived, is not a love affair but a business matter: her debt to the usurious merchant, Lheureux. When the bailiffs move in to attach the property, their inventory becomes a kind of autopsy. The household disintegrates before our eyes, as its component items are ticketed off, and we think of the auction in the *Sentimental Education.* This empty outcome— by the Flaubertian rule of opposites—is a sequel to the agricultural exhibition, where rural prosperity smugly dispenses its awards. And the lonely figure of Charles, left to brood among unpaid bills and faded love-letters, has been foreshadowed by Père Rouault after Emma's wedding, "as sad as an unfurnished house."

The vacuum her absence creates for her father and husband echoes the hollowness of her own misapplied affections. Rodolphe's gallantry, after meeting her desires half way, proves to be no more than a cynical technique of seduction. Léon's sentimentalism is quite sincere, until she seduces him, and then it vanishes like growing pains. "Every notary bears within him the ruins of a poet." Consequently, amid the most prosaic circumstances, there will still be some spark of poetry, and in Yonville-l'Abbaye it is Emma Bovary. It is not, alas, the Princesse de Clèves,[7] nor could that model of all the compunctions have flourished there; for her delicacy presupposes reciprocal behaviour on the part of others. Emma's dreams are destined, at the touch of reality, to wither into lies. Is that a critique of her or of reality? If she suffers for her mistakes, shall we infer that those who prosper are being rewarded for their merits? If we cannot, we can hardly assume—with the novel's apologists—that it preaches a self-evident moral. If it were a play our reactions would be clearer; we are more accustomed to facing her plight in the theatre; we disapprove of Hedda Gabler's[8] intrigues and pity and wistful Katerina in Ostrovsky's *Storm*. Though she possesses the qualities of both heroines, Emma is essentially a novelistic creation, set forth in all her internal complexities. Entrammelled by them, we cannot pretend to judge her, any more than we can judge ourselves. But, guided by Flaubert, perhaps we can understand her: *Madame Bovary c'est nous*. With her we look down from the town hall upon the exposition: a sordid rustic backdrop for Rodolphe's welcome advances. Again, at her rendezvous with Léon, the lovers occupy the foreground; but this time it is the massive cathedral of Rouen that looks down upon them; and its sculptured warriors and stained–glass saints, hastily passed by, are the mute upholders of higher standards than those which Emma and Léon are engaged in flouting. "Leave by the north portico, at any rate," the verger shouts after them, baffled by their indifference to Gothic antiquities, "and see the Resurrection, the Last Judgment, Paradise, King David, and the Condemned in Hellfire!"

The heavy judgment that Flaubert suspends, and which we too withhold, is implicit in this hurried exclamation. It affects the lovers as little as the extinct abbey affects Yonville, in whose name alone it survives. Yet oblique reference accomplishes what overt preaching would not, and those neglected works of art bear an ethical purport.

7. In Madame de Lafayette's famous novel about adultery (1678) [*Editor*].
8. The turbulent heroine of Ibsen's play (1890) whose life ends in suicide [*Editor*].

The category of *moraliste*, which is more comprehensive with the French than with us, since *mœurs* comprehends both morals and manners, applies to Flaubert *malgré lui*. Whereas he seemed immoral to those who confused him with his characters, and seems amoral to those who take at face-value an aloofness which is his mask for strong emotions, he protested too much when he claimed to be impersonal. If he deserves Maupassant's adjective "impassive," it is because all passion has crystallized beneath the lucent surfaces of his prose. He is not above making sententious and aphoristic pronouncements upon the behavior of his characters: "A request for money is the most chilling and blighting of all the winds that blow against love." Nor does he shrink from stigmatizing Emma's acts as phases of "corruption" and even "prostitution." More positively he betrays his sympathy, when it seems most needed, by the adjective *pauvre*. The crippled groom is a "poor devil," and so is the blind man; the luckless Charles is "poor boy," and the gestures of Emma's agony are made by "her poor hands." The word regains its economic overtones, and Flaubert's tone is uniquely humanitarian, when he pauses before the "poor garments" of Catherine Leroux. The hands of this aged peasant woman, in definitive contrast to Emma, are deformed with toil. On the platform "before those expansive bourgeois," personifying "half a century of servitude," her mute and ascetic presence strikes the single note of genuine dignity amid the pomposities and hypocrisies of the agricultural exhibition. Flaubert deliberately classifies her with the attendant livestock, for whose impassivity he reserves his compassion. His irony intervenes to measure her reward—twenty-five francs for a lifetime of service—against two pigs which have just gained prizes of sixty francs apiece. An earlier and more cruel twist, which Flaubert finally left out, pictures her deaf apprehension that the judges are accusing her of stealing the twenty-five francs.

Here is Flaubert's response to those who criticize *Madame Bovary* for its apparent lack of positive values. The human qualities he really admired, the stoic virtues of patience, devotion, work, are not less admirable when they go unrewarded. His careful portrait of Catherine Leroux—together with many landscapes, small and subdued, of his fog-tinted Normandy—belongs with the canvases then being painted by Courbet at Ornans and Millet at Barbizon. Peasant faces, though never conspicuous, are always in the background; they watch Emma through the broken window-panes of the Château. Animals, too, are sentient characters; her mysterious greyhound, Djali, is almost a demonic familiar. The people that Flaubert treats sympathetically are life's victims like the clubfooted Hippolyte: those whom Hugo would name *Les Misérables* and Dostoevsky *The Insulted and the Injured*. Surely the kindest person in the story is the druggist's errand-boy, Justin, whose dumb affection is the unwitting instrument of Emma's death, and whose illicit reading-matter is her ironic epitaph: a book entitled *Conjugal Love*. The meek do not inherit Flaubert's earth; the good, by definition, are the ones that suffer; and the unhappy ending, for poor little innocent Berthe, is grim child-labor in a textile factory. The most downtrodden creature of all, the doglike Blind Man, is linked by grotesque affinity with Emma herself. Conceiving him as a "monster," a *memento mori*, an incarnation of fleshly frailty, Flaubert had originally planned to use an armless and legless man; and accentuated Emma's disillusion by the swish of the driver's whip that knocks the helpless beggar off the coach. This, significantly, coincides with the critical stroke that once laid Flaubert prostrate on a muddy Norman road. His blind man dogs his heroine's footsteps to her very deathbed, with a terrible mimicry which is not unworthy of King Lear's fool; and there his unseasonable song, a lyric from Restif de la Bretonne[9] about young girls' dreams of love, finds its long awaited echo of relevance. Emma's eyes open to a recognition scene "like a person waking from a dream," like Don Quixote when death restores his aberrant sense of reality.

The counterpoint set up in the cathedral attains its fullest resolution—far from the Hotel-de-Boulogne—in Emma's bedchamber. There priestly rites alleviate clinical symptoms; the unction allays the poison; and, taking formal leave of her five senses one by one, Flaubert breaks off his prolonged sequence of associations between sacred and profane love. In so far as orchestration is based on arrangement rather than statement, Flaubert's can be best appreciated by comparing this episode with a remotely analogous one from Dickens, the famous sermon on the reiterated text: "Dear, gentle, patient, noble Nell was dead." Flaubert, who evokes what Dickens invokes and elaborates what the Englishman simplifies, dismisses his heroine more abruptly and absolutely: "She no longer existed." Thereafter Emma's deathwatch unites "in the same human weakness" Father Bournisien, with his holy water, and M. Homais, with his bottle of chlorine. Since religion is served by the priest as inadequately as science is by the pharmacist, it is not surprising that neither force has operated benignly on Emma's existence, or that the antagonists—as Bournisien predicts—"may end by understanding one another." Homais, the eternal quacksalver, is a would-be writer as well as a pseudo scientist, who practises the up-to-date art of journalism and is most adept at self-advertisement. Because his shop is the source of Emma's arsenic, he is an unconscious accomplice in her suicide; and he instigates the ill-advised surgery that

9. A prolific eighteenth-century disciple of Rousseau (1734–1806) of considerable interest. The song appears on pp. 193 and 238.

poisons Hippolyte's leg and blackens Charles's reputation. When his own prescription, the antiphlogistic pomade, fails to cure the Blind Man's scrofula, it is typical of him to add insult to injury, persecuting his patient while continuing to pose as the benefactor of mankind. M. Homais is definitively shown up by the retarded arrival of Dr. Larivière, just as the introduction of Catherine Leroux is a standing rebuke to Emma's course of conduct. Hereupon Flaubert, inspired by memories of his father, dedicates a strongly affirmative paragraph to the understanding physician, who pursues the compassionate calling of medicine as religiously as a medieval saint. But the doctor is no god-in-the-machine, and it is too late for an antidote. With a tear he immediately discerns the prognosis, and with a farewell pun he diagnoses the complaint of Homais. His difficulty is not *le sang* but *le sens*—neither anemia nor hypertension, nor indeed that lack of sense from which poor Emma suffered, but insensibility, the defect of her quality.

What is worse, the disease is contagious. With the rare exception of the stranger Larivière, and the dubious hope of agreement between the cleric and the anticlerical, nobody in Yonville seems to understand anybody else. And though collective misunderstanding is comic, failure to be understood is a personal tragedy. Though Emma, misunderstood by her husband and lovers and neighbours, misunderstands them and herself as well, at least she harbors a feeling of something missed; whereas the distinguishing mark of Homais is the bland assurance that he never misses anything. His Voltairean incantations, his hymns to progress, his faith in railroads and rubber, his fads and statistics, his optimism—a century afterwards—may seem as far-fetched as Emma's delusions of grandeur. His clichés, embedded like fossils in his newspaper articles, Flaubert was momentarily tempted to say, "would enable some future Cuvier of the moral sciences to reconstruct clearly all the ineptitude of the nineteenth-century middle class, if that race were not indestructible." Of that hardy breed M. Homais survives as our prime specimen. Neither a creation nor a discovery, he represents the fine flower of the species that pervaded the *Comédie humaine*, the ripe perfection of the philosophy whose accredited spokesman was M. Prudhomme. This was enthusiastically attested when Prudhomme's creator and actor, Henry Monnier,[1] sought permission to dramatize and enact Homais. The latter is more successful in attaining their common ambition, the decoration of the Legion of Honor; while his predecessor must content himself, when the curtain falls, with "a decorated son-in-law." The curtain-line of their spiritual

1. Joseph Prudhomme ("the upstanding man") is the satirical creation of Henri Monnier (1805–77); his name became part of the French language to designate the slightly sinister self-righteousness of the rising bourgeoisie [*Editor*].

relative, that famous father-in-law, M. Poirier,[2] is his resolve to be "peer of France in '48," a gesture which has meanwhile been thwarted by the revolution. But the unabashed Homais goes from strength to strength; the Empire will shower its accolades on him and his brethren; and the dazzling glimpse of him in his electric undervest is a veritable apotheosis.

When he equipped his bourgeois with a watchword, *"Il faut marcher avec son siècle!"* Flaubert may have remembered his newly decorated friends, Maxime DuCamp, whose *Chants modernes* were prefaced by a Whitmanesque declaration: *"Tout marche, tout grandit, tout s'augmente autour de nous. . . ."* Any endeavour which aims to "keep pace with one's century," as Flaubert realized better than his contemporaries, is bound to be outdistanced in the long run. He took the province for his ground because it was an available microcosm, because it exaggerated the ordinary, because its dearth of color sharpened its outlines; but he did not assume that provinciality was confined to the hinterland or, for that matter, to any territory. M. Homais is historically, rather than geographically, provincial. The habit of equating one's age with the apogee of civilization, one's town with the hub of the universe, one's horizons with the limits of human awareness, is paradoxically widespread: it is just what Russian novelists were attacking as *poshlost* or self-satisfied mediocrity. It is what stands between Emma Bovary and the all-too-easily-satisfied citizens of Yonville. Her capacity for dissatisfaction, had she been a man and a genius, might have led to Rimbaldian adventures or Baudelairean visions: "Anywhere out of this world." As things stand, her retribution is a triumph for the community, a vindication of the bourgeoisie. Flaubert, who does not always conceal his tenderness towards those who suffer, now and then reveals his bitterness towards those whose kingdom is of this world. We cannot sympathize with the prosperous Homais as we could with Balzac's bankrupt César Birotteau; for, unlike his prototypes on the comic stage, Flaubert's druggist is not just a harmless busybody, a well-meaning figure of fun; he is the formidable embodiment of a deeply satirical perception which was adumbrated in *le Garçon* and eventuates in *Bouvard and Pécuchet*. His Bovarism would be more illusive than Emma's, if the modern epoch did not conspire to support his bumptious ideology and to repay his flatteries with its honours. His *boutonnière*, like the one conferred on Tolstoy's Russian guardsman, symbolizes more than Napoleon intended—and less. For the symbol is an empty ornament, the

2. *Le Gendre de Monsieur Poirier* (1884), a comedy by Augier and Sandeau, is centered on the relation-ship between a bourgeois and his aristocratic son-in-law.

badge of society's approval is meaningless, when it is unsupported by reality.

What, then, is real? Not the tawdry medal awarded to Catherine Leroux, but the lifelong service that earned it so many times over. And what is realism? Not the pathology of Emma's case, but the diagnostic insight of Larivière. Charles Bovary, for all his shortcomings, remains the great doctor's disciple, and retains the peasant virtues of his own patients; he is led astray by other motives than his own, by sentimentalism through Emma and pretentiousness through Homais. As the thrice–injured party, conjugally betrayed, professionally humiliated, financially ruined, Dr. Bovary is the neglected protagonist. If Emma is a victim of the situation, he is her victim, and her revenge against the situation is to undermine his way of life. The depths of his ignominy can be gauged by the idealized achievements of Dr. Benassis in Balzac's *Country Doctor*. Flaubert's ideal, though more honored in the breach than in the observance, fortifies him against those negative values which triumph in his book, and rises to an unwonted pitch of affirmation with the character sketch of Dr. Larivière: his disinterested skill, his paternal majesty, his kindness to the poor, his scorn for all decorations, his ability to see through falsehood. His most revealing epithet is *hospitalier*, since it connotes not only hospitality but Flaubert's birthplace, his father's hospital at Rouen, and also the stained–glass figure of Saint Julian the Hospitaler, whom the verger of the cathedral pointed out in an earlier draft, and who would later be Flaubert's knightly hero. The hospital and the cathedral: such, in retrospect, are the substance and the form of *Madame Bovary*. The attitude that embraces the distance between them, that comprehends both the painful actualities and the grandiose aspirations, and that can therefore make each paragraph comment dynamically upon itself, is Flaubertian irony. Irony dominates life, so Flaubert asserted by precept and example. So it does, particularly for those who are occupied with art as well as life, and unflinchingly face the problems of their interrelationship. Hence the irony of ironies: a novel which is at once cautionary and exemplary, a warning against other novels and a model for other novelists, a classical demonstration of what literature gives and what literature takes.

JEAN PIERRE RICHARD

[Love and Memory in *Madame Bovary*]†

Flaubert is not, by nature, a compartmentalized creature; in his world all things communicate with each other. This coherence, which links together the inner experience, the concrete experience, and the metaphorical expression, is perhaps the most attractive aspect of his genius. The statistical study of the imagery undertaken by M. Demorest[1] reveals that love is most often expressed, especially in the most spontaneous works and in the early versions of the big novels, by images of water and fluidity. And M. Demorest rightly concludes that this preference indicates a certain unrest, an awareness of the fact that passion causes instability, almost a condemnation of love. It seems to us that it expresses even more clearly the essential truth that, in its nature as well as in its structure, love is a dissolution of the human personality. A psychoanalytical study would probably yield even more conclusive results.

But we have even better evidence: In Flaubert's everyday existence, at the root of his most commonplace tastes and habits as well as in the most ordinary scenes of his novels, we find this same obsessive concern with water, experienced as a dissolving and diluting force. The Turkish bath atmosphere, for instance, so well described by Charles du Bos in his marvelous essay on Flaubert,[2] should not merely be taken for a metaphor. Flaubert loved steam baths:

† From "La creation de la forme chez Flaubert" ("The creation of form in Flaubert") in *Littérature et sensation* (Paris: Editions du Seuil, 1954); reprinted by permission of the publisher. Translated by Paul de Man.

Our title is a made-up and somewhat distorting label designed to bring together two separate parts of a larger essay on the creation of form in Flaubert. The text should therefore be considered not as a closed statement on *Madame Bovary*, but as a demonstration of a specific method of literary analysis that characterizes the critical writing of Jean Pierre Richard and the group of critics to which he belongs (see the Introduction). It is part of a larger argument, too extensive to be summarized here, which attempts a description of the process of creation in Flaubert by tracing distinctive experiences similar to the ones described here throughout the entire work, including the letters, unpublished fragments, and drafts. The themes are, in turn, arranged into a coherent network, connected by links that establish a con-

sistent pattern of development, thus claiming to reproduce the movement of Flaubert's own literary consciousness. The passages have been selected because they deal primarily with *Madame Bovary*, but this manner of making excerpts tends to be misleading in this case. Critics like J. P. Richard do not take the finished form of completed works for their starting-point, nor do they consider them particularly meaningful structures; their interest focuses instead on the recurring, obsessive themes that appear most clearly before they have been hammered into form. In the case of Flaubert, where the "will to form" is particularly explicit, the critic's effort tends precisely to recapture the inchoate, purely subjective experience that precedes the final product. Hence the predilection for early drafts and versions, from which practically all the quotations are taken [*Editor*].

1. D. Demorest, *Symbolic and Figurative Expression in the Work of Gustave Flaubert* (Paris: Louis Conard, 1931).
2. See p. 360 of this edition [*Editor*].

The other day, I took a bath. I was alone at the bottom of the tub . . . Hot water was flowing all around me; stretched out like a calf, I let all kinds of thoughts go through my head; all my pores were quietly dilating. It was a highly voluptuous and gently melancholical experience to be thus taking a bath all by myself, lost among those large dark rooms in which the slightest noise echoed like a cannon shot, while the naked Kellaks called out to each other and handled me like embalmers preparing a body for the tomb.[3]

The body dilates and grows numb. Consciousness loses itself in the dark. We abandon ourselves to a happy passivity. Half disposssessed of all awareness, we become mummified.

At other moments, the same pleasure can grow more active, and water becomes like a body against which one rubs oneself, until total interpenetration is achieved:

I took a bath in the Red Sea. It was one of the most voluptuous pleasures in my life. I rolled myself in the water as on thousands of liquid teats that covered my entire body.[4]

Woman attracts as if she were water, and water caresses like a woman. In his bath, Flaubert experiences the voluptuous pleasure of a complete fusion, while remaining just conscious enough not to lose himself entirely, just powerful enough to let his muscles dominate the liquid element; the swimmer enters the water to which he abandons himself, while remaining poised on the surface. The bath is a prelude to lovemaking.

The *boat* is an even more detached experience. The full thickness of the hull protects one against the invading waters. The boat defies and conquers the water, even while being carried by it. Consequently, the boat-rides—near the end of *Madame Bovary*, for instance—suit the moment when love checks itself rather than overflows. Lost in the happy emptiness of their sensations, the two lovers allow themselves to be carried together by the languid movement of the moment, rather than losing themselves into each other. The flow of the river gives direction to the amorous effusion and orients its slow languor. Water makes them live *with* each other, makes them realize that, carried by the universal flux, they nevertheless exist and travel together.

More violently sensuous characters abandon themselves to less commonplace reveries. They feel themselves hampered by the hull of the boat, and resent the fact that, in the bath, they are not allowed to penetrate beyond the surface of the water. They dream of a deeper, underwater fusion. Louise Roche, for instance, in the *Sentimental Education* envies the *life of the fishes:*

3. *Correspondence,* II, 140.   4. *Ibid.,* 209.

It must be so sweet to roll oneself at ease in the water, to feel oneself caressed on all sides. And she trembles as with movements of sensuous play.[5]

The fish fits snugly in the liquid mass that surrounds him on all sides. He molds himself upon it in the full roundness of his shape. He is flexible. One could easily imagine him to be part of the water, a brother of the snake whose body mimics the motion of the waves and so often symbolizes, in Flaubert, the wavelike, languid movement of desire. A famous passage in *Madame Bovary* describes the refraction of a ray of moonlight in the river as follows: "and the silvery light seemed to spiral to the very bottom, like a headless serpent covered with scales."[6] The serpent is like a river in the river. The serpent in *Salammbo* is even more immediately reminiscent of the lunar deity: the reptile, flexible and clammy, in the same milky atmosphere, synthesizes all these material qualities into a common promise of total abandon to a liquid caress. In the *Temptation of Saint Anthony*, luxury crawls and spirals slowly, like a snake.

Running waters occupy only a minor part in Flaubert's dreams. They tear apart before they absorb, and he responds primarily to the slow *oozing* of one element into another. The continuity that wraps all things into one single entity fascinates him, and the most fascinating of all continuities, the most mysterious and the least visible, is the movement of water as it originates, its apparition at the surface of a solid object. Certain solids perspire in Flaubert's writing. It is not by chance that *Madame Bovary* takes place in an atmosphere of saturated humidity in which all things, sensations, feelings, houses, and landscapes make up a world of oozing waters. For it was to be the novel of "lascivious dampness," of "poor hidden souls, damp with melancholy, closed in like the courtyards in the provinces whose walls are covered with moss."[7] In Flaubert's own statement, he set out to reproduce "the musty color that surrounds the lives of lower insects."[8] Charles Bovary, for instance, literally oozes with boredom and greyness: "the long thin hairs that covered his cheeks like a blonde moisture . . . covered his expressionless face with a pale fuzz"[9]—a most effective image, showing stupidity grown visible, like a mushroom. Most of the time, this mildew does not coagulate enough to become moss or fungus. Instead, one sees the surface of things slowly swell and grow heavy, until a liquid *drop* comes into being and falls to the ground. This obscure operation awakens all kinds of dark responses in Flaubert's soul and he never ceases to meditate upon it.

5. *Sentimental Education*, p. 361.
6. *Madame Bovary* (Norton Critical Edition), p. 174. [Richard's citations have been altered to agree with our edition. *Editor*].
7. *Correspondence*, II, 17.
8. Goncourt, *Journal*, I, 283.
9. *Madame Bovary* (Pommier–Leleu edition), p. 134.

The drop is indeed a particularly mysterious entity, first of all because of its origin: it originates out of nothing, or rather, it grows like a pearl on elements with which it has nothing in common. The imagination can quite easily reconcile itself to the notion of an underground current coming to the surface; such an event is at least founded on a continuity that may not be visible, but is easily imagined. On the other hand, it is very difficult to account for the apparition of a drop on the flat surface of a wall or a rock. Everything on this flat plane seems to prohibit its formation; and yet, there it is, alive, born elsewhere, sign of the fact that one has to penetrate either beyond the wall or into the drop itself to capture the obscure power that brought it into existence. Maurice de Guérin,[1] in the furthest recess of the grotto where the Centaur comes to life, had strongly felt how gratuitous this experience appeared and saw it as a gift of the Gods, as an emanation of Being. The movement goes in the opposite direction in the case of Flaubert. The self oozes towards things and the drop is formed, not at the beginning, but at the climax of life. It appears when the inner self relaxes and lets go; it counteracts for a moment the excess of passivity by concentrating and objectifying it. It is like the avowal of weakness or the overflow of a saturation no longer able to keep itself in check. "In my heart," says Flaubert, "I feel something of the green oozings of the Norman cathedrals."[2] Consequently, drops appear in all the scenes of desire, of ennui and of death, in all the moments in which someone, on the verge of disappearing, has to gather himself into a moment of unity, albeit liquid and ephemeral, before vanishing into nothingness. This suspended state of saturation before one abandons oneself to desire, is perfectly represented by the drop; and when it falls to the ground, it renders the heavy explosion of pleasure.

When he falls in love with Emma, Charles watches the drops of a springlike rain fall on the young woman's umbrella:

> One day, during a thaw, the bark of the trees in the yard was oozing, the snow melted on the roofs of the buildings . . . She stood on the threshold; went to fetch her sunshade . . . Beneath it, she smiled at the gentle warmth; drops of water fell one by one on the taut silk.[3]

Elsewhere, in a scene of satisfied sensuality, Emma looks at the moonlight which is like "a monstrous candlestick, from which fell drops of melting diamond. . . ." These are the overflowings of a satisfied ripeness, echoing the manifestations of her tenderness; too,

1. The allusion is to the prose poem *The Centaur* by the French romantic writer Maurice de Guérin (1810–39).
2. *Correspondence,* III, 398.

3. *Madame Bovary* (Norton Critical Edition), p. 13.

there is the fall, in the night, "of a ripe peach that fell all by itself from the espalier."[4] The same movement of saturation followed by falling is present in the ripening fruit and the melting snow. During the horseback ride with Rodolphe, immediately prior to her un- doing, Emma's and Rodolphe's horses "kicked with their hooves fallen pinecones." When Emma, at the end of the novel, runs to Rodolphe's house to borrow money, "a warm wind blew in her face; melting snow fell drop by drop from the brave buds onto the grass . . ."[5]; the first draft added: "a weakening odor emanated from the damp tree-trunks, and she was about to faint with desire and apprehension."[6] We can go one step further still: ripeness turns into its own excess, the person bursts open like a rotten fruit, losing himself among all things. The dead Emma does not quite disappear forever: it seemed to Charles that "she slowly expanded beyond her own limits and diffused into all surrounding things, into the silence, into the night . . . and into the liquid drops that oozed from the walls. . . ."[7] Death and life come together in the same oozing drop.

But the symbolism of the drop goes even further: instead of imi- tating the mere movement of desire, it can recapture its very con- sciousness. Instead of concentrating on the origin and the end of desire, the imagination will focus on its renewal, its repetition. For any particular drop is only one element in a series of drops, and it necessarily lives within the continuity of this successive movement. It causes a moment of discontinuity, a momentary interruption that suspends the persistent flow of desire and thus awakens us from a state of torpor into a semiconsciousness. Letting oneself live, as it were, drop by drop, one feels satisfied; without losing touch alto- gether with the feeling of satisfaction, consciousness gains brief moments of relief while waiting for the next drop of desire to come into being, and this allows it to recover its strength and self-aware- ness. When Emma and Léon are frozen into mutual contempla- tion, they listen to the running water of a fountain:

> The water running in the courtyard, dripping from the pump into the watering can, kept time and created a palpitation.[8]

The regularity of the successive drops gives a semblance of life to feelings numbed by the monotony of desire; they awaken at least the consciousness of an inward palpitation and create an obscure feeling of duration. The rhythmical pattern of desire, alternating between rise and fulfillment, gives shape to the continuously ex-

4. *Ibid.*, p. 174.
5. *Ibid.*, p. 225.
6. *Madame Bovary* (Pommier–Leleu edition), p. 592.

7. *Ibid.*, p. 485.
8. *Ibid.*, p. 621.

panding movement of their love, as little shocks of self–awareness shake them, like the movements of the oars shake a boat on a river:

> The heavy boat advanced slowly, shaken by regular move-
> ments . . . The square oars tinkled against the irons and, with
> the breathing of the oarsman, this created an even, regular
> rhythm into the silence.[9]

Desire has at last found its deeper rhythm, its proper beat. Water is not only the element that absorbs and slides; it can also suggest an inner balance within the human being. After having given in to Rodolphe, Emma felt "her heart beginning to beat again, and her blood circulating within her like a river of milk." The happy rhythm of the body coincides at such moments with the powerful flow of free and life-giving rivers.

Every bath, whether it be dangerous or appealing, implies a risk of drowning. . . . The water symbolism in *Salammbo* culminates in a scene of drowning, reminiscent of the episode in Victor Hugo's novel *Les Miserables* in which Jean Valjean feels himself slowly drowning in the mud of a Paris sewer. The same experience, in Flaubert, stems from a more permanent form of anxiety. Hugo transcends it by his positive enjoyment of fullness, and by the image of flight into the void itself. For Flaubert, fullness is, from begin- ning to end, like the movement of a rising sea. When Emma has been betrayed by Rodolphe and wants to throw herself out of the window of her attic, she feels physically attracted by the void; she is possessed as by a liquid form of dizziness: "the ground of the village square seemed to tilt over and climb up the walls. . . ." She was "right at the edge, almost hanging, surrounded by vast space . . . She had but to yield, to let herself be taken."[1] Death is like a passive giving in to this liquid tide which has never ceased to be there, sustaining and absorbing life all along.

> What satisfaction she felt, when she leaned at last on something
> solid, something sturdier than love. . . .

Like Spendius and Mathô in *Salammbo*, Emma looks desperately for the rescuing pavement underneath that will stop her from drowning. "She tried naively to find support in something, in the love of her little girl, the cares of her household."[2] But these efforts are in vain, and she knows it: how to find support outside, if one is unable to find it within oneself? All Emma finds in herself are floating masses of feeling, like the ceaseless motion of dark waters, nothing solid or pure. She has no feelings which she can

9. *Ibid.*, p. 515.
1. *Madame Bovary* (Norton Critical Edition), p. 148.
2. *Madame Bovary* (Pommier–Leleu), p. 399.

take hold of, for feelings, by themselves, have no substantial existence; they merely represent the various affective tonalities through
which she moves with gliding motion. It is impossible to isolate a
definite part, to divide it by analysis. It is impossible to divide the
even flow of feeling; it runs along like an opaque mass that yields
nothing to the searching eye.

If Flaubert were nevertheless asked to explain how feelings can
originate, live and die, and what law governs the movement of their
existence, he would in all likelihood point to a kind of liquid
stirring-process, by means of which new psychological combinations
come into being:

> Literary reminiscences, mystical impulses, carnal ecstasies and
> ephemeral caresses, all were confused in the immensity of this
> passion. A heap of experiences, great and small, some ordinary
> some exotic, some insipid some succulent, reappeared there, giving
> the passion variety, like those Spanish salads where one finds fruits
> and vegetables, chunks of goat meat and slices of citron float-
> ing about in pale-blond oil.[3]

The sentence was deleted from the final version, probably because Flaubert considered the images too crude; its completion is
contained in an immediately preceding note: "Everything was
mixed together in the movement . . . It spilled over and carried
her away." The flow of inner duration draws together elements of
the most diverse origin and gathers them into a heterogeneous mass.
Feeling has no synthetic power in this case; it is the result of a
group of impulses that keep living side by side, without assimilation,
as long as the feeling lasts; they will resume their independent existence when the flow of feeling has subsided. When, at other moments, the driving force of an active passion is lacking, psychological changes occur by a kind of fermentation, due to the excessively
stagnant state of each separate feeling as it remains caught within
itself: "All was mixed together, all these frustrations, all these
fermentations turned into bitterness. . . ."[4] "Love *turned* into
melancholy."[5] This chemical transformation is not a change of
state, but merely a change into another liquid state, a change in the
consistency of the flow that keeps running incessantly within the
self.

At such moments, one lives as if carried by the current. "I am
driven from thought to thought, like a piece of dry grass on a river,
carried down the stream wave by wave. . . ."[6] This slow and
heavy water is like the stirrings of boredom. It drags us down carried by the impulse of a weakened imagination, an easy prey to the
most inauthentic, mechanical associations of ideas. Emma's imagi-

3. *Ibid.*, p. 383.   5. *Ibid.*, p. 396.
4. *Ibid.*, p. 298   6. *Correspondence*, II, 281.

nation wanders among the pages of the keepsake albums. No strong tie links the images together; the present is nowhere enriched by the imagination of the future. Whatever future there is, is considered to be beyond our reach, and in the middle of the most attractive dreams, she abandons herself to a kind of degradation of her being, of which she is aware, and which spoils even the pleasures of the imagination.

At other moments however, especially when it is directed towards the past, this same coagulating power of dreams can lead to valid and stable combinations. Experiences of time and of place come together, carried by the stream of memory. I no longer know where I am, who I am; the numbness that gains my senses makes me lose all awareness of my concrete situation. A drowsy state follows in which time and space are blurred. At times, this may happen before falling asleep. Just before dropping off, Emma dreams that she falls asleep in some other place, in a luxurious house that quickly grows into a reality:

> For, in a double and simultaneous perception, her thoughts mixed with the things that surrounded her, the cotton curtains became silk, the candlesticks on the chimney became silver, etc. . . .[7]

In this confusion of places and settings, the illusion, for an instant, is successful. More often, it is some exterior motion that causes the necessary drowsiness—for instance, the rocking motion of a carriage in which a traveller is being conveyed: Charles Bovary, seated in the cart that takes him, in the early hours of the morning, to the farm of old Rouault, Emma in the carriage taking her home after the dance at Vaubyessard or in the Yonville stagecoach after her days of lovemaking with Léon, Frédéric, in the *Sentimental Education*, going from Nogent to Paris, all drift off into the blurred world of semi-sleep. "His hopes, his memories, Nogent, the rue Choiseul, Madame Arnoux, his mother, everything became blurred and confused."[8] In the case of Charles Bovary, the sensations that are tightly fused together are even more specific:

> He would fall again into a tepid drowsiness, in which his most recent sensation came back to him. He saw himself *at the same time*, both husband and student, lying on his own bed beside his wife[9] as he had just left it, and walking busily about in an operating room. He felt under his elbow the sensation of a desk in an amphitheater which was also his pillow at home . . . He smelled the odor of cataplasms and of his wife's hair . . . And

7. *Madame Bovary* (Pommier–Leleu edition), p. 288.
8. *Sentimental Education.*
9. The passage refers to Charles Bo-

vary's first wife, not to Emma. The corresponding passage in the final version is on p. 9 [*Editor*].

it all mingled into one whole seeking for something with an uneasy longing, unable to lift its lead-weighted wings, while the confused memory turned round and round in place below.[1]

From this admirable text, which is itself like a pathetic effort to express the obscure something that lies hidden underneath the heavy and clumsy opacity of words, two main indications can be derived. The first concerns the concrete unity of original and repeated experience. Sensation and memory are experienced simultaneously, as if they were one and the same: "they (memory and sensation) oscillate, then blend together," as a correction to the above text puts it, like two liquid masses intimately blending together. But it would be hard to believe that such a perfect blending together could be a product of mere chance: there must be an essential analogy between the present sensation and the past memory, an analogy which, with the assistance of the half-sleep, actually caused both impressions to fuse into one. The smell of the cataplasms, which is also at the same time the smell of the hair, locates the sensation–memory in an area where sensation and disgust are one: both sensations (the hair and the cataplasms) bathe, as it were, into the same reaction of repulsion, each enriched by the particular quality of disgust that characterizes it: medical disgust in the first case, sexual disgust in the latter. We should remember that, in Flaubert, the pastelike texture of pommade suggests the very texture of desire; the smell of the cataplasms is thus closely linked to that of a pommade turned sour: Charles no longer feels any desire towards his first wife, who is constantly complaining and being ill. Elsewhere, in a more awake state of consciousness, subterranean relationships of the same type will be expressed by metaphors. But here, we are in an area that precedes that of metaphor, on the level where all substance is experienced as identical.[2]

Even more important is the emphasis, in this same passage, on the restless desire, the blurred memory that "turns round and round . . . below." Further corrections refer to it as a "loaded-down desire," "one with something persistent and obtuse . . . fighting in vain in the depths of consciousness . . . in order to come to the surface and find the light of day," in an effort akin to—and here is the clarifying metaphor—"that of his heavy eyelids that fell back by themselves."[3] The struggle is that of a half-stifled being, reaching in vain towards light and air, but incessantly dragged down again by its own apathy. The memory, which is itself

1. *Madame Bovary* (Pommier–Leleu edition), p. 152.
2. *"Au state de l'identité substantielle"*: this entire passage constitutes an important and revealing statement of the general relationship between language, sensation and consciousness on which J. P. Richard's critical method is based [*Editor*].
3. *Madame Bovary, Sketches and Unpublished Fragments*, I, 53–54.

penetrated with anxiety—"Charles tried to call to mind all the fractures he had seen, and how they were treated"—tries to pierce the opacity of the drowsy mind; it tries to fight the double tendency towards osmosis and towards horizontality, an evening out, which is characteristic of all liquid matter. Consciousness acts to attract it to the surface, force it into expression; but its own weight throws it back into the dark and drowsy sleep, the depths of which language can not penetrate. This desperate struggle to rise above one's own state of being resembles that of someone caught in quicksand or of an acrobat whose limbs are sheathed in lead: "in writing this book, I am like a man trying to play the piano with balls of lead attached to every articulation in my fingers."[4] Emerging from a bath, the body seems to have tripled in weight. Everything seemed to direct Flaubert towards the ease of a spontaneous fluidity, but he chooses instead to write the books "for which he is least gifted": writing is to him like an awakening of the mind, the emergence of consciousness.

And he will most effectively wake himself by taking his own drowsiness, his own experience, for the object of his description. Most of Flaubert's characters seem to exist in a state of drugged semi-awareness. They "stagger around like people suffering from exhaustion,"[5] overcome by some "irresistible torper like that of someone who has drunk a deadly beverage."[6] They are bewitched, "with a kind of mist in their head," which "neither the priest nor the doctor are able to dispell."[7] All these dazed characters end by devouring themselves out of sheer sloth. They collapse for good when they achieve their own deaths. Unlike Balzac's victims, she is not a victim of the mechanical power of money; she is defeated by weakness, by passivity, and most of all by lies, lies that are "like quicksand: one single step taken in that direction, and the heart itself is conquered . . ."[8] Her death is like a pathological drowning in quicksand: "it seemed to her that the stairs [of Rodolphe's house] gave way under her feet"; the furrows of the field look "like gigantic waves that broke all around her. The earth under her feet was weaker than water, and she was surprised not to be sinking away in it . . ." One should also refer to Flaubert's letter to Taine in which he describes the symptoms of the nervous disorders that plagued him: "his soul seemed to leave his body; all the memories, images and combinations of ideas that it contained exploded at once, in one single blow, like a thousand-piece fireworks." "She felt her soul escape."[9] Death is the final dissolution, prefigured in

4. *Correspondence*, III, 3.
5. *Ibid.*, III, 49.
6. *Salammbo*, p. 38.
7. *Madame Bovary* (Norton Critical Edition), p. 98.

8. *Madame Bovary* (Pommier–Leleu edition), p. 547.
9. *Ibid.*, p. 597.

sleep, sensation, and love. One says farewell, relinquishes all possessions. As in Bouvard and Pécuchet's dream, "one leaves in the dawn, in the breeze, among the stars."[1] Nothing, in fact, could be more familiar, more reassuring; ever since their birth, Flaubert's characters have been engaged in dying: their lives have been like a succession of fainting spells. As for death, it is called "a continuous fainting."[2] * * *

This immersion is followed by the awareness that something has been immersed: I can hold on to the memory of my metamorphoses. But this memory does not create a link with my past reality. To the contrary, the image of my past arises only to reveal the considerable distance that separates me from that past. It strengthens my isolation within the present moment, for it shows my past in an anonymous light, as if it consisted of episodes in the life of someone else. Upon arriving at Yonville just before falling asleep, Emma sees all her earlier memories parade before her eyes.

> The images followed each other with the continuous motion of a rotating cylinder; they appeared, disappeared, came back again. They seemed to exist on the same temporal plane, at equal distance from the present moment; and she considered them without joy or sadness, as if memory made her look at pictures painted on a wall.[3]

No intimate link exists between her and this spectacle. A region of total indifference, open only to the detached curiosity of the eye, stretches between her past and her present self. Some contact prevails, but it is devoid of all intimacy. The images parade at equal distance from the present, without any feeling of greater or lesser proximity. The absence of all gradation makes it impossible to create a perspective of depth, to build, as it were, a road inward that would allow descent, step by step, toward the depths of a reconstructed past. The equidistant and anonymous images allow for no architectural construction; they confine the act of memory to the space that separates the present from the flat horizon of all past experiences. This space becomes entirely negative, somewhat like the window-pane at Vaubyessard through which, at night, Emma perceives the faces of staring peasants that remind her of her own youth. "The brilliance of the present moment was such that her entire past life, so clear up till now, vanished to the point of making her doubt that she had lived it at all. There she was, and around

---

1. *Bouvard and Pécuchet*, p. 294.
2. J. P. Richard then pursues his analysis, using primarily examples taken from the *Correspondence*, and examines how Flaubert tries to overcome the original fluidity of his being. He shows how the novelist metamorphosizes himself into his various characters. But this attempt collapses as Flaubert realizes his inability to maintain these invented entities in existence [*Editor*].
3. *Madame Bovary* (Pommier–Leleu edition), p. 259.

her nothing existed but a darkness that engulfed all things."[4] The window is like a frozen surface through which no human warmth can penetrate. Only the eye can cross the obstacle, but this transparency precludes all direct participation in what lies on the other side. A spreading darkness reduces to a common impersonality all the faces and all the memories that lie on the far side of this fundamental obstacle. A first version of this same passage expressed this same feeling of distance by a different, but equally striking metaphor: "it seemed to her that her past life shrank more and more into itself, like an image seen through the small side of an operaglass. It took little space and seemed cut off from her, without anything in common with the present."[5] Memory disjoints the human personality; it can only confront us with the image of a past from which we are forever separated. "There she was," Flaubert writes. His heroes are always "there," while trying to reach their deep selves somewhere else. True, the liquid osmosis of semi-sleep, the blurred states of consciousness of reverie, allow these distances to melt into proximity, the "elsewhere" to become "here" by allowing the past sensation to coincide with the present one. But this passive subjugation by means of which the past returns to flood the present can hardly be called memory. The past is merely annulled, not recaptured. The suppression of the gap between past and present merely eliminates the past, and leaves the character as lonely as before. In this case also, Flaubert makes the cruel discovery that fusion with another entity fails to establish a real relationship: he is incapable of possession, in his relation toward himself as well as in that towards others or towards his characters.

Since nothing allows Flaubert to establish real links between the different stages of the metamorphoses he experiences, he will have to look elsewhere, outside himself, to fill in this void and give coherence to his destiny. Georges Poulet, in his study of temporality in Flaubert, has admirably described the various shapes which this near-pathological feeling of discontinuity can take. He comes to the conclusion that Flaubert finally settled for a deterministic method: caught in his own disorder, he chose to believe that his various inner states were coherently linked together. He chose order, but, Poulet adds, "this order can only be perceived and can perhaps only exist after it has been established. It can only be discovered in things that are entirely fulfilled, or in the postulate stating that they have fully come into being because of other things that allowed this to happen . . . The thought that occurs to you now has been brought to you . . . by successions, gradations, transformations and rebirths . . ."[6] It is an *a posteriori* construction that the mind

4. *Ibid.*, p. 72.
5. *Ibid.*, p. 213.

6. The quotation is from the *Temptation of Saint Anthony* [*Editor*].

forces upon the universe to make it seem coherent. It eliminates the empty void, it wipes out the discontinuities that separate things from each other, creating a gap between the present and the past. "We are in a purely immanent world . . . in which nothing remains concealed and everything can be expressed. The mind can imagine what the imagination is unable to revive."[7]

This analysis perfectly reveals how desperate and limited Flaubert's determinism actually is, as well as how far it is removed from his original sensitivity. Consequently, the option for order is bound to be frail and inconclusive. Forcefully bound to his own being, the character escapes neither from the rhythm of his metamorphoses, nor from the dissolving power of fluid inconsistency. The causal law will act as a dam, controlling the flow but without succeeding in stopping it: it changes the succession of events into a concatenation but fails to make them coherent or consistent. Once codified, the original fluidity becomes even more threatening: the main emphasis no longer falls on the liquidity of our being which, however unstable, nevertheless implied a certain kind of unity; it focuses instead on the sequence of dissolving acts. Reduced to a purely phenomenal existence, the character will consist of nothing but the succession of its different stages; in Bourget's words, characters become "associations of ideas on the march"; no inner rhythm animates the depth of their plasticity.

Flaubert himself knew the inadequacy of this solution and realized how little it satisfied his real desire: for how could the order to which he aspires affect a being on which it is merely superimposed? Like the "corset" he wants to impose on Madame Bovary, like the "Ciceronian mold" in which, at times, he wants to cast his sentences, the option for determinism is an aspect of Flaubert's intermittent temptation to overcome chaos by means of an arbitrary discipline, imposed from the outside. But this contrived solution solves none of the inner problems: underneath, things remain in a state of restless turmoil, all the more dangerous since the surface may now offer an appearance of solidity. The artificial order may overcome for an instant the deeper lack of coherence, but it is unable to create by itself the conditions in which a genuine order could come into being.

7. G. Poulet, *Studies in Human Time*, p. 331.

JEAN ROUSSET

Madame Bovary: Flaubert's Anti-Novel†

An Aspect of Flaubert's Technique: Point of View

We hear a lot today about the *anti-novel*. The expression was already in use during the seventeenth century: Sorel[1] applied it to the novels in the tradition of *Don Quixote*, written in reaction against the Romanesque excesses of current fiction. Sartre was instrumental in bringing the term back into fashion when, in his preface to Nathalie Sarraute's *Portrait of a Man Unknown*,[2] he wrote: "The anti-novels keep the appearance and outline of ordinary novels . . . But they do so in order to undermine the genre all the more effectively: they set out to undo the novel on its own terms; while seemingly constructing one, they destroy it before our eyes. . . ." This, he adds, indicates that "the novel is reflecting upon its own nature."

Extending the meaning of the term somewhat further, we can say that the anti-novel occurs whenever the novel loses faith in itself, becomes critical and self-critical, wishes to break with the established norms of the medium. A "crisis" of the novel then takes place; today we have a crisis of the fictional character, of its "psychology," even of the subject-matter. If by "subject" we mean the narrative, the plot, the sum of events that take place in the novel, it becomes clear that this "subject" tends increasingly to stand apart from the actual work, or even to disappear altogether. Robbe-Grillet recently admitted as much: "In my first book, *The Erasers*, there still was a conventional plot, imitated, in fact, from *Oedipus the King*. But it did not concern me in the least; I was not interested in making it consistent or plausible. Nor should the readers of *Jealousy* ask themselves whether or not the book contains autobiographical elements; this time, they have good reasons not to do so for, in this novel, nothing—or almost nothing—happens. . . . "[3]

† From *Forme et Signification, essais sur les structures littéraires de Corneille à Claudel* by Jean Rousset (Paris: Librairie José Corti, 1962), pp. 109–33; reprinted by permission of the publisher. Translated by Paul de Man.

1. Charles Sorel (1600?–74), author of *La vraie histoire comique de Francion*, is considered to be one of the founders of the realist novel in France [*Editor*].

2. The leading existentialist philosopher, author, and critic Jean-Paul Sartre has been interested in the experiments of Nathalie Sarraute in trying to bring the novel back to a more essential reality by stripping it of conventional forms of plot, dialogue, and description. With Alain Robbe-Grillet, Nathalie Sarraute is the leading representative of the so-called "new" French novel [*Editor*].

3. *Prétexte*, new series, n. 1, January 1958, p. 100.

Well before Robbe-Grillet and Nathalie Sarraute (different from each other as they are), Gide had his spokesman and protagonist Édouard say in *The Counterfeiters:* "My novel does not have a subject"; and George Moore used to warn Virginia Woolf:[4] "Mrs. Woolf, take my word for it, you'll never be able to write a good novel entirely without a subject." Such indeed was her dream, and who would deny that she made it come true?

Can we go back even further? The naturalists seem to be making similar claims, as when Goncourt tells Huret:[5] "Although more novels are being sold than ever before, I am convinced that the novel is a used up, dying genre. It has said all it had to say. I have done all I could to kill off the 'Romanesque,' all that has to do with adventure and sentiment for its own sake, to replace it by a kind of autobiography, memoirs of people to whom very little happens."[6] However, what is being eschewed here—and will also be rejected, in very similar terms, by Zola and Huysmans—is the plot and the fiction of earlier novels rather than the subject, the reference to the real world—a part of the novel that the naturalists were far from ready to relinquish. Yet there were readers, at the time, who complained that novels lacked subject-matter entirely, exactly as impressionistic painters were being blamed for making pictures without a subject.

In this context, one feels compelled to stress the importance of Flaubert, the pure novelist critic, brought up from infancy on that greatest ancestor of all anti-novels, *Don Quixote*. His ambition, expressed when he starts *Madame Bovary*, is well known: "What I deem beautiful, what I would want to do, is a book about nothing, a book without reference outside itself . . . , a book that would be almost without a subject, or in which the subject would be almost invisible, if such a thing is possible" (January 16, 1852). And, a little later: "If the book on which I am working with such difficulty can be brought to a successful conclusion, its existence will at least have proven the following two truths which I consider to be self–evident: first, that poetry is entirely subjective, that, in literature, there is no such thing as a beautiful subject—hence, that Yvetot will do just as well as Constantinople; and that, consequently, it makes no difference what one writes about" (June 25/26, 1853).

This century-old declaration of war against the intrinsic impor-

4. André Gide (1869–1951) and Virginia Woolf (1882–1941) both experimented boldly with the traditional form of the novel, especially by juxtaposing different events and loosening the conventional narrative sequence [*Editor*].
5. Edmond de Goncourt (1822–96) was the elder of the two Goncourt brothers, authors of naturalistic novels and of a famous journal. Jules Huret was a journalist whose interviews with prominent writers produced important documents on the history of nineteenth-century French literature [*Editor*].
6. J. Huret, *Enquête sur l'évolution littéraire*, 1891, p. 168.

tance of the subject[7] clearly shows that the novel was felt to be in a state of crisis and revolt well before 1950. When today's "new novelists" are up in arms against the "traditional novel," they are attacking a novel that was itself rebelling against its predecessors. Differences exist, not only between the products of this rebellion but also, less obviously, between the models that are being rejected: the non-subject of one generation often becomes the subject to be rejected by their successors.

This does not prevent Flaubert's experiments from being particularly meaningful for us today; he is the first in date of the non-figurative novelists. The subject—and the psychology—of *Madame Bovary* certainly still play their part, albeit a muted one, in the concert of the novel, which could not exist without them. Yet, we have the right, and perhaps the duty, to ignore them and to echo Flaubert's statement to Goncourt: "As for the story, the plot of a novel—I couldn't care less." We can add to this the very modern-sounding statement of beliefs: "The works of art that I admire above all others are those in which there is an *excess of Art*. In a picture, it is Painting that I like; in a poem, Poetry."[8] One could complete the statement: and in a novel, it is technique and style. Flaubert himself seems to invite us to read *Madame Bovary* as if it were a sonata. Thus we might escape the reproach he addressed to the greatest critics of his own time: "What shocks me in my friends Saint-Beuve and Taine is that they do not pay sufficient attention to *Art*, to the work in itself, to its construction, its style, all that makes up its beauty. . . ."[9]

Flaubert does not explicitly mention a principle of composition which must have concerned him to the highest degree: the "point of view" from which the novelist considers the events and the characters described in the novel. Is it the impartial and panoramic view of the ideal witness? One would expect this to be the case, remembering the author's declared intention in *Madame Bovary* to make himself as impersonal and objective as possible. This was, moreover, the usual technique in Balzac's novels. But Flaubert has no faith in impersonal knowledge. No such thing as objective reality exists for him; every vision, every perception is someone's particular illusion; there are as many "colored glasses" as there are observers. Does not this challenge the privileged position of the all-knowing author, endowed with divine and absolute vision?

---

7. We can go even further back in time to quote Mme. de la Fayette, who describes the *Princesse de Clèves* as a non–Romanesque novel, because it relinquishes the trappings of earlier novels: "It contains nothing adventurous or strikingly unusual; so it is not really a novel, much rather a memoir . . ." (Letter to Lescheraine, April 13, 1678).
8. *Correspondence*, LV, 397.
9. *Letters to Tourguenieff*, February 1869, Monaco, 1946, p. 15.

I. AN INTRODUCTORY CHARACTER: CHARLES BOVARY

The general organization of the book comes as a surprise: the main character is absent from the beginning as well as from the epilogue of the novel. This anomaly leads us directly to the problem of points of view.

The organization of the novel, which gives Charles Bovary a central position at the beginning and at the end, had been planned from the very first scenarios on. The only change that took place along the way is the growing importance of Homais in the final pages. These two characters are presented from the outside and from afar, almost as if they were things, opaque in their lack of self-awareness. The novel is thus framed by two episodes in which the point of view is very definitely that of the bystander watching the scene from a distance and from above, altogether detached from the inner motivations of characters which he treats as if they were puppets. At the one end, Charles first enters the field of our vision when he appears in the classroom observed by that curiously neutral "we" that will soon vanish from the novel; at the other end of the book, in a symmetrical construction so effective that it more than justifies the change in the original outline, we have the triumphantly grotesque exit of the pharmacist. At the two gates of his work, as he meets and as he leaves us, Flaubert has concentrated a maximum of sad irony and sarcasm, because these are the places in which his observation is most remote from its object. Thus the novel first moves from the outside inward, from the surface to the heart, from detachment to involvement, then returns from the inside to the periphery. Flaubert's first glance at the world always remains aloof, and only records the outside, the crust, the grotesque aspect of the mechanical gesture.[1]

But soon enough he penetrates beneath the surface. Homais remains seen from the outside throughout, thus making it possible to use him for the concluding passage, but the same is not true for Charles. From the start, while he holds the center of the stage for a relatively long time, the author draws much nearer to him and takes the reader with him. The puppet becomes human: a brief flashback tells us about his birth, his childhood and adolescence, thus opening the way for a more sympathetic insight. It is nevertheless with some feeling of surprise that we suddenly find ourselves intimately close to him, sharing in his reverie: "On the fine summer evenings . . . he opened his window and leaned out. The river . . . flowed beneath him . . . Opposite, beyond the roofs, spread the pure sky with the red sun setting. How pleasant it must be at home! How

1. See, for instance, the arrival in Egypt, in *Correspondence*, II, 119, 121–22, "I climbed in the crow's nest and saw this ancient Egypt. . . ."

fresh under the beech tree!"[2] One almost suspects a mistake on Flaubert's part: such nostalgic dreams before the window, such reveries directed towards open space, are usually associated with his heroine. He could not resist this slight token of identification, this brief moment during which he espouses the point of view of his character. As a temporary protagonist, Charles is allowed some of the benefits of this position. But the moment of insight is brief; the author at once withdraws again to the proper distance. The first drafts reveal that Flaubert had originally planned several pages of memories and dreams; he suppresses most of them, for they would definitely have made the character too close, too intimate. Yet he was unable to describe Bovary purely as if he were a mere object. Perhaps he didn't want to. The actual function of Charles Bovary in the novel and the explanation of his dominating presence in the introductory section can now be stated.

It is through Charles's eyes that we will first come upon Emma. Charles will be used as a reflector until the moment when the heroine, having been gradually introduced and then accepted, will occupy the front of the stage and become the central subject. But, like her future husband, she must first appear in the humbler guise of a character seen from the outside, as if she were a mere inanimate thing. Unlike Charles, however, the eye that perceives her is not critical, but dazzled, and the sensibility that reflects her image is familiar to us; the reader has even been allowed a glimpse of its inner workings, especially on the occasion of the doctor's early-morning visit to the Bertaux farm when, half asleep, we share in his split, double perceptions, just before Emma comes on the scene. Flaubert then uses Charles to introduce Emma, and to make us see her as she appears to him; we adopt strictly his point of view, his narrow field of vision, his subjective perception, as we follow him step by step in his discovery of an unknown woman. The author relinquishes the privileged position of the all-knowing novelist and gives us instead an image of his heroine that remains deliberately superficial and incomplete, in the sense that it records only successive and fragmentary impressions.[3]

Charles arrives at the farm: "A young woman, in a blue merino dress, with three flounces, appeared on the threshold . . ." A blue dress is what he notices first of all, is all that he shows us. One page later, he notices the whiteness of her nails, then her eyes; somewhat later still, on talking with her, he notes the "fullness of her lips."

2. *Madame Bovary* (Norton Critical Edition), p. 7.
3. Although Stendhal's and Flaubert's methods are entirely different and unrelated, one should consult the admirable study of Georges Blin, *Stendhal et les problèmes du roman* (Paris: Corti, 1954). Notice especially the second part.

When she turns her back on him, her hair on her neck swings in a movement "that the country doctor noticed there for the first time in his life." Instead of the full-sized portrait that exists out of time, and records what the author knows and perceives, as Balzac or, before him, Marivaux, would have given us, Flaubert draws a portrait composed of gradually emerging fragments—he lets such a portrait come into being from the pointillist[4] observations of a character who is emotionally stirred and involved. Other encounters with Emma will add further touches, always similarly scattered, as they originate in the confused and troubled consciousness of a man who is falling in love.

At times, Flaubert's first drafts allow us to recapture exactly his efforts to seize this vision and to render it faithfully. We have him writing, for instance, in his earliest version: "She wore neither shawl, nor cape, her white shoulders had a pink glow."[5] This is a beautiful impression of the effect of light in a kitchen on a summer day, but much too subtle for Charles Bovary. Retreating as author, Flaubert suppresses the passage and replaces it by an observation in keeping with the character behind which he is hiding: "He could see little drops of perspiration on her bare shoulders." One should add, however, that Flaubert doesn't rigorously adhere to the necessity of reflecting the limitations and distortions of his characters; he was still rather remote from Faulkner who locked himself hermetically within the interior monologue of a half-wit. Whether from lack of consistency or because he refuses to be over-systematic, Flaubert at times fills out Charles's usual perceptions, just as he sometimes puts in Emma's mind reflections or shades of irony that couldn't possibly be hers. The result is frequently a compromise in which it is difficult to discriminate between the contradictory viewpoints of the outside observer and the inner eye. Flaubert will not hesitate to commit the "error" for which Sartre so bitterly criticizes Mauriac (as if Mauriac were the first guilty of moving freely in and out of the consciousness of his characters):[6] "As for Charles, he didn't stay to ask himself why it was a pleasure to him to go to the Bertaux," or else: "Was she speaking seriously? Emma probably didn't even know herself. . . ."

There can be no question, however, that throughout the prologue Charles is deliberately used as a center and as a reflector. He is never absent, and Emma is seen only through his eyes. All we know

---

4. The pointillist technique in painting, whose main representatives are Seurat and Signac, proceeds by the juxtaposition of small dots in primary colors; the technique can be said to be analogous with the selection of minute details in Flaubert's description of the character [*Editor*].

5. *Madame Bovary, a New Version*, ed. Pommier and Leleu (Paris: Corti, 1949), p. 166.

6. The allusion is to an early article by Sartre (February 1939) entitled *Mr. François Mauriac and Freedom* that first appeared in the *Nouvelle revue française* and is now included in *Situations I*.

about her is what he finds out; the only words she speaks are those addressed to him. We don't have the slightest idea what she really thinks or feels. Emma is systematically shown us from the outside; Charles's point of view demands this. In this respect, Flaubert adheres strictly to his method. He even provides us with an extreme example: at the moment when the young girl makes the ominous decision to marry, a decision on which her entire miserable destiny and, therefore, the substance of the book hinges, the novelist hides her out of our sight; her conversation with her father, her inner reactions, and her answer are recorded indirectly and at great distance by Charles who is hiding behind the hedge and waiting for the window-blind to be pushed open against the wall. Only much later, when Flaubert moves closer to her and unlocks her thoughts, a set of refractions and juxtapositions will reveal something of what she thinks of Charles and her marriage, of her expectations, of what went on in her during that half hour. For the time being, however, she remains an opaque character contemplated from afar by Charles Bovary. All we know of her is what he knows—the outline of a face, a few gestures, a dress.

Soon enough, we discover what hides behind this surface and what kind of human being this young woman actually is, for the point of view is about to change. But Charles himself will never discover much more; to him, she will always remain that unknowable quantity that she will soon cease to be for us. He will never find out what hides behind this veil, for he totally lacks the novelist's power to penetrate into her inner self. From Chapter V on, the angle of vision slowly starts to revolve; from pure object, Emma becomes subject, the focus shifts from Charles to her, and the reader penetrates into a consciousness which, up till then, was as closed to him as it was to Charles.

This is probably the deeper reason for the country doctor's central position in the first chapters, as well as for the rigorous adherence to his point of view, including the occasional and surprising plumbing of his intimate self. Not only does it allow the reader to meet Emma first through a sensibility that is itself immersed in the flux of time; more than that, this organization of the perspective allows him to experience from the inside the type of knowledge that Charles will always possess of his wife. Thus prepared, the reader will remember it later, when Emma will have moved to the center, and this recollection will illuminate and enrich the fictional universe in which he immerses himself.

II. THE ART OF MODULATION

From Chapter VI on, Emma glides to the center of the novel, a place which she will never leave, except for some brief interruptions. There is nothing unusual about this. Balzac, master of the total and panoramic point of view, often chooses a central character, such as, for instance, Rastignac,[7] and organizes the action around him. Flaubert's originality resides in his combining the author's point of view with the heroine's. His perspectives alternate and interfere with each other, but the subjective vision of the character always predominates. His technical problem is to achieve the shifts in point of view and the transitions from one perspective to another without interrupting the movement, without disrupting the "tissue of the style."

Consider, for example, the transition from Charles to Emma, the gradual introduction, by almost unnoticeable steps, of the heroine's point of view. The point of departure and final destination of his itinerary are marked by the return of the same object, observed by two different sets of eyes: the garden of Tostes. "The garden, longer than wide, ran between two mud walls . . . to a thorn hedge that separated it from the field. In the middle was a slate sundial . . . ; four flower-beds . . . Right at the bottom, under the spruce bushes, a plaster priest was reading his breviary." This is a straightforward catalogue, an objective inventory of surfaces and materials, drawn up as by an outside observer,[8] altogether detached—without any anthropomorphic participation in things, as Robbe-Grillet would put it. The reason for this objectivity stems from the fact that Emma, when she is entering her new house, is still an utter stranger to whom Flaubert has not yet given us any access whatsoever. Thirty pages later, Emma's initiation accomplished, we come upon the same little garden, seen this time through the subjective glance of the disenchanted heroine, reacting fully to all the elements of stagnation, decline, and decay that reside in things: "The dew had left on the cabbages a silver lace with long transparent threads spreading from one to the other. No birds were to be heard; everything seemed asleep, the espalier covered with straw, and the vine, like a great sick serpent under the coping of the wall, along which, on drawing near, one saw the many-footed woodlice crawling. Under the spruce by the hedgerow, the curé in the three-cornered hat reading his breviary had lost his right foot, and the very plaster scaling off with the frost, had left white scabs on his face."

In the interval between the two passages everything has changed, not only in the situation and the mood of the heroine, but in the reader's position toward her as well. A skillful revolving movement has shifted the point of view, and the center of vision now gradually coincides with Emma's. We get a first glimpse into her dreams, followed, in flashback, by an analysis of the development that lead to

7. Rastignac, who appears throughout Balzac's *Human Comedy*, is the central figure in *Father Goriot* [*Editor*].
8. One reads in the first drafts at this point, "A third party, who would have observed them, facing each other . . ." (Pommier–Leleu), p. 182.

her present sensibility. Flaubert's hand is very apparent throughout; at this point, none of these insights could have been Emma's own. Then comes a more revealing insight in her dreams of another honeymoon: "She thought, some times . . ." leading to the long reverie under the beech trees which is by now altogether subjective and richly endowed with all the characteristics of Flaubert's inner ecstasies.[9]

Henry James, speaking of one of his novels, mentions "a planned rotation of aspects"; the expression could very well apply to Flaubert. It designates a subtle art of modulation in varying the point of view, an art of which Flaubert is a true master and which he puts to constant use. For if it is true that Emma never ceases to stand at the center of the novel, Flaubert nevertheless substitutes at times, for a brief moment, the outlook of another character. Such shifts are no easy matter to negotiate for an author who detests any trace of discontinuity, and wishes to avoid, at all cost, the tricks and manipulations of the novelist-stage director which abound in the first version of *The Sentimental Education*. When Flaubert relinquishes Emma's point of view in favor of that of Charles or Rodolphe, or gives the front of the stage for a moment to a minor character, he uses something resembling a closed-circuit system, without interrupting the flow of the narration. An example will show how the method works.

In the third chapter of Part II, immediately following the arrival at Yonville, Emma enters her new house; the reader goes with her, feeling "the cold of the plaster fall about her shoulders like damp linen. . . ." At this point, the novel has to impart miscellaneous bits of information about recently introduced characters such as Léon and Homais. Flaubert has to move away from the heroine without breaking the thread. He uses Emma's own outlook: "The next day, as she was getting up, she saw the clerk on the Square . . . Léon waited all day, etc. . . ."; the point of view has glided towards the clerk, where it stays for a while. From the clerk, whom M. Homais "respected for his education," we move almost imperceptibly over to the pharmacist, his habits, his attitude towards the new doctor, thus allowing a smooth transition to Charles. "Charles was depressed; he had no patients. . . ." Yet, in compensation, he rejoices in his wife's pregnancy. This glance cast by Charles on his pregnant wife closes the circle, returns us to Emma, happily concluding the full circuit of alternating viewpoints: "He looked at her undisturbed . . . Emma at first felt a great astonishment." Moreover, by juxtaposing the thoughts of Emma and Charles, Flaubert shows how distant they are from each other. He may, at times, de-

9. This is beautifully analyzed by Georges Poulet in "Gustave Flaubert: The Circle and the Center" (Norton Critical Edition), p. 392.

liberately forego his gradual transfers in order to reveal, as by a sudden gap, this divergence of their outlooks, the infinite distance that keeps them apart, even when they are sitting or lying side by side: "He saw himself dishonored . . . Emma, opposite, watched him; she did not share his humiliation, she felt another. . . ." But, as a rule, Flaubert puts a great deal of care in his art of modulation. Thus when Rodolphe and Emma end their last nocturnal dialogue, which the reader has experienced through the consciousness of the young woman:

> " 'Till tomorrow then!' said Emma in a last caress.
> And *she watched him* go.
> He didn't turn around . . . He was already on the other side of the river, walking fast across the meadows.
> After a few moments Rodolphe stopped. . . ."

Again, carried by Emma's eye, the reader leaves her for the object of her contemplation and joins Rodolphe; he hears him think and sees him write the letter that puts an end to the affair.

This art of modulation, this concern with smooth and gradual transition,[1] reflects in a distinctive manner Flaubert's general effort towards what he calls *style*. He conceives of style as a binding agent which reduces the diverse to the homogeneous. He strives for a unity of texture, as tight and even as possible, in order to create continuity: "Style is made of continuity, as virtue is made of constancy."[2] When he criticizes a poem by Louise Colet or Leconte de Lisle,[3] his strictures are aimed at unevenness of tone or of color. In his eyes, what makes for the quality of a work are not the pearls but the thread that holds them together, the uniform movement, the flow. Rereading the parts of *Madame Bovary* on which he has been working, he writes to Louise Colet: "I reread all this the day before yesterday, and I have been horrified by its inadequacy . . . Each paragraph is good enough by itself, and I am convinced that some pages are perfect. But just because of this, *it won't do*. It is a set of well-turned, static paragraphs which do not dovetail with each other. I'm going to have to loosen up a lot of screws and joints. . . ."[4] Those articulations will become the main concern of the artist; they must be made strong and flexible, while remaining invisible. Flaubert applies the mortar with infinite care, and he is not less careful in wiping away the last trace of its presence: "I've had to remove a lot of mortar that was showing between the bricks, and I

---

1. Cf. for instance: "I think I made a great step forward, namely in the *imperceptible* transition from the psychological to the dramatic part . . ." *Correspondence*, III, 423.

2. *Correspondence*, III, 401.

3. Flaubert's long-time mistress and confidante was also a poet of sorts, though certainly not of the calibre of Leconte de Lisle (1818–94) who was the leader of the Parnassian school of poetry [*Editor*].

4. *Correspondence*, III, 92.

had to rearrange the bricks to hide the joints from sight."[5]

Flaubert's imagination has always been captivated by the sight of large rocks, by vast arrangements of stones. At the end of his fine essay on Flaubert, Jean Pierre Richard shows how the deep fluidity of Flaubert's being leads him, in his creative effort, to strive for the firmness of rocks and stones; this sedimentation will be considered successful provided that the original plastic and humid mass is not allowed to dry up altogether. Flaubert remains faithful to himself when he defines his picture of "beauty" as being an entirely smooth surface, a *naked wall*. The term appears in a letter from 1876, but it goes back to a memory of his youth: "I remember how my heart beat and what pleasure I felt on looking at the wall of the Acropolis, a naked wall . . . I wonder whether a book, regardless of what it has to say, could not produce a similar impression? Is there not an intrinsic quality, a kind of divine power, in the precision of the construction, the economy of the means, the *polish of the surface*, the harmony of the whole . . . ?"[6] Elsewhere he writes: "Prose must stand erect from end to end, like a wall. . . ." What fascinates Flaubert in the picture of the wall is the homogeneous block, the compact, immobile, uninterrupted mass, the "great uniting line," the perfection of continuity created, as we have seen in the modulating passages.

This ideal of the "straight line" and of massive construction does not exclude variations of tonality and of movement in the inner texture of the novel, zones of greater or lesser intensity that determine the rhythm, the pulsation of the book.

In this respect, and without leaving the questions of point of view and field of vision with which we have been concerned, we should notice the important part that windows play in *Madame Bovary*. Léon Bopp has observed the importance of the frequent presence of the heroine before open windows. This allows for striking effects of depth perspective and panoramic vision, corresponding to phases of maximum subjectivity and extreme intensity.

III. WINDOWS AND PANORAMIC VISION

Maria, in the story *November*,[7] spent whole days at her window waiting, keeping a vigil over the empty space in which a customer might appear, or an event occur. The window is a favorite place for certain Flaubert characters who, though unable to move by themselves, are nevertheless swept away by the current of events. They are frozen by their own inertias while their minds wander forever. Caught in the closed space in which their souls dry up, they welcome the window as an escape which allows them to expand into

5. *Correspondence*, III, 264.
6. *Correspondence*, VII, 294.
7. *November* is a 120 page-long story written in 1842, when Flaubert was 21 years old, remarkable because it contains already so many of the stylistic and thematic devices of the later master [*Editor*].

space, without having to leave their chosen spots. The window combines open and enclosed space, represents an obstacle as well as an escape, a sheltering room as well as an area of endless expansion, a circumscribed infinity. Flaubert's main characters who, as Georges Poulet has so well shown, are always absent from where they live and present where they do not, vacillating between contraction and expansion, are bound to choose for their dwelling places borderline entities which allow for escape in immobility; no wonder they select windows as the ideal locale for their reveries.

Already in *Par le Champs et par les Grèves*[8] the following passage appears: "Ah! air! more air! give me space in which to breathe! Our oppressed souls are stifled and dying near the window. Our captive minds turn and turn upon themselves, like bears in cages, bumping against the walls that enclose them. Let my nostrils at least breathe in the scent of all winds that encircle the earth, and *let my eyes escape toward all the horizons.*"[9]

Emma Bovary, another captive locked within the walls of her cage, finds before her window an "escape towards all horizons": "She often stood there." In Tostes, she stands at the window to watch the rain fall and the monotonous round of the village days go by; in Yonville, the notary clerk as well as Rodolphe are first observed from a window; standing in the garden window, Emma hears the ringing of the angelus bells that will awaken a mystical longing in her, drawing her gaze upwards to lose itself among the clouds or among the meanderings of the river; the attic–window gives her the first dizzy temptation toward suicide; and after her illness, when she resumes contact with life, "they wheeled her arm chair by the window overlooking the Square. . . ." They are the windows of despair and of dreams.

On the other hand, we find in the novel closed windows, with all curtains drawn during the rare moments when Emma is no longer alienated from herself or from the place where she lives and, consequently, feels no need to scatter herself into the endless infinity of dreams. Instead, in the early and happy moment of her passions, she makes herself into the center of all things, as in Rouen, with Léon, "in the carriage with drawn blinds . . . more tightly closed than a tomb," then in the hotel room where they live locked up all day long "all curtains drawn, all doors locked . . . in a hothouse atmosphere," as one of the early scenarios expresses it. The same had happened with Rodolphe when Emma, at the onset of their affair, paid him surprise visits at la Huchette, in the room half–darkened by "the yellow curtains along the windows." But this first

8. "Along the Fields and the Sea Shores" is a journal kept by Flaubert during a trip he took with his friend Maxime DuCamp in 1847 through the Touraine and especially through Brittany [Editor].
9. *Par les champs et par les grèves*, ed. Conard, pp. 125–26.

passion is generally a passion in the open air, in garden or forest, where there are no windows at all. Flaubert thus contrasts the nature of the two lovers, while remaining faithful to the thematic meaning of the windows in his novel.

In conjunction with their special significance for Flaubert's characters, the windows provide the novelist-director with interesting technical opportunities in staging and ordering his scenes. Flaubert uses them frequently to vary the narrative perspective and to engineer interesting optical effects. The brilliant "symphonic" passage of the Agricultural Fair at once comes to mind, in which the point of view is that of the two future lovers, watching from the window on the second floor of the town hall. The panoramic view here offers a double advantage: in the first place, it reinforces the author's ironical detachment towards the goings-on below and towards the budding idyll that he treats in juxtaposition to the fair; more important still, it reflects the upward motion, the more elevated note struck at the moment of Emma's entrance upon the life of passion. The tone is picked up in the following episode: the same panoramic vision is used again a little later, during the horse ride when Rodolphe completes the conquest begun on the day of the fair. Arriving at the top of a hill, Flaubert gives us a panoramic outlook over the land similar to the one that Emma gains, at this same moment, over her life: "There was fog over the land. Hazy clouds hovered on the horizon between the outlines of the hills; others rent asunder, floated up and disappeared. Sometimes through a rift in the clouds, beneath a ray of sunshine, gleamed from afar the roofs of Yonville, with the gardens at the water's edge, the yards, the walls and the church steeple. Emma half closed her eyes to pick out her house, and never had this poor village where she lived appeared so small." The beginning of her love is marked by a rising above the habitual level of existence; the place where this existence occurred must first vanish before her eyes: Yonville must shrink away into a distance made infinite by the bird's-eye perspective, in order to make room for the imaginary space in which her love will take place, associated here with the image of evaporating water: "From the height on which they stood, the entire valley seemed an immense pale lake sending off its vapor into the air." At the moment when the author casts over the world the all-embracing glance of his heroine, as she is carried upward by her rising exaltation, the village and its houses have become a shapeless mirage, suspended in mid-air.

A few pages farther, on the evening of the same day, Emma dreams of this new life that dawns upon her. As if the high view of the afternoon had completely entered the inner landscape of her soul, she still thinks in terms of height and infinity, united against the lowliness of her common existence: "She was entering upon a marvelous world where all would be passion, ecstasy, endless rapture. A blue space surrounded her, the heights of sentiment sparkled under her thought, and ordinary existence appeared only intermittently between these heights, dark and far away underneath her."

Flaubert has made a different use of the same hilltop above the village, at a moment that is not less decisive, though oriented in the opposite direction. Madame Bovary has seen Rodolphe for the last time and she returns to Yonville, utterly dejected and about to kill herself. Instead of the ascent towards the ecstasy of passion, we now have the descent towards suicide. During this hallucinated walk at nightfall, we meet her at the top of a hill, the same perhaps as before. Suddenly, she is shaken out of her spellbound state:

> It all disappeared: she recognized the lights of the houses that shone through the fog.
> Now her plight, like an abyss, loomed before her . . . she ran down the hill . . .

The return from the world of the imagination to the world of reality is now a falling towards the village; this time, the village appears out of the fog instead of hiding beneath it; it is a descent into the abyss.

Thus, in two passages which, though quite far apart, are the symmetrical opposites of each other, Flaubert has placed his heroine, at the onset and at the end of her love-quest, in the same dominating position and has made her command the same panoramic outlook. It is up to the attentive reader to notice the structural link that unites the two episodes and to discover the wealth of meaning added by such a tightly controlled construction. One should compare to this another diptych, combining this time the use of the window with that of the carriage (which will play such an important part in the *Sentimental Education*): the two views of Rouen, on the arrival and at the departure of the stage coach, during Emma's Thursday encounters with Léon. We are given one more panoramic view: "Thus seen from above, the entire landscape seemed motionless like a painting. . . ." And here again, the landscape, at first frozen, will start to move, to vibrate and to expand under the impact of an imagination driven by impending passion. There is one important difference, however: instead of appearing remote and hidden by a veil that makes it shrink into near oblivion, the dwelling place of her desire will now, in a reverse optical illusion, appear out of the mist and start expanding into an immense capital—the only entity large enough to contain the ever widening space she projects before her: "Her love grew in the presence of this vastness, and filled with the tumult of the vague murmuring which rose from below. She poured it out, onto the squares, the avenues, the streets; and the old Norman city *spread out before her like some incredible Capital, a Babylon into which she was about to enter.*"

Windows and panoramic views, spatial reveries, opening up into infinite perspectives, make up the crucial centers around which the plot is organized; they are points of highest resistance that stop the flow of the narrative. They coincide with the adoption of a most unusual point of view: the author relinquishes his traditional god-like rights and leaves room instead for a totally subjective vision. He places himself behind his heroine and looks entirely through her eyes. Such moments occur at significant points in the book. They are unevenly distributed; entirely lacking during the periods of action, when the play of passion is acted out, they are more frequent during periods of stagnation and suspended waiting. So for instance at Tostes, after the invitation to the ball, when for the first time we see Emma, at the end of the evening, open the window and lean out.[1] From then on, in Tostes as well as in Yonville, the reverie will never cease, till the moment when she embarks upon her great adventure, returns to her husband, rejects him again after the clubfoot episode, prepares her elopement, gets involved in her financial dealings with Lheureux. After these chapters of action and accelerated movement, the end of the affair with Rodolphe brings back a slower tempo, a new period of stagnation and inertia. Again, this change of pace is introduced by a window opening up before the heroine; this time, however, the window is already a tragic one, suggesting the dizziness and loss of consciousness that is a prefiguration of the end. She reads Rodolphe's letter near the attic window, "opposite, beyond the roofs, the countryside stretched out as far as the eye could reach. . . ." She is about to return to a world of regrets and frustrated desires, in which she will try to expand beyond the limits of her confinement, to "float" in the airy realm which is that of her reverie and of her panoramic visions: "she was right at the edge, almost hanging, surrounded by vast space. The blue of the sky invaded her. . . ."[2]

Those repeated flights of reverie before the open window are always followed by a fall, a return to earth: " 'My wife! my wife!'

---

1. One knows that, in this passage, Flaubert had made sizeable deletions: the walk of the young woman, at dawn, in the park and her long contemplation of the countryside through colored window-panes. See pp. 216–17 of the Pommier–Leleu edition. It is a great pity that Flaubert chose to discard these passages, although, understandably enough, he considered them important. It is a perfect illus-

tration of subjective vision: seen through different colored glass, the landscape not only changes in color, but also in shape, in mood, even in structure. Emma's world will similarly be seen colored by the different shades of her passion.

2. The first draft reads: "She was going to float in the void, in order to annihilate herself . . ." (Pommier–Leleu edition), p. 444.

Charles called . . . and she had to *go down* and sit at the table!"
The book, like the inner life of the heroine, consists of this rhythmical succession of flights and falls. Thus, at the beginning of
Chapter VI of the second part, the open window through which
the ringing of the angelus is heard leads to a flow of memories and
to an ascent into a weightless, suspended state expressed by images
of flight, of swirling feathers: "she felt limp and helpless, like the
down of a bird whirled by the tempest"; then, on returning from
church, "she let *herself fall* into an armchair," recaptured by the
heavy and confining world of the room, by the monotonous weight
of time, by the opaque presence of creatures who "are there" as if
they were pieces of furniture: "the pieces of furniture seemed more
frozen in their places . . . , the clock went on ticking . . . little
Berthe was there, between the window and the sewing table . . .
Charles appeared. It was dinner time. . . ." Trying to reestablish
contact with daily life, after the moments of escape towards the beyond of the windows, is always an act of falling, a falling back into
confinement.

The same double movement recurs at other crucial passages, such
as the scene at the Agricultural Fair. Emma, stirred by a smell of
perfume and the "distant" sight of the stage coach, unites in a kind
of ecstasy lovers and experiences of the past before she returns
downward, to the crowd on the square and the official oratory. Or
again, in another ecstasy of a similarly erotic nature, the scene at
the opera in Rouen, which heralds the beginning of the affair with
Léon as the preceding one began the affair with Rodolphe. The box
from which Emma looks "from above" over the stage is an exact
equivalence of the window, a new amalgamation, a synthesis of
confinement and expansion towards a space on which an imaginary
destiny is being acted out. This time, it is not her own destiny that
is being played out, but somebody else's being performed for her
benefit; yet it doesn't take her long to recognize her own plight, to
identify with the main feminine part, to join her in her desire to
"*fly away* in an embrace" and to see another Rodolphe in the tenor
part: "A mad idea took possession of her: he was looking at her
right now! She longed to run to his arms . . . , and call out 'Take
me away!' . . . The curtain *fell* . . . and she *fell back* into her
seat. . . ." The sudden collapse of the dream and of the aerial perspective is followed after the flight, by the inevitable letdown. On
this occasion, Flaubert stresses at once the heaviness of the air and
the confinement of the space: "The smell of gas mingled with the
people's breath and the waving fans made the air even more suffocating. Emma wanted to go out; the crowd filled the corridors, and
she fell back in her armchair with palpitations that choked her."

One cannot fail to see in this scene a foreboding of Emma's last request when, during her death–struggle, gasping for air, she begs: "Open the window . . . I am suffocating." In her life, every ecstasy is followed by a smaller version of death; her actual, ultimate death harmoniously blends with the prefigurations that prepared it.

Moments of reverie, during which Flaubert's point of view comes closest to coinciding with that of his heroine and which allow us a glimpse into Emma's intimate self, abound in the slowest-moving parts of the novel, during the periods of inertia and spleen when time seems to stand still. They constitute the most original and striking aspects of the novel, the ones, also, that are most typical of Flaubert. During those moments, Flaubert relinquishes, to a considerable extent, the objective vision of the universal observer.

On the other hand, at times when the action must move forward, when new facts or characters have to be introduced, the author reclaims his sovereign rights and resorts to a panoramic perspective. Restoring the distance between himself and his characters, he can again show them from the outside. This happens, as we have shown, at the beginning and at the end of the novel, or in the opening chapters of a new part. Fresh beginnings demand the presence of the novelist-director, who sets the stage while introducing the cast of characters: so it is at the beginning of Part II, the big scene in the inn at Yonville or, in the introduction of Part III, the conversation between Emma and Léon in a Rouen hotel room, the rendezvous at the cathedral, the coach ride through the streets of Rouen. During the coach ride Flaubert takes advantage of the momentary distance that separates him from his heroine to achieve a surprising effect: the new lovers are in the coach, all curtains drawn, but the reader is not allowed to join them. In the foregoing pages, he was allowed no insight into their souls, but he could observe gestures and attitudes, catch the meaning of words that were spoken; here, even this privilege is taken from him—he can see nothing at all, and has to be satisfied with following the carriage from afar as it meanders through the streets. During this decisive episode, he finds himself confined to the narrowest point of view possible, that of the indifferent citizens of Rouen, for whom this woman is a total stranger. When she finally emerges from the carriage, he sees her in this very light: "a *woman* got out, walking with her veil down and without looking back." The effect is all the more uncanny since the reader has been allowed earlier intimate glimpses of Emma's soul, and this close knowledge makes it easy for him to guess what goes on behind the lowered veil.

A similar effect recurs somewhat later in the book, when the author adopts an equally distant point of view to narrate Emma's desperate call on Binet: the scene is shown through the eyes of the two prying neighbors as they watch through the attic window. We can hardly hear a word, we watch from afar; gestures and attitudes have to be guessed and interpreted—it is like a scene from a silent movie. One may assume that Flaubert, who has kept us in very close contact with his main character and made us share in her drama from the inside, feels so certain of our participation that he allows himself this sudden withdrawal to show us, for one brief moment, the heroine as she appears to the alien eye of the outside judge and observer. Immediately afterwards, we briefly lose sight of her altogether. The two gossips watch her disappear down the street in the direction of the graveyard, and we can only wonder with them what Emma is about to do. Then in a new and abrupt reversal, the novelist suddenly takes us back to Emma as she visits the nurse, letting us into her consciousness. Those violent manipulations of the reader, echoing the pathos that abounds in this part of the narrative, are the more effective since, at all other times, Flaubert, modulating and gliding from scene to scene in almost imperceptible transitions, has taken exactly the opposite approach.

In Flaubert's novel, the point of view and the subjective vision of the characters play a considerable part, at the expense of straightforward factual reporting. As a result, the importance of the slower movements increase as the outside impartial observer relinquishes his privileges, to a greater or lesser degree.[3]

This slowness of tempo combined with the use of inner perspective constitute the novelty and the originality of Flaubert's novels. He is the novelist of the inner vision and of a slow, almost stagnant action. Admirable and distinctive as those qualities are, Flaubert himself nevertheless discovers them only gradually by trial and error, more by instinct than by design, and not without some serious misgivings. We read in his letters that there is no "action," no "movement," "fifty pages without a single event." His concern about the shape his novel is taking (almost in spite of itself) stems from the awareness of his difference from his predecessors. He is thinking primarily of Balzac, for whom all is action, drama, and suspense. Then he resigns himself: "One must sing in one's own voice: and mine will never be dramatic or seductive. Besides, I am growing more and more convinced that all this is a matter of style, or, rather, of appearance, a way of presenting things."[4] The best he can do is to try to maintain a balance between action and inaction, between facts and dreams: "It will be a difficult task to make an almost equal division between adventure and thought."[5]

3. For a further development of these observations, one should read the outstanding passages in Erich Auerbach's *Mimesis* showing how it is Emma who sees, while it is the author who talks (Norton Critical Edition, p. 389).

4. *Correspondence*, III, 86.
5. *Correspondence*, III, 394.

Fortunately for us, he will never quite succeed in this.[6] The dreamy nature of his heroine and the natural bent of his literary talent pull in the same direction. The nature of Flaubert's genius is such that he prefers the reflected consciousness of an event to the event itself, the dream of passion to the actual experience, lack of action and emptiness to presence. This is where Flaubert's art really comes into its own. What is most beautiful in his novels bears little resemblance to ordinary fiction. It is found not in the events—for, in his hand, they tend to crumble and disappear—but in what lies between events, those wide empty regions, the vast areas of stagnation in which no movement occurs. To succeed in charging emptiness with so much existence and substance, to conjure up such fullness out of nothing, is the miracle.[7] But this reversal has still another consequence: in an objective narrative written in the third person, it magnifies the importance of the character's point of view and stresses the optics of his "thought"—the stage on which everything that matters takes place.

Flaubert is the great novelist of inaction, of ennui, of stagnation. He didn't know it, or didn't know it clearly, until he wrote *Madame Bovary*; he found out in the process, and not without some anxiety.

In so doing, he revealed (or confirmed) what is perhaps a law of literary invention: creation implies insecurity; whatever is new disturbs, and the first gesture of the innovator is a gesture of refusal. Yet it is this hesitant and tentative inquiry that leads the innovator to his real self. He comes to know himself for what he is in the act of composing. And this confirms another law: even with as deliberate a writer as Flaubert, as convinced as he was that everything could be made a matter of plan and of conception, true invention takes place in the course of the actual writing; the work completes its own conception in the concrete acts that make it come into being.

6. In comparing the scenarios with the final texts, one notices that, far from adding more action to his novels, Flaubert rather tends to make it sparser: in the first scenarios, Emma became Léon's mistress before embarking on the affair with Rodolphe; similarly, in the *Education,* he had first planned that Mme. Arnoux would become Frédéric's mistress (see M. J. Durry, *Flaubert et ses projets inédits,* Paris: Nizet, 1950, pp. 137 ff.). He will forego this episode later on.

In the first version of the *Sentimental Education,* Henry and Mme. Renaud elope and live in exile the life of their dreams; in *Madame Bovary,* Flaubert does away with the voyage and has Emma embark only on imaginary trips; the event is replaced by the dream of the event.
7. "Nothing happens, but that nothing has become a heavy, oppressive, threatening something," Auerbach, *op. cit.* (Norton Critical Edition, p. 389).

Selected Bibliography

The bibliography of Flaubert is very extensive: in his 1945 edition of *Madame Bovary*, René Dumesnil lists more than 500 titles directly relevant to the novel. We give only a highly selective list of interest for the American student; with very few exceptions, only texts that deal directly with *Madame Bovary*, and not with Flaubert in general, have been included. (Since practically all French books are published in Paris, we follow French bibliographical procedure in listing the publisher only, if the book was published in Paris; otherwise, the location is listed.)

I. EDITIONS

Madame Bovary, Vol. I in Gustave Flaubert, *Oeuvres complètes* (20 vols.), Louis Conard, 1910. [Contains variants, notes, a history of the publication of the novel, a bibliography and several extracts from early drafts.]

Madame Bovary, Vol. I in Gustave Flaubert, *Oeuvres complètes* and *Correspondance* known as Edition du Centenaire (9 vols.), Librairie de France, 1921–1925.

Madame Bovary, Vols. I and II in Gustave Flaubert, *Oeuvres complètes* (10 vols.), Collection des textes français de la Société des Belles-Lettres, edited by René Dumesnil, 1945–1948. [Contains a substantial introduction on the genesis and publication of the novel, a bibliography of over 500 titles, notes and variants.]

Aside from these three authoritative editions, innumerable editions of *Madame Bovary* are on the market. The two following editions are reliable and readily available:

Madame Bovary, edited by Edouard Maynial, Editions des Classiques Garnier, 1961.

Madame Bovary in G. Flaubert, *Oeuvres complètes*, edited by René Dumesnil and Albert Thibaudet, Bibliothèque de la Pléiade, 1946–1948.

Flaubert, Gustave. *Correspondance* (9 vols.), Louis Conard, 1926–1933.

II. BIBLIOGRAPHIES AND EARLY VERSIONS

Dumesnil, René. His edition of *Madame Bovary* listed above.

Dumesnil, René. *Gustave Flaubert. L'homme et l'oeuvre*, Desclée de Brouwer, 1932.

Dumesnil, René and Demorest, Don L. *Bibliographie de Gustave Flaubert*, L. Giraud-Badin, 1939. [Gives the full bibliographical history of the various editions of *Madame Bovary* between 1856 and 1873.]

Leleu, Gabrielle. *Madame Bovary. Ebauches et Fragments inédits*, L. Conard, 1936.

Leleu, Gabrielle and Pommier, Jean. *Madame Bovary. Nouvelle version précédée de scénarios inédits.* José Corti, 1949.

III. SOURCES AND HISTORY OF THE NOVEL

Consult the Conard and Dumesnil editions.

Dubosc, G. "La véritable *Madame Bovary*" in *Trois Normands* (*Corneille, Flaubert, Maupassant*), Rouen, 1917.

Du Camp, Maxime. *Souvenirs littéraires* (2 vols.), Hachette, 1882–1883. [Numerous references to Flaubert, starting from I, 218.]

Dumesnil, René. *La publication de Madame Bovary*, Malfère, 1927.

Dumesnil, René. "Une source inconnue de *Madame Bovary*," *Education nationale* (May, 1948).

Dumesnil, René. "La véritable Madame Bovary," *Mercure de France* CCCIV (November, 1948), 431.

Dumesnil, René. *La vocation de Gustave Flaubert*, Gallimard, 1961.

Leblanc, Georgette. *Un pèlerinage au pays de Madame Bovary*, Sansot, 1913.

Pommier, Jean. "Les maladies de Gustave Flaubert," *Progrès médical* (August 10–24, 1946).

Pommier, Jean and Leleu, Gabrielle. "Du nouveau sur Madame Bovary," *Revue d'histoire littéraire* (July–September, 1947), p. 211.

Pommier, Jean. "Noms et prénoms dans *Madame Bovary*," *Mercure de France* (June, 1949), p. 244.

Steegmuller, Francis. *Flaubert and Madame Bovary. A Double Portrait*, New York, 1947.

IV. CONTEMPORARY REACTIONS

Consult the Conard edition.

Barbey d'Aurevilly. *Les oeuvres et les hommes. Vol. IV: Les romanciers*, Amyot, 1865.

Baudelaire, Charles. *L'art romantique* (1857); also in *Oeuvres complètes*, ed. Y. G. de Dantec, Bibliothèque de la Pléiade, 1951, p. 995.

Cuvillier-Fleury, A. *Dernières études historiques et littéraires*, I, 352–66.

Sainte-Beuve. *Causeries du Lundi*, Garnier, XIII.

Weinberg, Bernard. *French Realism: The Critical Reaction 1830–1870*, MLA general series, Chicago, 1937.

V. CRITICAL STUDIES

Arnold, Matthew. "Anna Karenina and Madame Bovary" in *Essays in Criticism*, I, London, 1888.

Auerbach, Erich. *Mimesis: The Representation of Reality in Western Literature*, translated by Willard R. Trask, Princeton, N.J., 1953.

Bart, Benjamin F. "Balzac and Flaubert. Energy vs. Art," *Romanic Review*, XLII (1951), 198.

Bart, Benjamin F. "*Madame Bovary* after a Century," *French Review*, XXXI (January, 1958), 203.

Béguin, Albert. "Relire *Madame Bovary*," *Table ronde*, XXVII (1950), 160.

Bersani, Leo. "The Narrator and the Bourgeois Community in *Madame Bovary*," *French Review*, XXXII (1959), 527.

Blackmur, R. P. "*Madame Bovary*: Beauty Out of Place," *Kenyon Review*, XIII, 3 (Summer, 1951), 475.

Block, Haskell. "Theory of Language in Gustave Flaubert and James Joyce," *Revue de Littérature comparée*, XXXV (1941).

Bopp, Léon. *Commentaire sur Madame Bovary*, Neuchâtel, 1951.

du Bos, Charles. "Sur le 'milieu intérieur' chez Flaubert," *Approximations*, Plon, 1922.

Bourget, Paul. *Essais de psychologie contemporaine*, Plon, 1899.

Brunetière, Ferdinand. *Le roman naturaliste*, Calmann-Lévy, 1883.

Canu, Jean. "La 'couleur normande' de *Madame Bovary*," PMLA, XLVIII (March, 1933), 167.

Demorest, Don L. *L'expression figurée et symbolique dans l'oeuvre de Gustave Flaubert*, L. Conard, 1931.

Demorest, Don L. "Les suppressions dans le texte de *Madame Bovary*," *Mélanges Hugnet*, Boivin (1940).

Durry, Marie-Jeanne. *Flaubert et ses projets inédits*, Nizet, 1950.

Engstrom, Alfred G. "Flaubert's correspondence and the ironic and symbolic structure of *Madame Bovary*," *Studies in Philology*, XLVI (1949), 470.

Faguet, Emile. *Flaubert*, Hachette, 1899.

Fitch, Girdler W. "The comic sense of Flaubert in the light of Bergson's *Le Rire*," PMLA, LV (June, 1940), 511.

Friedrich, Hugo. *Die Klassiker des französischen Romans* (114–149), Leipzig, 1939.

Garcin, Philippe. "Madame Bovary ou l'imaginaire en défaut," *Cahiers du Sud*, 286 (1957), 980.

de Gaultier, Jules. *Le génie de Flaubert*, Mercure de France, 1913.

de Gaultier, Jules. *Le Bovarysme*, Mercure de France, 1921.

Gide, André. *Incidences*, Gallimard, 1924.

Girard, René. *Mensonge romantique et vérité romanesque*, Grasset, 1961.

de Goncourt, Edmond et Jules. *Journal*, Vol. IX, Charpentier, 1896.

de Gourmont, Remy. *Promenades littéraires*, 4ème série, Mercure de France, 1913.

Grounauer, Madeleine. "Notes en vue d'une étude sur la structure de *Madame Bovary*," *Trivium*, III (1945), 280.

Hatzfeld, Helmut. "Don Quixote und Madame Bovary," *Idealistische Philologie*, III (1927), 54, 116.

Hatzfeld, Helmut. *Initiation à l'explication de textes français*, Munich, 1957, p. 135.

James, Henry. *French Poets and Novelists*, London, 1876.

James, Henry. *Madame Bovary*, with critical introduction, London, 1902 [can be found in *The Future of the Novel*, ed. Leon Edel, New York, 1956].

Lapp, John. "Art and Hallucination in Flaubert," *French Studies* (October, 1956), p. 322.

Levin, Harry. *The Gates of Horn: a Study of Five French Realists*, New York, 1963.

Lubbock, Percy. *The Craft of Fiction*, New York and London, 1924.

Mauriac, François. *Trois grands hommes devant Dieu (Molière, Rousseau, Flaubert)*, Editions du Capitole, 1930.

Maynial, Edouard. *Gustave Flaubert*, Nouvelle Revue critique, 1930.

Moreau, Pierre. "L'art de la composition dans *Madame Bovary*," *Orbis Litterarum*, XII (1957), 171.

Pommier, Jean. "La création littéraire chez Gustave Flaubert," *Annuaire du Collège de France* (1947), p. 169.

Poulet, Georges. *Etudes sur le temps humain*, Plon, 1949 [also in *Studies in Human Time*, trans. Elliott Coleman, Baltimore, 1956].

Poulet, Georges. *La métamorphose du cercle*, Plon, 1961 [also in *Western Review*, XIX (Summer, 1955), 245].

Proust, Marcel. "A propos du 'style' de Flaubert," *Nouvelle revue française* (January, 1920). [See also Strauss, Walter A. *Proust and Literature: The Novelist as Critic*, Cambridge (Mass.), 1957.]

Richard, Jean-Pierre. *Littérature et sensation*, Editions du Seuil, 1954.

Rousset, Jean. *Forme et signification. Essai sur les structures littéraires de Corneille à Claudel*, José Corti, 1962.

Sand, George. *Questions d'art et de littérature*, Calmann-Lévy, 1878.

Sartre, Jean-Paul. *Being and Nothingness*, trans. Hazel A. Barnes, New York, 1956.

Sartre, Jean-Paul. *Search for a Method*, trans. Hazel A. Barnes, New York, 1963.

Seillère, Ernest. *Le romantisme des réalistes: G. Flaubert*, Plon, 1914.

Seznec, Jean. "*Madame Bovary* et la puissance des images," *Médecine de France*, VIII (1949), 37.

Shanks, Lewis Piaget. *Flaubert's Youth, 1821–1845*, Baltimore, 1927.

Thibaudet, Albert. "Sur le style de Flaubert," *Nouvelle revue française* (November, 1919), p. 942.

Thibaudet, Albert. *Gustave Flaubert. Sa vie, ses romans, son style*, Plon, 1922; revised edition, Gallimard, 1963.

Ullmann, Stephen. *Style in the French Novel*, Cambridge, 1957.

Valéry, Paul. *La tentation de (saint) Flaubert*, Daragnès, 1942; also in *Oeuvres*, ed. Jean Hytier, Bibliothèque de la Pléiade (1962), I, 613.

von Wartburg, Walter. *Evolution et structure de la langue française*, Leipzig, 1937.

Zola, Emile. *Le roman expérimental*, Charpentier, 1880, p. 226.

Zola, Emile. *Les romanciers naturalistes*, Charpentier, 1881, p. 125.